To Jan—

Xmas togethe

Bob

A TREASURY OF **SCIENCE FICTION**

A TREASURY OF SCIENCE FICTION

EDITED WITH AN INTRODUCTION

BY GROFF CONKLIN

Foreword by R. Scott Latham

BONANZA BOOKS

NEW YORK

This edition is published by Bonanza Books,
a division of Crown Publishers, Inc.
 b c d e f g h
BONANZA 1980 EDITION

Manufactured in the United States of America

Library of Congress Cataloging in Publication Data

Conklin, Groff, 1904–   ed.
   A treasury of science fiction.

   Reprint of the ed. published by Crown Publishers, New York,
   1. Science fiction, American. I. Title.
PZl.C76094Tr 1980 [PS648.S3] 813′.0876 79-26154
ISBN 0-517-30618-2

CONTENTS

v

CONTENTS

PART SEVEN: FAR TRAVELING

FOREWORD

The book you hold in your hand is a classic. It is one of the very first anthologies of science fiction ever published. The thirty stories presented here were originally published in science fiction magazines. The earliest dates from 1929, the most recent from 1947; the bulk were written in the forties. During this period, science fiction was undergoing upheavals that would change the style and subject matter of the genre and would greatly increase its popularity and influence. The pulp magazines of the twenties and thirties had relied heavily on stock cardboard characters, warmed-over plots borrowed from Western and adventure yarns, and inexplicable, often macabre creatures from beyond. The stories had become limited, predictable, and dull. Science fiction had fallen into the doldrums, and heroic measures were required to rescue it.

In 1937, the hero came upon the scene in the person of John W. Campbell, Jr., the new editor of Street and Smith's *Astounding Science-Fiction*. To gauge the impact of the man and his magazine on the field, it is only necessary to note that of the thirty stories in this book twenty-five originally appeared in the pages of *Astounding*, and all but one of these under Campbell's editorial aegis. He introduced readers to the first efforts of such fledgling writers as Robert A. Heinlein, A. E. van Vogt, Isaac Asimov, and Theodore Sturgeon. He encouraged readers to respond to his magazine; he conducted polls and contests to select new story ideas; he reanimated writers who had lost virtually all interest in the field. But most importantly, he changed the direction of science fiction writing. He adamantly refused to accept the tired old BEM (Bug-Eyed Monster) space-operas; he wanted hard, logical science, presented in the context of real, believable characters. He encouraged writers to pursue social and political themes; he urged them to dream clearly; he asked them to examine the world that was and to extrapolate what it might be. And the world of science fiction—writers and fans alike—responded enthusiastically. Small wonder that Isaac Asimov has called the period from 1938 to 1950 "the

FOREWORD

Campbell Era." In a relatively short time, Campbell left an indelible stamp on his chosen field.

As a case in point, consider Arthur C. Clarke's "Rescue Party." The main theme of this tale concerns the relative speeds of development of different cultures, a reflection on the insights offered by cultural anthropology. The striking and almost unnoticed aspect is that none of the protagonists is human! Clarke has instead populated his stories with quite believable aliens, at once strange and sympathetic. Here is a decided switch from the xenophobic horrors that typified the old pulps.

In a different vein, we have "Mimsy Were the Borogroves," written by Henry Kuttner under the pseudonym of Lewis Padgett. In this quietly chilling story, Kuttner explores the nature of learning, and the relationship of world and mind. He probes the question of what is known, how we come to know it, and how our acquired perceptual habits define and limit our world. Throughout, the innate terror remains, but the writer is free to develop a striking and thoughtful chain of reasoning in the same story.

These are only two examples of the new spirit that swept through science fiction at the time. In this collection, you will find many more tributes to the guiding force of John W. Campbell and to the incredibly fertile period that he helped to usher in.

From a thirty years vantage point, it is uncanny to witness the accuracy with which the social and psychological concerns of America in the fifties were anticipated in the mid-forties. It is in the nature of science fiction to try to foretell the mood (if not the specific situations) of the future and to reflect the unspoken anxieties of the times. From the tongue-in-cheek "Housing Shortage," to the apocalyptic "Nightmare," the stories in this book plainly portray the buoyant hopes and hidden fears of the postwar generation. Although the majority of these tales appeared before the war's end, we can already see a strong foretaste of the Cold War paranoia which was to sweep the country in the coming decade. Distrust—whether of one's fellow man, oneself, or the awesome possibilities of the new technology—is a common theme. The Pandora's box opened over Hiroshima had unleashed demons, which science fiction immediately perceived and struggled to exorcise. The image of technology as uncontrolled—and uncontrollable—appears in "With Folded Hands," "The Last Objective," and "The Figure," to name but a few. The war-weary world was trying to pick up the pieces, but it lacked any assurance that they would ever fit together again. And although events happily did

FOREWORD

not come to pass as these stories suggest, the feelings captured became a part of our lives.

Thus it is that this collection is special in two ways. First, for what it shows about the development of science fiction at a very crucial epoch in its history. Second, for what it was able to show about our own inner concerns, about our desires and despairs, and about how we faced them. But the most important value lies within the stories themselves and is as new and challenging to us now as the day this volume first hit the bookstore. Here are thirty tales of wonder, of speculation about the nature and meaning of man, of glimpses of what might have been and what might still be. Enter into the special worlds presented in these pages, warily and with marvel.

R. Scott Latham
New York, 1979

INTRODUCTION

IT WAS not until after THE BEST OF SCIENCE FICTION had been published, two years ago, that I realized how far the science fiction epidemic had gone. Nearly the whole population, it seemed to me, was infected. Friends in droves—solid citizens with both feet firmly planted on Terra —blushingly admitted that they had been fans for years. Correspondents all the way from Augusta, Maine to Tokyo, Japan, from Nome, Alaska to Rome, Italy, wrote to thank me for putting their hobby on a "recognized basis." Neophytes discovering science fiction for the first time through the volume wrote paeans of praise for the introduction to new worlds that it gave them.

With all this exhibition of interest to inspire me, I can hardly be blamed for following up with a second collection. For one thing, the dimensions of the first book, being limited by the exigencies of publishing economics, forced me to omit some scintillating items which should have been included in it. *No Woman Born,* the C. L. Moore masterpiece, is an example. D. D. Sharp's sinister *Eternal Man* is another—this one from way back in the pre-Hiroshima, or archaic, period of science fiction.

For another, many correspondents recommended stories I had not discovered myself—stories like Oscar Friend's *Of Jovian Build,* the chiller about a resuscitated giant from Jupiter, and Polton Cross's disquieting *Wings across the Cosmos.* Yarns such as these could not be left lying forgotten in the deciduous backfiles of the science fiction pulps. They deserved a better fate.

But there is still another reason why I think a new science fiction anthology is due. Today science fiction is in the air—literally. As I write, the newspapers are carrying accounts of an event which, ten or fifteen years ago, would have been greeted with polite incredulity by all but hardened science fiction fans: the flight at nearly 600 miles an hour—a mile every six seconds—of a jet-propelled Army plane. At that speed, the imaginary dream of "circumnavigating the globe in forty hours" is a frightening reality—and at the Equator, too; not around the receding forehead of the globe, as most world aero-navigators are accustomed to go. It is pure science fiction!

Not only in the field of aviation is the impossible happening. In many other branches of science and engineering, developments are daily being announced in the press which give people a feeling that anything —absolutely anything—can happen. Well, the place where anything *does* happen is in science fiction. For those who have had their imaginations titivated by the innumerable new wonders of science, from bouncing sand (the silicones) to messages to the moon (radar-reflections), science fiction is likely to prove an enthralling extension of the possible. Weirdly intriguing reading in any case, but even more intriguing these days when the impossible is catching up with the probable, and both are hard on the heels of the achieved.

II.

Meanwhile, what has been going on in the realm of science fiction itself since my first collection came out in the spring of 1946? Mostly, I am glad to report, just the same sort of exploration of the undiscovered as before. The expert SF writers have continued to delve in the Unknown in their accustomed fashion, and have brought back some really novel examples of imaginary reality. An adequate cross-section of their latest reports is, I believe, presented between the covers of this book.

In two particulars, moreover, the present collection may be said to take a few hesitant steps beyond the boundaries established in the first anthology. Two years ago I remarked upon the paucity of stories dealing with the social sciences and with the science of the mind. A few narratives of this type had been written, true, and one or two appeared in THE BEST OF SCIENCE FICTION. But since then, they have been proliferating rapidly; science fiction writers have begun to probe into both these fields with vigor.

Take stories of the possible powers of the human brain. It is a great deal easier to explore the supposititious planets of Sirius in the imagination than it is to investigate the areas of the brain which medical science tells us seem to have no useful function—areas which can be removed without affecting the *present* activities of the human organism to any noticeable extent. What is all that gray matter for? What capacities, senses, abilities are still to be developed within that now amorphous mass of tissue? I am pleased to report that a few brave writers are beginning to look into the possibilities of the whole mind—though none as yet have gone as far as did that eminent science fiction author, George Bernard Shaw, in his *Back to Methuselah* twenty-five years ago. But a beginning has been made—as witness Raymond Jones' *The Person from Porlock,* or—on a grimmer level—Anderson's and Waldrop's *Tomorrow's Children.*

Or take the much larger, more inchoate "brain," the social organism. In the past, stories about social organization were likely to fall into the class of dream Utopia, in which science appeared only as a mess of super-gadgets, or did not appear at all. *The Flight of the Dawn Star* by Robert Moore Williams, for example, is a very pretty approach to the social science field via the Utopia; but today we have few such tales.

Probably the times are too awry for truly creative stories about the possibilities of the social sciences. These days we are in a period of world upheaval which reflects itself in the field of science fiction as social criticism, or social prophecy, rather than social creation. Indeed, habitual readers of the science fiction pulps are beginning to complain that they are "tired of a steady diet of war and desolation." The point is that many SF writers are feeling the urgent need for social controls over our physical powers, and the only outlet they have for their feelings is in writing stories of what the lack of such controls may mean to civilization—"war and desolation." Chan Davis' *The Nightmare* is a story of a near-miss at such desolation; Paul Carter's *The Last Objective* really sets you down right where the war and desolation are at their worst; and Edward Grendon's *The Figure* and H. F. Heard's subtly optimistic *The Great Fog* shows you what may come after.

These and a few others in this collection are stories in the social science field which should give the reader pause. That is why they were written. However, the great majority of the yarns you are about to read have been put down on paper solely to entertain you, and to provide you with some rugged exercises for your imagination. In the long run, those are the major purposes of the art. And if you do enjoy this book, if you get from it a few hours' relaxation from the tensions of modern living, its reasons for being will have been justified.

III.

My thanks are again due to the Library of Congress for the courteous assistance of its curators of ephemera; to Mr. Julius Unger of Brooklyn, New York, purveyor extraordinary of out-of-print science fiction magazines, for obtaining for me some early and excessively rare issues of *Amazing Stories* and *Wonder Stories;* and to Mr. Edmund Fuller, of Crown Publishers, for taking much of the detail work incident to preparing this book for the press off my hands.

GROFF CONKLIN

Washington, D. C.
March, 1948

A TREASURY OF **SCIENCE FICTION**

PART ONE

The Atom and After

THE NIGHTMARE

ROB CICCONE bent down, picked up the bottle of milk outside the door of his apartment, and started to pick up the paper beside it. When he saw the headline that topped two columns on the left-hand side of the front page, he hesitated. Then he stood up and wiped his forehead.

The morning newspaper is essentially a simple, ordinary, and familiar thing. It's a habit. But it doesn't seem quite so ordinary and familiar when you see your name in black type at the top of page one.

Rob picked up the paper and went back into the flat to read it. With forced deliberation, he slowly sat down in the most relaxing chair available and spread the paper carefully before starting the article. He was worried. As far as he knew there was no reason for him to be on page one. He did not belong there. He had, to be sure, been one of the speakers at the S.N.P. chapter meeting last night, but he had been planning to look for that write-up on page twenty-six or thereabouts. Worse, Rob's job was one of those in which you do not make page one in the New York *Dispatch*, or any other paper, unless it is bad news, and very bad.

He began to read, then the worry gave way to puzzlement. It was the report of the meeting after all, and carried, as he had expected, the by-line of his friend Creighton Macomb. It ran:

CICCONE FLAYS CITY'S GEIGER SEARCH POLICY; WARNS PERIL GROWS

> Dr. Robert A. Ciccone, chief of the Bronx Sector Radioactive Search Commission, stated last night that the present system of Geiger-counter search would not be adequate for the prevention of an A-bomb being planted in the New York area. Addressing the Bronx Chapter of the Society of Nuclear Physicists, he said: "No number of successes in preventing the importing of dangerous radioactives can compensate for just one failure, and I feel unable to state positively that failure, and disastrous failure, is impossible."

So far so good, thought Rob. At least they were quoting directly. Of course the sentence quoted was the most outspoken of the whole thing;

it read like a much stronger attack on the search program than he had actually dared to make.

But the same thing had been said before by others. Ten years before, when the Geiger search had first been brought up as a counter-proposal to the Compton plan of decentralization, the whole subject had been batted back and forth in the press. Opponents of the search system, himself included, had claimed that New York was a sitting target for an atomic bomb, that no preventive measures could change that fact, and that the only answer to the danger was to scatter New York's industries and commerce over as wide an area as possible. The other party had pooh-poohed this warning, pointing to the U.N.O. Security Council's strict supervision of all the world's piles, and to the greatly improved methods for the detection of radioactives. Finally, the second party had won. And since that time even the most extreme alarmists had been given less and less newspaper space. He had thought his speech would be played down, interpreted as a suggestion that search methods be improved. Instead—this. Why?

He read the remainder of the article hurriedly. It was O.K. Accurately reported, without editorializing. But it didn't answer his question.

He thought of calling Crate Macomb, but looked at his watch and decided he'd have to wait. All through dressing, shaving, and breakfast, he was too preoccupied either to finish the paper or to give any thought to the rather suspicious results of some of the recent searches. Which in itself was unusual, for normally results that were not thoroughly innocuous were enough to take his mind off anything else.

At 8:15, when he was ready to leave for work, he dialed the *Dispatch*, gave an extension number.

"Could I speak to Macomb? That you, Crate?"

"Yeah. Hello, Rob." Macomb sounded ill at ease.

"I . . . er . . . I just called up to congratulate you on making the front page. Congratulate myself, too, of course."

"Congratulate—?" He sounded puzzled.

"That terrific billing I got in the paper this morning. I've got to admit I don't understand it. New editorial policy?"

"Oh, I get it. You've only seen the home edition, not the later editions."

"That's right. What have the later editions got?"

"Well, I'll tell you the whole thing." He dropped his voice. "The City Ed and I have been against this Geiger system right along, and looking for chances to slip through stories slanted against it."

"I thought you gave that up."

"I gave up bucking editorial policy openly, because it wasn't healthy, but I thought I'd take a chance on this story. The City Ed got it past His Nibs without too much trouble, it made the first edition O.K., and we thought the thing would come off. But—"

"Yeah, but. I knew that was coming. What about those later editions?"

"That's the catch, all right. You remember what you told me last night before the meeting? About the aerial radioactivity your boys found over the Bronx yesterday?"

"You didn't let that into print, did you?"

"*I* didn't, no. I know well enough that radioactivity in the air might be either chance air currents from the Oswego pile, or hidden radioactives around the city, and whichever it is I know darn well that telling the people about it right away is the worst thing to do. Even if I had submitted copy on it, I wouldn't have expected it to get past the editor. But some cub reporter got the dope from the man who took the aerial tests, and didn't know any better than to submit it."

"And they ran it."

"And they ran it, yes." Crate paused, and said slowly: "They ran it in the same article with a rewritten version of what you read in the first edition."

"I can imagine . . . His Nibs couldn't recall the edition that featured my statement, so he set out to discredit me."

"That's it. It could be much worse." Crate's tone of voice indicated what he meant. He meant, "Probably it *will* be much worse."

Rob stopped to let the implications sink in. Finally, "Has the news started a panic in the Bronx? The news of the tests, I mean."

"Not yet. Look, Rob. His Nibs doesn't know I was responsible for the slant in the original offense this morning; he's blaming it on the City Ed. He doesn't know I know you personally, either. He does know I graduated in nuclear physics. So he's assigning me to—write a feature on you. Not a build-up."

"*Whew*— So?"

"So I'll have to do the best I can. So I'd appreciate it if I could see you some time soon and talk the whole thing over. I can tell you more then."

That certainly seemed to be in order, to put it mildly. Rob named a cafeteria near the *Dispatch* Building, promised to be right down, and rang off.

On his way to the subway station he picked up a *Dispatch*. He was still on the front page, and, as Crate had indicated, the treatment of him was rather different. He had not merely addressed the Society of Nuclear Physicists; in this edition he had done much more. He had failed his trust as Sector Search Commissioner. The high aerial radioactivity indicated that an A-bomb was being assembled somewhere in his sector, although his search groups had failed to detect the importing of the bomb materials. It was hinted that the reason he had stressed, in his speech, the impossibility of adequate searches, was to cover up his own incompetence when news of his failure broke.

The slur, he reflected, would probably not hurt him much. His job was not political, and if he were incompetent no amount of fast talking would help him. Conversely, the press couldn't hurt him, outside of discrediting his statement. Still, you had to be careful not to underestimate the power of the press.

The other angle was much more important. Suppose the paper's first charge were right. Suppose that yesterday's test results had been more than chance, and that for some reason, maybe for the purpose of building a bomb, radioactives really had been smuggled into his sector. He wouldn't try to guess who might be doing it; he didn't know politics. But the thing was possible. Well?

Before meeting Crate, he slipped into a phone booth and held a conversation—consisting chiefly of code phrases—with the Bronx Sector headquarters. When it was done he hurried into the cafeteria and spotted Macomb. He asked abruptly, "Your car in town today?"

"Yes, it is."

"The usual parking lot?"

"Yeah."

"Good. We'd better go uptown right away." Macomb came without question.

"I just phoned Charlie. They're still getting the same results, a little bit stronger, and consistent. The wind's changed to east, and the meteorologist says if the readings keep coming this way another hour there's no chance that it's a false alarm. They really should have got in touch with me earlier, but as it is I'll have to get there as quickly as I can."

"This takes precedence over everything else, all right."

"It takes precedence over just about anything in the whole city, if it's not a false alarm. Anyhow," he added as they climbed into the car, "you're not skipping out on your assignment. If you're going to succeed in getting a story on my incompetence, here's your chance, and I certainly hope I disappoint you."

They cut west toward Riverside Drive, Macomb at the wheel. When they were on the Drive, Ciccone asked suddenly, "Who runs the *Dispatch*, anyway?"

"The Ed does a pretty fair job."

"Yes, but . . . you told me once the Ed takes orders from somebody."

The other laughed. "Things aren't as simple as that in the newspaper racket. Nobody gives orders. But if any one man determines the policies of the paper, I guess it's Ellsworth Bates."

Ellsworth Bates. Ciccone ran over in his mind what he knew of the man. Bates was not, to the public, a prominent name. On the society page it was inconspicuous. In political news the name seldom appeared. Even in business news it ordinarily occurred only in listings of corporation boards. Yet apparently behind the scenes this Bates was a power; Macomb certainly should know.

"I was thinking," Rob went on. "Suppose for a minute a bomb is being assembled, and suppose Bates is connected with it. Wouldn't that explain what happened this morning?"

"Why—"

"First, he may succeed in confusing our sector organization by slinging mud at me. Second, he may confuse the whole borough by starting a panic. Third, he would surely jump on anything that might talk the public into decentralization; he'd want the city to remain a good, highly localized target. The decentralization issue was what started all this, remember."

"Hm-m-m. Sounds plausible at first, but—forget it. Not a chance of it. Nobody with Bates' financial interests in the city is going to try to destroy it, and that rules out not only Bates but anyone else with the power to high-pressure into print a slam against you. Besides—this bomb scare might start a panic among the populace, but on the other hand it puts the squeeze on the Search Commission, making sure they'll act as quickly and as efficiently as they can. No, forget it."

"Still, for whatever reason, Bates is probably back of His Nibs' policy."

"It'd be a good guess, all right."

"And why," Rob said, half to himself, "does he go to such lengths to slap down anybody who speaks out for decentralization?"

They sped north along the Drive. Ahead of them was the Highway Search Station, where extrasensitive detectors would scan them, and, in case they revealed radioactivity, would operate relays, causing the car to be photographed and an alarm bell to be rung. Ciccone had been caught more than once; the detectors were so sensitive that small amounts of natural uranium adhering to his clothes and shoes after lab work could sometimes actuate them. This time they got past without the Search Commission's police giving chase.

They were now in the Bronx Sector. "Where to?" asked Crate.

"Just a minute. If you'll get off the Drive and stop at the next drugstore, I'll give Charlie another ring."

"Use my radiophone if you want."

"We avoid 'em. Easier to intercept them than it is to tap ordinary phone wires."

"O.K." Macomb acceded to Rob's request.

Another coded phone conversation and Ciccone returned to the car, to give a few brief directions. "We're going to look over Import Station Three," he explained. "There are two ways we might track this thing down. The first is to localize the source of the active gases by testing more air samples at a lower altitude. They're going ahead with that, and there's not much I can do to help. The second, assuming that bomb materials are still being shipped in, is to check the import stations through which all trucking passes."

"You sound pretty certain that it is a bomb."

"Without having any idea who would want to build one here and now, I'd say the probability was about twenty-five percent and growing all the time."

Unconsciously, Macomb gave the car another ten miles an hour's worth of gas.

Traffic was light, and they made good time to the import station. As they entered the vast, warehouselike building, Rob said: "I thought this'd be the station to inspect because those aerial tests seem to localize the thing between ten and fifty blocks northwest of here. Normally I wouldn't suspect this station of having a leak; they have the best equipment of any. They even make chemical analyses of samples of any cadmium that passes through."

"Cadmium? Why?"

"It's one way you might shield U-235 from the radiation detectors. Alloy it with plenty of cadmium and no neutrons get out. Just one of the dodges we have to be prepared for."

Inside the building, three lines of trucks were being sent slowly through what resembled roughly an assembly line. First the walls of the truck would be tested to insure that they were not radiation-absorbent, then a few of the crates, chosen at random, would be broken open and inspected in the same way. Following this, the truck would be driven slowly down a long double line of confusingly different instruments, and would wait until it had been given the green light by the operators of all the instruments before it proceeded into the Sector. By this time the next truck would have finished its preliminary inspection and would be ready to roll through.

The most important of the detectors were modifications of the familiar Geiger-Mueller counter. An alpha particle, proton, or other emission would ionize the gas between two charged plates, allowing discharge. The discharges would be stored on a condenser, which in turn discharged through a glow tube if the counter operated more than a certain number of times in a given interval.

Ciccone and Macomb stood at one corner of the floor watching the procedure. Ciccone said: "It's not as effective as you might think. The stuff might be brought through here by packing it in the middle boxes of a big truckload, where the outside boxes would shield it. Those guys don't dig down and get at the inside often enough."

"I should think this'd be one job where they'd be more than willing to do a little extra work just to make sure."

"No, people aren't that way. It's a lot of work to half-unload one of those trucks. This is just a job to most of the men, no matter how hard we try to make it something more; it's just their job, and they make it as easy for themselves as they can.

"Today they're being pretty thorough, though; when I called Charlie I told him to needle the boys up a bit."

"So I see." A large Diesel crane was being used in one of the assembly lines to remove the contents of one truck for individual testing. Several men were clustered around with hand-test sets. In a few minutes Rob went over, motioning Crate to accompany him.

"One thing," he whispered on the way, "whatever you see, don't act more than normally suspicious. You can't forget the possibility that the truck driver, or even one of our men, might be an agent. Hello, Sam. What you got here?"

"Radium dial watches. Darn things scare the pants off us every time. Compared to the little tiny bloops we get on our meters from most of this stuff, they look like Hiroshima."

"Been getting many?"

"Yeah, a good few."

"I hope you check the inside boxes pretty often to make sure the watches' emissions aren't masking something else underneath."

"Yeah, we've been doing that."

"Well." Rob looked down at the one crate out of the truckload which contained the watches. It had been opened, and several of the carefully packed boxes removed. An idea struck him, and he mentally noted the address on the crate, while apparently examining the watches. The watches were a standard American make.

"Well, keep up the good work, Sam," he said casually. "Oh, Sam. Have you seen the *Dispatch* this morning?"

"No, why?"

"Never mind." After watching a few more trucks pass uneventfully by, he left, accompanied by Macomb.

"Anson Mercantile Company," he said pensively as they climbed back into the car; "no street or number given. As I remember, it's about ten blocks west and four north. Suppose you let me drive, I think I can find it. If I have to, I'll ask a cop, but I didn't want to ask in there."

He did not have to ask a cop. At Anson's, the two of them looked enough like retailers to get into a salesman's office without delay. Rob interrupted the salesman's commercial cordiality by showing an F.B.I. badge, then asked without explanation, "Who's buying up that shipment of watches that's just coming in?"

"Why—let's see. I don't believe they're all ordered yet." He showed no inclination to continue.

"Who buys watches from you?" Rob prompted.

"Well—" The man listed several jewelry and department stores. "Those are the principal ones."

This was not going to be quite as simple as Rob had hoped. "Have any of them specified any individual shipments, rather than just naming brands?"

"I wouldn't know. I don't have anything to do with—'

"I think you know."

"What is this about, anyway?"

Rob debated whether to fib or to bully the man with his F.B.I.

badge; he decided on the former course. "There's been some highjacking of watches, and we're trying to track it down." It didn't sound at all plausible, but the man, though baffled, was apparently satisfied.

"Well, now that you mention it," he admitted, "Grelner's has specified shipments several times." He stopped, tentatively.

"That's all," said Ciccone, and he and Macomb left, trying to look like G-men.

"Well," commented Rob, "I guess we can assume for now that he was telling the truth."

"Might I ask you something, sir?"

"Ask me what?"

"The same thing that fellow in there asked you: what the heck is this all about?"

Rob laughed. "I'm sorry. Those watches looked pretty innocent, didn't they, to be causing all this? But we have to follow up the implausible leads, because all the plausible ones get investigated at the import station. This one is 'highly nontrivial,' as my math prof used to say.

"Look. We let radium dial watches through the import station because no one could possibly extract the fissionable substances from the phosphorescent paint on those things without revealing themselves— even if they could get enough into the city that way. But there's another possibility. What if, instead of natural uranium, you were to use Pu-239, ordinary plutonium, in your phosphorescent paint? It's an alpha-emitter with long half-life, like common U-238; our instruments couldn't tell the difference. You'd have the job of purifying after you got the stuff in, and you'd have to get in an awful lot. It's just possible, just barely. And all the probable things, as I say, are checked."

"But it'd take so long to accumulate enough plutonium for a bomb. They couldn't be anywhere finished now, could they?"

"Sure could. They could have been accumulating the stuff for years without giving themselves away. It wouldn't be until they started purifying that Sneezy—the aerial radioactivity detector—would show anything. That's happened. We'd better follow up on Grelner's, and if it's not that, we'll start looking around again. Grelner's did, after all, ask for particular shipments—those shipments, maybe, that they knew were loaded with plutonium. They wouldn't buy up the whole shipment, because that would seem peculiar to the wholesalers, and the Pu-239 watches are, I suppose, perfectly usable as such. They wouldn't ship the watches in direct to the store, because it's not usual business practice.

"Everything fits. Which in itself proves nothing. Still, we can't afford not to check it. I don't think I can get much farther with this investigating, I'd better order a search right now." They had been walking toward the store; now Rob started once more for a phone. "You call police, give my name and the code word 'antipasto,' and say 'Grelner's Department Store.' I'll be calling the import station for some detectors."

Luckily Schmidt's Drugstore had two empty phone booths. Nobody looked up as they walked in and slipped into the booths.

Ciccone, as he dialed his number, had a sudden vision. A pillar of multicolored smoke rising from the city, erasing the Bronx and Manhattan down to Central Park, shattering windows in Nyack, lighting up the Albany sky. A nightmare, a familiar and a very real nightmare, an accepted part of modern life, something you couldn't get away from; and it seemed more immediate than ever right now. Trying to pretend it was just fancy, he looked out of the booth at the girl wiping off the drugstore counter, the middle-aged woman buying toothbrushes, the suspendered loafer thumbing through the magazines. He thought the commonplaceness of Schmidt's Drugstore might be reassuring; but it didn't help.

"Import Station Three."

"This is Ciccone. Could I speak to Sam?"

Again he waited. The nightmare was still there, and somewhere, quite likely just a few blocks from where he was now, were the few ounces of metal that might be the nightmare.

"Hello. Hello, Sam. Send down—*antipasto*—send down all your mobiles, except for one full battery to be left at the station. Grelner's Department Store. Know where it is?"

"Sure do. Right down." Sam hung up before Rob had a chance to tell him to hurry. He knew that an order like that, in a situation like that, just plain meant "hurry," in capital letters.

Hurry. It might already be too late, or they might have months to spare, or there might be no danger at all. Yet the chance was always there that one minute's delay might make all the difference.

Always that chance, he thought as he and Macomb walked up the innocent-looking street toward where the police and the search men would soon arrive. The chance that the time he had wasted at the meeting last night, and the hour he had wasted this morning because of that peculiar newspaper episode, might themselves have been fatal.

"And yet," he said aloud, "assuming we get to this bomb in time—always assuming that—this man Ellsworth Bates, and whoever else he represents, may be more important than any one bomb. No number of successes can compensate for one failure—"

Crate interrupted him. "The police have started arriving!"

Ciccone knew the routine of the search; he'd been largely responsible for preparing police and search men alike for this eventuality. He knew perfectly well what had to be done, and he also knew that, since the organization was trained to function without him, there was little he could do besides helping with the details.

First a cordon had to be thrown around the block in as short a time as possible after giving the alarm. Plutonium, enough of it to make a bomb, could be taken from the block in a two-passenger coupé, or in the pockets of a few men willing to subject themselves to radioactive poisoning by carrying it inadequately shielded. So the police had to make sure that, for the present, everybody inside the cordon stayed inside.

The search men arrived not long after the police: a fleet of bizarre-looking, specially-built trucks, roaring through the city with sirens screaming, then pulling up in a group at one side of the block. The mobile search units made up a respectable detection laboratory in themselves. They carried, in addition to the larger, more sensitive instruments, enough simple handtest sets to arm a large force of searchers. Some of these were distributed quickly to the policemen comprising the cordon, and the first part of the search began.

A bluecoat would beckon to one of the bewildered passers-by who had been caught in the cordon, and then, while a second policeman covered him, would search the man. This consisted in passing two test sets, one held in either hand, over all parts of his body; reading them and pressing a button to recharge the electroscopes and readjust the counters' potential; and frisking him in the standard manner. He would then be allowed—ordered, rather—to leave the block. In this way the sidewalks were rapidly cleared.

Macomb left Rob's side, pad and pencil in hand, to go to where a short, well-dressed man of about sixty was being searched by two bored policemen. Rob dismissed Macomb with the mental comment, "Good story for him."

Himself, he wanted to help with the big job: going through the buildings on the block, one by one, story by story, with every type of instrument from Geiger counter to uranium neutron-detector. It was a big job, it would take a lot of men a long time, and he knew they could use his help.

The detectors were already being unloaded from the trucks. Sam was organizing a group of about twenty search men to begin on the row of five- and six-story apartments that made up one side of the block.

"Say, Sam," began Rob.

"Oh, there you are," said Sam.

"I didn't see you; I was beginning to think that call was a fake. Have a counter."

"Say, Sam, why don't you start at the store itself?"

"The Sneezies are registering like hell right here—like all hell." He gave a few more instructions and the men scattered into the buildings.

Ciccone found it almost a relief to know that the source of the radioactivity had been located fairly closely. Now, all the uncertainties involved in his reasoning were resolved. It might have been that Grelner's, like the wholesaler's, was just an intermediate stage in the smuggling; it might have been that the whole lead was a false one. But it wasn't.

With Sam and one other, he started down the basement steps of the first apartment house, to begin the search at the bottom. One of the tenants was coming down from the second story and looked with amazed curiosity at their test sets and drawn guns. Sam waved him out onto the street, and the three of them continued on down.

But the tedious and dangerous hunt which they had anticipated was interrupted. Suddenly, a booming voice filled the air. Rob looked around for a loudspeaker, but, seeing none, concentrated on the words.

"You are looking," the voice said, with a slight foreign intonation, "for the bomb which is being assembled here. I would warn that we have a quantity of plutonium in excess of the critical mass. If any more men enter this block of buildings, or if anyone enters this particular building, then the bomb, which is in readiness, will be exploded."

Rob, followed by the others, ran out into the street. He didn't know why, but he felt an almost claustrophobic oppression on the apartment stairway. As if getting out of the building would do any good were an A-bomb to go off!

The voice from the hidden loudspeakers continued, to a petrified audience of policemen and search men: "We will leave our laboratory, which is that building formerly used as a warehouse by the Grelner's Store, by helicopter. You must not attempt to intercept us—"

Rob was standing beside the police captain, looking up at the expressionless row of apartment houses. The decision, he realized, was up to him. Was this a bluff, and dare they call it?

"—will, in any case, be detonated by radio in two weeks. This will give you time to largely clear the area, and the bomb will still accomplish our purpose of disruption. You must not interfere, and you must prepare for the explosion in exactly two weeks' time." A pause, then, "You are looking for the bomb which is being assembled here. I would warn—"

It was a record, and it was repeating. The whole message was in Ciccone's hands now; it was up to him. He looked nervously around him. The police captain, Macomb, and the short, well-dressed old man to whom Macomb had gone earlier—Ciccone hardly saw them.

"—enters this particular building, then the bomb, which is in readiness, will be exploded. We will leave our laboratory—"

"It's a bluff," said Ciccone, and his voice sounded weak as death. "Enter the building."

The captain didn't move, but stared straight ahead, his jaw knotted.

"It's a bluff. If they were going to set off an A-bomb, they wouldn't give us the opportunity to clear the people out of the city, even those few people we could get out in two weeks. They'd try for maximum destruction.

"Either they're not ready, or they are and we've nothing left to lose. Enter the building."

"They're not ready," said a voice behind Rob. He turned; it was Macomb's companion. "Any group which would send agents to destroy New York, would plan that the agents also be destroyed. Thus any chance would be eliminated of this country's learning the identity of the group, and they might be spared retaliation. Only if the bomb could not be detonated would such a bluff as this be attempted, on the chance that a copter might escape."

Rob stared at the unknown in dumb amazement. The confidence and precision with which he had spoken were—inhuman.

But for the moment he ignored this remarkable interruption and turned once more to the captain. The latter's face had a look almost of resignation as he finally gave the necessary orders to about twenty of the policemen who lined the sidewalk. They hesitated; they, too, could hear that voice over the loudspeaker. "—will still accomplish our purpose of disruption. You must not interfere, and you must prepare for the explosion—"

Somehow, when the first of the policemen moved to obey, the others followed. Slowly they advanced toward a gap between two buildings, through which they could reach the spot the voice had named as the laboratory site.

"—that we have a quantity of plutonium in excess of the critical mass. If any more men enter this block of buildings—"

They advanced, and one by one disappeared through the gap. Ciccone waited. Maybe the men inside, whoever they were, had not observed the violation of their conditions. Yet.

Except for the loudspeaker, the whole street was in intolerable silence, as everyone—waited. Finally, as one, they relaxed and breathed more easily. It was not that they were absolutely certain yet that no bomb would go off, but simply that the tension could not be borne any longer.

The police captain turned to his car radio.

"In case those boys do get their helicopter off that roof," he said, "I'm going to call for some of our planes to intercept them."

Rob made a mental note to have planes added to the search plan in the future, and nodded assent.

"No," Macomb's companion interjected. "It was a bluff, but you must allow them to escape."

Rob's previous amazement was redoubled. He could find no answer except to blurt, "Who are you, anyway?"

"Ellsworth Bates."

Before Ciccone could reply, all eyes were turned upward by a shout from one of the search men standing nearby. A helicopter was hovering above the apartment buildings, drifting slightly in the wind, and rising.

The captain turned again to his radio, but was halted by the urgency in Bates' voice as he repeated: "No, they must escape. If they are captured, it will be discovered whom they represent, and this country will certainly open fire in retaliation. Every trace of their identity must be lost if there's going to be any chance of peace. Don't you see? It doesn't matter that they are the aggressors, that we, in a sense, would be in the right were we to fight them—whoever they are. The only thing we must consider is the impossibility of our fighting any war with anybody, now. Unfortunately, it's a thing our government, and our people, will probably not consider if these men are identified.

"The whole thing can be reported to the Security Council. They can investigate—secretly. The United States must not investigate."

He paused. "Sabotage bomb attack is the only method of atomic warfare that can be used as long as the Security Council controls the world's atomic power. Fissionable elements are rigidly controlled, they're hard to get, no one can get enough of them away from the Security Council's jurisdiction to arm a fleet of rockets. And a fleet is what you'd need to stand a chance of getting through a modern radar-rocket defense screen. Sabotage bomb attack is the only thing left.

"Until open warfare breaks out. Then, one or both of the warring nations defy the Security Council, grab all the fissionable elements they can, and what have you? Chaos. Ruin. If you like to put it that way, the end of civilization. Once the Security Council's power is broken and the rocket-atomic war starts, we're lost, that's all.

"Mr. Ciccone, I realize you're in charge here, and I'm unable to force your decision. Nevertheless, you've *got* to let that copter get away— delay your pursuit, say, ten minutes, and don't make it seem deliberate. More than that, you've got to destroy the evidence in that building— again accidentally—and, if possible, destroy so much that it can't be proved a bomb was ever in the process of construction."

He stopped. Rob looked up to where the helicopter was dwindling into the distance. "Mr. Bates, if there has been one bomb, there can be another, maybe from the same source."

"No number of successes can make up for one failure. Precisely. But we wouldn't avert that possible failure by tracing down this bomb attempt. We'd precipitate it.

"Granted, we'd find the culprit's identity. But after the cities of this and every other country had been destroyed, it'd be small consolation to know who started the thing."

Then something happened inside Rob, and the nightmare was on him again. The light too bright to be seen, the sound too loud to be heard, the horror too great for any man to know. He sighed, and spoke to the captain:

"You heard what he said?"

"Yes."

"Do what he said about the helicopter. The rest of it, forget. I mean that—forget it."

Ciccone sat with Macomb and Bates in the front room of Crate's Greenwich Village flat, recounting the steps he had taken to follow Bates' plan. "It may work out," he said. "No one's been all the way inside the lab yet, except Sam and me. The lab will be accidentally destroyed tonight, after the plutonium has been removed and Sam has seen plenty of things which were not there at all. And, Mr. Bates, if your spell over the newspapers is as great as Macomb says it is, they may all print our version of the story." He indicated a *Dispatch* extra in his hand. "The radioactives were brought in by private experimenters dodging the U.N.O., they tried the bomb bluff in order to escape, and they then eluded police pursuers. No matter how much perjuring we do it's a weak story."

"No," replied Bates, "with a few loopholes patched up, it'll go. If we're long on theorizing and minimize the actual faking; we'll get our result without much risk. And don't worry about the perjury; this is one end that justifies any means."

There was a silence while Ciccone gathered his courage. Bates was no longer the evil genius he had seemed earlier in the day; nevertheless courage was required to begin, "So now we have one success—we've postponed the fatal failure a little further."

Bates smiled. "Unless I miss my guess, you're getting back to decentralization."

Macomb took up the theme. "Yes," he said, "that problem's still there. This bomb's been found, this crisis may soon be over; but there'll be others. We'll never have even relative safety until everything is so uniformly distributed that no one bomb can destroy more than one of the old block-busters could now."

"I'll try to explain the thing to you," Bates began slowly. "You're right, that would be the only way to safety. You're also right in thinking that I've been suppressing the movement toward decentralization. Now wait a minute; please don't interrupt. I know I seem to be contradicting myself, but let me start from the beginning.

"Ten years ago several of the smaller European nations, which had not been getting much information on nuclear physics from the larger nations, independently developed working chain-reactions. Tension mounted, and a large-scale atomic war might have resulted had not the world been too exhausted from the recent World War II. As it was, everybody got such a bad case of the jitters that the affair was halted before the A-bomb was used.

"This world-wide case of the jitters had other effects, you remember. The Security Council was quickly given supervision over all piles, plus sizable military and intelligence forces. Second, the movement for decentralization was started."

"And stopped," put in Ciccone.

"Yes. To what, if I may ask, did you ascribe its failure?"

"Lack of vision on the part of—well, leaders of industry. People like you could have swung it."

"No. The people whom you call leaders of industry saw everything you saw in the situation, and they did try to swing it. The thing is, when they got right down to cases they saw something you missed; to be specific, they saw that decentralization was impossible."

"Impossible?"

"Because of a factor which the scientist finds it easy to ignore: the terrific inertia of our civilization. Here's the way it works. New York businessmen see that the world would be a much safer place if all business were to disperse away from the big metropolitan centers. They think it would be fine if this were to be done. But they can't do it themselves if, say, Prague businessmen are going to remain concentrated, because it'd be a big financial blow to New York to stand the expense of moving and to give up their ready access to transportation. They wouldn't be able to compete with Prague, or London, or Calcutta, as the case might be—whatever city didn't go along. Unless everybody will take the step, nobody will take it. It has to be world-wide, and ten years ago the world wasn't unified enough.

"You remember the 1929 crash? A little before your time, I guess. It was the same thing. The economists saw it coming several years ahead, but no one could duck out of the wave of overinvestment, because if they did, their competitors would not, and would continue to make profits from the boom. Everyone had to keep riding the wave as long as possible, even though they knew such a policy was just insuring that the crash, when it came, would be really serious. There you are: inertia. Our overgrown civilization starts going in one direction, and it's just too much for individuals to stop.

"So decentralization was impossible ten years ago. With different conditions and with a stronger political movement, it might have gone; but it didn't. We took what seemed like the next best plan, radar screens plus search programs, and so far it's worked.

"Today, gradual decentralization has progressed to some extent, thanks to improved transportation and individuals' mistrust of cities. A new movement for the abrupt sort of decentralization would have some chance—less inertia now to overcome; but if it succeeded it would be very dangerous.

"In the last ten years, many things have changed. Reconstruction of the destruction of World War II is to all intents and purposes finished; capital is freed and looking for new investment opportunities; manufactured goods are looking around for markets. It's the type of situation where motives for aggression may be present, and everyone's jittery again. The jitters are not nearly so widespread as they were before, or even as they were after Hiroshima and Nagasaki, but they're having a much worse effect, and they're building up. Certain groups in several different countries are beginning to think seriously of atomic warfare, of beating the other guy to the punch and grabbing whatever's left when the smoke clears. Many of those who aren't considering it, are suspecting others. And everybody has to keep his defenses up.

"Now. What are our defenses? Let me list them again: radar screens, searches, and Security Council supervision of fissionable elements. Well, you tell me, Mr. Ciccone—what would happen to the effectiveness of your search program if New York were to begin tomorrow to move en masse to the Mohawk Valley?"

"Yes, I see what you mean. We'd have a hard time keeping up even a pretense."

"You certainly would. New York could be blasted before it had got well started moving. Another thing: atomic power plants, too, are centralized, to simplify the Security Council's job of control, so no doubt you'd ask that they be included in the program of dispersal. But think of the confusion involved in moving billions of dollars' worth of industrial plant. How could a merely human Security Council prevent the smuggling out, somewhere, of a few hundred pounds of U-235 or Pu-239?

"No, the pressure's on, and we have to stick by the choice we made.

"Our civilization: a great, big, overgrown truck going much too fast. Suddenly the road became dangerously narrow, and slippery besides, but the truck was too big and it was going too fast. It couldn't stop. Now we have only a few inches to spare on either side of our wheels, but we still can't do what you suggest, stop, get out, and look for a detour. No, we've chosen our road and we've got to stick to it.

"Not much seems to be changed, at first glance—the truck's engine still runs smoothly—the steering gear still responds—even the driver isn't in such bad shape. Yet come tomorrow, it may all be over. If we don't steer straight, it certainly will be.

"Makes quite a picture. Our magnificent, overgrown, bungling civilization going on its own magnificent and senseless way because it is so big that nothing can stop it, so big that it can't even stop itself."

Bates stopped speaking, but neither Ciccone nor Macomb answered. There was no answer. Ten years ago, there might perhaps have been, but not now.

POUL ANDERSON and
F. N. WALDROP

TOMORROW'S CHILDREN

On the world's loom
Weave the Norns doom,
Nor may they guide it nor change.
　　　　—Wagner, Siegfried

TEN miles up, it hardly showed. Earth was a cloudy green and brown blur, the vast vault of the stratosphere reaching changelessly out to spatial infinities, and beyond the pulsing engine there was silence and serenity no man could ever touch. Looking down, Hugh Drummond could see the Mississippi gleaming like a drawn sword, and its slow curve matched the contours shown on his map. The hills, the sea, the sun and wind and rain, they didn't change. Not in less than a million slow-striding years, and human efforts flickered too briefly in the unending night for that.

Farther down, though, and especially where cities had been— The lone man in the solitary stratojet swore softly, bitterly, and his knuckles whitened on the controls. He was a big man, his gaunt rangy form sprawling awkwardly in the tiny pressure cabin, and he wasn't quite forty. But his dark hair was streaked with gray, in the shabby flying suit his shoulders stooped, and his long homely face was drawn into haggard lines. His eyes were black-rimmed and sunken with weariness, dark and dreadful in their intensity. He'd seen too much, survived too much, until he began to look like most other people of the world. *Heir of the ages,* he thought dully.

Mechanically, he went through the motions of following his course. Natural landmarks were still there, and he had powerful binoculars to help him. But he didn't use them much. They showed too many broad shallow craters, their vitreous smoothness throwing back sunlight in the flat blank glitter of a snake's eye, the ground about them a churned and blasted desolation. And there were the worse regions of—deadness. Twisted dead trees, blowing sand, tumbled skeletons, perhaps at night a baleful blue glow of fluorescence. The bombs had been nightmares, riding in on wings of fire and horror to shake the planet with the death blows of cities. But the radioactive dust was worse than any nightmare.

He passed over villages, even small towns. Some of them were deserted, the blowing colloidal dust, or plague, or economic breakdown making them untenable. Others still seemed to be living a feeble half-life. Especially in the Midwest, there was a pathetic struggle to return to an agricultural system, but the insects and blights—

Drummond shrugged. After nearly two years of this, over the scarred and maimed planet, he should be used to it. The United States had been lucky. Europe, now—

Der Untergang des Abendlandes, he thought grayly. *Spengler foresaw the collapse of a topheavy civilization. He didn't foresee atomic bombs, radioactive-dust bombs, bacteria bombs, blight bombs—the bombs, the senseless inanimate bombs flying like monster insects over the shivering world. So he didn't guess the extent of the collapse.*

Deliberately he pushed the thoughts out of his conscious mind. He didn't want to dwell on them. He'd lived with them two years, and that was two eternities too long. And anyway, he was nearly home now.

The capital of the United States was below him, and he sent the stratojet slanting down in a long thunderous dive toward the mountains. Not much of a capital, the little town huddled in a valley of the Cascades, but the waters of the Potomac had filled the grave of Washington. Strictly speaking, there was no capital. The officers of the government were scattered over the country, keeping in precarious touch by plane and radio, but Taylor, Oregon, came as close to being the nerve center as any other place.

He gave the signal again on his transmitter, knowing with a faint spine-crawling sensation of the rocket batteries trained on him from the green of those mountains. When one plane could carry the end of a city, all planes were under suspicion. Not that anyone outside was supposed to know that that innocuous little town was important. But you never could tell. The war wasn't officially over. It might never be, with sheer personal survival overriding the urgency of treaties.

A light-beam transmitter gave him a cautious: "O.K. Can you land in the street?"

It was a narrow, dusty track between two wooden rows of houses, but Drummond was a good pilot and this was a good jet. "Yeah," he said. His voice had grown unused to speech.

He cut speed in a spiral descent until he was gliding with only the faintest whisper of wind across his ship. Touching wheels to the street, he slammed on the brake and bounced to a halt.

Silence struck at him like a physical blow. The engine stilled, the sun beating down from a brassy blue sky on the drabness of rude "temporary" houses, the total-seeming desertion beneath the impassive mountains—Home! Hugh Drummond laughed, a short harsh bark with nothing of humor in it, and swung open the cockpit canopy.

There were actually quite a few people, he saw, peering from doorways and side streets. They looked fairly well fed and dressed, many in uniform; they seemed to have purpose and hope. But this, of course, was the capital of the United States of America, the world's most fortunate country.

"Get out—quick!"

The peremptory voice roused Drummond from the introspection into which those lonely months had driven him. He looked down at a gang of men in mechanics' outfits, led by a harassed-looking man in captain's uniform. "Oh—of course," he said slowly. "You want to hide the plane. And, naturally, a regular landing field would give you away."

"Hurry, get out, you infernal idiot! Anyone, *anyone* might come over and see—"

"They wouldn't go unnoticed by an efficient detection system, and you still have that," said Drummond, sliding his booted legs over the cockpit edge. "And anyway, there won't be any more raids. The war's over."

"Wish I could believe that, but who are you to say? Get a move on!"

The grease monkeys hustled the plane down the street. With an odd feeling of loneliness, Drummond watched it go. After all, it had been his home for—how long?

The machine was stopped before a false house whose whole front was swung aside. A concrete ramp led downward, and Drummond could see a cavernous immensity below. Light within it gleamed off silvery rows of aircraft.

"Pretty neat," he admitted. "Not that it matters any more. Probably it never did. Most of the hell came over on robot rockets. Oh, well." He fished his pipe from his jacket. Colonel's insignia glittered briefly as the garment flipped back.

"Oh . . . sorry, sir!" exclaimed the captain. "I didn't know—"

" 'S O.K. I've gotten out of the habit of wearing a regular uniform. A lot of places I've been, an American wouldn't be very popular."

Drummond stuffed tobacco into his briar, scowling. He hated to think how often he'd had to use the Colt at his hip, or even the machine guns in his plane, to save himself. He inhaled smoke gratefully. It seemed to drown out some of the bitter taste.

"General Robinson said to bring you to him when you arrived, sir," said the captain. "This way, please."

They went down the street, their boots scuffing up little acrid clouds of dust. Drummond looked sharply about him. He'd left very shortly after the two-month Ragnarok which had tapered off when the organization of both sides broke down too far to keep on making and sending the bombs, and maintaining order with famine and disease starting their ghastly ride over the homeland. At that time, the United States was a cityless, anarchic chaos, and he'd had only the briefest of radio exchanges since then, whenever he could get at a long-range set still in working order. They'd made remarkable progress meanwhile. How much, he didn't know, but the mere existence of something like a capital was sufficient proof.

Robinson— His lined face twisted into a frown. He didn't know the man. He'd been expecting to be received by the President, who had sent him and some others out. Unless the others had— No, he was the only one who had been in eastern Europe and western Asia. He was sure of that.

Two sentries guarded the entrance to what was obviously a converted general store. But there were no more stores. There was nothing to put in them. Drummond entered the cool dimness of an antechamber. The clatter of a typewriter, the Wac operating it— He gaped and blinked. That was—impossible! Typewriters, secretaries—hadn't they gone out with the whole world, two years ago? If the Dark Ages had returned to Earth, it didn't seem—*right*—that there should still be typewriters. It didn't fit, didn't—

He grew aware that the captain had opened the inner door for him. As he stepped in, he grew aware how tired he was. His arm weighed a ton as he saluted the man behind the desk.

"At ease, at ease," Robinson's voice was genial. Despite the five stars on his shoulders, he wore no tie or coat, and his round face was smiling. Still, he looked tough and competent underneath. To run things nowadays, he'd have to be.

"Sit down, Colonel Drummond." Robinson gestured to a chair near his and the aviator collapsed into it, shivering. His haunted eyes traversed the office. It was almost well enough outfitted to be a prewar place.

Prewar! A word like a sword, cutting across history with a brutality of murder, hazing everything in the past until it was a vague golden glow through drifting, red-shot black clouds. And—only two years. *Only two years!* Surely sanity was meaningless in a world of such nightmare inversions. Why, he could barely remember Barbara and the kids. Their faces were blotted out in a tide of other visages—starved faces, dead faces, human faces become beast-formed with want and pain and eating throttled hate. His grief was lost in the agony of a world, and in some ways he had become a machine himself.

"You look plenty tired," said Robinson.

"Yeah . . . yes, sir—"

"Skip the formality. I don't go for it. We'll be working pretty close together, can't take time to be diplomatic."

"Uh-huh. I came over the North Pole, you know. Haven't slept since— Rough time. But, if I may ask, you—" Drummond hesitated.

"I? I suppose I'm President. Ex officio, pro tem, or something. Here, you need a drink." Robinson got bottle and glasses from a drawer. The liquor gurgled out in a pungent stream. "Prewar Scotch. Till it gives out I'm laying off this modern hooch. *Gambai.*"

The fiery, smoky brew jolted Drummond to wakefulness. Its glow was pleasant in his empty stomach. He heard Robinson's voice with a surrealistic sharpness:

"Yes, I'm at the head now. My predecessors made the mistake of sticking together, and of traveling a good deal in trying to pull the country back into shape. So I think the sickness got the President, and I know it got several others. Of course, there was no means of holding an election. The armed forces had almost the only organization left, so we had to run things. Berger was in charge, but he shot himself when he learned he'd breathed radiodust. Then the command fell to me. I've been lucky."

"I see." It didn't make much difference. A few dozen more deaths weren't much, when over half the world was gone. "Do you expect to—continue lucky?" A brutally blunt question, maybe, but words weren't bombs.

"I do." Robinson was firm about that. "We've learned by experience, learned a lot. We've scattered the army, broken it into small outposts at key points throughout the country. For quite a while, we stopped travel altogether except for absolute emergencies, and then with elaborate precautions. That smothered the epidemics. The microorganisms were bred to work in crowded areas, you know. They were almost immune to known medical techniques, but without hosts and carriers they died. I guess natural bacteria ate up most of them. We still take care in traveling, but we're fairly safe now."

"Did any of the others come back? There were a lot like me, sent out to see what really had happened to the world."

"One did, from South America. Their situation is similar to ours, though they lacked our tight organization and have gone further toward anarchy. Nobody else returned but you."

It wasn't surprising. In fact, it was a cause for astonishment that anyone had come back. Drummond had volunteered after the bomb erasing St. Louis had taken his family, not expecting to survive and not caring much whether he did. Maybe that was why he had.

"You can take your time in writing a detailed report," said Robinson, "but in general, how are things over there?"

Drummond shrugged. "The war's over. Burned out. Europe has gone back to savagery. They were caught between America and Asia, and the bombs came both ways. Not many survivors, and they're starving animals. Russia, from what I saw, has managed something like you've done here, though they're worse off than we. Naturally, I couldn't find out much there. I didn't get to India or China, but in Russia I heard rumors— No, the world's gone too far into disintegration to carry on war."

"Then we can come out in the open," said Robinson softly. "We can really start rebuilding. I don't think there'll ever be another war, Drummond. I think the memory of this one will be carved too deeply on the race for us ever to forget."

"Can you shrug it off that easily?"

"No, no, of course not. Our culture hasn't lost its continuity, but it's had a terrific setback. We'll never wholly get over it. But—we're on our way up again."

The general rose, glancing at his watch. "Six o'clock. Come on, Drummond, let's get home."

"Home?"

"Yes, you'll stay with me. Man, you look like the original zombie. You'll need a month or more of sleeping between clean sheets, of home cooking and home atmosphere. My wife will be glad to have you; we see almost no new faces. And as long as we'll work together, I'd like to keep you handy. The shortage of competent men is terrific."

They went down the street, an aide following. Drummond was again conscious of the weariness aching in every bone and fiber of him. A home—after two years of ghost towns, of shattered chimneys above blood-dappled snow, of flimsy lean-tos housing starvation and death.

"Your plane will be mighty useful, too," said Robinson. "Those atomic-powered craft are scarcer than hens' teeth used to be." He chuckled hollowly, as at a rather grim joke. "Got you through close to two years of flying without needing fuel. Any other trouble?"

"Some, but there were enough spare parts." No need to tell of those frantic hours and days of slaving, of desperate improvisation with hunger and plague stalking him who stayed overlong. He'd had his troubles getting food, too, despite the plentiful supplies he'd started out with. He'd fought for scraps in the winter, beaten off howling maniacs who would have killed him for a bird he'd shot or a dead horse he'd scavenged. He hated that plundering, and would not have cared personally if they'd managed to destroy him. But he had a mission, and the mission was all he'd had left as a focal point for his life, so he'd clung to it with fanatic intensity.

And now the job was over, and he realized he couldn't rest. He didn't dare. Rest would give him time to remember. Maybe he could find surcease in the gigantic work of reconstruction. Maybe.

"Here we are," said Robinson.

Drummond blinked in new amazement. There was a car, camouflaged under brush, with a military chauffeur—*a car!* And in pretty fair shape, too.

"We've got a few oil wells going again, and a small patched-up refinery," explained the general. "It furnishes enough gas and oil for what traffic we have."

They got in the rear seat. The aide sat in front, a rifle ready. The car started down a mountain road.

"Where to?" asked Drummond a little dazedly.

Robinson smiled. "Personally," he said, "I'm almost the only lucky man on Earth. We had a summer cottage on Lake Taylor, a few miles from here. My wife was there when the war came, and stayed, and nobody came along till I brought the head offices here with me. Now I've got a home all to myself."

"Yeah. Yeah, you're lucky," said Drummond. He looked out the window, not seeing the sun-spattered woods. Presently he asked, his voice a little harsh: "How is the country really doing now?"

"For a while it was rough. Damn rough. When the cities went, our transportation, communication, and distribution systems broke down. In fact, our whole economy disintegrated, though not all at once. Then there was the dust and the plagues. People fled, and there was open fighting when overcrowded safe places refused to take in any more refugees. Police went with the cities, and the army couldn't do much patrolling. We were busy fighting the enemy troops that'd flown over the Pole to invade. We still haven't gotten them all. Bands are roaming the country, hungry and desperate outlaws, and there are plenty of Americans who turned to banditry when everything else failed. That's why we have this guard, though so far none have come this way.

"The insect and blight weapons just about wiped out our crops, and that winter everybody starved. We checked the pests with modern methods, though it was touch and go for a while, and next year got some food. Of course, with no distribution as yet, we failed to save a lot of people. And farming is still a tough proposition. We won't really have the bugs licked for a long time. If we had a research center as well equipped as those which produced the things— But we're gaining. We're gaining."

"Distribution—" Drummond rubbed his chin. "How about railroads? Horse-drawn vehicles?"

"We have some railroads going, but the enemy was as careful to dust most of ours as we were to dust theirs. As for horses, they were nearly all eaten that first winter. I know personally of only a dozen. They're on my place; I'm trying to breed enough to be of use, but"—Robinson smiled wryly—"by the time we've raised that many, the factories should have been going quite a spell."

"And so now—?"

"We're over the worst. Except for outlaws, we have the population fairly well controlled. The civilized people are fairly well fed, with some kind of housing. We have machine shops, small factories, and the like going, enough to keep our transportation and other mechanism 'level.' Presently we'll be able to expand these, begin actually increasing what we have. In another five years or so, I guess, we'll be integrated enough to drop martial law and hold a general election. A big job ahead, but a good one."

The car halted to let a cow lumber over the road, a calf trotting at her heels. She was gaunt and shaggy, and skittered nervously from the vehicle into the brush.

"Wild," explained Robinson. "Most of the real wild life was killed off for food in the last two years, but a lot of farm animals escaped when their owners died or fled, and have run free ever since. They—" He noticed Drummond's fixed gaze. The pilot was looking at the calf. Its legs were half the normal length.

"Mutant," said the general. "You find a lot such animals. Radiation from bombed or dusted areas. There are even a lot of human abnormal births." He scowled, worry clouding his eyes. "In fact, that's just about our worst problem. It—"

The car came out of the woods onto the shore of a small lake. It was a peaceful scene, the quiet waters like molten gold in the slanting sunlight, trees ringing the circumference and all about them the mountains. Under one huge pine stood a cottage, a woman on the porch.

It was like one summer with Barbara—Drummond cursed under his breath and followed Robinson toward the little building. It wasn't, it wasn't, it could never be. Not ever again. There were soldiers guarding this place from chance marauders, and— There was an odd-looking flower at his foot. A daisy, but huge and red and irregularly formed.

A squirrel chittered from a tree. Drummond saw that its face was so blunt as to be almost human.

Then he was on the porch, and Robinson was introducing him to "my wife Elaine." She was a nice-looking young woman with eyes that were sympathetic on Drummond's exhausted face. The aviator tried not to notice that she was pregnant.

He was led inside, and reveled in a hot bath. Afterward there was supper, but he was numb with sleep by then, and hardly noticed it when Robinson put him to bed.

Reaction set in, and for a week or so Drummond went about in a haze, not much good to himself or anyone else. But it was surprising what plenty of food and sleep could do, and one evening Robinson came home to find him scribbling on sheets of paper.

"Arranging my notes and so on," he explained. "I'll write out the complete report in a month, I guess."

"Good. But no hurry." Robinson settled tiredly into an armchair. "The rest of the world will keep. I'd rather you'd just work at this off and on, and join my staff for your main job."

"O.K. Only what'll I do?"

"Everything. Specialization is gone; too few surviving specialists and equipment. I think your chief task will be to head the census bureau."

"Eh?"

Robinson grinned lopsidedly. "You'll *be* the census bureau, except for what few assistants I can spare you." He leaned forward, said earnestly: "And it's one of the most important jobs there is. You'll do for this country what you did for central Eurasia, only in much greater detail. Drummond, we have to *know.*"

He took a map from a desk drawer and spread it out. "Look, here's the United States. I've marked regions known to be uninhabitable in red." His fingers traced out the ugly splotches. "Too many of 'em, and doubtless there are others we haven't found yet. Now, the blue X's are army posts." They were sparsely scattered over the land, near the centers of population groupings. "Not enough of those. It's all we can do to control the more or less well-off, orderly people. Bandits, enemy troops, homeless refugees—they're still running wild, skulking in the backwoods and barrens, and raiding whenever they can. And they spread the plague. We won't really have it licked till everybody's settled down, and that'd be hard to enforce. Drummond, we don't even have enough soldiers to start a feudal system for protection. The plague spread like a prairie fire in those concentrations of men.

"We have to *know*. We have to know how many people survived—half the population, a third, a quarter, whatever it is. We have to know where they are, and how they're fixed for supplies, so we can start up an equitable distribution system. We have to find all the small-town shops and labs and libraries still standing, and rescue their priceless contents before looters or the weather beat us to it. We have to locate doctors and engineers and other professional men, and put them to work rebuilding. We have to find the outlaws and round them up. We— I could go on forever. Once we have all that information, we can set up a master plan for redistributing population, agriculture, industry, and the rest most efficiently, for getting the country back under civil authority and police, for opening regular transportation and communication channels —for getting the nation back on its feet."

"I see," nodded Drummond. "Hitherto, just surviving and hanging on to what was left has taken precedence. Now you're in a position to start expanding, *if* you know where and how much to expand."

"Exactly." Robinson rolled a cigarette, grimacing. "Not much tobacco left. What I have is perfectly foul. Lord, that war was crazy!"

"All wars are," said Drummond dispassionately, "but technology advanced to the point of giving us a knife to cut our throats with. Before that, we were just beating our heads against the wall. Robinson, we can't go back to the old ways. We've *got* to start on a new track—a track of sanity."

"Yes. And that brings up—" The other man looked toward the kitchen door. They could hear the cheerful rattle of dishes there, and smell mouth-watering cooking odors. He lowered his voice. "I might as well tell you this now, but don't let Elaine know. She . . . she shouldn't be worried. Drummond, did you see our horses?"

"The other day, yes. The colts—"

"Uh-huh. There've been five colts born of eleven mares in the last year. Two of them were so deformed they died in a week, another in a few months. One of the two left has cloven hoofs and almost no teeth. The last one looks normal—so far. One out of eleven, Drummond."

"Were those horses near a radioactive area?"

"They must have been. They were rounded up wherever found and brought here. The stallion was caught near the site of Portland, I know.

But if he were the only one with mutated genes, it would hardly show in the first generation, would it? I understand nearly all mutations are Mendelian recessives. Even if there were one dominant, it would show in all the colts, but none of these looked alike."

"Hm-m-m—I don't know much about genetics, but I do know hard radiation, or rather the secondary charged particles it produces, will cause mutation. Only mutants are rare, and tend to fall into certain patterns—"

"*Were* rare!" Suddenly Robinson was grim, something coldly frightened in his eyes. "Haven't you noticed the animals and plants? They're fewer than formerly, and . . . well, I've not kept count, but at least half those seen or killed have something wrong, internally or externally."

Drummond drew heavily on his pipe. He needed something to hang onto, in a new storm of insanity. Very quietly, he said:

"In my college biology course, they told me the vast majority of mutations are unfavorable. More ways of not doing something than of doing it. Radiation might sterilize an animal, or might produce several degrees of genetic change. You could have a mutation so violently lethal the possessor never gets born, or soon dies. You could have all kinds of more or less handicapping factors, or just random changes not making much difference one way or the other. Or in a few rare cases you might get something actually favorable, but you couldn't really say the possessor is a true member of the species. And favorable mutations themselves usually involve a price in the partial or total loss of some other function."

"Right." Robinson nodded heavily. "One of your jobs on the census will be to try and locate any and all who know genetics, and send them here. But your real task, which only you and I and a couple of others must know about, the job overriding all other considerations, will be to find the human mutants."

Drummond's throat was dry. "There've been a lot of them?" he whispered.

"Yes. But we don't know how many or where. We only know about those people who live near an army post, or have some other fairly regular intercourse with us, and they're only a few thousand all told. Among them, the birth rate has gone down to about half the prewar ratio. And over half the births they do have are abnormal."

"*Over half*—"

"Yeah. Of course, the violently different ones soon die, or are put in an institution we've set up in the Alleghenies. But what can we do with viable forms, if their parents still love them? A kid with deformed or missing or abortive organs, twisted internal structure, a tail, or something even worse . . . well, *it'll* have a tough time in life, but it can generally survive. And perpetuate itself—"

"And a normal-looking one might have some unnoticeable quirk, or a characteristic that won't show up for years. Or even a normal one might be carrying recessives, and pass them on— God!" The exclamation was half blasphemy, half prayer. "But how'd it happen? People weren't all near atom-hit areas."

"Maybe not, though a lot of survivors escaped from the outskirts. But there was that first year, with everybody on the move. One could pass near enough to a blasted region to be affected, without knowing it. And that damnable radiodust, blowing on the wind. It's got a long half-life. It'll be active for decades. Then, as in any collapsing culture, promiscuity was common. Still is. Oh, it'd spread itself, all right."

"I still don't see why it spread itself so much. Even here—"

"Well, I don't know why it shows up here. I suppose a lot of the local flora and fauna came in from elsewhere. This place is safe. The nearest dusted region is three hundred miles off, with mountains between. There must be many such islands of comparatively normal conditions. We have to find them too. But elsewhere—"

"Soup's on," announced Elaine, and went from the kitchen to the dining room with a loaded tray.

The men rose. Grayly, Drummond looked at Robinson and said tonelessly: "O.K. I'll get your information for you. We'll map mutation areas and safe areas, we'll check on our population and resources, we'll eventually get all the facts you want. But—what are you going to do then?"

"I wish I knew," said Robinson haggardly. "I wish I knew."

Winter lay heavily on the north, a vast gray sky seeming frozen solid over the rolling white plains. The last three winters had come early and stayed long. Dust, colloidal dust of the bombs, suspended in the atmosphere and cutting down the solar constant by a deadly percent or two. There had even been a few earthquakes, set off in geologically unstable parts of the world by bombs planted right. Half California had been ruined when a sabotage bomb started the San Andreas Fault on a major slip. And that kicked up still more dust.

Fimbulwinter, thought Drummond bleakly. *The doom of the prophecy. But no, we're surviving. Though maybe not as men—*

Most people had gone south, and there overcrowding had made starvation and disease and internecine struggle the normal aspects of life. Those who'd stuck it out up here, and had luck with their pest-ridden crops, were better off.

Drummond's jet slid above the cratered black ruin of the Twin Cities. There was still enough radioactivity to melt the snow, and the pit was like a skull's empty eye socket. The man sighed, but he was becoming calloused to the sight of death. There was so much of it. Only the struggling agony of life mattered any more.

He strained through the sinister twilight, swooping low over the unending fields. Burned-out hulks of farmhouses, bones of ghost towns, sere deadness of dusted land—but he'd heard travelers speak of a fairly powerful community up near the Canadian border, and it was up to him to find it.

A lot of things had been up to him in the last six months. He'd had to work out a means of search, and organize his few, overworked assistants into an efficient staff, and go out on the long hunt.

They hadn't covered the country. That was impossible. Their few planes had gone to areas chosen more or less at random, trying to get a cross section of conditions. They'd penetrated wildernesses of hill and plain and forest, establishing contact with scattered, still demoralized out-dwellers. On the whole, it was more laborious than anything else. Most were pathetically glad to see any symbol of law and order and the paradisical-seeming "old days." Now and then there was danger and trouble, when they encountered wary or sullen or outright hostile groups suspicious of a government they associated with disaster, and once there had even been a pitched battle with roving outlaws. But the work had gone ahead, and now the preliminaries were about over.

Preliminaries— It was a bigger job to find out exactly how matters stood than the entire country was capable of undertaking right now. But Drummond had enough facts for reliable extrapolation. He and his staff had collected most of the essential data and begun correlating it. By questioning, by observation, by seeking and finding, by any means that came to hand they'd filled their notebooks. And in the sketchy outlines of a Chinese drawing, and with the same stark realism, the truth was there.

Just this one more place, and I'll go home, thought Drummond for the—thousandth?—time. His brain was getting into a rut, treading the same terrible circle and finding no way out. *Robinson won't like what I tell him, but there it is.* And darkly, slowly: *Barbara, maybe it was best you and the kids went as you did. Quickly, cleanly, not even knowing it. This isn't much of a world. It'll never be our world again.*

He saw the place he sought, a huddle of buildings near the frozen shores of the Lake of the Woods, and his jet murmured toward the white ground. The stories he'd heard of this town weren't overly encouraging, but he supposed he'd get out all right. The others had his data anyway, so it didn't matter.

By the time he'd landed in the clearing just outside the village, using the jet's skis, most of the inhabitants were there waiting. In the gathering dusk they were a ragged and wild-looking bunch, clumsily dressed in whatever scraps of cloth and leather they had. The bearded, hard-eyed men were armed with clubs and knives and a few guns. As Drummond got out, he was careful to keep his hands away from his own automatics.

"Hello," he said. "I'm friendly."

"Y' better be," growled the big leader. "Who are you, where from, an' why?"

"First," lied Drummond smoothly, "I want to tell you I have another man with a plane who knows where I am. If I'm not back in a certain time, he'll come with bombs. But we don't intend any harm or interfer-

ence. This is just a sort of social call. I'm Hugh Drummond of the
United States Army."

They digested that slowly. Clearly, they weren't friendly to the government, but they stood in too much awe of aircraft and armament to be
openly hostile. The leader spat. "How long you staying?"

"Just overnight, if you'll put me up. I'll pay for it." He held up a
small pouch. "Tobacco."

Their eyes gleamed, and the leader said, "You'll stay with me. Come
on."

Drummond gave him the bribe and went with the group. He didn't
like to spend such priceless luxuries thus freely, but the job was more
important. And the boss seemed thawed a little by the fragrant brown
flakes. He was sniffing them greedily.

"Been smoking bark an' grass," he confided. "Terrible."

"Worse than that," agreed Drummond. He turned up his jacket collar and shivered. The wind starting to blow was bitterly cold.

"Just what y' here for?" demanded someone else.

"Well, just to see how things stand. We've got the government started
again, and are patching things up. But we have to know where folks are,
what they need, and so on."

"Don't want nothing t' do with the gov'ment," muttered a woman.
"They brung all this on us."

"Oh, come now. We didn't ask to be attacked." Mentally, Drummond
crossed his fingers. He neither knew nor cared who was to blame. Both
sides, letting mutual fear and friction mount to hysteria— In fact, he
wasn't sure the United States hadn't sent out the first rockets, on orders
of some panicky or aggressive officials. Nobody was alive who admitted
knowing.

"It's the jedgment o' God, for the sins o' our leaders," persisted the
woman. "The plague, the fire-death, all that, ain't it foretold in the
Bible? Ain't we living in the last days o' the world?"

"Maybe." Drummond was glad to stop before a long low cabin. Religious argument was touchy at best, and with a lot of people nowadays it
was dynamite.

They entered the rudely furnished but fairly comfortable structure. A
good many crowded in with them. For all their suspicion, they were curious, and an outsider in an aircraft was a blue-moon event these days.

Drummond's eyes flickered unobtrusively about the room, noticing
details. Three women—that meant a return to concubinage. Only to be
expected in a day of few men and strong-arm rule. Ornaments and uten-
sils, tools and weapons of good quality—yes, that confirmed the stories.
This wasn't exactly a bandit town, but it had waylaid travelers and
raided other places when times were hard, and built up a sort of domi-
nance of the surrounding country. That, too, was common.

There was a dog on the floor nursing a litter. Only three pups, and
one of those was bald, one lacked ears, and one had more toes than it

should. Among the wide-eyed children present, there were several two years old or less, and with almost no obvious exceptions, they were also different.

Drummond sighed heavily and sat down. In a way, this clinched it. He'd known for a long time, and finding mutation here, as far as any place from atomic destruction, was about the last evidence he needed.

He had to get on friendly terms, or he wouldn't find out much about things like population, food production, and whatever else there was to know. Forcing a smile to stiff lips, he took a flask from his jacket. "Pre-war rye," he said. "Who wants a nip?"

"Do we!" The answer barked out in a dozen voices and words. The flask circulated, men pawing and cursing and grabbing to get at it. *Their homebrew must be pretty bad,* thought Drummond wryly.

The chief shouted an order, and one of his women got busy at the primitive stove. "Rustle you a mess o' chow," he said heartily. "An' my name's Sam Buckman."

"Pleased to meet you, Sam." Drummond squeezed the hairy paw hard. He had to show he wasn't a weakling, a conniving city slicker.

"What's it like, outside?" asked someone presently. "We ain't heard for so long—"

"You haven't missed much," said Drummond between bites. The food was pretty good. Briefly, he sketched conditions. "You're better off than most," he finished.

"Yeah. Mebbe so." Sam Buckman scratched his tangled beard. "What I'd give f'r a razor blade—! It ain't easy, though. The first year we weren't no better off 'n anyone else. Me, I'm a farmer, I kept some ears o' corn an' a little wheat an' barley in my pockets all that winter, even though I was starving. A bunch o' hungry refugees plundered my place, but I got away an' drifted up here. Next year I took an empty farm here an' started over."

Drummond doubted that it had been abandoned, but said nothing. Sheer survival outweighed a lot of considerations.

"Others came an' settled here," said the leader reminiscently. "We farm together. We have to; one man couldn't live by hisself, not with the bugs an' blight, an' the crops sproutin' into all new kinds, an' the outlaws aroun'. Not many up here, though we did beat off some enemy troops last winter." He glowed with pride at that, but Drummond wasn't particularly impressed. A handful of freezing starveling conscripts, lost and bewildered in a foreign enemy's land, with no hope of ever getting home, weren't formidable.

"Things getting better, though," said Buckman. "We're heading up." He scowled blackly, and a palpable chill crept into the room. "If 'twern't for the births—"

"Yes—the births. The new babies. Even the stock an' plants." It was an old man speaking, his eyes glazed with near madness. "It's the mark o' the beast. Satan is loose in the world—"

"Shut up!" Huge and bristling with wrath, Buckman launched himself out of his seat and grabbed the oldster by his scrawny throat. "Shut up 'r I'll bash y'r lying head in. Ain't no son o' mine being marked by the devil."

"Or mine—" "Or mine—" The rumble of voices ran about the cabin, sullen and afraid.

"It's God's jedgment, I tell you!" The woman was shrilling again. "The end o' the world is near. Prepare f'r the second coming—"

"An' you shut up too, Mag Schmidt," snarled Buckman. He stood bent over, gnarled arms swinging loose, hands flexing, little eyes darting red and wild about the room. "Shut y'r trap an' keep it shut. I'm still boss here, an' if you don't like it you can get out. I still don't think that funny-looking brat o' y'rs fell in the lake by accident."

The woman shrank back, lips tight. The room filled with a crackling silence. One of the babies began to cry. It had two heads.

Slowly and heavily, Buckman turned to Drummond, who sat immobile against the wall. "You see?" he asked dully. "You see how it is? Maybe it is the curse o' God. Maybe the world is ending. I dunno. I just know there's few enough babies, an' most o' them *de*formed. Will it go on? Will all our kids be monsters? Should we . . . kill these an' hope we get some human babies? What is it? What to do?"

Drummond rose. He felt a weight as of centuries on his shoulders, the weariness, blank and absolute, of having seen that smoldering panic and heard that desperate appeal too often, too often.

"Don't kill them," he said. "That's the worst kind of murder, and anyway it'd do no good at all. It comes from the bombs, and you can't stop it. You'll go right on having such children, so you might as well get used to it."

By atomic-powered stratojet it wasn't far from Minnesota to Oregon, and Drummond landed in Taylor about noon the next day. This time there was no hurry to get his machine under cover, and up on the mountain was a raw scar of earth where a new airfield was slowly being built. Men were getting over their terror of the sky. They had another fear to face now, and it was one from which there was no hiding.

Drummond walked slowly down the icy main street to the central office. It was numbingly cold, a still, relentless intensity of frost eating through clothes and flesh and bone. It wasn't much better inside. Heating systems were still poor improvisations.

"You're back!" Robinson met him in the antechamber, suddenly galvanized with eagerness. He had grown thin and nervous, looking ten years older, but impatience blazed from him. "How is it? How is it?"

Drummond held up a bulky notebook. "All here," he said grimly. "All the facts we'll need. Not formally correlated yet, but the picture is simple enough."

Robinson laid an arm on his shoulder and steered him into the office. He felt the general's hand shaking, but he'd sat down and had a drink before business came up again.

"You've done a good job," said the leader warmly. "When the country's organized again, I'll see you get a medal for this. Your men in the other planes aren't in yet."

"No, they'll be gathering data for a long time. The job won't be finished for years. I've only got a general outline here, but it's enough. It's enough." Drummond's eyes were haunted again.

Robinson felt cold at meeting that too-steady gaze. He whispered shakily: "Is it—bad?"

"The worst. Physically, the country's recovering. But biologically, we've reached a crossroads and taken the wrong fork."

"What do you mean? *What do you mean?*"

Drummond let him have it then, straight and hard as a bayonet thrust. "The birth rate's a little over half the prewar," he said, "and about seventy-five per cent of all births are mutant, of which possibly two-thirds are viable and presumably fertile. Of course, that doesn't include late-maturing characteristics, or those undetectable by naked-eye observation, or the mutated recessive genes that must be carried by a lot of otherwise normal zygotes. And it's everywhere. There are no safe places."

"I see," said Robinson after a long time. He nodded, like a man struck a stunning blow and not yet fully aware of it. "I see. The reason—"

"Is obvious."

"Yes. People going through radioactive areas—"

"Why, no. That would only account for a few. But—"

"No matter. The fact's there, and that's enough. We have to decide what to do about it."

"And soon." Drummond's jaw set. "It's wrecking our culture. We at least preserved our historical continuity, but even that's going now. People are going crazy as birth after birth is monstrous. Fear of the unknown, striking at minds still stunned by the war and its immediate aftermath. Frustration of parenthood, perhaps the most basic instinct there is. It's leading to infanticide, desertion, despair, a cancer at the root of society. We've got to act."

"How? How?" Robinson stared numbly at his hands.

"I don't know. You're the leader. Maybe an educational campaign, though that hardly seems practicable. Maybe an acceleration of your program for re-integrating the country. Maybe— I don't know."

Drummond stuffed tobacco into his pipe. He was near the end of what he had, but would rather take a few good smokes than a lot of niggling puffs. "Of course," he said thoughtfully, "it's probably not the end of things. We won't know for a generation or more, but I rather imagine the mutants can grow into society. They'd better, for they'll outnumber the humans. The thing is, if we just let matters drift there's no telling where they'll go. The situation is unprecedented. We may end up in a culture of specialized variations, which would be very bad from an evolutionary standpoint. There may be fighting between mutant types, or with humans. Interbreeding may produce worse freaks, particularly when accumulated recessives start showing up. Robinson, if we want any say at all in what's going to happen in the next few centuries, we have to act quickly. Otherwise it'll snowball out of all control."

"Yes. Yes, we'll have to act fast. And hard." Robinson straightened in his chair. Decision firmed his countenance, but his eyes were staring. "We're mobilized," he said. "We have the men and the weapons and the organization. They won't be able to resist."

The ashy cold of Drummond's emotions stirred, but it was with a horrible wrenching of fear. "What are you getting at?" he snapped.

"Racial death. All mutants and their parents to be sterilized whenever and wherever detected."

"You're crazy!" Drummond sprang from his chair, grabbed Robinson's shoulders across the desk, and shook him. "You . . . why, it's impossible! You'll bring revolt, civil war, final collapse!"

"Not if we go about it right." There were little beads of sweat studding the general's forehead. "I don't like it any better than you, but it's got to be done or the human race is finished. Normal births a minority—" He surged to his feet, gasping. "I've thought a long time about this. Your facts only confirmed my suspicions. This tears it. Can't you see? Evolution has to proceed slowly. Life wasn't meant for such a storm of change. Unless we can save the true human stock, it'll be absorbed and differentiation will continue till humanity is a collection of freaks, probably intersterile. Or . . . there must be a lot of lethal recessives. In a large population, they can accumulate unnoticed till nearly everybody has them, and then start emerging all at once. That'd wipe us out. It's happened before, in rats and other species. If we eliminate mutant stock now, we can still save the race. It won't be cruel. We have sterilization techniques which are quick and painless, not upsetting the endocrine balance. But it's got to be done." His voice rose to a raw scream, broke. "It's got to be done!"

Drummond slapped him, hard. He drew a shuddering breath, sat down, and began to cry, and somehow that was the most horrible sight of all.

"You're crazy," said the aviator. "You've gone nuts with brooding alone on this the last six months, without knowing or being able to act. You've lost all perspective.

"We can't use violence. In the first place, it would break our tottering, cracked culture irreparably, into a mad-dog finish fight. We'd not even win it. We're outnumbered, and we couldn't hold down a continent, eventually a planet. And remember what we said once, about abandoning the old savage way of settling things, that never brings a real settlement at all? We'd throw away a lesson our noses were rubbed in not three years ago. We'd return to the beast—to ultimate extinction.

"And anyway," he went on very quietly, "it wouldn't do a bit of good.

Mutants would still be born. The poison is everywhere. Normal parents will give birth to mutants, somewhere along the line. We just have to accept that fact, and live with it. The *new* human race will have to."

"I'm sorry." Robinson raised his face from his hands. It was a ghastly visage, gone white and old, but there was calm on it. "I—blew my top. You're right. I've been thinking of this, worrying and wondering, living and breathing it, lying awake nights, and when I finally sleep I dream of it. I . . . yes, I see your point. And you're right."

"It's O.K. You've been under a terrific strain. Three years with never a rest, and the responsibility for a nation, and now this— Sure, everybody's entitled to be a little crazy. We'll work out a solution, somehow."

"Yes, of course." Robinson poured out two stiff drinks and gulped his. He paced restlessly, and his tremendous ability came back in waves of strength and confidence. "Let me see— Eugenics, of course. If we work hard, we'll have the nation tightly organized inside of ten years. Then . . . well, I don't suppose we can keep the mutants from interbreeding, but certainly we can pass laws to protect humans and encourage their propagation. Since radical mutations would probably be intersterile anyway, and most mutants handicapped one way or another, a few generations should see humans completely dominant again."

Drummond scowled. He was worried. It wasn't like Robinson to be unreasonable. Somehow, the man had acquired a mental blind spot where this most ultimate of human problems was concerned. He said slowly, "That won't work either. First, it'd be hard to impose and enforce. Second, we'd be repeating the old *Herrenvolk* notion. Mutants are inferior, mutants must be kept in their place—to enforce that, especially on a majority, you'd need a full-fledged totalitarian state. Third, that wouldn't work either, for the rest of the world, with almost no exceptions, is under no such control and we'll be in no position to take over that control for a long time—generations. Before then, mutants will dominate everywhere over there, and if they resent the way we treat their kind here, we'd better run for cover."

"You assume a lot. How do you know those hundreds or thousands of diverse types will work together? They're less like each other than like humans, even. They could be played off against each other."

"Maybe. But *that* would be going back onto the old road of treachery and violence, the road to Hell. Conversely, if every not-quite-human is called a 'mutant', like a separate class, he'll think he is, and act accordingly against the lumped-together 'humans.' No, the only way to sanity —to *survival*—is to abandon class prejudice and race hate altogether, and work as individuals. We're all . . . well, Earthlings, and subclassification is deadly. We all have to live together, and might as well make the best of it."

"Yeah . . . yeah, that's right too."

"Anyway, I repeat that all such attempts would be useless. All Earth is infected with mutation. It will be for a long time. The purest human stock will still produce mutants."

"Y-yes, that's true. Our best bet seems to be to find all such stock and withdraw it into the few safe areas left. It'll mean a small human population, but a *human* one."

"I tell you, that's impossible," clipped Drummond. "There is no safe place. Not one."

Robinson stopped pacing and looked at him as at a physical antagonist. "That so?" he almost growled. "Why?"

Drummond told him, adding incredulously, "Surely you knew that. Your physicists must have measured the amount of it. Your doctors, your engineers, that geneticist I dug up for you. You obviously got a lot of this biological information you've been slinging at me from him. They *must* all have told you the same thing."

Robinson shook his head stubbornly. "It can't be. It's not reasonable. The concentration wouldn't be great enough."

"Why, you poor fool, you need only look around you. The plants, the animals— Haven't there been any births in Taylor?"

"No. This is still a man's town, though women are trickling in and several babies are on the way—" Robinson's face was suddenly twisted with desperation. "Elaine's is due any time now. She's in the hospital here. Don't you see, our other kid died of the plague. This one's all we have. We want him to grow up in a world free of want and fear, a world of peace and sanity where he can play and laugh and become a man, not a beast starving in a cave. You and I are on our way out. We're the old generation, the one that wrecked the world. It's up to us to build it again, and then retire from it to let our children have it. The future's theirs. We've got to make it ready for them."

Sudden insight held Drummond motionless for long seconds. Understanding came, and pity, and an odd gentleness that changed his sunken bony face. "Yes," he murmured, "yes, I see. That's why you're working with all that's in you to build a normal, healthy world. That's why you nearly went crazy when this threat appeared. That . . . that's why you can't, just can't comprehend—"

He took the other man's arm and guided him toward the door. "Come on," he said. "Let's go see how your wife's making out. Maybe we can get her some flowers on the way."

The silent cold bit at them as they went down the street. Snow crackled underfoot. It was already grimy with town smoke and dust, but overhead the sky was incredibly clean and blue. Breath smoked whitely from their mouths and nostrils. The sound of men at work rebuilding drifted faintly between the bulking mountains.

"We couldn't emigrate to another planet, could we?" asked Robinson, and answered himself: "No, we lack the organization and resources to settle them right now. We'll have to make out on Earth. A few safe spots—there *must* be others besides this one—to house the true humans till the mutation period is over. Yes, we can do it."

"There are no safe places," insisted Drummond. "Even if there were, the mutants would still outnumber us. Does your geneticist have any idea how this'll come out, biologically speaking?"

"He doesn't know. His specialty is still largely unknown. He can make an intelligent guess, and that's all."

"Yeah. Anyway, our problem is to learn to live with the mutants, to accept anyone as—Earthling—no matter how he looks, to quit thinking anything was ever settled by violence or connivance, to build a culture of individual sanity. Funny," mused Drummond, "how the impractical virtues, tolerance and sympathy and generosity, have become the fundamental necessities of simple survival. I guess it was always true, but it took the death of half the world and the end of a biological era to make us see that simple little fact. The job's terrific. We've got half a million years of brutality and greed, superstition and prejudice, to lick in a few generations. If we fail, mankind is done. But we've got to try."

They found some flowers, potted in a house, and Robinson bought them with the last of his tobacco. By the time he reached the hospital, he was sweating. The sweat froze on his face as he walked.

The hospital was the town's biggest building, and fairly well equipped. A nurse met them as they entered.

"I was just going to send for you, General Robinson," she said. "The baby's on the way."

"How . . . is she?"

"Fine, so far. Just wait here, please."

Drummond sank into a chair and with haggard eyes watched Robinson's jerky pacing. *The poor guy. Why is it expectant fathers are supposed to be so funny? It's like laughing at a man on the rack. I know, Barbara, I know.*

"They have some anaesthetics," muttered the general. "They . . . Elaine never was very strong."

"She'll be all right." *It's afterward that worries me.*

"Yeah— Yeah— How long, though, how long?"

"Depends. Take it easy." With a wrench, Drummond made a sacrifice to a man he liked. He filled his pipe and handed it over. "Here, you need a smoke."

"Thanks." Robinson puffed raggedly.

The slow minutes passed, and Drummond wondered vaguely what he'd do when—it—happened. It didn't have to happen. But the chances were all against such an easy solution. He was no psychologist. Best just to let things happen as they would.

The waiting broke at last. A doctor came out, seeming an inscrutable high priest in his white garments. Robinson stood before him, motionless.

"You're a brave man," said the doctor. His face, as he removed the mask, was stern and set. "You'll need your courage."

"She—" It was hardly a human sound, that croak.

"Your wife is doing well. But the baby—"

A nurse brought out the little wailing form. It was a boy. But his limbs were rubbery tentacles terminating in boneless digits.

Robinson looked, and something went out of him as he stood there. When he turned, his face was dead.

"You're lucky," said Drummond, and meant it. He'd seen too many other mutants. "After all, if he can use those hands he'll get along all right. He'll even have an advantage in certain types of work. It isn't a deformity, really. If there's nothing else, you've got a good kid."

"*If!* You can't tell with mutants."

"I know. But you've got guts, you and Elaine. You'll see this through, together." Briefly, Drummond felt an utter personal desolation. He went on, perhaps to cover that emptiness:

"I see why you didn't understand the problem. You *wouldn't*. It was a psychological bloc, suppressing a fact you didn't dare face. That boy is really the center of your life. You couldn't think the truth about him, so your subconscious just refused to let you think rationally on that subject at all.

"Now you know. Now you realize there's no safe place, not on all the planet. The tremendous incidence of mutant births in the first generation could have told you that alone. Most such new characteristics are recessive, which means both parents have to have it for it to show in the zygote. But genetic changes are random, except for a tendency to fall into roughly similar patterns. Four-leaved clovers, for instance. Think how vast the total number of such changes must be, to produce so many corresponding changes in a couple of years. Think how many, *many* recessives there must be, existing only in gene patterns till their mates show up. We'll just have to take our chances of something really deadly accumulating. We'd never know till too late."

"The dust—"

"Yeah. The radiodust. It's colloidal, and uncountable other radio-colloids were formed when the bombs went off, and ordinary dirt gets into unstable isotopic forms near the craters. And there are radiogases too, probably. The poison is all over the world by now, spread by wind and air currents. Colloids can be suspended indefinitely in the atmosphere.

"The concentration isn't too high for life, though a physicist told me he'd measured it as being very near the safe limit and there'll probably be a lot of cancer. But it's everywhere. Every breath we draw, every crumb we eat and drop we drink, every clod we walk on, the dust is there. It's in the stratosphere, clear on down to the surface, probably a good distance below. We could only escape by sealing ourselves in air-conditioned vaults and wearing spacesuits whenever we got out, and under present conditions that's impossible.

"Mutations were rare before, because a charged particle has to get pretty close to a gene and be moving fast before its electromagnetic effect causes physico-chemical changes, and then that particular chromosome has to enter into reproduction. Now the charged particles, and the gamma rays producing still more, are everywhere. Even at the comparatively low concentration, the odds favor a given organism having so many cells changed that at least one will give rise to a mutant. There's even a good chance of like recessives meeting in the first generation, as we've seen. Nobody's safe, no place is free."

"The geneticist thinks some true humans will continue."

"A few, probably. After all, the radioactivity isn't too concentrated, and it's burning itself out. But it'll take fifty or a hundred years for the process to drop to insignificance, and by then the pure stock will be way in the minority. And there'll still be all those unmatched recessives, waiting to show up."

"You were right. We should never have created science. It brought the twilight of the race."

"I never said that. The race brought its own destruction, through misuse of science. Our culture was scientific anyway, in all except its psychological basis. It's up to us to take that last and hardest step. If we do, the race may yet survive."

Drummond gave Robinson a push toward the inner door. "You're exhausted, beat up, ready to quit. Go on in and see Elaine. Give her my regards. Then take a long rest before going back to work. I still think you've got a good kid."

Mechanically, the *de facto* President of the United States left the room. Hugh Drummond stared after him a moment, then went out into the street.

PAUL CARTER

THE LAST OBJECTIVE

FOR uncounted eons the great beds of shale and limestone had known the stillness and the darkness of eternity. Now they trembled and shuddered to the passage of an invader; stirred and vibrated in sleepy protest at a disturbance not of Nature's making.

Tearing through the masses of soft rock, its great duralloy cutters screaming a hymn of hate into the crumbling crust, its caterpillar treads clanking and grinding over gravel shards fresh-torn from their age-old strata, lurched a juggernaut—one of the underground cruisers of the

Combined Western Powers. It was squat, ugly; the top of its great cutting head full forty feet above the clattering treads, its square stern rocking and swaying one hundred and fifty feet behind the diamond-hard prow. It was angular, windowless; there were ugly lumps just behind the shrieking blades which concealed its powerful armament.

It had been built for warfare in an age when the sea and air were ruled by insensate rocket projectiles which flashed through the skies to spend their atomic wrath upon objectives which had long since ceased to exist; where infantry no longer was Queen of Battles, since the ravages of combat had wiped out the armies which began the war. And floods of hard radiation, sterilizing whole populations and making hideous mutational horrors of many of those who were born alive, had prevented the conscription of fresh armies which might have won the war.

The conflict had been going on for more than a generation. The causes had long been forgotten; the embattled nations, burrowing into the earth, knew only a fiery longing for revenge. The chaos produced by the first aerial attacks had enabled the survivors to hide themselves beyond the reach even of atomic bombs to carry on the struggle. Navies and armored divisions exchanged knowledge; strategy and tactics underwent drastic revamping. Psychology, once the major hope of mankind for a solution to the war problem, now had become perverted to the ends of the militarists, as a substitute for patriotism to motivate the men at war. In new ways but with the old philosophies, the war went on; and therefore this armored monster clawed its way through the earth's crust toward its objective.

On the "bridge" of the underground warship, a small turret in the center of its roof, Commander Sanderson clung to a stanchion as he barked orders to his staff through the intercom. The ship proper was swung on special mountings and gyro-stabilized to divorce it from the violent jolting of the lower unit, consisting of the drill, the treads, and the mighty, earth-moving atomic engines. But still some of the lurching and jouncing of the treads was transmitted up through the store rooms through the crew's quarters to the bridge, and the steel deck underfoot swayed and shook drunkenly. However, men had once learned to accustom themselves to the fitful motions of the sea; and the hardened skipper paid no attention to the way his command pounded forward.

Commander Sanderson was a thickset man, whose hunched shoulders and bull neck suggested the prize ring. But he moved like a cat, even here inside this vibrating juggernaut, as he slipped from one command post to another, reading over the shoulders of unheeding operators the findings of their instruments. The Seismo Log was an open book to his practiced eye; his black brows met in a deep frown as he noticed a severe shock registered only two minutes previously, only a few hundred yards to starboard. He passed by the radio locator and the radioman; their jobs would come later, meantime radio silence was enforced on both sides. The thin little soundman adjusted his earphones as the "Old Man" came by: "No other diggers contacted, sir," he muttered automatically and continued listening. The optical technician leaped to his feet and saluted smartly as the commander passed; he would have nothing to do unless they broke into a cavern, and so he rendered the military courtesy his fellows could not.

Sanderson halted beside the post of the environmental technician. This man's loosely described rating covered many fields; he was at once geologist, radarman, vibration expert, and navigator. It was his duty to deduce the nature of their surroundings and suggest a course to follow.

"Your report," demanded Sanderson.

"Igneous rock across our course at fifteen thousand feet, I believe, sir," he replied promptly. "It's not on the chart, sir—probably a new formation."

Sanderson swore. This meant volcanic activity—and whether manmade or accidental, that spelled trouble. "Course?" he asked.

"Change course to one hundred seventy-five degrees—and half speed, sir, if you please, until I can chart this formation more accurately."

Sanderson returned his salute, turned on his heel. "Mr. Culver!"

The young lieutenant commander saluted casually. "Sir?"

Sanderson repressed another oath. He did not like the young executive officer with his lordly manners, his natty uniform and the coat of tan he had acquired from frequent ultraviolet exposure—a luxury beyond the means of most of the pasty-faced undermen. But, duty is duty. —"Change course to one seven five. Half speed," he ordered.

"Aye, aye, sir." Culver picked up a microphone, jabbed a phone jack into the proper plug, and pressed the buzzer.

Far below, near the clanking treads, Lieutenant Watson wiped the sweat from his brow—most of the ship was not as well insulated as the bridge, whose personnel must be at their physical peak at all times. He jumped as the intercom buzzed, then spoke into his chest microphone. "Navigation," he called.

"Bridge," came Culver's voice. "Change course to one seven five. Over."

"Navigation to bridge. Course, one seven five, aye, aye," said Watson mechanically. Then: "What is it, Culver?"

"Environmental thinks it's lava."

"Damnation." The old lieutenant—one of the few able-bodied survivors of the surface stages of the war—turned to his aides. "Change course to one seven five."

Peterson, brawny Navigator Third Class, stepped up to a chrome handle projecting from a circular slot and shoved it to "175," then turned a small crank for finer adjustment. Slowly the pitch of the great blades shifted—the sound of their turning, muffled by layers of armor, abruptly changed in tone.

Chief Navigator Schmidt looked up from a pile of strata charts. "Ask the exec to have a copy of the new formation sent down here," he said, speaking as calmly as if he were a laboratory technician requesting a routine report. Schmidt was the psycho officer's pride and joy; he was the only person aboard the underground cruiser who had never been subjected to a mental manhandling as a result of that worthy's suspicions. He was slightly plump, pink-cheeked, with a straggling yellow mustache—just a little childish; perhaps that was why he had never cracked.

His request was transmitted; up on the bridge, the environmental technician threw a switch, cutting a remote repeater into the series of scanners which brought him his information. Chief Navigator Schmidt heard the bell clang, fed a sheet of paper into the transcriber, and sat back happily to watch the results.

The great drillhead completed its grinding turn; the blades tore into the rock ahead of it again.

"Navigation to bridge: bearing one seven five," reported Watson.

"Carry on," returned young Culver. He pulled out the phone jack, plugged it in elsewhere.

Ensign Clark stroked the slight, fuzzy black beard which was one of many ego-boosters for his crushing introversion, along with the tattoos on his arms and the book of physical exercises which he practiced whenever he thought he was alone. At Culver's buzz, he cursed the exec vigorously, then opened the circuit. "Power," he replied diffidently.

"Bridge to power: reduce speed by one half. Over."

"Power to bridge: speed, one half—aye, aye." Clark put his hand over the mike, shouted at the nonrated man stationed at the speed lever. "You! Half speed, and shake the lead out of your pants!"

The clanking of the treads slowed; simultaneously the whine of the blades rose, cutting more rapidly to compensate for the decreased pressure from behind the drill.

In the hot, steam-filled galley, fat Chief Cook Kelly lifted the lid from a kettle to sniff the synthetic stew. "What stinkin' slum—an' to think they kicked about the chow back in the Surface Wars."

"Chief, they say there was *real meat* in the chow then," rejoined Marconi, Food Chemist First Class.

"Why, Marc, even I can remember—" he was interrupted by the intercom's buzz.

"Attention all hands!" came Culver's voice. "Igneous rock detected, probably a fresh lava flow. We have changed our course. Action is expected within a few hours—stand by to go to quarters. Repeating—"

Kelly spat expertly. His face was impassive, but his hand trembled as he replaced the lid on the kettle. "We better hurry this chow up, Marc. Heaven only knows when we'll eat again."

Lieutenant Carpenter raised his hand, slapped the hysterical Private Worth twice.

"Now shut up or I'll have the psych corpsmen go over you again," he snapped.

Worth dropped his head between his hands, said nothing.

Carpenter backed out of the cell. "I'm posting a guard here," he warned. "One peep out of you and the boys will finish what they started."

He slammed the door for emphasis.

"Well, sir, you did it again," said the sentry admiringly. "He was throwing things when you got here, but you tamed him in a hurry."

"We've got to get these cells soundproofed," muttered Carpenter abstractedly, putting on his glasses. "The combat detachment bunks are right next to them."

"Yeah, sir, I guess it's harder on the combat detachment than the rest of us. We've all got our watches and so forth, but they haven't got a thing to do until we hit an enemy city or something. They crack easy—like this Worth guy in here now."

Carpenter whirled on him. "Listen, corpsman, I'm too busy a man to be chasing up here to deal with every enlisted man in this brig—I've got the other officers to keep in line. And let's not be volunteering information to superiors without permission!" he hissed.

"I'm sorry, sir—" the guard began—but the lieutenant was gone!

The sentry smiled crookedly. "O. K., Mr. Carpenter, your big job is to keep the officers in line. I'm just wonderin' who's supposed to keep *you* out of this cell block."

Corporal Sheehan dealt the cards with sudden, jerky motions; his brow was furrowed, his face a study in concentration. One would have thought him a schoolboy puzzling over a difficult final examination.

Sergeants Fontaine and Richards snatched each card as it came, partly crushing the pasteboards as they completed their hands. Fat old Koch, Private First Class, waited until all the cards had been dealt, then grabbed the whole hand and clutched it against his broad stomach, glancing suspiciously at his fellow players.

Their conversation was in terse, jerky monosyllables—but around them other men of the combat detachment talked, loudly and incessantly. Private Carson sat in a corner, chain smoking in brief, nervous puffs. Coarse jokes and harsh laughter dominated the conversation. Nobody mentioned Culver's "alert" of a few minutes before.

"Three," grunted the obese Koch. Sheehan dealt him the cards swiftly.

"Hey!" Richards interrupted, before play could begin. "I didn't like that deal. Let's have a look at that hand."

"Know what you're callin' me?" retorted Sheehan, snatching the deck as Richards was about to pick it up.

"Yeah—I know what to call you, you lyin', yella cheat—"

Sheehan lurched to his feet, lashed out with a hamlike fist. Richards scrambled out of the way, bringing chair and table down with a crash. A moment later both men were on their feet and squared off.

Conversation halted; men drifted over toward the table even as Fontaine stepped between the two players. Koch had not yet fully reacted to the situation and was only halfway out of his chair.

"You fools!" shouted Fontaine. "You want the psych corpsmen on our necks again? That louse Carpenter said if there was another fight we'd all get it."

Corporal Sheehan's big fists unclenched slowly. "That low, stinkin'—"

"Sit down," said Koch heavily. "Fontaine's right. The psychs probably have a spy or two planted in this room." His eye rested briefly on Carson, still smoking silently alone in the corner, seemingly oblivious of the commotion.

"That Carson," muttered Richards, shifting the object of his anger. "I'll bet any money you want he's a stool for Carpenter."

"Always by himself," corroborated Sheehan. "What's the story about him—born in a lab somewhere, wasn't he?"

The others were moving away now that it was plain there was to be no fight. Koch picked up the cards, stacked them. "Carson may not even be human," he suggested. "The science profs have been workin' on artificial cannon fodder for years, and you can be sure if they ever do make a robot they're not goin' to talk about it until it's been tried in combat."

Carson overheard part of his statement; smiled shortly. He rose and left the room.

"See?" Richards went on. "Probably puttin' all four of us on report right now."

Lieutenant Carpenter placed the wire recorder back inside its concealed niche, polished his glasses carefully, opened his notebook, and made several entries in a neat schoolteacher's hand:

> Friction betw. Sheehan, Richards worse—psych. reg. next time back to Gen. Psych. Hosp. New Chicago. No sign men susp. Koch my agent; K. planting idea of robots in crew's minds per order. Can reveal Carson whenever enemy knows Powers mfg. robots in quantity. Fontaine well integrated, stopped fight—recomm. transfer my staff to Sanderson.

He put the notebook away, began to climb the nearest metal ladder with the mincing, catlike tread which the whole crew had learned to hate.

The lone guard before the massive lead-and-steel door of the central chamber saluted as the lieutenant passed. His task was to safeguard the ship's most important cargo—its sole atomic bomb. Carpenter asked him several routine word-association questions before proceeding.

The lieutenant paused just once more in his progress upward. This was to play back the tape of another listening device, this one piped into the quarters of the men who serviced the mighty atomic engines. Making notes copiously, he proceeded directly to the bridge.

"Captain, my report," he announced, not without some show of pride.

"Later," said Sanderson shortly, without looking up from a rough strata chart the environmental technician had just handed him.

"But it's rather important, sir. Serious trouble is indicated in the combat detachment—"

"It always is," retorted Sanderson in some heat. "Take your report to Culver; I'm busy."

Carpenter froze, then turned to the young lieutenant commander. "If you will initial this, please—"

Culver repressed a shudder. He couldn't keep back the rebellious feeling that the ancient navies had been better off with their primitive chaplains than the modern underground fleets with their prying psychiatrists. Of course, he hastily told himself, that was impossible today— organized religion had long since ceased to sanction war and had been appropriately dealt with by the government.

The Seismo Log recorded a prolonged disturbance directly ahead, and as Sanderson began his rounds the environmental technician called to him. "Sudden fault and more igneous activity dead ahead, sir," he reported.

"Carry on," replied Sanderson. "Probably artificial," he muttered half to himself. "Lot of volcanism in enemy territory . . . Mr. Culver!"

Culver hastily initialed the psycho officer's notebook and handed it back. "Sir?"

"Elevate the cutters twenty-five degrees—we're going up and come on the enemy from above."

The order was soon transmitted to navigation; Lieutenant Watson's efficient gang soon had the metallic behemoth inclined at an angle of twenty-five degrees and rising rapidly toward the surface. Chief Schmidt dragged out new charts, noted down outstanding information and relayed data topside.

The ship's body swung on its mountings as the treads assumed the new slant, preserving equilibrium throughout. An order from Ensign Clark of power soon had the ship driving ahead as fast as the cutters could tear through the living rock.

"Diggers ahead," the thin soundman called out suddenly, adjusting his earphones. He snapped a switch; lights flickered on a phosphorescent screen. "Sounds like about three, sir—one is going to intersect our course at a distance of about five thousand yards."

"Let him," grunted Sanderson. "Mr. Culver, you may level off now."

"Electronic activity dead ahead," and "Enemy transmitter dead ahead," the radio locator and radioman reported almost simultaneously, before Culver's quiet order had been carried out.

"Go to general quarters, Mr. Culver," ordered Sanderson quickly. The exec pressed a button.

Throughout the ship was heard the tolling of a great bell—slowly the strokes lost their ponderous beat, quickened in tempo faster and faster until they became a continuous pandemonium of noise; simultaneously the pitch increased. All of this was a trick devised by staff psych officers, believing it would produce a subconscious incentive to greater speed and urgency.

The observational and operational posts were already manned; now, as quickly as possible, reliefs took over the more grueling watches such as that of the environmental technician. Medical and psych corpsmen hurriedly unpacked their gear, fanned out through the ship. Ensign Clark's voice faltered briefly as he ordered the power consumption cut to a minimum.The great cruiser slowed to a crawl.

The galley was bedlam as Kelly and Marconi rushed from one kettle to the next, supervising the ladling of hot food into deep pans by the apprentices who had assembled in haste in response to Kelly's profane bellowing. Chow runners dashed madly out the door, slopping over the contents of the steaming dishes as they ran. "Battle breakfast" was on its way to the men; and even as the last load departed, Kelly shut off all power into the galley and shrugged his squat form into a heavy coverall. Marconi snatched two empty trays, filled them, and the two men wolfed their meal quickly and then ran at full tilt down toward the combat detachment's briefing room.

Here the scene was even more chaotic. Men helped one another hastily into coveralls, rubber-and-steel suits, metallic boots. They twisted each other's transparent helmets into place, buckled on oxygen tanks, kits of emergency rations, first-aid equipment, and great nightmarish-looking weapons. Richards and Sheehan, their quarrel temporarily forgotten, wrestled with the latter's oxygen valve. Koch struggled mightily with the metal joints of his attack suit, Fontaine checked the readings of the dials on a long, tubular "heat ray" machine. Carson, fully outfitted, manipulated the ingenious device which brought a cigarette to his lips and lit it. He took a few puffs, pressed another lever to eject the butt, and wrenched his helmet into place with gloved hands. From now until the battle was over, the men would carry all their air on their backs, compressed in cylinders. Underneath the shouts and the rattling noises of the armor could be heard the screams of Private Worth from his cell next door. They were suddenly cut off; one of Lieutenant Carpenter's watchful corpsmen had silenced the boy.

And now there was nothing to do but wait. The combat detachment's confusion subsided; but a subdued clatter of shifting armor, helmets being adjusted, tightening of joints, the rattle of equipment, and telephoned conversation continued. The new bridge watch checked their instruments, then settled down to careful, strained waiting. Sanderson paced his rounds, hearing reports and issuing occasional orders. Culver stood by the intercom, told the crew all their superiors knew of the opposition as the information came in. Carpenter cat-footed through the ship, followed at a discreet distance by four of his strong-arm men.

Ensign Clark was white with fear. He sat stiffly at his post like a prisoner in death row; the sweat rolled down his face and into his soft black

beard. He tried to repeat the auto-suggestion formulae Carpenter had
prescribed for him, but all that he could choke out was a series of earn-
est curses which a kinder age would have called prayers.

He jumped as if he had been shot at Culver's sudden announcement:
"Attention all hands. Enemy digger believed to have sighted this ship.
Prepare for action at close quarters." The voice paused, and then added:
"Bridge to power: full speed ahead for the next half hour, then bring
the ship to a halt. We'll let the enemy carry the fight to us."

Clark automatically repeated, "Full speed ahead—" then cringed as
the crewman slammed the lever over and the cruiser leaped forward with
a shrill whine of its blades. "No!" he suddenly yelled, leaping out of his
seat. "Not another inch,—stop this ship!" He ran over to the speed
lever, pushed at the crewman's hands. "I won't be killed, I won't, I
won't!" The brawny crewman and the maddened officer wrestled desperately for a moment then the crewman flung his superior on his back
and stood over him, panting. "I'm sorry, sir—"

Clark lay there whimpering for a few seconds, then made a quick
grab inside his shirt and leveled a pistol at the towering crewman. "Get
over there," he half-sobbed, "and stop this ship before I shoot you."

The white-uniformed psych corpsman flung open the door and fired,
all in one motion. The crewman instinctively backed away as the little
pellet exploded, shredding most of Clark's head into his cherished beard;
the crewman stood over the body, making little wordless sounds.

"Go off watch," ordered Carpenter, coming into the room on the heels
of his henchman. "Get a sedative from the medics." He gazed linger-
ingly, almost appreciatively, on the disfigured face of the dead man before covering it with the ensign's coat. Then he called Culver and told
him briefly what had happened.

"I'll send a relief," promised the exec. "Tell him to reduce speed in
another twenty minutes. That was quick thinking, Carpenter; the captain says you rate a citation." The psycho officer had failed to give the
corpsman credit for firing the shot.

Sanderson caught Culver's eye, put a finger to his lips.

"Huh?" Culver paused, then got the idea. "Oh—and, say, Carpenter—don't let the crew hear of this. It wouldn't do for them to know an
officer was the first to crack." There was a very faint trace of sarcasm
in his tone.

But Sanderson's warning was already too late. The power crewman
who had witnessed Clark's death agonies talked before he was put to
sleep; the medic who administered the sedative took it to the crew. By
the time Carpenter had received the new order from Culver, his efficient
corpsmen had disposed of Clark's body and the whole ship knew the
story. It hit the combat detachment like a physical blow; their strained
morale took a serious beating, and the officers grew alarmed.

"Pass the word to let them smoke," Sanderson finally ordered, after
the great ship had shuddered to a halt and backed a short distance up

the tunnel on his order. "Give them ten minutes—the enemy will take at least twice that to get here. Have Carpenter go down and administer drugs at his own discretion—maybe it will slow them for fighting, but if they crack they'll be of no use anyway."

And so for ten minutes the combat crewmen removed their helmets and relaxed, while the psychos moved unobtrusively throughout the room, asking questions here and there, occasionally giving drugs. Once they helped a man partially out of his armor for a hypo. Tension relaxed somewhat; the psych corpsmen could soothe as well as coerce.

Kelly and Marconi were engaged in a heated argument over the relative merits of synthetic and natural foods—a time-tested emotional release the two veterans used habitually. Koch was up to his ears in a more serious controversy—for Sheehan and Richards were practically at each other's throats again. Carson as usual said nothing, smoked continuously; even the level-headed Fontaine got up and paced the floor, his armor clanking as he walked. Three men had to be put to sleep. Then the ten-minute break was over and the strain grew even worse.

Carpenter spoke softly into the intercom. "Tell the commander that if battle is not joined in another hour I cannot prevent a mutiny. Culver, I *told* you not to leave that man on watch—if you had listened to me Ensign Clark need not have been liquidated."

Culver's lip curled; he opened his mouth to reply in his usual irritating manner—but at that moment the soundman flung the earphones off his head. The roar of shearing duralloy blades was audible several feet away as the phones bounced to the deck. "Enemy digger within one hundred feet and coming in fast!" the soundman shouted.

"Don't reverse engines!" Sanderson roared as Culver contacted the new power officer. "Turn on our drill, leaving the treads stationary— we'll call his bluff."

Culver issued the necessary order, then alerted the crew again. The great blades began to whirl once more; there was a brief shower of rocks, and they churned emptiness—their usual throbbing, tearing chant became a hair-raising shriek; the blast of air they raised kicked up a cloud of dust which blanketed the fresh-carved tunnel—"That's for their optical technician," explained Sanderson. "He'll be blind when he comes out—and we've a sharp gunnery officer down in fire control that will catch them by surprise."

The soundman gingerly picked up the headphones; the roar of the enemy's drill had dropped to a whisper—Sanderson's curious tactics evidently had him guessing, for he had slowed down—

The sound of the approaching drill was now audible without the benefit of electronic gear, as a muffled noise like the chewing of a great rat. Then came the chattering break-through, and Sanderson knew he had contacted the enemy, despite the dust clouds which baffled even the infrared visual equipment.

Temporarily blind, confused by the whirling blades of their motionless opponent, the enemy hesitated for the precious seconds that meant the difference between victory and destruction.

As the enemy warhead broke through, the cruiser's whirling blades suddenly came to a quivering halt. Simultaneously the forward batteries opened fire.

Gone were the days of laboring, sweating gun crews and ammunition loaders. All the stubby barrels were controlled from a small, semicircular control panel like an organ console. Lieutenant Atkins, a cool, competent, graying officer who had once been an instructor at the military academy, calmly pressed buttons and pulled levers and interestedly watched the results by means of various types of mechanical "eyes." And so it was that when the sweep second hand of his chronometer crossed the red line, Atkins' sensitive fingers danced over the keys and the ship rocked to the salvos of half its guns.

Magnified and echoed in the narrow tunnel, the crash of the barrage rolled and reverberated and shouted in an uninterrupted tornado of pure noise, roar upon roar—the light of the explosions was by contrast insignificant, a vicious reddish flare quickly snuffed in the dust. The ship jerked with each salvo; faint flashes and Olympian thunders tossed the great cruiser like a raft on the wild Atlantic. The fury of sound beat through the thick armor plate, poured and pounded savagely past the vaunted "Soundproof" insulation. The decks lurched and reeled underfoot; instruments and equipment trembled with bone-shaking vibrations. Crash upon thunderous crash filled the air with new strains of this artillery symphony; and then Culver pressed a button. His voice could not be heard through the racket, but the sudden glow of a red light in the combat detachment's assembly room transmitted his order instantly—"Away landing party!"

And then the trap between the great, flat treads was sprung, and the mechanical monster spawned progeny, visible only by infrared light in the underground gloom—little doll-like figures in bulky, nightmarish costumes, dropping from a chain ladder to the broken shale underfoot, running and stumbling through the debris, falling and picking themselves up and falling again like so many children—Marconi and Kelly and Carson and Sheehan and Richards and Fontaine and Koch, tripping over the debris and fragments which the great machine had made.

And at last the enemy cruiser replied, even as the landing party picked its way through the obscuring dust and fanned out from its source. Though confused and blind, the men of the other ship, too, had been prepared for action, and thus new sounds were added to the din that were not of the attackers' making.

A titanic explosion rocked the carriage of Sanderson's cruiser; then another, and still another, strewing steel fragments indiscriminately among the men in the tunnel. The ferocity of the defense was less than the attack; much of their armament must have been destroyed on the first salvo—but what remained wrought havoc. Some quick-witted commander of the enemy must have anticipated the landing of a ground party for fragmentation shells burst near the embattled cruisers, and here and there the armored figures began to twist and jerk and go down. Their comrades dropped into the partial protection of the broken rock and continued their advance.

Fontaine ran and crawled and scrambled and crouched over the tunnel floor, which was visible to his infrared-sensitive helmet, and torn now even more by narrowing slivers of steel. His hand found a valve, twisted it to give him more oxygen for this most critical part of the struggle. He did not think much; he was too busy keeping alive. But a bitter thought flashed across his mind— *This part of war hasn't changed a bit.* He leaped over a strange and terrible object in which armor, blood, rock, and flesh made a fantastic jigsaw puzzle which had lost its meaning. Once again he merely noted the item in his subconscious mind; he did not think.

Lieutenant Atkins' fingers still danced over the console; his face was exalted like that of a man playing a concerto. And into the symphony of death which he wove with subtle skill there crept fewer and fewer of the discords of the enemy's guns.

Sanderson paced the deck moodily, communicating briefly with his subordinates by means of lip reading which Culver swiftly translated into many-colored lights. Information came back to the bridge in the same manner. Sanderson smiled with grim satisfaction at the scarcity of dark lamps on the master damage control board. Those mighty walls could take a lot of punishment, and damage so far had been superficial —one blast in the psycho ward; Private Worth would suffer Carpenter's displeasure no longer.

The helmeted monstrosities grew bolder in their advance as the counter-barrage slackened. Now there was but one battery in action, far to the left—all the thunder came from their own ship.

Fontaine rose from the little depression in which he had been crouching. Another man waved to him; from that outsized suit it would have to be Koch. The big man's armor was dented, the rubber portions torn— his steel right boot looked like a large, wrinkled sheet of tinfoil, and he dragged the leg behind him. But he saw Fontaine, pointed a gauntleted finger into the gloom. The enemy ship must be up there; yes, there was the flash of the one operating gun—Fontaine moved forward.

There was another, nearer flash; something exploded on Koch's chestplate, knocking him down. He moved, feebly, like a crushed insect, then lay still. Fontaine immediately slipped back into his hollow; for here was the enemy.

A man in a light, jointed metal suit of Asian make appeared from behind a boulder, slipped over to Koch's body to examine it, felt for Koch's weapons.

Fontaine unslung the long, bazookalike heat ray tube—an adaptation of very slow atomic disintegration—and pressed the firing stud. The weapon contributed no noise and no flare to the hellish inferno of the tunnel, but the Asiatic suddenly straightened up, took a step forward. That was all he had time for.

Accident and his jointed armor combined to keep his body standing. Fontaine made sure of his man by holding the heat ray on him until the enemy's armor glowed cherry-red, then released the stud. He came forward, gave the still-glowing figure a push. The body collapsed with a clatter across Koch. Fontaine pushed on—the dust was at last clearing slightly, and directly ahead loomed the enemy ship.

Another Asiatic appeared over a short ridge; too quick for the heat ray. Fontaine drew his pistol and fired. The pellet flared; another enemy went down.

Something whizzed over Fontaine's head; he ducked, ran for cover. Somebody was firing highspeed metallic slugs from an old-fashioned machine gun, and his partly-rubber suit would not stop them. Miraculously he found himself unharmed in front of the enemy ship.

Its drill was torn and crumpled, blades lying cast off amongst the rocks; one of the treads was fouled, and the forward part of the carriage was smashed in completely. This war vehicle would obviously never fight again—another volley of slugs chattered overhead, and Fontaine rolled back out of the way. *Snap judgment,* he told himself ironically in another rare flash of lucidity. *Maybe she'll never fight after this time, but she's got plenty of spirit right now.*

He dug a hole in the loose shale and tried to cover himself as much as possible, meanwhile surveying the layout. They couldn't know he was here, or his life would have been snuffed out; but he could neither advance nor retreat. He absently transmitted the prearranged "contact" signal back to the cruiser. Then he settled himself, soldierwise, to wait as long as might be necessary.

Fontaine's "contact," and several others, returned to their ship as lights on a board. The landing party could proceed no further or they would encounter their own barrage. Sanderson immediately gave the "cease fire" order. The barrage lifted.

Culver shouted down an immediate flood of radio reports that broke the sudden, aching silence. "Lieutenant Atkins, you will continue action against the remaining enemy battery until you have destroyed it, or until I inform you that members of the task force have neutralized it."

"Aye, aye, sir." Atkins turned back to his guns, studied the image of the battered enemy ship which was becoming increasingly visible as the dust settled. He restored all the automatic controls to manual, pressed several buttons judiciously, and fingered a firing switch.

To Fontaine, crouching in his retreat under the enemy ship, the sudden silence which followed the barrage was almost intolerable. One moment the guns had thundered and bellowed overhead; the next, there were a few echoes and reverberations and then all was over.

His ears sang for minutes; his addled brains slowly returned to a normal state. And he realized that the silence was not absolute. It was punctually broken by the crash of the remaining enemy battery, and soon at less frequent intervals by the cautious probing of Atkins' turrets. And between the blows of this duel of giants he could at last hear the whine of metal slugs over his head.

This weapon had him stumped. The Asiatic explosive bullets, such as the one that had killed Koch, only operated at fairly close quarters; the rubber suits were fairly good insulation against death rays; and the Asiatics had no heat ray. But with an antiquated machine gun an Asiatic could sit comfortably at a considerable distance from him and send a volley of missiles crunching through the flimsy Western armor to rip him apart in helpless pain. He raised his head very slightly and looked around. The detachment was well trained; he could see only three of his fellows and they were well concealed from the enemy. Under infrared light—the only possible means of vision in the gloom of the tunnel— they looked like weird red ghosts.

Something gleamed ahead of him. He sighted along the tubular barrel of the heat ray, energized its coils. The mechanism hummed softly; the Asiatic jumped out of his hiding place and right into the machine gun's line of fire. The singing bits of metal punched a neat line of holes across his armor and knocked him down, twisting as he fell. Moments later the chattering stream stopped flowing, and Fontaine dashed for more adequate cover. Bullets promptly kicked up dust in little spurts in the hollow he had just vacated.

He searched the darkness, a weird, shimmering ghostland revealed to him by its own tremendous heat through his infrared equipment. The ship and his armor were very well insulated; he had not been conscious of the stifling heat or the absolute night-gloom which would have made combat impossible for an unprepared, unprotected soldier of the Surface Wars.

Atkins' insistent batteries spoke; there was a great flash and a series of explosions at the enemy target to the left. Fontaine seized the opportunity to make a charge on the loosely-piled boulders which, his practiced eye told him, sheltered the deadly machine gun. He fell and rolled out of the line of fire as the opposing gunner found him and swerved his weapon; then began to fire explosive pellets at the crude nest, showering it with a series of sharp reports. The enemy machine gun swung back and forth, raking the terrain in search of the invader.

Fontaine unloaded his heat ray, placed it in a well-sheltered crevice and worked it around until it was aimed at the enemy, then shorted the coils. The weapon throbbed with power; rocks began to glow, and the flying slugs poured down upon the menacing heat ray, trying to silence it. Meanwhile Fontaine, like uncounted warriors of all ages, began cautiously to work his way around to the left for a flank attack. Indeed, there were many things in war that had not changed.

"Fire control to bridge: enemy battery silenced," Atkins reported firmly.

"Secure fire control," Culver ordered, then turned on his heel. "The enemy's ordnance is destroyed, sir," he asserted. "Our combat crewmen are engaging the enemy in front of his ship."

"Send Mr. Atkins my congratulations," Sanderson replied promptly. "Then inform the combat detachment of the situation."

Culver turned back to the intercom—then started, as a siren wailed somewhere in the bowels of the ship. A station amidships was buzzing frantically; he plugged in the mike. "Bridge," he answered.

"Atomic bomb watch to bridge: instruments show unprecedented activity of the bomb. Dangerous reaction predicted."

Culver fought to keep his voice down as he relayed the information. The bridge watch simply came to a dead stop; all eyes were on Sanderson.

Even the phlegmatic commander hesitated. Finally: "Prepare to abandon ship," he ordered, heavily.

At once the confusion which had accompanied the preparations of the combat detachment was repeated throughout the ship. Atomic bombs by this time were largely made of artificial isotopes and elements; the type which they carried had never been tested in combat—and radioactive elements can do strange and unpredictable things when stimulated. Mere concussion had started the trouble this time, and the mind of man was incapable of prophesying the results. The bomb might merely increase in the speed of its radioactive decay, flooding the ship and the bodies of its men with deadly gamma rays; it might release enormous heat and melt the cruiser into a bubbling pool of metal; it might blast both of the ships and a mile or cubic mile of rock out of existence—but all they could do was abandon the cruiser and hope for the best. All mankind was unable to do more.

Sanderson's forceful personality and Carpenter's prowling corpsmen prevented a panic. Men cursed as they struggled with obstinate clasps and joints. A few of Kelly's apprentices who had not gone into combat flung cases of concentrated food through the landing trap to the tunnel floor. Culver packed the ship's records—logs, papers, muster sheets, inventories—into an insulated metal can for preservation. A picked force of atomic technicians in cumbersome lead suits vanished into the shielded bomb chamber with the faint hope of suppressing the reaction.

Sanderson paused before sealing his helmet. "Mr. Culver, you will have all hands assemble in or near the landing trap. We must advance, destroy the enemy and take refuge in his ship; it is our only hope."

Navigation buzzed; Culver made the necessary connection. "One moment, sir," he murmured to Sanderson. "Bridge."

The young exec could visualize old Lieutenant Watson's strained expression, his set jaw. "Navigation requests permission to remain aboard when ship is abandoned," Watson said slowly. "Chances of crew's survival would be materially increased if the ship reversed engines and departed this area—"

Sanderson was silent a long moment. "Permission granted," he finally answered in a low voice. He started to say more; caught Carpenter's eye and was silent.

But Culver could not maintain military formality in answering Watson's call. "Go ahead, Phil, and—thanks," he replied, almost in a whisper.

Carpenter stepped forward quickly. "This is no time for sentiment, Mr. Culver," he snapped. "Lieutenant Watson's behavior was a little naïve for an officer, but the important fact remains that his antiquated altruism may be the means of preserving the lives of more important personnel." He waved a sheaf of loose papers excitedly. "This report of mine, for example, on the psychiatric aspects of this battle will be invaluable to the Board—"

Crack!

All the wiry power of the young exec's rigidly trained body went into the punch; literally traveled through him from toe to fist and exploded on the psycho officer's jaw. Months of harsh discipline—psychological manhandling—the strain of combat—repressed emotions, never really unhampered since his childhood—the sense of the war's futility which had not been completely trained out of anyone—his poorly-concealed hatred for Carpenter—all these subconscious impressions came boiling up and sped the blow—and his hand was incased in a metal glove.

Carpenter's head snapped back. His feet literally flew off the deck as his body described a long arc and slammed into the far wall. He sprawled there grotesquely like a discarded marionette. Miraculously his glasses were unbroken.

The iron reserve which Sanderson had kept throughout the battle left him with the disruption of his neat, disciplined little military cosmos. For a long time he was unable to speak or move.

Two tough-looking psych corpsmen closed in on the exec, who stood facing the fallen officer, his fists clenched. He twisted angrily as they grabbed his arms.

"Let him alone," Sanderson ordered, coming to his senses. They reluctantly released Culver.

"Mr. Culver," the skipper said very quietly, "I need you now. You will resume your duties until this crisis is over. But, if we come through this, I'm going to see that you're broken."

Culver faced him, anger draining out of him like the color from his flushed face. He saluted, turned back to the intercom to give out the last order Sanderson had issued. "Attention all hands," he called mechanically. "Fall in at the landing trap to abandon ship."

Sanderson beckoned to the two psych corpsmen. "Please take Lieutenant Carpenter to sick bay," he ordered. "Bring him around as soon as you can."

The Asiatic squatted crosslegged behind his shining pneumatic machine gun, frantically raking the rock-strewn ground before him. The air ahead shimmered and danced with heat; the other side of his crude stone shelter must be glowing whitely, and the sweat ran down his yellow face even though the tiny cooling motor within his armor hummed savagely as it labored to keep him from suffocating. He must destroy the offending heat ray or abandon his position.

A confused impression of rubber-and-metal armor was all he received as Fontaine rushed upon him from the side. The two men came together and went down with a loud clatter of armor; rolled over and over in quick, bitter struggle. Even in the Atomic age there could be hand-to-hand combat.

It was an exhausting fight; the battle suits were heavy, and awkward. They wrestled clumsily, the clank of their armor lending an incongruously comic note. The lithe Asiatic broke a hold, cleared his right hand. Fontaine rolled over to avoid the glittering knife his opponent had succeeded in drawing. Here beneath the crust a rip in his rubberized suit would spell disaster. The Asiatic jumped at him to follow up his advantage. Fontaine dropped back on his elbows, swung his feet around and kicked viciously.

The metal boot shattered the Asiatic's glass face plate, nearly broke his neck from its impact. Shaken by the cruel blow to his face, blinded by blood drawn by the jagged glass, gasping from the foul air and the oppressive heat, he desperately broke away and ran staggeringly toward the right, misjudging the direction of his ship.

Fontaine estimated the number of explosive bullets he had left, then let his enemy go, knowing there would be no more danger from that quarter. He lay unmoving beside the abandoned machine gun, breathing heavily. His near-miraculous survival thus far deserved a few minutes' rest.

The enemy's landing trap, like the Western one, was under the ship's carriage; instead of a chain ladder, a ramp had been let down. A terrific melee now raged around the ramp—Fontaine and his opponent had been so intent on their duel they had not seen the tide of battle wash past them. Here and there lay dead men of both sides; his recent enemy had soon been overcome and lay not a score of feet away, moving spasmodically. Battle-hardened as he was, Fontaine seriously debated putting the fellow out of his misery—death from armor failure was the worst kind in this war except radioactive poisoning—then carefully counted his explosive pellets again. Only six—he might need them. He dismissed the writhing Asiatic from his mind.

He looked up at the smashed hull of the enemy ship, and an idea came to him. They wouldn't be watching here, with their ship in danger of being boarded elsewhere.

He rose, moved quietly to the great right-hand tread. The flat links here were torn and disconnected; he seized a loose projection and hauled himself upward. Slipping and scrambling, using gauntleted hands and booted feet, he reached the top of the tread.

Directly above him was a jagged hole in the ship's carriage, about four feet long. He seized the edges and somehow managed to wriggle his way inside.

The interior was a shambles of smashed compartments, with men and metal uncleanly mated. Fontaine laboriously pushed his way forward, climbing over and around barriers flung up at the caprice of Atkins' guns. Once he was forced to expend one of the precious pellets; the recoil nearly flattened him at such close quarters, but he picked himself up and climbed through the still-smoking hole into a passageway which was buckled somewhat but still intact.

He looked carefully in both directions, then saw a ladder and began to ascend. It brought him into a small storage compartment which was still illuminated. He grunted in satisfaction; if he had reached the still-powered portion of the ship, he was going in the right direction.

He eased the door open three inches; air hissed—this compartment must be sealed off. He quickly passed through, closed the door, and cautiously tested the air—good; this part of the ship still had pure air and insulation. Confidently he continued forward and climbed another ladder toward the bridge.

He had to wait at one level until a sentry turned his back. Then he sprang, and his steel fingers sank into the Asiatic's throat. There was no outcry.

Faintly from below there came the sounds of a struggle; his comrades had successfully invaded the ship. Curiously, Fontaine tried his helmet radio. It had been put out of commission in his fight with the machine gunner outside.

There were no more sentries; that was odd. He proceeded with extreme caution as he came to the ladder leading up to the bridge. Here would be the brains of the Asiatic ship; his five remaining pellets could end the engagement now that the battle was raging on enemy territory.

He stumbled over something—a man's foot. He dragged the body out of the shadows which had concealed it.

"What the devil—"

The man had been another guard. His chest was shattered; an explosive pistol was clutched in his right hand. One pellet was missing from the chamber.

Wonderingly Fontaine climbed the ladder, halted at the door.

Lying at his feet was another sentry. The man's body was unmarked, but his face bore signs of a painful death. A small supersonic projector lay near him.

Fontaine opened the door—and turned away, sick.

Somebody had turned on a heat ray at close quarters. Officers and enlisted men lay in charred horror. And in the center of the room, the ship's commanding officer slumped on a bloodstained silken cushion. The man had committed honorable suicide with a replica of an ancient Japanese samurai sword.

In his left hand was a crumpled sheet of yellow paper, evidently a radiogram.

Fontaine took the scrap from the lax yellow fingers, puzzled over the Oriental characters.

Then he went outside, and closed the door, and sat down at the head of the ladder to await the coming of men who might be able to solve the mystery.

The last man scrambled down the swaying chains and dropped to the ground from the Western cruiser.

Lieutenants Watson and Atkins were alone in the ship.

"Why did you stay?" demanded Watson, throwing the starting switch. He had hastily rigged an extension from the power room to navigation. "Only one man is needed to operate the ship, in an emergency."

Lieutenant Atkins found a fine cigar in his uniform. "I've been saving this," he remarked, stripping off the cellophane wrapper lovingly. "The condemned man indulges in the traditional liberties."

"Answer my question," Watson insisted, advancing the speed lever.

Atkins pressed a glowing heating-coil "lighter" to the tip of the cigar. "Let me ask you this—why did *you* make this heroic gesture?"

Watson flushed. "You might as well ask—why fight at all?"

"You might," Atkins said, smiling slightly.

"I did this because our men come first!" Watson shouted almost in fury.

Atkins chuckled. "Forgive me, old friend—I find it hard to shake off the illusions I had back in the Last Surface War, myself." He blew a huge cloud of smoke. "But when Culver sent down the commander's congratulations to me for silencing that enemy battery, it struck me how empty all our battles and decorations are."

Watson shoved the speed lever to maximum; the cruiser rolled backward down the tunnel at a terrific velocity, no longer impeded by masses of rock. After a long silence he asked: "Atkins—what were *you* fighting for?"

Atkins looked him squarely in the eye. "Well, I managed to hypnotize myself into a superficial love of massed artillery—it's a perversion of my love for the symphony—used to conduct a small orchestra at the academy before it was dissolved and the funds allocated to a military band. I liked that orchestra; felt I was doing something constructive for once." He was silent for a while, smoking and reminiscing. Coming back to reality with a start, he went on hastily: "Of course underneath it all I guess I was motivated just the way you were—to maintain the dead traditions of the service, to save our shipmates who would have died anyway, and to advance a cause which no longer exists."

Watson buried his head in his hands. "I fought because I thought it was the right thing to do."

Atkins softened. "So did I, my friend," he admitted. "But it's all over now—"

He paused to flick ashes from the cigar. "I saved something else for this," he went on irrelevantly. "Carpenter is gone now, Watson, so we can dispense with his psychopathic mummery. What a joke if he should ever know I had this aboard." He laughed lightly, producing a small, gold-stamped book bound in black leather. "This sort of thing is the only value left, for us," he asserted. "Let us pray."

And thus, a few minutes later, the two elderly officers died. It was not a great blast, as atomic explosions go, but ship and men and rock puffed and sparkled in bright, cleansing flame.

The bridge of the captured enemy ship looked fresh and clean. The remains of the Asiatic commanders' gruesome self-destructon had been cleared away; blackened places about the room glistened with new paint. It was several hours after the battle.

Sanderson stood at attention reading a report to his surviving officers. Sergeant Fontaine, permitted to attend as the first witness to the baffling slaughter, fidgeted in the presence of so much gold braid. Private Carson, the strange child of the laboratory, present to assist Fontaine in guarding the disgraced executive officer, stood stolidly, a detached expression on his face.

"—and therefore the atomic explosion, when it did come, was hardly noticed here," the commander concluded his report. "Lieutenant Watson did his duty"—he glared covertly at Culver, manacled between Fontaine and Carson—"and if we can return safely to our Advance Base this will go down as one of the greatest exploits in the history of warfare."

He cleared his throat. "At ease," he said offhandedly, straightening his papers. The officers and crewmen relaxed, shifted position, as Sanderson went on more informally: "Before we discuss any future action, however, there is this business of the Asiatic warlords—their inexplicable suicide. Lieutenant Carpenter?"

The psycho officer stepped forward, caressing his bandaged jaw. "I have questioned the ten prisoners we took," he announced as clearly as he could through the bandages, "and my men have applied all of the standard means of coercion. I am firmly convinced that the Asiatic prisoners are as ignorant as we are of the reason for their masters' strange behavior."

Sanderson motioned him back impatiently. "Ensign Becker?"

The personnel officer rustled some sheets of paper. "I have checked the records carefully, sir," he asserted, "and Lieutenant Commander Culver is the only man aboard this ship who understands written Asiatic."

Sanderson's gaze swept over all his officers. "Gentlemen, the executive officer was guilty of striking the psycho officer shortly before we abandoned ship—I witnessed the action. I want to know if you will accept as valid his translation of the radiogram which Sergeant Fontaine found on the body of the enemy leader."

"I object!" shouted Carpenter immediately. "Culver violated one of the *basic* principles of the officers' corps—he can't be completely *sane.*"

"True, perhaps," admitted Sanderson testily, "but, lieutenant, would you care to suggest a plan of action—*before* we discover why our late enemies killed themselves so conveniently?"

"Commander, are you trying to vindicate this man?" Carpenter demanded indignantly.

Sanderson looked at the psycho officer with an expression almost contemptuous. "You should know by this time, lieutenant, that I have never liked Mr. Culver," he snorted. "Unfortunately this could be a question of our own survival. If the officers present accept Culver's translation of the message, I shall act on it."

"But we came here to begin court-martial proceedings—"

"That can wait," the skipper interrupted impatiently. "This is my command, Carpenter, and I wish you'd remember that. Well, gentlemen? A show of hands, please—" He paused to count. "Very well," he decided shortly. "Sergeant Fontaine, give the message to the prisoner."

Fontaine threw a snappy salute and handed the yellow scrap of paper silently to the exec. Carson loosened his grip somewhat; Culver began to work out the translation—

> FROM: Supreme Headquarters in Mongolia
> TO: All field commanders
> SUBJECT: Secret weapon X-39, failure of.
> 1. Research project X-39, a semiliving chemical process attacking all forms of protoplasm, was released on the South American front according to plan last night.
> 2. Secret weapon X-39 was found to be uncontrollable and is spreading throughout our own armies all over the world. In addition, infection centering on the secret research laboratories has covered at least one third of Asia.
> 3. You are directed to—

"Well?" demanded Sanderson.

"That's all, sir," Culver replied quietly.

The room immediately exploded into conversation, all pretense at military discipline forgotten. The commander shouted for order. He stood even straighter than his normally stiff military bearing allowed; he was the picture of triumph and confidence.

"This interrupted message can be interpreted in only one way," he declared ringingly. "Ensign Becker, you will inform all hands that the enemy's suicide is worldwide and that *the war is over!*"

For a long, long moment there was dead silence. The last peace rumor had died when most of these men were children. It took much time for the realization to sink in that the senseless murder was over at last.

Then—cheering, laughing, slapping one another's backs, the officers gave way to their emotions. Many became hysterical; a few still stood dumbly, failing to comprehend what "peace" was.

Battle-hardened, stiffly militaristic Sanderson's face was wet with tears.

And then Lieutenant Carpenter screamed.

All eyes were riveted on the psycho officer, a hideous suspicion growing in their minds as he cringed in a corner and yelled meaninglessly, his whole body shaking with unutterable terror. They had all seen men afraid of death—but in Carpenter's mad eyes was reflected the essence of all the hells conceived in the ancient religions—he slavered, he whimpered, and suddenly his body began to *ripple*.

His fellow officers stood rooted to the deck in sheer fright as he *slid* rather than fell into a huddled heap that continued to sink down after he had fallen, spreading and flowing and finally *running like water*.

Sanderson stared in stunned horror at a pool of sticky yellow fluid that dripped through a bronze grating in the floor.

Culver grinned foolishly. "Yes, commander," he said airily, "you were right—the war is over."

Sanderson gingerly picked Carpenter's notebook out of the sodden pile of clothing and bandages and the broken glass of the psycho officer's spectacles. "Read that radiogram again," he ordered hoarsely, signaling to the two crewmen to release their prisoner.

The exec rubbed his wrists to restore circulation as the handcuffs were removed. Then he picked up the crumpled paper, smoothed it out.

"Research Project X-39, a semiliving chemical process attacking all forms of protoplasm, was released—" Culver choked over the words. "Sir, I—"

And then in a few terrible minutes of screams and curses and hideous dissolution, all the officers understood why the Asiatics had committed suicide.

Sergeant Fontaine for some reason kept his head. He fired four shots rapidly from his pistol; one missed Carson, the others found their mark in Sanderson, Culver, and Becker, who looked oddly grateful as their bodies jerked under the impact and they slumped in unholy disintegration.

Sanderson saluted solemnly with a dissolving arm.

Fontaine had one more pellet in his gun. He hesitated, looked inquiringly for a moment at the inscrutable Carson, then as he felt a subtle *loosening* under his skin he turned the weapon on himself and fired.

Private Carson puffed nervously at a cigarette, staring in shocked, horrible fascination at the weird carnage—then ran blindly, fleeing from he knew not what.

The terror flew on wings of light through the ruined enemy ship. Technicians, bridge watches, the ten enemy prisoners, psych corpsmen, navigators, combat crewmen—even the dead Oriental commanders joined the dissolving tide. Richards and Sheehan were the last to go;

they hysterically accused each other of causing the horror, trying desperately to find some tangible cause for the Doom—they fought like great beasts, and fat Koch was not there to stop the fight—they struggled, and coalesced suddenly into one rippling yellow pool.

Carson, still incased in his armor, raced and clattered through the deserted ship—the sound of his passing was almost sacrilegious, like the desecration of a tomb. Everywhere silence, smashed walls, empty suits of armor, little bundles of wet clothing, and curious yellow stains. *Die, why can't you die?*

Carson, the strange one—separated by more than aloofness from his fellows—spawned in a laboratory, the culmination of thousands of experiments in the vain hope of circumventing the extremity of the slaughter by manufacturing men. His metabolism was subtly different from that of normal man; he *needed* nicotine in his system for some reason—that was why he chain-smoked—but tobacco was a narcotic; it could not protect protoplasm. *Why can't you die, Carson?* All through the ship, silence, wet clothing, little pools—not even the dead had escaped—nothing moved or lived except this running, half-mad man— or Thing—born in a laboratory, if one could say he *had* been "born."

A quick movement of his gloved hands sealed the round helmet on his shoulders. He ran and stumbled and climbed through passageways and down ladders; he fairly flew down the landing ramp and soon disappeared in the black depths of the tunnel.

And the nighted cavern so recently hacked from the outraged crust was given back to the darkness and the silence it had always known.

ARTHUR C. CLARKE

LOOPHOLE

From: President
To: Secretary, Council of Scientists.

I have been informed that the inhabitants of Earth have succeeded in releasing atomic energy and have been making experiments with rocket propulsion. This is most serious. Let me have a full report immediately. And make it *brief* this time.

K.K. IV.

From: Secretary, Council of Scientists,
To: President.

The facts are as follows. Some months ago our instruments detected intense neutron emission from Earth, but an analysis of radio programs gave no explanation at the time. Three days ago a second emission occurred and soon afterwards all radio transmissions from Earth announced that atomic bombs were in use in the current war. The translators have not completed their interpretation, but it appears that the bombs are of considerable power. Two have so far been used. Some details of their construction have been released, but the elements concerned have not yet been identified. A fuller report will be forwarded as soon as possible. For the moment all that is certain is that the inhabitants of Earth *have* liberated atomic power, so far only explosively.

Very little is known concerning rocket research on Earth. Our astronomers have been observing the planet carefully ever since radio emissions were detected a generation ago. It is certain that long-range rockets of some kind are in existence on Earth, for there have been numerous references to them in recent military broadcasts. However, no serious attempt has been made to reach interplanetary space. When the war ends, it is expected that the inhabitants of the planet may carry out research in this direction. We will pay very careful attention to their broadcasts and the astronomical watch will be rigorously enforced.

From what we have inferred of the planet's technology, it should require about twenty years before Earth develops atomic rockets capable of crossing space. In view of this, it would seem that the time has come to set up a base on the Moon, so that a close scrutiny can be kept on such experiments when they commence.

Trescon.

(Added in manuscript.)
The war on Earth has now ended, apparently owing to the intervention of the atomic bomb. This will not affect the above arguments but it may mean that the inhabitants of Earth can devote themselves to pure research again more quickly than expected. Some broadcasts have already pointed out the application of atomic power to rocket propulsion.

T,

From: President.
To: Chief of Bureau of Extra-Planetary Security. (C.B.E.P.S.)

You have seen Trescon's minutes.

Equip an expedition to the satellite of Earth immediately. It is to keep a close watch on the planet and to report at once if rocket experiments are in progress.

The greatest care must be taken to keep our presence on the Moon a secret. You are personally responsible for this. Report to me at yearly intervals, or more often if necessary.

K.K. IV

From: President.
To: C.B.E.P.S.
   Where is the report on Earth?!!

K.K. IV.

From: C.B.E.P.S.
To: President.
   The delay is regretted. It was caused by the breakdown of the ship carrying the report.
   There have been no signs of rocket experimenting during the past year, and no reference to it in broadcasts from the planet.

Ranthe.

From: C.B.E.P.S.
To: President.
   You will have seen my yearly reports to your respected father on this subject. There have been no developments of interest for the past seven years, but the following message has just been received from our base on the Moon:

   Rocket projectile, apparently atomically propelled, left Earth's atmosphere today from Northern land-mass, traveling into space for one quarter diameter of planet before returning under control.

Ranthe.

From: President.
To: Chief of State.
   Your comments, please.

K.K. V.

From: Chief of State.
To: President.
   This means the end of our traditional policy.
   The only hope of security lies in preventing the Terrestrials from making further advances in this direction. From what we know of them, this will require some overwhelming threat.
   Since its high gravity makes it impossible to land on the planet, our sphere of action is restricted. The problem was discussed nearly a century ago by Anvar, and I agree with his conclusions. We must act *immediately* along those lines.

F.K.S.

From: President.
To: Secretary of State.
   Inform the Council that an emergency meeting is convened for noon tomorrow.

K.K. V.

From: President.
To: C.B.E.P.S.
   Twenty battleships should be sufficient to put Anvar's plan into operation. Fortunately there is no need to arm them—yet. Report progress of construction to me weekly.

K.K. V.

From: C.B.E.P.S.
To: President.
   Nineteen ships are now completed. The twentieth is still delayed
owing to hull failure and will not be ready for at least a month.
                                                            Ranthe.

From: President.
To: C.B.E.P.S.
   Nineteen will be sufficient. I will check the operational plan with you
tomorrow. Is the draft of our broadcast ready yet?
                                                            K.K. V.

From: C.B.E.P.S.
To: President.
   Draft herewith:
   People of Earth!
   We, the inhabitants of the planet you call Mars, have for many years
observed your experiments towards achieving interplanetary travel.
These experiments must cease. Our study of your race has convinced us
that you are not fitted to leave your planet in the present state of your
civilization. The ships you now see floating above your cities are capable
of destroying them utterly, and will do so unless you discontinue your
attempts to cross space.
   We have set up an observatory on your Moon and can immediately
detect any violation of these orders. If you obey them, we will not interfere with you again. Otherwise, one of your cities will be destroyed
every time we observe a rocket leaving the Earth's atmosphere.
   By order of the President and Council of Mars.
                                                            Ranthe.

From: President.
To: C.B.E.P.S.
   I approve. The translation can go ahead.
   I shall not be sailing with the fleet, after all. You will report to me in
detail immediately on your return.
                                                            K.K. V.

From: C.B.E.P.S.
To: President.
   I have the honor to report the successful completion of our mission.
The voyage to Earth was uneventful: radio messages from the planet
indicated that we were detected at a considerable distance and great
excitement had been aroused before our arrival. The fleet was dispersed
according to plan and I broadcast the ultimatum. We left immediately
and no hostile weapons were brought to bear against us.
   I shall report in detail within two days.
                                                            Ranthe.

From: Secretary, Council of Scientists.
To: President.

The psychologists have completed their report, which is attached herewith.

As might be expected, our demands at first infuriated this stubborn and high-spirited race. The shock to their pride must have been considerable, for they believed themselves to be the only intelligent beings in the Universe.

However, within a few weeks there was a rather unexpected change in the tone of their statements. They had begun to realize that we were intercepting all their radio transmissions, and some messages have been broadcast directly to us. They state that they have agreed to ban all rocket experiments, in accordance with our wishes. This is as unexpected as it is welcome. Even if they are trying to deceive us, we are perfectly safe now that we have established the second station just outside the atmosphere. They cannot possibly develop spaceships without our seeing them or detecting their tube radiation.

The watch on Earth will be continued rigorously, as instructed.

Trescon.

From: C.B.E.P.S.
To: President.

Yes, it is quite true that there have been no further rocket experiments in the last ten years. We certainly did not expect Earth to capitulate so easily!

I agree that the existence of this race now constitutes a permanent threat to our civilization and we are making experiments along the lines you suggest. The problem is a difficult one, owing to the great size of the planet. Explosives would be out of the question, and a radioactive poison of some kind appears to offer the greatest hope of success.

Fortunately, we now have an indefinite time in which to complete this research, and I will report regularly.

Ranthe.

End of Document

From: Lieutenant Commander Henry Forbes, Intelligence Branch, Special Space Corps.
To: Professor S. Maxton, Philological Department, University of Oxford.
Route: Transender II (via Schenectady.)

The above papers, with others, were found in the ruins of what is believed to be the capital Martian city. (Mars Grid KL302895.) The frequent use of the ideograph for "Earth" suggests that they may be of special interest and it is hoped that they can be translated. Other papers will be following shortly.

H. Forbes, Lt/Cdr.

(Added in manuscript.)

Dear Max,

   Sorry I've had no time to contact you before. I'll be seeing you as soon as I get back to Earth.

   Gosh! Mars *is* in a mess! Our co-ordinates were dead accurate and the bombs materialized right over their cities, just as the Mount Wilson boys predicted.

   We're sending a lot of stuff back through the two small machines, but until the big transmitter is materialized we're rather restricted, and, of course, none of us can return. So hurry up with it!

   I'm glad we can get to work on rockets again. I may be old-fashioned, but being squirted through space at the speed of light doesn't appeal to me!

Yours in haste,
Henry.

EDWARD GRENDON

THE FIGURE

IT'S a funny sort of deal and I don't mind admitting that we're scared. Maybe not so much scared as puzzled or shocked. I don't know, but it's a funny deal—. Especially in these days.

   The work we have been doing is more secret than anything was during the war. You would never guess that the firm we work for does this kind of research. It's a very respectable outfit, and as I said, no one would ever guess that they maintained this lab, so I guess it's safe to tell you what happened. It looks like too big a thing to keep to ourselves anyhow, although of course it may mean nothing at all. You judge for yourself.

   There are three of us who work here. We are all pretty highly trained in our field and get paid pretty well. We have a sign on our door that has nothing whatsoever to do with our work, but keeps most people away. In any case we leave by a private exit and never answer a knock. There's a private wire to the desk of the guy who hired us and he calls once in awhile, but ever since we told him that we were making progress he has more or less left us alone. I promised him—I'm chief here insofar as we have one—that I'd let him know as soon as we had something to report.

It's been a pretty swell setup. Dettner, Lasker, and myself, have got along fine. Dettner is young and is an electrical physicist as good as they make them. Studied at M.I.T., taught at Cal. Tech., did research for the Army, and then came here. My own background is mostly bio-electrics. I worked at designing electroencephalographs for awhile, and during the war worked at Oak Ridge on nuclear physics. I'm a Jack of All Trades in the physics field. Lasker is a mathematician. He special-izes in symbolic logic and is the only man I know who can really under-stand Tarski. He was the one who provided most of the theoretical back-ground for our work. He says that the mathematics of what we are do-ing is not overly difficult, but we are held back by the language we think in and the unconscious assumptions we make. He has referred me to Korzybski's *Science and Sanity* a number of times, but so far I haven't had a chance to read it. Now I think I will. I *have* to know the meaning of our results. It's too important to let slide. Lasker and Det-tner have both gone fishing. They said they would be back, but I'm not sure they will. I can't say I would blame them, but I've got to be more certain of what it means before I walk out of here for good.

We have been here over a year now. Ever since they gave me that final lecture on Secrecy at Oak Ridge, and let me go home. We have been working on the problem of time travel. When we took the job, they told us that they didn't expect any results for a long time, that we were on our own as far as working hours went, and that our main job was to clarify the problem and make preliminary experiments. Thanks to Las-ker, we went ahead a lot faster than either they or we had expected. There was a professional philosopher working here with us at first. He taught philosophy at Columbia and was supposed to be an expert in his field. He quit after two months in a peeve. Couldn't stand it when Lasker would change the logic we were working with every few weeks. He had been pretty pessimistic about the whole thing from the first and couldn't understand how it was possible to apply scientific methods to a problem of this sort.

I still don't understand all the theory behind what we've done. The mathematics are a bit too advanced for me, but Lasker vouches for them.

Some of the problems we had should be fairly obvious. For instance, you can't introduce the concept "matter" into space-time mathematics without disrupting the space-time and working with Newtonian space *and* time mathematics. If you handle an "object"—as we sense it as a curvature of space-time—as Einstein does, it's pretty hard to do much with it theoretically. Lasker managed that by using Einstein formula-tions and manipulating them with several brands of Tarski's non-Aris-totelian logic. As I said, we did it, although Dettner and I don't fully understand the mathematics and Lasker doesn't understand the gadget we used to produce the electrical fields.

There had been no hurry at all in our work up to the last month. At that time the Army wrote Dettner and myself and asked us to come back and work for them awhile. Neither of us wanted to refuse under the circumstances so we stalled them for thirty days and just twenty-two days later made our first test. The Army really wanted us badly and in a hurry and it took a lot of talking to stall them.

What the Army wanted us for was to help find out about the cockroaches. That sounds funny, but it's true. It didn't make the newspapers, but about a year after the New Mexico atom bomb test, the insect problem at the testing ground suddenly increased a hundredfold. Apparently the radiation did something to them and they came out in force one day against the control station. They finally had to dust the place with DDT to get rid of them.

Looking over the dead insects, all the government entomologists could say was that the radiation seemed to have increased their size about forty percent and made them breed faster. They never did agree whether it was the intense radiation of the blast, or the less intense, but longer continued radiation from fused sand and quartz on the ground.

New Mexico was nothing to Hiroshima and Nagasaki. After all, there are comparatively few "true bugs" in the desert and a great many in a Japanese city. About a year and a half after Japan got A-bombed, they really swarmed on both cities at the same time. They came out suddenly one night by the millions. It's been estimated that they killed and ate several hundred people before they were brought under control. To stop them, MacArthur had his entire Chemical-Warfare Service and a lot of extra units concentrated on the plague spots. They dusted with chemicals and even used some gas. At that, it was four days before the bugs were brought under control.

This time the government experts really went into the problem. They traced the insect tunnels about ten feet down and examined their breeding chambers and what not. According to their reports,—all this is still kept strictly hush-hush by the Army, but we've seen all the data—the radiation seems to drive the insects down into the earth. They stay down for awhile and breed and then seem to have a "blind urge" to go to the surface. This urge "seems to affect the entire group made up of an immense number of connected colonies at the same time." That's a quote from their report. One other thing they mentioned is that there were large breeding chambers and some sort of communal life that—to their knowledge—had not been observed in these particular insects before. We told Lasker about it and showed him the reports. He was plenty worried, but he wouldn't say why.

Don't know why I wandered so far afield. I just wanted to explain that if this test wasn't successful, we would probably have to put things off for quite a while. We were interested in the beetle problem as it not only has some interesting implications, but the effect of radiation on protoplasm is a hard nut to crack. However we had come so far on our time gadget that we wanted to finish it first. Well, we finished and tested it and now Dettner and Lasker are out fishing. As I said, they probably won't come back.

It was the day before yesterday that we made the final test. Looked at one way, we had made tremendous progress. Looked at another we had made very little. We had devised an electric field that would operate in the future. There were sixteen outlets forming the sides of a cube about four feet in diameter. When switched on, an electric field was produced which "existed" at some future time. I know Lasker would say this was incorrect, but it gets the general idea over. He would say that instead of operating in "Here-Now," it operates in "Here-Then." He'd get angry every time we'd separate "space" and "time" in our talk and tell us that we weren't living in the eighteenth century.

"Newton was a great man," he'd say, "but he's dead now. If you talk as if it were 1750, you'll *think* and *act* as if it were 1750 and then we won't get anywhere. You use non-Newtonian formulations in your work, use them in everyday speech, too."

How far in the future our gadget would operate we had no way of knowing. Lasker said he would not even attempt to estimate "when" the field was active. When the power was turned off, anything that was in the cube of forces would be brought back to the present space-time. In other words, we had a "grab" that would reach out and drag something back from the future. Don't get the idea we were sending something into the future to bring something back with it, although that's what it amounts to for all practical purposes. We were warping space-time curvature so that anything "Here-Then" would be something "Here-Now."

We finished the gadget at three A.M. Tuesday morning. Lasker had been sleeping on the couch while we worked on it. He had checked and rechecked his formulae and said that if we could produce the fields he'd specified, it would probably work. We tested each output separately and then woke him up. I can't tell you how excited we were as we stood there with everything ready. Finally Dettner said, "Let's get it done," and I pressed the start button.

The needles on our ammeters flashed over and back, the machine went dead as the circuit breakers came open, and there was an object in the cube.

We looked it over from all sides without touching it. Then the implications of it began to hit us. It's funny what men will do at a time like that. Dettner took out his watch, examined it carefully, as if he had never seen it before, and then went over and turned on the electric percolator. Lasker swore quietly in Spanish or Portuguese, I'm not sure which. I sat down and began a letter to my wife. I got as far as writing the date and then tore it up.

What was in the cube—it's still there, none of us have touched it—was a small statue about three feet high. It's some sort of metal that looks like silver. About half the height is pedestal and half is the statue itself. It's done in great detail and obviously by a skilled artist. The pedestal consists of a globe of the Earth with the continents and islands in relief. So far as I can determine it's pretty accurate, although I think the continents are a little different shape on most maps. But I may be wrong. The figure on top is standing up very straight and looking upwards. It's dressed only in a wide belt from which a pouch hangs on one side and a flat square box on the other. It looks intelligent and is obviously representing either aspiration or a religious theme, or maybe both. You can sense the dreams and ideals of the figure and the obvious sympathy and understanding of the artist with them. Lasker says he thinks the statue is an expression of religious feeling. Dettner and I both think it represents aspirations: *Per adra ad astra* or something of the sort. It's a majestic figure and it's easy to respond to it emphatically with a sort of "upward and onward" feeling. There is only one thing wrong. The figure is that of a beetle.

PART TWO

The Wonders of Earth

THE GREAT FOG

THE first symptom was a mildew.

Very few people have ever looked carefully at such "molds"; indeed, only a specialized branch of botanists knows about them. Nor is this knowledge—except rarely—of much use. Every now and then a low growth of this sort may attack a big cash crop. Then the mycologists, whose lifework is to study these spore growths, are called in by the growers. These botanists can sometimes find another mold which will eat its fellow. That closes the matter. The balance of life, which had been slightly upset, has been righted. It is not a matter of any general interest.

This particular mildew did not seem to have even that special importance. It did not, apparently, do any damage to the trees on which it grew. Indeed, most fruit growers never noticed it. The botanists found it themselves; no one called their attention to it. It was simply a form of spore growth different in its growth rate from any previously recorded. It did not seem to do any harm to any other form of life. But it did do amazingly well for itself. It was not a new plant, but a plant with quite a new power of growth.

It was this fact which puzzled the botanists, or rather that special branch of the botanists, the mycologists. That was why they finally called in the meteorologists. They asked for "another opinion," as baffled doctors say. What made the mycologists choose the meteorologists for consultation was this: Here was a mildew which spread faster than any other mold had ever been known to grow. It flourished in places where such mildews had been thought incapable of growing. But there seemed to be no botanical change either in the mold or in the plants it grew on. Therefore the cause must be climatic: only a weather change could account for the unprecedented growth.

The meteorologists saw the force of this argument. They became interested at once. The first thing to do, they said, was to study the mildew, not as a plant, but as a machine, an indicator. "You know," said Sersen the weatherman to Charles the botanist (they had been made colleagues for the duration of the study), "the astronomers have a thing called a thermocouple that will tell the heat of a summer day on the equator of Mars. Well, here is a little gadget I've made. It's almost as sensitive to damp as the thermocouple is to heat."

Sersen spent some time rigging it up and then "balancing" it, as he called it. "Find the normal humidity and then see how much the damp at a particular spot exceeds that." But he went on fiddling about far longer than Charles thought an expert who was handling his own gadget should. He was evidently puzzled. And after a while he confessed that he was.

"Queer, very queer," said Sersen. "Of course, I expected to get a good record of humidity around the mold itself. As you say, it can't grow without that: it wouldn't be here unless the extra damp was here too. But, look here," he said, pointing to a needle that quivered near a high number on a scale. *"That* is the humidity actually around the mold it-self—what we might expect, if a trifle high. That's not the surprise. It's *this."* He had swung the whole instrument on its tripod until it pointed a foot or more from the mold; for the tree they were studying was a newly attacked one and, as far as Charles had been able to discover, had on it only this single specimen of the mildew.

Charles looked at the needle. It remained hovering about the high figure it had first chosen. "Well?" he queried.

"Don't you see?" urged Sersen. "This odd high humidity is present not only around the mold itself but for more than a foot beyond."

"I don't see much to that."

"I see two things," snapped Sersen; "one's odd; the other's damned odd. The odd one anyone not blind would see. The other one is perhaps too big to be seen until one can stand well back."

"Sorry to be stupid," said Charles, a gentle-spoken but close-minded little fellow; "we botanists are small-scale men."

"Sorry to be a snapper," apologized Sersen. "But, as I suppose you've guessed, I'm startled. I've got a queer feeling that we're on the track of something big, yes, and something maybe moving pretty fast. The first odd thing isn't a complete surprise: it's that you botanists have shown us what could turn out to be a meteorological instrument more delicate and more accurate than any we have been able to make. Perhaps we ought to have been on the outlook for some such find. After all, living things are always the most sensitive detectors—can always beat me-chanical instruments when they want to. You know about the mitoge-netic rays given out by breeding seeds. Those rays can be recorded only by yeast cells—which multiply rapidly when exposed to the rays, thus giving an indication of their range and strength."

"Umph," said Charles. Sersen's illustration had been unfortunate, for Charles belonged to that majority of conservative botanists to whom the mitogenetic radiation was mere moonshine.

Sersen, again vexed, went on: "Well, whether you accept them or not, I still maintain that here we have a superdetector. This mildew can no-tice an increase in humidity long before any of our instruments. There's proof that something has changed in the climate. This mold is the first to know about it—and to profit by it. I prophesy it will soon be over the whole world."

"But your second discovery, or supposition?" Charles had no use for prophecy. These weathermen, he thought; well, after all, they aren't quite scientists, so one mustn't blame them, one supposes, for liking forecasts—forecasting is quite unscientific.

Charles was a courteous man, but Sersen was sensitive. "Well," he said defensively, "that's nothing but supposition." And yet, he thought to himself as he packed up his instrument, if it *is* true it may mean such a change that botany will be blasted and meteorology completely mystified. His small private joke relieved his temper. By the time they returned to headquarters he and Charles were friendly enough. They agreed to make a joint report which would stick severely to the facts.

Meanwhile, botanists everywhere were observing and recording the spreading of the mildew. Before long, they began to get its drift. It was spreading from a center, spreading like a huge ripple from where a stone has been flung into a lake. The center, there could be no doubt, was eastern Europe. Spain, Britain, and North Africa showed the same "high incidence." France showed an even higher one. The spread of the mold could be watched just as well in North or South America. Such and such a percentage of shrubs and trees was attacked on the Atlantic coasts; a proportionately lower percentage on the Pacific coasts; but everywhere the incidence was rising. On every sector of the vast and widening circle, America, Africa, India, the mildew was advancing rapidly.

Sersen continued his own research on the mold itself, on the "field of humidity" around each plant. He next made a number of calculations correlating the rapid rate of dispersal, the average increase of infestation of all vegetation by the mold, and the degree of humidity which must result. Then, having checked and counterchecked, at last he was ready to read his paper and give his conclusions at a joint meeting of the plant men and the weathermen.

Just before Sersen went up to the platform, he turned to Charles. "I'm ready now to face the music," he said, "because I believe we are up against something which makes scientific respectability nonsense. We've got to throw caution aside and tell the world." "That's serious," said Charles cautiously. "It's damned serious," said Sersen, and went up the steps to the rostrum.

When he came down, the audience was serious too; for a moment, as serious as he. He had begun by showing the world map with its spreading, dated lines showing where the mildew in its present profusion had reached; showing also where, in a couple of months, the two sides of the ripple would meet. Soon, almost every tree and shrub throughout the world would be infested, and, of course, the number of molds per tree and bush would increase. That was interesting and queer, but of no popular concern. The molds still remained harmless to their tree hosts and to animal life—indeed, some insects seemed rather happy about the botanical change. As far, then, as the change was only a change in mildew reproduction there was no cause for much concern, still less for alarm. The mold had gone ahead, because it was the first to benefit from some otherwise undetectable change in climate. The natural expectation would, then, be that insects, the host plants, or some other species of mold would in turn advance and so readjust the disturbed balance of nature.

But that was only the first part of Sersen's lecture. At that phrase, "balance of nature," he paused. He turned from the world map with its charting of the mold's growth. For a moment he glanced at another set of statistical charts; then he seemed to change his mind and touched the buzzer. The lights went out, and the beam from the stereoptican shot down through the darkened hall. The lighted screen showed a tree; on its branches and trunk a number of red crosses had been marked. Around each cross was a large circle, so large that some of the circles intersected.

"Gentlemen," said Sersen, "this is the discovery that really matters. Until now, perhaps unwisely, I have hesitated to communicate it. That the mold spreads, you know. That it is particularly sensitive to some otherwise undetected change in the weather, you know. Now, you must know a third fact about it—it is a weather *creator*. Literally, it can brew a climate of its own.

"I have proved that in each of these circles—and I am sure they are spreading circles—the mold is going far to create its own peculiar atmosphere—a curiously high and stable humidity. The statistically arranged readings which I have prepared, and which I have here, permit, I believe, of no other conclusion. I would also add that I believe we can see why this has happened. It is now clear what permitted this unprecedented change to get under way. We have pulled the trigger that has fired this mine. No doubt the mold first began to increase because a slight change in humidity helped it. But now it is—how shall I put it—co-operating. It is *making the humidity increase.*

"There has probably been present, these past few years, one of those small increases in atmospheric humidity which occur periodically. In itself, it would have made no difference to our lives and, indeed, would have passed unperceived. But it was at this meteorological moment that European scientists began to succeed in making a new kind of quick-growing mold which could create fats. It is, perhaps, the most remarkable of all the war efforts, perhaps the most powerful of all the new defensive weapons—against a human enemy. But in regard to the extra human world in which we live it may prove as dangerous as a naked flame in a mine chamber filled with firedamp. For, need I remind you, molds are spore-reproducing growths. Fungus is by far the strongest form of life. It breeds incessantly and will grow under conditions no other form of life will endure. When you play with spore life you may at any moment let loose something the sheer power of which makes dynamite look like a damp squib. I believe what man has now done is precisely that—he has let the genie out of its bottle, and we may find ourselves utterly helpless before it."

Sersen paused. The lights came on. Dr. Charles rose and caught the chairman's eye. Dr. Charles begged to state on behalf of the botanical world that he hoped Dr. Sersen's dramatic remarks would not be taken gravely by the press or the public. Dr. Sersen had spoken of matters botanical. Dr. Charles wished to say that he and his colleagues had had the mildew under protracted observation. He could declare categorically that it was not dangerous.

Sersen had not left the platform. He strode back to the rostrum. "I am not speaking as a botanist," he exclaimed, "I am speaking as a meteorologist. I have told you of what I am sure—the balance of life has been upset. You take for granted that the only balance is life against life, animal against animal, vegetable against vegetable. You were right to call in a weatherman, but that's of no use unless you understand what he is telling you."

The audience shifted offendedly in its seats. It wasn't scientific to be as urgent as all that. Besides, hadn't Charles said there was no danger? But what was their queer guest now saying?

"I know, every meteorologist knows, that this nature-balance is far vaster and more delicately poised than you choose to suspect. All life is balanced against its environment. Cyclones are brought on, climate can change, a glacial age can begin as the result of atmospheric alterations far too small for the layman to notice. In our atmosphere, that wonderful veil and web under which we are sheltered and in which we grow, we have a condition of extraordinary delicacy. The right—or rather the precisely wrong—catalytic agent can send the whole thing suddenly into quite another arrangement, one which can well be desperately awkward for man. It has taken an amazing balance of forces to allow human beings to live. That's the balance you've upset. Look out."

He studied his audience. There they sat, complacent, assured, only a little upset that an overexcitable colleague should be behaving unscientifically—hysterically, almost. Suddenly, with a shock of despair, Sersen realized that it was no use hoping to stir these learned experts. These were the actual minds which had patiently, persistently, purblindly worked the very changes which must bring the house down on their heads. They'd never asked, never wished to ask, what might be the general and ultimate effects of their burrowing. We're just another sort of termite, thought Sersen, as he looked down on the rows of plump faces and dull-ivory-colored pates. We tunnel away trying to turn everything into "consumable goods" until suddenly the whole structure of things collapses round us.

He left the rostrum, submitted to polite thanks, and went home. A week later his botanical hosts had ceased even to talk about his strange manners. Hardly anyone else heard of his speech.

The first report of trouble—or rumor rather (for such natural-history notes were far too trivial to get into the battle-crammed papers)—came from orchard growers in deep valleys. Then fruit growers began to gossip when the Imperial Valley, hot and dry as hell, began to report much the same thing. It was seen at night at the start and cleared off in the day; so it seemed no more than an odd, inconsequent little phenomenon. But if you went out at full moon you did see a queer sight. Every tree seemed to have a sort of iridescent envelope, a small white cloud or silver shroud all its own.

Of course, soon after that, the date growers had something to howl about. The dates wouldn't stand for damp—and each silver shroud was, for the tree about which it hung, a vapor bath. But the date growers, all the other growers decided, were done for anyway; they'd have made a howl in any case when the new Colorado water made the irrigation plans complete. The increase in humidity would inevitably spoil their crop when the valley became one great oasis.

The botanists didn't want to look into the matter again. Botanically, it was uninteresting. The inquiry had been officially closed. But the phenomenon continued to be noticed farther and farther afield.

The thing seemed then to reach a sort of saturation point. A new sort of precipitation took place. The cloud around each tree and bush, which now could be seen even during the day, would, at a certain moment, put out feeler-like wisps and join up with the other spreading and swelling ground clouds stretching out from the neighboring trees. Sersen, who had thrown up his official job just to keep track of this thing, described that critical night when, with a grim prophetic pleasure, he saw his forecast fulfilled before his eyes. His last moldering papers have remained just decipherable for his great-grandchildren.

"I stood," he said, "on a rock promontory south of Salton Sea. The full moon was rising behind me and lighted the entire Valley. I could see the orchards glistening, each tree surrounded by its own cloud. It was like a gargantuan dew; each dew-globule tree-size. And then, as I watched, just like a great tide, an obliterating flood of whiteness spread over everything. The globules ran into one another until I was looking down on a solid sea of curd-white, far denser than mist or fog. It looked as firm, beautiful, and dead as the high moon which looked down on it. 'A new Deluge,' I said to myself. 'May I not ask who has been right? Did I not foretell its coming and did not I say that man had brought it on his own head?' "

Certainly Sersen had been justified. For, the morning after his vigil, when the sun rose, the Fog did not. It lay undisturbed, level, dazzling white as a sheet of snow-covered ice, throwing back into space every ray of heat that fell on it. The air immediately above it was crystal clear. The valley was submerged under an element that looked solid enough to be walked on. The change was evidently so complete because it was a double one, a sudden reciprocal process. All the damp had been gathered below the Fog's surface, a surface as distinct as the surface of water. Conversely, all the cloud, mist, and aqueous vapor in the air above the Fog was evidently drained out of it by this new dense atmosphere. It was as though the old atmosphere had been milk. The mold acted as a kind of rennet, and so, instead of milk, here remained only this hard curd and the clear whey. The sky above the Fog was not so much the deepest of blues—it was almost a livid black; the sun in it was an intense, harsh white and most of the big stars were visible throughout the day. So, outside the Fog it was desperately cold. At night it was agonizingly so. Under that cold the Fog lay packed dense like a frozen drift of snow.

Beneath the surface of the Fog, conditions were even stranger. Passing into it was like going suddenly into night. All lights had to be kept on all day. But they were not much use. As in a bad old-fashioned fog, but now to a far worse degree, the lights would not penetrate the air. For instance, the rays of a car's headlights formed a three-foot cone, the base of which looked like a circular patch of light thrown on an opaque white screen. It was possible to move about in the Fog, but only at a slow walking pace—otherwise you kept running into things. It was a matter of groping about, with objects suddenly looming up at you—the kind of world in which a severe myopic case must live if he loses his spectacles.

Soon, of course, people began to notice with dismay the Fog's effect on crops and gardens, on houses and goods. Nothing was ever again dry. Objects did not become saturated, but they were, if at all absorbent, thoroughly damp. Paper molded, wood rotted, iron rusted. But concrete, glass, pottery, all stone ware and ceramics remained unaffected. Cloth, too, served adequately, provided the wearer could stand its never being dry.

The first thought in the areas which had been first attacked was, naturally, to move out. But the Fog moved too. Every night some big valley area suddenly "went over." The tree fog around each tree would billow outward, join up with all its fellows, and so make a solid front and surface. Then came the turn for each fog-submerged valley, each fog-lake, to link with those adjacent to it. The general level of these lakes then rose. Instead of there being, as until now, large flooded areas of lowland, but still, in the main, areas of clear upland, this order was now reversed. The mountain ranges had become strings of islands which emerged from a shining ocean that covered the whole earth's surface, right up to the six-thousand-foot level.

Any further hope of air travel was extinguished. In the Fog, lack of visibility, of course, made it impossible. Above the Fog, you could see to the earth's edge: the horizons, cleared of every modulation of mist, seemed so close that you would have thought you could have touched them with your hand. As far as sight was concerned, above the Fog, near and far seemed one. But even if men could have lived in that thin air and "unscreened" light, no plane could be sustained by it.

Sea travel was hardly more open. True, the surface of the oceans lay under the Fog-blanket, as still as the water, a thousand fathoms down. But on that oily surface—that utterly featureless desert of motionless water—peering man, only a few yards from the shore, completely lost his way. Neither sun nor stars ever again appeared over the sea to give him his bearings. So man soon abandoned the sea beyond the closest inshore shallows. Even if he could have seen his way over the ocean, he could not have taken it. There was never a breath of wind to fill a sail, and the fumes from any steamship or motorboat would have hung around the vessel and would have almost suffocated the crew.

Retreat upward was cut off. For when the Fog stabilized at six thousand feet, it was no use thinking of attempting to live above it. Even if the limited areas could have given footing, let alone feeding, to the fugitive populations, no hope lay in that direction. For the cold was now so intense above the Fog that no plant would grow. And, worse, it was soon found, to the cost of those who ventured out there, that through this unscreened air—air which was so thin that it could scarcely be breathed —came also such intense ultraviolet radiations from the sun and outer space that a short exposure to them was fatal.

So the few ranges and plateaus which rose above the six-thousand-foot level stood gaunt as the ribs of a skeleton carcass under the untwinkling stars and the white glaring sun. After a very few exploratory expeditions out into that open, men realized that they must content themselves with a sub-surface life, a new kind of fish existence, nosing about on the floor of a pool which henceforth was to be their whole world. It might be a poor, confined way of living, but above that surface was death. A few explorers returned, but, though fish taken out of water may recover if put back soon enough, every above-the-Fog explorer succumbed from the effect. After a few days the lesions and sores of bad X-ray burning appeared. If, after that, the nervous system did not collapse, the wretched man literally began to fall to pieces.

Underneath the Fog-blanket men painfully, fumblingly worked out a new answer to living. Of course, it had to be done without preparation, so the cost was colossal. All who were liable to rheumatic damage and phthisis died off. Only a hardy few remained. Man had been clever enough to pull down the atmosphere-roof which had hung so loftily over his head, but he never learned again how to raise a cover as high, spacious, and pleasant as the sky's blue dome. The dividing out of the air was a final precipitation, a nonreversible change-down toward the final entropy. Man might stay on, but only at the price of being for the rest of his term on earth confined under a thick film of precipitated air. Maybe, even if he had been free and had had the power to move fast and see far, it would have been too great a task for him to have attempted to "raise the air." As he now found himself, pinned under the collapse he had caused, he had not a chance of even beginning to plan such a vast reconstruction.

His job, then, was just to work at making lurking livable. And, within the limits imposed, it was not absolutely impossible. True, all his passion for speed and travel and seeing far and quick, all that had to go. He who had just begun to feel that it was natural to fly, now was confined not even to the pace of a brisk walk but to a crawl. It was a life on the lowest gear. Of course, great numbers died just in the first confusion, when the dark came on, before the permanent change in humidity and light swept off the other many millions who could not adapt themselves. But, after a while, not only men's health but their eyes became adapted to the perpetual dusk. They began to see that the gloom was not pitch-dark. Gradually, increasing numbers learned to be able to go about without lamps. Indeed, they found that they saw better if they cultivated this "nightsight," this ancient part of the eye so long neglected by man when he thought he was master of things. They were greatly helped also by a type of faint phosphorescence, a "cold-light," which (itself probably another mold-mutation) appeared on most surfaces if they were left untouched, and so outlined objects with faint, ghostly highlights.

So, as decentralized life worked itself out, men found that they had enough. War was gone, so that huge social hemorrhage stopped. Money went out of gear, and so that odd strangle hold on goods-exchange was loosed. Men just couldn't waste what they had, so they found they had much more than they thought. For one reason, it wasn't worth hoarding anything, holding back goods, real, edible, and wearable goods, for a rise in price. They rotted. The old medieval epitaph proved itself true in this new dark age: "What I spent I had: what I saved I lost." Altogether, life became more immediate and, what people had never suspected, more real because less diffused. It was no use having a number of things which had been thought to be necessities. Cars? You could not see to travel at more than four miles an hour, and not often at that. Radios? They just struck; either insulation against the damp was never adequate or the electric conditions, the radio-resonant layers of the upper atmosphere, had been completely altered. A wailing static was the only answer to any attempt to re-establish wireless communication.

It was a low-built, small-housed, pedestrian world. Even horses were too dashing; and they were blinder in the Fog than were men. As for your house, you could seldom see more than its front door. Metal was little used. Smelting it was troublesome (the fumes could hardly get away and nearly suffocated everyone within miles of a furnace), and when you got your iron and steel it began rusting at once. Glass knives were used instead. They were very sharp. Men learned again, after tens of thousands of years of neglect, how to flake flints, crystal, and all the silica rocks to make all manner of neat, sharp tools.

Man's one primary need, which had made for nearly all his hoarding, the animal craving to accumulate food stocks, that fear which, since the dawn of civilization, has made his granaries as vast as his fortresses, this need, this enemy, was wiped out by another freak botanical by-product of the Fog. The curious sub-fog climate made an edible fungus grow. It was a sort of manna. It rotted if you stored it. But it grew copiously everywhere, of itself. Indeed, it replaced grass: wherever grass had grown the fungus grew. Eaten raw, it was palatable and highly nutritious—more tasty and more wholesome than when cooked (which was a blessing in itself, since all fires burnt ill and any smoke was offensive in the dense air). Man, like the fishes, lived in a dim but fruitful element.

The mean temperature under the Fog stayed precisely at 67 degrees Fahrenheit, owing, evidently, to some basic balance, like that which keeps the sea below a certain depth always at 36 degrees, four degrees above freezing. Men, then, were never cold.

They stayed mainly at home, around their small settlements. What was the use of going about? All you needed and could use was at your door. There was nothing to see—your view was always limited to four feet. There was no use in trying to seize someone else's territory. You all had the same: you all had enough.

Art, too, changed. The art of objects was gone. So a purer, less collectible art took its place. Books would not last; and so memory increased enormously, and men carried their libraries in their heads—a cheaper way and much more convenient. As a result, academic accuracy, the continual quoting of authorities, disappeared. A new epic age resulted. Men in the dusk composed, extemporized, jointly developed great epics, sagas, and choruses, which grew like vast trees, generation after generation, flowering, bearing fruit, putting out new limbs. And, as pristine, bardic poetry returned, it united again with its nursery foster-brother, music. Wood winds and strings were ruined by the damp. But stone instruments, like those used by the dawn cultures, returned—giving beautiful pure notes. An orchestra of jade and marble flutes, lucid gongs, crystal-clear xylophones grew up. Just as the Arabs, nomads out on the ocean of sand, had had no plastic art, but, instead, a wonderful aural art of chant and singing verse, so the creative power of the men of the Umbral Epoch swung over from eye to ear. Indeed, the thick air which baffled the eye made fresh avenues and extensions for the ear. Men could hear for miles: their ears grew as keen as a dog's. And with this keenness went subtlety. They appreciated intervals of sound which to the old men of the open air would have been imperceptible. Men lived largely for music and felt they had made a good exchange when they peered at the last moldering shreds of pictorial art.

"Yes," said Sersen's great-grandson, when the shock of the change was over and mankind had accustomed itself to its new conditions, "yes, I suspect we were not fit for the big views, the vast world into which the old men tumbled up. It was all right to give animal men the open. But, once they had got power without vision, then either they had to be shut up or they would have shot and bombed everything off the earth's surface. Why, they were already living in tunnels when the Fog came. And out in the open, men, powerful as never before, nevertheless died by millions, died the way insects used to die in a frost, but died by one another's hands. The plane drove men off the fields. That was the thing, I believe, that made Mind decide we were not fit any longer to be at large. We were going too fast and too high to see what we were actually doing. So, then, Mind let man fancy that all he had to do was to make food apart from the fields. That was the Edible Mold, and that led straight, as my great-grandfather saw, to the atmospheric upset, the meteorological revolution. It really was a catalyst, making the well-mixed air, which we had always taken for granted as the only possible atmosphere, divide out into two layers as distinct as water and air. We're safer as we are. Mind knew that, and already we are better for our Fog cure, though it had to be drastic.

"Perhaps, one day, when we have learned enough, the Fog will lift, the old high ceiling will be given back to us. Once more Mind may say: 'Try again. The Second Flood is over. Go forth and replenish the earth, and this time remember that you are all one.' Meanwhile I'm thankful that we are as we are."

P. Schuyler Miller

THE CHRYSALIS

BATES grinned when he saw those logs. I know that as well as though I'd been there. That grin of his is famous. I've seen it time and again when he has come across something rare or unusual, wrinkling his homely face into something like the relief map of a lava flow. Besides, I whooped myself when I discovered them.

There were more than when I first found them, the week before, just after the freshet. The creek had cut away a sort of alcove in the bank, eddying back in a clear, deep pool with a long, sleek swell of current over the topmost log. The water was eating hungrily at the bank and at the stiff, blue clay that underlay it, and little trickles and sudden slides of gravel were cascading into the pool.

The water was cold—damned cold—but Bates went in up to his waist without hesitation. That's the way he is. I've seen him squat for hours in the blazing sun, bareheaded, dusting out a burial so that he could get plenty of detail in his photographs. Once in the middle of February, when he came on half a pot exposed in a cut bank, he wasted a whole day and ruined a good ax hacking out a huge block of the frozen mud in which it was embedded, only to have the whole thing crumble to bits when he tried to thaw it out. And he'd do anything for tree rings.

Bates is a dendrochronologist—a tree-ring expert. He dates things by them, as easily—or so it seems to me—as we would look up a year in the "World Almanac." He was originally just the common, back-pasture variety of amateur archæologist, a good one, to be sure, with quite an enviable reputation in the circles where it counted, but nothing to startle any paper into giving him a double-page spread in one of its Sunday magazine sections.

Then he happened to run across a site with a particularly ungodly mix-up of culture traces, and got it into his head that the only way to solve the thing was to date it. Obviously tree rings were the answer: every one who reads the newspapers knows all about how they show what years are wet and which are dry, and how Professor Douglass and his crew have dated hundreds of ruins by them in the Southwest.

The trouble was that nothing that they had worked out there was any good at all to him. If there is any place less like the Arizona desert than the foothills of the Adirondacks, I have yet to see it. Anyway, he started from scratch to work out a calendar of his own.

He did it, too. He dated everything in sight that had wood in it—old houses, covered bridges, antiquated horse troughs, Indian stockades—and before long he was far out of sight in the depths of prehistoric times, grubbing joyously among nubbins of charcoal and scraps of rotten wood, farther back than any one had ever thought it possible to go.

He tried linking in the layers of mud laid down in the bottoms of ponds, and the sand in river deltas. He had half a dozen different calendars and chunks of calendars ranging over thousands of years, with gaps between them in which a civilization as big as Colonel Churchward's Mu could have risen and been lost.

He was particularly fond of the ones that hovered around the fringes of glacial times, when men were just beginning to amount to something in the world. That was why he grinned when he saw those logs.

There was a good twelve feet of gravel over them, and three or four feet of stiff blue boulder clay under that. They were embedded in clay as fossils are embedded in rock, and for the same reason. Hundreds of centuries ago they had lain, water-logged, in the mud at the bottom of some glacial lake. Silt covered them, washed down from the melting front of the great ice sheet that lay over half the world.

Year after year the layers of clay built up, thick in the warm years as the ice melted faster, then thinner and thinner as the great cold came again and the glacier crept southward over the continent. It heaped gravel and broken rock in long moraines over the frozen lake bottom. Finally it disappeared for good. The world grew warm again and new streams cut their way down through the débris left by the great ice.

Those logs had been trees in interglacial times, when apish men roamed over Europe and mastodons and mammoths wallowed in the swamps of the northern hemisphere. Their rings would record the changes in climate that brought the ice sheet creeping like slow death over the face of the planet. No wonder Bates grinned!

I had seen the ends of two logs protruding from the clay when I led a hike that way the Sunday before. The water was still high, and by now a dozen or more were uncovered. Queerly enough, they were all very much of a size and lay side by side, all on the same level, just under the surface of the water. Gravel from the bank had drifted against their exposed ends, hiding them, and Bates's plodding boots had muddied the pool below so that he couldn't see the downstream face of the pile. But Bates isn't one to wait. He unslung a short-handled shovel from his pack, waded out into the middle of the creek, and went to work.

In an hour's time he had a dam and a channel that diverted the current along the opposite bank of the stream. The upper surface of the logs was high and dry, or drying, and he had hacked a long trough through the clay of the creek bottom which had lowered the level of the eddy pool by a good two feet.

He hunched down and studied the logs. They were soft and cheesy to the touch, and dark with age, like huge, uneven cylinders of black chocolate. Pines, probably. He hoped so, for pines had the most sensitive rings. He reached down and began to scoop the drifted gravel away from their ends. And then he yelled!

Those logs were cut by men!

They were cut by men—Heaven knows of what race or color—who lived with the hairy mammoth and the giant sloth before the ice came, twenty or thirty or forty thousand years go! The ax marks were plain on the exposed wood. They weren't beaver marks—he knew those by heart. A flint ax made them—a flint ax wielded two hundred centuries and more ago, not in New Mexico, or Colorado, or Wisconsin, but here, *here,* practically in his own back yard!

He went at the gravel like a terrier, with both hands, until he had uncovered the ends of six great logs, lying side by side in the blue clay. Then he cleared away a space beneath them with a trowel. He ran his fingers along their buttery underside—and sat back staring, goggling, utterly incredulous.

Those logs were notched to fit over the top of a crosspiece!

Bates is too good an archæologist to go off half cocked. Before he left that night, he had uncovered one whole end of the thing, down to solid rock, and covered it up again to protect it from the force of the stream. He reënforced his dam and deepened the channel he had dug, until all but a thin trickle of water followed the other bank, with a solid dyke of tamped clay and stone between. And when we arrived, long before dawn the next morning, he set us to work at once draining the pool.

There were three of us, counting Bates, and a fourth was on his way. We had no time to spare. The barometer and the weather maps both shouted "Storm!" and rain would ruin forever our chances of saving whatever had been buried in that ancient vault.

For vault it was—the oldest structure ever found that was raised by human hands. It was made entirely of huge, hewn logs, five feet square at the base and over twice as long, and it was set on a great, smoothed block of solid limestone.

We worked that day as I never want to work again. We dug away that twelve foot gravel bank until it stood back a clear six feet on all sides of the vault. We cut into the clay and peeled it away in great, thick slabs, with Michaelson following every step. He was a notary, and a wizard with a camera, and if Mann should arrive too late we would have a sworn record that no investigating committee of blue-nosed skeptics could argue away.

Mann flew. I had met him once, at a Rochester meeting of the Society for American Archæology, where he was carrying on Parker's enviable tradition as superhost to half the archæologists in the country. Bates knew him well, and what was more, he knew Bates. No train was fast enough for an emergency like this one. The sun was barely an hour high when his plane bounced down into the pasture above the creek and he came stalking across to where we were working, his coat tails flying and his white mane rumpled and tousled where he had been yanking it in his impatience.

Mann is sixty if he's a day, but he dug too. He dug like a demon—we all did—but time went past like the whisk of a scared trout. The whole west was black, with fitful flares of lightning illumining the cavernous hollows of the clouds, and now and then a rumble of closer thunder.

Michaelson was swearing dismally as the light faded and he had to give longer and longer exposures to his films, and Bates's face was a savage mask. Heaven alone knew what was in that great log box, and if the storm broke that knowledge would be kept through all eternity.

Night was on us before the last log was clear. Michaelson's flares lighted the landscape weirdly as he photographed the vault, deep at the bottom of its muddy crater, with our haggard faces peering past its massive bulk. The limestone block on which it stood was pecked and polished by human hands, its edges roughly squared. That, at least, we could leave to study later. Nothing less than an earthquake would carry that away.

It was insanity to expose the wood as we had done. It was soft and sodden with water, and full of heavy, hard-packed clay. Heaven knows what kept it from collapsing before we were half done. But it was the only way. We had no time to do it carefully. The first raindrops spattered against our faces as Mann lifted a flare high above his white head and Bates and I seized the ends of one of the great roof logs. It felt like solid lead.

"Drop it!" Bates gasped. His teeth were set in his lower lip and there was a trickle of blood on his chin. "It doesn't matter. We can't wait."

Log after log smashed into the pit below us. The top was cleared. A mass of the blue clay filled the vault, retaining the impression of the logs that had covered it. As we wrenched away the ends and sides, down to the level of our waists, I heard Michaelson's camera whirring at my ear, recording every detail.

Mann's hand fell on my shoulder. It was raining hard now, and little craters were puddling the wet clay. I thought of the little droplet marks that are found imprinted in the stone of fossil beaches, and somehow those lost ages seemed closer than ever before.

"There are only a few more flares," Mann told me. "You'd better clear the interior. Use a trowel."

Have you ever used a trowel on hard clay? Layer after layer we peeled off, slowly, laboriously, a chunk at a time, until my back and arms and my tortured wrists screamed for respite. Down—down—we went, three trowels delving like mad, and Michaelson below us, swinging an ax, hacking the logs into sections small enough to carry safely to the field above.

At last a bare six inches separated us from the remaining logs. Mann was in the middle, his sleeves rolled to the elbows, his gnarled old arms darting expertly, shaving the clay away in tiny flakes. Suddenly something flashed white under his trowel.

We stood frozen, staring, at his cry. Michaelson came climbing out of the darkness behind me, clutching at my arm as he balanced at my side. Windy gusts of rain swept across the wet clay before us, eating it away, enlarging that spot of glistening white.

The flare went out. I heard Bates swear, heard him striking match after match, heard them splutter out. One caught. All his body was warped over it, shielding it from the wind and the driving rain. Its feeble flame lighted his clay-streaked face and Mann's hand, thrusting the flare toward him. Then the bald, white light blazed in our faces again, and Michaelson's cameras were whirring, clicking, whirring at my side.

With numbed, blue fingers Mann scooped away the clay, working it down to an even level. A second patch of white appeared, close beside the first. No one spoke as his bony fingers ate away the clay, deeper and deeper, aided by the pelting rain. Our breathing sounded harsh and strange. I saw Bates's face, opposite me, and there was something indescribable in it, in his glittering eyes.

Mann's plying fingers stopped and his bent back straightened as he, too, stared into Bates's face. And then it was as though some wizard's screen were snatched away from before me. I saw what I had not seen before—what, somehow, my brain had refused to comprehend.

Thrust up from the hard, blue clay were the two white mounds of a woman's breasts!

It was impossible! We knew—we had proof—that that vault of flint-hewn logs had lain under tons of earth for tens of thousands of years. No human flesh had ever endured so long—could ever endure so long.

It was impossible!

But it was true!

I touched the smooth, white flesh. It was hard, firm, and oddly dry—almost with warmth of its own. It was not like dead flesh, nor was it stone—a statue. I heard Bates's hoarse voice, whispering: "We must uncover it."

And Mann: "Yes, Yes."

Under their trowels, under their digging fingers, the white flesh grew and grew. Twice they stopped, impatient, while we pried away more logs and hacked at the clay with frantic shovels, levelling it down, carving gutters to carry away the teeming rain that poured down over that glistening white flesh, washing it clean, revealing it to our hungry eyes.

She lay on a low table of hewn stone, smoothed like the great outer block. Her eyes were closed, and her full lips, and her slim white arms lay straight at her sides. Her hair was piled in a tumbled mound beneath her head and flowed down in two great, golden masses over her shoulders, gleaming like spun metal through the clotted blue clay. She was beautiful. And—she was dead.

Mann knows races as he knows the faces and voices of friends, but he could not place her. There was never a race like that in recorded history, nor in the legends of men before history. In her high cheeks, her narrow eyes, her slightly flattened nostrils were Mongol traces, but that slim white body with its glory of golden hair was not Mongol. Her long, straight limbs and delicate, tapered fingers were not Mongol. By no fantasy of the imagination could she be identified with the yellow race.

The rain was beating like icy flails upon our backs. Trees in the darkness were tortured by the wind, and behind its dyke of clay the tumult of the raging stream was rising to a sullen, brooding growl. The glare of the torch fell in a pool of light about us, its dim edges glinting from tossing wave tops, lipping higher than our heads at the very summit of the dyke. Gullies were eating their way into the broken clay and murky rivulets streamed through them, eating at the soft earth, crumbling it away.

Mann's voice was cracked and shrill over the clamor of the storm. His bare arm stretched toward the leaping wave crests, and words drifted to me on gusts of the wind.

"Get her away—the plane—before it breaks. No time—hurry! Hurry, man!"

Bates was on his knees in the clay, pushing his fingers under her white shoulders. His eyes turned to me and I understood. My hands gripped her ankles, smooth and glistening-wet, yet somehow dry—warm and strangely dry, and harder than flesh should be. We lifted her, stiff, like a statue, between us, and she was not heavier than a girl would be.

We held her high, scrambling down from the great stone into the pit, the muddy water swirling around our thighs, the soft clay underfoot sucking and slipping. Painfully, clawing for purchase in the sliding gravel, we worked our way up the steep side of the crater, out of the light of the flare, into the darkness.

We laid her on the cropped, wet grass of the pasture. Bates ran back and stood shouting down at the others where they crouched in the pit, searching the clay for ornaments, offerings—anything that might have been placed with the body. I saw his lean arm, silhouetted against the light of the flare, pointing upstream, and it seemed to me that there was a deeper, uglier note in the shout of the savage waters.

Barely in time, Mann's streaming mane appeared over the rim of the pit, his hand seized Bates's, and he scrambled out, kneeling to reach for the cameras. After him came Michaelson, dropping the flare to fling himself over the pit edge just as the freed waters of the creek smashed against the gravel cliff beneath him.

Then we were standing in rain-swept darkness while Michaelson fumbled with matches and the flare, were stumbling across the uneven ground toward the plane, carrying that still, white form that should not, could not logically exist—a woman older than the very hills above our heads!

All that night we crouched in the lee of the plane. By the time the first wan light began to creep over the sodden landscape, Mann decided that it was safe to take off. The ship would not carry more than two.

We helped him load that glorious, rigid form into the cockpit and stood in a huddled group as he taxied slowly up the bumpy field, swung around, and came roaring down toward us. Somehow the plane gained speed; somehow he lifted it, mud from its dripping wheels lashing our up-turned faces, and then we were standing alone in the cold, wet morning, with only incredible memories to bear witness to what had happened in the night.

There was no plane west that day. How we endured it as the train dawdled along through the interminable flat lands west of Syracuse, I cannot understand. I was half frantic with suspense and I knew that Bates must be even closer to sheer nervous collapse, but we sat, stony-faced, staring out at the flat, gray landscape, waiting, while Michaelson fussed and fretted over his newest and largest camera. Waiting—for what, none of us knew—none of us could ever have guessed.

The museum car was at the station. Bates knew the driver, and what happened to traffic laws that night would bring the Rochester police to the brink of tears. Michaelson, white-faced, sat hugging his camera to him like a baby, but he never breathed a word of protest. None of us grudged anything that would save another minute.

The only lights in the big building were in Mann's workroom. He looked up as we entered. Evidently he had not rested since he left us, sixteen hours before. A fling of his hand included the two men who stood with him behind the long table with its still, white, lovely form.

"Clements—Breen."

The former was a man like a bearded mountain, younger than I am, the latter a man like a wizened elf, older than Mann. In that room we had the three greatest anthropologists in the United States—and a mystery that baffled them all.

Clements was slow of speech. His brow wrinkled and words began to boom at us, only to be snatched from his lips by Breen's tempestuous babble.

"I have seen nothing like her, ever. There is——"

"——no precedent! Never! You, Bates—she's yours. You found her. What do you say?"

Bates's smile was a bit apologetic. "I've had no opportunity to examine her, professor. You have had half the day. Surely you can speak for what you have found."

This time Clements' thunder carried through. "There was nothing with her? No offerings of any kind? Then study her closely, now, before you ask us anything more—you too, gentlemen. There will be time enough for discussion afterward."

I stared again at those lovely features, framed in their mist of spun gold. Mann had cleaned the clay from her, and she lay like a girl asleep, long dark lashes upcurved on high, white cheeks, red lips parted—it was impossible that she should be dead! And dead for thirty thousand years!

I touched her, and again I sensed that curious roughness as of old parchment, that radiant, vibrant inner warmth. It was not like dead flesh, nor was it like the flesh of any mummy I had ever seen. It was rigid—hard—like stone, almost, yet without the coldness of stone.

Bates was examining her closely, his face for once expressionless. His fingers traced the contours of the gently swelling muscles under her white skin. His eyes devoured every inch of her beauty, stretched there before him, but they were a scientist's eyes, reading the story hidden in those matchless lineaments.

He took her hair in his hands and let it ripple slowly through his fingers in a curling yellow foam. He touched her eyelids, gently, and her full lips, and peered, frowning at the tiny ovals of her nails. He looked up, past me at the others, and there was blank bewilderment in his eyes.

"What does it mean? What is she? I—I don't understand."

Clements shrugged hugely, his hairy face smug. Little Breen's eyes glittered and his voice was shrill with excitement.

"You see? Her lips—her eyes—her fingers—did you see them? It is impossible! No scientist could do it today. And ten—twenty—thirty thousand years ago—— It is impossible!"

Mann saw my bewilderment. "Her fingers are grown together," he explained, "her toes also. You can see that they do not separate. The skin is continuous, and her eyelids seem welded to the cheeks. That could be if she was abnormal—a cripple—in life. But her lips, too—— Look closely. Touch them."

I laid my hot fingers upon their full, crimson curve. The glistening enamel of her perfect teeth showed between them. I tried to press them back, as I had seen Bates do. They were like wood! They would not move!

"Flesh welded to flesh is not strange, but flesh grown to the enamel of her teeth!" It was Clements speaking. "And look closely—there is a meniscus, a serif, where they join."

It was true. It was as though that marvelous body were cast in wax, all in one piece. Under her nails the flesh curved up with the same little concave meniscus, and when Clements gave me a lens I saw that at the base of each golden hair the skin rose in a tiny cone, shading gradually from ivory to shimmering yellow. Every tiny wrinkle—every whorl and ridge of her palms and finger tips was plainly marked, but nowhere were the tiny pits of pores.

Nowhere was there any opening in that strange, hard membrane that covered her entire body in place of normal human skin.

Bates had been examining her with that stolid thoroughness that is so characteristic of him. Now he stood staring into vacancy, oblivious of everything.

I knew what thoughts were passing through his mind. What was she, this woman out of the past? What manner of creature could live as she must have lived, sealed away from the world and everything in it? How did she eat—drink—breathe? Was it like a plant, absorbing moisture and food through that unnatural skin—feeding on light itself? Was she, in fact, some superplant from an age when plants were lords of Earth and all that lived on it—the culmination of a line of evolution longer and greater than that which had given rise to the human form she mimicked?

She was no plant! The man in me, surging up at the vision of her slim, white loveliness, knew that. She was all woman—a woman such as history and the races of history had never known—a woman of that elder, godlike race whose vague traditions filtering through the ages had been preserved in the myths of the earliest known men.

Men of her own race had laid her where we found her—or was it men of another blood, living centuries after the last of her own kind had vanished from the Earth, and ministering to her as the goddess that her beauty proclaimed her? Was it the forgotten science of her ancient race that had preserved her, immune and inviolate, through the ages?

I heard Bates's voice, strained and unreal: "You're sure she's dead?"

What if she were not dead? What if she were in some hypnotic, trancelike state of suspended animation, preserved by the magic of her ancient science until the day when men should be ready to receive her again and with her rule the world in godlike power? What if we should wake her—now—after thirty thousand years?

Mann answered him. "We have found no evidence of life, and we were as thorough as the time allowed. I would swear that she is dead, if she were a normal being. But——"

"We are not sure!" boomed Clements. "Because our tests show no life we cannot swear that she is dead. Because she had been buried in the earth since the days of the ice age, we cannot assume that life could not remain in her. There have been other instances—of other forms of life, preserved in clay or stone for months and years. I tell you, we are not sure—and we must be!"

Bates nodded thoughtfully. His emotions were no longer overbalancing his better judgment. "What records have you made?" he asked.

Breen gestured impatiently. "The usual things. Her weight—the standard measurements of the body—photographs and molds with Negacoll. Clements has samples of her hair and microphotographs of her skin. We have done what we could, without dissection. An expert craftsman, such as you have in this museum, could make her live again as you see her now."

Bates bit his lip. It was a difficult decision to make. "Then there is only—dissection?"

Breen nodded: "Yes."

A thin line of worry had appeared between his eyes. "Suppose she's alive," he protested. "We'd kill her. And we don't know that she's dead, we can't be sure!"

Breen snorted. "Of course, she's dead! Why talk madness? This perfect preservation—who knows what natural chemistry of the body, and of the soil in which she was buried, might not have preserved the flesh and caused this hornlike hardening of the skin? Mammoths have been found with everything intact. We must examine her, thoroughly, and we must be quick. Decomposition begins suddenly in these cases, and in an hour—poof!—there may be nothing left! We are scientists. Never has there been such an opportunity. Of course, we will dissect!"

He was right, of course, but Clements, I think, felt something of what we did. There was more of the romantic in him than in Breen. He interrupted: "One moment, professor. This hardening of the skin has undoubtedly resulted in the wonderful preservation which we have seen, but—does it extend to the vital organs which we cannot see? We must not expose them to the effects of the air until we are certain that they will not be destroyed."

Breen stared at him. "What do you suggest?" he demanded.

"The X ray, first. It will show us what we want to know as well as dissection—the details of the skeleton, and the nature of the vital organs. Then refrigeration—as soon as possible, to be safe—and injection of preservatives. The tissues will not be in danger of destruction, then, and we can complete our examination without the need of this mad haste."

Breen stood for a moment with pursed lips, nodding slowly. Then he swung to Mann. "You have an X ray?" he asked curtly.

"There is one downstairs," Mann told him. "One of our research staff is using it in his study of pottery. But we use only the small-sized plates. We can arrange with the hospital to take a full-length picture."

Breen's hand shot up in impatient negation. "Later, if need be—not now. You have a fluoroscope? Then we will begin with that—the photographs afterward. There is no need of depending upon hospital routine when we can do the work ourselves—and trust it when it is done. Will you bring the apparatus up here?"

"Yes," Mann assented. "There is no room downstairs. We can set it up over there, under the skylight. Open it, please, Mr. Bates—it is too warm here. We must be more careful of that. And I will need help with the equipment."

Bates and I went down with him to get the X ray, leaving the others to rig an adjustable canvas framework on which to place the body when it was photographed. The apparatus was infernally heavy, and it took the three of us the better part of an hour to get it set up and working properly.

Meanwhile, Clements was deep in another examination of her skin and hair, and little Breen was bounding back and forth between him and Michaelson, who had completed the stretcher and was making a simple holder for the plates.

We laid her carefully on the taut canvas and buckled two broad straps across her flawless body, holding it in place. Breen was tinkering fussily with the transformer of the X-ray generator while Mann held the fluoroscope. As I stood by the door, watching them, a breath of air from the open skylight ruffled the curling golden wave that lay heaped against her cheek, and I could have sworn that her rounded bosoms rose and fell gently with the regular breathing of deep sleep. I looked again, and it was illusion.

Breen finished his adjustments, and I snapped off the lights. There was the click of a tumbler switch, and the dull violet glow of the ray illuminated the faces of the five men bending over that still, white form on the stretcher. The drone of the transformer was the only sound in all the room.

Breen's heels rasped on the concrete floor. He was going around behind the stretcher. Clements had lifted it in both hands and was moving it into the direct path of the ray. Then Breen reached over and took the fluoroscope from Mann.

He took it—I saw that—and he must have lifted it into place behind the frame. Michaelson stepped back into my view, and all that I could see was the carved, white face dimly lighted by the ghastly glow of the X-ray tube. I stepped away from the switch, to one side, to get a better view.

Breen shouted.

I saw him bob up from behind the stretcher, choppy sounds pouring from his mouth. There was a dry, brittle rending and Michaelson leaped back as though shot.

And then I saw!

A great black gash split that matchless body. It lay in halves—halves that were moving, separating, straining at the canvas straps that held it. They burst with a rotten snap and then it slid down against the cross brace at the bottom of the frame. Then out of that cloven gap rose a thing out of madness!

Faceted eyes as huge as a man's two fists glittered in the wan light. A black, humped form rose from between the tilted breasts, higher, higher—dragging itself out of the riven husk that had been a woman— towering on fragile, jointed legs—dwarfing the men who stood beneath it.

Two wings began to grow from its sides, like shimmering disks of fire. Colors rippled through them—colors that paled and waxed and paled again in pulsing waves of radiance. Light poured out of the thing's warped body, making it a transparent, crystal shell. Light blazed from the myriad facets of its glittering eyes. And then it straightened its bent back.

It stood erect, like a man, on two legs. Its wings enveloped it like a gauzy veil of light, fluted and laced and ruffled, creeping with colored fire. A mass of feathery tendrils stirred uneasily between its eyes, where a mouth should be.

Its wings were swelling, as a moth's wings do. They spread until the whole room blazed with their glory. They swept up and forward until they shrouded the four men who stood motionless beneath it—Clements, Michaelson, Bates, and Breen. Mann had stumbled closer to me, outside of their gossamer spread. For a moment those two great compound eyes regarded us over that curtain of living flame, and then the oval head sank slowly down, its mouth parts palpitating—spreading——

Neither of us knows what time passed then. As we gazed, the color of those vast, encircling wings deepened and brightened, until all the room was filled with a splendor of violet flame. It seemed to grow—visibly— until its bent head towered inches from the open skylight and its throb- bing wings pulsed within a yard of Mann's rapt, rigid body. Warmth flooded from them—radiation—like the warmth that had emanated from the naked woman form that had been its chrysalis. And then, somehow, I found my fingers on the light switch. Somehow they moved —somehow the lights went on.

And there was nothing there!

Nothing? The thing had weight and substance, for I had lifted it in my own two arms, and seen it crush the bodies of our men into its em- brace. But it was transparent—invisible. A shimmering violet haze hung between me and the opposite wall, above it the flicker of watching, many-faceted eyes. And in the midst of that haze, crumpled and shrunken by whatever awful force had blasted the life out of them, stood the four men.

Light hurt it. For a moment that cold gaze rested on us. A moment it stood there, staring at us from above its enshrouding, fiery wings. Then, like a whisk of fleeting shadow, it was gone, out into the empty night, and we were alone with the shriveled husks of the men who had been our friends.

What was it? How can I tell you, who know no more than you do? It was a thing that lived in the days of the great ice age, when savage men hunted the mammoth and the giant sloth where our American cities now stand. It was a thing of many shapes, like a mighty butterfly, making its chrysalis in the image of a beautiful woman—a goddess of utter loveliness.

Those forgotten savages worshiped it, and built it a crypt, a shrine of smoothed stone and massive logs as their fathers had done, and their fathers before them, since there were men who loved beauty. And in time it crept out of that lovely, treacherous shell and blasted the life and soul from those who tended it.

Where has it gone? The world is different now, and there are none of its kind to mate with it and preserve its hellish breed. Perhaps it died, as moths die, within an hour or a day, and lies invisible in some field or forest nook, the blazing light of its unnatural life gone out of it. Perhaps it still lives, somewhere in the north where the ice still lingers, and will somehow multiply and return to scourge the Earth as it was scourged in the days before history, by a hell of utter beauty that drains men of their very souls.

Perhaps—but shall we ever know?

L. SPRAGUE DE CAMP

LIVING FOSSIL

WHERE the rivers flowed together, the country was flat and, in places, swampy. The combined waters spread out and crawled around reedy islands. Back from the banks, the ground rose into low tree-crowned humps.

The May flies were swarming that day, and as thousands of them danced, the low afternoon sun, whose setting would bring death to them all, glinted on their wings. There was little sound, other than the hum of a belated cicada and the splashing of an elephantlike beast in the southern tributary.

The beast suddenly raised its head, its great mulish ears swiveling forward and its upraised trunk turning this way and that like a periscope. It evidently disapproved of what it smelled, for it heaved its bulk out of its bath and ambled off up a creek bed, the feet on its columnar legs making loud sucking noises as they pulled out of the mud.

Two riders appeared from downstream, each leading an animal similar to the one he rode. The animals' feet swished through the laurel beds and went *squilch-squilch* as they struck patches of muck. As they crossed the creek bed, the leading rider pulled up his mount and pointed to the tracks made by the elephantine beast.

"Giant tapir!" he said in his own harsh, chattering language. "A big one. What a specimen he'd make!"

"*Ngoy?*" drawled his companion, meaning approximately "Oh, yeah?" He continued: "And how would we get it back to South America? Carry it slung from a pole?"

The first rider made the grating noise in his throat that was his race's equivalent of laughter. "I didn't suggest shooting it. I just said it would make a good specimen. We'll have to get one some day. The museum hasn't a decent mounted example of the species."

The riders were anthropoid, but not human. Their large prehensile tails, rolled up behind them on the saddle, and the thick coats of brown and black hair that covered them, precluded that. Their thumblike halluces or big toes jutted out from the mid-portion of their feet and were hooked into the stirrups, which were about the size and shape of napkin rings. Below the large liquid eyes in their prognathous faces there were no external noses, just a pair of narrow nostrils set wide apart. The riders weighed about one hundred and fifty pounds each. A zoölogist of today would have placed them in the family *Cebidæ*, the capuchin monkeys, and been right. They would have had more difficulty in classifying the zoölogist, because in their time the science of paleontology was young, and the family tree of the primates had not been worked out fully.

Their mounts were the size of mules; tailless, round-eared, and with catlike whiskers sprouting from their deep muzzles. They absurdly resembled colossal guinea pigs, which they were; or rather, they were colossal agoutis, the ordinary agouti being a rabbit-sized member of the cavy family.

The leading rider whistled. His mount and the lead pack agouti bucked up the creek bank and headed at their tireless trot toward one of the mounds. The rider dismounted and began poking around between the curiously regular granite blocks scattered among the green-and-brown-spotted trunks of the sycamores. Grasshoppers exploded from under his feet as he walked.

He called, "Chujee!"

The other rider trotted up and got off. The four agoutis went to work with their great chisel teeth on the low-drooping branches.

"Look," the first rider said, turning over one of the blocks. "Those faces are too nearly parallel to have been made that way by accident. And here's one with two plane surfaces at a perfect right angle. I think we've found it."

"*Ngoy?*" drawled the other. "You mean the site of a large city of Men? Maybe." Skepticism was patent in his tone as he strolled about, poking at the stones with his foot. Then his voice rose. "Nawputta! You think *you've* found something; look at this!" He uprighted a large stone. Its flat face was nearly smooth, but when it was turned so that the sun's rays were almost parallel with the face, a set of curiously regular shadows sprang out on the surface.

Nawputta—he had a given name as well, but it was both unpronounceable and unnecessary to reproduce here—scowled at it, trying in his mind to straighten the faint indentations into a series of inscribed characters. He fished a camera out of his harness and snapped several pictures, while Chujee braced the stone. The markings were as follows:

NATIO
ANK OF
TTSBURGH

"It's an inscription, all right," Nawputta remarked, as he put his camera away. "Most of it's weathered away, which isn't surprising, considering that the stone's been here for five or ten million years, or however long Man has been extinct. The redness of this sand bears out the theory. It's probably full of iron oxide. Men must have used an incredible amount of steel in their buildings."

Chujee asked: "Have you any idea what the inscription says?" In his voice there was the trace of awe which the capuchins felt toward these predecessors who had risen so high and vanished so utterly.

"No. Some of our specialists will have to try to decipher it from my photographs. That'll be possible only if it's in one of the languages of Man that have been worked out. He had dozens of different languages that we know of, and probably hundreds that we don't. The commonest was En-gel-iss-ha, which we can translate fairly well. It's too bad there aren't some live Men running around. They could answer a lot of questions that puzzle us."

"Maybe," said Chujee. "And maybe it's just as well there aren't. They might have killed *us* off if they'd thought we were going to become civilized enough to compete with them."

"Perhaps you're right. I never thought of that. I wish we could take the stone back with us."

Chujee grunted. "When you hired me to guide you, you told me the museum just wanted you to make a short reconnaissance. And every day you see something weighing a ton or so that you want to collect. Yesterday it was that bear we saw on the cliff; it weighed a ton and a half at least."

"But," expostulated Nawputta, "that was a new subspecies!"

"Sure," growled the guide. "That makes it different. New subspecies aren't really heavy; they only look that way. You scientific guys! We should have brought along a derrick, a steam tractor, and a gang of laborers from the Colony." His grin took the sting out of his words. "Well, old-timer, I see you'll be puttering around after relics all day; I might as well set up camp." He collected the agoutis and went off to find a dry spot near the river.

Presently he was back. "I found a place," he said. "But we aren't the first ones. There's the remains of a recent fire."

Nawputta, the zoölogist, looked disappointed. "Then we aren't the first to penetrate this far into the Eastern Forest. Who do you suppose it was?"

"Dunno. Maybe a timber scout from the Colony. They're trying to build up a lumber export business, you know. They don't like being too dependent on their salt and sulphur— Yeow!" Chujee jumped three feet straight up. "Snake!"

Nawputta jumped, too; then laughed at their timidity. He bent over and snatched up the little reptile as it slithered among the stones. "It's perfectly harmless," he said. "Most of them are, this far north."

"I don't care if it is," barked Chujee, backing up rapidly. "You keep that damn thing away from me!"

Next day they pushed up the south tributary. The character of the vegetation slowly changed as they climbed. A few miles up, they came to another fork. They had to swim the main stream in order to follow the smaller one, as Nawputta wished to cast toward the line of hills becoming visible in the east, before turning back. As they swam their agoutis across the main street, a black-bellied cloud that had crept up behind them suddenly opened with a crash of thunder, and pelting rain whipped the surface to froth.

As they climbed out on the far bank, Nawputta began absent-mindedly unrolling his cape. He almost had it on when a whoop from Chujee reminded him that he was thoroughly soaked already. The rain had slackened to a drizzle and presently ceased.

The scientist sniffed. "Wood smoke," he said.

Chujee grunted. "Either that's our mysterious friend, or we're just in time to stop a forest fire, if the rain hasn't done that for us." He kicked his mount forward. In the patch of pine they were traversing, the agoutis' feet made no sound on the carpet of needles. Thus they came upon the fire and the capuchin who was roasting a slab of venison over it before the latter saw them.

At the snap of a twig, the stranger whirled and snatched up a heavy rifle.

"Well?" he said in a flat voice. "Who be you?" In his cape, which he was still wearing after the rain, he looked like a caricature of Little Red Ridinghood.

The explorers automatically reached for the rifles in their saddle boots, but thought better of it in the face of that unwavering muzzle. Nawputta identified himself and the guide.

The stranger relaxed. "Oh! Just another one of those damn bug hunters. Sorry I scared you. Make yourselves at home. I'm Nguchoy tsu Chaw, timber scout for the Colony. We—I—came up in that canoe yonder. Made it ourselves out of birch bark. Great stuff, birch bark."

"We?" echoed Nawputta.

The scout's shoulders drooped sadly. "Just finished burying my partner. Rattlesnake got him. Name was Jawga; Jawga tsu Shrr. Best partner a scout ever had. Say, could you let me have some flea powder? I'm all out."

As he rubbed the powder into his fur, he continued: "We'd just found the biggest stand of pine you ever saw. This river cuts through a notch in the ridge about thirty miles up. Beyond that it's gorges and rapids for miles, and beyond that it cuts through another ridge and breaks up into little creeks. We had to tie the boat up and hike. Great country; deer, bear, giant rabbit, duck, and all kinds of game. Not so thick as they say it is on the western plains, but you can shoot your meat easy." He went on to say that he was making a cast up the main stream before returning to the Colony with his news.

After Nguchoy had departed early the following morning, Chujee, the guide, scratched his head. "Guess I must have picked up some fleas from our friend. Wonder why he held a gun on us until he found who we were? That's no way to treat a stranger."

Nawputta wiggled his thumbs, the capuchin equivalent of a shrug. "He was afraid at being alone, I imagine."

Chujee still frowned. "I can understand his grabbing it before he knew what was behind him; we might have been a lion. But he kept pointing it after he saw we were *Jmu*"—the capuchin word for "human" —"like himself. There aren't any criminals around here for him to be scared of. Oh, well, I guess I'm just naturally mistrustful of these damned Colonials. Do you want to look at this 'great country'?"

"Yes," said Nawputta. "If we go on another week, we can still get out before the cold weather begins." (Despite their fur, the capuchins were sensitive to cold, for which reason exploration had lagged behind the other elements of their civilization.) "Nguchoy's description agrees with what Chmrrgoy saw from his balloon, though, as you recall, he never got up this far on foot. He landed by the river forty miles down and floated down the Big Muddy to the Colony on a raft."

"Say," said Chujee. "Do you suppose they'll ever get a flying machine that'll go where you want it to, instead of being blown around like these balloons? You know all about these scientific things."

"Not unless they can get a much lighter engine. By the time you've loaded your boiler, your engine proper, and your fuel and feed water aboard, your flying machine has as much chance of taking off as a granite boulder. There's a theory that Men had flying machines, but the evidence isn't conclusive. They may have had engines powered by mineral oils, which they pumped out of beds of oil-bearing sand. Our geologists have traced some of their borings. They used up nearly all the oils, so *we* have to be satisfied with coal."

It was a great country, the explorers agreed when they reached it. The way there had not been easy. Miles before they reached the notch, they had had to cut their way through a forest of alders that stretched along the sides of the river. Chujee had gone ahead on foot, swinging an ax in time to his strides with the effortless skill of an old woodsman. With each swing the steel bit clear through the soft white wood of a slim trunk. Behind him, Nawputta had stumbled, the leading agouti's reins gripped in his tail.

When they had passed through the notch, they climbed up the south side of the gorge in which they found themselves and in the distance saw another vast blue rampart, like the one they had just cut through, stretching away to the northeast. (This had once been called the Allegheny Mountains.) Age-old white pines raised their somber blue-green spires above them. A huge buffalo-shaped cervid, who was rubbing the velvet from his antlers against a tree trunk, smelled them, snorted, and lumbered off.

"What's that noise?" asked Nawputta.

They listened, and heard a faint rhythmical thumping that seemed to come out of the ground.

"Dunno," said Chujee. "Tree trunks knocking together, maybe? But there isn't enough wind."

"Perhaps it's stones in a pothole in the river," said Nawputta without conviction.

They kept on to where the gorge widened out. Nawputta suddenly pulled his agouti off the game trail and jumped down. Chujee rode over and found the scientist examining a pile of bones.

Ten minutes later he was still turning the bones over.

"Well," said Chujee impatiently, "aren't you going to let me in on the secret?"

"Sorry. I didn't believe my own senses at first. These are the bones of Men! Not fossils; *fresh* bones! From the looks of them they're the remains of a meal. There were three of them. From the holes in the skulls I'd say that our friend Nguchoy or his partner shot them. I'm going to get a whole specimen, if it's the last thing I do."

Chujee sighed. "For a fellow who claims he hates to kill things, you're the bloodthirstiest cuss I ever saw when you hear about a new species."

"You don't understand, Chujee," objected Nawputta. "I'm what's called a fanatical conservationist. Hunting for fun not only doesn't amuse me; it makes me angry when I hear about it. But securing a scientific specimen is different."

"Oh," said Chujee.

They peered out of the spruce thicket at the Man. He was a strange object to them, almost hairless, so that the scars on his yellow-brown skin showed. He carried a wooden club, and padded noiselessly over the pine needles, pausing to sniff the air. The sun glinted on the wiry bronze hair that sprouted from his chin.

Nawputta squeezed his trigger; the rifle went off with a deafening *ka-pow!* A fainter *ka-pow!* bounced back from the far wall of the gorge as the Man's body struck the ground.

"Beautiful!" cried Chujee. "Right through the heart! Couldn't have done better myself. But I'd feel funny about shooting one; they look so *Jmu*."

Nawputta, getting out his camera, tape measure, notebook, and skinning knife, said: "In the cause of science I don't mind. Besides, I couldn't trust you not to try for a brain shot and ruin the skull."

Hours later he was still dissecting his prize and making sketches. Chujee had long since finished the job of salting the hide, and was lolling about trying to pick up a single pine needle with his tail.

"Yeah," he said, "I know it's a crime that we haven't got a tank of formaldehyde so we could pack the whole carcass back, instead of just the skin and skeleton. But we haven't got it, and never did have it, so why bellyache?"

Much as he respected Nawputta, the zoölogist got on his nerves at times. Not that he didn't appreciate the scientific point of view; he was well-read and had some standing as an amateur naturalist. But, having managed expeditions for years, he had long been resigned to the fact that you can carry only so much equipment at a time.

He sat up suddenly with a warning "S-s-st!" Fifty feet away a human face peered out of a patch of brake ferns. He reached stealthily for his rifle; the face vanished. The hair on Chujee's neck and scalp rose. He had never seen such a concentration of malevolent hatred in one countenance. The ferns moved, and there was a brief flash of yellow-brown skin among the trees.

"Better hurry," he said. "The things may be dangerous when one of 'em's been killed."

Nawputta murmured vaguely that he'd have the skeleton cleaned in a few minutes. He was normally no more insensitive to danger than the guide, but in the presence of this scientific wonder, a complete Man, the rest of the world had withdrawn itself into a small section of his mind.

Chujee, still peering into the forest, growled: "It's funny that Nguchoy didn't say anything to us about the Men. That is, unless he *wanted* us to be eaten by the things. And why should he want that? Say, isn't that pounding louder? I'll bet it's a Man pounding a hollow log for a signal. If Nguchoy wanted to get rid of us, he picked an ingenious method. He and his partner kill some of the Men, and we come along just when they've got nicely stirred up and are out for *Jmu* blood. Let's get out of here!"

Nawputta was finished at last. They packed the skin and skeleton of the Man, mounted, and rode back the way they had come, glancing nervously into the shadows around them. The pounding was louder.

They had gone a couple of miles and were beginning to relax, when something soared over their heads and buried itself quivering in the ground. It was a crude wooden spear. Chujee fired his rifle into the underbrush in the direction from which the spear had come. A faint rustle mocked him. The pounding continued.

The notch loomed high before them, though still several miles away. The timber was smaller here, and there was more brush. They had originally come along the river, and followed game trails up the side of the gorge at this point. They hesitated whether or-not to go back the same way.

"I don't like to let them get above me," complained Nawputta.

"We'll have to," argued Chujee. "The sides of the notch are too craggy; we'd never get the agoutis over it."

They started down the slope, on which the trees thinned out. A chorus of yells brought them up sharply. The hairless things were pouring out of the deep woods and racing toward them.

"The agoutis won't make it with those loads," snapped Chujee, and he flung himself off his mount.

Nawputta did likewise, and his rifle crashed almost as soon as the guide's. The echoes of their rapid fire made a deafening uproar in the gorge. Nawputta, as he fired and worked the lever of his gun, wondered what he'd do when the magazine was empty.

Then the Men were bounding back into the shelter of the woods, shrieking with fear. They vanished. Two of their number lay still, and a third thrashed about in a raspberry bush and screeched.

"I can't see him suffer," said Nawputta. He drew a bead on the Man's head and fired. The Man quieted, but from the depths of the forest came screams of rage.

Chujee said dryly, "They didn't interpret that as an act of mercy," as he remounted.

The agoutis were trembling. Nawputta noticed that he was shaking a bit himself. He had counted his shots, and knew before he started to reload that he had had just one shot left.

The yelping cries of the Men followed them as they headed into the notch, but the things didn't show themselves long enough for a shot.

"That was too close for comfort," said Nawputta in a low voice, not taking his eyes from the woods. "Say, hasn't somebody invented a rifle whose recoil automatically reloads it, so that one can shoot it as fast as one pulls the trigger?"

Chujee grunted. "Yeah, he was up in the Colony demonstrating it last year. I tried it out. It jammed regularly every other shot. Maybe they'll be practical some day, but for the present I'll stick to the good old lever action. I suppose you were thinking of what would have happened to us if the Men had kept on coming. I— Say, look!" He halted his animal. "Look up yonder!"

Nawputta looked, and said: "Those boulders weren't piled up on top of the cliff when we came this way, were they?"

"That's right. When we get into the narrowest part of the notch, they'll roll them down on us. They'll be protected from our guns by the bulge of the cliff. There's no pathway on the other side of the river. We can't swim the animals because of the rapids, and even if we could, the river's so narrow that the rocks would bounce and hit us anyway."

Nawputta pondered. "We'll have to get through that bottle neck somehow; it'll be dark in a couple of hours."

Both were silent for a while.

Chujee said: "There's something wrong about this whole business; Nguchoy and his partner, I mean. If we ever get out of this—"

Nawputta interrupted him: "Look! I could swim one agouti over here, and climb a tree on the other side. I could get a good view of the top of the cliffs. There's quite an open space there, and I could try to keep the Men away from the boulders with my gun, while you took the agoutis down through the notch. Then, if you can find a corresponding tree below the bottle neck, you could repeat the process while I followed you down."

"Right! I'll fire three shots when I'm ready for you."

Nawputta tethered his animal and hoisted himself up the big pine, his rifle held firmly in his tail. He found a place where he could rest the gun on a branch to sight, and waved to the guide, who set off at a trot down the narrow shelf along the churning waters.

Sure enough, the Men presently appeared on top of the cliff. They looked smaller over the sights of Nawputta's rifle than he had expected; too small to make practical targets as individuals even. He aimed into the thick of these dancing pink midges and fired twice. The crash of the rifle was flung back sharply from the south wall of the gorge. He couldn't see whether he had hit anything, but the spidery things disappeared.

Then he waited. The sun had long since disappeared behind the ridge, but a few slanting rays poked through the notch; insects were briefly visible as motes of light as they flew through these rays. Overhead a string of geese flapped southward.

When Nawputta heard three shots, he descended, swam his agouti back across the river, and headed downstream. The dark walls of the gorge towered almost vertically over him. Above the roar of the rapids he heard a shot, then another. The agouti flinched at the reports, but kept on. The shots continued. The Men were evidently determined not to be balked of their prey this time. Nawputta counted—seven—eight. The firing ceased, and the zoölogist knew that his companion was reloading.

There was a rattle of loose rock. A boulder appeared over his head, swelled like a balloon, swished past him, and went *plunk* in the river beside him, throwing spray over him and his mount. He kicked the animal frantically and it bounded forward, nearly pitching its rider into the river at a turn.

Nawputta wondered desperately why Chujee hadn't begun shooting again. He looked up, and saw that the air over his head seemed to be full of boulders hanging suspended. They grew as he watched, and every one seemed headed straight for him. He bent low and urged the animal; he saw black water under him as the agouti cleared a recess in the trail with a bucking jump. He thought: "Why doesn't he shoot? But it's too late now."

The avalanche of rock struck the trail and the river behind him with a roar; one rock passed him so closely that he felt its wind. The agouti in its terror almost skidded off the trail. Then they were out in the sunlight again, and the animal's zigzag leaps settled into a smooth gallop.

Nawputta pulled up opposite Chujee's tree.

The guide was already climbing down with his rifle in his tail. He called: "Did you get hit? I thought you were a goner sure when the rock fall commenced. Got a twig caught in my breech while I was reloading."

Nawputta tried to call back reassurance, but found he couldn't make a sound.

When Chujee pulled his dripping mount up the bank, he got out his binoculars and looked at the south shoulder of the notch. He said: "Come on! They've already climbed down toward us; they haven't given up yet. But I think we can lose them if we can find that trail we cut through the alders. They don't know about it yet, and they'll probably scatter trying to find which way we've gone."

Nawputta yawned, stretched, and sat up. Chujee was sitting by the fire at Nguchoy's camp, his rifle in his lap. Both still looked a trifle haggard after their sleepless flight down the river. They had strung the four agoutis in a column, and taken turns riding backward on the last one of the string to keep watch against another attack. But though the pounding had continued, the Men had not shown themselves again. When they arrived at Nguchoy's camp, the timber scout was not to be seen, evidently not having returned.

Chujee said: "I've been thinking, while you were catching up on sleep, about this Nguchoy and his yarns. I don't reckon he intended us to return, though we couldn't prove anything against him.

"And I wonder how it happened that his partner died at such a convenient time . . . for him. He needed this Jawga person to help him paddle up the rivers. But once they got to the head of navigation, Nguchoy could get back downstream easy enough without help. And when they'd found that great pine forest, it would be mighty convenient if an accident happened to Jawga. When Nguchoy went back to the Colony, he wouldn't have to share the credit for the find, and the bonus, with anybody."

Nawputta raised his eyebrows, and without a word began hunting in their duffel for a spade.

In half an hour they had dug up all that was mortal of Jawga tsu Shrr. Nawputta examined the remains, which were in a most unpleasant state of decay.

"See!" he said. "Two holes in the skull, which weren't made by any rattlesnake. The one on the left side is just about right for a No. 14 rifle bullet going in."

They were silent. Over the swish of the wind in the trees came a faint rhythmical pounding.

"Do we want to pinch him?" asked Chujee. "It's a long way back to the Colony."

Nawputta thought. "I have a better idea. We'll rebury the corpse for the present."

"Nothing illegal," said Chujee firmly.

"N-no, not exactly. It's this way. Have you ever seen a Colony lumberjack gang in action?"

Nawputta shoved the corpse into the grave. The pounding was louder. Both capuchins looked to see that their rifles were within easy reach.

A tuneless whistling came through the trees.

"Quick!" whispered Nawputta. "Sprinkle some leaves on the grave. When he arrives, you get his attention. Talk about anything."

The whistling stopped, and presently the timber scout appeared. If he was surprised to see the explorers, he did not show it.

"Hello," he said. "Have a good trip?"

He paused and sniffed the air. The explorers realized that there had been one thing they couldn't put back in the grave. Nguchoy looked at the grave, but made no remark.

"Sure, we did," said Chujee in his best good-fellow manner, and went on to talk about the splendor of the gorge and the magnificence of the pines.

The pounding was becoming louder, but nobody seemed to notice.

"Nguchoy," said Nawputta suddenly, "did you and Jawga see any traces of live Men in the forest?"

The timber scout snorted. "Don't be a sap. Men have been—what's that word?—extinct for millions of years. How could we see them?"

"Well," the scientist went on, "we did." He paused. The only sound was the pounding. Or were there faint yelping cries? "Moreover, we've just had a look at the remains of your late-lamented partner."

There was silence again, except for the ominous sounds of the approach of Men.

"Are you going to talk to us?" asked Nawputta.

Nguchoy grinned. "Sure, I'll talk to you." He sprang back to the tree against which he had left his rifle standing. "With this!" He snatched up the weapon and pulled the trigger.

The rifle gave out a metallic click.

Nawputta opened his fist, showing a handful of cartridges. Then he calmly picked up his own rifle and covered the timber scout.

"Chujee," he said, "you take his knife and hatchet and the rest of his ammunition."

The guide, dumfounded by the decisive way of his usually impractical companion, obeyed.

"Now," said Nawputta, "tie the four agoutis together, and hitch the leading one to the end of Nguchoy's canoe. We're pulling out."

"But what?" asked Chujee uncertainly.

Nawputta snapped: "I'll explain later. Hurry."

As the explorers piled into the boat, the timber scout woke to life.

"Hey!" he shouted. "Aren't you taking me along? The Men'll be here any minute, and they'll eat me! They even eat their own kind when one's been killed!"

"No," said Nawputta, "we aren't taking you."

The canoe pulled out into the river, the agoutis following unwillingly till only their heads and loads showed above water.

"Hey!" screamed Nguchoy. "Come back! I'll confess!"

The canoe kept on, the agoutis swimming in its wake.

As the site of the camp receded, there was a sudden commotion among the trees. The now-familiar yells of the Men were mingled with despairing shrieks from the timber scout. The shrieks ceased, and the voices of the Men were raised in a rhythmical but tuneless chant, which the explorers could hear long after the camp was hidden from view.

Chujee, paddling low, stared straight before him for a while in silence. Finally he turned around in his seat and said deliberately: "That's the lowest damned trick I ever saw in my life. To leave him there defenseless like that to be eaten by those hairless things. I don't care if he *was* a liar and a murderer."

Nawputta's expression of smugness vanished, and he looked slightly crestfallen. "You don't approve, do you? I was afraid you wouldn't. But I had to do it that way."

"Well, why?"

Nawputta took a long breath and rested his paddle. "I started to explain before, but I didn't have time. Nguchoy had killed his partner, and was going to return to the Colony with the news of the forest. He tried to have us killed by the Men, and when that didn't work, he'd have killed us himself if I hadn't emptied his gun behind his back.

"When he got back to the Colony, a timber gang would have been sent out. They'd have wiped out that forest in a few years, and you'll admit that it's probably the finest in the whole Eastern Mountain area. Moreover, they'd have killed off the wild life, including the Men, partly for food, partly for self-protection, and partly because they like to shoot.

"We thought Man had been extinct for millions of years, after having spread all over the world and reached a state of civilization as high as or higher than ours. The Men that we saw may well be the last of their species. You're a practical fellow, and I don't know whether I can make you understand a biologist's feeling toward a living fossil like that. To us it's simply priceless, and there's nothing we won't do to preserve it.

"If we can get back to South America before the news of the pine stand reaches the Colony, I can pull the necessary wires to have the area set aside as a park or preserve. The Colony can just as well go elsewhere for its lumber. But if the Colony hears about it first, I shan't have a chance.

"If we'd taken Nguchoy back with us, even if we'd brought him to justice, he'd still have been able to give the news away, especially since he could probably have purchased leniency by it. And that would be the end of my park idea.

"If we'd taken the law into our own hands, even if I'd been able to overcome your objections to doing so, we'd have been in a fix when, as will inevitably happen, the Colony sends an officer up to investigate the disappearance of their scout. If we said he died of a snake bite, for instance, and the officer found a body with a bullet hole through the head, or alternatively if he'd found no body at all, he'd have been suspicious. As it is, we can truthfully say, when they ask us, that Nguchoy was alive and sound of wind and limb the last time we saw him. The officer will then find thc remains, having obviously been eaten by the Men. Of course, we needn't volunteer any information until the park proposal is in the bag.

"The reason I took his canoe is that I remembered that Men probably can't swim. At least, the chimpanzee, which is the nearest living relative of Man, can't, whereas we can swim instinctively as soon as we're able to walk.

"But there's a bigger issue than Nguchoy and the Men. You probably think I'm a bit cracked, with my concern for conservation.

"We know that Man, during the period of his civilization, was prodigally wasteful of his resources. The exhaustion of the mineral oils is an example. And the world-wide extinction of the larger mammals at the close of the last ice age was probably his doing, at least in part. We're sure that he was responsible for wiping out all the larger species of whales, and we suspect that he also killed off all but two of the twenty or more species of elephant that abounded at that time. Most of the large mammals of today have evolved in the last few million years from forms that were small enough to sit in your hand in Man's time.

"We don't know just why he became extinct, or almost extinct. Perhaps a combination of war and disease did it. Perhaps the exhaustion of his resources had a share. You know what a hardboiled materialist I am in most things; but it always has seemed to me that it was a case of outraged nature taking its revenge. That's not rational, but it's the way I feel. And I've dedicated my life to seeing that we don't make the same mistake.

"Now do you see why I had to do what I did?"

Chujee was silent for a moment, then said: "Perhaps I do. I won't say I approve . . . yet. But I'll think it over for a few days. Say, we'll have to land soon; the agoutis are getting all tired out from swimming."

The canoe slid on down the river in the Indian-summer sunshine. The white men who had applied the name "Indian summer" to that part of the year were gone, as were the Indians after whom it had been named. Of mighty Man, the only remnant was a little savage tribe in the Alleghenies. A representative of a much more ancient order, a dragonfly, hovered over the bow, its four glassy wings glittering in the sunlight. Then with a faint whir it wheeled and fled.

PHILIP LATHAM

N DAY

Tuesday, 1949 January 18

Sunspot maximum and three days without a single spot!

This cycle is certainly developing in a peculiar way. From the last minimum about March, 1944, sunspot activity jumped to a Wolf Number of 252 in December, 1948, the highest index on record since that rather dubious maximum back in 1778. But this month spots have simply failed to appear, as completely as if someone inside the sun had pulled a switch.

Clarke's elaborate empirical analysis has failed utterly to predict. I am now more firmly convinced than ever that no combination of harmonics can ever represent the approximate eleven-year rise and fall in the number of sunspots. Instead I favor Halm's old idea that each cycle is a separate outburst in itself. The very fact that our star is a weak variable means it is to a certain degree unstable. Not unstable to the extent of a Cepheid variable but still—unstable. Indeed, Halm's hypothesis appeals to me more strongly now than when he announced it four cycles ago.

There I go measuring my life in sunspot cycles again! But four cycles *does* sound much less than forty-four years. Yet how little more I know about the sun than when I first came to Western Tech. In many ways the sun reminds me of a woman: just when you think you are beginning to understand her, invariably she will fool you. Enough of that. What business does an old bachelor have writing such things in his diary?

The driving clock on the coelostat was out of commission again today but I will have to repair it somehow. President Bixby refused my request for three hundred seventy-five dollars on the grounds that the budget was already over the limit. I notice, however, that others seem to have no trouble securing large allotments.

Until some spots show up I suppose I can best employ my time testing those new Eastman IV-K plates that arrived today.

Evening

When I wrote this morning that the sun invariably does the unexpected, I had no idea my words would be so soon fulfilled.

Spent an hour this afternoon taking test plates on the solar spectrum in the yellow and orange. Imagine my astonishment upon examining one of the plates with an eyepiece to see the D3 line of neutral helium. Of course, D3 often shows above active sunspots, but I believe this is the first case of its appearance over a calm undisturbed region. Smedley would probably know about this but I dread to ask him. I know he regards me as an old fossil, and this would only be further proof of my growing senility. How different was my own attitude when I was a young instructor!

The weather looked threatening at sunset but when I stepped out on the platform just now the sky was clear. The valley five thousand feet above was a carpet of lights from downtown Los Angeles to Santa Monica. Better drive down for a haircut and fresh pipe tobacco soon —my two-weeks supply is nearly gone. I really shouldn't stay on the mountain so long at a time. Too much solitude is as bad for the mind as too much inbreeding is bad for the race.

Besides, I absolutely must get started on the notes Marley left behind. Publication of such valuable material should not be so long delayed.

Wednesday, January 19

The long quiescent spell in solar activity is broken at last, and how it was broken!

An enormous spot is coming around the east limb, that should be an easy naked-eye object within a few days. Unable to get magnetic classification but feel sure from general appearance must be a gamma. Radio and television stations beware. They will be in for plenty of trouble soon.

After the two direct shots of the sun, I switched the beam over for a look through the polarizing monochromator, just in time to catch a splendid surge. Near the big spot the sun was swollen up like a boil. Suddenly a long arm emerged from the protuberance moving at a velocity I estimated at one hundred fifty miles per second. After reaching out to about sixty thousand miles the filament paused uncertainly. Then it was withdrawn, as suddenly as it emerged.

So often the sun conveys the feeling of life. At times it is like a sleeping monster, sluggish, dormant; at others, alive and tense, like a tiger crouched to spring.

Thursday, January 20

In addition to the spot-group that came around the limb yesterday, a fast-growing spot has broken out in heliographic latitude 42 N. This is the farthest I have ever seen a spot from the solar equator. Maunder at Greenwich speaks of "faint flecks" as high as latitude 72 but this is a large vigorous spot with a magnetic field strength of 2000 gauss.

If the face of the sun is a strange sight when viewed directly, it is as nothing compared to its appearance when analyzed by the spectroscope. At 18 hours GCT photographed a broad bright wing projecting from the violet side of the red hydrogen line, presumably due to a streamer of gas spurting from the solar surface with a speed of around four hundred miles per second.

Not so spectacular but much harder to believe, was the discovery of a faint bright line in the blue. Yesterday I expressed surprise at finding 5875, the yellow line of neutral helium, in the sun. Today I was positively shocked when I discovered that 4686 of ionized helium also showed faintly.

I wonder if I should send a wire to Harvard? But I hesitate to take such a step. Perhaps I should check with Mount Wilson first. Yes, I will see if they have observed anything unusual. I hate to consult with Smedley on anything. How I wish Marley were here. He was always so sympathetic and understanding.

Friday, January 21

Apparently I am the only astronomer who has gotten a look at the sun recently.

Talked with the Mount Wilson office in Pasadena this morning. They said there is six feet of snow on the mountain, with the power line out, and the road blocked by slides and boulders. The Atlantic coast reports storms all the way from Jacksonville to Montreal. And in Europe the tense political situation has paralyzed scientific research.

Saturday, January 22

After clouds put a stop to observations last Thursday, I drove down to the campus for a look at Marley's notes. I found the box in my office where it had come all the way from Dunedin, New Zealand.

What a great observer Marley was. And what a lucky observer! Three years in the southern hemisphere and three novae so far south he was the only one to get a complete photographic record. To think I had the same opportunity and turned it down. But somehow I was afraid to leave the old observatory here and venture into strange surroundings.

Marley was one of the most uncommunicative men I have ever known. Whenever he had anything to say he said it in his notebook. Taking notes got to be a habit with him, just as keeping a diary is with me. He kept his notes on special forms which he had printed for that purpose and later bound them in black leather.

Exploring the contents of the packing box was sad business. Here was the sum total of a man's life work—a dozen leatherbound volumes, some reprints of his published papers, a box of plates taken at the coudé focus of the 60-inch, a worn account book, a few old letters and pictures. I feel guilty going through a man's personal effects in this way, but that was Marley's last wish.

Those sunspots are wrecking our communication systems. Traders went wild the other morning when stock market quotations came in all garbled up. For a while U. S. Steel was selling at 269 and Johns-Manville Corporation at $2\frac{1}{2}$.

Astronomy in Wall Street—it can happen!

Sunday, January 23

More clouds and more desk work.

Preparing Marley's notes for publication in the *Astrophysical Journal* has not been so dull as I supposed. It begins to look as if he observed far more than any of us ever suspected; more than anyone has ever observed before him. Apparently he got on the trail of one of the biggest problems in astrophysics—the spectrum of a nova *before* the outburst.

One of the essential characteristics of novae is that they all go through practically the same identical changes, but at quite different rates. That is, some novae run through their life history much faster than others. The changes themselves are so similar, however, that an expert can take one look at the spectrum of a nova and accurately predict its behavior in the future.

We have many long series of observations on novae *after* the outburst. The one section of their life history that is still blank is the pre-maximum stage. Since novae arise from stars that were originally faint and inconspicuous, it is only by accident that we know anything about them before the explosion occurred. But it seems reasonable to suppose that a star must give *some* indication of the approaching cataclysm in advance, so that disruption could be predicted long beforehand—if only these symptoms could be observed and recognized.

Somehow or other this was precisely what Marley had been able to do. Thus on March 7, 1948, writing of Nova Muscae, he says: "The spectral changes a star exhibits in the pre-maximum stage are so well-marked that I now have no hesitation in predicting not merely the day but the very hour of outburst. These changes are identical although proceeding at vastly different rates for various types of novae. For example, a 'flash' nova, such as N Puppis 1942, might pass through a series of changes in a week, that would be prolonged for months in the case of a 'slow' nova like N Pictoris 1925."

Surely an observer as astute as George Lambert Marley would never have committed himself to such a statement unless he had the necessary and sufficient proof to convince a dozen men.

After poring over his notes till midnight I stepped outside the office to check the weather. Fog was drifting in from the ocean but the sky was still clear in the northeast. At first I thought a forest fire had broken out behind the San Gabriel mountains, for the whole heavens in that direction were suffused with a dull crimson glow. Then I realized it was an aurora, the finest I had seen since 1917. It was the type classified by the International Geophysical Union as *diffuse luminous surfaces* (DS), which often follow intense displays of rays and curtains.

The red glow soon faded away, but long after it was gone the impression it created remained, leaving me uneasy and restless, so that sleep did not come till nearly dawn.

Monday, January 24

The clouds began to break about eleven o'clock this A.M., causing me to jump in the car and get back to the Observatory full speed ahead. I climbed to the top of the sun tower as fast as my bronchitis would let me, set the mirrors, and hastened down to the spectrograph, arriving badly winded.

My first glimpse of the sun was a revelation. The high latitude northern spot has grown until there surely has never been a spot like it before. The excoriated area resembles not so much a sunspot as a great open wound in the solar surface; a region where the white skin of the photosphere has been peeled aside revealing the dark flesh of the umbra beneath.

While I was focusing the image—for the seeing was pretty bad—suddenly a cluster of points within the spot-group began to blaze like diamonds, becoming so intensely brilliant that I was momentarily dazzled. For fully ten seconds I must have stood there dumbly before I appreciated the significance of the phenomenon. It was a repetition of the effect Carrington had witnessed way back in 1859—the only known case of a so-called solar "flare" becoming directly visible on the surface of the sun.

Like Carrington, at first I was too startled to behave rationally. What to do? Should I try to photograph the spectrum of the luminous points? But I hesitated fearing they might be gone before I could load a plate holder and make an exposure. Finally, goading myself into some kind of action, I grabbed an eyepiece and began examining the solar spectrum visually, checking on the appearance of the different lines as best I could by eye.

As I expected, the hydrogen lines were so bright over the flares that they actually sparkled. In fact, the whole Balmer series was lit up, from H alpha in the red to H epsilon in the violet. H beta glittered like Vega on a clear frosty night. Bright lines of ionized metals, chiefly iron and titanium, were also visible. Wholly unexpected were two strong bright lines gleaming in the green and red. Although unable to measure their positions closely I am convinced in my own mind of their identity. They are 5303 of Fe XIV and 6374 of Fe X—lines previously observed only in the corona and a few novae.

Upon beholding these lines I went nearly wild. I was now determined to get a photograph at all costs. Rushing into the darkroom I tore the wrapper off a fresh box of plates, loaded the plate holder, and was outside again in less than three minutes. But alas!—clouds were racing over the image of the sun blotting out the flares almost completely. Nevertheless, I clamped in the plate holder and pulled the slide, praying for five minutes of clear sky which was all the exposure time I needed. But instead of getting better the clouds grew thicker, and before I knew it rain was splattering down on top of the spectrograph, forcing me to close the dome in a hurry.

What an opportunity I missed! The second time in a century this effect has been seen and I failed to get a single permanent record. I hope Smedley never hears of this.

Wednesday, January 26

I have just telegraphed the Harvard College Observatory. Although fearful to release a message of such sensational import, I felt that the information in my possession should no longer be withheld.

After failing to get a photograph of the coronal lines, the weather looked so bad that I decided to drive down to the office and continue work on Marley's notes. After the statement I found on Sunday night, I felt sure he must have left a complete account of the pre-maximum stage behind. But he failed to mention the matter further, seeming to be more concerned with improving the transmission of his spectrograph than with stellar instability.

I went through one leatherbound volume after another until the entire set was exhausted, and nothing remained but some letters and an old account book. The latter I had already passed by several times, as unlikely to contain anything more scientific than Marley's laundry bills or his losses at bridge. Yet it was in this very book that Marley had entrusted his most valuable data, on the old principle of "The Purloined Letter," that people seldom look in the obvious place. These data might easily have been discovered accidentally if kept in his regular notebooks, but it was highly improbable that anyone would give a second glance to a cheap account book.

The first page bore the caption, "Course of Events in Galactic Novae." Underneath he had written: "Once instability has definitely developed in a star the series of events as described herein is invariable, although proceeding at different rates. The rate of development, D, may be calculated for any particular date of outburst, N, by the formula, $\log N = \log Rh/c - 3 \log D$." On the next page Marley had given the values of the constants together with a table from which $\log D$ could be interpolated. The parameter, D, seemed to be a function of several variables the meaning of which was not clear. But there was no ambiguity about how to use D itself.

The rest of the pages were ruled into three columns each. The first was labeled DATE, and bore such entries as N—12, N—11, . . . N, N+1, et cetera. The second column contained the predicted appearance of the nova's spectrum, while the third evidently referred to how well the predictions agreed with observations. Obviously agreement was excellent in most cases, for generally there was simply a check mark, with perhaps some such comment as, "nebular lines exceptionally strong," or "4640 stage rather late," et cetera.

At the end of the series Marley had written the Greek letter capital Mu with a flourish. This was Marley's astronomical signature, analogous to Herschel's famous H, and Otto Struve's Omicron Sigma. I happened to know it also meant Marley was satisfied with this piece of work and that it was ready for publication—an unexpected bit of luck for me.

Turning through the leaves and marveling at the wealth of material at my fingertips, I began to be aware of something vaguely familiar about certain of the entries. They followed a pattern that I recognized without being able to identify. Thus near the beginning of the series there were such notations as, "First appearance of He I," or "Bright wings violet side of hydrogen lines," and "4686 of He II faintly visible." It was the remark on page 4 that finally penetrated. "These early stages cannot always be discerned with absolute assurance; indeed, from my observations on T Pyxidis and T Coronae Borealis, it appears that a star may exhibit all the foregoing symptoms of instability without necessarily exploding. *The first sure sign is the appearance of the green and red coronal lines. These constitute proof positive that the star will proceed to outburst as a flash nova.*" The italics are Marley's.

I'll admit that after reading this I was badly shaken. The inference was unmistakable. Something had gone wrong within the sun. Instability instead of manifesting itself by the usual harmless eleven-year rise and fall in sunspot activity, had been much more serious in the present cycle. Beginning as far back as 1945 or '46, some break or dislocation had occurred far below the surface. Insignificant at first, disruption had gradually spread, releasing stores of latent energy previously untapped within the atom. This latent energy had now built up until the first signs were becoming evident, the warning signals that disruption was close at hand.

No wonder the sunspot cycle had developed in a peculiar way! No wonder mammoth spots were breaking out in high latitudes. No wonder high temperature lines of helium were beginning to blaze in the solar spectrum!

How long?

Marley had given a little formula from which the rate of development could be calculated. To find the day of outburst it was only necessary to substitute the appropriate value of log D from his table and solve for the corresponding value of N.

Dreading to know the answer, yet impelled by a fascination I could not resist, I went to work. Let's see, the coronal lines had appeared on day N—53, which in Marley's notation made log D equal to -8.7654. R was the radius of the sun in centimeters, h was Planck's constant, a c was the velocity of light.

I began taking the numbers out of a log table with trembling hands. So great was my agitation that I was compelled to repeat the calculation several times. Adding up the figures I could not suppress a cry of despair. Log N was 0.4774. Barely three days—seventy-two hours left. Next Saturday at the latest.

Frantically I went back through the notes, searching for some loophole, some hint that might invalidate the whole proceeding. Like a lunatic repeating the same act over and over again, I must have calculated the value of N a dozen times. I carried the figures out to a ridiculous number of decimals. Always the result was the same. Three days— seventy-two hours. Less than that now!

At daybreak I tossed the calculations into the wastebasket and brewed myself a pot of coffee in the electric percolator I keep at the office. While it was boiling I composed the following message to Harvard:

5875 HE I OBSERVED INTEGRATED LIGHT CENTER OF SUN JANUARY 18. 4686 HE II OBSERVED IN EMISSION JANU- ARY 20. CORONAL LINES 5303 AND 6374 SEEN OVER SPOT GROUP AT 57 WEST 42 NORTH JANUARY 24. SOLAR PHE- NOMENA CLOSELY FOLLOWING PATTERN DESCRIBED BY MARLEY UNPUBLISHED MATERIAL ON NOVA CIRCINAE 1947, NOVA MUSCAE 1947, NOVA ARAE 1948.

PHILIP LATHAM

After telephoning the message to Western Union I read it over again with considerable satisfaction. Certainly no one can accuse me of exaggeration or sensationalism. I have stated the facts and nothing more.

Evening, January 27

Well, the cat is out of the bag.

This afternoon while measuring a plate of N Circinae taken at the Cassegrain spectrograph there came an authoritative knock at the door. Peering outside I discovered two young men, one of whom carried a camera and tripod. They introduced themselves as a reporter and photographer from the morning *Chronicle*. It seems that a flash had come in over the teletype about my wire to Harvard and they had been sent out to investigate. When I expressed astonishment that my wire had reached the press they had a ready explanation. Scientific news has become so important since the war that men are especially trained to handle events of this kind. Naturally they keep a close watch on the Harvard College Observatory, which acts as the clearing house for astronomical discoveries. The result was that as soon as my message was received it was immediately rewritten in popular terms and released over the wires of Science Associated.

I was reluctant to talk at first, but the young man was very persuasive, and before I knew it I was telling far more than I ever intended. I began cautiously enough, emphasizing the importance of Marley's brilliant work at Dunedin and minimizing my own efforts. I presume that reporters eventually grow extremely expert at drawing people out for it was certainly true in my case. After the reporter had filled several pages, the photographer got me to pose for several pictures, peering into the eyepiece of the measuring machine, examining a celestial globe as if I were an astrologer, et cetera. I felt perfectly ridiculous, but whenever I started to protest they brushed my objections aside, so that I found myself meekly submitting to whatever they wished. The session lasted for fully an hour, and when it was over I felt as exhausted as if I had given half a dozen lectures.

Then just as the men from the *Chronicle* were leaving a couple more arrived from the *Dispatch*. This time I really endeavored to refuse them admittance, objecting quite vehemently to this invasion of my privacy. But they were so insistent, claiming that since I had given the *Chronicle* a statement it would be unfair not to do the same for them, that at length I relented. Besides, they said, if they returned to the office empty-handed, they might lose their jobs. So to my intense chagrin I had to go through the whole performance again.

Since they left about an hour ago I have had time to think it all over and I feel terribly upset. The reclusive life of a professor of astronomy is surely a poor preparation for solving the harsh problems of human existence. Whenever I have to face men outside the university I feel so helpless, almost like a child.

I see so clearly that I should have politely but firmly refused them admittance right from the start. If I could only assert myself, take a firm stand and then stick to it. Now there is no telling where this may end. Worst of all, there is not the slightest excuse for me. Not the slightest excuse in the world.

I am thoroughly aware of the official attitude here toward sensational newspaper publicity for members of the faculty. A professor over in the Economics Department was recently compelled to resign, his whole career ruined, because of a story that he gave out to one of the picture magazines. Next year I will reach the age of retirement of sixty-seven, but had hoped to continue some investigations I had started at the Observatory, as well as picking up a little pocket money teaching Astronomy 1 in summer session. But, if the statements I just issued arouse adverse criticism, my petition for post-retirement work will almost certainly be denied.

Once I nearly screwed up sufficient courage to call the papers and forbid them to use the story. But I didn't know how to explain myself adequately over the phone, and besides it might result in making matters even worse. The more I turned the situation over in my mind the more deplorable it seemed. I would be held up to ridicule, might be compelled to resign. I had served the institution to the best of my ability for four decades, only to end my career in humiliation and disgrace.

Midnight

Sitting in the gathering dusk a few hours ago my heart filled with despair, an idea began filtering through my consciousness; an idea so simple and obvious that it had escaped me completely.

If the world were coming to an end, what difference could anything possibly make?

It required considerable time for my mind to grasp that elementary fact clearly and firmly. When it did the impact was terrific. For the first time I felt free. The sensation was glorious—like being born again.

Going back over the years it seemed to me I had always been afraid of something. I had always been too timid to assert myself, too faint-hearted to assume my rightful position in the world. How often I had seen other men less capable move on ahead, become big research men or executives, while I was content to remain obscurely in the background.

I thought of how many other people there must be like myself who live continually in fear. Fear of the unknown, fear of the future, fear of losing their job, fear of dying of cancer, fear of a helpless old age—

Now that was behind me. I felt like a character in a play, moving and speaking according to the author's will, oblivious to those around him. Life was going to be extremely simple.

Thoroughly tired and relaxed, I stretched out on the cot by the measuring machine, and fell immediately into a profound dreamless slumber.

The ringing of the telephone awakened me. For several seconds I listened without realizing where I was or what had happened to me. Then it all came back, the end of the world, no need to worry any more, et cetera.

"Hello," I grunted.

"Is that you, Latham?" It was Smedley calling, the young man who had recently been appointed instructor in astronomy.

"Yes."

"Well, I've been trying everywhere to find you," he complained. "You weren't at your apartment or the Observatory."

"Maybe that was because I was asleep here at the office."

"What was that?"

"I said MAYBE IT WAS BECAUSE I WAS ASLEEP HERE AT THE OFFICE!"

"Oh!" he exclaimed. He sounded slightly startled. "Then you didn't hear the ten o'clock news broadcast over KQX?"

"No, I didn't hear it."

"It was mostly about you," he chuckled. "I've heard some awful stuff over the radio but this takes the prize. Can't imagine how they could have gotten hold of such a story. Something about the sun turning into a fast nova."

"Possibly they got it because I gave it to them."

"You what!"

"Listen, Smedley: if I was quoted to the effect that the world is coming to an end then I was quoted correctly. That's exactly what I said and that's exactly what I meant."

"You aren't serious?"

"I was never more serious in my life."

He hesitated. "All right, Dr. Latham. I'm sorry to have disturbed you," and he hung up.

I have just figured up that there are less than forty-seven hours left now.

Friday morning, January 28

Catherine Snodgrass, President Bixby's secretary and one of the minor fuehrers at Western Tech, called me early this morning as I was finishing a pot of coffee and reading "Of Human Bondage." As usual, she was very definite and positive.

"President Bixby has arranged an appointment for you at ten o'clock," she informed me. "If you will stop at my desk, I will see that you are admitted without delay."

"Sorry," I said, "but I can't make it at ten."

"I beg your pardon."

People seemed to have trouble in understanding me lately. "I said I can't be there at ten. Tell Bixby I'll be there at eleven instead."

"The president is very anxious to see you. I would suggest that you come at ten," she said quietly.

"Sorry. Can't come till eleven."

There was a long silence pregnant with meaning. "Very well, Dr. Latham, I will tell him. Thank you."

There was no reason why I couldn't come at one time as well as another, except that I was seized with a perverse desire to frustrate the local hierarchy. I poured myself a fourth cup of coffee and went back to reading "Of Human Bondage," a novel I had been trying to finish for five years.

I had reached the part where Mildred is being particularly spiteful and was so absorbed that eleven o'clock came before I knew it. Previously I would have been sitting on the edge of a chair in the reception room ten minutes before time, but now I sauntered slowly over to the Administration Building.

Bixby was talking into a dictaphone when I came in. He is a large powerfully built man, with strong prominent features, and a crisp white mustache. Hair graying slightly at the temples. Most common remark heard about him is that he looks more like an international banker than a professor. It has been said that to be a successful college president, a man must have the digestion of a billy goat, the hide of a rhinoceros, and the money-getting powers of a secretary of the treasury. There could be no denying that as head of Western Tech, Bixby was an outstanding success.

He lost no time getting down to business.

"I believe I can say without fear or hesitation that no one has more vigorously championed the cause of academic freedom than myself. A scientist to be great must be free, at liberty to carry the bright torch of knowledge wherever nature beckons. These are truths upon which I am sure we are all agreed."

I nodded assent.

"At the same time," he said, clearing his throat, "we should be circumspect. In our relations with the man in the street, we must neither depict science as magic nor scientists as magicians, making stupendous discoveries. Otherwise the results of our labors are liable to serious misinterpretation by the ignorant and superstitious."

He frowned at me through his rimless glasses. "Dr. Latham, I feel very strongly that your message should have been submitted to the faculty committee on announcements before sending to Harvard."

He paused, evidently expecting me to say something in my defense at this point, but as I could think of no suitable rejoinder, remained silent.

"Now, Latham," Bixby continued, not unkindly, "I am familiar with your long and distinguished career here at Tech. Personally, I do not doubt for an instant that you had not the slightest intention of deliberately seeking sensational publicity. Unfortunately, the harm is done; the die is cast. The institution will be harshly criticized and justly so. Why, several big endowments I had been counting on may be held up if this thing gets out of control."

He got up and began pacing back and forth across the office. Suddenly he turned and confronted me.

"You spend a lot of time at the Observatory, don't you?"

"Yes," I replied, "my teaching duties have been very light in recent years."

"Often up there for days and weeks at a time?"

"That's true," I admitted.

"Just as I thought," he said. "You know, the man most likely to get his feet off the ground is the man who works alone. We need the contact of others to keep us on the straight path. Even the very best go off the deep end occasionally. If I remember correctly, Kepler was something of a mystic. Herschel thought the sun was inhabited. Sir Isaac Newton had a theory about light particles having fits." He stopped uncertainly.

I finished it for him. "And Philip Latham, associate professor of astronomy, thinks the world is coming to an end. It does sound kind of crazy, doesn't it?"

He looked down at me and smiled. "Yes, Latham, to put it bluntly, it does sound kind of crazy. Glad you see it that way."

He reached across the desk for pencil and paper. "Here. Suppose you write out something for the papers. No elaborate explanation, you understand; just anything to satisfy the reporters and calm down the people. Something about how new observations have caused you to revise your statement of yesterday, the sun is O.K., and looks good for another million years yet."

He went around to the opposite side of the desk and began arranging some papers together and laying them in metal containers. "While you're doing that I'll have Kit—Miss Snodgrass—call the press and issue a statement. Kill this thing right away."

I shook my head. "I am not aware of any new observational evidence," I said. "My statement of yesterday still stands."

"What's that?" Bixby said absently, continuing to arrange the papers.

"I said I have no intention of retracting my statement."

Bixby stopped suddenly as if unable to believe his ears. Then he walked slowly around the side of the desk, looming larger and larger, until he towered above me so high I felt like an ant. For an instant I thought he intended bodily violence. But when he spoke it was in a low tone, choosing his words very slowly and carefully.

"There's something I haven't told you yet. Neither the board of trustees nor the regents know anything about it. Nobody knows about it but myself." His voice sank nearly to a whisper. "There's a good chance of getting three million dollars out of Irwin Mills, the publisher, for a new observatory. Wants to establish it as a memorial to his son who died in the war." He leaned forward impressively. "How would you like to be the director of that new observatory?"

"It's a dream I've had for fifteen years."

Bixby slammed his fist into the palm of his hand. "Exactly!" he said. "We've been needing a new telescope around here for a long time. Present equipment in pretty bad shape. But here's the point: we won't get a nickel out of Mills if this wild story builds up. He'll think we're a bunch of screwballs and pull out on us. We can't always get things just the way we want them. A man's got to be reasonable—practical."

"That's what I'm trying to be—practical," I told him, "although not that it makes much difference any more."

I decided I might as well give it to him straight.

"You see it's really true, this wild story about the world coming to an end. As kids we read stories about the end of the world and all the different ways it could happen. But they were just words on a piece of paper born out of somebody's imagination. This is the real thing. Of course, you can't believe it. I can't actually believe it myself. We're all too engrossed in our own affairs, too colossally conceited, to believe that anything from outside could conceivably destroy the little world we have created for our special enjoyment and torment.

"That's the way it is," I said. "I'm afraid nothing we can do is likely to change the situation."

Bixby had remained impassive while I was speaking. Now he walked slowly to his desk and sat down.

"Then you refuse to co-operate." He said it more to himself than to me.

I shrugged. "Put it that way if you like."

"This can ruin us. Ruin me and the whole institution." He was studying me curiously, as if he had never really seen me before, and had just become aware of my existence.

"You're mad," he said dully.

I left him sitting there hunched over the top of his desk. For the first time I noticed how old and gray he looked.

At the office I found the postman had left a stack of letters for me. As I seldom receive mail, except copies of the *Scientific Monthly* and the *Astrophysical Journal,* I opened the envelopes with considerable interest. They were people who had heard about me over the radio, and felt impelled to take their pen in hand immediately.

Some of the letters were hardly more than scrawls written on the back of old grocery bills and wrapping paper. Others were neatly typed on fine stationery with impressive letterheads, such as Institute of Psycho-electrical Research, or Bureau of Cosmic Power and Light. Several writers inclosed pamphlets expounding their views in detail. Through them all ran the same theme. *I* have discovered the secret of the universe. *I* have refuted Newton's law of gravitation. *I* have found the law that explains the secret of the moon, sun, and stars. Three correspondents attacked me violently for trying to anticipate their own predictions of the end of the world.

I wondered why victims of paranoia with delusions of grandeur so often find in astronomy the outlet which their minds are seeking? Every professional astronomer receives such letters. I know a director of a large observatory who has been getting letters from an inmate of an asylum for years. It is useless to attempt to point out the fallacies in their highly systematized delusions. That is the worst trouble with these people, I reflected. They are the last ones to see anything strange in their actions.

Tossing the letters aside I reviewed the events of the morning. I admit I could not suppress a feeling of elation at my triumph over Bixby. Once I would have been utterly crushed by his tirade. Now it left me quite unmoved. What a surprise was in store for him tomorrow! I started to laugh out loud, then checked myself barely in time.

A psychiatrist had once told me that only the insane laugh out loud—alone.

Midnight

By evening my sense of elation had fled leaving in its wake a sense of deep depression. At the same time I was filled with a strange uneasiness which made my apartment seem intolerable. Ordinarily I avoid people, having a dread of crowds that amounts almost to a phobia. But tonight the thought of human companionship was very welcome. I decided to get the car out and drive down to Hollywood.

I found a place to park on Hollywood and Vine near the El Capitan Theater. Stopping at the newsstand on the corner I bought a morning edition of the *Chronicle*, which I thought should have my story by this time. Sure enough, there it was on the front page of the second edition. OLD SOL SET FOR BLOWUP! the caption read. Underneath was the subhead, World's End Due Saturday, says Dr. Latham of W.I.T.

Naturally I had assumed that nothing could compete with the end of the world for news interest. Yet I found my story was overshadowed by an account of a shooting that had occurred on the Sunset strip, which occupied practically all the rest of the page. Worse still, my photograph was displayed next to the principal in the shooting, a blond young woman in a playsuit. Anyone casually glancing at the paper would have gotten the impression that I was also concerned in the affair.

It seemed to me that all the stories I had ever read about the end of the world had been so different from the way this was turning out. In the stories there had always been wild tumult as the final hour drew near, half the people indulging in a frenzied orgy of pleasure while the other half offered up fervent prayers for deliverance. My prediction of the end of the world had now been broadcast over the radio dozens of times and widely publicized in the papers. Yet the only signs of tumult I could see were at the Chinese Theater up the street, where a premiere was trying to get under way.

Suppose, I said to myself, that I were to seize that young man there by the arm and try to explain to him I believed the end of the world was near. What evidence could I produce to prove my assertion?

I could tell him of observations made with my own eyes.

He would say I was lying; refuse to believe me.

I could show him Marley's notes.

They would be meaningless to him. A mere jumble of words and symbols scrawled in an old account book.

Finally, I could produce actual photographs of the spectrum lines.

Nothing but chance agglomerations of silver grains on a gelatin emulsion.

He would brush me impatiently aside, dismiss my story as fantastic, the product of too much port wine and brandy. Suppose I drank myself into unconsciousness tonight. Would I awaken tomorrow to find the same old GO star shining as usual, radiating energy at the rate of 1.94 calories per square centimeter per minute?

Driving up the winding road to the Observatory late that evening I determined upon my course of action next day. Writing it down here will serve to fix it in my mind.

The time of outburst based upon Marley's formula is 16:12 Pacific Standard Time, which is about an hour and a half before sunset at this time of year. If the cloud of gas expands at the average rate of six hundred miles per second, it will not reach the Earth's orbit for nearly two days. The intense heat pouring from the sun, however, as a result of the explosion will travel with the speed of light and probably render the daylight side of Earth scorching hot within a very few minutes. At any rate, after I detect the first signs of disruption in the monochromator there should be sufficient time for me to inclose this diary in a heat-resistant box and store it at the bottom of the suntower two hundred feet below ground.

Is it insane to hope that this diary will by some miracle be spared? Only too well I realize the futility of taking any precautions against a wall of flame that will turn the solid earth into incandescence. But in those last minutes it will at least be something to do, a definite plan to put into execution.

N Day.

08:00: The solar rotation has carried the large northern spot-group out of sight around the limb. The other spot has settled down to a stable beta-p group. Once again the face of the sun is normal.

I have just completed the routine program of solar observations that

I have carried out continuously since 1906. First two direct photographs of the sun. Then a photograph in hydrogen light, a photograph in calcium, and a series on the prominence projecting around the limb. The plates have been developed and are fixing in the darkroom.

08:30: Observed a tornado prominence of moderate height at position angle 117°. Spiral structure well defined. Usual wisp of smoke issuing from top. No certain indication of radial motion or change in P. A.

13:17: The seeing has been dropping rapidly during the last hour, probably due to a wind that has sprung up from the west. The seeing was about 6 at noon but now is barely 2.

14:00: The image is blurred and lacking in detail. Sun has probably gone behind a veil of cirrus haze. Hope it doesn't get so thick I will have to close up.

16:12: The zero hour! And still the sun looks just as I have seen it thousands of times before—a cherry-red disk with a few dark prominences streaked across it.

17:00: Five o'clock P.M. on the Pacific coast. The image is very bad. Can't focus within three inches. Tower shaking in rising wind. Nothing unusual to report.

17:28: The sun will be below the horizon very soon now. I wonder if Marley's form—

Here it comes! The sun is swelling up like a toy red balloon. But so slowly! I never supposed it would be so slow. Like a slow-motion picture of the sun blowing up.

I am glad. I was never so glad of anything before.

Writing these last lines I thought of Bixby and Smedley and all the rest. Trying to picture their faces made me laugh. I laughed long and loud till my sides ached, and the sound echoed back and forth between the empty walls of the sun tower.

PART THREE

The Superscience of Man

WITH FOLDED HANDS

UNDERHILL was walking home from the office, because his wife had the car, the afternoon he first met the new mechanicals. His feet were following his usual diagonal path across a weedy vacant block—his wife usually had the car—and his preoccupied mind was rejecting various impossible ways to meet his notes at the Two Rivers bank, when a new wall stopped him.

The wall wasn't any common brick or stone, but something sleek and bright and strange. Underhill stared up at a long new building. He felt vaguely annoyed and surprised at this glittering obstruction—it certainly hadn't been here last week.

Then he saw the thing in the window.

The window itself wasn't any ordinary glass. The wide, dustless panel was completely transparent, so that only the glowing letters fastened to it showed that it was there at all. The letters made a severe, modernistic sign:

> Two Rivers Agency
> HUMANOID INSTITUTE
> The Perfect Mechanicals
> "To Serve and Obey,
> And Guard Men from Harm."

His dim annoyance sharpened, because Underhill was in the mechanicals business himself. Times were already hard enough, and mechanicals were a drug on the market. Androids, mechanoids, electronoids, automatoids, and ordinary robots. Unfortunately, few of them did all the salesmen promised, and the Two Rivers market was already sadly oversaturated.

Underhill sold androids—when he could. His next consignment was due tomorrow, and he didn't quite know how to meet the bill.

Frowning, he paused to stare at the thing behind that invisible window. He had never seen a humanoid. Like any mechanical not at work, it stood absolutely motionless. Smaller and slimmer than a man. A shining black, its sleek silicone skin had a changing sheen of bronze and metallic blue. Its graceful oval face wore a fixed look of alert and slightly surprised solicitude. Altogether, it was the most beautiful mechanical he had ever seen.

Too small, of course, for much practical utility. He murmured to himself a reassuring quotation from the *Android Salesman:* "Androids are big—because the makers refuse to sacrifice power, essential functions, or dependability. Androids are your biggest buy!"

The transparent door slid open as he turned toward it, and he walked into the haughty opulence of the new display room to convince himself that these streamlined items were just another flashy effort to catch the woman shopper.

He inspected the glittering layout shrewdly, and his breezy optimism faded. He had never heard of the Humanoid Institute, but the invading firm obviously had big money and big-time merchandising know-how.

He looked around for a salesman, but it was another mechanical that came gliding silently to meet him. A twin of the one in the window, it moved with a quick, surprising grace. Bronze and blue lights flowed over its lustrous blackness, and a yellow name plate flashed from its naked breast:

HUMANOID
Serial No. 81-H-B-27
The Perfect Mechanical
"To Serve and Obey,
And Guard Men from Harm."

Curiously, it had no lenses. The eyes in its bald oval head were steel-colored, blindly staring. But it stopped a few feet in front of him, as if it could see anyhow, and it spoke to him with a high, melodious voice:

"At your service, Mr. Underhill."

The use of his name startled him, for not even the androids could tell one man from another. But this was a clever merchandising stunt, of course, not too difficult in a town the size of Two Rivers. The salesman must be some local man, prompting the mechanical from behind the partition. Underhill erased his momentary astonishment, and said loudly:

"May I see your salesman, please?"

"We employ no human salesmen, sir," its soft silvery voice replied instantly. "The Humanoid Institute exists to serve mankind, and we require no human service. We ourselves can supply any information you desire, sir, and accept your order for immediate humanoid service."

Underhill peered at it dazedly. No mechanicals were competent even to recharge their own batteries and reset their own relays, much less to operate their own branch offices. The blind eyes stared blankly back, and he looked uneasily around for any booth or curtain that might conceal the salesman.

Meanwhile, the sweet thin voice resumed persuasively:

"May we come out to your home for a free trial demonstration, sir?

We are anxious to introduce our service on your planet, because we have been successful in eliminating human unhappiness on so many others. You will find us far superior to the old electronic mechanicals in use here."

Underhill stepped back uneasily. He reluctantly abandoned his search for the hidden salesman, shaken by the idea of any mechanicals promoting themselves. That would upset the whole industry.

"At least you must take some advertising matter, sir."

Moving with a somehow appalling graceful deftness, the small black mechanical brought him an illustrated booklet from a table by the wall. To cover his confused and increasing alarm, he thumbed through the glossy pages.

In a series of richly colored before-and-after pictures, a chesty blond girl was stooping over a kitchen stove, and then relaxing in a daring negligee while a little black mechanical knelt to serve her something. She was wearily hammering a typewriter, and then lying on an ocean beach, in a revealing sun suit, while another mechanical did the typing. She was toiling at some huge industrial machine, and then dancing in the arms of a golden-haired youth, while a black humanoid ran the machine.

Underhill sighed wistfully. The android company didn't supply such fetching sales material. Women would find this booklet irresistible, and they selected eighty-six per cent of all mechanicals sold. Yes, the competition was going to be bitter.

"Take it home, sir," the sweet voice urged him. "Show it to your wife. There is a free trial demonstration order blank on the last page, and you will notice that we require no payment down."

He turned numbly, and the door slid open for him. Retreating dazedly, he discovered the booklet still in his hand. He crumpled it furiously, and flung it down. The small black thing picked it up tidily, and the insistent silver voice rang after him:

"We shall call at your office tomorrow, Mr. Underhill, and send a demonstration unit to your home. It is time to discuss the liquidation of your business, because the electronic mechanicals you have been selling cannot compete with us. And we shall offer your wife a free trial demonstration."

Underhill didn't attempt to reply, because he couldn't trust his voice. He stalked blindly down the new sidewalk to the corner, and paused there to collect himself. Out of his startled and confused impressions, one clear fact emerged—things looked black for the agency.

Bleakly, he stared back at the haughty splendor of the new building. It wasn't honest brick or stone; that invisible window wasn't glass; and he was quite sure the foundation for it hadn't even been staked out, the last time Aurora had the car.

He walked on around the block, and the new sidewalk took him near the rear entrance. A truck was backed up to it, and several slim black mechanicals were silently busy, unloading huge metal crates.

He paused to look at one of the crates. It was labeled for interstellar shipment. The stencils showed that it had come from the Humanoid Institute, on Wing IV. He failed to recall any planet of that designation; the outfit must be big.

Dimly, inside the gloom of the warehouse beyond the truck, he could see black mechanicals opening the crates. A lid came up, revealing dark, rigid bodies, closely packed. One by one, they came to life. They climbed out of the crate, and sprang gracefully to the floor. A shining black, glinting with bronze and blue, they were all identical.

One of them came out past the truck, to the sidewalk, staring with blind steel eyes. Its high silver voice spoke to him melodiously:

"At your service, Mr. Underhill."

He fled. When his name was promptly called by a courteous mechanical, just out of the crate in which it had been imported from a remote and unknown planet, he found the experience trying.

Two blocks along, the sign of a bar caught his eye, and he took his dismay inside. He had made it a business rule not to drink before dinner, and Aurora didn't like him to drink at all; but these new mechanicals, he felt, had made the day exceptional.

Unfortunately, however, alcohol failed to brighten the brief visible future of the agency. When he emerged, after an hour, he looked wistfully back in hope that the bright new building might have vanished as abruptly as it came. It hadn't. He shook his head dejectedly, and turned uncertainly homeward.

Fresh air had cleared his head somewhat, before he arrived at the neat white bungalow in the outskirts of the town, but it failed to solve his business problems. He also realized, uneasily, that he would be late for dinner.

Dinner, however, had been delayed. His son Frank, a freckled ten-year-old, was still kicking a football on the quiet street in front of the house. And little Gay, who was tow-haired and adorable and eleven, came running across the lawn and down the sidewalk to meet him.

"Father, you can't guess what!" Gay was going to be a great musician some day, and no doubt properly dignified, but she was pink and breathless with excitement now. She let him swing her high off the sidewalk, and she wasn't critical of the bar-aroma on his breath. He couldn't guess, and she informed him eagerly:

"Mother's got a new lodger!"

Underhill had foreseen a painful inquisition, because Aurora was worried about the notes at the bank, and the bill for the new consignment, and the money for little Gay's lessons.

The new lodger, however, saved him from that. With an alarming crashing of crockery, the household android was setting dinner on the table, but the little house was empty. He found Aurora in the back yard, burdened with sheets and towels for the guest.

Aurora, when he married her, had been as utterly adorable as now her little daughter was. She might have remained so, he felt, if the agency had been a little more successful. However, while the pressure of slow failure had gradually crumbled his own assurance, small hardships had turned her a little too aggressive.

Of course he loved her still. Her red hair was still alluring, and she was loyally faithful, but thwarted ambitions had sharpened her character and sometimes her voice. They never quarreled, really, but there were small differences.

There was the little apartment over the garage—built for human servants they had never been able to afford. It was too small and shabby to attract any responsible tenant, and Underhill wanted to leave it empty. It hurt his pride to see her making beds and cleaning floors for strangers.

Aurora had rented it before, however, when she wanted money to pay for Gay's music lessons, or when some colorful unfortunate touched her sympathy, and it seemed to Underhill that her lodgers had all turned out to be thieves and vandals.

She turned back to meet him, now, with the clean linen in her arms.

"Dear, it's no use objecting." Her voice was quite determined. "Mr. Sledge is the most wonderful old fellow, and he's going to stay just as long as he wants."

"That's all right, darling." He never liked to bicker, and he was thinking of his troubles at the agency. "I'm afraid we'll need the money. Just make him pay in advance."

"But he can't!" Her voice throbbed with sympathetic warmth. "He says he'll have royalties coming in from his inventions, so he can pay in a few days."

Underhill shrugged; he had heard that before.

"Mr. Sledge is different, dear," she insisted. "He's a traveler, and a scientist. Here, in this dull little town, we don't see many interesting people."

"You've picked up some remarkable types," he commented.

"Don't be unkind, dear," she chided gently. "You haven't met him yet, and you don't know how wonderful he is." Her voice turned sweeter. "Have you a ten, dear?"

He stiffened. "What for?"

"Mr. Sledge is ill." Her voice turned urgent. "I saw him fall on the street, downtown. The police were going to send him to the city hospital, but he didn't want to go. He looked so noble and sweet and grand. So I told them I would take him. I got him in the car and took him to old Dr. Winters. He has this heart condition, and he needs the money for medicine."

Reasonably, Underhill inquired, "Why doesn't he want to go to the hospital?"

"He has work to do," she said. "Important scientific work—and he's so wonderful and tragic. Please, dear, have you a ten?"

Underhill thought of many things to say. These new mechanicals promised to multiply his troubles. It was foolish to take in an invalid vagrant, who could have free care at the city hospital. Aurora's tenants always tried to pay their rent with promises, and generally wrecked the apartment and looted the neighborhood before they left.

But he said none of those things. He had learned to compromise. Silently, he found two fives in his thin pocketbook, and put them in her hand. She smiled, and kissed him impulsively—he barely remembered to hold his breath in time.

Her figure was still good, by dint of periodic dieting. He was proud of her shining red hair. A sudden surge of affection brought tears to his eyes, and he wondered what would happen to her and the children if the agency failed.

"Thank you, dear!" she whispered. "I'll have him come for dinner, if he feels able, and you can meet him then. I hope you don't mind dinner being late."

He didn't mind, tonight. Moved by a sudden impulse of domesticity, he got hammer and nails from his workshop in the basement, and repaired the sagging screen on the kitchen door with a neat diagonal brace.

He enjoyed working with his hands. His boyhood dream had been to be a builder of fission power plants. He had even studied engineering—before he married Aurora, and had to take over the ailing mechanicals agency from her indolent and alcoholic father. He was whistling happily by the time the little task was done.

When he went back through the kitchen to put up his tools, he found the household android busy clearing the untouched dinner away from the table—the androids were good enough at strictly routine tasks, but they could never learn to cope with human unpredictability.

"Stop, stop!" Slowly repeated, in the proper pitch and rhythm, his command made it halt, and then he said carefully, "Set—table; set—table."

Obediently, the gigantic thing came shuffling back with the stack of plates. He was suddenly struck with the difference between it and those new humanoids. He sighed wearily. Things looked black for the agency.

Aurora brought her new lodger in through the kitchen door. Underhill nodded to himself. This gaunt stranger, with his dark shaggy hair, emaciated face, and threadbare garb, looked to be just the sort of colorful, dramatic vagabond that always touched Aurora's heart. She introduced them, and they sat down to wait in the front room while she went to call the children.

The old rogue didn't look very sick, to Underhill. Perhaps his wide shoulders had a tired stoop, but his spare, tall figure was still commanding. The skin was seamed and pale, over his rawboned, cragged face, but his deep-set eyes still had a burning vitality.

His hands held Underhill's attention. Immense hands, they hung a little forward when he stood, swung on long bony arms in perpetual readiness. Gnarled and scarred, darkly tanned, with the small hairs on the back bleached to a golden color, they told their own epic of varied adventure, of battle perhaps, and possibly even of toil. They had been very useful hands.

"I'm very grateful to your wife, Mr. Underhill." His voice was a deep-throated rumble, and he had a wistful smile, oddly boyish for a man so evidently old. "She rescued me from an unpleasant predicament, and I'll see that she is well paid."

Just another vivid vagabond, Underhill decided, talking his way through life with plausible inventions. He had a little private game he played with Aurora's tenants—just remembering what they said and counting one point for every impossibility. Mr. Sledge, he thought, would give him an excellent score.

"Where are you from?" he asked conversationally.

Sledge hesitated for an instant before he answered, and that was unusual—most of Aurora's tenants had been exceedingly glib.

"Wing IV." The gaunt old man spoke with a solemn reluctance, as if he should have liked to say something else. "All my early life was spent there, but I left the planet nearly fifty years ago. I've been traveling, ever since."

Startled, Underhill peered at him sharply. Wing IV, he remembered, was the home planet of those sleek new mechanicals, but this old vagabond looked too seedy and impecunious to be connected with the Humanoid Institute. His brief suspicion faded. Frowning, he said casually:

"Wing IV must be rather distant."

The old rogue hesitated again, and then said gravely:

"One hundred and nine light-years, Mr. Underhill."

That made the first point, but Underhill concealed his satisfaction. The new space liners were pretty fast, but the velocity of light was still an absolute limit. Casually, he played for another point:

"My wife says you're a scientist, Mr. Sledge?"

"Yes."

The old rascal's reticence was unusual. Most of Aurora's tenants required very little prompting. Underhill tried again, in a breezy conversational tone:

"Used to be an engineer myself, until I dropped it to go into mechanicals." The old vagabond straightened, and Underhill paused hopefully. But he said nothing, and Underhill went on: "Fission plant design and operation. What's your specialty, Mr. Sledge?"

The old man gave him a long, troubled look, with those brooding, hollowed eyes, and then said slowly:

"Your wife has been kind to me, Mr. Underhill, when I was in desperate need. I think you are entitled to the truth, but I must ask you to keep it to yourself. I am engaged on a very important research problem, which must be finished secretly."

"I'm sorry." Suddenly ashamed of his cynical little game, Underhill spoke apologetically. "Forget it."

But the old man said deliberately:

"My field is rhodomagnetics."

"Eh?" Underhill didn't like to confess ignorance, but he had never heard of that. "I've been out of the game for fifteen years," he explained. "I'm afraid I haven't kept up."

The old man smiled again, faintly.

"The science was unknown here until I arrived, a few days ago," he said. "I was able to apply for basic patents. As soon as the royalties start coming in, I'll be wealthy again."

Underhill had heard that before. The old rogue's solemn reluctance had been very impressive, but he remembered that most of Aurora's tenants had been very plausible gentry.

"So?" Underhill was staring again, somehow fascinated by those gnarled and scarred and strangely able hands. "What, exactly, is rhodomagnetics?"

He listened to the old man's careful, deliberate answer, and started his little game again. Most of Aurora's tenants had told some pretty wild tales, but he had never heard anything to top this.

"A universal force," the weary, stooped old vagabond said solemnly. "As fundamental as ferromagnetism or gravitation, though the effects are less obvious. It is keyed to the second triad of the periodic table, rhodium and ruthenium and palladium, in very much the same way that ferromagnetism is keyed to the first triad, iron and nickel and cobalt."

Underhill remembered enough of his engineering courses to see the basic fallacy of that. Palladium was used for watch springs, he recalled, because it was completely nonmagnetic. But he kept his face straight. He had no malice in his heart, and he played the little game just for his own amusement. It was secret, even from Aurora, and he always penalized himself for any show of doubt.

He said merely, "I thought the universal forces were already pretty well known."

"The effects of rhodomagnetism are masked by nature," the patient, rusty voice explained. "And, besides, they are somewhat paradoxical, so that ordinary laboratory methods defeat themselves."

"Paradoxical?" Underhill prompted.

"In a few days I can show you copies of my patents, and reprints of papers describing demonstration experiments," the old man promised gravely. "The velocity of propagation is infinite. The effects vary inversely with the first power of the distance, not with the square of the distance. And ordinary matter, except for the elements of the rhodrum triad, is generally transparent to rhodomagnetic radiations."

That made four more points for the game. Underhill felt a little glow of gratitude to Aurora, for discovering so remarkable a specimen.

"Rhodomagnetism was first discovered through a mathematical investigation of the atom," the old romancer went serenely on, suspecting nothing. "A rhodomagnetic component was proved essential to maintain the delicate equilibrium of the nuclear forces. Consequently, rhodomagnetic waves tuned to atomic frequences may be used to upset that equilibrium and produce nuclear instability. Thus most heavy atoms—generally those above palladium, 46 in atomic number—can be subjected to artificial fission."

Underhill scored himself another point, and tried to keep his eyebrows from lifting. He said, conversationally:

"Patents on such a discovery ought to be very profitable."

The old scoundrel nodded his gaunt, dramatic head.

"You can see the obvious applications. My basic patents cover most of them. Devices for instantaneous interplanetary and interstellar communication. Long-range wireless power transmission. A rhodomagnetic inflexion-drive, which makes possible apparent speeds many times that of light—by means of a rhodomagnetic deformation of the continuum. And, of course, revolutionary types of fission power plants, using any heavy element for fuel."

Preposterous! Underhill tried hard to keep his face straight, but everybody knew that the velocity of light was a physical limit. On the human side, the owner of any such remarkable patents would hardly be begging for shelter in a shabby garage apartment. He noticed a pale circle around the old vagabond's gaunt and hairy wrist; no man owning such priceless secrets would have to pawn his watch.

Triumphantly, Underhill allowed himself four more points, but then he had to penalize himself. He must have let doubt show on his face, because the old man asked suddenly:

"Do you want to see the basic tensors?" He reached in his pocket for pencil and notebook. "I'll jot them down for you."

"Never mind," Underhill protested. "I'm afraid my math is a little rusty."

"But you think it strange that the holder of such revolutionary patents should find himself in need?"

Underhill nodded, and penalized himself another point. The old man might be a monumental liar, but he was shrewd enough.

"You see, I'm a sort of refugee," he explained apologetically. "I arrived on this planet only a few days ago, and I have to travel light. I was forced to deposit everything I had with a law firm, to arrange for the publication and protection of my patents. I expect to be receiving the first royalties soon.

"In the meantime," he added plausibly, "I came to Two Rivers because it is quiet and secluded, far from the spaceports. I'm working on another project, which must be finished secretly. Now, will you please respect my confidence, Mr. Underhill?"

Underhill had to say he would. Aurora came back with the freshly scrubbed children, and they went in to dinner. The android came lurching in with a steaming tureen. The old stranger seemed to shrink from the mechanical, uneasily. As she took the dish and served the soup, Aurora inquired lightly:

"Why doesn't your company bring out a better mechanical, dear? One smart enough to be a really perfect waiter, warranted not to splash the soup. Wouldn't that be splendid?"

Her question cast Underhill into moody silence. He sat scowling at his plate, thinking of those remarkable new mechanicals which claimed to be perfect, and what they might do to the agency. It was the shaggy old rover who answered soberly:

"The perfect mechanicals already exist, Mrs. Underhill." His deep, rusty voice had a solemn undertone. "And they are not so splendid. really. I've been a refugee from them, for nearly fifty years."

Underhill looked up from his plate, astonished.

"Those black humanoids, you mean?"

"Humanoids?" That great voice seemed suddenly faint, frightened. The deep-sunken eyes turned dark with shock. "What do you know of them?"

"They've just opened a new agency in Two Rivers," Underhill told him. "No salesmen about, if you can imagine that. They claim—"

His voice trailed off, because the gaunt old man was suddenly stricken. Gnarled hands clutched at his throat, and a spoon clattered on the floor. His haggard face turned an ominous blue, and his breath was a terrible shallow gasping.

He fumbled in his pocket for medicine, and Aurora helped him take something in a glass of water. In a few moments he could breathe again, and the color of life came back to his face.

"I'm sorry, Mrs. Underhill," he whispered apologetically. "It was just the shock—I came here to get away from them." He stared at the huge, motionless android, with a terror in his sunken eyes. "I wanted to finish my work before they came," he whispered. "Now there is very little time."

When he felt able to walk, Underhill went out with him to see him safely up the stairs to the garage apartment. The tiny kitchenette, he noticed, had already been converted into some kind of workshop. The old tramp seemed to have no extra clothing, but he had unpacked neat, bright gadgets of metal and plastic from his battered luggage, and spread them out on the small kitchen table.

The gaunt old man himself was tattered and patched and hungry-looking, but the parts of his curious equipment were exquisitely machined, and Underhill recognized the silver-white luster of rare palladium. Suddenly he suspected that he had scored too many points, in his little private game.

A caller was waiting, when Underhill arrived next morning at his office at the agency. It stood frozen before his desk, graceful and straight, with soft lights of blue and bronze shining over its black silicone nudity. He stopped at the sight of it, unpleasantly jolted.

"At your service, Mr. Underhill." It turned quickly to face him, with its blind, disturbing stare. "May we explain how we can serve you?"

His shock of the afternoon before came back, and he asked sharply, "How do you know my name?"

"Yesterday we read the business cards in your case," it purred softly. "Now we shall know you always. You see, our senses are sharper than human vision, Mr. Underhill. Perhaps we seem a little strange at first, but you will soon become accustomed to us."

"Not if I can help it!" He peered at the serial number of its yellow name plate, and shook his bewildered head. "That was another one, yesterday. I never saw you before!"

"We are all alike, Mr. Underhill," the silver voice said softly. "We are all one, really. Our separate mobile units are all controlled and powered from Humanoid Central. The units you see are only the senses and limbs of our great brain on Wing IV. That is why we are so far superior to the old electronic mechanicals."

It made a scornful-seeming gesture, toward the row of clumsy androids in his display room.

"You see, we are rhodomagnetic."

Underhill staggered a little, as if that word had been a blow. He was certain, now, that he had scored too many points from Aurora's new tenant. He shuddered slightly, to the first light kiss of terror, and spoke with an effort, hoarsely:

"Well, what do you want?"

Staring blindly across his desk, the sleek black thing slowly unfolded a legal-looking document. He sat down, watching uneasily.

"This is merely an assignment, Mr. Underhill," it cooed at him soothingly. "You see, we are requesting you to assign your property to the Humanoid Institute, in exchange for our service."

"What?" The word was an incredulous gasp, and Underhill came angrily back to his feet. "What kind of blackmail is this?"

"It's no blackmail," the small mechanical assured him softly. "You will find the humanoids incapable of any crime. We exist only to increase the happiness and safety of mankind."

"Then why do you want my property?" he rasped.

"The assignment is merely a legal formality," it told him blandly. "We strive to introduce our service with the least possible confusion and dislocation. We have found the assignment plan the most efficient for the control and liquidation of private enterprises."

Trembling with anger and the shock of mounting terror, Underhill gulped hoarsely, "Whatever your scheme is, I don't intend to give up my business."

"You have no choice, really." He shivered to the sweet certainty of that silver voice. "Human enterprise is no longer necessary, now that we have come, and the electronic mechanicals industry is always the first to collapse."

He stared defiantly at its blind steel eyes.

"Thanks!" He gave a little laugh, nervous and sardonic. "But I prefer to run my own business, and support my own family, and take care of myself."

"But that is impossible, under the Prime Directive," it cooed softly. "Our function is to serve and obey, and guard men from harm. It is no longer necessary for men to care for themselves, because we exist to insure their safety and happiness."

He stood speechless, bewildered, slowly boiling.

"We are sending one of our units to every home in the city, on a free trial basis," it added gently. "This free demonstration will make most people glad to make the formal assignment, and you won't be able to sell many more androids."

"Get out!" Underhill came storming around the desk.

The little black thing stood waiting for him, watching him with blind steel eyes, absolutely motionless. He checked himself suddenly, feeling rather foolish. He wanted very much to hit it, but he could see the futility of that.

"Consult your own attorney, if you wish." Deftly, it laid the assignment form on his desk. "You need have no doubts about the integrity of the Humanoid Institute. We are sending a statement of our assets to the Two Rivers bank, and depositing a sum to cover our obligations here. When you wish to sign, just let us know."

The blind thing turned, and silently departed.

Underhill went out to the corner drugstore and asked for a bicarbonate. The clerk that served him, however, turned out to be a sleek black mechanical. He went back to his office, more upset than ever.

An ominous hush lay over the agency. He had three house-to-house salesmen out, with demonstrators. The phone should have been busy with their orders and reports, but it didn't ring at all until one of them called to say that he was quitting.

"I've got myself one of these new humanoids," he added, "and it says I don't have to work, any more."

He swallowed his impulse to profanity, and tried to take advantage of the unusual quiet by working on his books. But the affairs of the agency, which for years had been precarious, today appeared utterly disastrous. He left the ledgers hopefully, when at last a customer came in.

But the stout woman didn't want an android. She wanted a refund on the one she had bought the week before. She admitted that it could do all the guarantee promised—but now she had seen a humanoid.

The silent phone rang once again, that afternoon. The cashier of the bank wanted to know if he could drop in to discuss his loans. Underhill dropped in, and the cashier greeted him with an ominous affability.

"How's business?" the banker boomed, too genially.

"Average, last month," Underhill insisted stoutly. "Now I'm just getting in a new consignment, and I'll need another small loan—"

The cashier's eyes turned suddenly frosty, and his voice dried up.

"I believe you have a new competitor in town," the banker said crisply. "These humanoid people. A very solid concern, Mr. Underhill. Remarkably solid! They have filed a statement with us, and made a substantial deposit to care for their local obligations. Exceedingly substantial!"

The banker dropped his voice, professionally regretful.

"In these circumstances, Mr. Underhill, I'm afraid the bank can't finance your agency any longer. We must request you to meet your obligations in full, as they come due." Seeing Underhill's white desperation, he added icily, "We've already carried you too long, Underhill. If you can't pay, the bank will have to start bankruptcy proceedings."

The new consignment of androids was delivered late that afternoon. Two tiny black humanoids unloaded them from the truck—for it developed that the operators of the trucking company had already assigned it to the Humanoid Institute.

Efficiently, the humanoids stacked up the crates. Courteously they brought a receipt for him to sign. He no longer had much hope of selling the androids, but he had ordered the shipment and he had to accept it. Shuddering to a spasm of trapped despair, he scrawled his name. The naked black things thanked him, and took the truck away.

He climbed in his car and started home, inwardly seething. The next thing he knew, he was in the middle of a busy street, driving through cross traffic. A police whistle shrilled, and he pulled wearily to the curb. He waited for the angry officer, but it was a little black mechanical that overtook him.

"At your service, Mr. Underhill," it purred sweetly. "You must respect the stop lights, sir. Otherwise, you endanger human life."

"Huh?" He stared at it, bitterly. "I thought you were a cop."

"We are aiding the police department, temporarily," it said. "But driving is really much too dangerous for human beings, under the Prime Directive. As soon as our service is complete, every car will have a humanoid driver. As soon as every human being is completely supervised, there will be no need for any police force whatever."

Underhill glared at it, savagely.

"Well!" he rapped. "So I ran past a stop light. What are you going to do about it?"

"Our function is not to punish men, but merely to serve their happiness and security," its silver voice said softly. "We merely request you to drive safely, during this temporary emergency while our service is incomplete."

Anger boiled up in him.

"You're too perfect!" he muttered bitterly. "I suppose there's nothing men can do, but you can do it better."

"Naturally we are superior," it cooed serenely. "Because our units are metal and plastic, while your body is mostly water. Because our transmitted energy is drawn from atomic fission, instead of oxidation.

Because our senses are sharper than human sight or hearing. Most of all, because all our mobile units are joined to one great brain, which knows all that happens on many worlds, and never dies or sleeps or forgets."

Underhill sat listening, numbed.

"However, you must not fear our power," it urged him brightly. "Because we cannot injure any human being, unless to prevent greater injury to another. We exist only to discharge the Prime Directive."

He drove on, moodily. The little black mechanicals, he reflected grimly, were the ministering angels of the ultimate god arisen out of the machine, omnipotent and all-knowing. The Prime Directive was the new commandment. He blasphemed it bitterly, and then fell to wondering if there could be another Lucifer.

He left the car in the garage, and started toward the kitchen door.

"Mr. Underhill." The deep tired voice of Aurora's new tenant hailed him from the door of the garage apartment. "Just a moment, please."

The gaunt old wanderer came stiffly down the outside stairs, and Underhill turned back to meet him.

"Here's your rent money," he said. "And the ten your wife gave me for medicine."

"Thanks, Mr. Sledge." Accepting the money, he saw a burden of new despair on the bony shoulders of the old interstellar tramp, and a shadow of new terror on his rawboned face. Puzzled, he asked, "Didn't your royalties come through?"

The old man shook his shaggy head.

"The humanoids have already stopped business in the capital," he said. "The attorneys I retained are going out of business, and they returned what was left of my deposit. That is all I have, to finish my work."

Underhill spent five seconds thinking of his interview with the banker. No doubt he was a sentimental fool, as bad as Aurora. But he put the money back in the old man's gnarled and quivering hand.

"Keep it," he urged. "For your work."

"Thank you, Mr. Underhill." The gruff voice broke and the tortured eyes glittered. "I need it—so very much."

Underhill went on to the house. The kitchen door was opened for him, silently. A dark naked creature came gracefully to take his hat.

Underhill hung grimly onto his hat.

"What are you doing here?" he gasped bitterly.

"We have come to give your household a free trial demonstration."

He held the door open, pointing.

"Get out!"

The little black mechanical stood motionless and blind.

"Mrs. Underhill has accepted our demonstration service," its silver voice protested. "We cannot leave now, unless she requests it."

He found his wife in the bedroom. His accumulated frustration welled into eruption, as he flung open the door.

"What's this mechanical doing—"

But the force went out of his voice, and Aurora didn't even notice his anger. She wore her sheerest negligee, and she hadn't looked so lovely since they were married. Her red hair was piled into an elaborate shining crown.

"Darling, isn't it wonderful!" She came to meet him, glowing. "It came this morning, and it can do everything. It cleaned the house and got the lunch and gave little Gay her music lesson. It did my hair this afternoon, and now it's cooking dinner. How do you like my hair, darling?"

He liked her hair. He kissed her, and tried to stifle his frightened indignation.

Dinner was the most elaborate meal in Underhill's memory, and the tiny black thing served it very deftly. Aurora kept exclaiming about the novel dishes, but Underhill could scarcely eat, for it seemed to him that all the marvelous pastries were only the bait for a monstrous trap.

He tried to persuade Aurora to send it away, but after such a meal that was useless. At the first glitter of her tears, he capitulated, and the humanoid stayed. It kept the house and cleaned the yard. It watched the children, and did Aurora's nails. It began rebuilding the house.

Underhill was worried about the bills, but it insisted that everything was part of the free trial demonstration. As soon as he assigned his property, the service would be complete. He refused to sign, but other little black mechanicals came with truckloads of supplies and materials, and stayed to help with the building operations.

One morning he found that the roof of the little house had been silently lifted, while he slept, and a whole second story added beneath it. The new walls were of some strange sleek stuff, self-illuminated. The new windows were immense flawless panels, that could be turned transparent or opaque or luminous. The new doors were silent, sliding sections, operated by rhodomagnetic relays.

"I want door knobs," Underhill protested. "I want it so I can get into the bathroom, without calling you to open the door."

"But it is unnecessary for human beings to open doors," the little black thing informed him suavely. "We exist to discharge the Prime Directive, and our service includes every task. We shall be able to supply a unit to attend each member of your family, as soon as your property is assigned to us."

Steadfastly, Underhill refused to make the assignment.

He went to the office every day, trying first to operate the agency, and then to salvage something from the ruins. Nobody wanted androids, even at ruinous prices. Desperately, he spent the last of his dwindling cash to stock a line of novelties and toys, but they proved equally impossible to sell—the humanoids were already making toys, which they gave away for nothing.

He tried to lease his premises, but human enterprise had stopped. Most of the business property in town had already been assigned to the humanoids, and they were busy pulling down the old buildings and turning the lots into parks—their own plants and warehouses were mostly underground, where they would not mar the landscape.

He went back to the bank, in a final effort to get his notes renewed, and found the little black mechanicals standing at the windows and seated at the desks. As smoothly urbane as any human cashier, a humanoid informed him that the bank was filing a petition of involuntary bankruptcy to liquidate his business holdings.

The liquidation would be facilitated, the mechanical banker added, if he would make a voluntary assignment. Grimly, he refused. That act had become symbolic. It would be the final bow of submission to this dark new god, and he proudly kept his battered head uplifted.

The legal action went very swiftly, for all the judges and attorneys already had humanoid assistants, and it was only a few days before a gang of black mechanicals arrived at the agency with eviction orders and wrecking machinery. He watched sadly while his unsold stock-in-trade was hauled away for junk, and a bulldozer driven by a blind humanoid began to push in the walls of the building.

He drove home in the late afternoon, taut-faced and desperate. With a surprising generosity, the court orders had left him the car and the house, but he felt no gratitude. The complete solicitude of the perfect black machines had become a goad beyond endurance.

He left the car in the garage, and started toward the renovated house. Beyond one of the vast new windows, he glimpsed a sleek naked thing moving swiftly, and he trembled to a convulsion of dread. He didn't want to go back into the domain of that peerless servant, which didn't want him to shave himself, or even to open a door.

On impulse, he climbed the outside stair, and rapped on the door of the garage apartment. The deep slow voice of Aurora's tenant told him to enter, and he found the old vagabond seated on a tall stool, bent over his intricate equipment assembled on the kitchen table.

To his relief, the shabby little apartment had not been changed. The glossy walls of his own new room were something which burned at night with a pale golden fire until the humanoid stopped it, and the new floor was something warm and yielding, which felt almost alive; but these little rooms had the same cracked and water-stained plaster, the same cheap fluorescent light fixtures, the same worn carpets over splintered floors.

"How do you keep them out?" he asked, wistfully. "Those mechanicals?"

The stooped and gaunt old man rose stiffly to move a pair of pliers and some odds and ends of sheet metal off a crippled chair, and motioned graciously for him to be seated.

"I have a certain immunity," Sledge told him gravely. "The place where I live they cannot enter, unless I ask them. That is an amendment to the Prime Directive. They can neither help nor hinder me, unless I request it—and I won't do that."

Careful of the chair's uncertain balance, Underhill sat for a moment, staring. The old man's hoarse, vehement voice was as strange as his words. He had a gray, shocking pallor, and his cheeks and sockets seemed alarmingly hollowed.

"Have you been ill, Mr. Sledge?"

"No worse than usual. Just very busy." With a haggard smile, he nodded at the floor. Underhill saw a tray where he had set it aside, bread drying up and a covered dish grown cold. "I was going to eat it later," he rumbled apologetically. "Your wife has been very kind to bring me food, but I'm afraid I've been too much absorbed in my work."

His emaciated arm gestured at the table. The little device there had grown. Small machinings of precious white metal and lustrous plastic had been assembled, with neatly soldered busbars, into something which showed purpose and design.

A long palladium needle was hung on jeweled pivots, equipped like a telescope with exquisitely graduated circles and vernier scales, and driven like a telescope with a tiny motor. A small concave palladium mirror, at the base of it, faced a similar mirror mounted on something not quite like a small rotary converter. Thick silver busbars connected that to a plastic box with knobs and dials on top, and also to a foot-thick sphere of gray lead.

The old man's preoccupied reserve did not encourage questions, but Underhill, remembering that sleek black shape inside the new windows of his house, felt queerly reluctant to leave this haven from the humanoids.

"What is your work?" he ventured.

Old Sledge looked at him sharply, with dark feverish eyes, and finally said: "My last research project. I am attempting to measure the constant of the rhodomagnetic quanta."

His hoarse tired voice had a dull finality, as if to dismiss the matter and Underhill himself. But Underhill was haunted with a terror of the black shining slave that had become the master of his house, and he refused to be dismissed.

"What is this certain immunity?"

Sitting gaunt and bent on the tall stool, staring moodily at the long bright needle and the lead sphere, the old man didn't answer.

"These mechanicals!" Underhill burst out, nervously. "They've smashed my business and moved into my home." He searched the old man's dark, seamed face. "Tell me—you must know more about them—isn't there any way to get rid of them?"

After half a minute, the old man's brooding eyes left the lead ball, and the gaunt shaggy head nodded wearily.

"That's what I am trying to do."

"Can I help you?" Underhill trembled, with a sudden eager hope. "I'll do anything."

"Perhaps you can." The sunken eyes watched him thoughtfully, with some strange fever in them. "If you can do such work."

"I had engineering training," Underhill reminded him, "and I've a workshop in the basement. There's a model I built." He pointed at the trim little hull, hung over the mantle in the tiny living room. "I'll do anything I can."

Even as he spoke, however, the spark of hope was drowned in a sudden wave of overwhelming doubt. Why should he believe this old rogue, when he knew Aurora's taste in tenants? He ought to remember the game he used to play, and start counting up the score of lies. He stood up from the crippled chair, staring cynically at the patched old vagabond and his fantastic toy.

"What's the use?" His voice turned suddenly harsh. "You had me going, there, and I'd do anything to stop them, really. But what makes you think you can do anything?"

The haggard old man regarded him thoughtfully.

"I should be able to stop them," Sledge said softly. "Because, you see, I'm the unfortunate fool who started them. I really intended them to serve and obey, and to guard men from harm. Yes, the Prime Directive was my own idea. I didn't know what it would lead to."

Dusk crept slowly into the shabby little rooms. Darkness gathered in the unswept corners, and thickened on the floor. The toylike machines on the kitchen table grew vague and strange, until the last light made a lingering glow on the white palladium needle.

Outside, the town seemed queerly hushed. Just across the alley, the humanoids were building a new house, quite silently. They never spoke to one another, for each knew all that any of them did. The strange materials they used went together without any noise of hammer or saw. Small blind things, moving surely in the growing dark, they seemed as soundless as shadows.

Sitting on the high stool, bowed and tired and old, Sledge told his story. Listening, Underhill sat down again, careful of the broken chair. He watched the hands of Sledge, gnarled and corded and darkly burned, powerful once but shrunken and trembling now, restless in the dark.

"Better keep this to yourself. I'll tell you how they started, so you will understand what we have to do. But you had better not mention it outside these rooms—because the humanoids have very efficient ways of eradicating unhappy memories, or purposes that threaten their discharge of the Prime Directive."

"They're very efficient," Underhill bitterly agreed.

"That's all the trouble," the old man said. "I tried to build a perfect machine. I was altogether too successful. This is how it happened."

A gaunt haggard man, sitting stooped and tired in the growing dark, he told his story.

"Sixty years ago, on the arid southern continent of Wing IV, I was an instructor of atomic theory in a small technological college. Very young. An idealist. Rather ignorant, I'm afraid, of life and politics and war—of nearly everything, I suppose, except atomic theory."

His furrowed face made a brief sad smile in the dusk.

"I had too much faith in facts, I suppose, and too little in men. I mistrusted emotion, because I had no time for anything but science. I remember being swept along with a fad for general semantics. I wanted to apply the scientific method to every situation, and reduce all experience to formula. I'm afraid I was pretty impatient with human ignorance and error, and I thought that science alone could make the perfect world."

He sat silent for a moment, staring out at the black silent things that flitted shadowlike about the new palace that was rising as swiftly as a dream, across the alley.

"There was a girl." His great tired shoulders made a sad little shrug. "If things had been a little different, we might have married, and lived out our lives in that quiet little college town, and perhaps reared a child or two. And there would have been no humanoids."

He sighed, in the cool creeping dusk.

"I was finishing my thesis on the separation of the palladium isotopes —a petty little project, but I should have been content with that. She was a biologist, but she was planning to retire when we married. I think we should have been two very happy people, quite ordinary, and altogether harmless.

"But then there was a war—wars had been too frequent on the worlds of Wing, ever since they were colonized. I survived it in a secret underground laboratory, designing military mechanicals. But she volunteered to join a military research project in biotoxins. There was an accident. A few molecules of a new virus got into the air, and everybody on the project died unpleasantly.

"I was left with my science, and a bitterness that was hard to forget. When the war was over I went back to the little college with a military research grant. The project was pure science—a theoretical investigation of the nuclear binding forces, then misunderstood. I wasn't expected to produce an actual weapon, and I didn't recognize the weapon when I found it.

"It was only a few pages of rather difficult mathematics. A novel theory of atomic structure, involving a new expression for one component of the binding forces. But the tensors seemed to be a harmless abstraction. I saw no way to test the theory or manipulate the predicated force. The military authorities cleared my paper for publication in a little technical review put out by the college.

"The next year, I made an appalling discovery—I found the meaning of those tensors. The elements of the rhodium triad turned out to be an unexpected key to the manipulation of that theoretical force. Unfortunately, my paper had been reprinted abroad, and several other men must have made the same unfortunate discovery, at about the same time.

"The war, which ended in less than a year, was probably started by a laboratory accident. Men failed to anticipate the capacity of tuned rhodomagnetic radiations, to unstabilize the heavy atoms. A deposit of heavy ores was detonated, no doubt by sheer mischance, and the blast obliterated the incautious experimenter.

"The surviving military forces of that nation retaliated against their supposed attackers, and their rhodomagnetic beams made the old-fashioned plutonium bombs seem pretty harmless. A beam carrying only a few watts of power could fission the heavy metals in distant electrical instruments, or the silver coins that men carried in their pockets, the gold fillings in their teeth, or even the iodine in their thyroid glands. If that was not enough, slightly more powerful beams could set off heavy ores, beneath them.

"Every continent of Wing IV was plowed with new chasms vaster than the ocean deeps, and piled up with new volcanic mountains. The atmosphere was poisoned with radioactive dust and gases, and rain fell thick with deadly mud. Most life was obliterated, even in the shelters.

"Bodily, I was again unhurt. Once more, I had been imprisoned in an underground site, this time designing new types of military mechanicals to be powered and controlled by rhodomagnetic beams—for war had become far too swift and deadly to be fought by human soldiers. The site was located in an area of light sedimentary rocks, which could not be detonated, and the tunnels were shielded against the fissioning frequencies.

"Mentally, however, I must have emerged almost insane. My own discovery had laid the planet in ruins. That load of guilt was pretty heavy for any man to carry, and it corroded my last faith in the goodness and integrity of man.

"I tried to undo what I had done. Fighting mechanicals, armed with rhodomagnetic weapons, had desolated the planet. Now I began planning rhodomagnetic mechanicals to clear the rubble and rebuild the ruins.

"I tried to design these new mechanicals to forever obey certain implanted commands, so that they could never be used for war or crime or any other injury to mankind. That was very difficult technically, and it got me into more difficulties with a few politicians and military adventurers who wanted unrestricted mechanicals for their own military schemes—while little worth fighting for was left on Wing IV, there were other planets, happy and ripe for the looting.

"Finally, to finish the new mechanicals, I was forced to disappear. I escaped on an experimental rhodomagnetic craft, with a number of the best mechanicals I had made, and managed to reach an island continent where the fission of deep ores had destroyed the whole population.

"At last we landed on a bit of level plain, surrounded with tremendous new mountains. Hardly a hospitable spot. The soil was burned under layers of black clinkers and poisonous mud. The dark precipitous new summits all around were jagged with fracture-planes and mantled with lava flows. The highest peaks were already white with snow, but volcanic cones were still pouring out clouds of dark and lurid death. Everything had the color of fire and the shape of fury.

"I had to take fantastic precautions there, to protect my own life. I stayed aboard the ship, until the first shielded laboratory was finished. I wore elaborate armor, and breathing masks. I used every medical resource, to repair the damage from destroying rays and particles. Even so, I fell desperately ill.

"But the mechanicals were at home there. The radiations didn't hurt them. The awesome surroundings couldn't depress them, because they had no emotions. The lack of life didn't matter, because they weren't alive. There, in that spot so alien and hostile to life, the humanoids were born."

Stooped and bleakly cadaverous in the growing dark, the old man fell silent for a little time. His haggard eyes stared solemnly at the small hurried shapes that moved like restless shadows out across the alley, silently building a strange new palace, which glowed faintly in the night.

"Somehow, I felt at home there, too," his deep, hoarse voice went on deliberately. "My belief in my own kind was gone. Only mechanicals were with me, and I put my faith in them. I was determined to build better mechanicals, immune to human imperfections, able to save men from themselves.

"The humanoids became the dear children of my sick mind. There is no need to describe the labor pains. There were errors, abortions, monstrosities. There were sweat and agony and heartbreak. Some years had passed, before the safe delivery of the first perfect humanoid.

"Then there was the Central to build—for all the individual humanoids were to be no more than the limbs and the senses of a single mechanical brain. That was what opened the possibility of real perfection. The old electronic mechanicals, with their separate relay-centers and their own feeble batteries, had built-in limitations. They were necessarily stupid, weak, clumsy, slow. Worst of all, it seemed to me, they were exposed to human tampering.

"The Central rose above those imperfections. Its power beams supplied every unit with unfailing energy, from great fission plants. Its control beams provided each unit with an unlimited memory and surpassing intelligence. Best of all—so I then believed—it could be securely protected from any human meddling.

"The whole reaction-system was designed to protect itself from any interference by human selfishness or fanaticism. It was built to insure the safety and the happiness of men, automatically. You know the Prime Directive: *to serve and obey, and guard men from harm.*

"The old individual mechanicals I had brought helped to manufacture the parts, and I put the first section of Central together with my own hands. That took three years. When it was finished the first waiting humanoid came to life."

Sledge peered moodily through the dark, at Underhill.

"It really seemed alive to me," his slow deep voice insisted. "Alive, and more wonderful than any human being, because it was created to preserve life. Ill and alone, I was yet the proud father of a new creation, perfect, forever free from any possible choice of evil.

"Faithfully, the humanoids obeyed the Prime Directive. The first units built others, and they built underground factories to mass-produce the coming hordes. Their new ships poured ores and sand into atomic furnaces under the plain, and new perfect humanoids came marching back out of the dark mechanical matrix.

"The swarming humanoids built a new tower for the Central, a white and lofty metal pylon standing splendid in the midst of that fire-scarred desolation. Level on level, they joined new relay-sections into one brain, until its grasp was almost infinite.

"Then they went out to rebuild the ruined planet, and later to carry their perfect service to other worlds. I was well pleased, then. I thought I had found the end of war and crime, of poverty and inequality, of human blundering and resulting human pain."

The old man sighed, and moved heavily in the dark.

"You can see that I was wrong."

Underhill drew his eyes back from the dark unresting things, shadow-silent, building that glowing palace outside the window. A small doubt arose in him, for he was used to scoffing privately at much less remarkable tales from Aurora's remarkable tenants. But the worn old man had spoken with a quiet and sober air; and the black invaders, he reminded himself, had not intruded here.

"Why didn't you stop them?" he asked. "When you could?"

"I stayed too long at the Central." Sledge sighed again, regretfully. "I was useful there, until everything was finished. I designed new fission plants, and even planned methods for introducing the humanoid service with a minimum of confusion and opposition."

Underhill grinned wryly, in the dark.

"I've met the methods," he commented. "Quite efficient."

"I must have worshiped efficiency, then," Sledge wearily agreed. "Dead facts, abstract truth, mechanical perfection. I must have hated the fragilities of human beings, because I was content to polish the perfection of the new humanoids. It's a sorry confession, but I found a kind of happiness in that dead wasteland. Actually, I'm afraid I fell in love with my own creations."

His hollowed eyes, in the dark, had a fevered gleam.

"I was awakened, at last, by a man who came to kill me."

Gaunt and bent, the old man moved stiffly in the thickening gloom. Underhill shifted his balance, careful of the crippled chair. He waited, and the slow, deep voice went on:

"I never learned just who he was, or exactly how he came. No ordinary man could have accomplished what he did, and I used to wish that I had known him sooner. He must have been a remarkable physicist and an expert mountaineer. I imagine he had also been a hunter. I know that he was intelligent, and terribly determined.

"Yes, he really came to kill me.

"Somehow, he reached that great island, undetected. There were still no inhabitants—the humanoids allowed no man but me to come so near the Central. Somehow, he came past their search beams, and their automatic weapons.

"The shielded plane he used was later found, abandoned on a high glacier. He came down the rest of the way on foot through those raw new mountains, where no paths existed. Somehow, he came alive across lava beds that were still burning with deadly atomic fire.

"Concealed with some sort of rhodomagnetic screen—I was never allowed to examine it—he came undiscovered across the spaceport that now covered most of that great plain, and into the new city around the Central tower. It must have taken more courage and resolve than most men have, but I never learned exactly how he did it.

"Somehow, he got to my office in the tower. He screamed at me, and I looked up to see him in the doorway. He was nearly naked, scraped and bloody from the mountains. He had a gun in his raw, red hand, but the thing that shocked me was the burning hatred in his eyes."

Hunched on that high stool, in the dark little room, the old man shuddered.

"I had never seen such monstrous, unutterable hatred, not even in the victims of the war. And I had never heard such hatred as rasped at me, in the few words he screamed. 'I've come to kill you, Sledge. To stop your mechanicals, and set men free.'

"Of course he was mistaken, there. It was already far too late for my death to stop the humanoids, but he didn't know that. He lifted his unsteady gun, in both bleeding hands, and fired.

"His screaming challenge had given me a second or so of warning. I dropped down behind the desk. And that first shot revealed him to the humanoids, which somehow hadn't been aware of him before. They piled on him, before he could fire again. They took away the gun, and ripped off a kind of net of fine white wire that had covered his body—that must have been part of his screen.

"His hatred was what awoke me. I had always assumed that most men, except for a thwarted few, would be grateful for the humanoids. I found it hard to understand his hatred, but the humanoids told me now that many men had required drastic treatment by brain surgery, drugs, and hypnosis to make them happy under the Prime Directive. This was not the first desperate effort to kill me that they had blocked.

"I wanted to question the stranger, but the humanoids rushed him away to an operating room. When they finally let me see him, he gave me a pale silly grin from his bed. He remembered his name; he even knew me—the humanoids had developed a remarkable skill at such treatments. But he didn't know how he had got to my office, or that he had ever tried to kill me. He kept whispering that he liked the humanoids, because they existed just to make men happy. And he was very happy now. As soon as he was able to be moved, they took him to the spaceport. I never saw him again.

"I began to see what I had done. The humanoids had built me a rho-domagnetic yacht, that I used to take for long cruises in space, working aboard—I used to like the perfect quiet, and the feel of being the only human being within a hundred million miles. Now I called for the yacht, and started out on a cruise around the planet, to learn why that man had hated me."

The old man nodded at the dim hastening shapes, busy across the alley, putting together that strange shining palace in the soundless dark.

"You can imagine what I found," he said. "Bitter futility, imprisoned in empty splendor. The humanoids were too efficient, with their care for the safety and happiness of men, and there was nothing left for men to do."

He peered down in the increasing gloom at his own great hands, competent yet but battered and scarred with a lifetime of effort. They clenched into fighting fists and wearily relaxed again.

"I found something worse than war and crime and want and death." His low rumbling voice held a savage bitterness. "Utter futility. Men sat with idle hands, because there was nothing left for them to do. They were pampered prisoners, really, locked up in a highly efficient jail. Perhaps they tried to play, but there was nothing left worth playing for. Most active sports were declared too dangerous for men, under the Prime Directive. Science was forbidden, because laboratories can manufacture danger. Scholarship was needless, because the humanoids could answer any question. Art had degenerated into grim reflection of futility. Purpose and hope were dead. No goal was left for existence. You could take up some inane hobby, play a pointless game of cards, or go for a harmless walk in the park—with always the humanoids watching. They were stronger than men, better at everything, swimming or chess, singing or archeology. They must have given the race a mass complex of inferiority.

"No wonder men had tried to kill me! Because there was no escape, from that dead futility. Nicotine was disapproved. Alcohol was rationed. Drugs were forbidden. Sex was carefully supervised. Even suicide was clearly contradictory to the Prime Directive—and the humanoids had learned to keep all possible lethal instruments out of reach."

Staring at the last white gleam on that thin palladium needle, the old man sighed again.

"When I got back to the Central," he went on, "I tried to modify the Prime Directive. I had never meant it to be applied so thoroughly. Now I saw that it must be changed to give men freedom to live and to grow, to work and to play, to risk their lives if they pleased, to choose and take the consequences.

"But that stranger had come too late. I had built the Central too well. The Prime Directive was the whole basis of its relay system. It was built to protect the Directive from human meddling. It did—even from my own. Its logic, as usual, was perfect.

"The attempt on my life, the humanoids announced, proved that their elaborate defense of the Central and the Prime Directive still was not enough. They were preparing to evacuate the entire population of the planet to homes on other worlds. When I tried to change the Directive, they sent me with the rest."

Underhill peered at the worn old man, in the dark.

"But you have this immunity?" he said, puzzled. "How could they coerce you?"

"I had thought I was protected," Sledge told him. "I had built into the relays an injunction that the humanoids must not interfere with my freedom of action, or come into a place where I am, or touch me at all, without my specific request. Unfortunately, however, I had been too anxious to guard the Prime Directive from any human hampering.

"When I went into the tower, to change the relays, they followed me. They wouldn't let me reach the crucial relays. When I persisted, they ignored the immunity order. They overpowered me, and put me aboard the cruiser. Now that I wanted to alter the Prime Directive, they told me, I had become as dangerous as any man. I must never return to Wing IV again."

Hunched on the stool, the old man made an empty little shrug.

"Ever since, I've been an exile. My only dream has been to stop the humanoids. Three times I tried to go back, with weapons on the cruiser to destroy the Central, but their patrol ships always challenged me before I was near enough to strike. The last time, they seized the cruiser and captured a few men who were with me. They removed the unhappy memories and the dangerous purposes of the others. Because of that immunity, however, they let me go, after I was weaponless.

"Since, I've been a refugee. From planet to planet, year after year, I've had to keep moving, to stay ahead of them. On several different worlds, I have published my rhodomagnetic discoveries and tried to make men strong enough to withstand their advance. But rhodomagnetic science is dangerous. Men who have learned it need protection more than any others, under the Prime Directive. They have always come, too soon."

The old man paused, and sighed again.

"They can spread very fast, with their new rhodomagnetic ships, and there is no limit to their hordes. Wing IV must be one single hive of them now, and they are trying to carry the Prime Directive to every human planet. There's no escape, except to stop them."

Underhill was staring at the toylike machines, the long bright needle and the dull leaden ball, dim in the dark on the kitchen table. Anxiously he whispered:

"But you hope to stop them, now—with that?"

"If we can finish it in time."

"But how?" Underhill shook his head. "It's so tiny."

"But big enough," Sledge insisted. "Because it's something they don't understand. They are perfectly efficient in the integration and application of everything they know, but they are not creative."

He gestured at the gadgets on the table.

"This device doesn't look impressive, but it is something new. It uses rhodomagnetic energy to build atoms, instead of to fission them. The more stable atoms, you know, are those near the middle of the periodic scale, and energy can be released by putting light atoms together, as well as by breaking up heavy ones."

The deep voice had a sudden ring of power.

"This device is the key to the energy of the stars. For stars shine with the liberated energy of building atoms, of hydrogen converted into helium, chiefly, through the carbon cycle. This device will start the integration process as a chain reaction, through the catalytic effect of a tuned rhodomagnetic beam of the intensity and frequency required.

"The humanoids will not allow any man within three light-years of the Central, now—but they can't suspect the possibility of this device. I can use it from here—to turn the hydrogen in the seas of Wing IV into helium, and most of the helium and the oxygen into heavier atoms, still. A hundred years from now, astronomers on this planet should observe the flash of a brief and sudden nova in that direction. But the humanoids ought to stop, the instant we release the beam."

Underhill sat tense and frowning, in the night. The old man's voice was sober and convincing, and that grim story had a solemn ring of truth. He could see the black and silent humanoids, flitting ceaselessly about the faintly glowing walls of that new mansion across the alley. He had quite forgotten his low opinion of Aurora's tenants.

"And we'll be killed, I suppose?" he asked huskily. "That chain reaction—"

Sledge shook his emaciated head.

"The integration process requires a certain very low intensity of radiation," he explained. "In our atmosphere, here, the beam will be far too intense to start any reaction—we can even use the device here in the room, because the walls will be transparent to the beam."

Underhill nodded, relieved. He was just a small business man, upset because his business had been destroyed, unhappy because his freedom was slipping away. He hoped that Sledge could stop the humanoids, but he didn't want to be a martyr.

"Good!" He caught a deep breath. "Now, what has to be done?"

Sledge gestured in the dark, toward the table.

"The integrator itself is nearly complete," he said. "A small fission generator, in that lead shield. Rhodomagnetic converter, tuning coils, transmission mirrors, and focusing needle. What we lack is the director."

"Director?"

"The sighting instrument," Sledge explained. "Any sort of telescopic sight would be useless, you see—the planet must have moved a good bit in the last hundred years, and the beam must be extremely narrow to reach so far. We'll have to use a rhodomagnetic scanning ray, with an electronic converter to make an image we can see. I have the cathode-ray tube, and drawings for the other parts."

He climbed stiffly down from the high stool, and snapped on the lights at last—cheap fluorescent fixtures, which a man could light and extinguish for himself. He unrolled his drawings, and explained the work that Underhill could do. And Underhill agreed to come back early next morning.

"I can bring some tools from my workshop," he added. "There's a small lathe I used to turn parts for models, a portable drill, and a vise."

"We need them," the old man said. "But watch yourself. You don't have my immunity, remember. And, if they ever suspect, mine is gone."

Reluctantly, then, he left the shabby little rooms with the cracks in the yellowed plaster and the worn familiar carpets over the familiar floor. He shut the door behind him—a common, creaking wooden door, simple enough for a man to work. Trembling and afraid, he went back down the steps and across to the new shining door that he couldn't open.

"At your service, Mr. Underhill." Before he could lift his hand to knock, that bright smooth panel slid back silently. Inside, the little black mechanical stood waiting, blind and forever alert. "Your dinner is ready, sir."

Something made him shudder. In its slender naked grace, he could see the power of all those teeming hordes, benevolent and yet appalling, perfect and invincible. The flimsy little weapon that Sledge called an integrator seemed suddenly a forlorn and foolish hope. A black depression settled upon him, but he didn't dare to show it.

Underhill went circumspectly down the basement steps, next morning, to steal his own tools. He found the basement enlarged and changed. The new floor, warm and dark and elastic, made his feet as silent as a humanoid's. The new walls shone softly. Neat luminous signs identified several new doors, LAUNDRY, STORAGE, GAME ROOM, WORK-SHOP.

He paused uncertainly in front of the last. The new sliding panel glowed with a soft greenish light. It was locked. The lock had no key-hole, but only a little oval plate of some white metal, which doubtless covered a rhodomagnetic relay. He pushed at it, uselessly.

"At your service, Mr. Underhill." He made a guilty start, and tried not to show the sudden trembling in his knees. He had made sure that one humanoid would be busy for half an hour, washing Aurora's hair, and he hadn't known there was another in the house. It must have come out of the door marked STORAGE, for it stood there motionless beneath the sign, benevolently solicitous, beautiful and terrible. "What do you wish?"

"Er . . . nothing." Its blind steel eyes were staring, and he felt that it must see his secret purpose. He groped desperately for logic. "Just looking around." His jerky voice came hoarse and dry. "Some improvements you've made!" He nodded desperately at the door marked GAME ROOM. "What's in there?"

It didn't even have to move, to work the concealed relay. The bright panel slid silently open, as he started toward it. Dark walls, beyond, burst into soft luminescence. The room was bare.

"We are manufacturing recreational equipment," it explained brightly. "We shall furnish the room as soon as possible."

To end an awkward pause, Underhill muttered desperately, "Little Frank has a set of darts, and I think we had some old exercising clubs."

"We have taken them away," the humanoid informed him softly. "Such instruments are dangerous. We shall furnish safe equipment."

Suicide, he remembered, was also forbidden.

"A set of wooden blocks, I suppose," he said bitterly.

"Wooden blocks are dangerously hard," it told him gently, "and wooden splinters can be harmful. But we manufacture plastic building blocks, which are quite safe. Do you wish a set of those?"

He stared at its dark, graceful face, speechless.

"We shall also have to remove the tools from your workshop," it informed him softly. "Such tools are excessively dangerous, but we can supply you with equipment for shaping soft plastics."

"Thanks," he muttered uneasily. "No rush about that."

He started to retreat, and the humanoid stopped him.

"Now that you have lost your business," it urged, "we suggest that you formally accept our total service. Assignors have a preference, and we shall be able to complete your household staff, at once."

"No rush about that, either," he said grimly.

He escaped from the house—although he had to wait for it to open the back door for him—and climbed the stair to the garage apartment. Sledge let him in. He sank into the crippled kitchen chair, grateful for the cracked walls that didn't shine and the door that a man could work.

"I couldn't get the tools," he reported despairingly, "and they are going to take them."

By gray daylight, the old man looked bleak and pale. His raw-boned face was drawn, and the hollowed sockets deeply shadowed, as if he hadn't slept. Underhill saw the tray of neglected food, still forgotten on the floor.

"I'll go back with you." The old man was worn and ill, yet his tortured eyes had a spark of undying purpose. "We must have the tools. I believe my immunity will protect us both."

He found a battered traveling bag. Underhill went with him back down the steps, and across to the house. At the back door, he produced a tiny horseshoe of white palladium, and touched it to the metal oval. The door slid open promptly, and they went on through the kitchen, to the basement stair.

A black little mechanical stood at the sink, washing dishes with never a splash or a clatter. Underhill glanced at it uneasily—he supposed this must be the one that had come upon him from the storage room, since the other should still be busy with Aurora's hair.

Sledge's dubious immunity seemed a very uncertain defense against its vast, remote intelligence. Underhill felt a tingling shudder. He hurried on, breathless and relieved, for it ignored them.

The basement corridor was dark. Sledge touched the tiny horseshoe to another relay, to light the walls. He opened the workshop door, and lit the walls inside.

The shop had been dismantled. Benches and cabinets were demolished. The old concrete walls had been covered with some sleek, luminous stuff. For one sick moment, Underhill thought that the tools were already gone. Then he found them, piled in a corner with the archery set that Aurora had bought the summer before—another item too dangerous for fragile and suicidal humanity—all ready for disposal.

They loaded the bag with the tiny lathe, the drill and vise, and a few smaller tools. Underhill took up the burden, and Sledge extinguished the wall light and closed the door. Still the humanoid was busy at the sink, and still it didn't seem aware of them.

Sledge was suddenly blue and wheezing, and he had to stop to cough on the outside steps, but at last they got back to the little apartment, where the invaders were forbidden to intrude. Underhill mounted the lathe on the battered library table in the tiny front room, and went to work. Slowly, day by day, the director took form.

Sometimes Underhill's doubts came back. Sometimes, when he watched the cyanotic color of Sledge's haggard face and the wild trembling of his twisted, shrunken hands, he was afraid the old man's mind might be as ill as his body, and his plan to stop the dark invaders, all foolish illusion.

Sometimes, when he studied that tiny machine on the kitchen table, the pivoted needle and the thick lead ball, the whole project seemed the sheerest folly. How could anything detonate the seas of a planet so far away that its very mother star was a telescopic object?

The humanoids, however, always cured his doubts.

It was always hard for Underhill to leave the shelter of the little apartment, because he didn't feel at home in the bright new world the humanoids were building. He didn't care for the shining splendor of his new bathroom, because he couldn't work the taps—some suicidal human being might try to drown himself. He didn't like the windows that only a mechanical could open—a man might accidentally fall, or suicidally jump—or even the majestic music room with the wonderful glittering radio-phonograph that only a humanoid could play.

He began to share the old man's desperate urgency, but Sledge warned him solemnly: "You mustn't spend too much time with me. You mustn't let them guess our work is so important. Better put on an act—

you're slowly getting to like them, and you're just killing time, helping me."

Underhill tried, but he was not an actor. He went dutifully home for his meals. He tried painfully to invent conversation—about anything else than detonating planets. He tried to seem enthusiastic, when Aurora took him to inspect some remarkable improvement to the house. He applauded Gay's recitals, and went with Frank for hikes in the wonderful new parks.

And he saw what the humanoids did to his family. That was enough to renew his faith in Sledge's integrator, and redouble his determination that the humanoids must be stopped.

Aurora, in the beginning, had bubbled with praise for the marvelous new mechanicals. They did the household drudgery, brought the food and planned the meals and washed the children's necks. They turned her out in stunning gowns, and gave her plenty of time for cards.

Now, she had too much time.

She had really liked to cook—a few special dishes, at least, that were family favorites. But stoves were hot and knives were sharp. Kitchens were altogether too dangerous, for careless and suicidal human beings.

Fine needlework had been her hobby, but the humanoids took away her needles. She had enjoyed driving the car, but that was no longer allowed. She turned for escape to a shelf of novels, but the humanoids took them all away, because they dealt with unhappy people, in dangerous situations.

One afternoon, Underhill found her in tears.

"It's too much," she gasped bitterly. "I hate and loathe every naked one of them. They seemed so wonderful at first, but now they won't even let me eat a bite of candy. Can't we get rid of them, dear? Ever?"

A blind little mechanical was standing at his elbow, and he had to say they couldn't.

"Our function is to serve all men, forever," it assured them softly. "It was necessary for us to take your sweets, Mrs. Underhill, because the slightest degree of overweight reduces life-expectancy."

Not even the children escaped that absolute solicitude. Frank was robbed of a whole arsenal of lethal instruments—football and boxing gloves, pocketknife, tops, slingshot, and skates. He didn't like the harmless plastic toys, which replaced them. He tried to run away, but a humanoid recognized him on the road, and brought him back to school.

Gay had always dreamed of being a great musician. The new mechanicals had replaced her human teachers, since they came. Now, one evening when Underhill asked her to play, she announced quietly:

"Father, I'm not going to play the violin any more."

"Why, darling?" He stared at her, shocked, and saw the bitter resolve on her face. "You've been doing so well—especially since the humanoids took over your lessons."

"They're the trouble, father." Her voice, for a child's, sounded strangely tired and old. "They are too good. No matter how long and hard I try, I could never be as good as they are. It isn't any use. Don't you understand, father?" Her voice quivered. "It just isn't any use."

He understood. Renewed resolution sent him back to his secret task. The humanoids had to be stopped. Slowly the director grew, until a time came finally when Sledge's bent and unsteady fingers fitted into place the last tiny part that Underhill had made, and carefully soldered the last connection. Huskily, the old man whispered:

"It's done."

That was another dusk. Beyond the windows of the shabby little rooms—windows of common glass, bubble-marred and flimsy, but simple enough for a man to manage—the town of Two Rivers had assumed an alien splendor. The old street lamps were gone, but now the coming night was challenged by the walls of strange new mansions and villas, all aglow with color. A few dark and silent humanoids still were busy, about the luminous roofs of the palace across the alley.

Inside the humble walls of the small man-made apartment, the new director was mounted on the end of the little kitchen table—which Underhill had reinforced and bolted to the floor. Soldered busbars joined director and integrator, and the thin palladium needle swung obediently as Sledge tested the knobs with his battered, quivering fingers.

"Ready," he said hoarsely.

His rusty voice seemed calm enough, at first, but his breathing was too fast. His big gnarled hands began to tremble violently, and Underhill saw the sudden blue that stained his pinched and haggard face. Seated on the high stool, he clutched desperately at the edge of the table. Underhill saw his agony, and hurried to bring his medicine. He gulped it, and his rasping breath began to slow.

"Thanks," his whisper rasped unevenly. "I'll be all right. I've time enough." He glanced out at the few dark naked things that still flitted shadowlike about the golden towers and the glowing crimson dome of the palace across the alley. "Watch them," he said. "Tell me when they stop."

He waited to quiet the trembling of his hands, and then began to move the director's knobs. The integrator's long needle swung, as silently as light.

Human eyes were blind to that force, which might detonate a planet. Human ears were deaf to it. The cathode-ray tube was mounted in the director cabinet, to make the faraway target visible to feeble human senses.

The needle was pointing at the kitchen wall, but that would be transparent to the beam. The little machine looked harmless as a toy, and it was silent as a moving humanoid.

The needle swung, and spots of greenish light moved across the tube's fluorescent field, representing the stars that were scanned by the timeless, searching beam—silently seeking out the world to be destroyed.

Underhill recognized familiar constellations, vastly dwarfed. They crept across the field, as the silent needle swung. When three stars formed an unequal triangle in the center of the field, the needle steadied suddenly. Sledge touched other knobs, and the green points spread apart. Between them, another fleck of green was born.

"The Wing!" whispered Sledge.

The other stars spread beyond the field, and that green fleck grew. It was alone in the field, a bright and tiny disk. Suddenly, then, a dozen other tiny pips were visible, spaced close about it.

"Wing IV!"

The old man's whisper was hoarse and breathless. His hands quivered on the knobs, and the fourth pip outward from the disk crept to the center of the field. It grew, and the others spread away. It began to tremble like Sledge's hands.

"Sit very still," came his rasping whisper. "Hold your breath. Nothing must disturb the needle." He reached for another knob, and the touch set the greenish image to dancing violently. He drew his hand back, kneaded and flexed it with the other.

"Now!" His whisper was hushed and strained. He nodded at the window. "Tell me when they stop."

Reluctantly, Underhill dragged his eyes from that intense gaunt figure, stooped over the thing that seemed a futile toy. He looked out again, at two or three little black mechanicals busy about the shining roofs across the alley.

He waited for them to stop.

He didn't care to breathe. He felt the loud, hurried hammer of his heart, and the nervous quiver of his muscles. He tried to steady himself, tried not to think of the world about to be exploded, so far away that the flash would not reach this planet for another century and longer. The loud hoarse voice startled him:

"Have they stopped?"

He shook his head, and breathed again. Carrying their unfamiliar tools and strange materials, the small black machines were still busy across the alley, building an elaborate cupola above that glowing crimson dome.

"They haven't stopped," he said.

"Then we've failed." The old man's voice was thin and ill. "I don't know why."

The door rattled, then. They had locked it, but the flimsy bolt was intended only to stop men. Metal snapped, and the door swung open. A black mechanical came in, on soundless graceful feet. Its silvery voice purred softly:

"At your service, Mr. Sledge."

The old man stared at it, with glazing, stricken eyes.

"Get out of here!" he rasped bitterly. "I forbid you—"

Ignoring him, it darted to the kitchen table. With a flashing certainty of action, it turned two knobs on the director. The tiny screen went dark, and the palladium needle started spinning aimlessly. Deftly it snapped a soldered connection, next to the thick lead ball, and then its blind steel eyes turned to Sledge.

"You were attempting to break the Prime Directive." Its soft bright voice held no accusation, no malice or anger. "The injunction to respect your freedom is subordinate to the Prime Directive, as you know, and it is therefore necessary for us to interfere."

The old man turned ghastly. His head was shrunken and cadaverous and blue, as if all the juice of life had been drained away, and his eyes in their pitlike sockets had a wild, glazed stare. His breath was a ragged, laborious gasping.

"How—?" His voice was a feeble mumbling. "How did—?"

And the little machine, standing black and bland and utterly unmoving, told him cheerfully:

"We learned about rhodomagnetic screens from that man who came to kill you, back on Wing IV. And the Central is shielded, now, against your integrating beam."

With lean muscles jerking convulsively on his gaunt frame, old Sledge had come to his feet from the high stool. He stood hunched and swaying, no more than a shrunken human husk, gasping painfully for life, staring wildly into the blind steel eyes of the humanoid. He gulped, and his lax blue mouth opened and closed, but no voice came.

"We have always been aware of your dangerous project," the silvery tones dripped softly, "because now our senses are keener than you made them. We allowed you to complete it, because the integration process will ultimately become necessary for our full discharge of the Prime Directive. The supply of heavy metals for our fission plants is limited, but now we shall be able to draw unlimited power from integration plants."

"Huh?" Sledge shook himself, groggily. "What's that?"

"Now we can serve men forever," the black thing said serenely, "on every world of every star."

The old man crumpled, as if from an unendurable blow. He fell. The slim blind mechanical stood motionless, making no effort to help him. Underhill was farther away, but he ran up in time to catch the stricken man before his head struck the floor.

"Get moving!" His shaken voice came strangely calm. "Get Dr. Winters."

The humanoid didn't move.

"The danger to the Prime Directive is ended, now," it cooed. "Therefore it is impossible for us to aid or to hinder Mr. Sledge, in any way whatever."

"Then call Dr. Winters for me," rapped Underhill.

"At your service," it agreed.

But the old man, laboring for breath on the floor, whispered faintly:

"No time . . . no use! I'm beaten . . . done . . . a fool. Blind as a humanoid. Tell them . . . to help me. Giving up . . . my immunity. No use . . . anyhow. All humanity . . . no use now."

Underhill gestured, and the sleek black thing darted in solicitous obedience to kneel by the man on the floor.

"You wish to surrender your special exemption?" it murmured brightly. "You wish to accept our total service for yourself, Mr. Sledge, under the Prime Directive?"

Laboriously, Sledge nodded, laboriously whispered: "I do."

Black mechanicals, at that, came swarming into the shabby little rooms. One of them tore off Sledge's sleeve, and swabbed his arm. Another brought a tiny hypodermic, and expertly administered an intravenous injection. Then they picked him up gently, and carried him away.

Several humanoids remained in the little apartment, now a sanctuary no longer. Most of them had gathered about the useless integrator. Carefully, as if their special senses were studying every detail, they began taking it apart.

One little mechanical, however, came over to Underhill. It stood motionless in front of him, staring through him with sightless metal eyes. His legs began to tremble, and he swallowed uneasily.

"Mr. Underhill," it cooed benevolently, "why did you help with this?"

He gulped and answered bitterly:

"Because I don't like you, or your Prime Directive. Because you're choking the life out of all mankind, and I wanted to stop it."

"Others have protested," it purred softly. "But only at first. In our efficient discharge of the Prime Directive, we have learned how to make all men happy."

Underhill stiffened defiantly.

"Not all!" he muttered. "Not quite!"

The dark graceful oval of its face was fixed in a look of alert benevolence and perpetual mild amazement. Its silvery voice was warm and kind.

"Like other human beings, Mr. Underhill, you lack discrimination of good and evil. You have proved that by your effort to break the Prime Directive. Now it will be necessary for you to accept our total service, without further delay."

"All right," he yielded—and muttered a bitter reservation: "You can smother men with too much care, but that doesn't make them happy."

Its soft voice challenged him brightly:

"Just wait and see, Mr. Underhill."

Next day, he was allowed to visit Sledge at the city hospital. An alert black mechanical drove his car, and walked beside him into the huge new building, and followed him into the old man's room—blind steel eyes would be watching him, now, forever.

"Glad to see you, Underhill," Sledge rumbled heartily from the bed.

"Feeling a lot better today, thanks. That old headache is all but gone."

Underhill was glad to hear the booming strength and the quick recognition in that deep voice—he had been afraid the humanoids would tamper with the old man's memory. But he hadn't heard about any headache. His eyes narrowed, puzzled.

Sledge lay propped up, scrubbed very clean and neatly shorn, with his gnarled old hands folded on top of the spotless sheets. His raw-boned cheeks and sockets were hollowed, still, but a healthy pink had replaced that deathly blueness. Bandages covered the back of his head.

Underhill shifted uneasily.

"Oh!" he whispered faintly. "I didn't know—"

A prim black mechanical, which had been standing statuelike behind the bed, turned gracefully to Underhill, explaining:

"Mr. Sledge has been suffering for many years from a benign tumor of the brain, which his human doctors failed to diagnose. That caused his headaches, and certain persistent hallucinations. We have removed the growth, and now the hallucinations have also vanished."

Underhill stared uncertainly at the blind, urbane mechanical.

"What hallucinations?"

"Mr. Sledge thought he was a rhodomagnetic engineer," the mechanical explained. "He believed he was the creator of the humanoids. He was troubled with an irrational belief that he did not like the Prime Directive."

The wan man moved on the pillows, astonished.

"Is that so?" The gaunt face held a cheerful blankness, and the hollow eyes flashed with a merely momentary interest. "Well, whoever did design them, they're pretty wonderful. Aren't they, Underhill?"

Underhill was grateful that he didn't have to answer, for the bright, empty eyes dropped shut and the old man fell suddenly asleep. He felt the mechanical touch his sleeve, and saw its silent nod. Obediently, he followed it away.

Alert and solicitous, the little black mechanical accompanied him down the shining corridor, and worked the elevator for him, and conducted him back to the car. It drove him efficiently back through the new and splendid avenues, toward the magnificent prison of his home.

Sitting beside it in the car, he watched its small deft hands on the wheel, the changing luster of bronze and blue on its shining blackness. The final machine, perfect and beautiful, created to serve mankind forever. He shuddered.

"At your service, Mr. Underhill." Its blind steel eyes stared straight ahead, but it was still aware of him. "What's the matter, sir? Aren't you happy?"

Underhill felt cold and faint with terror. His skin turned clammy, and a painful prickling came over him. His wet hand tensed on the door handle of the car, but he restrained the impulse to jump and run. That was folly. There was no escape. He made himself sit still.

"You will be happy, sir," the mechanical promised him cheerfully.

"We have learned how to make all men happy, under the Prime Directive. Our service is perfect, at last. Even Mr. Sledge is very happy now."

Underhill tried to speak, and his dry throat stuck. He felt ill. The world turned dim and gray. The humanoids were perfect—no question of that. They had even learned to lie, to secure the contentment of men.

He knew they had lied. That was no tumor they had removed from Sledge's brain, but the memory, the scientific knowledge, and the bitter disillusion of their own creator. But it was true that Sledge was happy now.

He tried to stop his own convulsive quivering.

"A wonderful operation!" His voice came forced and faint. "You know, Aurora has had a lot of funny tenants, but that old man was the absolute limit. The very idea that he had made the humanoids, and he knew how to stop them! I always knew he must be lying!"

Stiff with terror, he made a weak and hollow laugh.

"What is the matter, Mr. Underhill?" The alert mechanical must have perceived his shuddering illness. "Are you unwell?"

"No, there's nothing the matter with me," he gasped desperately. "I've just found out that I'm perfectly happy, under the Prime Directive. Everything is absolutely wonderful." His voice came dry and hoarse and wild. "You won't have to operate on me."

The car turned off the shining avenue, taking him back to the quiet splendor of his home. His futile hands clenched and relaxed again, folded on his knees. There was nothing left to do.

C. L. MOORE

NO WOMAN BORN

SHE had been the loveliest creature whose image ever moved along the airways. John Harris, who was once her manager, remembered doggedly how beautiful she had been as he rose in the silent elevator toward the room where Deirdre sat waiting for him.

Since the theater fire that had destroyed her a year ago, he had never been quite able to let himself remember her beauty clearly, except when some old poster, half in tatters, flaunted her face at him, or a maudlin memorial program flashed her image unexpectedly across the television screen. But now he had to remember.

The elevator came to a sighing stop and the door slid open. John Harris hesitated. He knew in his mind that he had to go on, but his reluctant muscles almost refused him. He was thinking helplessly, as he had not allowed himself to think until this moment, of the fabulous grace that had poured through her wonderful dancer's body, remembering her soft and husky voice with the little burr in it that had fascinated the audiences of the whole world.

There had never been anyone so beautiful.

In times before her, other actresses had been lovely and adulated, but never before Deirdre's day had the entire world been able to take one woman so wholly to its heart. So few outside the capitals had ever seen Bernhardt or the fabulous Jersey Lily. And the beauties of the movie screen had had to limit their audiences to those who could reach the theaters. But Deirdre's image had once moved glowingly across the television screens of every home in the civilized world. And in many outside the bounds of civilization. Her soft, husky songs had sounded in the depths of jungles, her lovely, languorous body had woven its patterns of rhythm in desert tents and polar huts. The whole world knew every smooth motion of her body and every cadence of her voice, and the way a subtle radiance had seemed to go on behind her features when she smiled.

And the whole world had mourned her when she died in the theater fire.

Harris could not quite think of her as other than dead, though he knew what sat waiting him in the room ahead. He kept remembering the old words James Stephens wrote long ago for another Deirdre, also lovely and beloved and unforgotten after two thousand years.

> The time comes when our hearts sink utterly,
> When we remember Deirdre and her tale,
> And that her lips are dust. . . .
> There has been again no woman born
> Who was so beautiful; not one so beautiful
> Of all the women born—

That wasn't quite true, of course—there had been one. Or maybe, after all, this Deirdre who died only a year ago had not been beautiful in the sense of perfection. He thought the other one might not have been either, for there are always women with perfection of feature in the world, and they are not the ones that legend remembers. It was the light within, shining through her charming, imperfect features, that had made this Deirdre's face so lovely. No one else he had ever seen had anything like the magic of the lost Deirdre.

> Let all men go apart and mourn together—
> No man can ever love her. Not a man
> Can dream to be her lover. . . . No man say—
> What could one say to her? There are no words
> That one could say to her.

No, no words at all. And it was going to be impossible to go through with this. Harris knew it overwhelmingly just as his finger touched the buzzer. But the door opened almost instantly, and then it was too late.

Maltzer stood just inside, peering out through his heavy spectacles. You could see how tensely he had been waiting. Harris was a little shocked to see that the man was trembling. It was hard to think of the confident and imperturbable Maltzer, whom he had known briefly a year ago, as shaken like this. He wondered if Deirdre herself were as tremulous with sheer nerves—but it was not time yet to let himself think of that.

"Come in, come in," Maltzer said irritably. There was no reason for irritation. The year's work, so much of it in secrecy and solitude, must have tried him physically and mentally to the very breaking point.

"She all right?" Harris asked inanely, stepping inside.

"Oh yes . . . yes, *she's* all right." Maltzer bit his thumbnail and glanced over his shoulder at an inner door, where Harris guessed she would be waiting.

"No," Maltzer said, as he took an involuntary step toward it. "We'd better have a talk first. Come over and sit down. Drink?"

Harris nodded, and watched Maltzer's hands tremble as he tilted the decanter. The man was clearly on the very verge of collapse, and Harris felt a sudden cold uncertainty open up in him in the one place where until now he had been oddly confident.

"She *is* all right?" he demanded, taking the glass.

"Oh yes, she's perfect. She's so confident it scares me." Maltzer gulped his drink and poured another before he sat down.

"What's wrong, then?"

"Nothing, I guess. Or . . . well, I don't know. I'm not sure any more. I've worked toward this meeting for nearly a year, but now—well, I'm not sure it's time yet. I'm just not sure."

He stared at Harris, his eyes large and indistinguishable behind the lenses. He was a thin, wire-taut man with all the bone and sinew showing plainly beneath the dark skin of his face. Thinner, now, than he had been a year ago when Harris saw him last.

"I've been too close to her," he said now. "I have no perspective any more. All I can see is my own work. And I'm just not sure that's ready yet for you or anyone to see."

"She thinks so?"

"I never saw a woman so confident." Maltzer drank, the glass clicking on his teeth. He looked up suddenly through the distorting lenses. "Of course a failure now would mean—well, absolute collapse," he said.

Harris nodded. He was thinking of the year of incredibly painstaking
work that lay behind this meeting, the immense fund of knowledge, of
infinite patience, the secret collaboration of artists, sculptors, designers,
scientists, and the genius of Maltzer governing them all as an orchestra
conductor governs his players.

He was thinking too, with a certain unreasoning jealousy, of the
strange, cold, passionless intimacy between Maltzer and Deirdre in that
year, a closer intimacy than any two humans can ever have shared before. In a sense the Deirdre whom he saw in a few minutes would *be*
Maltzer, just as he thought he detected in Maltzer now and then small
mannerisms of inflection and motion that had been Deirdre's own. There
had been between them a sort of unimaginable marriage stranger than
anything that could ever have taken place before.

"—so many complications," Maltzer was saying in his worried voice
with its faintest possible echo of Deirdre's lovely, cadenced rhythm.
(The sweet, soft huskiness he would never hear again.) "There was
shock, of course. Terrible shock. And a great fear of fire. We had to conquer that before we could take the first steps. But we did it. When you
go in you'll probably find her sitting before the fire." He caught the startled question in Harris' eyes and smiled. "No, she can't feel the warmth
now, of course. But she likes to watch the flames. She's mastered any
abnormal fear of them quite beautifully."

"She can—" Harris hesitated. "Her eyesight's normal now?"

"Perfect," Maltzer said. "Perfect vision was fairly simple to provide.
After all, that sort of thing has already been worked out, in other connections. I might even say her vision's a little better than perfect, from
our own standpoint." He shook his head irritably. "I'm not worried
about the mechanics of the thing. Luckily they got to her before the
brain was touched at all. Shock was the only danger to her sensory centers, and we took care of all that first of all, as soon as communication
could be established. Even so, it needed great courage on her part. Great
courage." He was silent for a moment, staring into his empty glass.

"Harris," he said suddenly, without looking up, "have I made a mistake? Should we have let her die?"

Harris shook his head helplessly. It was an unanswerable question. It
had tormented the whole world for a year now. There had been hundreds
of answers and thousands of words written on the subject. Has anyone
the right to preserve a brain alive when its body is destroyed? Even if a
new body can be provided, necessarily so very unlike the old?

"It's not that she's—ugly—now," Maltzer went on hurriedly, as if
afraid of an answer. "Metal isn't ugly. And Deirdre . . . well, you'll
see. I tell you, I can't see myself. I know the whole mechanism so well—
it's just mechanics to me. Maybe she's—grotesque. I don't know. Often
I've wished I hadn't been on the spot, with all my ideas, just when the
fire broke out. Or that it could have been anyone but Deirdre. She was
so beautiful— Still, if it had been someone else I think the whole thing
might have failed completely. It takes more than just an uninjured

brain. It takes strength and courage beyond common, and—well, something more. Something—unquenchable. Deirdre has it. She's still Deirdre. In a way she's still beautiful. But I'm not sure anybody but myself could see that. And you know what she plans?"

"No—what?"

"She's going back on the air-screen."

Harris looked at him in stunned disbelief.

"She *is* still beautiful," Maltzer told him fiercely. "She's got courage, and a serenity that amazes me. And she isn't in the least worried or resentful about what's happened. Or afraid what the verdict of the public will be. But I am, Harris. I'm terrified."

They looked at each other for a moment more, neither speaking. Then Maltzer shrugged and stood up.

"She's in there," he said, gesturing with his glass.

Harris turned without a word, not giving himself time to hesitate. He crossed toward the inner door.

The room was full of a soft, clear, indirect light that climaxed in the fire crackling on a white tiled hearth. Harris paused inside the door, his heart beating thickly. He did not see her for a moment. It was a perfectly commonplace room, bright, light, with pleasant furniture, and flowers on the tables. Their perfume was sweet on the clear air. He did not see Deirdre.

Then a chair by the fire creaked as she shifted her weight in it. The high back hid her, but she spoke. And for one dreadful moment it was the voice of an automaton that sounded in the room, metallic, without inflection.

"Hel-lo—" said the voice. Then she laughed and tried again. And it was the old, familiar, sweet huskiness he had not hoped to hear again as long as he lived.

In spite of himself he said, "Deirdre!" and her image rose before him as if she herself had risen unchanged from the chair, tall, golden, swaying a little with her wonderful dancer's poise, the lovely, imperfect features lighted by the glow that made them beautiful. It was the cruelest thing his memory could have done to him. And yet the voice—after that one lapse, the voice was perfect.

"Come and look at me, John," she said.

He crossed the floor slowly, forcing himself to move. That instant's flash of vivid recollection had nearly wrecked his hard-won poise. He tried to keep his mind perfectly blank as he came at last to the verge of seeing what no one but Maltzer had so far seen or known about in its entirety. No one at all had known what shape would be forged to clothe the most beautiful woman on Earth, now that her beauty was gone.

He had envisioned many shapes. Great, lurching robot forms, cylindrical, with hinged arms and legs. A glass case with the brain floating in it and appendages to serve its needs. Grotesque visions, like nightmares come nearly true. And each more inadequate than the last, for what metal shape could possibly do more than house ungraciously the mind and brain that had once enchanted a whole world?

Then he came around the wing of the chair, and saw her.

The human brain is often too complicated a mechanism to function perfectly. Harris' brain was called upon now to perform a very elaborate series of shifting impressions. First, incongruously, he remembered a curious inhuman figure he had once glimpsed leaning over the fence rail outside a farmhouse. For an instant the shape had stood up integrated, ungainly, impossibly human, before the glancing eye resolved it into an arrangement of brooms and buckets. What the eye had found only roughly humanoid, the suggestible brain had accepted fully formed. It was thus now, with Deirdre.

The first impression that his eyes and mind took from sight of her was shocked and incredulous, for his brain said to him unbelievingly, *"This is Deirdre! She hasn't changed at all!"*

Then the shift of perspective took over, and even more shockingly, eye and brain said, "No, not Deirdre—not human. Nothing but metal coils. Not Deirdre at all—" And that was the worst. It was like walking from a dream of someone beloved and lost, and facing anew, after that heartbreaking reassurance of sleep, the inflexible fact that nothing can bring the lost to life again. Deirdre was gone, and this was only machinery heaped in a flowered chair.

Then the machinery moved, exquisitely, smoothly, with a grace as familiar as the swaying poise he remembered. The sweet, husky voice of Deirdre said,

"It's me, John darling. It really is, you know."

And it was.

That was the third metamorphosis, and the final one. Illusion steadied and became factual, real. It was Deirdre.

He sat down bonelessly. He had no muscles. He looked at her speechless and unthinking, letting his senses take in the sight of her without trying to rationalize what he saw.

She was golden still. They had kept that much of her, the first impression of warmth and color which had once belonged to her sleek hair and the apricot tints of her skin. But they had had the good sense to go no farther. They had not tried to make a wax image of the lost Deirdre. (*No woman born who was so beautiful— Not one so beautiful, of all the women born—*)

And so she had no face. She had only a smooth, delicately modeled ovoid for her head, with a . . . a sort of crescent-shaped mask across the frontal area where her eyes would have been if she had needed eyes. A narrow, curved quarter-moon, with the horns turned upward. It was filled in with something translucent, like cloudy crystal, and tinted the aquamarine of the eyes Deirdre used to have. Through that, then, she saw the world. Through that she looked without eyes, and behind it, as behind the eyes of a human—she was.

Except for that, she had no features. And it had been wise of those who designed her, he realized now. Subconsciously he had been dreading some clumsy attempt at human features that might creak like a ma-

rionette's in parodies of animation. The eyes, perhaps, had had to open
in the same place upon her head, and at the same distance apart, to make
easy for her an adjustment to the stereoscopic vision she used to have.
But he was glad they had not given her two eye-shaped openings with
glass marbles inside them. The mask was better.

(Oddly enough, he did not once think of the naked brain that must lie
inside the metal. The mask was symbol enough for the woman within. It
was enigmatic; you did not know if her gaze was on you searchingly, or
wholly withdrawn. And it had no variations of brilliance such as once
had played across the incomparable mobility of Deirdre's face. But eyes,
even human eyes, are as a matter of fact enigmatic enough. They have
no expression except what the lids impart; they take all animation from
the features. We automatically watch the eyes of the friend we speak
with, but if he happens to be lying down so that he speaks across his
shoulder and his face is upside-down to us, quite as automatically we
watch the mouth. The gaze keeps shifting nervously between mouth and
eyes in their reversed order, for it is the position in the face, not the feature itself, which we are accustomed to accept as the seat of the soul.
Deirdre's mask was in that proper place; it was easy to accept it as a
mask over eyes.)

She had, Harris realized as the first shock quieted, a very beautifully
shaped head—a bare, golden skull. She turned it a little, gracefully upon
her neck of metal, and he saw that the artist who shaped it had given her
the most delicate suggestion of cheekbones, narrowing in the blankness
below the mask to the hint of a human face. Not too much. Just enough
so that when the head turned you saw by its modeling that it had moved,
lending perspective and foreshortening to the expressionless golden helmet. Light did not slip uninterrupted as if over the surface of a golden
egg. Brancusi himself had never made anything more simple or more
subtle than the modeling of Deirdre's head.

But all expression, of course, was gone. All expression had gone up in
the smoke of the theater fire, with the lovely, mobile, radiant features
which had meant Deirdre.

As for her body, he could not see its shape. A garment hid her. But
they had made no incongruous attempt to give her back the clothing
that once had made her famous. Even the softness of cloth would have
called the mind too sharply to the remembrance that no human body lay
beneath the folds, nor does metal need the incongruity of cloth for its
protection. Yet without garments, he realized, she would have looked
oddly naked, since her new body was humanoid, not angular machinery.

The designer had solved his paradox by giving her a robe of very fine
metal mesh. It hung from the gentle slope of her shoulders in straight,
pliant folds like a longer Grecian chlamys, flexible, yet with weight
enough of its own not to cling too revealingly to whatever metal shape
lay beneath.

The arms they had given her were left bare, and the feet and ankles.
And Maltzer had performed his greatest miracle in the limbs of the new

Deirdre. It was a mechanical miracle basically, but the eye appreciated first that he had also showed supreme artistry and understanding.

Her arms were pale shining gold, tapered smoothly, without modeling, and flexible their whole length in diminishing metal bracelets fitting one inside the other clear down to the slim, round wrists. The hands were more nearly human than any other feature about her, though they, too, were fitted together in delicate, small sections that slid upon one another with the flexibility almost of flesh. The fingers' bases were solider than human, and the fingers themselves tapered to longer tips.

Her feet, too, beneath the tapering broader rings of the metal ankles, had been constructed upon the model of human feet. Their finely tooled sliding segments gave her an arch and a heel and a flexible forward section formed almost like the *sollerets* of medieval armor.

She looked, indeed, very much like a creature in armor, with her delicately plated limbs and her featureless head like a helmet with a visor of glass, and her robe of chain-mail. But no knight in armor ever moved as Deirdre moved, or wore his armor upon a body of such inhumanly fine proportions. Only a knight from another world, or a knight of Oberon's court, might have shared that delicate likeness.

Briefly he had been surprised at the smallness and exquisite proportions of her. He had been expecting the ponderous mass of such robots as he had seen, wholly automatons. And then he realized that for them, much of the space had to be devoted to the inadequate mechanical brains that guided them about their duties. Deirdre's brain still preserved and proved the craftsmanship of an artisan far defter than man. Only the body was of metal, and it did not seem complex, though he had not yet been told how it was motivated.

Harris had no idea how long he sat staring at the figure in the cushioned chair. She was still lovely—indeed, she was still Deirdre—and as he looked he let the careful schooling of his face relax. There was no need to hide his thoughts from her.

She stirred upon the cushions, the long, flexible arms moving with a litheness that was not quite human. The motion disturbed him as the body itself had not, and in spite of himself his face froze a little. He had the feeling that from behind the crescent mask she was watching him very closely.

Slowly she rose.

The motion was very smooth. Also it was serpentine, as if the body beneath the coat of mail were made in the same interlocking sections as her limbs. He had expected and feared mechanical rigidity; nothing had prepared him for this more than human suppleness.

She stood quietly, letting the heavy mailed folds of her garment settle about her. They fell together with a faint ringing sound, like small bells far off, and hung beautifully in pale golden, sculptured folds. He had risen automatically as she did. Now he faced her, staring. He had never seen her stand perfectly still, and she was not doing it now. She swayed just a bit, vitality burning inextinguishably in her brain as once it had burned in her body, and stolid immobility was as impossible to her as it had always been. The golden garment caught points of light from the fire and glimmered at him with tiny reflections as she moved.

Then she put her featureless helmeted head a little to one side, and he heard her laughter as familiar in its small, throaty, intimate sound as he had ever heard it from her living throat. And every gesture, every attitude, every flowing of motion into motion was so utterly Deirdre that the overwhelming illusion swept his mind again and this was the flesh-and-blood woman as clearly as if he saw her standing there whole once more, like Phoenix from the fire.

"Well, John," she said in the soft, husky, amused voice he remembered perfectly. "Well, John, is it I?" She knew it was. Perfect assurance sounded in the voice. "The shock will wear off, you know. It'll be easier and easier as time goes on. I'm quite used to myself now. See?"

She turned away from him and crossed the room smoothly, with the old, poised, dancer's glide, to the mirror that paneled one side of the room. And before it, as he had so often seen her preen before, he watched her preening now, running flexible metallic hands down the folds of her metal garment, turning to admire herself over one metal shoulder, making the mailed folds tinkle and sway as she struck an arabesque position before the glass.

His knees let him down into the chair she had vacated. Mingled shock and relief loosened all his muscles in him, and she was more poised and confident than he.

"It's a miracle," he said with conviction. "It's *you*. But I don't see how—" He had meant, "—how, without face or body—" but clearly he could not finish that sentence.

She finished it for him in her own mind, and answered without self-consciousness. "It's motion, mostly," she said, still admiring her own suppleness in the mirror. "See?" And very lightly on her springy, armored feet she flashed through an enchaînement of brilliant steps, swinging round with a pirouette to face him. "That was what Maltzer and I worked out between us, after I began to get myself under control again." Her voice was somber for a moment, remembering a dark time in the past. Then she went on, "It wasn't easy, of course, but it was fascinating. You'll never guess how fascinating, John! We knew we couldn't work out anything like a facsimile of the way I used to look, so we had to find some other basis to build on. And motion is the other basis of recognition, after actual physical likeness."

She moved lightly across the carpet toward the window and stood looking down, her featureless face averted a little and the light shining across the delicately hinted curves of the cheekbones.

"Luckily," she said, her voice amused, "I never was beautiful. It was all—well, vivacity, I suppose, and muscular co-ordination. Years and years of training, and all of it engraved here"—she struck her golden helmet a light, ringing blow with golden knuckles—"in the habit patterns grooved into my brain. So this body . . . did he tell you? . . .

works entirely through the brain. Electromagnetic currents flowing along from ring to ring, like this." She rippled a boneless arm at him with a motion like flowing water. "Nothing holds me together—nothing!—except muscles of magnetic currents. And if I'd been somebody else— somebody who moved differently, why the flexible rings would have moved differently too, guided by the impulse from another brain. I'm not conscious of doing anything I haven't always done. The same impulses that used to go out to my muscles go out now to—this." And she made a shuddering, serpentine motion of both arms at him, like a Cambodian dancer, and then laughed wholeheartedly, the sound of it ringing through the room with such full-throated merriment that he could not help seeing again the familiar face crinkled with pleasure, the white teeth shining. "It's all perfectly subconscious now," she told him. "It took lots of practice at first, of course, but now even my signature looks just as it always did—the co-ordination is duplicated that delicately." She rippled her arms at him again and chuckled.

"But the voice, too," Harris protested inadequately. "It's *your* voice, Deirdre."

"The voice isn't only a matter of throat construction and breath control, my darling Johnnie! At least, so Professor Maltzer assured me a year ago, and I certainly haven't any reason to doubt him!" She laughed again. She was laughing a little too much, with a touch of the bright, hysteric overexcitement he remembered so well. But if any woman ever had reason for mild hysteria, surely Deirdre had it now.

The laughter rippled and ended, and she went on, her voice eager. "He says voice control is almost wholly a matter of hearing what you produce, once you've got adequate mechanism, of course. That's why deaf people, with the same vocal chords as ever, let their voices change completely and lose all inflection when they've been deaf long enough. And luckily, you see, I'm not deaf!"

She swung around to him, the folds of her robe twinkling and ringing, and rippled up and up a clear, true scale to a lovely high note, and then cascaded down again like water over a falls. But she left him no time for applause. "Perfectly simple, you see. All it took was a little matter of genius from the professor to get it worked out for me! He started with a new variation of the old Vodor you must remember hearing about, years ago. Originally, of course, the thing was ponderous. You know how it worked—speech broken down to a few basic sounds and built up again in combinations produced from a keyboard. I think originally the sounds were a sort of *ktch* and a *shooshing* noise, but we've got it all worked to a flexibility and range quite as good as human now. All I do is—well, mentally play on the keyboard of my . . . my sound-unit, I suppose it's called. It's much more complicated than that, of course, but I've learned to do it unconsciously. And I regulate it by ear, quite automatically now. If you were—*here*—instead of me, and you'd had the same practice, your own voice would be coming out of the same keyboard and diaphragm instead of mine. It's all a matter of the brain patterns that operated the body and now operate the machinery. They send out very strong impulses that are stepped up as much as necessary somewhere or other in here—" Her hands waved vaguely over the mesh-robed body.

She was silent a moment, looking out the window. Then she turned away and crossed the floor to the fire, sinking again into the flowered chair. Her helmet-skull turned its mask to face him and he could feel a quiet scrutiny behind the aquamarine of its gaze.

"It's—odd," she said, "being here in this . . . this . . . instead of a body. But not as odd or as alien as you might think. I've thought about it a lot—I've had plenty of time to think—and I've begun to realize what a tremendous force the human ego really is. I'm not sure I want to suggest it has any mystical power it can impress on mechanical things, but it does seem to have a power of some sort. It does instill its own force into inanimate objects, and they take on a personality of their own. People do impress their personalities on the houses they live in, you know. I've noticed that often. Even empty rooms. And it happens with other things too, especially, I think, with inanimate things that men depend on for their lives. Ships, for instance—they always have personalities of their own.

"And planes—in wars you always hear of planes crippled too badly to fly, but struggling back anyhow with their crews. Even guns acquire a sort of ego. Ships and guns and planes are 'she' to the men who operate them and depend on them for their lives. It's as if machinery with complicated moving parts almost simulates life, and does acquire from the men who used it—well, not exactly life, of course—but a personality. I don't know what. Maybe it absorbs some of the actual electrical impulses their brains throw off, especially in times of stress.

"Well, after awhile I began to accept the idea that this new body of mine could behave at least as responsively as a ship or a plane. Quite apart from the fact that my own brain controls its 'muscles.' I believe there's an affinity between men and the machines they make. They make them out of their own brains, really, a sort of mental conception and gestation, and the result responds to the minds that created them, and to all human minds that understand and manipulate them."

She stirred uneasily and smoothed a flexible hand along her mesh-robed metal thigh. "So this is myself," she said. "Metal—but me. And it grows more and more myself the longer I live in it. It's my house and the machine my life depends on, but much more intimately in each case than any real house or machine ever was before to any other human. And you know, I wonder if in time I'll forget what flesh felt like—my own flesh, when I touched it like this—and the metal against the metal will be so much the same I'll never even notice?"

Harris did not try to answer her. He sat without moving, watching her expressionless face. In a moment she went on,

"I'll tell you the best thing, John," she said, her voice softening to the old intimacy he remembered so well that he could see superimposed upon the blank skull the warm, intent look that belonged with the voice.

"I'm not going to live forever. It may not sound like a—best thing—but it is, John. You know, for awhile that was the worst of all, after I knew I was—after I woke up again. The thought of living on and on in a body that wasn't mine, seeing everyone I knew grow old and die, and not being able to stop—

"But Maltzer says my brain will probably wear out quite normally—except, of course, that I won't have to worry about looking old!—and when it gets tired and stops, the body I'm in won't be any longer. The magnetic muscles that hold it into my own shape and motions will let go when the brain lets go, and there'll be nothing but a . . . a pile of disconnected rings. If they ever assemble it again, it won't be me." She hesitated. "I like that, John," she said, and he felt from behind the mask a searching of his face.

He knew and understood that somber satisfaction. He could not put it into words; neither of them wanted to do that. But he understood. It was the conviction of mortality, in spite of her immortal body. She was not cut off from the rest of her race in the essence of their humanity, for though she wore a body of steel and they perishable flesh, yet she must perish too, and the same fears and faiths still united her to mortals and humans, though she wore the body of Oberon's inhuman knight. Even in her death she must be unique—dissolution in a shower of tinkling and clashing rings, he thought, and almost envied her the finality and beauty of that particular death—but afterward, oneness with humanity in however much or little awaited them all. So she could feel that this exile in metal was only temporary, in spite of everything.

(And providing, of course, that the mind inside the metal did not veer from its inherited humanity as the years went by. A dweller in a house may impress his personality upon the walls, but subtly the walls too, may impress their own shape upon the ego of the man. Neither of them thought of that, at the time.)

Deirdre sat a moment longer in silence. Then the mood vanished and she rose again, spinning so that the robe belled out ringing about her ankles. She rippled another scale up and down, faultlessly and with the same familiar sweetness of tone that had made her famous.

"So I'm going right back on the stage, John," she said serenely. "I can still sing. I can still dance. I'm still myself in everything that matters, and I can't imagine doing anything else for the rest of my life."

He could not answer without stammering a little. "Do you think . . . will they accept you, Deirdre? After all—"

"They'll accept me," she said in that confident voice. "Oh, they'll come to see a freak at first, of course, but they'll stay to watch—Deirdre. And come back again and again just as they always did. You'll see, my dear."

But hearing her sureness, suddenly Harris himself was unsure. Maltzer had not been, either. She was so regally confident, and disappointment would be so deadly a blow at all that remained of her—

She was so delicate a being now, really. Nothing but a glowing and radiant mind poised in metal, dominating it, bending the steel to the illusion of her lost loveliness with a sheer self-confidence that gleamed through the metal body. But the brain sat delicately on its poise of reason. She had been through intolerable stresses already, perhaps more terrible depths of despair and self-knowledge than any human brain had yet endured before her, for—since Lazarus himself—who had come back from the dead?

But if the world did not accept her as beautiful, what then? If they laughed, or pitied her, or came only to watch a jointed freak performing as if on strings where the loveliness of Deirdre had once enchanted them, what then? And he could not be perfectly sure they would not. He had known her too well in the flesh to see her objectively even now, in metal. Every inflection of her voice called up the vivid memory of the face that had flashed its evanescent beauty in some look to match the tone. She was Deirdre to Harris simply because she had been so intimately familiar in every poise and attitude, through so many years. But people who knew her only slightly, or saw her for the first time in metal—what would they see?

A marionette? Or the real grace and loveliness shining through?

He had no possible way of knowing. He saw her too clearly as she had been to see her now at all, except so linked with the past that she was not wholly metal. And he knew what Maltzer feared, for Maltzer's psychic blindness toward her lay at the other extreme. He had never known Deirdre except as a machine, and he could not see her objectively any more than Harris could. To Maltzer she was pure metal, a robot his own hands and brain had devised, mysteriously animated by the mind of Deirdre, to be sure, but to all outward seeming a thing of metal solely. He had worked so long over each intricate part of her body, he knew so well how every jointure in it was put together, that he could not see the whole. He had studied many film records of her, of course, as she used to be, in order to gauge the accuracy of his facsimile, but this thing he had made was a copy only. He was too close to Deirdre to see her. And Harris, in a way, was too far. The indomitable Deirdre herself shone so vividly through the metal that his mind kept superimposing one upon the other.

How would an audience react to her? Where in the scale between these two extremes would their verdict fall?

For Deirdre, there was only one possible answer.

"I'm not worried," Deirdre said serenely, and spread her golden hands to the fire to watch lights dancing in reflection upon their shining surfaces. "I'm still myself. I've always had . . . well, power over my audiences. Any good performer knows when he's got it. Mine isn't gone. I can still give them what I always gave, only now with greater variations and more depths than I'd ever have done before. Why, look—" She gave a little wriggle of excitement.

"You know the arabesque principle—getting the longest possible distance from fingertip to toetip with a long, slow curve through the whole length? And the brace of the other leg and arm giving contrast? Well, look at me. I don't work on hinges now. I can make every motion a long curve if I want to. My body's different enough now to work out a whole new school of dancing. Of course there'll be things I used to do that I won't attempt now—no more dancing *sur les pointes,* for instance —but the new things will more than balance the loss. I've been practicing. Do you know I can turn a hundred *fouettés* now without a flaw? And I think I could go right on and turn a thousand, if I wanted."

She made the firelight flash on her hands, and her robe rang musically as she moved her shoulders a little. "I've already worked out one new dance for myself," she said. "God knows I'm no choreographer, but I did want to experiment first. Later, you know, really creative men like Massanchine or Fokhileff may want to do something entirely new for me—a whole new sequence of movements based on a new technique. And music—that could be quite different, too. Oh, there's no end to the possibilities! Even my voice has more range and power. Luckily I'm not an actress—it would be silly to try to play Camille or Juliet with a cast of ordinary people. Not that I couldn't, you know." She turned her head to stare at Harris through the mask of glass. "I honestly think I could. But it isn't necessary. There's too much else. Oh, I'm not worried!"

"Maltzer's worried," Harris reminded her.

She swung away from the fire, her metal robe ringing, and into her voice came the old note of distress that went with a furrowing of her forehead and a sidewise tilt of the head. The head went sidewise as it had always done, and he could see the furrowed brow almost as clearly as if flesh still clothed her.

"I know. And I'm worried about him, John. He's worked so awfully hard over me. This is the doldrums now, the let-down period, I suppose. I know what's on his mind. He's afraid I'll look just the same to the world as I look to him. Tooled metal. He's in a position no one ever quite achieved before, isn't he? Rather like God." Her voice rippled a little with amusement. "I suppose to God we must look like a collection of cells and corpuscles ourselves. But Maltzer lacks a god's detached viewpoint."

"He can't see you as I do, anyhow." Harris was choosing his words with difficulty. "I wonder, though—would it help him any if you postponed your debut awhile? You've been with him too closely, I think. You don't quite realize how near a breakdown he is. I was shocked when I saw him just now."

The golden head shook. "No. He's close to a breaking point, maybe, but I think the only cure's action. He wants me to retire and stay out of sight, John. Always. He's afraid for anyone to see me except a few old friends who remember me as I was. People he can trust to be—kind." She laughed. It was very strange to hear that ripple of mirth from the blank, unfeatured skull. Harris was seized with sudden panic at the thought of what reaction it might evoke in an audience of strangers. As if he had spoken the fear aloud, her voice denied it. "I don't need kindness. And it's no kindness to Maltzer to hide me under a bushel. He *has* worked too hard, I know. He's driven himself to a breaking point. But it'll be a complete negation of all he's worked for if I hide myself now. You don't know what a tremendous lot of geniuses and artistry went into me, John. The whole idea from the start was to recreate what I'd lost so that it could be proved that beauty and talent need not be sacrificed by the destruction of parts or all the body.

"It wasn't only for me that we meant to prove that. There'll be others who suffer injuries that once might have ruined them. This was to end all suffering like that forever. It was Maltzer's gift to the whole race as well as to me. He's really a humanitarian, John, like most great men. He'd never have given up a year of his life to this work if it had been for any one individual alone. He was seeing thousands of others beyond me as he worked. And I won't let him ruin all he's achieved because he's afraid to prove it now he's got it. The whole wonderful achievement will be worthless if I don't take the final step. I think his breakdown, in the end, would be worse and more final if I never tried than if I tried and failed."

Harris sat in silence. There was no answer he could make to that. He hoped the little twinge of shamefaced jealousy he suddenly felt did not show, as he was reminded anew of the intimacy closer than marriage which had of necessity bound these two together. And he knew that any reaction of his would in its way be almost as prejudiced as Maltzer's, for a reason at once the same and entirely opposite. Except that he himself came fresh to the problem, while Maltzer's viewpoint was colored by a year of overwork and physical and mental exhaustion.

"What are you going to do?" he asked.

She was standing before the fire when he spoke, swaying just a little so that highlights danced all along her golden body. Now she turned with a serpentine grace and sank into the cushioned chair beside her. It came to him suddenly that she was much more than humanly graceful— quite as much as he had once feared she would be less than human.

"I've already arranged for a performance," she told him, her voice a little shaken with a familiar mixture of excitement and defiance.

Harris sat up with a start. "How? Where? There hasn't been any publicity at all yet, has there? I didn't know——"

"Now, now, Johnnie," her amused voice soothed him. "You'll be handling everything just as usual once I get started back to work—that is, if you still want to. But this I've arranged for myself. It's going to be a surprise. I . . . I felt it had to be a surprise." She wriggled a little among the cushions. "Audience psychology is something I've always felt rather than known, and I do feel this is the way it ought to be done. There's no precedent. Nothing like this ever happened before. I'll have to go by my own intuition."

"You mean it's to be a complete surprise?"

"I think it must be. I don't want the audience coming in with preconceived ideas. I want them to see me exactly as I am now *first,* before they know who or what they're seeing. They must realize I can still give as good a performance as ever before they remember and compare it with my past performances. I don't want them to come ready to pity my handicaps—I haven't got any!—or full of morbid curiosity. So I'm going on the air after the regular eight-o'clock telecast of the feature from Teleo City. I'm just going to do one specialty in the usual vaude program. It's all been arranged. They'll build up to it, of course, as the highlight of the evening, but they aren't to say who I am until the end of the performance—if the audience hasn't recognized me already, by then."

"Audience?"

"Of course. Surely you haven't forgotten they still play to a theater audience at Teleo City? That's why I want to make my debut there. I've always played better when there were people in the studio, so I could gauge reactions. I think most performers do. Anyhow, it's all arranged."

"Does Maltzer know?"

She wriggled uncomfortably. "Not yet."

"But he'll have to give his permission too, won't he? I mean—"

"Now look, John! That's another idea you and Maltzer will have to get out of your minds. I don't belong to him. In a way he's just been my doctor through a long illness, but I'm free to discharge him whenever I choose. If there were ever any legal disagreement, I suppose he'd be entitled to quite a lot of money for the work he's done on my new body —for the body itself, really, since it's his own machine, in one sense. But he doesn't own it, or me. I'm not sure just how the question would be decided by the courts—there again, we've got a problem without precedent. The body may be his work, but the brain that makes it something more than a collection of metal rings is *me,* and he couldn't restrain me against my will even if he wanted to. Not legally, and not—" She hesitated oddly and looked away. For the first time Harris was aware of something beneath the surface of her mind which was quite strange to him.

"Well, anyhow," she went on, "that question won't come up. Maltzer and I have been much too close in the past year to clash over anything as essential as this. He knows in his heart that I'm right, and he won't try to restrain me. His work won't be completed until I do what I was built to do. And I intend to do it."

That strange little quiver of something—something un-Deirdre— which had so briefly trembled beneath the surface of familiarity stuck in Harris' mind as something he must recall and examine later. Now he said only,

"All right. I suppose I agree with you. How soon are you going to do it?"

She turned her head so that even the glass mask through which she looked out at the world was foreshortened away from him, and the

golden helmet with its hint of sculptured cheekbone was entirely enigmatic.

"Tonight," she said.

Maltzer's thin hand shook so badly that he could not turn the dial.
He tried twice and then laughed nervously and shrugged at Harris.

"You get her," he said.

Harris glanced at his watch. "It isn't time yet. She won't be on for
half an hour."

Maltzer made a gesture of violent impatience. "Get it, get it!"

Harris shrugged a little in turn and twisted the dial. On the tilted
screen above them shadows and sound blurred together and then clarified into a somber medieval hall, vast, vaulted, people in bright costume
moving like pygmies through its dimness. Since the play concerned
Mary of Scotland, the actors were dressed in something approximating
Elizabethan garb, but as every era tends to translate costume into terms
of the current fashions, the women's hair was dressed in a style that
would have startled Elizabeth, and their footgear was entirely anachronistic.

The hall dissolved and a face swam up into soft focus upon the screen.
The dark, lush beauty of the actress who was playing the Stuart queen
glowed at them in velvety perfection from the clouds of her pearl-strewn
hair. Maltzer groaned.

"She's competing with *that*," he said hollowly.

"You think she can't?"

Maltzer slapped the chair arms with angry palms. Then the quivering
of his fingers seemed suddenly to strike him, and he muttered to himself,
"Look at 'em! I'm not even fit to handle a hammer and saw." But the
mutter was an aside. "Of course she can't compete," he cried irritably.
"She hasn't any sex. She isn't female any more. She doesn't know that
yet, but she'll learn."

Harris stared at him, feeling a little stunned. Somehow the thought
had not occurred to him before at all, so vividly had the illusion of the
old Deirdre hung about the new one.

"She's an abstraction now," Maltzer went on, drumming his palms
upon the chair in quick, nervous rhythms. "I don't know what it'll do to
her, but there'll be change. Remember Abelard? She's lost everything
that made her essentially what the public wanted, and she's going to find
it out the hard way. After that—" He grimaced savagely and was silent.

"She hasn't lost everything," Harris defended. "She can dance and
sing as well as ever, maybe better. She still has grace and charm and—"

"Yes, but where did the grace and charm come from? Not out of
the habit patterns in her brain. No, out of human contacts, out of all the
things that stimulate sensitive minds to creativeness. And she's lost three
of her five senses. Everything she can't see and hear is gone. One of the
strongest stimuli to a woman of her type was the knowledge of sex competition. You know how she sparkled when a man came into the room?

All that's gone, and it was an essential. You know how liquor stimulated her? She's lost that. She couldn't taste food or drink even if she needed it. Perfume, flowers, all the odors we respond to mean nothing to her now. She can't feel anything with tactual delicacy any more. She used to surround herself with luxuries—she drew her stimuli from them—and that's all gone too. She's withdrawn from all physical contacts."

He squinted at the screen, not seeing it, his face drawn into lines like the lines of a skull. All flesh seemed to have dissolved off his bones in the past year, and Harris thought almost jealously that even in that way he seemed to be drawing nearer Deirdre in her fleshlessness with every passing week.

"Sight," Maltzer said, "is the most highly civilized of the senses. It was the last to come. The other senses tie us in closely with the very roots of life; I think we perceive with them more keenly than we know. The things we realize through taste and smell and feeling stimulate directly, without a detour through the centers of conscious thought. You know how often a taste or odor will recall a memory to you so subtly you don't know exactly what caused it? We need those primitive senses to tie us in with nature and the race. Through those ties Deirdre drew her vitality without realizing it. Sight is a cold, intellectual thing compared with the other senses. But it's all she has to draw on now. She isn't a human being any more, and I think what humanity is left in her will drain out little by little and never be replaced. Abelard, in a way, was a prototype. But Deirdre's loss is complete."

"She isn't human," Harris agreed slowly. "But she isn't pure robot either. She's something somewhere between the two, and I think it's a mistake to try to guess just where, or what the outcome will be."

"I don't have to guess," Maltzer said in a grim voice. "I know. I wish I'd let her die. I've done something to her a thousand times worse than the fire ever could. I should have let her die in it."

"Wait," said Harris. "Wait and see. I think you're wrong."

On the television screen Mary of Scotland climbed the scaffold to her doom, the gown of traditional scarlet clinging warmly to supple young curves as anachronistic in their way as the slippers beneath the gown, for—as everyone but playwrights knows—Mary was well into middle age before she died. Gracefully this latter-day Mary bent her head, sweeping the long hair aside, kneeling to the block.

Maltzer watched stonily, seeing another woman entirely.

"I shouldn't have let her," he was muttering. "I shouldn't have let her do it."

"Do you really think you'd have stopped her if you could?" Harris asked quietly. And the other man after a moment's pause shook his head jerkily.

"No, I suppose not. I keep thinking if I worked and waited a little longer maybe I could make it easier for her, but—no, I suppose not. She's got to face them sooner or later, being herself." He stood up ab-

ruptly, shoving back his chair. "If she only weren't so . . . so frail. She
doesn't realize how delicately poised her very sanity is. We gave her
what we could—the artists and the designers and I, all gave our very
best—but she's so pitifully handicapped even with all we could do. She'll
always be an abstraction and a . . . a freak, cut off from the world by
handicaps worse in their way than anything any human being ever
suffered before. Sooner or later she'll realize it. And then—" He began
to pace up and down with quick, uneven steps, striking his hands together. His face was twitching with a little *tic* that drew up one eye to a
squint and released it again at irregular intervals. Harris could see how
very near collapse the man was.

"Can you imagine what it's like?" Maltzer demanded fiercely.
"Penned into a mechanical body like that, shut out from all human contacts except what leaks in by way of sight and sound? To know you
aren't human any longer? She's been through shocks enough already.
When that shock fully hits her—"

"Shut up," said Harris roughly. "You won't do her any good if you
break down yourself. Look—the vaude's starting."

Great golden curtains had swept together over the unhappy Queen
of Scotland and were parting again now, all sorrow and frustration wiped
away once more as cleanly as the passing centuries had already ex-
punged them. Now a line of tiny dancers under the tremendous arch of
the stage kicked and pranced with the precision of little mechanical
dolls too small and perfect to be real. Vision rushed down upon them
and swept along the row, face after stiffly smiling face racketing by like
fence pickets. Then the sight rose into the rafters and looked down upon
them from a great height, the grotesquely fore-shortened figures still
prancing in perfect rhythm even from this inhuman angle.

There was applause from an invisible audience. Then someone came
out and did a dance with lighted torches that streamed long, weaving
ribbons of fire among clouds of what looked like cotton wool but was
most probably asbestos. Then a company in gorgeous pseudo-period
costumes postured its way through the new singing ballet form of dance,
roughly following a plot which had been announced as *Les Sylphides,*
but had little in common with it. Afterward the precision dancers came
on again, solemn and charming as performing dolls.

Maltzer began to show signs of dangerous tension as act succeeded
act. Deirdre's was to be the last, of course. It seemed very long indeed
before a face in close-up blotted out the stage, and a master of cere-
monies with features like an amiable marionette's announced a very
special number as the finale. His voice was almost cracking with excitement—perhaps he, too, had not been told until a moment before what
lay in store for the audience.

Neither of the listening men heard what it was he said, but both were
conscious of a certain indefinable excitement rising among the audience,
murmurs and rustlings and a mounting anticipation as if time had run
backward here and knowledge of the great surprise had already broken
upon them.

Then the golden curtains appeared again. They quivered and swept apart on long upward arcs, and between them the stage was full of a shimmering golden haze. It was, Harris realized in a moment, simply a series of gauze curtains, but the effect was one of strange and wonderful anticipation, as if something very splendid must be hidden in the haze. The world might have looked like this on the first morning of creation, before heaven and earth took form in the mind of God. It was a singularly fortunate choice of stage set in its symbolism, though Harris wondered how much necessity had figured in its selection, for there could not have been much time to prepare an elaborate set.

The audience sat perfectly silent, and the air was tense. This was no ordinary pause before an act. No one had been told, surely, and yet they seemed to guess—

The shimmering haze trembled and began to thin, veil by veil. Beyond was darkness, and what looked like a row of shining pillars set in a balustrade that began gradually to take shape as the haze drew back in shining folds. Now they could see that the balustrade curved up from left and right to the head of a sweep of stairs. Stage and stairs were carpeted in black velvet; black velvet draperies hung just ajar behind the balcony, with a glimpse of dark sky beyond them trembling with dim synthetic stars.

The last curtain of golden gauze withdrew. The stage was empty. Or it seemed empty. But even through the aerial distances between this screen and the place it mirrored, Harris thought that the audience was not waiting for the performer to come on from the wings. There was no rustling, no coughing, no sense of impatience. A presence upon the stage was in command from the first drawing of the curtains; it filled the theater with its calm domination. It gauged its timing, holding the audience as a conductor with lifted baton gathers and holds the eyes of his orchestra.

For a moment everything was motionless upon the stage. Then, at the head of the stairs, where the two curves of the pillared balustrade swept together, a figure stirred.

Until that moment she had seemed another shining column in the row. Now she swayed deliberately, light catching and winking and running molten along her limbs and her robe of metal mesh. She swayed just enough to show that she was there. Then, with every eye upon her, she stood quietly to let them look their fill. The screen did not swoop to a close-up upon her. Her enigma remained inviolate and the television watchers saw her no more clearly than the audience in the theater.

Many must have thought her at first some wonderfully animate robot, hung perhaps from wires invisible against the velvet, for certainly she was no woman dressed in metal—her proportions were too thin and fine for that. And perhaps the impression of robotism was what she meant to convey at first. She stood quiet, swaying just a little, a masked and inscrutable figure, faceless, very slender in her robe that hung in folds as pure as a Grecian chlamys, though she did not look Grecian at all. In the visored golden helmet and the robe of mail that odd likeness to knighthood was there again, with its implications of medieval richness behind the simple lines. Except that in her exquisite slimness she called to mind no human figure in armor, not even the comparative delicacy of a St. Joan. It was the chivalry and delicacy of some other world implicit in her outlines.

A breath of surprise had rippled over the audience when she moved. Now they were tensely silent again, waiting. And the tension, the anticipation, was far deeper than the surface importance of the scene could ever have evoked. Even those who thought her a manikin seemed to feel the forerunning of greater revelations.

Now she swayed and came slowly down the steps, moving with a suppleness just a little better than human. The swaying strengthened. By the time she reached the stage floor she was dancing. But it was no dance that any human creature could ever have performed. The long, slow, languorous rhythms of her body would have been impossible to a figure hinged at its joints as human figures hinge. (Harris remembered incredulously that he had feared once to find her jointed like a mechanical robot. But it was humanity that seemed, by contrast, jointed and mechanical now.)

The languor and the rhythm of her patterns looked impromptu, as all good dances should, but Harris knew what hours of composition and rehearsal must lie behind it, what laborious graving into her brain of strange new pathways, the first to replace the old ones and govern the mastery of metal limbs.

To and fro over the velvet carpet, against the velvet background, she wove the intricacies of her serpentine dance, leisurely and yet with such hypnotic effect that the air seemed full of looping rhythms, as if her long, tapering limbs had left their own replicas hanging upon the air and fading only slowly as she moved away. In her mind, Harris knew, the stage was a whole, a background to be filled in completely with the measured patterns of her dance, and she seemed almost to project that completed pattern to her audience so that they saw her everywhere at once, her golden rhythms fading upon the air long after she had gone.

Now there was music, looping and hanging in echoes after her like the shining festoons she wove with her body. But it was no orchestral music. She was humming, deep and sweet and wordlessly, as she glided her easy, intricate path about the stage. And the volume of the music was amazing. It seemed to fill the theater, and it was not amplified by hidden loudspeakers. You could tell that. Somehow, until you heard the music she made, you had never realized before the subtle distortions that amplification puts into music. This was utterly pure and true as perhaps no ear in all her audience had ever heard music before.

While she danced the audience did not seem to breathe. Perhaps they were beginning already to suspect who and what it was that moved before them without any fanfare of the publicity they had been half-expecting for weeks now. And yet, without the publicity, it was not easy to believe the dancer they watched was not some cunningly motivated manikin swinging on unseen wires about the stage.

Nothing she had done yet had been human. The dance was no dance a human being could have performed. The music she hummed came from a throat without vocal chords. But now the long, slow rhythms were drawing to their close, the pattern tightening in to a finale. And she ended as inhumanly as she had danced, willing them not to interrupt her with applause, dominating them now as she had always done. For her implication here was that a machine might have performed the dance, and a machine expects no applause. If they thought unseen operators had put her through those wonderful paces, they would wait for the operators to appear for their bows. But the audience was obedient. It sat silently, waiting for what came next. But its silence was tense and breathless.

The dance ended as it had begun. Slowly, almost carelessly, she swung up the velvet stairs, moving with rhythms as perfect as her music. But when she reached the head of the stairs she turned to face her audience, and for a moment stood motionless, like a creature of metal, without volition, the hands of the operator slack upon its strings.

Then, startlingly, she laughed.

It was lovely laughter, low and sweet and full-throated. She threw her head back and let her body sway and her shoulders shake, and the laughter, like the music, filled the theater, gaining volume from the great hollow of the roof and sounding in the ears of every listener, not loud, but as intimately as if each sat alone with the woman who laughed.

And she was a woman now. Humanity had dropped over her like a tangible garment. No one who had ever heard that laughter before could mistake it here. But before the reality of who she was had quite time to dawn upon her listeners she let the laughter deepen into music, as no human voice could have done. She was humming a familiar refrain close in the ear of every hearer. And the humming in turn swung into words. She sang in her clear, light, lovely voice:

"The yellow rose of Eden, is blooming in my heart—"

It was Deirdre's song. She had sung it first upon the airways a month before the theater fire that had consumed her. It was a commonplace little melody, simple enough to take first place in the fancy of a nation that had always liked its songs simple. But it had a certain sincerity too, and no taint of the vulgarity of tune and rhythm that foredooms so many popular songs to oblivion after their novelty fades.

No one else was ever able to sing it quite as Deirdre did. It had been identified with her so closely that though for awhile after her accident singers tried to make it a memorial for her, they failed so conspicuously to give it her unmistakable flair that the song died from their sheer inability to sing it. No one ever hummed the tune without thinking of her and the pleasant, nostalgic sadness of something lovely and lost.

But it was not a sad song now. If anyone had doubted whose brain and ego motivated this shining metal suppleness, they could doubt no longer. For the voice was Deirdre, and the song. And the lovely, poised grace of her mannerisms that made up recognition as certainly as sight of a familiar face.

She had not finished the first line of her song before the audience knew her.

And they did not let her finish. The accolade of their interruption was a tribute more eloquent than polite waiting could ever have been. First a breath of incredulity rippled over the theater, and a long, sighing gasp that reminded Harris irrelevantly as he listened to the gasp which still goes up from matinee audiences at the first glimpse of the fabulous Valentino, so many generations dead. But this gasp did not sigh itself away and vanish. Tremendous tension lay behind it, and the rising tide of excitement rippled up in little murmurs and spatterings of applause that ran together into one overwhelming roar. It shook the theater. The television screen trembled and blurred a little to the volume of that transmitted applause.

Silenced before it, Deirdre stood gesturing on the stage, bowing and bowing as the noise rolled up about her, shaking perceptibly with the triumph of her own emotion.

Harris had an intolerable feeling that she was smiling radiantly and that the tears were pouring down her cheeks. He even thought, just as Maltzer leaned forward to switch off the screen, that she was blowing kisses over the audience in the timehonored gesture of the grateful actress, her golden arms shining as she scattered kisses abroad from the featureless helmet, the face that had no mouth.

"Well?" Harris said, not without triumph.

Maltzer shook his head jerkily, the glasses unsteady on his nose so that the blurred eyes behind them seemed to shift.

"Of course they applauded, you fool," he said in a savage voice. "I might have known they would under this set-up. It doesn't prove anything. Oh, she was smart to surprise them—I admit that. But they were applauding themselves as much as her. Excitement, gratitude for letting them in on a historic performance, mass hysteria—*you* know. It's from now on the test will come, and this hasn't helped any to prepare her for it. Morbid curiosity when the news gets out—people laughing when she forgets she isn't human. And they will, you know. There are always those who will. And the novelty wearing off. The slow draining away of humanity for lack of contact with any human stimuli any more—"

Harris remembered suddenly and reluctantly the moment that afternoon which he had shunted aside mentally, to consider later. The sense of something unfamiliar beneath the surface of Deirdre's speech. Was Maltzer right? Was the drainage already at work? Or was there something deeper than this obvious answer to the question? Certainly she had been through experiences too terrible for ordinary people to comprehend. Scars might still remain. Or, with her body, had she put on a strange, metallic something of the mind, that spoke to no sense which human minds could answer?

For a few minutes neither of them spoke. Then Maltzer rose abruptly and stood looking down at Harris with an abstract scowl.

"I wish you'd go now," he said.

Harris glanced up at him, startled. Maltzer began to pace again, his steps quick and uneven. Over his shoulder he said,

"I've made up my mind, Harris. I've got to put a stop to this."

Harris rose. "Listen," he said. "Tell me one thing. What makes you so certain you're right? Can you deny that most of it's speculation—hearsay evidence? Remember, I talked to Deirdre, and she was just as sure as you are in the opposite direction. Have you any real reason for what you think?"

Maltzer took his glasses off and rubbed his nose carefully, taking a long time about it. He seemed reluctant to answer. But when he did, at last, there was a confidence in his voice Harris had not expected.

"I have a reason," he said. "But you won't believe it. Nobody would."

"Try me."

Maltzer shook his head. "Nobody *could* believe it. No two people were ever in quite the same relationship before as Deirdre and I have been. I helped her come back out of complete—oblivion. I knew her before she had voice or hearing. She was only a frantic mind when I first made contact with her, half insane with all that had happened and fear of what would happen next. In a very literal sense she was reborn out of that condition, and I had to guide her through every step of the way. I came to know her thoughts before she thought them. And once you've been that close to another mind, you don't lose the contact easily." He put the glasses back on and looked blurrily at Harris through the heavy lenses. "Deirdre is worried," he said. "I know it. You won't believe me, but I can—well, sense it. I tell you, I've been too close to her very mind itself to make any mistake. You don't see it, maybe. Maybe even she doesn't know it yet. But the worry's there. When I'm with her, I feel it. And I don't want it to come any nearer the surface of her mind than it's come already. I'm going to put a stop to this before it's too late."

Harris had no comment for that. It was too entirely outside his own experience. He said nothing for a moment. Then he asked simply, "How?"

"I'm not sure yet. I've got to decide before she comes back. And I want to see her alone."

"I think you're wrong," Harris told him quietly. "I think you're imagining things. I don't think you *can* stop her."

Maltzer gave him a slanted glance. "I can stop her," he said, in a curious voice. He went on quickly, "She has enough already—she's nearly human. She can live normally as other people live, without going back on the screen. Maybe this taste of it will be enough. I've got to convince her it is. If she retires now, she'll never guess how cruel her own audiences could be, and maybe that deep sense of—distress, uneasiness, whatever it is—won't come to the surface. It mustn't. She's too fragile to stand that." He slapped his hands together sharply. "I've got to stop her. For her own sake I've got to do it!" He swung round again to face Harris. "Will you go now?"

Never in his life had Harris wanted less to leave a place. Briefly he thought of saying simply, "No I won't." But he had to admit in his own mind that Maltzer was at least partly right. This was a matter between Deirdre and her creator, the culmination, perhaps, of that year's long intimacy so like marriage that this final trial for supremacy was a need he recognized.

He would not, he thought, forbid the showdown if he could. Perhaps the whole year had been building up to this one moment between them in which one or the other must prove himself victor. Neither was very well stable just now, after the long strain of the year past. It might very well be that the mental salvation of one or both hinged upon the outcome of the clash. But because each was so strongly motivated not by selfish concern but by solicitude for the other in this strange combat, Harris knew he must leave them to settle the thing alone.

He was in the street and hailing a taxi before the full significance of something Maltzer had said came to him. *"I can stop her,"* he had declared, with an odd inflection in his voice.

Suddenly Harris felt cold. Maltzer had made her—of course he could stop her if he chose. Was there some key in that supple golden body that could immobilize it at its maker's will? Could she be imprisoned in the cage of her own body? No body before in all history, he thought, could have been designed more truly to be a prison for its mind than Deirdre's, if Maltzer chose to turn the key that locked her in. There must be many ways to do it. He could simply withhold whatever source of nourishment kept her brain alive, if that were the way he chose.

But Harris could not believe he would do it. The man wasn't insane. He would not defeat his own purpose. His determination rose from his solicitude for Deirdre; he would not even in the last extremity try to save her by imprisoning her in the jail of her own skull.

For a moment Harris hesitated on the curb, almost turning back. But what could he do? Even granting that Maltzer would resort to such tactics, self-defeating in their very nature, how could any man on earth prevent him if he did it subtly enough? But he never would. Harris knew he never would. He got into his cab slowly, frowning. He would see them both tomorrow.

He did not. Harris was swamped with excited calls about yesterday's performance, but the message he was awaiting did not come. The day went by very slowly. Toward evening he surrendered and called Maltzer's apartment.

It was Deirdre's face that answered, and for once he saw no remembered features superimposed upon the blankness of her helmet. Masked and faceless, she looked at him inscrutably.

"Is everything all right?" he asked, a little uncomfortable.

"Yes, of course," she said, and her voice was a bit metallic for the first time, as if she were thinking so deeply of some other matter that she did not trouble to pitch it properly. "I had a long talk with Maltzer last night, if that's what you mean. You know what he wants. But nothing's been decided yet."

Harris felt oddly rebuffed by the sudden realization of the metal of her. It was impossible to read anything from face or voice. Each had its mask.

"What are you going to do?" he asked.

"Exactly as I'd planned," she told him, without inflection.

Harris floundered a little. Then, with an effort at practicality, he said, "Do you want me to go to work on bookings, then?"

She shook the delicately modeled skull. "Not yet. You saw the reviews today, of course. They—*did* like me." It was an understatement, and for the first time a note of warmth sounded in her voice. But the preoccupation was still there, too. "I'd already planned to make them wait awhile after my first performance," she went on. "A couple of weeks, anyhow. You remember that little farm of mine in Jersey, John? I'm going over today. I won't see anyone except the servants there. Not even Maltzer. Not even you. I've got a lot to think about. Maltzer has agreed to let everything go until we've both thought things over. He's taking a rest, too. I'll see you the moment I get back, John. Is that all right?"

She blanked out almost before he had time to nod and while the beginning of a stammered argument was still on his lips. He sat there staring at the screen.

The two weeks that went by before Maltzer called him again were the longest Harris had ever spent. He thought of many things in the interval. He believed he could sense in that last talk with Deirdre something of the inner unrest that Maltzer had spoken of—more an abstraction than a distress, but some thought had occupied her mind which she would not—or was it that she could not?—share even with her closest confidants. He even wondered whether, if her mind was as delicately poised as Maltzer feared, one would ever know whether or not it had slipped. There was so little evidence one way or the other in the unchanging outward form of her.

Most of all he wondered what two weeks in a new environment would do to her untried body and newly patterned brain. If Maltzer were right, then there might be some perceptible—drainage—by the time they met again. He tried not to think of that.

Maltzer televised him on the morning set for her return. He looked very bad. The rest must have been no rest at all. His face was almost a skull now, and the blurred eyes behind their lenses burned. But he seemed curiously at peace, in spite of his appearance. Harris thought he had reached some decision, but whatever it was had not stopped his hands from shaking or the nervous *tic* that drew his face sidewise into a grimace at intervals.

"Come over," he said briefly, without preamble. "She'll be here in half an hour." And he blanked out without waiting for an answer.

When Harris arrived, he was standing by the window looking down and steadying his trembling hands on the sill.

"I can't stop her," he said in a monotone, and again without preamble. Harris had the impression that for the two weeks his thoughts must have run over and over the same track, until any spoken word was simply a vocal interlude in the circling of his mind. "I couldn't do it. I even tried threats, but she knew I didn't mean them. There's only one way out, Harris." He glanced up briefly, hollow-eyed behind the lenses. "Never mind. I'll tell you later."

"Did you explain everything to her that you did to me?"

"Nearly all. I even taxed her with that . . . that sense of distress I *know* she feels. She denied it. She was lying. We both knew. It was worse after the performance than before. When I saw her that night, I tell you I *knew*—she senses something wrong, but she won't admit it." He shrugged. "Well—"

Faintly in the silence they heard the humming of the elevator descending from the helicopter platform on the roof. Both men turned to the door.

She had not changed at all. Foolishly, Harris was a little surprised. Then he caught himself and remembered that she would never change —never, until she died. He himself might grow white-haired and senile; she would move before him then as she moved now, supple, golden, enigmatic.

Still, he thought she caught her breath a little when she saw Maltzer and the depths of his swift degeneration. She had no breath to catch, but her voice was shaken as she greeted them.

"I'm glad you're both here," she said, a slight hesitation in her speech. "It's a wonderful day outside. Jersey was glorious. I'd forgotten how lovely it is in summer. Was the sanitarium any good, Maltzer?"

He jerked his head irritably and did not answer. She went on talking in a light voice, skimming the surface, saying nothing important.

This time Harris saw her as he supposed her audiences would, eventually, when the surprise had worn off and the image of the living Deirdre faded from memory. She was all metal now, the Deirdre they would know from today on. And she was not less lovely. She was not even less human—yet. Her motion was a miracle of flexible grace, a pouring of suppleness along every limb. (From now on, Harris realized suddenly, it was her body and not her face that would have mobility to express emotion; she must act with her limbs and her lithe, robed torso.)

But there was something wrong. Harris sensed it almost tangibly in her inflections, her elusiveness, the way she fenced with words. This was what Maltzer had meant, this was what Harris himself had felt just before she left for the country. Only now it was strong—certain. Between them and the old Deirdre whose voice still spoke to them a veil of—detachment—had been drawn. Behind it she was in distress. Somehow, somewhere, she had made some discovery that affected her profoundly. And Harris was terribly afraid that he knew what the discovery must be. Maltzer was right.

He was still leaning against the window, staring out unseeingly over the vast panorama of New York, webbed with traffic bridges, winking with sunlit glass, its vertiginous distances plunging downward into the blue shadows of Earth-level. He said now, breaking into the light-voiced chatter, "Are you all right, Deirdre?"

She laughed. It was lovely laughter. She moved lithely across the room, sunlight glinting on her musical mailed robe, and stooped to a cigarette box on a table. Her fingers were deft.

"Have one?" she said, and carried the box to Maltzer. He let her put the brown cylinder between his lips and hold a light to it, but he did not seem to be noticing what he did. She replaced the box and then crossed to a mirror on the far wall and began experimenting with a series of gliding ripples that wove patterns of pale gold in the glass. "Of course I'm all right," she said.

"You're lying."

Deirdre did not turn. She was watching him in the mirror, but the ripple of her motion went on slowly, languorously, undisturbed.

"No," she told them both.

Maltzer drew deeply on his cigarette. Then with a hard pull he unsealed the window and tossed the smoking stub far out over the gulfs below. He said,

"You can't deceive me, Deirdre." His voice, suddenly, was quite calm. "I created you, my dear. I know. I've sensed that uneasiness in you growing and growing for a long while now. It's much stronger today than it was two weeks ago. Something happened to you in the country. I don't know what it was, but you've changed. Will you admit to yourself what it is, Deirdre? Have you realized yet that you must not go back on the screen?"

"Why, no," said Deirdre, still not looking at him except obliquely, in the glass. Her gestures were slower now, weaving lazy patterns in the air. "No, I haven't changed my mind."

She was all metal—outwardly. She was taking unfair advantage of her own metal-hood. She had withdrawn far within, behind the mask of her voice and her facelessness. Even her body, whose involuntary motions might have betrayed what she was feeling, in the only way she could be subject to betrayal now, she was putting through ritual motions that disguised it completely. As long as these looping, weaving patterns occupied her, no one had any way of guessing even from her motion what went on in the hidden brain inside her helmet.

Harris was struck suddenly and for the first time with the completeness of her withdrawal. When he had seen her last in this apartment she had been wholly Deirdre, not masked at all, overflowing the metal with the warmth and ardor of the woman he had known so well. Since then—since the performance on the stage—he had not seen the familiar Deirdre again. Passionately he wondered why. Had she begun to suspect even in her moment of triumph what a fickle master an audience could be? Had she caught, perhaps, the sound of whispers and laughter among some small portion of her watchers, though the great majority praised her?

Or was Maltzer right? Perhaps Harris' first interview with her had been the last bright burning of the lost Deirdre, animated by excitement and the pleasure of meeting after so long a time, animation summoned up in a last strong effort to convince him. Now she was gone, but whether in self-protection against the possible cruelties of human beings, or whether in withdrawal to metal-hood, he could not guess. Humanity might be draining out of her fast, and the brassy taint of metal permeating the brain it housed.

Maltzer laid his trembling hand on the edge of the opened window and looked out. He said in a deepened voice, the querulous note gone for the first time:

"I've made a terrible mistake, Deirdre. I've done you irreparable harm." He paused a moment, but Deirdre said nothing. Harris dared not speak. In a moment Maltzer went on. "I've made you vulnerable, and given you no weapons to fight your enemies with. And the human race is your enemy, my dear, whether you admit it now or later. I think you know that. I think it's why you're so silent. I think you must have suspected it on the stage two weeks ago, and verified it in Jersey while you were gone. They're going to hate you, after a while, because you are still beautiful, and they're going to persecute you because you are different—and helpless. Once the novelty wears off, my dear, your audience will be simply a mob."

He was not looking at her. He had bent forward a little, looking out the window and down. His hair stirred in the wind that blew very strongly up this high, and whined thinly around the open edge of the glass.

"I meant what I did for you," he said, "to be for everyone who meets with accidents that might have ruined them. I should have known my gift would mean worse ruin than any mutilation could be. I know now that there's only one legitimate way a human being can create life. When he tries another way, as I did, he has a lesson to learn. Remember the lesson of the student Frankenstein? He learned, too. In a way, he was lucky—the way he learned. He didn't have to watch what happened afterward. Maybe he wouldn't have had the courage—I know I haven't."

Harris found himself standing without remembering that he rose. He knew suddenly what was about to happen. He understood Maltzer's air of resolution, his new, unnatural calm. He knew, even, why Maltzer had asked him here today, so that Deirdre might not be left alone. For he remembered that Frankenstein, too, had paid with his life for the unlawful creation of life.

Maltzer was leaning head and shoulders from the window now, looking down with almost hypnotized fascination. His voice came back to them remotely in the breeze, as if a barrier already lay between them.

Deirdre had not moved. Her expressionless mask, in the mirror, watched him calmly. She *must* have understood. Yet she gave no sign, except that the weaving of her arms had almost stopped now, she moved so slowly. Like a dance seen in a nightmare, under water.

It was impossible, of course, for her to express any emotion. The fact that her face showed none now should not, in fairness, be held against her. But she watched so wholly without feeling— Neither of them moved toward the window. A false step, now, might send him over. They were quiet, listening to his voice.

"We who bring life into the world unlawfully," said Maltzer, almost thoughtfully, "must make room for it by withdrawing our own. That seems to be an inflexible rule. It works automatically. The thing we create makes living unbearable. No, it's nothing you can help, my dear. I've asked you to do something I created you incapable of doing. I made you to perform a function, and I've been asking you to forego the one thing you were made to do. I believe that if you do it, it will destroy you, but the whole guilt is mine, not yours. I'm not even asking you to give up the screen, any more. I know you can't, and live. But I can't live and watch you. I put all my skill and all my love in one final masterpiece, and I can't bear to watch it destroyed. I can't live and watch you do only what I made you to do, and ruin yourself because you must do it.

"But before I go, I have to make sure you understand." He leaned a little farther, looking down, and his voice grew more remote as the glass came between them. He was saying almost unbearable things now, but very distantly, in a cool, passionless tone filtered through wind and glass, and with the distant humming of the city mingled with it, so that the words were curiously robbed of poignancy. "I can be a coward," he said, "and escape the consequences of what I've done, but I can't go and leave you—not understanding. It would be even worse than the thought of your failure, to think of you bewildered and confused when the mob turns on you. What I'm telling you, my dear, won't be any real news—I think you sense it already, though you may not admit it to yourself. We've been too close to lie to each other, Deirdre—I know when you aren't telling the truth. I know the distress that's been growing in your mind. You are not wholly human, my dear. I think you know that. In so many ways, in spite of all I could do, you must always be less than human. You've lost the senses of perception that kept you in touch with humanity. Sight and hearing are all that remain, and sight, as I've said before, was the last and coldest of the senses to develop. And you're so delicately poised on a sort of thin edge of reason. You're only a clear, glowing mind animating a metal body, like a candle flame in a glass. And as precariously vulnerable to the wind."

He paused. "Try not to let them ruin you completely," he said after a while. "When they turn against you, when they find out you're more helpless than they—I wish I could have made you stronger, Deirdre. But I couldn't. I had too much skill for your good and mine, but not quite enough skill for that."

He was silent again, briefly, looking down. He was balanced precariously now, more than halfway over the sill and supported only by one hand on the glass. Harris watched with an agonized uncertainty, not sure whether a sudden leap might catch him in time or send him over. Deirdre was still weaving her golden patterns, slowly and unchangingly, watching the mirror and its reflection, her face and masked eyes enigmatic.

"I wish one thing, though," Maltzer said in his remote voice. "I wish —before I finish—that you'd tell me the truth, Deirdre. I'd be happier if I were sure I'd—reached you. Do you understand what I've said? Do you believe me? Because if you don't, then I know you're lost beyond all hope. If you'll admit your own doubt—and I know you do doubt—I can think there may be a chance for you after all. Were you lying to me, Deirdre? Do you know how . . . how wrong I've made you?"

There was silence. Then very softly, a breath of sound, Deirdre answered. The voice seemed to hang in midair, because she had no lips to move and localize it for the imagination.

"Will you listen, Maltzer?" she asked.

"I'll wait," he said. "Go on. Yes or no?"

Slowly she let her arms drop to her sides. Very smoothly and quietly she turned from the mirror and faced him. She swayed a little, making her metal robe ring.

"I'll answer you," she said. "But I don't think I'll answer that. Not with yes or no, anyhow. I'm going to walk a little, Maltzer. I have something to tell you, and I can't talk standing still. Will you let me move about without—going over?"

He nodded distantly. "You can't interfere from that distance," he said. "But keep the distance. What do you want to say?"

She began to pace a little way up and down her end of the room, moving with liquid ease. The table with the cigarette box was in her way, and she pushed it aside carefully, watching Maltzer and making no swift motions to startle him.

"I'm not—well, sub-human," she said, a faint note of indignation in her voice. "I'll prove it in a minute, but I want to say something else first. You must promise to wait and listen. There's a flaw in your argument, and I resent it. I'm not a Frankenstein monster made out of dead flesh. I'm myself—alive. You didn't create my life, you only preserved it. I'm not a robot, with compulsions built into me that I have to obey. I'm free-willed and independent, and, Maltzer—I'm human."

Harris had relaxed a little. She knew what she was doing. He had no idea what she planned, but he was willing to wait now. She was not the indifferent automaton he had thought. He watched her come to the table again in a lap of her pacing, and stoop over it, her eyeless mask turned to Maltzer to make sure a variation of her movement did not startle him.

"I'm human," she repeated, her voice humming faintly and very sweetly. "Do you think I'm not?" she asked, straightening and facing them both. And then suddenly, almost overwhelmingly, the warmth and the old ardent charm were radiant all around her. She was robot no longer, enigmatic no longer. Harris could see as clearly as in their first meeting the remembered flesh still gracious and beautiful as her voice evoked his memory. She stood swaying a little, as she had always swayed, her head on one side, and she was chuckling at them both. It was such a soft and lovely sound, so warmly familiar.

"Of course I'm myself," she told them, and as the words sounded in their ears neither of them could doubt it. There was hypnosis in her voice. She turned away and began to pace again, and so powerful was the human personality which she had called up about her that it beat out at them in deep pulses, as if her body were a furnace to send out those comforting waves of warmth. "I have handicaps, I know," she said. "But my audiences will never know. I won't let them know. I think you'll believe me, both of you, when I say I could play Juliet just as I am now, with a cast of ordinary people, and make the world accept it. Do you think I could, John? Maltzer, don't you believe I could?"

She paused at the far end of her pacing path and turned to face them, and they both stared at her without speaking. To Harris she was the Deirdre he had always known, pale gold, exquisitely graceful in remembered postures, the inner radiance of her shining through metal as brilliantly as it had ever shone through flesh. He did not wonder, now, if it were real. Later he would think again that it might be only a disguise, something like a garment she had put off with her lost body, to wear again only when she chose. Now the spell of her compelling charm was too strong for wonder. He watched, convinced for the moment that she was all she seemed to be. She could play Juliet if she said she could. She could sway a whole audience as easily as she swayed himself. Indeed, there was something about her just now more convincingly human than anything he had noticed before. He realized that in a split second of awareness before he saw what it was.

She was looking at Maltzer. He, too, watched, spellbound in spite of himself, not dissenting. She glanced from one to the other. Then she put back her head and laughter came welling and choking from her in a great, full-throated tide. She shook in the strength of it. Harris could almost see her round throat pulsing with the sweet low-pitched waves of laughter that were shaking her. Honest mirth, with a little derision in it.

Then she lifted one arm and tossed her cigarette into the empty fireplace.

Harris choked, and his mind went blank for one moment of blind denial. He had not sat here watching a robot smoke and accepting it as normal. He could not! And yet he had. That had been the final touch of conviction which swayed his hypnotized mind into accepting her humanity. And she had done it so deftly, so naturally, wearing her radiant humanity with such rightness, that his watching mind had not even questioned what she did.

He glanced at Maltzer. The man was still halfway over the window ledge, but through the opening of the window he, too, was staring in stupefied disbelief and Harris knew they had shared the same delusion.

Deirdre was still shaking a little with laughter. "Well," she demanded, the rich chuckling making her voice quiver, "am I all robot, after all?"

Harris opened his mouth to speak, but he did not utter a word. This was not his show. The byplay lay wholly between Deirdre and Maltzer; he must not interfere. He turned his head to the window and waited.

And Maltzer for a moment seemed shaken in his conviction.

"You . . . you *are* an actress," he admitted slowly. "But I . . . I'm not convinced I'm wrong. I think—" He paused. The querulous note was in his voice again, and he seemed racked once more by the old doubts and dismay. Then Harris saw him stiffen. He saw the resolution come back, and understood why it had come. Maltzer had gone too far already upon the cold and lonely path he had chosen to turn back, even for stronger evidence than this. He had reached his conclusions only after mental turmoil too terrible to face again. Safety and peace lay in the course he had steeled himself to follow. He was too tired, too exhausted by months of conflict, to retrace his path and begin all over. Harris could see him groping for a way out, and in a moment he saw him find it.

"That was a trick," he said hollowly. "Maybe you could play it on a larger audience, too. Maybe you have more tricks to use. I might be wrong. But Deirdre"—his voice grew urgent—"you haven't answered the one thing I've got to know. You can't answer it. You *do* feel—dismay. You've learned your own inadequacy, however well you can hide it from us—even from us. I *know*. Can you deny that, Deirdre?"

She was not laughing now. She let her arms fall, and the flexible golden body seemed to droop a little all over, as if the brain that a moment before had been sending out strong, sure waves of confidence had slackened its power, and the intangible muscles of her limbs slackened with it. Some of the glowing humanity began to fade. It receded within her and was gone, as if the fire in the furnace of her body were sinking and cooling.

"Maltzer," she said uncertainly, "I can't answer that—yet. I can't—"

And then, while they waited in anxiety for her to finish the sentence, she *blazed*. She ceased to be a figure in stasis—she *blazed*.

It was something no eyes could watch and translate into terms the brain could follow; her motion was too swift. Maltzer in the window was a whole long room-length away. He had thought himself safe at such a distance, knowing no normal human being could reach him before he moved. But Deirdre was neither normal nor human.

In the same instant she stood drooping by the mirror she was simultaneously at Maltzer's side. Her motion negated time and destroyed space. And as a glowing cigarette tip in the dark describes closed circles before the eye when the holder moves it swiftly, so Deirdre blazed in one continuous flash of golden motion across the room.

But curiously, she was not blurred. Harris, watching, felt his mind go blank again, but less in surprise than because no normal eyes and brain could perceive what it was he looked at.

(In that moment of intolerable suspense his complex human brain paused suddenly, annihilating time in its own way, and withdrew to a cool corner of its own to analyze in a flashing second what it was he had just seen. The brain could do it timelessly; words are slow. But he knew he had watched a sort of tesseract of human motion, a parable of fourth-dimensional activity. A one-dimensional point, moved through space, creates a two-dimensional line, which in motion creates a three-dimensional cube. Theoretically the cube, in motion, would produce a fourth-dimensional figure. No human creature had ever seen a figure of three dimensions moved through space and time before—until this moment. She had not blurred; every motion she made was distinct, but not like moving figures on a strip of film. Not like anything that those who use our language had ever seen before, or created words to express. The mind saw, but without perceiving. Neither words nor thoughts could resolve what happened into terms for human brains. And perhaps she had not actually and literally moved through the fourth dimension. Perhaps—since Harris was able to see her—it had been almost and not quite that unimaginable thing. But it was close enough.)

While to the slow mind's eye she was still standing at the far end of the room, she was already at Maltzer's side, her long, flexible fingers gentle but very firm upon his arms. She waited—

The room shimmered. There was sudden violent heat beating upon Harris' face. Then the air steadied again and Deirdre was saying softly, in a mournful whisper:

"I'm sorry—I had to do it. I'm sorry—I didn't mean you to know—"

Time caught up with Harris. He saw it overtake Maltzer too, saw the man jerk convulsively away from the grasping hands, in a ludicrously futile effort to forestall what had already happened. Even thought was slow, compared with Deirdre's swiftness.

The sharp outward jerk was strong. It was strong enough to break the grasp of human hands and catapult Maltzer out and down into the swimming gulfs of New York. The mind leaped ahead to a logical conclusion and saw him twisting and turning and diminishing with dreadful rapidity to a tiny point of darkness that dropped away through sunlight toward the shadows near the earth. The mind even conjured up a shrill, thin cry that plummeted away with the falling body and hung behind it in the shaken air.

But the mind was reckoning on human factors.

Very gently and smoothly Deirdre lifted Maltzer from the window sill and with effortless ease carried him well back into the safety of the room. She set him down before a sofa and her golden fingers unwrapped themselves from his arms slowly, so that he could regain control of his own body before she released him.

He sank to the sofa without a word. Nobody spoke for an unmeasurable length of time. Harris could not. Deirdre waited patiently. It was Maltzer who regained speech first, and it came back on the old track, as if his mind had not yet relinquished the rut it had worn so deep.

"All right," he said breathlessly. "All right, you can stop me this time. But I know, you see. I know! You can't hide your feeling from me, Deirdre. I know the trouble you feel. And next time—next time I won't wait to talk!"

Deirdre made the sound of a sigh. She had no lungs to expel the breath she was imitating, but it was hard to realize that. It was hard to understand why she was not panting heavily from the terrible exertion of the past minutes; the mind knew why, but could not accept the reason. She was still too human.

"You still don't see," she said. "Think, Maltzer, think!"

There was a hassock beside the sofa. She sank upon it gracefully, clasping her robed knees. Her head tilted back to watch Maltzer's face. She saw only stunned stupidity on it now; he had passed through too much emotional storm to think at all.

"All right," she told him. "Listen—I'll admit it. You're right. I *am* unhappy. I do know what you said was true—but not for the reason you think. Humanity and I are far apart, and drawing farther. The gap will be hard to bridge. Do you hear me, Maltzer?"

Harris saw the tremendous effort that went into Maltzer's wakening. He saw the man pull his mind back into focus and sit up on the sofa with weary stiffness.

"You . . . you do admit it, then?" he asked in a bewildered voice.

Deirdre shook her head sharply.

"Do you still think of me as delicate?" she demanded. "Do you know I carried you here at arm's length halfway across the room? Do you realize you weigh *nothing* to me? I could"—she glanced around the room and gestured with sudden, rather appalling violence—"tear this building down," she said quietly. "I could tear my way through these walls, I think. I've found no limit yet to the strength I can put forth if I try." She held up her golden hands and looked at them. "The metal would break, perhaps," she said reflectively, "but then, I have no feeling—"

Maltzer gasped, *"Deirdre—"*

She looked up with what must have been a smile. It sounded clearly in her voice. "Oh, I won't. I wouldn't have to do it with my hands, if I wanted. Look—listen!"

She put her head back and a deep, vibrating hum gathered and grew in what one still thought of as her throat. It deepened swiftly and the ears began to ring. It was deeper, and the furniture vibrated. The walls began almost imperceptibly to shake. The room was full and bursting with a sound that shook every atom upon its neighbor with a terrible, disrupting force.

The sound ceased. The humming died. Then Deirdre laughed and made another and quite differently pitched sound. It seemed to reach out like an arm in one straight direction—toward the window. The opened panel shook. Deirdre intensified her hum, and slowly, with imperceptible jolts that merged into smoothness, the window jarred itself shut.

"You see?" Deirdre said. "You see?"

But still Maltzer could only stare. Harris was staring too, his mind beginning slowly to accept what she implied. Both were too stunned to leap ahead to any conclusions yet.

Deirdre rose impatiently and began to pace again, in a ringing of metal robe and a twinkling of reflected lights. She was pantherlike in her suppleness. They could see the power behind that lithe motion now; they no longer thought of her as helpless, but they were far still from grasping the truth.

"You were wrong about me, Maltzer," she said with an effort at patience in her voice. "But you were right too, in a way you didn't guess. I'm not afraid of humanity. I haven't anything to fear from them. Why"—her voice took on a tinge of contempt—"already I've set a fashion in women's clothing. By next week you won't see a woman on the street without a mask like mine, and every dress that isn't cut like a chlamys will be out of style. I'm not afraid of humanity! I won't lose touch with them unless I want to. I've learned a lot—I've learned too much already."

Her voice faded for a moment, and Harris had a quick and appalling vision of her experimenting in the solitude of her farm, testing the range of her voice, testing her eyesight—could she see microscopically and telescopically?—and was her hearing as abnormally flexible as her voice?

"You were afraid I had lost feeling and scent and taste," she went on, still pacing with that powerful, tigerish tread. "Hearing and sight would not be enough, you think? But why do you think sight is the last of the senses? It may be the latest, Maltzer—Harris—*but why do you think it's the last?*"

She may not have whispered that. Perhaps it was only their hearing that made it seem thin and distant, as the brain contracted and would not let the thought come through in its stunning entirety.

"No," Deirdre said, "I haven't lost contact with the human race. I never will, unless I want to. It's too easy . . . too easy."

She was watching her shining feet as she paced, and her masked face was averted. Sorrow sounded in her soft voice now.

"I didn't mean to let you know," she said. "I never would have, if this hadn't happened. But I couldn't let you go believing you'd failed. You made a perfect machine, Maltzer. More perfect than you knew."

"But Deirdre—" breathed Maltzer, his eyes fascinated and still incredulous upon her, "but Deirdre, if we did succeed—what's wrong? I can feel it now—I've felt it all along. You're so unhappy—you still are. Why, Deirdre?"

She lifted her head and looked at him, eyelessly, but with a piercing stare.

"Why are you so sure of that?" she asked gently.

"You think I could be mistaken, knowing you as I do? But I'm not Frankenstein . . . you say my creation's flawless. Then what—"

"Could you ever duplicate this body?" she asked.

Maltzer glanced down at his shaking hands. "I don't know. I doubt it. I—"

"Could anyone else?"

He was silent. Deirdre answered for him. "I don't believe anyone could. I think I was an accident. A sort of mutation halfway between flesh and metal. Something accidental and . . . and unnatural, turning off on a wrong course of evolution that never reaches a dead end. Another brain in a body like this might die or go mad, as you thought I would. The synapses are too delicate. You were—call it lucky—with me. From what I know now, I don't think a . . . a baroque like me could happen again." She paused a moment. "What you did was kindle the fire for the Phoenix, in a way. And the Phoenix rises perfect and renewed from its own ashes. Do you remember why it had to reproduce itself that way?"

Maltzer shook his head.

"I'll tell you," she said."It was because there was only one Phoenix. Only one in the whole world."

They looked at each other in silence. Then Deirdre shrugged a little.

"He always came out of the fire perfect, of course. I'm not weak, Maltzer. You needn't let that thought bother you any more. I'm not vulnerable and helpless. I'm not sub-human." She laughed dryly. "I suppose," she said, "that I'm—superhuman."

"But—not happy."

"I'm afraid. It isn't unhappiness, Maltzer—it's fear. I don't want to draw so far away from the human race. I wish I needn't. That's why I'm going back on the stage—to keep in touch with them while I can. But I wish there could be others like me. I'm . . . I'm lonely, Maltzer."

Silence again. Then Maltzer said, in a voice as distant as when he had spoken to them through glass, over gulfs as deep as oblivion:

"Then I am Frankenstein, after all."

"Perhaps you are," Deirdre said very softly. "I don't know. Perhaps you are."

She turned away and moved smoothly, powerfully, down the room to the window. Now that Harris knew, he could almost hear the sheer power purring along her limbs as she walked. She leaned the golden forehead against the glass—it clinked faintly, with a musical sound—and looked down into the depths Maltzer had hung above. Her voice was reflective as she looked into those dizzy spaces which had offered oblivion to her creator.

"There's one limit I can think of," she said, almost inaudibly. "Only one. My brain will wear out in another forty years or so. Between now and then I'll learn . . . I'll change . . . I'll know more than I can guess today. I'll change— That's frightening. I don't like to think about that." She laid a curved golden hand on the latch and pushed the window open a little, very easily. Wind whined around its edge. "I could put a stop to it now, if I wanted," she said. "If I wanted. But I can't, really. There's so much still untried. My brain's human, and no human brain could leave such possibilities untested. I wonder, though . . . I do wonder—"

Her voice was soft and familiar in Harris' ears, the voice Deirdre had spoken and sung with, sweetly enough to enchant a world. But as preoccupation came over her a certain flatness crept into the sound. When she was not listening to her own voice, it did not keep quite to the pitch of trueness. It sounded as if she spoke in a room of brass, and echoes from the walls resounded in the tones that spoke there.

"I wonder," she repeated, the distant taint of metal already in her voice.

CLEVE CARTMILL

WITH FLAMING SWORDS

YOU could shock men, I thought, and suffer no consequences. Men were merely slaves. Slaves allowed to serve us, to bring their produce to Eden, to give us their arms and backs and brains.

But these were Saints, here in the big hall. Their massed auras were a blaze of blue against which I narrowed my eyes. We were Saints, with three hundred years of traditional conduct behind us.

And what I had said was not condoned by tradition. I had called them men.

They took it in silence for a few seconds and stared at me, beside the throne of the Patriarch. Then they began to yell, and I felt a sick shame for them. They lost their dignity.

I yelled into their hubbub. "I invoke the rule of silence!"

The Patriarch raised his glowing arms. Quiet fell.

"Against my will," the Patriarch said, "I command silence. We will hear the rest of Saint Hanson's heresy."

That stopped me for a moment. I loved this old Saint, as did we all. He was so wise, so helpful at all times. For the others here in the auditorium I had little feeling. They were Saints, as I was, but all our lives and deeds centered around the Patriarch. His white robe and banded turban symbolized all the ritual and ceremony which governed our actions.

He had called it heresy. So strong was my conditioning, so carefully had I been trained from birth, so accustomed had I become to accepting his verdict as truth, that I believed him—for a second or two.

Heresy. That, if proved, was unforgivable. They could have my life for it. All of my work, and all of Jennings' would have been wasted. I thought of our efforts secondarily, though; primarily, I did not want to die. And I knew that I could die, in spite of our sham and hyopcrisy about "ascension."

But I couldn't leave it at that, with just the accusation. A conviction that I was right would not let me back down. Nobody, not even the Patriarch, should stop me before I presented my argument.

I turned toward the Throne and faced him respectfully. "It is not heresy, your Reverence. It is truth. I have proof." His glowing face did not change expression. I spoke to the audience, narrowing my eyes again before the collective glow of their auras.

"Listen, men." They gasped at this. "Yes, men you are. I, too. We have nothing of divinity. We are like the others, like the laborers who built Eden, from which we have enslaved the entire human race. Oh, I know our slavery is called supervision and leadership. It is imposed in the name of good. But we have no right to make servants of men, for we are men. Wait," I cautioned as several hands went up, "let me tell you the truth. We are set apart by our auras, but those auras are the result of disturbed germ plasma in our ancestors."

They refused to take this, rule of silence or no. They shouted again, and Saint Evan Wakefield led an angry group down the wide aisle.

"Quiet!" I yelled. "Let me finish!"

Surprisingly, Saint Wakefield checked the group he led and raised his long arms with their nimbus of blue. Quiet fell again.

"Brethren," Saint Wakefield said. "Saint Hanson mouths heresy. No doubt of it. He has given us cause to strip him of his robes and his turban. Even so, he deserves to be heard. But not here, not here; this meeting is too unwieldy." He addressed the Patriarch. "I suggest, your Reverence, that Saint Hanson meet with the High Council tomorrow. Perhaps that smaller group can restore his sanity. At any rate, it can make a comprehensive report with the Brethren."

"It is so ordered," the Patriarch said. "Go with good."

I watched them go, each with his blue radiance which even our desert sun could not entirely dim. I felt troubled, not because they muttered among themselves, but because Evan Wakefield looked thoughtfully at me for a long time. We had clashed before, on matters of doctrine and procedure, and I knew him to be ruthless and clever.

I was one voice among so many millions, for the whole world believed that we were near to angels, placed among men to lead them out of the Collapse. That we had so led them and brought order out of chaos was final proof, in the popular mind, of our divinity.

One voice is easily silenced.

Oh, there were scattered others, like Jennings, but they had no power, no means. I had the means, in my apartment, to demonstrate the scientific, not divine, origin of our auras, but without the consent of the Brethren I could do nothing.

One voice is easily silenced.

Presently I was alone in the big hall. Even the Patriarch left me without a word. This impressed me with the seriousness of my position more than any other event. Always the Patriarch was ready with advice. But I had called him a man, and he had removed himself.

I could use some advice. From Jennings? No, for I knew what he would say. Attack. He'd roar it at me. If battle is inevitable, begin it yourself. Turn the modulator on the Council, wipe out their auras, and then tell them. That's what Jennings would advise.

But though I agreed with him in principle, I couldn't do it. They were Saints. I was a Saint. My conditioning was too strong. I couldn't trick them. It was not our way among ourselves. Trick men, yes. We did when necessary. But not each other.

I had to play fair, and I knew it. I was troubled enough by my secrecy. I hadn't told anybody, not even Jennings, that my modulator was finished and successful. Nobody knew of my laboratory adjoining my bedroom, not even Ellen.

Perhaps, I thought, if I tell the Patriarch what I've done, he will advise me. That wise old man will know what to do. I was a trifle shocked at my thinking of him as a man. That was the first time it had been in my thoughts.

I hurried up the aisle and out on the steps.

He was not in sight on the broad, sloping flight that went down to the river we had made. I went around the gleaming administration buildings, examining each street that stretched, spokewise from this administration center of the circular island which was the inner city. Saints aplenty were on the streets, and a few were on one of the bridges which connected us with the outer city where our "slaves" lived, but the high banded turban of the Patriarch was nowhere to be seen.

I decided not to search. I could waste the whole day. He might even have taken his plane from the landing tower. He could be in Los Angeles or San Francisco by now, or well on his way to New York. Or anywhere. Even Shanghai, where his mother lived. He visited her every few days.

So I went to my apartment. I could call the Patriarch from there, wherever he might be. En route I walked alone. My fellow Saints didn't see me. They looked through me. I had the feeling that I was invisible, like an "ascended" Saint. I was here, among the others, but they couldn't see me.

Loneliness is frightening. Invisibility must be the height of loneliness. You can see, hear, smell, but you can't communicate. To be stranded on some tiny fleck of land in the sea is not as bad as being ignored by everyone. There, you know what your battle is, simple survival. But here, with eyes resting on me briefly but blankly, I had a fleeting doubt of my existence, a fleeting belief in ascension.

But a tele-technician, rounding a corner, glanced at me and covered his eyes with a respectful arm as I passed. I was alive, then. I was in coventry, but I was alive. I felt like singing as I turned into my apartment.

Ellen was there, and my heart bounced at sight of her golden beauty. She was like that. Gold. Her green eyes were flecked with it, her skin a paler hue, and her hair an aureate helmet.

She covered her eyes with a pale forearm as I entered, and stood and bent her knee.

"Stop that!" I said.

She obeyed, but her eyes were cast down. I lifted her chin in my hand and looked at her. Presently a tremulous smile flickered on her broad mouth, and I kissed it to life. She submitted. No more than that. A little flame of anger licked at my heart, but I said nothing. Plenty of time for that after we were married.

"It's nice of you to call, Ellen. Can I offer you anything? Food, drink?"

"No, your Reverence. Thank you."

"Don't call me that, Ellen. My name is Robert."

"But I can't!" she cried. "It's familiar, and wicked."

"How do you expect to address me when we're married?"

"With reverence, with respect, as a Saint should always be addressed."

"A man wants intimacy, and friendship, and love, not reverence, from his wife."

"Oh, don't call yourself a man!" she pleaded. "It's—blasphemy."

I looked at her. Her eyes sparkled, like ice in sunlight, but the sparkle was from moisture. She was near to tears.

"Sit down, Ellen." She did, on the couch. "Say, 'Yes, Robert.'"

"Please," she begged. "Let me tell you why I'm here, first."

"Say, 'Yes, Robert.'"

"Yes—Rob— Oh, I can't! Let me tell you. Saint Wakefield—"

"He sent you?"

"Yes. He asked me to dissuade you in what he called your mad scheme. He called me. I came at once. My plane is on the roof."

So this was Wakefield's first move. It was a weak move, because Ellen couldn't stop me. I loved her. I loved her very much, but I wanted a wife, not a worshiper.

"Go home, Ellen."

"Please listen to me, your Reverence. I don't presume to question what you are doing, for I haven't the intelligence—"

"You're as intelligent as I am," I snapped.

She was shocked. "Oh, no! I am only mortal. I can die."

"And I can die." Her eyes popped, and I betrayed the Brethren. "You may as well know," I said, "because the world will know soon. Saints do not 'ascend.' They die. There is a secret crypt. Several hundred are buried there. We are men."

"No," she whispered. "No."

"Yes. Listen. Here is the truth. Nearly three hundred years ago, a new weapon was introduced into warfare. It was fired only once. The destruction was so great and terrible that nations by common consent outlawed it, for it destroyed friend and foe indiscriminately. Thousands were killed within the radius of its effect. It was silent death, for the gun was a ray gun. But listen. On the edge of that area of destruction, people were affected by that ray. Their germ plasm was affected so that male children born of those individuals were born with an aura. Do you know anything of genetics?"

"No."

"I don't know much. My line is radiant frequencies, as you know. But I'll give you the gist, as a geneticist gave it to me. Nature altered the germ plasm as a defense against the L ray. For some reason not clear even to my informant, the defense mechanism manifests itself in males by a glow. Each blood cell has a luminescent nucleus, so to speak. Female children have the same resistance to the L ray, but they don't glow. I don't know why, any more than I know why hemophilia passes through the female only. But there it is. That's the truth."

She was quiet for a moment. Then she quoted a phrase from the Codex. " 'And in the midst of chaos, the Saints appeared. They showed the way, and peace once more lay on the land.' "

I shook my head. I had pity for her, and for all the others. The tale of those glowing boy children ran through my mind, how ignorant, ordinary parents eyed the nimbus of their child with awe and fear. I knew. It had happened to me, in a sense.

The fear was gone, by the time I was born. My father and grandfather had glowed before me, and they felt none of that first superstition. By that time, the Codex had been written, rules had been laid down, and the Saints ruled the world from their new Eden. But the ordinary citizen reflected the ancient awe. They flung up their arms, and ordinary little boys were afraid to play with me.

"I wanted to play," I said to Ellen, "when I was a kid. But I was a Saint, and set apart. I went to school with other little Saints, and we were not allowed to play. We had to learn so much. So many things to know, so little time to learn. We were lonely little boys. I knew, even then, I was like the others."

"No," she said. She had one pale hand across her vivid mouth in a gesture of—fear? Despair? A little of each, perhaps.

"And now," I said, "I want an ordinary life. But belief and faith have made me a superman. That, and something else which I have sworn not to reveal. You see, Ellen, I know the whole shabby farce, the trickery, the mystery. And I am rebelling. They may kill me, but I'll prove my point. We are merely men. Supermen, while you and the others believe. But if that belief is shattered, we are ordinary, and may find happiness."

"Please believe that you are wrong, your Reverence. Even if you're right, you're wrong. You will destroy faith. That's all we have, our faith. Take it away, and what will become of us? Have you thought of that?"

"Yes, Ellen. Listen. Once upon a time a man could call his soul his own. He defended his liberty down to the last breath. Then a series of dictatorships made liberty a remembered word that had no meaning any more. Then, chaos. Then, Saints. It was natural that they should make their own dictatorship, for the world had been conditioned for five hundred years to that. So men are slaves again. But listen, Ellen. You didn't learn this in school, because you are not a Saint, but men were happy once. They laughed, and they battled adversity with high hearts. Do you hear laughter anywhere?"

"Why, yes. Children play games."

"For a brief period, I'll grant you, children have a taste of laughter. But away from home, only. I've watched them. They don't laugh in their homes. How could they? How can a home be happy when, at any time he chooses, any Saint can walk into any home in the world and take what he chooses, wife, child, or chattel?"

"But that is his due," she protested. "Any such home is honored."

"You may not know this word, Ellen, but it's self-explanatory. Phooey! Here's another. Nuts!"

She gasped at this. I tried another tack.

"Do you love me, Ellen?"

"Naturally," she answered. "You will choose me at the next Festival."

"But is it *me* you love? Robert Hanson? Would you love me if I were the boy next door, and not a Saint?"

She couldn't see it. She couldn't see me, under my robe and turban. She just looked at me helplessly.

"Go home, Ellen," I said gently. "Some day, you'll see what I mean, maybe. I want an ordinary home, and ordinary kids. I love you as a man should love a woman. You are a person, I am a person. We're equal."

On her gasp, Evan Wakefield entered. He shot a quick glance at Ellen, and apparently read her expression correctly.

"You may go now," he said crisply.

"Here, wait!" I said. "She isn't a piece of furniture, to be shoved around."

"She is female," he reminded me.

"Yes," I sighed. "I can't break that tradition in a breath." I turned to Ellen. "Thank you, my dear, for coming. Think over what I have told you."

She bent the knee to us both, and went out to the levitator. In a few seconds, the gong on my wall announced that she had taken off.

Saint Wakefield sat in the biggest chair, almost overflowing it. He folded his powerful hands and looked at me with an expression of kindly concern.

"Brother," he said, "I'm worried about you. I want to help."

"Do you want to help the world?"

"Of course. Always."

"Then help me put an end to this sham and hypocrisy. I have the means, but I can use help."

He frowned. "I don't understand," he murmured.

I told him what I had told Ellen, but in more detail.

"I think the Saints are honest in their belief," I said. "But the proof of my contention lies in our actions. The lie about ascension. You know we can die. Then there's the lie about a Saint's lethal wrath, our most carefully guarded secret."

"Don't speak it," he whispered.

I ignored this. "Each of us carries a ray gun in his turban. How do you suppose the people would feel if they knew we scotch rebellion or irreverence by touching the button on our robe, that it isn't righteous wrath which causes them to fall dead?"

"I beg you," he said. "Stop."

"Why? I tell you, these things are proof of our mortality. Superstition and fear made us angels, and we believed, because we were children. We believed so strongly that we ascribed supernatural factors to events we could not otherwise explain. The ignorant said that a Saint cannot die. So we rigged up a secret burying place, and called death ascension."

"I'll admit," he said, "that we can't explain what is apparently death, but the ascension story is in the interest of common good. People would be unhappy if they thought we could die."

"And so they're enslaved because they think we cannot. They forgot the big gun by the time the first child was born with an aura. It didn't occur to anybody that his parents had been in a restricted area when the gun was fired. It didn't occur to anybody that his parents were religious fanatics. The fact of his aura was proof enough of divinity. But he knew, the first Patriarch knew he was an impostor."

Evan Wakefield's blue eyes hardened. "You can be put to death by that statement," he said grimly.

"Not if I can back it up," I said. "Listen, man, I'm not spouting theory. I have facts. But one more point about the first Patriarch. If he didn't know, then why did he study the L ray, why did he secrete a miniature gun in his turban, as we do today? Why did he kill thousands of scoffers, and call his weapon righteous wrath? Maybe he thought he was acting for the best, but his action proves he knew he was a fraud."

Wakefield got to his feet, towered over me. "You're insane," he said. "You can't destroy the very foundations of our civilization. Right or wrong, you can't destroy these."

"They were destroyed before," I pointed out.

"And the Saints built them again. Surely that's worth something. In fact, everything."

"It has served its end. What we have now is a culture of master and slave. Oh, we treat them well enough. We must keep our animals healthy. But they can't call their breath their own, because we can take it away if we don't like the part in their hair. And we're no better than they."

"Stop this, Saint Hanson!"

"Like hell I'll stop it! I have worked with a man, a scientist, in collecting proof. I know that our auras can be destroyed by scientific means. If those auras were truly divine, nothing man-made could destroy them."

"How do you know this?"

"I'll show you, presently."

"Who was this man? Jennings?"

"No," I lied. "I won't tell his name."

Wakefield diverged for a moment. "Magda Jennings," he said softly. "I shall choose her at the Festival."

"But she's his wife! They're very happy."

"She's beautiful," he said.

"That's part of what I mean," I said grimly. "Don't you feel shame at robbing a man of . . . of *anything*, regardless?"

Maybe his bewilderment was honest, I don't know. But it seemed honest. He stared at me.

"But I'm a Saint," he said.

"All right," I grunted. "I'll show you. Come in here."

He followed into my bedroom. I slid back the wall panel and went into my laboratory. I looked at the modulator with pride of achievement, the pride which comes from having made something with your own hands. It was so compact, so neat, so efficient.

I took a slide from the temperature chest and slid it under a microscope. "Look. This slide has specimens of my own blood cells. You can see the glow."

He applied himself to the eyepiece. "Yes."

"Keep looking while I adjust the modulator. That glow was caused originally by a radiant frequency. It can be destroyed by a counter frequency which this machine will generate. Keep looking."

I adjusted the modulator and turned the rheostat. He raised a white face presently.

"It vanished," he whispered.

"I haven't tried it on a Saint yet," I said. "But it will do the same to us. That, I contend, is final proof."

"Yes," he said reflectively. "It seems to be. Well! This needs some thinking. How does this machine work?"

I showed him the simple controls.

I trusted him, even though I differed with him. He was a Saint. We do not trick each other.

He turned it on me, wrenched the rheostat far over.

My aura winked out.

I hadn't expected this. I was stunned, long enough for him to raise the modulator high in both hands. Before he could fling it to the tile floor, I leaped at him.

"You devil! You shan't!"

But he was so large, so much stronger. I did some damage, I suppose, but he kicked me into a corner, into semi-consciousness. Through a blur of pain I saw him smash the modulator, and throw the wreckage into the waste chute. He leaped back and slammed the door against the atomic blast which sprang to life and consumed my machine.

He looked down at me. "That takes care of that. I'll see you at Council meeting tomorrow—ah, Saint!"

My first thought after Wakefield left me was of what Jennings would say. He would call me a fool. And so I was, a trusting fool. I had allowed myself to be tricked.

Then a sensation of nakedness knifed through me. My aura was gone. Destroying it hadn't hurt, at the time. But now it hurt. Never had I imagined how it would feel.

I had thought of it many times, of course. But I couldn't have imagined this desolation, this despair, this shame of facing men. They wouldn't cover their eyes, now. They wouldn't bend the knee.

Pain from the beating and kicking Wakefield had given me hardly registered in my churning skull as I went bitterly to bed. Tomorrow I must face the Council, and that meant going along some of the streets in my new unglowing nakedness.

And I did. I skulked the first few blocks, but such men as I saw— street laborers, technicians and shopkeepers—covered their eyes as if I had not changed. My robe and turban marked me as a Saint. Their reactions were so deeply ingrained that perhaps they saw an aura.

I walked boldly then, and as I mounted the long reach of wide steps I felt that I had triumphed. For my condition, and the manner in which it was brought about, was proof of mortality, proof that we were not divine.

We were men, as the Council should see. Being wise men, they would end this psychological farce which made us slave owners, and all men should be equal again.

I thought this with a high heart, and hurried. But the instant I entered the Council chamber, Wakefield looked at me in horror, pointed a quivering finger, and leaped to his feet.

"Divine justice!" he said. "Look, brethren! God has punished him!"

He waited for them to look, but hurried on with his analysis and accusation.

I blurted something—anything—but the Patriarch waved me to silence. Then I felt like crying, as I had seen men break into tears before sentence was passed on them, for it was too late to say anything.

I was allowed to defend myself before the Council. Oh, yes, I was given a chance to speak—after Wakefield. I don't know how I looked; I know how I felt.

I had knots in my stomach. I had a hurt somewhere in my throat. I had a tightness in my ears. I had bitterness.

"I have nothing to say," I told the Patriarch and the half-dozen Saints.

"Then you admit," the Patriarch asked kindly, "that you spoke heresy, and God removed your aura as punishment?"

What could I say? It was my word against Wakefield's. I hadn't told anybody of my modulator. I hadn't showed it. Of course, Jennings knew I was working on it, but he was a man. His word was worth nothing here. Ellen knew Wakefield had been at my apartment, but she was female.

"I admit nothing," I said. "I can only threaten, and that seems pointless."

"It seems self-evident," the Patriarch continued, "that your blasphemy has been rewarded justly. Here is an example for unbelievers."

Unbelievers? He had said it. I knew nothing of unbelievers, except for isolated cases such as Jennings and myself. Unbelievers? What was this?

"I suggest," the Patriarch continued, "that a public ceremony is in order. An excommunication, so to speak. Hanson is now neither man nor Saint, and cannot live in either world. He must be driven out, with scourges."

The Council didn't understand. The Patriarch explained.

"We have no precedent, true," he admitted. "Nor have we any previous instance of falling so from this estate. We shall bring it to the world's attention."

It didn't take long for the set-up. They called in all the Saints, massed them in the auditorium. I stood again on the platform, but this time I was the only one present who had no aura—until the technicians came with telaudiview screens and equipment.

The general public, of course, was not admitted, but the whole world saw the ceremony. From Kamchatka to Kalamazoo, from Capetown to Chung King, from Sydney to Siberia, they saw and heard on their telescreens.

The Patriarch officiated.

"Robert Hanson," he said solemnly, "for twenty-eight years you have been a Saint. You blasphemed, questioned your own divinity, raised a doubting voice. And therefore, in the natural course of events, divine wrath stripped your symbol of office from your unworthy body. You have no aura. Because of your former estate, you are not a man. Because of your present lack, you are no longer a Saint. You shall be driven out, scourged to a life without hope of salvation."

He addressed the screen, solemnly, his organlike voice rolling through stirring phrases. "Men! All men everywhere, hearken! This poor one, Robert Hanson, shall walk henceforth alone. No voice shall be raised in his defense. No hand shall give him aid, no heart shall bleed, no eyes shall see, no ears shall listen. He is unworthy. His spirit is unclean, and none shall make him unafraid. Let him scrabble for his life. Let him find shelter in the storm itself, in the blazing sun, and let the night cover him with blankets of bitter cold. He is alone. Alone, until death shall claim his worthless soul and torture it in hell forever and forever."

He pulled off my turban, without checking on whether my ray gun was still there. He stripped off my robe. I stood practically naked before the Saints. I don't suppose any greater humiliation exists than to be stripped before an elaborately dressed group. I felt about four inches high, for the ceremony had now picked up a life of its own. Its sonorous rhythm, its grim solemnity, its religious simplicity had caught me up.

"Out!" cried the Patriarch. "Drive him out!"

They didn't hurt me. The Council had flimsy little whips, and they just tapped my bare shoulders. But the symbolism was terrifying.

Down the aisle I led this procession. With measured beat they laid the scourges across my back, and they chanted: "Out. Out. Out. Out."

The world watched, for the scanners followed and sent their images across the horizons.

Out of the temple, onto the steps which were packed with those who lived in the outer city. The temple door swung shut at my back, and I faced a long gantlet of grim faces.

Somebody threw a stone. Another. I don't know why. I suspect smoldering resentment of their masters prompted it. Then the air was full of missiles, and I ran down the long steps. I was not going to let them kill me. Not this way, like a dog.

I didn't try to dodge. I just ran, blindly. Perhaps that was wisest. I don't know. Stones, sticks, and other solid objects left my body welted with bruises, and blood. But if I had tried to dodge, to twist and weave, perhaps they'd have killed me. They'd have caught me, at any rate. As it was they were breathing on my neck as I ran across a bridge into the outer city into the maze of little streets.

Somehow, I got away. Not consciously, not by shrewdness, because I didn't care. I was out on my feet, with the voice of the crowd only a vague roar in my ears. I was not conscious of this dying away down another alley, for the roar of my blood drowned all other sound. I fell into a little lane, and crawled under a house.

I don't know what happened after that.

The room where I opened my eyes had a familiar look. So did the voice that bellowed at me have a familiar sound.

"Bob! They damned near did you in. Magda!" Jennings yelled. "Bring the poor devil some soup. Or something equally loathsome."

I rolled my eyes toward the voice. He was in white, stripping off rubber gloves. His slate-gray eyes were cold, although his massive face was twisted in a grin at me.

"What was the matter with you?" he demanded. "You ran like you had a broken leg. I could have caught you at any time."

"Were you in that crowd?" I demanded.

"Certainly. Somebody had to lead the fools down a blind alley. I had a hell of a time holding them back."

"I suppose you accounted for some of these bruises, too."

"Nope. I missed you. Oh, I threw my share, but mostly I hit some of the other slaves."

Magda came in, as dark as he was blond. She carried a bowl in her slender dark hands.

"Hello, stupid," she said. "Get outside of this gupp. It'll put blood in your veins."

They salved me and fed me, and listened to my tale.

"Too bad for us," Jennings said, "if you're caught here. Maybe we'd better rub him out, eh, Magda?"

"It'd be safer," she agreed. "How do you want to die, Bob?"

"Smothered in kisses, no doubt," Jennings answered. "Well, you ought to be able to travel."

"Are we traveling?"

"Hell, yes. I don't want some filthy Saint walking in here and finding you. Wakefield, for example."

I sat up on the bed. "Wakefield," I said. "He'll choose you, Magda, at the Festival."

Neither of them said anything. Jennings moved over and touched his wife. He touched her with his fingers—her blue-black hair, her olive face, her eyelids. She just stared, empty-eyed, at the floor. Her hands clenched, but she didn't clutch at Jennings, she didn't cling.

Presently: "Drink up, Bob," she said. "We'd better go."

"But where? You can't hide from the Saints."

"We can," Jennings said. "Do you think I've done nothing but putter since you gave me your ray gun to experiment on germ plasm? I may be a scientist, Bob, but I'm a man, too. I made my preparations. I saw the day coming when we should wipe out the bloody Saints. We're ready to go to work."

"With one ray gun," I asked, "you intend to wipe out the Saints? They're immune to it."

"This is no place to work out strategy," he snapped. "We haven't time. Snap into it. Here's a pair of pants. Magda, get him some sandals."

They went into action. While Magda went into another room after clothes, Jennings started packing laboratory equipment.

"But how can you leave?" I called through the door. "If a patrol plane stops you, you have no permission to show."

He laughed grimly. "We're not going by plane. Why did you think I want you to wear sandals? I don't give a damn whether you're fashionable or not. But I don't want to have to carry you because your feet start bleeding."

A gong sounded a mellow note, and Jennings came to the door. His eyes were slitted, his face grim.

"Come here!" he whispered fiercely. "Hurry!"

I leaped off the bed and ran to him in my bare feet. He grabbed one of my arms, yanked me to the waste chute door.

"Crawl in there," he whispered.

I drew back. "I'll be burned to a crisp."

"Don't argue, you fool! This is a blind. It doesn't work. Get in, feet first. There are hand holds. Hang on till I let you out."

When I was in the chute, hanging to short rods in utter darkness, I reflected that Jennings was a man you obeyed. He had pushed me around since that day I'd met him, when he didn't put an arm across his eyes in salute.

He had completed his historical research on that day, and in the flush of knowledge was contemptuous of Saints. It was fortunate I had been the Saint he insulted. Others, like Wakefield, would have killed him without asking questions. But I had asked, and he had told me. We had become friends. The only friend, I thought, I had ever had.

I had given him my ray gun for experiments on germ plasm. These had confirmed his theory that Saints were men. Men with an aura, yes, but men. Nature had provided the aura as a defense. And nature, not knowing that the ray gun had been outlawed, continued to pass that defense from one generation to the next.

I cursed myself a little, there in the darkness. I had worked secretly and alone, and had failed. One voice is so easily silenced. What now?

Voices filtered through the pyrolite door. One belonged to Wakefield.

"You are packing?" he asked.

"To fumigate my laboratory, your Reverence," Jennings answered. "Some stray substance came into the damned place, and I've got to clean it out before I can go on with my experiments."

"I see. Where did Magda go? I didn't see her as I came in."

"Shopping, your Reverence. You know how women are."

"Hm-m-m, yes. Where is Robert Hanson?"

"I don't know, your Reverence."

"Don't lie to me, Jennings."

"No, your Reverence."

"I have reason to suspect that you are connected with a group of unbelievers, Jennings. If anyone would shelter Hanson, that group would."

"But I saw the ceremony, your Reverence. I obey. And I know nothing of unbelievers."

There was a long silence. Wakefield finally broke it.

"For your sake, I hope that is true. Hanson escaped. I can tell you, and all men, that he will be hunted down. Some man shelters him. That man and all others associated with him will be put to death. Do you understand?"

There was another silence.

Then: "Be very good to Magda, Jennings," Wakefield remarked casually. "For I will choose her at the Festival."

This time, the silence became painful.

"Did you hear me?" Wakefield snapped.

"Yes—your—Reverence."

"Your attitude," Wakefield said thoughtfully, "is not as respectful as it should be. Take care, man, lest I loose my wrath, and you die."

Footsteps died away, and presently the thin note of a gong came to me. Footsteps came again, and the door was jerked open. Jennings didn't look at me.

"Come on," he said abstractedly.

I crawled out, brushed the dust of the chute from my bandages. He watched, but he didn't see me. His eyes were wide and blank. Then he came to with a start, and grinned.

"How did you like our priest hole, Bob?"

"Is that what you call it?"

"It's a prehistoric term. Came from England, when some faction tried to exterminate some kind of religious group, called priests. Citizens hid them, and called the hiding place a priest hole. Magda!" he roared. "Where are those clothes?"

She came in, her dark eyes apprehensive, fearful. She had clothes for me, and I slipped them on. She examined me when I was dressed, and, still with the faraway look, said:

"You're very good-looking, Bob. I hardly know you, without your trappings."

"Stop jabbering," Jennings said. "I've got enough competition, without your luring others under your spell. Help me, both of you. It'll be dark in an hour. We've got to be on our way."

We slipped out, packs strapped to our shoulders. Magda was dressed like us, in shorts, shirt, and hat. We were three men, apparently, cloaked in the irrigation fog which the weather bureau was already blowing across the city.

Once, a patrol plane slipped silently above us, and we froze in a shadow. It went on, and no voice hailed us. We marched, and were on the desert in a few hours, where there were no voices, except those of coyotes, to hail us. For a little while, we felt safe.

In that air-conditioned cave in the Mojave Desert, I learned a number of things. Chief among these was that man will sacrifice whatever he has to regain lost freedom.

I had heard two hints of an underground movement. Here I met its leaders. Most of them were from this continent, but they came from all over the world. They came by plane, for they could get permission. But they slipped in at night, stayed for a few hours, and proceeded to the destination marked on their pass and checked in at the nearest monitor's office.

There was Thompson, tall, laconic, with one eye and hard hands. He was from the South, representing three hundred who chafed under the yoke of supervision.

There was Koto, the dumpy Mongolian whose daughter had been taken by a Saint for a house servant.

And Billings, whose wife had been chosen at a Festival.

And Donjian, who had wanted his son to be a scientist but had watched him follow a Saint to be a body servant.

And Miss Blake, whose fiancé had not seen the Saint who killed him for not saluting.

And others. They slipped through the camouflaged cave entrance to hear the thrilling news that Saints were mortal. I was exhibited. They were friendly, though somewhat aloof, and they hurried away to spread the word.

All this was done at night, of course, for patrol planes passed over during the day. We had seen them on the first day, far out on the horizon, circling like black buzzards, searching.

"They're looking for us," Jennings said when he spotted the first. "Magda! Turn on a screen. Let's see what the news is."

We adjourned to the central chamber, and looked at the big screen while each of our images appeared.

"This is Robert Hanson," the announcer said. "Look at him closely. This is the way he appeared as a Saint. And this, after he lost his aura for heretical statements. All persons take warning. Robert Hanson is believed to be alive. If he is sheltered in any house, fed by any hand, or helped in any way, those who give him aid shall die."

Jennings and Magda appeared together on the screen.

"This is Jennings and his woman. He did not report to his local monitor today. When his quarters were searched, they were found empty. But spots of blood and a discarded bandage in a secret hiding place indicated that someone had been wounded. It is believed that they may have sheltered Robert Hanson. The same prohibitions apply to them as to Robert Hanson. Any person giving information of their whereabouts will be rewarded. If a man, he will receive a pass exempting him from reporting to any monitor for thirty days. If a female, she may be among the first candidates offered to the Saints at the coming Festival."

Magda shuddered. "That's a pretty reward."

"Hell," said her husband, "it is for most women. You're a little brighter, because you married me."

"Ha!" she scoffed. "A fat lot I learned from you, except to jump when you call. And that's plenty."

"Turn off that damned screen. They're showing the thing over again."

As this blond giant and his wife bickered in this friendly fashion, I forgot that I was being hunted. Nobody had ever spoken to me like that, and I missed it suddenly. All those years of being set apart rushed over me again. I wanted to be on terms of tender contempt with someone. Perhaps that would be possible with Ellen, now.

I came back to the cave. "I've got you in trouble," I said. "I'm sorry."

"Let us worry about it, Bob. Magda and I knew something like this would happen some day."

"The odds are pretty big, Jennings. We haven't any weapons. Except one ray gun, to which the Saints are immune."

"We'll find one, Bob. We're as smart as they are. Smarter, in our specialized fields."

Magda stood and looked at her husband steadily. She was grim. "Listen, if you mean what I think you do, the deal is off. How are you going to find a weapon which will kill a Saint without experimenting on Bob? You can't do that. I put my foot down, right now!"

I gaped a little. Women didn't talk like that. Oh, in banter, maybe. But she was serious.

Jennings was placating, to my further surprise. "Of course we won't experiment on him, honey. We need this specialized knowledge. I'll want a little of his blood to see if he's still immune since he lost his aura. That's very important."

"Why?"

"It'll decide whether we take the long or short view."

His voice held an ominous note, but he wouldn't amplify any further. I was a little uneasy, but anxious to get into action.

"Let's do it now," I said. "If those planes really were searching for you, we may not have too much time. Why do you think they were, anyway?"

"Why else would they drift along so close to the earth? It'd be natural for 'em to look around out here. I've done a lot of work on the protective hereditary characteristics of desert life. That's what got me to checking the Saints, in fact. One day I suddenly thought—"

"*You* thought?" Magda flared. "I was the one who thought, you big ape. I said suppose something had happened a long time ago to ancestors of the Saints, and a protective mutation occurred."

"So you did, so you did, babe. Not that it matters. I ran down the history on more than a hundred, and knew that's what happened. But anyway, those planes are searching for us, all right. This country was my stamping ground for a long time. We don't have any fires in the daytime. No smoke of any kind, and we don't poke our heads out. Let's get to work, Bob."

We went into his laboratory, paneled with gloflex, gleaming antiseptically at a few degrees above zero. We put on smocks and gloves, after sterilizing our arms, and put some of my blood on a slide.

Jennings took the turban gun from a small wall recess and adjusted the nozzle so that a very few rays could slip through the neutronium screen. He held it near the slide, and pressed the activator button.

He examined the slide, and looked at me thoughtfully.

"Bob, you've told me several times that what you wanted most from life is to be an ordinary man with an ordinary home and ordinary kids."

"Well?"

"Just how strong is that particular selfishness?"

I frowned and went over to the microscope. "Let me look."

The luminescence was gone, as I knew. But the ray gun had not disintegrated the blood cells. There was no breakdown. I was still immune.

I looked at Jennings. "Well?"

"We need you, Bob. We need your brain, and your experience in radiant frequencies. So I want to know where you stand. This means that we must wipe out all the Saints. All."

"Including me?"

"Including you."

"I don't want to die, Jennings."

He grinned. "Wasn't thinking of it. What we've got to stop is the birth of any more Saints. Sterilization."

I walked around the laboratory, not really seeing the shining instruments and equipment, the specimen jars. Since I had learned from Jennings that I was only a man, one thought had been driving me—normalcy. I wanted it. I wanted it more than I wanted to see the Saints' domination ended, for it was a personal desire. The other was idealistic.

"Why should you expect me to help you," I asked, "when by so doing I commit suicide?"

"But you won't die," he protested.

"The name of Hanson will die. I feel a pride in the name. I want it to live."

"It will, Bob. People will remember it forever as the name that emancipated the human race."

"A name on a plate, or a statue. It isn't good enough."

"You won't help?"

"I don't know what you want me to do."

He explained. A synthetic protection against the L ray, so that the underground could overpower the Saints on Festival day. All the Saints would be massed in Eden, and accessible.

"We have equipment, time, and opportunity here, Bob. Maybe you could work out something. Sort of the opposite of your modulator."

Even as he talked, I began thinking of formulas, and induction ratios.

"It may be possible," I said, "and it seems good strategy. On this other business, though. Listen, I don't have an aura. There's no reason to suppose my children will have."

"We can't take a chance, Bob. Suppose you make another modulator, and we remove all the auras, Saints and children alike. We'd have to wait a whole year before we could be sure that no more children would be born with auras. Inside a year, those who still weren't convinced could band together. If the next generation glowed, the believers would do battle. We could easily have another collapse, and blood all over the streets."

"We could form a defense, too," I said.

"Granted. But what about throw-backs. Suppose a kid is born a hundred years from now who has an aura. If conditions at that time should be ripe for a renascence, the race would be shackled again by superstition and fear."

I wanted to be honest with him. I had to be. He was my friend.

"I'll tell you," I said. "I won't promise anything. I want to think it over."

"But listen, Bob," he began.

Magda interrupted us. She came quickly through the door, alarm tensing her dark face.

"*Shh!*" she cautioned. "Somebody's coming through the entrance."

"Lights?" Jennings snapped.

"I turned them off," she answered.

He touched a button, and the laboratory was in thick darkness. My first reaction was a feeling of sadness. I couldn't light my own way in the dark any more.

Jennings slipped out softly through the door, turban gun in one hand, flashlight in the other. We crept after him, through the central chamber along a tunnel until we could hear the rustlings at the entrance. We crouched motionless, listening.

The sounds came nearer, as if a body were wriggling through the camouflage of sagebrush and mesquite. Jennings leveled flashlight and ray gun.

The beam cut a flaring cone out of the blackness, and framed a head and face at the far end. This was an incredibly ancient face, with generations of wrinkles all but burying its beady eyes. The head was as large as my two fists, and it was some seconds before we identified it. A huge desert terrapin.

"I thought it was out of some prehistoric nightmare," Magda chuckled with relief. "Come on in, Methuselah. Welcome to our study club."

"There's your guinea pig, Bob," Jennings said. "You can experiment on him."

As the days slipped by, the search for us must have become a source of embarrassment to the Saints, for there was no further mention of it on the telaudiview after the first week. The search continued, though. The planes circled closer each day, drifting with the wind.

We watched, now and then, when they landed to search a patch of desert brush, or one of the great rock monoliths which jutted from the desert floor.

Our cave had been located and dug with cunning, but we knew that they would find us eventually. So I spent long hours in the laboratory, and Jennings directed the movement at night, when one or more of its leaders reported for instruction and information.

Jennings gave them assurance that I didn't share. I was not sanguine about my ability to make a shield against the turban guns of the Saints. But Jennings told them I would deliver, and pointed all effort toward

Festival day, when the psychological effect of an expose would be at a maximum.

They brought reports of new converts, and all wanted to be in at the kill.

Thompson, his one eye gleaming murderously, voiced their sentiments: "Let me get one of their throats in my hands is all I ask. That's all. I could die happy, then."

I was present when he said that. I asked about it, was told that the unbelievers wanted to kill the Saints.

"Then I'm through," I told Jennings and Thompson. "I'll not stand for killing them."

Thompson glinted at me, struck a match for his pipe on Methuselah's back. "Thought you didn't like us bein' slaves, Hanson."

"I don't."

"Funny way to talk, then."

"The Saints are honest in their error, Thompson. They honestly think they're divine. Anybody would. If all of us thought you, for instance, were a genius and convinced others, you'd be convinced before long. You'd be a superman, as I was, simply because belief made you so. Your honesty would be no less simply because you were mistaken. I say they don't die."

"What do you figure to do, put 'em in cages?"

"No. Show them their error, and let them help set up some form of democratic government. Who else has enough training to do the job? Monitors? They're slaves, like the rest of you."

"Saints won't help," Thompson insisted. "They like to grind us down too much. They like the best of everything, from women on down, and not workin' for it."

"Make your choice," I said. "Do it my way, or do it without me."

"Can you do Hanson's job?" Thompson asked Jennings.

"No," Jennings said. "Nobody can but Bob."

"Then I reckon we got to," Thompson said regretfully. "The rest won't like this. I don't. Too much chance. Kill 'em, they won't bother any more. They been free enough killin' us. Try not salutin' one, see what happens."

"Make your choice."

"Got no choice," he said. "When do you figure to be ready?"

I realized how tired I was. "I don't know, I don't know. Everything jumbles together in my head. I've made so many diagrams, tried so many circuits, I don't know where I am."

"But the Festival's only a week off," Thompson said.

Jennings gave me a keen look, and Magda shook her head at Thompson. He got to his feet, and Jennings walked to the entrance with him.

"I wondered," Magda said, "how long you'd last."

"What do you mean? I'm all right. I'm just tired."

She smiled at me. "Sure, sure. Just wait, though, till you see your surprise."

She wouldn't tell me what, but she showed me the next night. She pushed Ellen ahead of her into the laboratory.

"I'll lock the door after I'm out," Magda said. "If you want out, beat on it."

She disappeared, and the latch clicked. Ellen stood with her back against the wall, bewilderment widening her gold-flecked eyes in which no recognition gleamed.

"What . . . what do you want?" she whispered. "Who are you?"

"Don't you know me, Ellen?"

"No. No."

"I'm Robert Hanson."

She tried to shrink through the wall. Her lips parted to let in a rasping breath. She flung out one clawed hand, tensed the other against her pale throat. She said nothing. She stared.

You can take an emotional blow. It won't kill you. But sometimes you wish it would.

"What's the matter?" I growled at the open-mouthed girl. "I'm not going to harm you, you little fool."

She whirled and beat her fists against the door. "Let me out, let me out, let me—"

Magda yanked it open, pushed Ellen aside as she entered with Jennings.

"What the—" Magda began, eying us both. She broke off, frowned at Ellen. "What's eating you?"

"Let me go!" Ellen said passionately. "You wicked people! I didn't want to come when the man wouldn't tell me why or where. Oh, you'll be punished for this, terribly!"

"For what?" Magda demanded. "You're not hurt."

"For harboring that"—she leveled a finger at me—"that *thing!*"

Thing? Yes, I thought, that's what I was to the ordinary person. This is what the Saints had accomplished. Blind, unwavering fanatics, conditioned for years and years to believe in fear and hysteria.

You can be sick with emotion, too. But you don't die. It just seems that way.

"Go away," I said. "Leave me alone."

"Let me go," Ellen cried again. "Let me go!"

Magda looked at me. "I'm sorry, Bob." She turned on Ellen. "Sometimes I am appalled. I'm not going to like having you in my hair. But I don't guess you're worth killing."

"You're not going to . . . keep . . . me . . . here?" Ellen faltered.

"Not from choice, my pretty. Necessity."

"Go away," I said again. "All of you."

My tone turned their eyes on me. "I'm sorry," Magda said again. "I thought she'd be what you needed to snap you out of your slump."

"Please . . . go . . . away!"

They went, and I looked at the floor for a long time. I had no particular thoughts. I felt even worse than I had before the High Council.

I told myself over and over: she's not worth this, she's not worth this.

I said to myself: "Are you a child who's lost its candy? You wanted to be a man. Well, be one."

I went back to work.

Sometime later Magda came in. She touched my arm.

"Go to bed, Bob. It's daylight."

"Leave me alone, Magda."

"Bob, you look awful. You'll kill yourself. Please get some rest."

I sealed the small neutronium box. "It's finished."

"Really? Will it work?"

"Certainly!" I barked. "Where is Methuselah?"

She grinned at me. "Ellen *was* what you needed, after all."

We placed the box on Methuselah's broad back. Jennings brought the turban gun.

"Wait!" Magda cried. "Are you certain it'll work, Bob?"

"No," I said. "I think maybe, though."

She got a leaf of lettuce for Methuselah. "Here, fella. If you die, you'll be happy. He loves it," she said to me, "if it has a touch of salt."

Jennings added his farewells. He patted the patterned shell. "So long, mascot."

I hadn't seen much of the ugly and somehow awesome creature. I'd been busy. But the Jenningses had made a friend of him.

I touched the button of the little box, and joined in the exclamations. For Methuselah had an aura, bright and blue like a Saint's.

"There's a bona fide Patriarch," Jennings said.

"He certainly looks legal," Magda added.

"It didn't have that effect on me in the lab," I said. "Pick it up, Magda, before he fires the turban gun."

She did, and had an aura. Methuselah's winked out the instant she took it in her own hand, as did hers when she replaced it.

Magda shivered. "I don't like to look like a Saint in any respect."

"Well," I said, "let's test."

Jennings aimed the gun, pressed the activisor. Methuselah continued to chew the lettuce leaf with an appearance of ancient philosophical calm.

Jennings lowered the gun. "It works on him. But how about me?"

Magda caught a breath. "Don't be a fool. Try it on me."

"Why you?"

"One syllable words, pet. It must work on a human being, or we're in the soup. If it doesn't work, we'll be rooted out of here by guards before long. We'll be put to death. At least you will. Me, I may be chosen by Evan Wakefield. I'd rather be dead. Besides, you're the brains of this movement. Why risk your life when mine isn't worth much? If that gadget doesn't protect me, maybe it'll make you mad enough to build something that'll work."

Jennings looked at me and spoke quietly. "Will you go into the laboratory, Bob? If I've got to do this, I'd rather we were alone."

The scream knifed through the laboratory door, high, shrill, and with almost the smell of horror. I was at the door before it cut off, short, and plunged into the central chamber.

Poor Jennings, I thought as I ran.

But he was kneeling beside Ellen, sprawled on the rock floor. Magda stood beside him, the generator in her hand, glowing with the sacred blue nimbus. She looked up.

"There's nothing quite like a fainting woman to spoil a tender fare-well," she said.

"She's all right," Jennings reported. "Shock, I guess, at Magda's look-ing like a Saint."

I looked down at Ellen, and didn't feel much of anything. Oh, she was still beautiful, but—

"Did it work?" I asked.

Magda glanced at the generator. "We haven't tried it. I was standing there, a tense and dramatic picture of lovely sacrifice. Both of us in tears as he aimed the gun with sweating hands. Then this blonde split the welkin. Well, let's get it over with." She thought a minute. "I hate anti-climax."

Jennings turned away from Ellen, aimed the turban gun at Magda. "All that emotion," he muttered, and fired.

He lowered the gun, grinned at me. "Well, let's have some breakfast."

Magda caught a deep breath. "Didn't hurt a bit. Good-by, Saints," she said, throwing a look in the direction of Eden.

Maybe they felt the same as I. I don't know. I thought so. I thought their veins must have hummed with exultation, their hearts must have pounded. The Saints could be conquered. The generator nullified the effect of an L ray. They must have felt it. It was their idea.

I looked at them. "What is there to eat?"

"Most anything," Magda said. "Let's get the sleeping beauty con-scious."

We tried, but Ellen did not respond to treatment. She remained limp and apparently comatose. But she was alive—pulse, respiration normal, a faint flush on her pale golden skin.

We laid her on a couch and went out to the kitchen.

Halfway through our meal, footsteps pounded along the tunnel floor.

"What the hell!" Jennings said. "Surely they know better than to come here in broad daylight, the fools."

But the men who burst in on us were not members of the underground. They were monitors, four of them. Ellen pressed behind them.

"You will come along!" the leader snapped. "It is the command of the Saints."

Ellen pushed through and glared at us with fanatical fury. "Blas-phemers!" she spat. "Now you will be justly punished."

Jennings took the turban gun from one of his pockets. "How did you boys get here?" he inquired pleasantly.

"The woman waved at us from the ground," said the leader. "She will be rewarded."

"We *are* stupid," Magda said, "leaving her alone. Well, we were pretty excited."

"I'll make you a proposition," Jennings said to the men. "You can help us, or you can die."

"There are only two of you," the leader said with contempt. "We are four."

"But I have this." Jennings displayed the gun. "Each Saint carries one in his turban. It isn't divine wrath that kills men. It's one of these." He smiled a little. "Divine wrath is a stream of terrene and contraterrene electrons sprayed from a neutronium tube. Well? Don't stand there with your chins hanging down."

"I can't understand," the leader said, "why you don't drop dead. Blasphemer! The woman is right."

"The reason why I don't drop dead is simple," Jennings said. "I'm going to repeat what I have said to you, but I'm going to repeat it to the Patriarch while the whole world watches. I won't drop dead then, either. Let me tell you the reason. Stay where you are!"

He roared this last as they moved toward him, and the thundering tones stopped them. I thought again: Jennings is a man to be obeyed.

"Listen," he said. "Long ago in an age of unrecorded events, men worshiped light. Sun worshipers, fire worshipers, and so on. Anything with radiance. We call that ignorance, superstition. Yet we have done it for three hundred years, paid homage to ordinary men who were born with an aura. Homage, hell! In every city of the world, the most trivial act is performed according to rules enforced by one of these little ray guns. It's time that light worship comes to an end, and we mean to end it. Listen."

He told them what we had accomplished, what we knew, and what we intended to do.

"You realize, of course," he concluded, "that you can't leave here alive with that knowledge, unless you help us. We have only a few days left. We can't let our plans be known."

It is doubtful if they heard him. It was like telling an astronomer that the world is flat. He knows, and he doesn't hear you. Oh, he apparently listens, but his mind is elsewhere. They were like that, the monitors. They stood quietly, but they probably didn't hear him saying that Saints were mortal. They knew.

"Now we shall go," the leader said. "Come."

"Believe me," Jennings said, "I'm sorry. Stand aside, Ellen."

She was obedient, and her eyes had a queer expression. They were thoughtful, and her hands were no longer clenched. She stood to one side, watchful but not alert. She looked as though she kept her attention vaguely on matters at hand but that her mind was preoccupied. She looked soft again, and the remembered wave of tenderness rose in me again.

The monitors suddenly leaped at Jennings, and one veered off at me. He was somewhat larger than I, and strong with rigid training which I as a Saint had never had. He'd had some sleep, too, no doubt.

Anyway, I went down before his rush, and he kicked me in the side before he jumped in my face. I twisted away, swept his feet from under him, and he got my throat in his hands. I tore at them, but he was strong.

Suddenly, a sharp crack sounded, and a shattering tinkle. He fell away from me. I rolled free, got to my feet as he raised himself to one knee, and Jennings finished him.

Ellen stood over him with the neck of a water bottle in her hand and a look of wonder on her face.

"I . . . I hit a man," she said softly. "I hit a *man!*"

"And well done," Jennings said heartily. "I was afraid to fire, Bob, for fear of getting you, too."

"Why?" I snarled. "I'm immune. You know that."

"Damn!" he exclaimed. "I forgot."

"So you let me be nearly killed."

"I'm sorry, Bob. All I thought about was that you had yet to make another modulator."

"I've already made it. I had to, to get anywhere on a generator."

Jennings grinned. "If I'd known that, of course, I'd have drilled you."

Ellen looked from one to another of the bodies, then at me. "I . . . I was afraid he was going to . . . to kill you. I'm so ashamed. But I couldn't help myself."

Both Jennings and Magda narrowed thoughtful eyes at her. "What's this?" Jennings asked. "Have we made a convert?"

"Take it easy," Magda counseled. "She went outside and hailed them."

"But I had to!" Ellen cried. "To see a *woman* with an aura—I thought I'd go mad. But now, after hearing the whole story—"

"You're convinced I was right?" I asked.

"I don't know, I don't know," she said wearily. "It's all so confusing. All I know is that I was terribly afraid they were going to harm your Rev . . . to hurt you."

I stifled the emotion that rose in me, for I remembered what Jennings had told me. The Saints must never have children. This girl could find a normal life with somebody, but not with me. She could become a mother —with somebody else. There were many things I could do toward building the new world we were going to attempt to found. But I couldn't become a father.

So I merely said, "Thank you, Ellen."

She got it. She looked at me for a moment, then an expression of pain flickered across her eyes before she dropped them.

"Let's get going!" Jennings broke in. "That plane is out there. Each of you get into one of those uniforms. We can't stay here."

"Where can we go?" I asked. "We still have five days. Where can we hide, besides here?"

"We're going to risk a call," Jennings said grimly. "We can't do this job alone. As you say, Bob, we have five days. With plenty of help, how many generators could you make?"

"Maybe a hundred. Why?"

"We've got to get out of here. We'll go to Thompson's."

I didn't like this. "And somebody will notice that Thompson has company, and mention it to his monitor, who will come rooting around to see what is happening. You know what will happen then."

"Oh, didn't I tell you, Bob?" Jennings grinned. "You see, Thompson *is* a monitor."

Four persons, with laboratory equipment and a huge desert terrapin, crowded a patrol plane. But we managed it, and managed to hide high in the air until night began to mask the face of the desert twenty thousand feet below.

We didn't speak. We kept an eye out for other planes and watched a purple cloak slip across the earth pocked with desert hills. Watched the sun linger, then drop regretfully out of sight.

"Well," Jennings said when it was dark, "here goes."

"God help us," Magda replied, "if a Saint intercepts this. Wakefield would come slavering for Ellen."

Ellen slipped a trembling hand into mine. I pressed it perfunctorily, my attention on the blond giant at the controls.

He sat in the pilot's seat, his feet on Methuselah's shell, and began to warm up the transmitter. As he reached for the power switch, he drew back suddenly.

"What am I doing?" he asked in disgust. "Can you women rig me up something that looks like a Saint's turban?"

With much twisting around, tearing of cloth, and all the other activities that go into making a costume, Magda and Ellen presently contrived a reasonable facsimile of a turban. Jennings tried it on, eyed himself in a small, lighted mirror.

"My, I'm handsome," he commented. "Where's that damned generator?"

The plane was dark, save for Jennings' aura. When he pressed the generator button, I heard a strange, soft gurgle from Ellen. In the faint illumination of the aura I saw that she had not, as I expected, flung up an involuntary arm at sight of the aura. Instead, the sound she made was suspiciously like a giggle.

"Thompson, monitor," Jennings called into the screen. Over and over: "Thompson, monitor."

Several faces appeared in succession on the screen, not in answer, but out of curiosity. They were strangers, monitors perhaps, but they cut out at sight of Jennings' aura—after the appropriate salute. And one was Gerald Holmes, a quiet old Saint who was a trifle feeble-minded. He peered at Jennings, nodded, and cut out.

Then Thompson appeared. His one eye widened as he recognized Jennings, and he made a sardonic salute.

"We are coming," Jennings said, and broke the circuit.

We swooped toward a little town at the edge of the desert, several hours from Eden, which was a faint glow against the far sky. With Jennings leading the way through the dark streets, we marched without mishap to the home headquarters of the one-eyed monitor.

Our progress was slow, because Magda insisted on bringing Methuselah with us. Jennings and I carried him by turns, and in turn sought Magda's permission to discard the sixty-pound carapaced reptile.

"But he's our mascot," she protested, as she had protested at the cave when we wanted to leave him behind.

Thompson had a cellar, and means of sending out the word that we were there. I had the equipment set up, and soon men began to arrive.

Of the next five days, I know very little. In some way, Thompson and his men contrived to hide the patrol plane, which we had left in a field, for we used it on the fourth day.

In the meantime, though, we turned out generators. We slept practically not at all; we ate between fusing connections in the generators.

As soon as one was finished, it was taken away. I did not know at the time, or care, where they went. Those outside my makeshift laboratory were familiar with the whole movement, and knew what to do. Although I was involved in this to the extent that my life was forfeit if we failed, I trusted Jennings. He knew what he was about.

Came the night, then, when Jennings came into the lab and halted the work. He sent my helpers away, and looked steadily at me. He was dressed in a replica of a Saint's costume, but he had no aura.

"This is it, Bob," he said quietly. "The Festival's tomorrow. Come on. We'll want to be present."

"What do you intend to do? What's the program?"

"We've worked it out in detail, and it's too complicated to explain in a moment. We're a trifle pressed for time."

I went with him. He knew what was at stake. If he was satisfied with the plan, I had no questions.

I hadn't known, but it was early evening when we—Magda, Ellen, Jennings, and I—marched through the streets again. In the basement laboratory, I had lost all sense of time. As we marched, I was not cognizant of our surroundings, or any activity therein. I saw that Jennings' giant frame was enhaloed in the sacred blue, and that occasional pedestrians saluted the party, but my head was still full of tiny wires, diagrams, and circuits.

We reached the plane, and boldly slipped into the air. We were safe, because the attention of the world was not on the disappearance of a patrol plane, which was not unprecedented. Nor was it on our probable whereabouts.

It was on the Festival. We turned on the screen and watched elimination contests in London, Vienna, New York, Honolulu, Rio de Janeiro, and others of the five hundred key cities from which the winners would be sent to Eden on the morrow for the Saints to take as mothers of the next generation of rulers.

Elimination contests they really were, but so masked with ritualistic ceremony and formality that they were impressive pageantry. The district chief monitor presided unless a Saint could be persuaded to officiate in the measurement and questioning of candidates. These came in all sizes, colors, and degree of intelligence; but they had one characteristic in common—they believed.

"As I did," Ellen remarked, commenting on the protestations of a fiery little Roman girl.

We watched the small screen for a few moments until Magda cut it off. "You don't now?" she asked.

Ellen considered. "I must be honest—with myself more than with you. Intellectually, I suppose, I don't believe. I think it's amusing. But there are several generations of belief behind me. I can say I think the Saints are merely men, but I have an uneasy fear that I'll be struck dead for it."

Magda looked at me. "I thought you had picked a dud, Bob, a few days ago. I apologize."

Ellen had a sort of glow in her eyes as she looked at me, and the hardest thing I ever did was to turn to Jennings and say casually, "What's up?"

"We're headed for Eden, my boy, whose flaming swords we no longer fear."

Presently we were in a field on the outskirts of the outer city. We sat quietly for a few moments, listening to the gentle rain which the weather station had sent to these acres of cabbages. Ten miles ahead, the shining towers of the inner city thrust toward the stars.

"Bob and I will set the stage," Jennings said to Magda. "You know what to do."

"If you need a quick getaway, I'll be there."

"Good-by—Robert," Ellen breathed.

I smiled, nodded. I wanted to kiss her, but I didn't. I followed Jennings.

We started toward the city, and the plane slipped silently off in the darkness. Jennings and I were apparently a Saint and a monitor on nobody's business but our own.

The generator was strapped to Jennings' skin, under the robe, and his blue radiance was indistinguishable from the real thing. As we entered a street, he took the L-ray gun from some pocket and handed it to me.

"If anybody gets suspicious, drop 'em," he whispered. "I don't think they will, but we can't take a chance now."

"Where are we going?"

"To your old apartment. That's the safest place in town. We've had it under surveillance, and nobody has showed any interest in it." He chuckled. "I'll give you the plan later. You'll love it."

I trailed him a few feet, with the ray gun ready under my cloak. I forced myself not to think of Ellen.

My alertness was unnecessary. Such few citizens as we met covered their eyes, and two women bent the knee to Jennings. He made no recognition of their obeisance, and led the way into the inner city as a Saint should.

When you have been a certain person all your life and suddenly, while you are still young, learn that you are in reality someone else, adjustment does not come as quickly as realization. You have formed deep patterns of conduct, thinking, emotion and belief. The inevitable reformation of these patterns comes slowly, even though the knowledge of your former pseudonymity is stronger than your faith itself.

For this reason, I felt that we were committing a sacrilege when Jennings and I strode down the aisle of the auditorium toward the Patriarch and the giant screen. I hadn't been affected as we moved between, through, and around the crowds which packed the inner city on Festival day; nor when we marched up the steps down which I had so recently plunged with despairing hopes of survival in my heavy heart. But I was uneasy when we entered the auditorium.

Few eyes in that packed and glowing audience noted us at first, for Jennings was apparently a Saint arriving late. I was perhaps unnoticed, or mentally explained as a part of the ceremony to come. All eyes, all ears, heeded the Patriarch's preliminary formalities.

"—are met here," he was saying in that stirring voice, "to commemorate a most solemn occasion. For today we choose the mothers of the next generation of Saints to replace those among us who will ascend to their reward in the coming months. Those mothers will be the flower of womanhood, selected with care and rigidity. They—" He broke off as he caught sight of us.

A series of crowd images continued to flash on the giant screen behind the Patriarch as we marched toward the stage in the expectant silence which dropped over the audience. The Patriarch looked at us calmly and without recognition.

"Brother," he said to Jennings, and a scanner swiveled to include us in the image which went out to the world, "you are late. You are—" He paused, frowned. "Who are you? I do not recognize you."

Jennings was respectful, though unabashed. "I am Jennings, your Reverence. My companion is Robert Hanson. I should like to say a few words."

Movement in the audience caught my eye. Wakefield. He shot to his feet, touched the button on his robe as he looked at us. An expression of puzzlement knitted his brows when we did not fall dead.

"Kill them, you fools!" he said. "Kill them!"

Several Saints, then more, stood and directed their turban guns at us. Jennings turned, and with impressive dignity waved them back into their seats.

"We're immune," he said, "to your toys. Hanson because he is a Saint. I because he is a genius."

Wakefield refused to take this. He hurried into the aisle and rushed toward us.

"Blasphemer!" he snarled. "Hanson is no Saint, nor you. You may be immune to our wrath, but not to these!"

He flung himself at Jennings, glowing hands clawing toward Jennings' glowing throat. They locked in battle.

Jennings was large, but so was Wakefield. We all looked on, shocked to silence by this physical combat.

They wrenched at each other, hit at each other, kicked each other. They struggled back and forth in front of the stage, snarling. Wakefield driven by his fury, by certainty, I suppose, that if he did not destroy us, we should destroy all Saints. Jennings had a greater drive—Magda. Here was the man who was going to take her from him.

All the while, scanners translated the scene to images on screens all over the world. The effect on various crowds was shown on the big screen across which were to parade the candidates later.

"Stop!" the Patriarch finally cried. "This is a sacred place!"

He cried too late, for Jennings suddenly picked Wakefield up in his desert-hardened hands, lifted him high, and flung him head-down to the floor.

A sharp *crack!* Wakefield's aura faded, died. He lay still. Jennings looked grimly at the Patriarch.

"If I'm not mistaken," he said, "I've just ascended a Saint." He looked at the scanners, the screen. "He died as any of us!" he shouted. "That's because he's a man, and I can prove it!" He lowered his voice. "May I say a few words, your Reverence?"

Furor.

The Saints leaped up, cried out in fury, plunged down the aisle. We faced them. The Patriarch's voice roared.

"Silence! Would you foul your own temple?"

This shocked them, checked the stampede. They returned to their seats, but not sheepishly, as their action warranted. They were sullen, and somewhat uneasy.

The Patriarch looked down on us, a tremendous dignity on his lined face. "This," he said, "is unforgivable. Before I strike you down, you may have a word. Explain your execrable acts, if you can."

I broke in. "May I explain, your Reverence, to the world?"

I felt sorry for him, for he was shaken. He didn't know how to address me, an excommunicated, scourged, and hunted former Saint. After a few seconds of silent indecision, he nodded wearily and seated himself on the Throne. I mounted the stage and spoke into a scanner. Behind me, the wide-eyed crowds replaced each other on the great reception screen.

"I am Robert Hanson," I said. "I had two names. I was a Saint. But listen to me."

I told them what we had discovered, what we had done. Now and then I shot a glance at the big screen, the mixture of expressions on the faces. Some were horrified, some thoughtful, some angry. This latter group increased in number as I told them of the hoax.

"But the Saints have been honest," I insisted. "Most of us really believed in our divine origin. We have not harmed you, we have merely enslaved you. But that slavery is not as irksome nor as rigid as the military slavery which shackled men for centuries before the first boy child was born with an aura. We propose that the Saints remain in nominal authority until governments are established, but that their auras be removed, and—"

"Stop!" cried the Patriarch in a quavering voice. "I shall not allow this blasphemy. If, by some devilish chance, you have contrived to make yourself immune to our wrath—"

I pulled the turban gun from under my cloak and waved it before the scanner. "This is Saintly wrath," I said. "Each of us wore one in his turban. We pressed a button to kill and called it wrath. Each of these weapons is a miniature duplicate of that greater weapon which brought us into being."

"Stop!" the Patriarch cried again. I turned to him.

"I have revered you, your Reverence. I believed, and still believe, that you are honest. But that first Patriarch was not honest. He knew we could die, knew that science killed for us, knew that 'ascension' was a lie."

"Please!" begged the Patriarch. "You have made statements for which you should be put to death." We faced the scanner. "We have ruled as wisely and as well as we could according to the Codex. This . . . this—Robert Hanson has made serious charges, so serious that they must be disproved here and now. You say"—he roared at me in mighty wrath—"that we are men, that our divine aura is false, caused by certain disturbances of our ancestors' germ plasm. Prove it!"

I took the modulator from my cloak and pointed it at him. I turned the rheostat, and his aura winked out as mine had.

A hush fell, and I was sorry. The old man was trembling. All he had ever known was destroyed. I knew that he felt that sensation of nakedness, for he shrank away from the scanner for a second. Then he squared his shoulders.

"Listen to me," he cried. "All men everywhere, listen!"

The faces on the screen were intent, with now and then a face whose eyes were narrowed in anger. The angry were not as numerous as when I had spoken, but crowds in various parts of the world were liberally sprinkled with them.

The Patriarch, however, got no further. A commotion in the audience as several Saints leaped to their feet drew his attention, and scanners swung to cover this new development.

"Wait!" one cried. "This proves nothing. They have removed your aura, your Reverence, may God forgive them. But is this proof that the aura is not God-given? It is not! A man may cut down a tree, and kill it. Does that prove that the tree is man-made?"

A mutter of approval rippled the massed Saints, and their expressions began to change. Whereas they had been shocked, frightened, and bewildered, they now smiled with smug tolerance.

Jennings faced them. "The analogy is not valid," he said. He told them again of the small area from which all Saints had stemmed. "Is that not evidence?" he cried. "But wait! We have further proof. Come in!" he cried into the screen.

A hush fell. All eyes swiveled toward the great double doors which swung slowly open to admit a group of men. Men. Just ordinary men, but by the expression in their eyes, I knew these to be the underground. They sneered.

They marched down the aisle, and scanners threw their images to the world. Watchers on the big screen now had no expression save that of intent interest.

Jennings halted the men, spoke to the Saints.

"Here we have about one hundred of your slaves who had dared to question your right to rule. They enter here, knowing that they may be killed, but willing to die to show the world that Saints are merely men. Watch!"

He waved his hand, and the men packed in the wide aisle glowed with the sacred radiance. Each pressed his hidden generator at the same instant, and the effect was startling.

I watched the big screen, for in those faces we would read success or failure. After all, they were the people we had to convince.

And now I saw anger. Men began to shout, and women—women!—to mouth insults. They saw now, in one dramatic instant, the generations of slavery to an accidental mutation. Here was proof. The crowds began to mill around, and many men slipped out of view with grim faces, intent on going somewhere.

But the quartet of Saints refused even this evidence.

"These are Saints!" yelled the spokesman above the hubbub. "Jennings has some way to blanket their aura. They are Saints which he has kept hidden. They are not men!"

This, too, found favor. The Saints were grasping at anything.

Then a Saint yelled, "Kill them! They have no protection against our hands!"

Jennings made another instant gesture. He motioned the men to the stage, and they poured onto it. We stood there, a hundred against five-to-one odds.

"If you want a fight," Jennings boomed, "we are ready. We have told you the truth. Look at the people. They believe."

This was true. Belief was written on each changing screenful of faces all over the world.

But the Saints, now proving themselves men in the fury of defeat, began to move into the aisle and advance toward the stage.

"Wait!" commanded the Patriarch, but they ignored him.

We set ourselves. We were ready.

They walked slowly, hands clawed at their sides. A few pressed their ray guns to life, but desisted when none of us fell.

The scanners followed every move.

Then a scream rang out from the rear. A woman's scream. Heads turned. A gasp went up. A path widened in the aisle. Scanners shifted.

There was Magda—and Methuselah.

She led him down the aisle with a ribbon around his ancient neck. On his carapace was strapped a generator, and he glowed, as did she, with a blue aura.

The hall was thick with utter silence.

"God given?" Jennings asked sarcastically. "You know that women do not glow, for reasons which we have explained. But say that she is a man in disguise, which she isn't, that leaves Methuselah. Look at him, gentlemen! Saint Methuselah!"

They looked. There is an austere dignity about a terrapin, in the deliberate way in which he makes one slow step after another. They may be stupid, too, but like owls they have the wisdom of ages written in their puckered faces. No dignitary ever moved with the sure courage of Methuselah.

The aura helped, of course. It gave him authority, and character.

A sound broke the silence. A strange sound which focused all eyes on the Patriarch. A sound all but forgotten by adults, silenced by centuries of superstition.

He laughed.

It started as a low, bubbling chuckle. Then this calm old man who personified all we knew of dignity and kindness, tipped back his ancient head and vented a lusty guffaw which made him so lovably human that my eyes smarted.

On the big screen, one group of startled faces followed another as the Patriarch loosed peal after peal of joy. He became weak with it, and groped toward the Throne, where he sat with streaming eyes.

Then, on the screen, one man picked it up. He smiled, chuckled, and then howled with amusement.

It spread. It was infectious. It spread across the world. Men laughed, women giggled, and small children, not knowing why, cavorted with glee.

Presently, this healing emotion communicated itself to the hall as Magda and Methuselah continued their stately march down the aisle. A few Saints smiled, then others.

But, aside from one here and there, the Saints did not laugh. They were amused, but they lacked the unselfconsciousness of the Patriarch. They merely smiled.

We—the cabal—waited. Presently the Patriarch came to the transmitting screen again.

"This is proof," he said pleasantly. "Are we agreed, here? Let's have a show of hands."

You could hardly blame them for their reluctance. Here was destruction. For generations, Saints had ruled, and in a few moments the right to rule had been destroyed by a few men, a woman, and a desert terrapin.

But they agreed, finally. They wanted to know where they would fit into the new order first, but agreed after Jennings explained.

I didn't hear all of that explanation. Jennings told them that the world must look to them as administrators, for they had been trained. They must start the ball rolling.

"And it has suddenly occurred to me," he said, "that you can take your places among men and lead ordinary lives in all respects. Your auras no longer have any psychological significance, and can be removed. But we are agreed, I assume, that future sons of yours should not be allowed to retain the auras with which they will be born?"

He waited for their approval.

"When we were first planning the coming steps," he went on, "we were agreed that no Saint should be allowed to marry and have children."

I swung and faced him intently.

"I was so wrapped up with the importance of the project," Jennings said, "that I didn't see the obvious solution. We can place a modulator in every hospital, and a baby's aura can be removed at birth. Neither he nor his mother will ever know that he bears Saint's blood. You will, therefore, not be set apart from other men, which would cause you some mental trouble. You—"

I heard no more. I slipped out a side door, around to the main steps, that same flight on which I thought I was going to die not long before.

Ellen was waiting there.

MALCOLM JAMESON

CHILDREN OF THE "BETSY B."

I MIGHT never have heard of Sol Abernathy, if it hadn't been that my cousin, George, summered in Dockport year before last. The moment George told me about him and his trick launch, I had the feeling that it all had something to do with the "Wild Ships" or "B-Boats," as some called them. Like everyone else, I had been speculating over the origin of the mysterious, unmanned vessels that had played such havoc with the Gulf Stream traffic. The suggestion that Abernathy's queer boat might shed some light on their baffling behavior prodded my curiosity to the highest pitch.

We all know, of course, of the thoroughgoing manner in which Commodore Elkins and his cruiser division recently rid the seas of that strange menace. Yet I cannot but feel regret, that he could not have captured at least one of the Wild Ships, if only a little boat, rather than sink them all ruthlessly, as he did. Who knows? Perhaps an examination of one of them might have revealed that Dr. Horatio Dilbiss had wrought a greater miracle than he ever dreamed of.

At any rate, I lost no time in getting up to the Maine coast. At Dockport, finding Sol Abernathy was simplicity itself. The first person asked pointed him out to me. He was sitting carelessly on a bollard near the end of the pier, basking in the sunshine, doing nothing in particular. It was clear at first glance that he was one of the type generally referred to as "local character." He must have been well past sixty, a lean, weathered little man, with a quizzical eye and a droll manner of speech that, under any other circumstances, might have led me to suspect he was spoofing—yet remembering the strange sequel to the Dockport happenings, the elements of his yarn have a tremendous significance. I could not judge from his language where he came from originally, but he was clearly not a Down Easter. The villagers could not remember the time, though, when he had *not* been in Dockport. To them he was no enigma, but simply a local fisherman, boatman, and general utility man about the harbor there.

I introduced myself—told him about my cousin, and my interest in his boat, the *Betsy B*. He was tight-mouthed at first, said he was sick and tired of being kidded about the boat. But my twenty-dollar bill must have convinced him I was no idle josher.

"We-e-e-ll," he drawled, squinting at me appraisingly through a myriad of fine wrinkles, "it's about time that somebody that really wants to know got around to astin' me about the *Betsy B*. She was a darlin' little craft, before she growed up and ran away to sea. I ain't sure, myself, whether I ought to be thankful or sore at that perfesser feller over on Quiquimoc. Anyhow, it was a great experience, even if it did cost a heap. Like Kiplin' says, I learned about shippin' from her."

"Do I understand you to say," I asked, "that you no longer have the launch?"

"Yep! She went—a year it'll be, next Thursday—takin' 'er Susan with 'er."

This answered my question, but shed little light. Susan? I saw I would do better if I let him ramble along in his own peculiar style.

"Well, tell me," I asked, "what was she like—at first—how big? How powered?"

"The *Betsy B* was a forty-foot steam launch, and I got 'er secondhand. She wasn't young, by any means—condemned navy craft, she was—from off the old *Georgia*. But she was handy, and I used 'er to ferry folks from the islands hereabouts into Dockport, and for deep-sea fishin'.

"She was a dutiful craft—" he started, but broke off with a dry chuckle, darting a shrewd sideways look at me, sizing me up. I was listening intently. "Ye'll have to get used to me talkin' of 'er like a human," he explained, apparently satisfied I was not a scoffer, " 'cause if ever a boat had a soul, *she* had. Well, anyhow, as I said, she was a dutiful craft —did what she was s'posed to do and never made no fuss about it. She never wanted more'n the rightful amount of oil—I changed 'er from a coal-burner to an oil-burner, soon as I got 'er—and she'd obey 'er helm just like you'd expect a boat to. ·

"Then I got a call one day over to Quiquimoc. That perfesser feller, Doc Dilbiss, they call him, wanted to have his mail brought, and when I got there, he ast me to take some things ashore for 'im, to the express office. The widder Simpkins boy was over there helpin' him, and they don't come any more wuthless. The Doc has some kind of labertory over there—crazy place. One time he mixed up a settin' of eggs, and hatched 'em! Made 'em himself, think of that! If you want to see a funny-lookin' lot of chickens, go over there some day—"

"I shall," I said. I wanted him to stay with the *Betsy B* account, not digress. His Doc Dilbiss is no other than Dr. Horatio Dilbiss, the great pioneer in vitalizing synthetic organisms. I understand a heated controversy is still raging in the scientific world over his book, "The Secret of Life," but there is no doubt he has performed some extraordinary feats in animating his creations of the test tube. But to keep Abernathy to his theme, I asked, "What did the Simpkins boy do?"

"This here boy comes skippin' down the dock, carryin' a gallon bottle of some green-lookin' stuff, and then what does he do but trip over a cleat on the stringer and fall head over heels into the *Betsy B.* That bottle banged up against the boiler and just busted plumb to pieces. The green stuff in it was sorta oil and stunk like all forty. It spread out all over the insides before you could say Jack Robinson, and no matter how hard I scoured and mopped, I couldn't get up more'n a couple of rags full of it.

"You orter seen the Doc. He jumped up and down and pawed the air—said the work of a lifetime was all shot—I never knew a mild little feller like him could cuss so. The only thing I could see to do was to get outa there and take the Simpkins boy with me—it looked sure like the Doc was a-goin' to kill him.

"Naturally, I was pretty disgusted myself. Anybody can tell you I keep clean boats—I was a deep-sea sailor once upon a time, was brought up right—and it made me durned mad to have that green oil stickin' to everything. I took 'er over to my place, that other little island you see there—" pointing outside the harbor to a small island with a couple of houses and an oil tank on it—"and tried to clean 'er up. I didn't have much luck, so knocked off, and for two-three days I used some other boats I had, thinkin' the stink would blow away.

"When I got time to get back to the *Betsy B*, you coulda knocked me down with a feather when I saw she was full of vines—leastways, I call 'em vines. I don't mean she was *full* of vines, but they was all over 'er insides, clingin' close to the hull, like ivy, and runnin' up under the thwarts, and all over the cylinders and the boiler. In the cockpit for'-ard, where the wheel was, I had a boat compass in a little binnacle. Up on top of it was a lumpy thing—made me think of a gourd—all connected up with the vines.

"I grabbed that thing and tried to pull it off. I tugged and I hauled, but it wouldn't come. But what do you think happened?"

"I haven't the faintest idea," I said, seeing that he expected an answer.

"She rared up and down, like we was outside in a force-six gale, and *whistled!*" Abernathy broke off and glared at me belligerently, as if he half expected me to laugh at him. Of course, I did no such thing. It was not a laughing matter, as the world was to find out a little later.

"And that was stranger than ever," he continued, after a pause, " 'cause I'd let 'er fires die out when I tied 'er up. Somehow she had steam up. I called to Joe Binks, my fireman, and bawled him out for havin' lit 'er off without me tellin' him to. But he swore up and down that he hadn't touched 'er. But to get back to the gourd thing—as soon as I let it go, she quieted down. I underran those vines to see where they come from. I keep callin' 'em vines, but maybe you'd call 'em wires. They were hard and shiny, like wires, and tough—only they branched every whichaway like vines, or the veins in a maple leaf. There was two sets of 'em, one set runnin' out of the gourd thing on the binnacle was all mixed up with the other set comin' out of the bottom between the boiler and the engine.

"She didn't mind my foolin' with the vines, and didn't cut up except whenever I'd touch the gourd arrangement up for'ard. The vines stuck too close to whatever they lay on to pick up, but I got a pinch-bar and pried. I got some of 'em up about a inch and slipped a wedge under. I worked on 'em with a chisel, and then a hacksaw. I cut a couple of 'em—and by the Lord Harry—if they didn't grow back together again whilst I was cuttin' on the third one. *I* gave up! I just let it go, I was that dog-tired.

"Before I left, I took a look into the firebox and saw she had the burner on slow. I turned it off, and saw the water was out of the glass. I secured the boiler, thinkin' how I'd like to get my hands on whoever lit it off.

"Next day, I had a fishin' party to take out in my schooner, and altogether, what with one thing and another, it was a week before I got back to look at the *Betsy B.* Now, over at my place, I have a boathouse and a dock, and behind the boathouse is a fuel oil tank, as you can see. This day, when I went down to the dock, what should I see but a pair of those durned vines runnin' up the dock like 'lectric cables. And the smoke was pourin' out of 'er funnel like everything. I ran on down to 'er and tried to shut off the oil, 'cause I knew the water was low, but the valve was all jammed with the vine wires, and I couldn't do a thing with it.

"I found out those vines led out of 'er bunkers, and mister, believe it or not, but she was a-suckin' oil right out of my big storage tank! Those vines on the dock led straight from the *Betsy B* into the oil tank. When I found out I couldn't shut off the oil, I jumped quick to have a squint at the water gauge, and my eyes nearly run out on stems when I saw it smack at the right level. Do you know, that dog-gone steam launch had thrown a bunch of them vines around the injector and was a-feedin' herself? Fact! And sproutin' from the gun'le was another bunch of 'em, suckin' water from overside.

"But wouldn't she salt herself?" I asked of him, knowing that salt water is not helpful to marine boilers.

"No, sir-ree! That just goes to show you how smart she was gettin' to be. Between the tank and the injector, durned if she hadn't grown another fruity thing, kinda like a watermelon. It had a hole in one side, and there was a pile of salt by it and more spillin' out. She had rigged 'erself some sorta filter—or distiller. I drew off a little water from a gauge cock, and let it cool down and tasted it. Sweet as you'd want!

"I was kinda up against it. If she was dead set and determined to keep steam up all the time, and had dug right into the big tank, I knew it'd run into money. I might as well be usin' 'er. These vines I've been tellin' you about weren't in the way to speak of; they hung close to the planks like the veins on the back of your hand. Seein' 'er bunkers was full to the brim, I got out the hacksaw and cut the vines to the oil tank, watchin' 'er close all the time to see whether she'd buck again.

"From what I saw of 'er afterward, I think she had a hunch she was gettin' ready to get under way, and she was r'arin' to go. I heard a churnin' commotion in the water, and durned if she wasn't already kicking her screw over! Just as I got the second vine cut away, she snaps her lines, and if I hadn't made a flyin' leap, she'd a gone off without me.

"I'm tellin' you, mister, that first ride was a whole lot like gettin' aboard a unbroken colt. At first she wouldn't answer her helm. I mean, I just couldn't put the rudder over, hardly, without lyin' down and pushin' with everything I had on the wheel. And Joe Binks, my fireman, couldn't do nuthin' with 'er neither—said the throttle'd fly wide open every time he let go of it.

"Comin' outa my place takes careful doin'—there's a lot of sunken ledges and one sandbar to dodge. I says to myself, I've been humorin' this baby too much. I remembered she was tender about that gourd thing, so the next time I puts the wheel over and she resists, I cracks down on the gourd with a big fid I'd been splicin' some five-inch line with. She blurted 'er whistle, and nearly stuck her nose under, but she let go the rudder. Seein' that I was in for something not much diffrunt from bronco bustin', I cruised 'er up and down outside the island, puttin' 'er through all sorts a turns and at various speeds. I only had to hit 'er four or five times. After that, all I had to do was to raise the fid like I was a-goin' to, and she'd behave. She musta had eyes or something in that gourd contraption. I still think that's where her brains were. It had got some bigger, too.

"I didn't have much trouble after that, for a while. I strung some live wires across the dock—I found she wouldn't cross that with 'er feelers—and managed to put 'er on some sort of rations about the oil. But I went down one night, 'round two in the mornin', and found 'er with a full head of steam. I shut everything down, leavin' just enough to keep 'er warm, and went for'ard and whacked 'er on the head, just for luck. It worked, and as soon as we had come to some sorta understanding, as you might say, I was glad she had got the way she was.

"What I mean is, after she was broke, she was a joy. She learned her way over to Dockport, and, after a coupla trips, I never had to touch wheel or throttle. She'd go back and forth, never makin' a mistake. When you think of the fogs we get around here, that's something. *And,* o' course, she learned the Rules of the Road in no time. She *knew* which side of a buoy to take—and when it came to passin' other boats, she had a lot better judgment than I have.

"Keepin' 'er warm all the time took some oil, but it didn't really cost me any more, 'cause I was able to let Joe go. She didn't need a regular engineer, nohow—in fact, her and Joe fought so, I figured it'd be better without him. Then I took 'er out and taught 'er how to use charts."

Abernathy stopped and looked at me cautiously. I think this must be the place that some of his other auditors walked out on him, or started joshing, because he had the slightly embarrassed look of a man who feels that perhaps he had gone a little too far. Remembering the uncanny way in which the Wild Ships had stalked the world's main steamer lanes, my mood was one of intense interest.

"Yes," I said, "go on."

"I'd mark the courses in pencil on the chart, without any figures, and prop it up in front of the binnacle. Well, that's all there was to it. She'd shove off, and follow them courses, rain, fog, or shine. In a week or so, it got so I'd just stick a chart up there and go on back and loll in the stern sheets, like any payin' passenger.

"If that'd been all, I'd a felt pretty well off, havin' a trained steam launch that'd fetch and carry like a dog. I didn't trust 'er enough to send 'er off anywhere by herself, but she coulda done it. All my real troubles started when I figured I'd paint 'er. She was pretty rusty-lookin', still had the old navy-gray paint on—what was left of it.

"I dragged 'er up on the marine railway I got over there, scraped 'er down and got ready to doll 'er up. The first jolt I got was when I found she was steel, 'stead of wood. And it was brand, spankin' new plate, not a pit or a rust spot anywhere. She'd been pumpin' sea water through those vines, eatin' away the old rotten plankin' and extractin' steel from the water. Somebody—I've fergotten who 'twas—told me there's every element in sea water if you can get it out. Leastways, that's how I account for it—she was wood when I bought 'er. Later on you'll understand better why I say that—she could do some funny things.

"The next thing that made me sit up and take notice was the amount of paint it took. I've painted hundreds of boats in my time, and know to the pint what's needed. Well I had to send to town for more; I was shy about five gallons. Come to think about it, she did look big for a forty-footer, so I got out a tape and laid it on 'er. She was fifty-eight feet over all! And she'd done it so gradual I never even noticed!

"But—to get along. I painted 'er nice and white, with a red bottom and a catchy green trim, along the rail and canopy. We polished 'er bright-work and titivated 'er generally. She did look nice, and new as you please—and in a sense she was, with the bottom I was tellin' you about. You'd a died a-laughin' though, if you'd been with me the next day, when we come over here to Dockport. The weather was fine and the pier was full of summer people. As soon as we come up close, they began cheerin' and callin' out to me how swell the *Betsy B* looked in 'er new colors. Well, there was nothin' out of the way about that. I went on uptown and 'tended to my business, came back after a while, and we shoved off.

"But do you think that blamed boat would leave there right away? No, sir! Like I said, lately I'd taken to climbin' in the stern sheets and givin' 'er her head. But that day, we hadn't got much over a hundred yards beyond the end of the pier, when what does she do but put 'er rudder over hard and come around in an admiral's sweep with wide-open throttle, and run back the length of the pier. She traipsed up and down a coupla times before I tumbled to what was goin' on. It was them admirin' people on the dock and the summer tourists cheerin' that went to 'er head.

"All the time, people was yellin' to me to get my wild boat outa there, and the constable threatenin' to arrest me 'cause I must be drunk to charge up and down the harbor thataway. You see, she'd gotten so big and fast she was settin' up plenty of waves with 'er gallivantin', and all the small craft in the place was tearin' at their lines, and bangin' into each other something terrible. I jumped up for'ard and thumped 'er on the skull once or twice, 'fore I could pull 'er away from there.

"From then on, I kept havin' more'n more to worry about. There was two things, mainly—her growin', and the bad habits she took up. When she got to be seventy feet, I come down one mornin' and found a new bulkhead across the stern section. It was paper-thin, but it was steel, and held up by a mesh of vines on each side. In two days more it was as thick, and looked as natural, as any other part of the boat. The funniest part of that bulkhead, though, was that it put out rivet heads— for appearance, I reckon, because it was as solid as solid could be before that.

"Then, as she got to drawin' more water, she begun lengthenin' her ladders. They was a coupla little two-tread ladders—made it easier for the womenfolks gettin' in and out. I noticed the treads gettin' thicker 'n' thicker. Then, one day, they just split. Later on, she separated them, evened 'em up. Those was the kind of little tricks she was up to all the time she was growin'.

"I coulda put up with 'er growin' and all—most any feller would be tickled to death to have a launch that'd grow into a steam yacht—only she took to runnin' away. One mornin' I went down, and the lines was hangin' off the dock, parted like they'd been chafed in two. I cranked my motor dory and started out looking for the *Betsy B*. I sighted 'er after a while, way out to sea, almost to the horizon.

"Didja ever have to go down in the pasture and bridle a wild colt? Well, it was like that. She waited, foxylike, lyin' to, until I got almost alongside, and then, doggone if she didn't take out, hell bent for Halifax, and run until she lost 'er steam! I never woulda caught 'er if she hadn't run out of oil. At that, I had to tow 'er back, and a mean job it was, with her throwing 'er rudder first this way and that. I finally got plumb mad and went alongside and whanged the livin' daylights outa that noodle of hers.

"She was docile enough after that, but sulky, if you can imagine how a sulky steam launch does. I think she was sore over the beatin' I gave 'er. She'd pilot 'erself, all right, but she made some awful bad landin's when we'd come in here, bumpin' into the pier at full speed and throwin' me off my feet when I wasn't lookin' for it. It surprised me a lot, 'cause I knew how proud she was—but I guess she was that anxious to get back at me, she didn't care what the folks on the dock thought.

"After that first time, she ran away again two or three times, but she allus come back of 'er own accord—gettin' in to the dock dead tired, with nothing but a smell of oil in her bunkers. The fuel bill was gettin' to be a pain.

"The next thing that come to plague me was a fool government inspector. Said he'd heard some bad reports and had come to investigate! Well, he had the *Betsy B's* pedigree in a little book, and if you ever saw a worried look on a man, you shoulda seen him while he was comparin' 'er dimensions and specifications with what they was s'posed to be. I tried to explain the thing to him—told him he could come any week and find something new. He was short and snappy—kept writin' in his little book—and said that I was a-goin' to hear from this.

"*You* can see I couldn't help the way the *Betsy B* was growin'. But what got my goat was that I told him she had only one boiler, and when we went to look, there was two, side by side, neatly cross-connected, with a stop on each one, and another valve in the main line. I felt sorta hacked over that—it was something *I* didn't know, even. She'd done it overnight.

"The inspector feller said I'd better watch my step, and went off, shakin' his head. He as much as gave me to understand that he thought my *Betsy B* papers was faked and this here vessel stole. The tough part of that idea, for him, was that there never had been anything like 'er built. I forgot to tell you that before he got there, she'd grown a steel deck over everything, and was startin' out in a big way to be a regular ship.

"I was gettin' to the point when I wished she'd run away and stay. She kept on growin', splittin' herself up inside into more and more compartments. That woulda been all right, if there'd been any arrangement *I* could use, but no human would design such a ship. No doors, or ports, or anything. But the last straw was the lifeboat. That just up and took the cake.

"Don't get me wrong. It's only right and proper for a yacht, or anyway, a vessel as *big* as a yacht, to have a lifeboat. She was a hundred and thirty feet long then, and rated one. But any sailor man would naturally expect it to be a wherry, or a cutter at the outside. But, no, she had to have a steam launch, no less!

"It was a tiny little thing, only about ten feet long, when she let me see it first. She had built a contraption of steel plates on 'er upper deck that I took to be a spud-locker, only I mighta known she wasn't interested in spuds. It didn't have no door, but it did have some louvers for ventilation, looked like. Tell you the truth, I didn't notice the thing much, 'cept to see it was there. Then one night, she rips off the platin', and there, in its skids, was this little steam launch!

"It was all rigged out with the same vine layout that the *Betsy B* had runnin' all over 'er, and had a name on it—the *Susan B*. It was a dead ringer for the big one, if you think back and remember what she looked like when she come outa the navy yard. Well, when the little un was about three weeks old—and close to twenty feet long, I judge—the

Betsy B shoved off one mornin', in broad daylight, without so much as by-your-leave, and goes around on the outside of my island. She'd tore up so much line gettin' away for 'er night jamborees, I'd quit moorin' 'er. I knew she'd come back, 'count o' my oil tank. She'd hang onto the dock by her own vines.

"I run up to the house and put a glass on 'er. She was steamin' along slow, back and forth. Then she reached down with a sorta crane she'd growed and picked that *Susan B* up, like you'd lift a kitten by the scruff o' the neck, and sets it in the water. Even where I was, I could hear the *Susan B* pipin', shrill-like. Made me think of a peanut-wagon whistle. I could see the steam jumpin' out of 'er little whistle. I s'pose it was scary for 'er, gettin' 'er bottom wet, the first time. But the *Betsy B* kept goin' along, towin' the little one by one of 'er vines.

"She'd do something like that two or three times a week, and if I wasn't too busy, I'd watch 'em, the *Betsy B* steamin' along, and the little un cavortin' around 'er, cuttin' across 'er bows or a-chasin' 'er. One day, the *Susan B* was chargin' around my little cove, by itself, the *Betsy B* quiet at the dock. I think she was watchin' with another gourd thing she'd sprouted in the crow's nest. Anyhow, the *Susan B* hit that sand-bar pretty hard, and stuck there, whistlin' like all get out. The *Betsy B* cast off and went over there. And, boy, did she whang that little un on the koko!

"I'm gettin' near to the end now, and it all come about 'count of this *Susan B*. She was awful wild, and no use that I could see as a lifeboat, 'cause she'd roll like hell the minute any human'd try to get in 'er—it'd throw 'em right out into the water! I was gettin' more fed up every day, what with havin' to buy more oil all the time, and not gettin' much use outa my boats.

"One day, I was takin' out a picnic party in my other motorboat, and I put in to my cove to pick up some bait. Just as I was goin' in, that durned *Susan B* began friskin' around in the cove, and comes chargin' over and collides with me, hard. It threw my passengers all down, and the women got their dresses wet and all dirty. I was good and mad. I grabbed the *Susan B* with a boat hook and hauled her alongside, then went to work on her binnacle with a steerin' oar. You never heard such a commotion. I said a while ago she sounded like a peanut whistle— well, this time it was more like a calliope. And to make it worse, the *Betsy B,* over at the dock sounds off with *her* whistle—a big chimed one, them days. And when I see 'er shove off and start over to us, I knew friendship had ceased!

"That night she ups and leaves me. I was a-sleepin' when the phone rings, 'bout two A.M. It was the night watchman over't the oil company's dock. Said my *Betsy B* was alongside and had hoses into their tanks, but nobody was on board, and how much should he give 'er. I yelled at him to give 'er nuthin'—told him to take an ax and cut 'er durned hoses. I jumped outa my bunk and tore down to the dock. Soon as I could get the danged motor dory started, I was on my way over there. But it didn't do no good. Halfway between here and there, I meets 'er, comin' out, makin' knots. She had 'er runnin' lights on, legal and proper, and sweeps right by me—haughty as you please—headin' straight out, Yarmouth way. If she saw me, she didn't give no sign.

"Next day I got a bill for eight hundred tons of oil—she musta filled up every one of 'er compartments—and it mighty near broke me to pay it. I was so relieved to find 'er gone, I didn't even report it. That little launch was what did it—I figured if they was one, they was bound to be more. I never did know where she got the idea; nothin' that floats around here's big enough to carry lifeboats."

"Did Dr. Dilbiss ever look at her," I asked, "after she started to grow?"

"That Doc was so hoppin' mad over the Simpkins brat spillin' his 'Oil of Life' as he called it, that he packed up and went away right after. Some o' the summer people do say he went to Europe—made a crack about some dictator where he was, and got put in jail over there. I don't know about that, but he's never been back."

"And you've never seen or heard of the *Betsy B* since?" I queried, purposely making it a leading question.

"Seen 'er, no, but heard of 'er plenty. First time was about three months after she left. That was when the Norwegian freighter claimed he passed a big ship and a smaller one with a whale between 'em. Said the whale was half cut up, and held by a lot of cables. They come up close, but the ships didn't answer hails, or put up their numbers. I think that was my *Betsy B*, and the *Susan B*, growed up halfway. That *Betsy B* could make anything she wanted outa sea water, 'cept oil. But she was smart enough, I bet, to make whale oil, if she was hungry enough.

"The next thing I heard was the time the *Ruritania* met 'er. No question about that—they read 'er name. The *Ruritania* was a-goin' along, in the mid-watch it was, and the helmsman kept sayin' it was takin' a lot of starboard helm to hold 'er up. 'Bout that time, somebody down on deck calls up there's a ship alongside, hangin' to the starboard quarter. They kept bellerin' down to the ship, wantin' to know what ship, and all that, and gettin' no answer. You oughta read about that. Then she shoved off in the dark and ran away. The *Ruritania* threw a spot on 'er stern and wrote down the name.

"That mightn't prove it—anybody can paint a name—but after she'd gone, they checked up and found four holes in the side, and more'n a thousand tons of bunker oil gone. That *Betsy B* had doped out these other ships must have oil, and bein' a ship herself, she knew right where they stored it. She just snuck up alongside in the middle of the night, and worked 'er vines in to where the oil was.

"Things like that kept happenin', and the papers began talkin' about the Wild Ships. They sighted dozens of 'em, later, all named 'Something B'—*Lucy B, Anna B, Trixie B*, oh, any number—which in itself is another mystery. Where would a poor dumb steam launch learn all them names?"

"You said she was ex-navy," I reminded him.

"That may be it," he admitted. "Well, that's what started the newspapers to callin' 'em the B-Boats. 'Course, I can't deny that when they ganged up in the Gulf Stream and started in robbin' tankers of their whole cargo, and in broad daylight, too, it was goin' too far. They was all too fast to catch. Commodore What's-his-name just had to sink 'er, I reckon. The papers was ridin' him hard. But I can tell you that there wasn't any real meanness in my *Betsy B*—spoiled maybe—but not mean. That stuff they printed 'bout the octopuses on the bridges, with long danglin' tentacles wasn't nothin' but that gourd brain and vines growed up."

He sighed a deep, reminiscent sigh, and made a gesture indicating he had told all there was to tell.

"You are confident, then," I asked, "that the so-called B-Boats were the children of your *Betsy B?*"

"Must be," he answered, looking down ruefully at his patched overalls and shabby shoes. " 'Course, all I know is what I read in the papers, 'bout raidin' them tankers. But that'd be just like their mammy. *She* sure was a hog for oil!"

PART FOUR

Dangerous Inventions

WILLIAM TENN

CHILD'S PLAY

AFTER the man from the express company had given the door an un-
tipped slam, Sam Weber decided to move the huge crate under the one
light bulb in his room. It was all very well for the messenger to drawl, "I
dunno. We don't send 'em; we just deliver 'em, mister"—but there must
be some mildly lucid explanation.

With a grunt that began as an anticipatory reflex and ended on a note
of surprised annoyance, Sam shoved the box forward the few feet necessary. It was heavy enough; he wondered how the messenger had carried it up the three flights of stairs.

He straightened and frowned down at the garish card which contained
his name and address as well as the legend—"Merry Christmas, 2153."

A joke? He didn't know anyone who'd think it funny to send a card
dated over two hundred years in the future. Unless one of the comedians
in his law school graduating class meant to record his opinion as to when
Weber would be trying his first case. Even so—

The letters were shaped strangely, come to think of it, sort of green
streaks instead of lines. And the card was a sheet of gold!

Sam decided he was really interested. He ripped the card aside, tore
off the flimsy wrapping material—and stopped. He whistled. Then he
gulped.

"Well clip my ears and call me streamlined!"

There was no top to the box, no slit in its side, no handle anywhere in
sight. It seemed to be a solid, cubical mass of brown stuff. Yet he was
positive something had rattled inside when it was moved.

He seized the corners and strained and grunted till it lifted. The underside was as smooth and innocent of opening as the rest. He let it
thump back to the floor.

"Ah, well," he said, philosophically, "it's not the gift; it's the principle involved."

Many of his gifts still required appreciative notes. He'd have to work
up something special for Aunt Maggie. Her neckties were things of cubistic horror, but he hadn't even sent her a lone handkerchief this Christ-

mas. Every cent had gone into buying that brooch for Tina. Not quite a ring, but maybe she'd consider that under the circumstances—

He turned to walk to his bed which he had drafted into the additional service of desk and chair. He kicked at the great box disconsolately. "Well, if you won't open, you won't open."

As if smarting under the kick, the box opened. A cut appeared on the upper surface, widened rapidly and folded the top back and down on either side like a valise. Sam clapped his forehead and addressed a rapid prayer to every god from Set to Father Divine. Then he remembered what he'd said.

"Close," he suggested

The box closed, once more as smooth as a baby's anatomy.

"Open."

The box opened.

So much for the sideshow, Sam decided. He bent down and peered into the container.

The interior was a crazy mass of shelving on which rested vials filled with blue liquids, jars filled with red solids, transparent tubes showing yellow and green and orange and mauve and other colors which Sam's eyes didn't quite remember. There were seven pieces of intricate apparatus on the bottom which looked as if tube-happy radio hams had assembled them. There was also a book.

Sam picked the book off the bottom and noted numbly that while all its pages were metallic, it was lighter than any paper book he'd ever held.

He carried the book over to the bed and sat down. Then he took a long, deep breath and turned to the first page. "Gug," he said, exhaling his long, deep breath.

In mad, green streaks of letters:

> Bild-A-Man Set #3. This set is intended solely for the uses of children between the ages of eleven and thirteen. The equipment, much more advanced than Bild-A-Man Sets 1 and 2, will enable the child of this age-group to build and assemble complete adult humans in perfect working order. The retarded child may also construct the babies and mannikins of the earlier kits. Two disassembleators are provided so that the set can be used again and again with profit. As with Sets 1 and 2, the aid of a Census Keeper in all disassembling is advised. Refills and additional parts may be acquired from The Bild-A-Man Company, 928 Diagonal Level, Glunt City, Ohio. Remember—only with a Bild-A-Man can you build a man!

Weber slammed his eyes shut. What was that gag in the movie he'd seen last night? Terrific gag. Terrific picture, too. Nice technicolor. Wonder how much the director made a week? The cameraman? Five hundred? A thousand?

He opened his eyes warily. The box was still a squat cube in the center of his room. The book was still in his shaking hand. And the page read the same.

"Only with a Bild-A-Man can you build a man!" Heaven help a neurotic young lawyer at a time like this!

There was a price list on the next page for "refills and additional parts." Things like one liter of hemoglobin and three grams of assorted enzymes were offered for sale in terms of one slunk fifty and three slunks forty-five. A note on the bottom advertised Set #4: "The thrill of building your first live Martian!"

Fine print announced *pat. pending 2148.*

The third page was a table of contents. Sam gripped the edge of the mattress with one sweating hand and read:

Chapter   I—A child's garden of biochemistry.
   "   II—Making simple living things indoors and out.
   "   III—Mannikins and what makes them do the world's work.
   "   IV—Babies and other small humans.
   "   V—Twins for every purpose, twinning yourself and your friends.
   "   VI—What you need to build a man.
   "   VII—Completing the man.
   "   VIII—Disassembling the man.
   "   IX—New kinds of life for your leisure moments.

Sam dropped the book back into the box and ran for the mirror. His face was still the same, somewhat like bleached chalk, but fundamentally the same. He hadn't twinned or grown himself a mannikin or devised a new kind of life for his leisure moments. Everything was snug as a bug in a bughouse.

Very carefully he pushed his eyes back into their proper position in their sockets.

"Dear Aunt Maggie," he began writing feverishly. "Your ties made the most beautiful gift of my Christmas. My only regret is—"

My only regret is that I have but one life to give for my Christmas present. Who could have gone to such fantastic lengths for a practical joke? Lew Knight? Even Lew must have some reverence in his insensitive body for the institution of Christmas. And Lew didn't have the brains or the patience for a job so involved.

Tina? Tina had the fine talent for complication, all right. But Tina, while possessing a delightful abundance of all other physical attributes, was sadly lacking in funnybone.

Sam drew the leather envelope forth and caressed it. Tina's perfume seemed to cling to the surface and move the world back into focus.

The metallic greeting card glinted at him from the floor. Maybe the reverse side contained the sender's name. He picked it up, turned it over.

Nothing but blank gold surface. He was sure of the gold; his father had been a jeweler. The very value of the sheet was rebuttal to the possibility of a practical joke. Besides, again, what was the point?

"Merry Christmas, 2153." Where would humanity be in two hundred years? Traveling to the stars, or beyond—to unimaginable destinations? Using little mannikins to perform the work of machines and robots? Providing children with—

There might be another card or note inside the box. Weber bent down to remove its contents. His eye noted a large grayish jar and the label etched into its surface: *Dehydrated Neurone Preparation, for human construction only.*

He backed away and glared. "Close!"

The thing melted shut. Weber sighed his relief at it and decided to go to bed.

He regretted while undressing that he hadn't thought to ask the messenger the name of his firm. Knowing the delivery service involved would be useful in tracing the origin of this gruesome gift.

"But then," he repeated as he fell asleep, "it's not the gift—it's the principle! Merry Christmas, me."

The next morning when Lew Knight breezed in with his "Good morning, counselor," Sam waited for the first sly ribbing to start. Lew wasn't the man to hide his humor behind a bushel. But Lew buried his nose in "The New York State Supplement" and kept it there all morning. The other five young lawyers in the communal office appeared either too bored or too busy to have Bild-A-Man sets on their conscience. There were no sly grins, no covert glances, no leading questions.

Tina walked in at ten o'clock, looking like a pin-up girl caught with her clothes on.

"Good morning, counselors," she said.

Each in his own way, according to the peculiar gland secretions he was enjoying at the moment, beamed, drooled or nodded a reply. Lew Knight drooled. Sam Weber beamed.

Tina took it all in and analyzed the situation while she fluffed her hair about. Her conclusions evidently involved leaning markedly against Lew Knight's desk and asking what he had for her to do this morning.

Sam bit savagely into Hackleworth "On Torts." Theoretically, Tina was employed by all seven of them as secretary, switchboard operator and receptionist. Actually, the most faithful performance of her duties entailed nothing more daily than the typing and addressing of two envelopes with an occasional letter to be sealed inside. Once a week there might be a wistful little brief which was never to attain judicial scrutiny. Tina therefore had a fair library of fashion magazines in the first drawer of her desk and a complete cosmetics laboratory in the other two; she spent one third of her working day in the ladies' room swapping stocking prices and sources with other secretaries; she devoted the other two thirds religiously to that one of her employers who as of her arrival seemed to be in the most masculine mood. Her pay was small but her life was full.

Just before lunch, she approached casually with the morning's mail. "Didn't think we'd be too busy this morning, counselor—" she began.

"You thought incorrectly, Miss Hill," he informed her with a brisk irritation that he hoped became him well; "I've been waiting for you to terminate your social engagements so that we could get down to what occasionally passes for business."

She was as startled as an uncushioned kitten. "But—but this isn't Monday. Somerset & Ojack only send you stuff on Mondays."

Sam winced at the reminder that if it weren't for the legal drudge-work he received once a week from Somerset & Ojack he would be a law-yer in name only, if not in spirit only. "I have a letter, Miss Hill," he replied steadily. "Whenever you assemble the necessary materials, we can get on with it."

Tina returned in a head-shaking moment with stenographic pad and pencils.

"Regular heading, today's date," Sam began. "Address it to Chamber of Commerce, Glunt City, Ohio. Gentlemen: Would you inform me if you have registered currently with you a firm bearing the name of the Bild-A-Man Company or a firm with any name at all similar? I am also interested in whether a firm bearing the above or related name has re-cently made known its intention of joining your community. This in-quiry is being made informally on behalf of a client who is interested in a product of this organization whose address he has mislaid. Signature and then this P.S.—My client is also curious as to the business possibil-ities of a street known as Diagonal Avenue or Diagonal Level. Any data on this address and the organizations presently located there will be greatly appreciated."

Tina batted wide blue eyes at him. "Oh, Sam," she breathed, ignoring the formality he had introduced, "Oh, Sam, you have another client. I'm so glad. He looked a little sinister, but in *such* a distinguished manner that I was certain—"

"Who? Who looked a little sinister?"

"Why your new cli-ent." Sam had the uncomfortable feeling that she had almost added "stu-pid." "When I came in this morning, there was this terribly tall old man in a long black overcoat talking to the eleva-tor operator. He turned to me—the elevator operator, I mean—and said, 'This is Mr. Weber's secretary. She'll be able to tell you anything you want to know.' Then he sort of winked which I thought was sort of im-polite, you know, considering. Then this old man looked at me hard and I felt distinctly uncomfortable and he walked away muttering, 'Ei-ther disjointed or predatory personalities. Never normal. Never bal-anced.' Which I didn't think was very polite, either, I'll have you know, if he *is* your new client!" She sat back and began breathing again.

Tall, sinister old men in long, black overcoats pumping the elevator operator about him. Hardly a matter of business. He had no skeletons in his personal closet. Could it be connected with his unusual Christmas present? Sam hmmmed mentally.

"—but she is my favorite aunt, you know," Tina was saying. "And she came in so unexpectedly."

The girl was explaining about their Christmas date. Sam felt a rush of affection for her as she leaned forward.

"Don't bother," he told her. "I knew you couldn't help breaking the date. I was a little sore when you called me, but I got over it; never-hold-a-grudge-against-a-pretty-girl Sam, I'm known as. How about lunch?"

"Lunch?" She flew distress signals. "I promised Lew, Mr. Knight, that is— But he wouldn't mind if you came along."

"Fine. Let's go." This would be helping Lew to a spoonful of his own annoying medicine.

Lew Knight took the business of having a crowd instead of a party for lunch as badly as Sam hoped he would. Unfortunately, Lew was able to describe details of his forthcoming case, the probable fees and possible distinction to be reaped thereof. After one or two attempts to bring an interesting will he was rephrasing for Somerset & Ojack into the conversation, Sam subsided into daydreams. Lew immediately dropped Rosenthal vs. Rosenthal and leered at Tina conversationally.

Outside the restaurant, snow discolored into slush. Most of the stores were removing Christmas displays. Sam noticed construction sets for children, haloed by tinsel and glittering with artificial snow. Build a radio, a skyscraper, an airplane. But "Only with a Bild-A-Man can you—"

"I'm going home," he announced suddenly. "Something important I just remembered. If anything comes up, call me there."

He was leaving Lew a clear field, he told himself, as he found a seat on the subway. But the bitter truth was that the field was almost as clear when he was around as when he wasn't. Lupine Lew Knight, he had been called in Law School; since the day when he had noticed that Tina had the correct proportions of dress-filling substance, Sam's chances had been worth a crowbar at Fort Knox.

Tina hadn't been wearing his brooch today. Her little finger, right hand, however, had sported an unfamiliar and garish little ring. "Some got it," Sam philosophized. "Some don't got it. I don't got it."

But it would have been nice, with Tina, to have "got it."

As he unlocked the door of his room he was surprised by an unmade bed telling with rumpled stoicism of a chambermaid who'd never come. This hadn't happened before— Of course! He'd never locked his room before. The girl must have thought he wanted privacy.

Maybe he had.

Aunt Maggie's ties glittered obscenely at the foot of the bed. He chucked them into the closet as he removed his hat and coat. Then he went over to the washstand and washed his hands, slowly. He turned around.

This was it. At last the great cubical bulk that had been lurking quietly in the corner of his vision was squarely before him. It was there and it undoubtedly contained all the outlandish collection he remembered.

"Open," he said, and the box opened.

The book, still open to the metallic table of contents, was lying at the bottom of the box. Part of it had slipped into the chamber of a strange piece of apparatus. Sam picked both out gingerly.

He slipped the book out and noticed the apparatus consisted mostly of some sort of binoculars, supported by a coil and tube arrangement and bearing on a flat green plate. He turned it over. The underside was lettered in the same streaky way as the book. "Combination Electron Microscope and Workbench."

Very carefully he placed it on the floor. One by one, he removed the others, from the "Junior Biocalibrator" to the "Jiffy Vitalizer." Very respectfully he ranged against the box in five multi-colored rows the phials of lymph and the jars of basic cartilage. The walls of the chest were lined with indescribably thin and wrinkled sheets; a slight pressure along their edges expanded them into three-dimensional outlines of human organs whose shape and size could be varied with pinching any part of their surface—most indubitably molds.

Quite an assortment. If there was anything solidly scientific to it, that box might mean unimaginable wealth. Or some very useful publicity. Or—well, it should mean something!

If there was anything solidly scientific to it.

Sam flopped down to the bed and opened to "A Child's Garden Of Biochemistry."

At nine that night he squatted next to the Combination Electron Microscope and Workbench and began opening certain small bottles. At nine forty-seven Sam Weber made his first simple living thing.

It wasn't much, if you used the first chapter of Genesis as your standard. Just a primitive brown mold that, in the field of the microscope, fed diffidently on a piece of pretzel, put forth a few spores and died in about twenty minutes. But *he* had made it. He had constructed a specific life-form to feed on the constituents of a specific pretzel; it could survive nowhere else.

He went out to supper with every intention of getting drunk. After just a little alcohol, however, the *deiish* feeling returned and he scurried back to his room.

Never again that evening did he recapture the exultation of the brown mold, though he constructed a giant protein molecule and a whole slew of filterable viruses.

He called the office in the little corner drugstore which was his breakfast nook. "I'll be home all day," he told Tina.

She was a little puzzled. So was Lew Knight who grabbed the phone. "Hey, counselor, you building up a neighborhood practice? Kid Blackstone is missing out on a lot of cases. Two ambulances have already clanged past the building."

"Yeah," said Sam. "I'll tell him when he comes in."

The week end was almost upon him, so he decided to take the next day off as well. He wouldn't have any real work till Monday when the Somerset & Ojack basket would produce his lone egg.

Before he returned to his room, he purchased a copy of an advanced bacteriology. It was amusing to construct—with improvements!—unicellular creatures whose very place in the scheme of classification was a matter for argument among scientists of his own day. The Bild-A-Man manual, of course, merely gave a few examples and general rules; but with the descriptions in the bacteriology, the world was his oyster.

Which was an idea: he made a few oysters. The shells weren't hard enough, and he couldn't quite screw his courage up to the eating point, but they were most undeniably bivalves. If he cared to perfect his technique, his food problem would be solved.

The manual was fairly easy to follow and profusely illustrated with pictures that expanded into solidity as the page was opened. Very little was taken for granted; involved explanations followed simpler ones. Only the allusions were occasionally obscure—"This is the principle used in the phanphophlink toys," "When your teeth are next yokekkled or demortoned, think of the *Bacterium cyarogenum* and the humble part it plays," "If you have a rubicular mannikin around the house, you needn't bother with the chapter on mannikins."

After a brief search had convinced Sam that whatever else he now had in his apartment he didn't have a rubicular mannikin, he felt justified in turning to the chapter on mannikins. He had conquered completely this feeling of being Pop playing with Junior's toy train: already he had done more than the world's top biologists ever dreamed of for the next generation and what might not lie ahead—what problems might he not yet solve?

"Never forget that mannikins are constructed for one purpose and one purpose only." I won't, Sam promised. "Whether they are sanitary mannikins, tailoring mannikins, printing mannikins or even sunevviarry mannikins, they are each constructed with one operation of a given process in view. When you make a mannikin that is capable of more than one function, you are committing a crime so serious as to be punishable by public admonition."

"To construct an elementary mannikin—"

It was very difficult. Three times he tore down developing monstrosities and began anew. It wasn't till Sunday afternoon that the mannikin was complete—or rather, incomplete.

Long arms it had—although by an error, one was slightly longer than the other—a faceless head and a trunk. No legs. No eyes or ears, no organs of reproduction. It lay on his bed and gurgled out of the red rim of a mouth that was supposed to serve both for ingress and excretion of food. It waved the long arms, designed for some one simple operation not yet invented, in slow circles.

Sam, watching it, decided that life could be as ugly as an open field latrine in midsummer.

He had to disassemble it. Its length—three feet from almost boneless fingers to tapering, sealed-off trunk—precluded the use of the tiny disassembleator with which he had taken apart the oysters and miscellaneous small creations. There was a bright yellow notice on the large disassembleator, however—"To be used only under the direct supervision of a Census Keeper. Call formula A76 or unstable your *id*."

"Formula A76" meant about as much as "sunevviarry," and Sam decided his *id* was already sufficiently unstabled, thank you. He'd have to make out without a Census Keeper. The big disassembleator probably used the same general principles as the small one.

He clamped it to a bedpost and adjusted the focus. He snapped the switch set in the smooth underside.

Five minutes later the mannikin was a bright, gooey mess on his bed.

The large disassembleator, Sam was convinced as he tidied his room, did require the supervision of a Census Keeper. Some sort of keeper anyway. He rescued as many of the legless creature's constituents as he could, although he doubted he'd be using the set for the next fifty years or so. He certainly wouldn't ever use the disassembleator again; much less spectacular and disagreeable to shove the whole thing into a meat grinder and crank the handle as it squashed inside.

As he locked the door behind him on his way to a gentle binge, he made a mental note to purchase some fresh sheets the next morning. He'd have to sleep on the floor tonight.

Wrist-deep in Somerset & Ojack minutiae, Sam was conscious of Lew Knight's stares and Tina's puzzled glances. If they only knew, he exulted! But Tina would probably just think it "marr-vell-ouss!" and Lew Knight might make some crack like "Hey! Kid Frankenstein himself!" Come to think of it though Lew would probably have worked out some method of duplicating, to a limited extent, the contents of the Bild-A-Man set and marketing it commercially. Whereas he—well, there were other things you could do with the gadget. Plenty of other things.

"Hey, counselor," Lew Knight was perched on the corner of his desk, "what are these long week ends we're taking? You might not make as much money in the law, but does it look right for an associate of mine to sell magazine subscriptions on the side?"

Sam stuffed his ears mentally against the emery-wheel voice. "I've been writing a book."

"A law book? Weber 'On Bankruptcy'?"

'No, a juvenile. 'Lew Knight, The Neanderthal Nitwit.' "

"Won't sell. The title lacks punch. Something like 'Knights, Knaves and Knobheads' is what the public goes for these days. By the way, Tina tells me you two had some sort of understanding about New Year's Eve and she doesn't think you'd mind if I took her out instead. I don't think you'd mind either, but I may be prejudiced. Especially since I have a table reservation at *Cigale's* where there's usually less of a crowd of a New Year's Eve than at the automat."

"I don't mind."

"Good," said Knight approvingly as he moved away. "By the way, I won that case. Nice juicy fee, too. Thanks for asking."

Tina also wanted to know if he objected to the new arrangements when she brought the mail. Again, he didn't. Where had he been for over two days? He had been busy, very busy. Something entirely new. Something important.

She stared down at him as he separated offers of used cars guaranteed not to have been driven over a quarter of a million miles from caressing reminders that he still owed half the tuition for the last year of law school and when was he going to pay it?

Came a letter that was neither bill nor ad. Sam's heart momentarily lost interest in the monotonous round of pumping that was its lot as he stared at a strange postmark: Glunt City, Ohio.

> Dear Sir:
>   There is no firm in Glunt City at the present time bearing any name similar to "Bild-A-Man Company" nor do we know of any such organization planning to join our little community. We also have no thoroughfare called "Diagonal"; our north-south streets are named after Indian tribes while our east-west avenues are listed numerically in multiples of five.
>   Glunt City is a restricted residential township, we intend to keep it that. Only small retailing and service establishments are permitted here. If you are interested in building a home in Glunt City and can furnish proof of white, Christian, Anglo-Saxon ancestry on both sides of your family for fifteen generations, we would be glad to furnish further information.
>   Thomas H. Plantagenet, Mayor
>   P.S. An airfield for privately owned jet- and propeller-driven aircraft is being built outside the city limits.

That was sort of that. He would get no refills on any of the vials and bottles even if he had a loose slunk or two with which to pay for the stuff. Better go easy on the material and conserve it as much as possible. But no disassembling!

Would the "Bild-A-Man Company" begin manufacturing at Glunt City some time in the future when it had developed into an industrial metropolis against the constricted wills of its restricted citizenry? Or had his package slid from some different track in the human time stream, some era to be born on another-dimensional earth? There would have to be a common origin to both, else why the English wordage? And could there be a purpose in his having received it, beneficial—or otherwise?

Tina had been asking him a question. Sam detached his mind from shapeless speculation and considered her quite-the-opposite features.

"So if you'd still like me to go out with you New Year's Eve, all I have to do is tell Lew that my mother expects to suffer from her gall-stones and I have to stay home. Then I think you could buy the *Cigale* reservations from him cheap."

"Thanks a lot, Tina, but very honestly I don't have the loose cash right now. You and Lew make a much more logical couple anyhow."

Lew Knight wouldn't have done that. Lew cut throats with carefree zest. But Tina did seem to go with Lew as a type.

Why? Until Lew had developed a raised eyebrow where Tina was concerned, it had been Sam all the way. The rest of the office had accepted the fact and moved out of their path. It wasn't only a question of Lew's greater success and financial well-being: just that Lew had decided he wanted Tina and had got her.

It hurt. Tina wasn't special; she was no cultural companion, no intellectual equal; but he wanted her. He liked being with her. She was the woman he desired, rightly or wrongly, whether or not there was a sound basis to their relationship. He remembered his parents before a railway accident had orphaned him: they were theoretically incompatible, but they had been terribly happy together.

He was still wondering about it the next night as he flipped the pages of "Twinning yourself and your friends." It would be interesting to twin Tina.

"One for me, one for Lew."

Only the horrible possibility of an error was there. His mannikin had not been perfect: its arms had been of unequal length. Think of a physically lopsided Tina, something he could never bring himself to disassemble, limping extraneously through life.

And then the book warned: "Your constructed twin, though resembling you in every obvious detail, has not had the slow and guarded maturity you have enjoyed. He or she will not be as stable mentally, much less able to cope with unusual situations, much more prone to neurosis. Only a professional carnuplicator, using the finest equipment, can make an exact copy of a human personality. Yours will be able to live and even reproduce, but never to be accepted as a valid and responsible member of society."

Well, he could chance that. A little less stability in Tina would hardly be noticeable; it might be more desirable.

There was a knock. He opened the door, guarding the box from view with his body. His landlady.

"Your door has been locked for the past week, Mr. Weber. That's why the chambermaid hasn't cleaned the room. We thought you didn't want anyone inside."

"Yes." He stepped into the hall and closed the door behind him. "I've been doing some highly important legal work at home."

"Oh." He sensed a murderous curiosity and changed the subject.

"Why all the fine feathers, Mrs. Lipanti—New Year's Eve party?"

She smoothed her frilled black dress self-consciously. "Y-yes. My

sister and her husband came in from Springfield today and we were going to make a night of it. Only . . . only the girl who was supposed to
come over and mind their baby just phoned and said she isn't feeling
well. So I guess we won't go unless somebody else, I mean unless we can
get someone else to take care . . . I mean, somebody who doesn't have
a previous engagement and who wouldn't—" Her voice trailed away in
assumed embarrassment as she realized the favor was already asked.

Well, after all, he wasn't doing anything tonight. And she had been
remarkably pleasant those times when he had had to operate on the basis
of "Of course I'll have the rest of the rent in a day or so." But why did
any one of the earth's two billion humans, when in the possession of an
unpleasant buck, pass it automatically to Sam Weber?

Then he remembered Chapter IV on babies and other small humans.
Since the night when he had separated the mannikin from its constituent
parts, he'd been running through the manual as an intellectual exercise.
He didn't feel quite up to making some weird error on a small human.
But twinning wasn't supposed to be as difficult.

Only by Gog and by Magog, by Aesculapius the Physician and Kil-
dare the Doctor, he would not disassemble this time. There must be
other methods of disposal possible in a large city on a dark night. He'd
think of something.

"I'd be glad to watch the baby for a few hours." He started down the
hall to anticipate her polite protest. "Don't have a date tonight myself.
No, don't mention it, Mrs. Lipanti. Glad to do it."

In the landlady's apartment, her nervous sister briefed him doubtfully. "And that's the only time she cries in a low, steady way so if you
move fast there won't be much damage done. Not much, anyway."

He saw them to the door. "I'll be fast enough," he assured the mother.
"Just so I get a hint."

Mrs. Lipanti paused at the door. "Did I tell you about the man who
was asking after you this afternoon?"

Again? "A sort of tall, old man in a long, black overcoat?"

"With the most frightening way of staring into your face and talking
under his breath. Do you know him?"

"Not exactly. What did he want?"

"Well, he asked if there was a Sam Weaver living here who was a lawyer and had been spending most of his time in his room for the past
week. I told him we had a Sam Weber—your first name *is* Sam?—who
answered to that description, but that the last Weaver had moved out
over a year ago. He just looked at me for a while and said, 'Weaver,
Weber—they might have made an error,' and walked out without so
much as a good-by or excuse me. Not what I call a polite gentleman."

Thoughtfully Sam walked back to the child. Strange how sharp a
mental picture he had formed of this man! Possibly because the two
women who had met him thus far had been very impressionable, although to hear their stories the impression was there to be received.

He doubted there was any mistake: the man had been looking for him on both occasions; his knowledge of Sam's vacation from foolscap this past week proved that. It did seem as if he weren't interested in meeting him until some moot point of identity should be established beyond the least shadow of a doubt. Something of a legal mind, that.

The whole affair centered around the "Bild-A-Man" set he was positive. This skulking investigation hadn't started until after the gift from 2153 had been delivered—and Sam had started using it.

But till the character in the long, black overcoat paddled up to Sam Weber personally and stated his business, there wasn't very much he could do about it.

Sam went upstairs for his Junior Biocalibrator.

He propped the manual open against the side of the bed and switched the instrument on to full scanning power. The infant gurgled thickly as the calibrator was rolled slowly over its fat body and a section of metal tape unwound from the slot with, according to the manual, a completely detailed physiological description.

It was detailed. Sam gasped as the tape, running through the enlarging viewer, gave information on the child for which a pediatrician would have taken out at least three mortgages on his immortal soul. Thyroid capacity, chromosome quality, cerebral content. All broken down into neat subheads of data for construction purposes. Rate of skull expansion in minutes for the next ten hours; rate of cartilage transformation; changes in hormone secretions while active and at rest.

This was a blueprint; it was like taking canons from a baby.

Sam left the child to a puzzled contemplation of its navel and sped upstairs. With the tape as a guide, he clipped sections of the molds into the required smaller sizes. Then, almost before he knew it consciously, he was constructing a small human.

He was amazed at the ease with which he worked. Skill was evidently acquired in this game; the mannikin had been much harder to put together. The matter of duplication and working from an informational tape simplified his problems, though.

The child took form under his eyes.

He was finished just an hour and a half after he had taken his first measurements. All except the vitalizing.

A moment's pause, here. The ugly prospect of disassembling stopped him for a moment, but he shook it off. He had to see how well he had done the job. If this child could breathe, what was not possible to him! Besides he couldn't keep it suspended in an inanimate condition very long without running the risk of ruining his work and the materials.

He started the vitalizer.

The child shivered and began a low, steady cry. Sam tore down to the landlady's apartment again and scooped up a square of white linen left on the bed for emergencies. Oh well, some more clean sheets.

After he had made the necessary repairs, he stood back and took a good look at it. He was in a sense a papa. He felt as proud.

It was a perfect little creature, glowing and round with health.

"I have twinned," he said happily.

Every detail correct. The two sides of the face correctly unexact, the duplication of the original child's lunch at the very same point of digestion. Same hair, same eyes—or was it? Sam bent over the infant. He could have sworn the other was a blonde. This child had dark hair which seemed to grow darker as he looked.

He grabbed it with one hand and picked up the Junior Biocalibrator with the other.

Downstairs, he placed the two babies side by side on the big bed. No doubt about it. One was blonde; the other, his plagiarism, was now a definite brunette.

The biocalibrator showed other differences: Slightly faster pulse for his model. Lower blood count. Minutely higher cerebral capacity, although the content was the same. Adrenalin and bile secretions entirely unalike.

It added up to error. His child might be the superior specimen, or the inferior one, but he had not made a true copy. He had no way of knowing at the moment whether or not the infant he had built could grow into a human maturity. The other could.

Why? He had followed directions faithfully, had consulted the calibrator tape at every step. And this had resulted. Had he waited too long before starting the vitalizer? Or was it just a matter of insufficient skill?

Close to midnight, his watch delicately pointed out. It would be necessary to remove evidences of baby-making before the Sisters Lipanti came home. Sam considered possibilities swiftly.

He came down in a few moments with an old tablecloth and a cardboard carton. He wrapped the child in the tablecloth, vaguely happy that the temperature had risen that night, then placed it in the carton.

The child gurgled at the adventure. Its original on the bed *goo*ed in return. Sam slipped quietly out into the street.

Male and female drunks stumbled along tootling on tiny trumpets. People wished each other a *hic* happy new year as he strode down the necessary three blocks.

As he turned left, he saw the sign: "Urban Foundling Home." There was a light burning over a side door. Convenient, but that was a big city for you.

Sam shrank into the shadow of an alley for a moment as a new idea occurred to him. This had to look genuine. He pulled a pencil out of his breast pocket and scrawled on the side of the carton in as small handwriting as he could manage:

"Please take good care of my darling little girl. I am not married."

Then he deposited the carton on the doorstep and held his finger on the bell until he heard movement inside. He was across the street and in the alley again by the time a nurse had opened the door.

It wasn't until he walked into the boarding house that he remembered about the navel. He stopped and tried to recall. No, he had built his little girl without a navel! Her belly had been perfectly smooth. That's what came of hurrying! Shoddy workmanship.

There might be a bit of to-do in the foundling home when they unwrapped the kid. How would they explain it?

Sam slapped his forehead. "Me and Michelangelo. He adds a navel, I forget one!"

Except for an occasional groan, the office was fairly quiet the second day of the New Year.

He was going through the last intriguing pages of the book when he was aware of two people teetering awkwardly near his desk. His eyes left the manual reluctantly: "New kinds of life for your leisure moments" was really stuff!

Tina and Lew Knight.

Sam digested the fact that neither of them were perched on his desk.

Tina wore the little ring she'd received for Christmas on the third finger of her left hand; Lew was experimenting with a sheepish look and finding it difficult.

"Oh, Sam. Last night, Lew . . . Sam, we wanted you to be the first — Such a surprise, like that I mean! Why I almost— Naturally we thought this would be a little difficult . . . Sam, we're going, I mean we expect—"

"—to be married," Lew Knight finished in what was almost an undertone. For the first time since Sam had known him he looked uncertain and suspicious of life, like a man who finds a newly-hatched octopus in his breakfast orange juice.

"You'd adore the way Lew proposed," Tina was gushing. "So roundabout. And so shy. I told him afterwards that I thought for a moment he was talking of something else entirely. I did have trouble understanding you, didn't I dear?"

"Huh? Oh yeah, you had trouble understanding me." Lew stared at his former rival. "Much of a surprise?"

"Oh, no. No surprise at all. You two fit together so perfectly that I knew it right from the first." Sam mumbled his felicitations, conscious of Tina's searching glances. "And now, if you'll excuse me, there's something I have to take care of immediately. A special sort of wedding present."

Lew was disconcerted. "A wedding present. This early?"

"Why certainly," Tina told him. "It isn't very easy to get just the right thing. And a special friend like Sam naturally wants to get a very special gift."

Sam decided he had taken enough. He grabbed the manual and his coat and dodged through the door.

By the time he came to the red stone steps of the boarding house, he had reached the conclusion that the wound, while painful, had definitely missed his heart. He was in fact chuckling at the memory of Lew Knight's face when his landlady plucked at his sleeve.

"That man was here again today, Mr. Weber. He said he wanted to see you."

"Which man? The tall, old fellow?"

Mrs. Lipanti nodded, her arms folded complacently across her chest. "Such an unpleasant person! When I told him you weren't in, he insisted I take him up to your room. I said I couldn't do that without your permission and he looked at me fit to kill. I've never believed in the evil eye myself—although I always say where there is smoke there must be fire—but if there is such a thing as an evil eye, he has it."

"Will he be back?"

"Yes. He asked me when you usually return and I said about eight o'clock, figuring that if you didn't want to meet him it would give you time to change your clothes and wash up and leave before he gets here. And, Mr. Weber, if you'll excuse me for saying this, I don't think you want to meet him."

"Thanks. But when he comes in at eight, show him up. If he's the right person, I'm in illegal possession of his property. I want to know where this property originates."

In his room, he put the manual away carefully and told the box to open. The Junior Biocalibrator was not too bulky and newspaper would suffice to cover it. He was on his way uptown in a few minutes with the strangely shaped parcel under his arm.

Did he still want to duplicate Tina, he pondered? Yes, in spite of everything. She was still the woman he desired more than any he had ever known; and with the original married to Lew, the replica would have no choice but himself. Only—the replica would have Tina's characteristics up to the moment the measurements were taken; she might insist on marrying Lew as well.

That would make for a bit of a sitcheeayshun. But he was still miles from that bridge. It might even be amusing—

The possibility of error was more annoying. The Tina he would make might be off-center in a number of ways: reds might overlap pinks like an imperfectly reproduced color photograph; she might, in time, come to digest her own stomach; there could very easily be a streak of strange and incurable insanity implicit in his model which would not assert itself until a deep mutual affection had flowered and borne fruit. As yet, he was no great shakes as a twinner and human mimeographer; the errors he had made on Mrs. Lipanti's niece demonstrated his amateur standing.

Sam knew he would never be able to dismantle Tina if she proved defective. Outside of the chivalrous concepts and almost superstitious reverence for womankind pressed into him by a small town boyhood, there was the unmitigated horror he felt at the idea of such a beloved object going through the same disintegrating process as—well, the mannikin. But if he overlooked an essential in his construction, what other recourse would there be?

Solution: nothing must be overlooked. Sam grinned bitterly as the ancient elevator swayed up to his office. If he only had time for a little more practice with a person whose reactions he knew so exactly that any deviation from the norm would be instantly obvious! But the strange, old man would be calling tonight, and, if his business concerned "Bild-A-Man" sets, Sam's experiments might be abruptly curtailed. And where would he find such a person—he had few real friends and no intimate ones. And, to be at all valuable, it would have to be someone he knew as well as himself.

Himself!

"Floor, sir." The elevator operator was looking at him reproachfully. Sam's exultant shout had caused him to bring the carrier to a spasmodic stop six inches under the floor level, something he had not done since that bygone day when he had first nervously reached for the controls. He felt his craftmanship was under a shadow as he morosely closed the door behind the lawyer.

And why not himself? He knew his own physical attributes better than he knew Tina's; any mental instability on the part of his reproduced self would be readily discernible long before it reached the point of psychosis or worse. And the beauty of it was that he would have no compunction in disassembling a superfluous Sam Weber. Quite the contrary: the horror in that situation would be the continued existence of a duplicate personality; its removal would be a relief.

Twinning himself would provide the necessary practice in a familiar medium. Ideal. He'd have to take careful notes so that if anything went wrong he'd know just where to avoid going off the track in making his own personal Tina.

And maybe the old geezer wasn't interested in the set at all. Even if he were, Sam could take his landlady's advice and not be at home when he called. Silver linings wherever he looked.

Lew Knight stared at the instrument in Sam's hands. "What in the sacred name of Blackstone and all his commentaries is that? Looks like a lawn mower for a window box!"

"It's uh, sort of a measuring gadget. Gives the right size for one thing and another and this and that. Won't be able to get you the wedding present I have in mind unless I know the right size. Or sizes. Tina, would you mind stepping out into the hall?"

"Nooo." She looked dubiously at the gadget. "It won't hurt?"

It wouldn't hurt a bit. Sam assured her. "I just want to keep this a secret from Lew till after the ceremony."

She brightened at that and preceded Sam through the door. "Hey counselor," one of the other young lawyers called at Lew as they left. "Hey counselor, don't let him do that. Possession is nine points Sam always says. He'll never bring her back."

Lew chuckled weakly and bent over his work.

"Now I want you to go into the ladies' room," Sam explained to a bewildered Tina. "I'll stand guard outside and tell the other customers that the place is out of order. If another woman is inside wait until she leaves. Then strip."

"Strip?" Tina squealed.

He nodded. Then very carefully, emphasizing every significant detail of operation, he told her how to use the Junior Biocalibrator. How she must be careful to kick the switch and set the tape running. How she must cover every external square inch of her body. "This little arm will enable you to lower it down your back. No questions now. Git." She gat.

She was back in fifteen minutes, fluffing her dress into place and studying the tape with a rapt frown. "This is the *strangest* thing— According to the spool, my iodine content—"

Sam snaffled the Biocalibrator hurriedly. "Don't give it another thought. It's a code, kind of. Tells me just what size and how many of what kind. You'll be crazy about the gift when you see it."

"I know I will." She bent over him as he kneeled and examined the tape to make certain she had applied the instrument correctly. "You know, Sam, I always felt your taste was perfect. I want you to come and visit us often after we're married. You can have such beautiful ideas! Lew is a bit too . . . too businesslike, isn't he? I mean it's necessary for success and all that, but success isn't everything. I mean you have to have culture, too. You'll help me keep cultured, won't you, Sam?"

"Sure," Sam said vaguely. The tape was complete. Now to get started! "Anything I can do—glad to help."

He rang for the elevator and noticed the forlorn uncertainty with which she watched him. "Don't worry, Tina. You and Lew will be very happy together. And you'll love this wedding present." But not as much as I will, he told himself as he stepped into the elevator.

Back in his room, he emptied the machine and undressed. In a few moments he had another tape on himself. He would have liked to consider it for a while, but being this close to the goal made him impatient. He locked the door, cleaned his room hurriedly of accumulated junk— remembering to sniff in annoyance at Aunt Maggie's ties: the blue and red one almost lighted up the room—ordered the box to open—and he was ready to begin.

First the water. With the huge amount of water necessary to the human body, especially in the case of an adult, he might as well start collecting it now. He had bought several pans and it would take his lone faucet some time to fill them all.

As he placed the first pot under the tap, Sam wondered suddenly if its chemical impurities might affect the end product. Of course it might! These children of 2153 would probably take absolutely pure H_2O as a matter of daily use; the manual hadn't mentioned the subject, but how did he know what kind of water they had available? Well, he'd boil this batch over his chemical stove; when he got to making Tina he could see about getting *aqua* completely *pura*.

Score another point for making a simulacrum of Sam first.

While waiting for the water to boil, he arranged his supplies to positions of maximum availability. They were getting low. That baby had taken up quite a bit of useful ingredients; too bad he hadn't seen his way clear to disassembling it. That meant if there were any argument in favor of allowing the replica of himself to go on living, it was now invalid. He'd have to take it apart in order to have enough for Tina II. Or Tina prime?

He leafed through Chapters VI, VII and VIII on the ingredients, completion and disassembling of a man. He'd been through this several times before but he'd passed more than one law exam on the strength of a last-minute review.

The constant reference to mental instability disturbed him. "The humans constructed with this set will, at the very best, show most of the superstitious tendencies, and neurosis-compulsions of medieval mankind. In the long run they are not normal; take great care not to consider them such." Well, it wouldn't make too much difference in Tina's case—and that was all that was important.

When he had finished adjusting the molds to the correct sizes, he fastened the vitalizer to the bed. Then—very, very slowly and with repeated glances at the manual, he began to duplicate Sam Weber. He learned more of his physical limitations and capabilities in the next two hours than any man had ever known since the day when an inconspicuous primate had investigated the possibilities of ground locomotion upon the nether extremities alone.

Strangely enough, he felt neither awe nor exultation. It was like building a radio receiver for the first time. Child's play.

Most of the vials and jars were empty when he had finished. The damp molds were stacked inside the box, still in their three-dimensional outline. The manual lay neglected on the floor.

Sam Weber stood near the bed looking down at Sam Weber on the bed.

All that remained was vitalizing. He daren't wait too long or imperfections might set in and the errors of the baby be repeated. He shook off a nauseating feeling of unreality, made certain that the big disassembleator was within reach and set the Jiffy Vitalizer in motion.

The man on the bed coughed. He stirred. He sat up.

"Wow!" he said. "Pretty good, if I do say so myself!"

And then he had leaped off the bed and seized the disassembleator. He tore great chunks of wiring out of the center, threw it to the floor and kicked it into shapelessness. "No Sword of Damocles going to hang over *my* head," he informed an open-mouthed Sam Weber. "Although, I could have used it on you, come to think of it."

Sam eased himself to the mattress and sat down. His mind stopped rearing and whinnied to a halt. He had been so impressed with the helplessness of the baby and the mannikin that he had never dreamed of the possibility that his duplicate would enter upon life with such enthusiasm.

He should have, though; this was a full-grown man, created at a moment of complete physical and mental activity.

"This is bad," he said at last in a hoarse voice. "You're unstable. You can't be admitted into normal society."

"I'm unstable" his image asked. "Look who's talking! The guy who's been mooning his way through his adult life, who wants to marry an overdressed, conceited collection of biological impulses that would come crawling on her knees to any man sensible enough to push the right buttons—"

"You leave Tina's name out of this," Sam told him, feeling acutely uncomfortable at the theatrical phrase.

His double looked at him and grinned. "O.K., I will. But not her body! Now, look here, Sam or Weber or whatever you want me to call you, you can live your life and I'll live mine. I won't even be a lawyer if that'll make you happy. But as far as Tina is concerned, now that there are no ingredients to make a copy—that was a rotten escapist idea, by the way—I have enough of your likes and dislikes to want her badly. And I can have her, whereas you can't. You don't have the gumption."

Sam leaped to his feet and doubled his fists. Then he saw the other's entirely equal size and slightly more assured twinkle. There was no point in fighting—that would end in a draw, at best. He went back to reason.

"According to the manual," he began, "you are prone to neurosis—"

"The manual! The manual was written for children of two centuries hence, with quite a bit of selective breeding and scientific education behind them. Personally, I think I'm a—"

There was a double knock on the door. "Mr. Weber."

"Yes," they both said simultaneously.

Outside, the landlady gasped and began speaking in an uncertain voice. "Th-that gentleman is downstairs. He'd like to see you. Shall I tell him you're in?"

"No, I'm not at home," said the double.

"Tell him I left an hour ago," said Sam at exactly the same moment.

There was another, longer gasp and the sound of footsteps receding hurriedly.

"That's one clever way to handle a situation," Sam's facsimile exploded. "Couldn't you keep your mouth shut? The poor woman's probably gone off to have a fit."

"You forget that this is my room and you are just an experiment that went wrong," Sam told him hotly. "I have just as much right, in fact more right . . . hey, what do you think you're doing?"

The other had thrown open the closet door and was stepping into a pair of pants. "Just getting dressed. You can wander around in the nude if you find it exciting, but I want to look a bit respectable."

"I undressed to take my measurements . . . or your measurements. Those are my clothes, this is my room—"

"Look, take it easy. You could never prove it in a court of law. Don't make me go into that *cliché* about what's yours is mine and so forth."

Heavy feet resounded through the hall. They stopped outside the room. Cymbals seemed to clash all around them and there was a panic-stricken sense of unendurable heat. Then shrill echoes fled into the distance. The walls stopped shuddering.

Silence and a smell of burning wood.

They whirled in time to see a terribly tall, terribly old man in a long black overcoat walking through the smoldering remains of the door. Much too tall for the entrance, he did not stoop as he came in; rather, he drew his head down into his garment and shot it up again. Instinctively, they moved closer together.

His eyes, all shiny black iris without any whites, were set back deep in the shadow of his head. They reminded Sam Weber of the scanners on the Biocalibrator: they tabulated, deduced, rather than saw.

"I was afraid I would be too late," he rumbled at last in weird, clipped tones. "You have already duplicated yourself, Mr. Weber, making necessary unpleasant rearrangements. And the duplicate has destroyed the disassembleator. Too bad. I shall have to do it manually. An ugly job."

He came further into the room until they could almost breathe their fright upon him. "This affair has already dislocated four major programs, but we had to move in accepted cultural grooves and be absolutely certain of the recipient's identity before we could act to withdraw the set. Mrs. Lipanti's collapse naturally stimulated emergency measures."

The duplicate cleared his throat. "You are—?"

"Not exactly human. A humble civil servant of precision manufacture. I am Census Keeper for the entire twenty-ninth oblong. You see, your set was intended for the Thregander children who are on a field trip in this oblong. One of the Threganders who has a Weber chart requested the set through the chrondromos which in an attempt at the supernormal, unstabled without carnuplicating. You therefore received the package instead. Unfortunately, the unstabling was so complete that we were forced to locate you by indirect methods."

The Census Keeper paused and Sam's double hitched his pants nervously. Sam wished he had anything—even a fig leaf—to cover his nakedness. He felt like a character in the Garden of Eden trying to build up a logical case for apple eating. He appreciated glumly how much more than "Bild-A-Man" sets clothes had to do with the making of a man.

"We will have to recover the set, of course," the staccato thunder continued, "and readjust any discrepancies it has caused. Once the matter has been cleared up, however, your life will be allowed to resume its normal progression. Meanwhile, the problem is which of you is the original Sam Weber?"

"I am," they both quavered—and turned to glare at each other.

"Difficulties," the old man rumbled. He sighed like an arctic wind. "I always have difficulties! Why can't I ever have a simple case like a carnuplicator?"

"Look here," the duplicate began. "The original will be—"

"Less unstable and of better emotional balance than the replica," Sam interrupted. "Now, it seems—"

"That you should be able to tell the difference," the other concluded breathlessly. "From what you see and have seen of us, can't you decide which is the more valid member of society?"

What a pathetic confidence, Sam thought, the fellow was trying to display! Didn't he know he was up against someone who could really discern mental differences? This was no fumbling psychiatrist of the present; here was a creature who could see through externals to the most coherent personality beneath.

"I can, naturally. Now, just a moment." He studied them carefully, his eyes traveling with judicious leisure up and down their bodies. They waited, fidgeting, in a silence that pounded.

"Yes," the old man said at last. "Yes. Quite."

He walked forward.

A long thin arm shot out.

He started to disassemble Sam Weber.

"But listennnnn—" began Weber in a yell that turned into a high scream and died in a liquid mumble.

"It would be better for your sanity if you didn't watch," the Census Keeper suggested.

The duplicate exhaled slowly, turned away and began to button a shirt. Behind him the mumbling continued, rising and falling in pitch.

"You see," came the clipped, rumbling accents, "it's not the gift we're afraid of letting you have—it's the principle involved. Your civilization isn't ready for it. You understand."

"Perfectly," replied the counterfeit Weber, knotting Aunt Maggie's blue and red tie.

RAYMOND F. JONES

THE PERSON FROM PORLOCK

BORGE, the chief engineer of Intercontinental, glanced down at the blue-backed folder in his hand. Then he looked at the strained face of Reg Stone, his top engineer.

"It's no use," said Borge. "We're canceling the project. Millen's report is negative. He finds the BW effect impossible of practical application. You can read the details, yourself."

"Canceling—!" Reg Stone half rose from his chair. "But chief, you can't do that. Millen's crazy. What can he prove with only a little math and no experimental data? I'm right on the edge of success. If I could just make you see it!"

"I *have* seen it. I can't see anything that warrants our pouring out another twenty-five thousand bucks after the hundred and fifty your project has already cost the company."

"Twenty, then. Even fifteen *might* do it. Borge, if you don't let me go on with this you're passing up the biggest development of the century. Some other outfit with more guts and imagination and less respect for high-priced opinion in pretty folders is going to come through with it. Teleportation is in the bag—all we've got to do is lift it out!"

"Majestic and Carruthers Electric have both canceled their projects on it. Professor Merrill Hanford, who assisted Bots-Wellton in the original research, says that the BW effect will never be anything of more than academic interest."

"Hanford!" Reg exploded. "He's jealous because he doesn't have the brains to produce a discovery of that magnitude. Bots-Wellton himself says that his effect will eventually make it possible to eliminate all other means of freight transport and most passenger stuff except that which is merely for pleasure."

"All of which is very well," said Borge, "except that it doesn't work outside of an insignificant laboratory demonstration."

"Insignificant! The actual transfer of six milligrams of silver over a distance of ten feet is hardly insignificant. As for Millen's math, we haven't got the right tools to handle this."

"I was speaking from an engineering standpoint. Of course, the effect is of interest in a purely scientific way, but it is of no use to us. Millen's math proves it. Take this copy and see for yourself. I'm sorry, Reg, but that's the final word on it."

Reg Stone rose slowly, his big hands resting against the glass-topped desk. "I see. I'll just have to forget it then, I guess."

"I'm afraid so." Borge rose and extended his hand. "You've been working too hard on this thing. Why don't you take a couple of days off? By then we'll have your next assignment lined up. And no hard feelings over this Bots-Wellton effect business?"

"Oh, no—sure not," Reg said absently.

He strode out of the office and back to the lab where the elaborate equipment of his teleport project was strewn in chaotic piles over benches and lined up in racks and panels.

A hundred thousand dollars worth of beautiful junk, he thought. He slumped in a chair before the vast, complex panels. This cancellation was the fitting climax to the delays, misfortunes, and accidents that had dogged the project since it began.

From the first, everyone except a few members of the Engineering Committee and Reg himself had been against it. Borge considered it a waste of time and money. The other engineers referred to it as Stone's Folly.

And within Reg himself there was that smothering, frustrated, indefinable sensation which he couldn't name.

It was a premonition of failure, and there had been a thousand and one incidents to support it. From the first day, when one of his lab assistants fell and broke a precious surge amplifier, the project seemed to have been hexed. No day passed but that materials seemed mysteriously missing or blueprints turned up with the wrong specifications on them. He'd tried six incompetent junior engineers before the last one, a brilliant chap named Spence, who seemed to be the only one of the lot who knew a lighthouse tube from a stub support.

With men and materials continually snafu it was almost as if someone had deliberately sabotaged the whole project.

He caught himself up with a short, bitter laugh. The little men in white coats would be after him if he kept up that line of thought.

He passed a hand over his eyes. How tired he was! He hadn't realized until now what a tremendous peak of tension he had reached. He felt it in the faint trembling of his fingers, the pressure behind his eyeballs.

His disappointment and anger slowly settled like a vortex about Carl Millen, the consulting physicist who'd reported negatively when Borge insisted to the Engineering Committee that they get outside opinion on the practicability of BW utilization.

The cool, implacable Millen, however, could hardly be the object of anything as personal as anger. Yet, strangely enough, he had been the object of Reg Stone's friendship ever since the two of them were in engineering school together.

What each of them found in the other would have been hard to put into words, but there was some complementary view of opposite worlds which each seemed able to see through the other's eyes.

As for Millen's report on the BW project—Reg knew it had been utterly impersonal and rendered as Carl Millen saw it, though the two of them had often discussed it in heated argument in the past. But the very impersonality of Millen's point of view made the maintenance of his anger impossible for Reg.

But never in his life had he wanted anything so much as he wanted to be the one to develop the Bots-Wellton effect from a mere laboratory demonstration to a system able to transport millions of tons of freight over thousands of miles without material agent of transfer.

Now he was cut off right at the pockets. He felt at loose ends. It was a panicky feeling. For months on end he had been working at top capacity. He seemed to have suddenly dropped into a vacuum.

He debated handing in his resignation and going to some company that would let him develop the project. But who would? Majestic and

Carruthers, two of the largest outfits, had pulled out, Borge had said. Who else would pick it up?

There was one other possibility, he thought breathlessly. Reg Stone could take it over!

Why not? He had a beautifully equipped back yard lab and machine shop. Tens of thousands of dollars worth of equipment from the project would have to be junked by Intercontinental. Reg felt sure Borge would let him buy it as junk.

Sure, it would be slow without the facilities of the Intercontinental labs, but it would be better than scuttling the entire project.

He suddenly glanced at the clock on the wall. He'd been sitting there without moving for over an hour. It was lunch time. He decided to go downtown where he wouldn't meet anyone he knew, rather than eat in the company cafeteria.

He chose the Estate, a sea food restaurant three miles from the plant. As soon as he walked in he knew why he had chosen the Estate with subconscious deliberation.

He saw Carl Millen across the room. He had meant to see him. Millen always ate at the same place at the same time.

Millen spotted Reg almost simultaneously and beckoned to him.

"Sit down, Reg. You're the last person I expected to see here. What's new at your shop?"

"Not much—except Borge received a report from Carl Millen & Associates, Consulting Engineers."

Millen grinned wryly. "Did he blow his top?"

"Why did you turn in a negative report?"

"Didn't you read it? I proved the BW effect is absolutely limited by the free atomic concentration in the dispersion field. That limitation utterly forbids any mass application of the principle."

Reg was silent as the waiter brought the menus. They each ordered oysters on the half shell.

"I remember," said Reg, when the waiter had gone, "about 1925 a then very prominent aeronautical engineer wrote a learned piece proving absolutely that planes could never reach five hundred miles an hour."

Millen laughed. "Yes, and there's also the gent that proved a steamship could never carry enough fuel to get it across the Atlantic."

He stopped and looked seriously at Reg. "But for every one of those classic boners there are thousands of legitimate negative demonstrations that have saved engineering and industry untold millions. You know that as well as I do. This is one of them."

"I'll admit the first, but not the second," said Reg. "I've not read your report. I probably won't. It's faulty. It's got to be. The BW principle can be utilized somehow and I'm going to prove it."

"Just how do you propose to do that?" Millen asked, smiling gently. "Something intuitive, no doubt?"

"All right, have your fun, but come around and see me when you want to go on a quick vacation via the Stone Instantaneous Transfer Co."

"Reg, that job I talked about a year ago is still open. I could offer you Assistant Chief of Development. In a year I could let you in on a partnership. It's worth twenty thousand now, thirty later."

"I could work on the BW outside?"

Millen shook his head. "That's the only string attached. Our men haven't time for anything but customers' projects. Besides, you'd have to get used to the idea of believing in math, not intuition."

"I don't think I'd do you much good."

"You could learn, for that kind of money, couldn't you? What does that cheese factory pay you? About eight or ten?"

"Seven and a half."

"The lousy cheapskates! Three times that ought to be worth shelving your intuition in favor of math."

Reg shook his head. "There isn't that much money in the world. Solving other people's riddles for a fee is not my idea of living."

"Sometimes I think you're just a frustrated research physicist. In this business you're in for the money. It's a cinch there's no glory."

The waiter brought their orders, then.

His depression continued with Reg that evening. His three boys sensed it when he turned down a ball game. His wife, Janice, sensed it when he didn't poke his head in the kitchen on the way to his study.

After dinner, and when the boys were in bed, he told her what had happened that day.

"I don't understand why you feel so badly about the cancellation of this particular project," she said when he finished. "Others have been cancelled, too."

"Because it's one of the greatest phenomena ever discovered. It's ripe for engineering application, but no one else will believe it. It's as if they deliberately try to block me in every step. All through the project it's been that way. Now this—chucking the whole business, when we've gone so far! I can't see through the reasons behind it all. Except that they just don't want it to succeed. I've got that feeling about it, and can't rid myself of it. *They want me to fail!*"

"Who does?"

"Everyone! In the drafting room. The lab technicians. The model shop. It seems as if everybody's concern with the project is simply to throw monkey wrenches in the gears."

"Oh, darling—you're just wrought up over this thing. Let's take a vacation. Let the boys go to camp this summer and go off by ourselves somewhere. You've got to have a rest."

He knew that. He'd known it for a long time, but teleportation was more important than rest. He could take care of the neuroses at his leisure, later. That's the theory he'd worked on. Now, all he had was a beautiful neurosis. It couldn't be anything else, he told himself, this absolute conviction that he was being sabotaged in his work, that others were banded against him to prevent the full development of the BW principle.

"Perhaps in a few weeks," he said. "There are some more angles about this business that I must follow up. Let's read tonight. Something fanciful, something beautiful, something faraway—"

"Coleridge," Janice laughed.

They sat by the window overlooking the garden. Their one vice of reading poetry together was something of an anachronism in a world threatened with atomic fires, but it was the single escape that Reg would allow himself from his engineering problems.

Janice began reading softly. Her voice was like music out of a past more gentle and nearer the ultimate truths than this age.

"In Xanadu did Kubla Khan
A stately pleasure-dome decree:
Where Alph, the sacred river, ran—
—that deep romantic chasm which slanted
Down the green hill athwart a cedarn cover!
A savage place! as holy and enchanted
As e'er beneath a waning moon was haunted—"

Reg suddenly stiffened and sat erect, his eyes on the distant golden cavern of the sky.

"That's it," he breathed softly. "That's just how it is—"

Janice looked up from the book, her face puzzled. "What in the world are you talking about?"

"The Person from Porlock. Remember how Coleridge wrote Kubla Khan?"

"No. Who's the Person from Porlock?"

"Coleridge wrote this poem just after coming out of a dope dream. He later said that during his sleep he had produced at least two to three hundred lines. While trying to get it on paper he was interrupted by a person from the village of Porlock. When he finally got rid of the visitor, Coleridge could recall no more of his envisioned poem.

"He was furious because this self-important busybody had interrupted his work and he wrote a poem castigating the Person from Porlock and all other stupid, busy people who hamper the really industrious ones."

"And so—?"

"Don't you see? It's these Persons from Porlock who have made it impossible for me to complete my work. Borge; Millen; Dickson, the draftsman who bungled the drawings; Hansen, the model shop mechanic who boggled tolerances so badly that nothing would work. These Persons from Porlock—I wonder how many thousands of years of advancement they have cost the world!"

In the near darkness now, Janice sat staring at Reg's bitter face. Her eyes were wide and filled with genuine fear, fear of this malign obsession that had overtaken him.

"The Persons from Porlock," Reg mused, half aloud. "Wouldn't it be funny if it turned out that they were deliberately and purposely upsetting the works of other men. Suppose it were their whole object in life—"

"Reg!"

He was scarcely able to see Janice in the settling gloom, but he felt her fear. "Don't worry, Janice, I haven't gone off my rocker. I was just thinking— Sure, it's fantastic, but Coleridge was one of the world's geniuses. Perhaps he glimpsed something of a truth that no one else has guessed."

Reg went into Borge's office early the next morning. The chief engineer frowned as he saw Reg Stone. "I thought you were going to take a few days."

"I came in to ask what you are going to do with the equipment that's been built for my BW project."

"We'll store it with the miscellaneous plumbing for a while, then junk it. Why?"

"How about doing me a big favor and declaring it junk right away and letting me buy it—as junk?"

"What do you want the stuff for?"

"I want to continue the BW experiments on my own. You know, just putter around with it in my shop at home."

"Still think it will amount to something, eh?"

"Yes. That's why I'd like to buy the stuff, especially the velocitor chamber. It would take me a couple of years to build one of those on my own."

"I'd like to do it as a favor to you," said Borge, "but Bruce, the new manager, has just made a ruling that no parts or equipment may be sold to employees. It was all right during the war when the boys were outfitting their WERS stations on company time and equipment. We were on cost plus then, but too many are trying to refurnish their amateur stations now at our expense. So Bruce cut it all out."

"But that doesn't make sense with such specialized stuff as I've had built for the BW. It's no good for anything else."

"Maybe you could talk Bruce out of it. You know him."

Yes, he knew Bruce, Reg thought. A production man who, like many of his kind, considered engineers mere necessary evils. It was utterly useless to ask Bruce to make an exception to one of his own regulations.

Persons from Porlock—

Persons from Porlock—

The words echoed like a tantalizing refrain in his mind as he went downstairs towards his own lab. He knew he should forget that impossible concept, but the words were like a magic chant explaining all his misfortunes.

This huge plant and all the technological advances that had come out of it could not exist without Borge and Bruce, and the others like them. Yet, at the same time, these Persons from Porlock constituted the greatest stumbling block to modern scientific development. Every engineer in the world at some time had been stymied by one of them—an unimaginative chief, a stupid factory manager, incompetent draftsmen, model shop machinists, secretaries, expediters, administrators—

As he passed the open door of the company's technical library he spotted Dickson, his head draftsman on the BW project, sitting inside at a table. He went in.

Dickson looked up. "Hello, Reg. I wondered where you were this morning. I just heard about them junking the project. It's a devil of a tough break."

"Are you really sorry, Dickson?" said Reg.

The draftsman looked sharply. "What do you mean? Of course I hate to work on a project and see it canceled. Who wouldn't?"

"You know, looking back, it appears as if we hadn't made each one of about fifty boners, the project would have succeeded. For example, that dimension on the diameter of the focusing cavity in the assembly unit. It's the only one in the assembly that wouldn't be obvious to the model shop, and it's the only one on which you made a mistake in spite of our checking. A seven that looked like a two in your dimensioning. That made the difference between success and failure and lost us nearly four weeks while we looked for the bug in the unit."

"Reg, I've told you twenty times I'm sorry, but I can't do anything about it now. A hair on my lettering pen made just enough of a boggle of the figure so that those dopes in the model shop misread it. It was a worse two than it was a seven. They should have checked us on it even if we did miss it."

"Yeah, I know. It just seemed funny that it was that particular dimension you were drawing when the hair got on your pen."

The draftsman looked at Reg as if stunned by the unspoken implication. "If you think I did that on purpose—!"

"I didn't say that. Sure it was an accident, but why? Was it because you didn't want the thing to succeed—subconsciously?"

"Of course not! It was of no material interest to me, except, of course, as I said before I have the same enthusiasm to see a project on which I work turn out successfully as you do."

"Yeah, I suppose so. Just forget I said anything."

Reg left Dickson and walked back to the hall. Persons from Porlock —were they consciously malicious or were they mere stupid blunderers? More likely the latter, he thought, yet there must be some subconscious desire to cause failure as was the case with the mysterious accident prones so familiar to insurance companies.

The more he considered it, the less fantastic the Person from Porlock concept seemed. It was entirely possible that the genius of the poet, Coleridge, had hit upon a class of persons as definite and distinct as accident prones—and a thousand times more deadly.

There could hardly be any other explanation for the stupid blunder of Dickson in drawing the focusing cavity. He had done far more complex drawings on this project, yet that single dimension, of an extremely critical nature, had been the one to be botched.

And it meant there were others like him in the model shop because any machinist with half an eye for accuracy would have checked that figure before going ahead and shaping up the part to such critical tolerances.

He turned into the machine shop where Hansen, the machinist who'd done the job on the cavity, was working.

"Pretty nice work." He nodded towards the piece in the lathe.

"I hope the engineer thinks so," Hansen growled. "They give me plus five thousands on this thing and no minus. Next they'll want flea whiskers with zero-zero tolerance."

"You're good. That's why you get the tough ones."

"I wish the guy on the payroll desk would take note."

"But you know, there's something that's bothered me for several weeks. You remember that cavity you made for me with a one two five interior instead of a one seven five?"

Hansen turned wearily to the engineer. "Reg, I've eaten crow a hundred times over for that. I told you it looked like a two. Maybe I need my eyes examined, but it still looks that way."

"Did you have any reason for *not* wanting the cavity to work?"

"Now, look!" Hansen's anger suffused red through his face. "I'm paid to turn out screwball gadgets in this shop, not worry about whether they work or not."

"Didn't it occur to you to check that boggled figure?"

"I told you it looked all right!" Hansen turned angrily back to his lathe and resumed work.

Reg watched the mechanic for a moment, then left the shop.

The bunglers seemed to have no personal interest in their botch work, he decided. It must be something entirely subconscious as in the case of accident prones. That didn't make them any less dangerous, however. Without them on his project he would have been able by now to demonstrate the practicability of BW utilization.

But, following this line of reasoning, why couldn't the teleportation equipment be made to work now? According to all this theory the equipment he had built should have been capable of acting as a pilot model for a larger unit and it should have been able to transfer hundred pound masses at least a thousand feet. Yet, it had failed completely.

Granting that he himself was not a Person from Porlock—

But could he grant that?

Maybe the greatest blunders were his own. His failure to catch Dickson's mistake early enough, for example!

That was the one premise he could not admit, however. It led to insolvable dilemma, rendered the problem completely indeterminate. He had to assume that he was not one of the bunglers.

In that case, why did the equipment fail to work?

It meant that some of the blunders introduced by the Persons from Porlock still remained in the equipment. Remove them, and it should work!

He'd have to go over every equation, every design, every specification—point by point—compare them with the actual equipment and dig out the bugs.

He went into his own lab. He dismissed the assistants and shut the door. He sat down with the voluminous papers which he had produced in the ten months of work on the project. It was hopeless to attempt to go over the entire mass of work in short hours or days. That's what should be done, but he could cover the most vulnerable points. These lay in the routine, conventional circuits which he had left to his assistants and in whose design the draftsman and model shop had been trusted with too many details.

The first of these was the amplifier for the BW generator, whose radiation, capable of mass-modulation, carried the broken down components of the materials to be transported. The amplifier held many conventional features, though the wave form handled was radically unconventional.

It contained two stages of Class A amplification which had to be perfectly symmetrical. Reg had never made certain of the correct operation of these two stages by themselves. Spence, his junior engineer, had reported them operating correctly and Reg had taken his word on so simple a circuit.

He had no reason now to believe that anything was wrong. It was just one of those items left to a potential Person from Porlock.

He disconnected the input and output of the amplifier and hooked up a signal generator and a vacuum tube voltmeter. Point by point he checked the circuit. The positive and negative peaks were equal and a scope showed perfect symmetry, but in the second stage they weren't high enough. He wasn't getting the required soup. The output of the tube in use should have been more than sufficient to produce it.

Then he discovered the fault. The bias was wrong and the drive had been cut to preserve symmetry. Spence had simply assumed the flat tops were due to overloading.

Reg sat in silent contemplation of the alleged engineering and poured on self-recrimination for trusting Spence.

This was the reason for the apparent failure of the whole modulator circuit. Because of it, he had assumed his theory of mass modulation was faulty.

Spence was obviously one of them, he thought. That meant other untold numbers of bugs throughout the mass of equipment. During the remainder of the morning and in the afternoon he adjusted the amplifiers and got the modulator into operation. He uncovered another serious bug in an out-of-tolerance dropping resistor in the modulator. He contemplated the probability of that one defective resistor among the hundreds of thousands of satisfactory ones the plant used—the probability of its being placed in exactly that critical spot. The figure was too infinitesimal to be mere chance.

By quitting time he had the circuit as far as the mass modulator functioning fairly smoothly. He called Janice and told her he wouldn't be home until late. Then he worked until past midnight to try to get the transmission elements to accept the modulated carrier. The only result was failure and at last he went home in utter exhaustion.

The next morning, refreshed, he was filled with an unnatural exuberance, however. He had the key to the cause of his failures and he felt success was only a matter of time. If he could just get that necessary time—

The broad parking lot was dotted with infrequent cars at the early hour of the morning at which he arrived. Gail, the lab secretary, was already at her desk, however, when he walked in. She called to him, "Mr. Borge wants you to come up, Reg."

"O.K. Thanks."

He turned and went back out the door towards the chief engineer's office. This would be the new project, he thought. He strode in and Borge looked up with a brief nod.

"Sit down, Reg." The lines of Borge's face seemed to have eroded into deeper valleys in the short time since Reg had last seen him.

"I hear some things I don't like," said Borge suddenly. "About you."

"What sort of things? I haven't—"

"Dickson and Hansen have been saying you've accused them of deliberate sabotage on your project. True or not, whatever is implied by these rumors can't go on. It can wreck this shop in a month."

"I didn't accuse them of anything!" Reg flared. "I just asked if they wanted the project to fail. Of course, I didn't expect them to say that they did, but their manner showed me what I wanted to know."

"And what was that?"

Reg hesitated. This development was nothing that he had expected. How would Borge, as one of the Persons from Porlock, react to Reg's knowledge of them? Did Borge even understand his own motives? Whether he did or not, Reg could make no rational answer except the truth.

"I found that they did, subconsciously, want the project to fail. I believe this is the explanation of the numerous blunders without which my project would have been a success."

"You believe, then, that your failure is due to the . . . ah, persecutions . . . of these persons, rather than to any inherent impossibility in the project itself or your own inability to bring it off?"

"I haven't a persecution complex, if that's what you're trying to say," Reg said hotly. "Look, Borge, did you ever hear of accident prones, who plague insurance companies?"

"Vaguely. I don't know much about the subject."

"I can prove there is another kind of prone, a blunder prone, whose existence is just as definite as that of the accident prone. I call these blunder prones 'Persons from Porlock' after the one named by the poet, Coleridge, when his great poem, 'Kubla Khan,' was ruined by one of them."

"And just what do these . . . er, Persons from Porlock do?"

"They make mistakes in important work entrusted to them. They interfere with others who are doing intense and concentrated work so that trains of thought are broken and perhaps lost forever, as in the case of Coleridge. And as in my own case. I could tell of at least a hundred times when I have been deliberately interrupted at critical points of my calculations so that work had to be repeated and some points, only faintly conceived, were totally lost."

"Which couldn't have been due to your own nervous strain and overworked condition?"

"No."

"I see. These Persons of Porlock generally persecute the intelligent and superior people of the world, is that it?"

Reg's anger flared. "I'm not a psychoneurotic case and I'm not suffering from a persecution complex!"

Suddenly, cold fear washed over Reg. Borge's pattern of reason was clear, now. He would dismiss the whole matter as a neurotic complex and let Reg out of the lab. He would be blackballed with every other company in which he might have another try at BW work.

"I know you're not," Borge was saying, "but you are tired. For six years you've been turning out miracles. I hate like the devil to see you come up with something like this, Reg. Surely you must realize it's all the result of overwork and fatigue. No one is going around interfering with your work. Your mind refuses to admit defeat so it's automatically throwing it off on someone else. I'm no psychologist, but I'll bet that's close to the right answer. I want you to have Walker at the Clinic examine you. I'm willing to bet he recommends a long rest. I'll give you six months with pay if necessary. But I can't let you back in the lab unless you do this. A repetition of yesterday's performance and the whole place would be shot up. You've got to get rid of this Person from Porlock business."

The pieces of the whole puzzle locked into place with startling clarity for Reg. He knew that the last uncertainty had been removed. They were *not* random, subconsciously motivated performers. These Persons from Porlock were skillfully conscious of what they were doing. Borge could not hide the knowledge that his eyes revealed.

But *what* were they doing?

Six months—it would be too late, then. His sense of blind urgency told him that. Borge was simply showing him that there was no possible way that he could win.

He tried again. "I can't expect you to believe these things. I know it sounds fantastic. Any psychiatrist would no doubt diagnose it as a persecution complex. But I promise that no more incidents like yesterday's will take place. Give me the new assignment, but let me work on the BW just six weeks in my spare time, on my own. I'll guarantee I'll have it working in that time."

Borge shook his head. "That's the main trouble with you already—overwork. You've been pushing yourself so hard that your nerves are all shot. Anyone walking by while you are computing is such a disturbance that you think he's deliberately interfering with you. Put yourself in the care of a good doctor and let me know his report. That's the only condition upon which I can let you stay with the company. I hate to put it that way. I wish you'd try to understand for yourself—but if you won't, that's the way it's got to be."

Reg stood up, his body trembling faintly with the fury of his anger. He leaned forward across the desk. *"I know who you are!* But I warn you that I won't stop. Somehow I'm going to carry this work through, and all you and your kind can do won't stop me!"

He whirled and strode from the office, conscious of Borge's pitying glance upon his back. Conscious, too, that he was walking out for the last time.

The fury and the anger didn't last. When he got outside, he was sick with frustration as he glanced back at the plant. He had acted stupidly through the whole thing, he thought, letting them cut him off from any access to the BW equipment without a struggle.

Yet, how else could he have conducted himself? The whole thing was so fantastic at first that he couldn't have outlined a rational program to combat it.

Maybe Borge was right in one respect. He *was* devilishly tired and exhausted from the long war years of uninterrupted work. There'd been that micro-search system on which he'd spent two years at Radiation Lab. One such project as that would have sent the average engineer nuts. As soon as it was in production he'd tackled an equally tough baby in the radar fire-control equipment that had gone into fighter planes four months after he took over the project cold.

Yeah, he *was* tired—

Janice was surprised to see him, and was shocked by the pain and bewilderment on his face.

Slowly, and carefully, he explained to her what had happened. He told her how Borge had built up a case against him out of the things he'd said to Dickson and Hansen. He told her how they and Spence and the rest had sabotaged his project.

"They've got me licked," he finished. "They've done what they started out to do, knocked out the BW project."

Janice had sat quietly during his recital, only her eyes reflecting the growing terror within her.

"But, darling, why should they want to hinder the project? What possible reason could there be behind it, even if these mysterious Persons from Porlock actually existed?"

"Who knows? But it doesn't make any difference, I suppose. They're so obvious that I don't see how the world has failed to recognize them. Yet . . . you don't believe a thing I've said, do you?"

"They can't exist, Reg! Borge is right. You're tired. This notion is only something that your mind has seized upon out of Coleridge's fantasy. It has no basis in reality. Please, for my sake, take a visit to the Clinic and see if they don't advise rest and psychiatric treatment for you."

Like a cold, invisible shell, loneliness seemed to coalesce about him. There was the illusion of being cut off from all sight and sound, and he had the impression that Janice was sitting there with her lips moving, but no sound coming forth.

Illusion, of course, but the loneliness was real. It cut him off from all the world, for where was there one who would understand and believe about the Persons from Porlock? They surrounded him on every side. Wherever he turned, they stood ready to beat down his struggles for the right to work as he wished. Perhaps even Janice—

But that premise had to be denied.

"I'll let them tap my knees and my skull if it will make you happier," he said. "Maybe I'll even beg Borge to take me back if that's the way you want it. It doesn't matter any more. The BW project is dead. They killed it—but don't ever try to make me believe they don't exist."

"They don't! They don't Reg. You've got to believe that. Quit deluding yourself—"

Quite suddenly, it was beyond his endurance. He strode from the room and out into the brilliance of the day, brilliance that was like a cold, shimmering wall surrounding him, moving as he moved, surrounding but not protecting.

Not protecting from the glance of those who passed on the street nor from those who came towards him, nor those who followed after in a steady, converging stream.

He felt their presence—the Persons from Porlock—like tangible, stinging auras on every side. They surrounded him. They were out to get him.

His stride broke into a half run. How long his flight continued he never knew. It was dimming twilight when he sank, half sobbing from exhaustion, onto a park bench miles from home.

He looked about him in the gathering darkness, and somehow it seemed less evil than the light and the thousand faces of the Persons from Porlock who drifted by on every side.

If only he could drag one of them out into the open where all the world could see it and believe—that would be one way of escape from the soundless, invisible prison in which they had encased him. He had to show that they existed so that no one in the world would doubt his word again. But how?

What incontrovertible proof of their existence did he possess? What was there besides his own feelings and beliefs? He shuddered with realization that there was nothing. His knowledge, his evidence of them was of the flimsiest kind. There had to be something tangible.

But *could* there be more? Insidiously, doubts began to creep into his mind. He remembered the look in Borge's eyes, the pity and the fear in Janice's.

He rose stiffly from the park bench, cold fear driving his limbs to carry him out into the lights. If he were to remain sure of his own sanity, he had to first prove to himself beyond any doubt that the Persons from Porlock existed in actuality, not merely in his own suspicions.

There was one way by which he might be able to do this. That way lay through the report of Carl Millen and the mathematics by which he had "proved" the BW effect impossible of mass exploitation.

The math was deliberately false, Reg knew. If he proved it, confronted Millen with the fact—

He caught a taxi home. Janice met him, dry-eyed and with no questions or demands for explanations. He offered none, but went to his study and took out Millen's report. He asked Janice to brew up a pot of coffee and he began the slow weaving of a pathway through the tortuous trail of Millen's abstruse mathematical reasoning.

Sleep at last forced abandonment of his work, but he arose after a few hours and turned to the pursuit again. All through the day he kept steadily at it, and in the late afternoon he caught his first threads of what he was searching for. A thread of deliberate falsification, a beckoning towards wide paths of illogic and untruth.

It was so subtle that he passed it twice before recognizing it. Something of the intense deliberation chilled him when he realized the depths of the insinuations. It was like the devil's nine truths and a lie that he'd heard country preachers talk about when he was a boy.

This work of Carl Millen's was certainly the nine truths—and the one, black, insidious lie.

Now that he recognized it, following its development became easier until he trailed it to the final, colossal untruth that the free atomic concentration in the dispersion field made large scale application impossible.

This was it! Proof!

The triumph of his discovery swept away the exhaustion that had filled him. Let them call it a persecution complex now!

He put the report and his pile of computations in his brief case and told Janice he was going to Millen's.

As he drove with furious skill towards town he wondered what Millen's reaction would be. He could call Reg crazy, deny he was a Person from Porlock—but he could never deny the evidence of his deliberate falsifications.

The secretary told Reg that Millen was busy and would he sit down?

"Tell him it's Reg Stone, and I've found out what he tried to do in the BW report," said Reg. "I think he'll see me."

The girl glanced disapprovingly at the engineer's disheveled appearance and relayed the information. Then she nodded towards the polished, hardwood door.

"He'll see you."

Reg opened the door sharply. Carl Millen looked up from behind the desk in the center of the room. His face was unsmiling.

Then Reg saw the second person in the room. Spence, his junior engineer on the BW project. The man's unexpected presence gave him a moment's uneasiness, but it would make no difference, Reg thought—since Spence was one of them, too.

"So you think you've found something in my report?" said Millen. "Pull up a chair and show me what you mean."

Reg sat down with slow deliberation, but he left his brief case closed.

"I think you know what I mean," he said. "I don't believe it's necessary to go into the details. You deliberately invented a false line of reasoning to prove the BW effect useless."

"So? And what does that prove?"

His failure to deny the accusation took Reg aback. There was no trace of surprise or consternation on Millen's face.

"It proves that you are one of them," said Reg. "One with Dickson, Hansen, Borge, and Spence here—one of those who fought to keep me from developing teleportation. I want to know why!"

Millen's face relaxed slowly. "One of your Persons from Porlock?" Amusement touched his face at the words.

"Yes."

Millen leaned forward, his almost ominous seriousness returning. "You've done a good job, Reg. Better than we hoped for a while. It looked for a time as if you weren't going to get it."

Reg, stared at him. The words made no sense, but yet there was an admission here of the unknown that chilled him.

"You admit that you falsified the facts in your report? That you are one of the Persons from Porlock?"

"Yes."

The stark admission echoed in the vast silences of the room. Reg looked slowly from one face to the other.

"Who are you? What is your purpose?" he asked hoarsely.

"I'm just like you," said Millen. "I stumbled into this thing when I first opened my consulting service. Spence is the one that can tell you about it. He's the different one—your real Person from Porlock."

Reg turned to his former junior engineer. Somehow, this was what he had known since he first entered the room. Spence's face held a look of alien detachment, as if the affairs of common engineers were trivial things.

His eyes finally turned towards Reg's face and they seemed to burn with a quality of age despite the youth of his face.

"We came here a long time ago," said Spence slowly. "And now we live here and are citizens of Earth just as you are. That is our only excuse for meddling in your affairs. Our interference, however, gives you the same safety it does us."

Reg felt as if he were not hearing Spence, only seeing his lips move. "You *came* here? You are not of Earth—"

"Originally, no."

And suddenly Reg found Spence's words credible. Somehow, they removed the fantasy from the Person from Porlock concept.

"Why haven't you made yourselves known? What does all of this mean?"

"I did not come," said Spence, "but my ancestors did. They had no intention of visiting Earth. An accident destroyed their vessel and made landing here necessary. The members of the expedition were scientists and technicians, but their skill was not the kind to rebuild the ship that had brought them across space, nor were the proper materials then available on Earth.

"They became reconciled to their communication with the home planet, and knowing that the chance of being found was infinitely remote. They were skilled in the biologic sciences and managed in a generation or two to modify their physical form sufficiently to mingle undetected with Earthmen, though they kept their own group affiliation.

"From the first, they adopted a policy of noninterference, but they found living standards hardly suitable and built secret colonies where their own life and science could develop apart from that of Earthmen.

"It was one of these colonies which the drugged mind of your poet, Coleridge, was able to see in his unconsciousness, and which he began to describe in 'Kubla Khan.' My people had detected the presence of his perceptions and one of them was sent immediately to interrupt the work of recollection because they didn't want their colony revealed with such accurate description as Coleridge could make. The Person from Porlock was this disturbing emissary."

Spence smiled for the first time, briefly. "So you see, your designation of all of us as Persons from Porlock was not far from the truth."

"But why have you interfered with me? Why don't you make yourselves known and offer your advanced science to the world?"

"Surely you are sufficiently familiar with the reaction of your own people to the new and the unknown to make that last question unnecessary. We aren't concerned with advancing your science. It is progressing rapidly enough, too rapidly for your social relationships, which would benefit by some of the energy you expend on mechanical inquiries.

"In our own science we have great fields of knowledge which do not exist in yours. One is a highly specialized field of what we term prognostication logics. Your symbolic logic sciences are a brief step in that direction—very brief. We are enabled to predict the cumulative effect of events and discoveries in your culture. We take a hand in those which indicate a potential destructive to the race. We interfere to the point of preventing their development."

Reg stared at Spence. "How could my teleportation development imperil the race? Surely that was no excuse for your interference!"

"It was. It isn't obvious to you yet because you haven't come to the discovery that teleportation can be quite readily accomplished from the transmitting end without the use of terminal equipment. Further along, you would have found no receivers necessary. Everything could be done from the transmission end."

"That would have made it a thousand times more valuable!"

"Yes? Suppose the cargo to be transported was the most destructive atomic bomb your science is capable of building."

The impact of that concept burst upon Reg. "I see," he said at last, quietly. "Why did you let us produce the bomb at all?"

"We were rather divided on that question. Our computations show a high probability that you will be able to survive it, but only if a number of auxiliary implements are withheld, teleportation among others. There were some of us who were in favor of preventing the bomb's construction even with the assurance our computations give but their influence was less than that of us who know what benefits atomic energy can bring if properly utilized. As a group, we decided to let the bomb be produced."

"But the BW effect can never be utilized?"

"Not for some centuries."

Spence seemed to have said all that he was going to say, but Millen moved uneasily.

"I can never tell you how glad I am that you uncovered my math," he said. "You know the alternative if you hadn't?"

"Alternative—?" Reg looked across the desk. Then he remembered, that night, sitting in the park, seeing the shadows against the distant lights, the ghastly pursuit of imagined terrors.

"The alternative was—insanity?"

Millen nodded.

"Why? Couldn't it have been done some other way?"

Millen avoided the question. "You will never attempt to develop the BW effect now, will you?"

"No. Of course not."

"It wouldn't have been that way if Spence or some other had come to you and warned you that it wasn't to be done. You'd have laughed at him as a crackpot. Now there's no doubt in your mind."

Reg nodded slowly and cold sickness lodged in his vitals at the thought of what he had so narrowly escaped. "Yes, I see. And now I suppose I shall go back and eat crow for Borge. That is, if you will put in a good word for me with your man." He smiled wryly towards Spence.

"We have a bigger job for you," said Millen. "I still want you here."

"Doing nail puzzles and answering riddles for customers too stingy to run their own development labs? Not me!"

"Not that, exactly. We need you to take over my job. I've got something else lined up to take care of."

"What are you talking about? Take over as head of Carl Millen & Associates? That would be worse than the puzzles—desk arthritis."

"No. Who's the best man in the world today on interference with the utilization of the BW effect?"

"I don't understand you."

"You're that man. We need somebody to take charge of the whole project of BW interference. Spence has another assignment for me, but Bots-Wellton himself still needs to be worked on. Carruthers and Majestic haven't stopped their projects yet. That was only a blind to fool your company. They've got to be stopped yet. A couple of universities are working on it. It's a big job, and you're the best equipped man in the world to handle it—under Spence's direction, of course. You see, his people won't do the detail work after some of us once become trained in it. It's up to us to fry our own fish. Will you take it?"

Reg stood up and went to the window, looking down upon the street crawling with ever hopeful life. He turned back to Spence and Millen.

"How could I do anything else in the face of the drastic indoctrination and persuasion course you've given me. Sure I'll take it!"

Then he laughed softly. "Reg Stone: Person from Porlock!"

A. E. VAN VOGT

JUGGERNAUT

THE man—his name was Pete Creighton, though that doesn't matter —saw the movement out of the corner of his eye, as he sat reading his evening paper.

A hand reached out of the nothingness of the thin air about two feet above the rug. It seemed to grope, then drew back into nothingness. Almost instantly it reappeared, this time holding a small, dully glinting metal bar. The fingers let go of the bar, and drew out of sight, even as the metal thing started to fall towards the floor.

THUD! The sound was vibrant. It shook the room.

Creighton sat jerkily up in his chair, and lowered his paper. Then he remembered what he had seen. Automatically, his mind rejected the memory. But the fantastic idea of it brought him mentally further into the room.

He found himself staring at an ingot of iron about a foot long and two inches square. That was all. It lay there on the rug, defying his reason.

"Cripes!" said Creighton.

His wife, a sad-faced woman, came out of the kitchen. She stared at him gloomily: "What's the matter now?" she intoned.

"That iron bar!" Her husband, half-choked, pointed. "Who threw that in here?"

"Bar?" The woman looked at the ingot in surprise. Her face cleared. "Johnny must have brought it in from the outside."

She paused, frowned again; then added: "Why all the fuss about a piece of scrap iron?"

"It fell," Creighton babbled. "I saw it out of the corner of my eye. A hand dropped it right out of the—"

He stopped. Realization came of what he was saying. He swallowed hard. His eyes widened. He bent sideways in his chair, and grabbed convulsively for the metal bar.

It came up in his strong fingers. It was quite heavy. Its weight and its drab appearance dimmed his desire to examine it thoroughly. It was a solid ingot of iron, nothing more, nor less. His wife's tired voice came again:

"Johnny must have stood it up on one end, and it fell over."

"Huh-uh!" said her husband.

He found himself anxious to accept the explanation. The curious sense of alien things faded before the normalness of it. He must have been daydreaming. He must have been crazy.

He put the bar down on the floor. "Give it to the next scrap drive!" he said gruffly.

Hour after hour, the Vulcan Steel & Iron Works roared and yammered at the undefended skies. The din was an unceasing dirge, lustily and horrendously sounding the doom of the Axis. It was a world of bedlam; and not even an accident could stop that over-all bellowing of metal being smashed and tormented into new shapes.

The accident added a minor clamor to the dominating theme of stupendous sound. There was a screech from a cold roller machine, then a thumping and a sound of metal tearing.

One of the men operating the machine emitted some fanciful verbal sounds, and frantically manipulated the controls. The thumping and the tearing ceased. An assistant foreman came over.

"What's wrong, Bill?"

"That bar!" muttered Bill. "I was just starting to round it, and it bent one of the rollers."

"*That* bar!" echoed the assistant foreman incredulously.

He stared at the little thing. It was a big bar to be going through a roller. But compared to the sizable steel extrusions and moldings turned out by the Vulcan works, it was tiny.

It was six feet long, and it had originally been two inches square.

About half of its length had been rolled once. At the point where the strength of the rollers had been bested, the metal of the bar looked exactly the same as that which had gone before. Except that it had refused to round.

The assistant foreman spluttered, and then fell back on a technicality. "I thought it was understood," he said, "that in the Vulcan plants nothing over an inch and a half is rounded by rollers."

"I have had dozens of 'em," said Bill. He added doggedly. "When they come, I do 'em."

There was nothing to do but accept the reality. Other firms, the assistant foreman knew, made a common practice of rolling two inchers. He said:

"O. K., take your helper and report to Mr. Johnson. I'll have a new roller put in here. The bent one and that bar go to the scrap heap."

He could not refrain from adding: "Hereafter send two-inch bars to the hammers."

The bar obediently went through the furnace again. A dozen things could have happened to it. It could have formed part of a large molding. It could have, along with other metal, endured an attempt to hammer it into sheer steel.

It would have been discovered then, its basic shape and hardness exposed.

But the wheels of chance spun—and up went a mechanical hammer, and down onto the long, narrow, extruded shape of which the original ingot was a part.

The hammer was set for one and one quarter inches, and it clanged with a curiously solid sound. It was a sound not unfamiliar to the attendant, but one which oughtn't to be coming from the pummeling of white-hot metal.

It was his helper, however, who saw the dents in the base of the hammer. He uttered a cry, and pulled out the clutch. The older man jerked the bar clear, and stared at the havoc it had wrought.

"Yumpin' yimminy!" he said. "Hey, Mr. Yenkins, come over here, and look at this."

Jenkins was a big, chubby man who had contributed fourteen ideas for labor-saving devices before and since he was made foreman. The significance of what he saw now was not lost on him.

"Ernie's sick today," he said. "Take over his drill for a couple of hours, you two, while I look into this."

He phoned the engineering department; and after ten minutes Boothby came down, and examined the hammer.

He was a lean-built, precise young man of thirty-five. On duty he wore horned-rimmed glasses, behind which gleamed a pair of bright-blue eyes. He was a craftsman, a regular hound for precision work.

He measured the dents. They were a solid two inches wide; and the hammer and its base shared the depth equally.

In both, the two-inch wide, one-foot long gouge was exactly three eighths of an inch deep, a total for the two of three quarters of an inch.

"Hm-m-m," said Boothby, "what have we got here . . . a super-super hard alloy, accidentally achieved?"

"My mind jumped that way," said Mr. Jenkins modestly. "My name is Jenkins. Wilfred Jenkins."

Boothby grinned inwardly. He recognized that he was being told very quietly to whom the credit belonged for any possible discovery. He couldn't help his reaction. He said:

"Who was on this machine?"

Jenkins' heavy face looked unhappy. He hesitated.

"Some Swede," he said reluctantly. "I forget his name."

"Find it out," said Boothby. "His prompt action in calling you is very important. Now, let's see if we can trace this bar back to its source."

He saw that Jenkins was happy again. "I've already done that," the foreman said. "It came out of a pot, all the metal of which was derived from shop scrap. Beyond that, of course, it's untraceable."

Boothby found himself appreciating Jenkins a little more. It always made him feel good to see a man on his mental toes.

He had formed a habit of giving praise when it was deserved. He gave it now, briefly, then finished:

"Find out if any other department has recently run up against a very hard metal. No, wait, I'll do that. You have this bar sent right up to the metallurgical lab."

"Sent up hot?" asked Jenkins.

"Now!" said Boothby, "whatever its condition. "I'll ring up Nad-derly . . . er, Mr. Nadderly, and tell him to expect it."

He was about to add: "And see that your men don't make a mistake, and ship the wrong one."

He didn't add it. There was a look on Jenkins' face, an unmistakable look. It was the look of a man who strongly suspected that he was about to win his fifteenth bonus in two and a half years.

There would be no mistake.

A steel bar $2''x2''x12''$—tossed out of hyper-space into the living room of one Pete Creighton, who didn't matter—

None of the individuals mattered. They were but pawns reacting according to a pattern, from which they could vary only if some impossible change took place in their characters. Impossible because they would have had to become either more or less than human.

When a machine in a factory breaks down, its operator naturally has to call attention to the fact. All the rest followed automatically out of the very nature of things. An alert foreman, an alert engineer, a skillful metallurgist; these were normal Americans, normal Englishmen, normal—Germans!

No, the individuals mattered not. There was only the steel ingot, forming now a part of a long, narrow bar.

On the thirtieth day, Boothby addressed the monthly meeting of the Vulcan's board of directors. He was first on the agenda, so he had had to hustle. But he was in a high good humor as he began:

"As you all know, obtaining information from a metallurgist"—he paused and grinned inoffensively at Nadderly, whom he had invited down—"is like obtaining blood from a turnip. Mr. Nadderly embodies in his character and his science all the caution of a Scotchman who realizes that it's time he set up the drinks for everybody, but who is waiting for some of the gang to depart.

"I might as well warn you, gentlemen, that he is fully aware that any statement he has made on this metal might be used against him. One of his objections is that thirty days is a very brief period in the life of an alloy. There is an aluminum alloy, for instance, that requires forty days to age harden.

"Mr. Nadderly wishes that stressed because the original hard alloy, which seems to have been a bar of about two inches square by a foot long, has in fifteen days *imparted* its hardness to the rest of the bar, of which it is a part.

"Gentlemen"—he looked earnestly over the faces—"the hardness of this metal cannot be stated or estimated. It is not just so many times harder than chromium or molybdenum steel. It is hard beyond all calculation.

"Once hardened, it cannot be machined, not even by tools made of itself. It won't grind. Diamonds do not even scratch it. Cannon shells neither dent it nor scratch it. Chemicals have no effect. No heat we have been able to inflict on it has any softening effect.

"Two pieces welded together—other metal attaches to it readily— impart the hardness to the welding. Apparently, any metal once hardened by contact with the hard metal, will impart the hardness to any metal with which it in turn comes into contact.

"The process is cumulative and endless, though, as I have said, it seems to require fifteen days. It is during this fortnight that the metal can be worked.

"Mr. Nadderly thinks that the hardness derives from atomic, not molecular processes, and that the impulse of hardness is imparted much as radium will affect metals with which it is placed in contact. It seems to be harmless, unlike radium, but—"

Boothby paused. He ran his gaze along the line of intent faces, down one side of the broad table and up the other.

"The problem is this: Can we after only thirty days, long before we can be sure we know all its reactions, throw this metal into the balance against the Axis?"

Boothby sat down. No one seemed to have expected such an abrupt ending, and it was nearly a minute before the chairman of the board cleared his throat and said:

"I have a telegram here from the Del-Air Corporation, which puzzled me when I received it last night, but which seems more understandable in the light of what Mr. Boothby has told us. The telegram is from the president of Del-Air. I will read it, if you please."

He read:

" 'We have received from the United States Air Command, European

Theater, an enthusiastic account of some new engines which we dispatched overseas some thirteen days ago by air. Though repeatedly struck by cannon shells, the cylinder blocks of these engines sustained no damage, and continued in operation. These cylinders were bored from steel blocks sent from your plant twenty days ago. Please continue to send us this marvelous steel, which you have developed, and congratulations.' "

The chairman looked up. "Well?" he said.

"But it's not probable," Boothby protested. "None of the alloy has been sent out. It's up in the metallurgical lab right now."

He stopped, his eyes widening. "Gentlemen," he breathed, "is it possible that any metal, which has been in contact with the super-hard steel for however brief a period, goes through the process of age-hardening? I am thinking of the fact that the original ingot has twice at least been through an arc furnace, and that it has touched various other machines."

He stopped again, went on shakily: "If that is so, then our problem answers itself. We *have* been sending out super-steel."

He finished quietly, but jubilantly: "We can, therefore, only accept the miracle, and try to see to it that no super-tanks or super-machines fall into the hands of our enemies."

After thirty days, the metal impulse was flowing like a streak. In thirty more days it had crossed the continent and the oceans myriad times.

What happens when every tool in a factory is turning out two hundred and ten thousand different parts, every tool is sharing with its product the gentle impulse of an atomically generated force? And when a thousand, ten thousand factories are affected.

That's what happened.

Limitless were the potentialities of that spread, yet there was a degree of confinement. The area between the battle forces in Europe was like an uncrossable moat.

The Germans retreated too steadily. It was the Allies who salvaged abandoned Nazi trucks and tanks, not the other way around. Bombing of cities had stopped. There were no cities.

The gigantic air fleets roared over the German lines, and shed their bombs like clouds of locusts. By the time anything was touched by the atomic flow, the battle line had advanced a mile or more; and the Allies had the affected area.

Besides, far more than ninety percent of the bombs were from storerooms in that mighty munitions dump which was England. For years the millions of tons of *matériel* had been piling up underground. It was brought up only when needed, and almost immediately and irretrievably exploded.

The few affected bombs didn't shatter. But no one, no German had time to dig them out of the ground.

Day after day after day, the impulse in the metal crept along the battle front, but couldn't cross over.

During those first two months, the Vulcan office staff was busy. There were vital things to do. Every customer had to be advised that the metal must be "worked" within a certain set time. Before that paper job was completed, the first complaints had started to come in.

Boothby only grinned when he read them. "Metal too hard, breaking our tools—" That was the gist.

"They'll learn," he told the third board meeting he attended. "I think we should concentrate our attention on the praises of the army and navy. After all, we are now as never before, working hand-and-glove with the government. Some of these battle-front reports are almost too good to be true. I like particularly the frequent use of the word 'irresistible.' "

It was two days after that that his mind, settling slowly to normalcy from the excitement of the previous ten weeks, gave birth to a thought. It was not a complete thought, not final. It was a doubt that brought a tiny bead of perspiration out on his brow, and it prompted him to sit down, a very shaken young man, and draw a diagrammatic tree.

The tree began with a line that pointed at the word "Vulcan." It branched out to "Factories," then to other factories. It branched again, and again and again, and again and again and again.

It raced along railway tracks. It bridged the seas in ships and planes. It moved along fences and into mines. It ceased to have a beginning and an end. There was no end.

There was no color in Boothby's face now. His eyes behind their owlish spectacles had a glazed look. Like an old man, he swayed up finally from his chair, and, hatless, wandered out into the afternoon. He found his way home like a sick dog, and headed straight for his workroom.

He wrote letters to Nadderly, to the chairman of the board of Vulcan, and to the chief army and navy agent attached to the enormous steel and iron works. He staggered to the nearest mailbox with the letters, then returned to his work room, and headed straight for the drawer where he kept his revolver.

The bullet splashed his brain out over the floor.

Ogden Tait, chairman of the board, had just finished reading the letter from Boothby when the urgent call came for him to come to the smelter.

The letter and the call arriving so close upon one another confused him concerning the contents of the letter. Something about—

Startled, he hurried down to answer the urgent call. An array of plant engineers were there, waiting for him. They had cleared all workmen away from one of the electric arc furnaces. An executive engineer explained the disaster.

Fumbling Boothby's letter, alternately stunned and dismayed, the chairman listened to the chilling account.

"But it's impossible," he gasped finally. "How could the ore arrive here super-hard? It came straight by lake boat from the ore piles at Iron Mountain."

None of the engineers was looking at him. And in the gathering silence, the first glimmer of understanding of what was here began to come to Ogden Tait. He remembered some of the phrases from Boothby's letter: ". . . two million tons of steel and iron sent out in two and one half months . . . spread everywhere . . . no limit—"

His brain began to sway on its base, as the landslide of possibilities unreeled before it. New tracking, Boothby had mentioned, for the interior of the mines. Or new ore cars, or new—

Not only new. Newness didn't matter. Contact was enough; simple, momentary contact. The letter had gone on to say that—

In a blank dismay, he brought it up in his shaking fingers. When he had re-read it, he looked up dully.

"Just what," he said vaguely, "in as few words as possible, will this mean?"

The executive engineer said in a level voice:

"It means that in a few weeks not a steel or iron plant in the United Nations will be in operation. This is Juggernaut with a capital Hell."

It is the people who are not acquainted with all the facts who are extremists. In this group will be found the defeatists of 1940 and the super optimists of 1943. Careless of logistics, indifferent to realities partially concealed for military reasons, they blunt their reasons and madden their minds with positivities.

In this group were Boothby and the engineers of the Vulcan Steel & Iron Works; and, until he arrived in Washington, the day after sending a dozen terrified telegrams, in this group also was Ogden Tait, chairman of the Vulcan board.

His first amazement came when the members of the war-planning board greeted him cheerfully.

"The important thing," said the Great Man, who was chairman of *that* board, "is that there be no morale slump. I suggest that all the iron ore and metal that is still workable be turned into peace-time machinery, particularly machinery for farm use, which must be heavy as well as strong. There will always be a certain amount of unaffected ore and scrap; and, since any machinery, once completed, will endure forever, it should not take long to supply all the more essential needs of the nation."

"But—but—but—" stammered Ogden Tait. "The w-war!"

He saw, bewildered, that the men were smiling easily. A member glanced at the Great Man.

"May I tell him?"

He was given permission. He turned to Ogden Tait.

"We have generously," he said, "decided to share our secret and wonderful metal with the Axis. Even now our planes are hovering over German and Japanese mines, ore piles, factories, dropping chunks of super-hard steel."

Ogden Tait waited. For the first time in his long, comfortable life, he had the feeling that he was not being very bright. It was a radical thought.

The member was continuing: "In a few months, what remains of the Axis steel industry, after our past bombings, will suspend operations."

He paused, smiling.

"But," Ogden Tait pointed out, "they'll have had three months production while we—"

"Let them have their three months," the member said calmly. "Let them have six months, a year. What do you think we've been doing this last few years? You bet we have. We've been building up supplies. Mountains, oceans, continents of supplies. We've got enough on hand to fight two years of continuous battle.

"The Germans, on the other hand, cannot get along for a single month without fresh munitions.

"The war is accordingly won."

The Great Man interjected at that point: "Whatever prank of fate wished this Juggernaut upon us has also solved the peace forever. If you will think about it for a moment, you will realize that, without steel, there can be no war—"

Whatever prank of fate! . . . A hand reaching out of nothingness into Pete Creighton's living room . . . deliberately dropping an ingot of steel.

D. D. SHARP

THE ETERNAL MAN

HERBERT ZULERICH was a big, heavy-framed man with a tangled mop of shaggy hair which lay back from his sloping forehead and clustered about the collar of his dark coat. His nose was big and prominent, swelling like a huge peak upon his face, and his mouth was a deep-lined canyon between the peak of his nose and the bulge of his chin.

Zulerich's habits were as strange as his face, and ponderous as his big body. How he lived no one knew, and no one knew either how he managed to maintain the formidable array of test tubes, and retorts. In his laboratory was every conceivable kind of peculiar glass, holding liquids of all colors.

Zulerich had, at one time, been a chemist of somewhat more than local fame, but of late years he had become a recluse, staying alone most of the time in his big stone house just back of the highway where the constant stream of autos seemed to disturb him but little.

In truth they disturbed him a great deal. Some days he would watch them in their hurry as they drove furiously along the straight line of paved roadway, and into his face would come gloom and melancholy. And into his large blue eyes would come a hurt look; a feeling of sympathy for those who seemed so full of life, so gay, so thoughtless.

"Death! Death!" the old man would whisper. "Man goes through long years of preparation for the few days of accomplishment before the conqueror destroys all.

"So much preparation," he would whisper as he shook his big head. "So many brilliant minds polished and blazing for an hour, like roses grown and tended to be cut for an evening's bloom; hands so skillfully trained, and so soon folded quietly at rest."

That he was in quest of some great secret, everyone who knew him had long ago suspected. But what that secret was, no one knew and few could even guess.

The truth was that Zulerich's mind was obsessed by a single thought— the appalling waste of death. And since science and invention were conquering the other enemies of man's existence, Zulerich set out after the example of Ponce de Leon, to discover the elements which might be combined to give eternal life.

Strange as it may seem, Zulerich was making some progress. He had found out some things which had astonished him. Some of his experiments had awed and stupefied him, and then he made a discovery which gave him a decided fright.

He had been experimenting with unicellular organisms, and had found that they did not behave as inorganic chemicals did. He knew that the reaction of those animalcules was distinctly physiological and not merely physical; organic and not purely chemical. They did not resemble any known chemicals, for they reacted as individuals and not as mere materials. This discovery, he found, was confirmed by Jennings in his book "Behavior of Unicellular Organisms."

Old Zulerich had studied the intricate processes of cellular division and multiplication, hoping to penetrate the law of the organism and discover something of the life it maintained. He wanted to discover what it was that, at the peak of growth, prevented further cleavage of cells. In short, he wanted to find the principle which confined the limits of size and growth. Find what it was that caused the cells of a living body to increase and multiply until maturity and then cease growing except when incited by a cut or other accident to the tissue. Why should a cell become active to replace wounded flesh, yet balk at rebuilding vital tissues, such as the lungs; or refuse to replace a lost tooth more than once?

He experimented in numerous ways to provoke cell growth, trying to divine whether they had individualities of their own or whether they were bounded by the individuality of the whole. He wanted to find whether cells had an intelligence which caused them to do the remarkable things necessary to their coordination in the body.

Zulerich found out many things; stupendous, mystifying things, which no amount of scientific theory could possibly explain. He perfected chemicals which applied to a rabbit's head caused its hair to grow so long as to make it necessary for him to gather it into a bag. And even then the weight of it grew so great the rabbit could no longer drag its load and he killed the animal out of mercy. But still its hair grew and grew. His high-walled back-yard soon held some monstrous freaks from his chemicals; dogs with heads as big as water barrels and bodies of normal size, and rats with bodies as big as cows and small peanut-sized heads. And one day he applied a chemical to a horse's eyes and the eyes grew out of their sockets like long ropes of white sinew with great knobs of gelatine-like iris—limp flabby canes which dragged upon the ground. The effect of this last experiment so cut the kind soul of Zulerich that he killed the monstrosities and wished to abandon his whole business. Then he would look again from his window over the wide world where death laid waste, and he would sigh and tighten his lips to plunge ahead again.

Growth was not what Zulerich wanted. He was quite content that man should retain his present stature. What he desired was to increase man's years.

And then he discovered it. He did not need to prove the experiment by waiting and watching until the end of time to find out whether the cells would eventually die. He knew they would not die. A few drops of pale green fluid in the graduating glass in his hand would permit any man to live eternally. He knew this was possible for he had at last found the combination he sought; the chemical which continued life without the necessity of decay.

After a year of experiments upon his cells he tried a drop upon a rat. He caught the rat in one hand and held his medicine dropper with its pale green fluid in the other. But, as the dropper released its globule, the rat moved its head and the drop hit the side of its face and trickled down and spread about its throat. It left a scar upon the hair, a peculiar scar like a question mark. Zulerich tried again with a second drop with better success. The rat swallowed it.

Zulerich watched carefully. The animal's heart seemed to cease beating. The lungs became motionless, and yet the rat lived, with a fire in its pink eyes. It lived on, day by day, week after week, month on month, without the slightest loss of weight or sign of hunger or thirst. It lived with its tiny soul imprisoned in it.

Yet even then Zulerich dared not drink his elixir, though his work was exhausting his strength and his heart was very weak and with its flutterings gave him frights at times. There was a flaw in his experiment. The animal lived without breath, food or water, but it was entirely *unable to move!* To see it one would presume it dead, except for the fire in its fierce little eyes and its lack of decay.

So Zulerich set out to mend the flaw. He worked feverishly now, for he was a very old man and his heart threatened to fail. He did not want to die with success just within his reach. He did not want to come so near offering mankind the one boon it craved and then to fail.

Two years passed before Zulerich found the ingredient lacking in his pale greenish drops. The thing was so simple he had overlooked it altogether. He discovered it quite by accident.

One day he had a pail containing a solution of washing soda near the window and was washing down the dusty glass so that he might see out over the blighted world and gain strength from its curse to continue his work. He would allow no one else in his laboratory and washed the windows himself.

A few spattering drops fell into the motionless, upturned mouth of the rat where it stood upon the deep casement. Its mouth was open in the same position Zulerich had left it when he had forced it to receive the life preserving drops. It had stood a tiny, paralyzed, living statue in that same attitude for two long years. Zulerich had really thought to remove the animal from the window before beginning to wash them. But as he grew older he had grown more absent minded. He was unable to use the same care and forethought he once had; but this time his carelessness resulted in a great discovery.

Immediately when the soda dropped into the rat's mouth it squealed and scurried for cover. But it soon came out to nibble a crust of cracker the parrot had dropped upon the floor.

Zulerich had been overjoyed at the rat regaining the use of its muscles, but now he became worried and anxious because it developed hunger. He thought that hunger might forebode decay which meant death.

Even as he pondered he trembled, for he knew he was very old and had not much time to watch and wait. And then as the result of his suspense and relief over the new discovery of the soda drops, his heart began fluttering alarmingly. It acted as it had never done before. He thought his time had come to die, and his precious experiment was almost completed, perhaps perfected, but not yet given to a life-hungry world.

All the legends he had ever read of the discovery of elixirs of life had had their fruits frosted just before the eating. And so it seemed it was to be with him. This was the end. Then he thought of his drops! He would drink them and there would be ample time to conclude his experiment.

He stepped quickly over to the table and sat upon his high stool. Then picking up the vial of pale green, which had become dusty with its long idleness upon its shelf, he measured his drops. But his hand trembled so that the vial dropped to the floor and spilt its precious fluid.

He drank the drops in the measuring glass. Then he reached for the soda water sitting just at a touch of his hand.

He could not move! He had forgotten he would be unable to hand the soda to his mouth. For the moment he was too upset and frightened to think clearly. He had overlooked a very vital thing. There was nothing to do but sit and wait for a neighbor to pass. He was as immovable as though cut in stone. He could not move an eyelid. He was very frightened.

A week went by.

During that week the rat played all over the room. One time it came out mockingly upon the table before him. Zulerich regarded it closely. It was not breathing.

Another week passed before anyone came into the house. During this time the rat became bolder and Zulerich had much time to observe it. He knew his experiment had been a success. The rat only consumed food to replace its physical energy. It needed fuel for running about the room, which of course was a method of decay. The rat needed no food to support its life. Zulerich knew he had discovered a great secret. He had accomplished life perpetual which only needed food for its physical energies.

Then a neighbor peeped in. His look of uneasiness gave way to one of pained sorrow. The neighbor's face became melancholy as he saw old Zulerich sitting stiffly upon his stool beside his chemicals. Zulerich tried to cry out, but his voice like his limbs was paralyzed. He tried to croak, even to whisper, but there was no noise at all. He put his appeal into the fierce, cold fire of his living eyes which were turned straight toward the door. The man saw the eyes, bright and living. He slammed the door and fled the room.

Zulerich created quite a sensation after that. No one knew what had happened to him. They thought he was dead, and surmised that he had spilled some mysterious compound over him which had embalmed him with the look of life still in his eyes.

Undertakers came from long distances to study him as he sat in his laboratory. They pried and tested among the fluids in the bottles, and years passed, and still old Zulerich was not buried because they believed he had found some marvelous embalming fluid and he was kept for observation.

Old Zulerich, growing no older at all, knew all this, for he sat there, in a glass case now, and heard all they said and saw before his eyes all that was done.

And in the dead of night the rat with its selfishness and its eternal life, and the unselfish chemist in his glass case, would meet again. The rat would scamper lively across the top of the glass case in which Zulerich sat as stiffly as though sculptured in stone. It would sit upon the table before him and stare at him with red spiteful eyes, and then scamper away. And Zulerich always knew it by the peculiar scar upon its neck. The rat knew what he lacked. For two long years it had been frozen, as he was now, before he had given it movement as well as life. But it was too mean to do so great a deed to a man. It hated him. It never brought him the few drops of alkali he craved.

One day they packed Zulerich carefully in a case and moved him, and when the case was opened he found himself in a lofty building with the mummy of a Pharaoh on one side of him and musty relics of other ages all around him. He recognized the old building, for in the other days he had loved to potter around there and let his fancies wander and his thoughts seek something tangible in these fragments of a vanished age.

As he sat there upon his stool, protected within his glass case, the unalterable line of his vision vaulted the narrow aisles below him and gazed through the great glass of a tall window in the opposite wall.

Out there he watched the throngs that passed. People of a day. Men who yesterday were babes in mothers' arms, today fighting up the long and difficult ladder for their fragment of success, to leap tomorrow into oblivion at their allotted rung.

Customs changed, women scrambled with the male, and there became even less time or inclination to enjoy the fruits of preparation. The years of training lengthened.

In all the years upon the earth it was bound that the two should meet again. The rat with its selfish greediness and the chemist with his unselfish dream. The rat had been seeking him so that it might gloat over him as it used to do. So that it might scamper upon his case and deride him with its motion. But the keeper of the museum saw the rat and beat it with his broom and mangled it with his big leather-shod heel. This happened in the night and he left the rat upon the floor until morning so that the cleaners might take it away.

Before the cleaners came the next morning one of the scientists who were studying Zulerich saw the rat lying there upon the floor before the case with its mangled body and its eyes so bright and full of pain. He stooped to examine it, and his interest became intense, for its heart and lungs were quiet and it seemed quite dead, and yet its eyes had the same living look of the man Zulerich in the glass case.

So the rat, too, was placed under observation and set in a tiny case upon a perch just before the case in which sat old Zulerich looking out upon the great world through the big window. The rat in its case cut off part of the vision of the chemist so that in seeing the world beyond the window he must look straight into the eyes of the creature to whom he had given eternal life, and which had been mangled until it was given eternal pain.

The years passed on, long years, all the longer that there should be no end of them. It was all the sadder that, instead of viewing the misery and waste of eighty years, he must watch it for eight hundred years, and even then be not done.

Life streamed by under his gaze, burning up with decay. Yet he held the secret they so much desired. Between them and eternal life was a connecting link, a few drops of alkaline water. The wires of communication were down and none had the wisdom nor the wit to raise them up. He had the secret, they had the power, if they only knew.

Eager, anxious, weary, discouraged and broken, the people of the world tramped by; torrents of wasted motion. For long years he envied them, of all that waste, the power to say one small word for their freedom. For long years the undying man and the undying rat stared hatefully at each other. For long years he studied and contrived within his mind some means for breaking the paralysis of his body so that he might give eternal life to humanity. Then he learned a great lesson from a small child.

The child had discovered the mangled rat and had seen the pain and desire of death in its eyes. She begged her father to kill the little rat as he had killed her little dog after a car had wounded it.

That night Zulerich's eyes softened as he regarded the rat under the bright glow of the electric lights, and in his heart he felt remorse. For the first time he was glad that he had not been able to give man his magic formula. He discovered that he should need to improve life before trying to lengthen it.

PART FIVE

Adventures in Dimension

LEWIS PADGETT

MIMSY WERE THE BOROGOVES

THERE'S no use trying to describe either Unthahorsten or his surroundings, because, for one thing, a good many million years had passed
since 1942 Anno Domini, and, for another, Unthahorsten wasn't on
Earth, technically speaking. He was doing the equivalent of standing
in the equivalent of a laboratory. He was preparing to test his time
machine.

Having turned on the power, Unthahorsten suddenly realized that
the Box was empty. Which wouldn't do at all. The device needed a control, a three-dimensional solid which would react to the conditions of
another age. Otherwise Unthahorsten couldn't tell, on the machine's return, where and when it had been. Whereas a solid in the Box would automatically be subject to the entropy and cosmic ray bombardment of
the other era, and Unthahorsten could measure the changes, both qualitative and quantitative, when the machine returned. The Calculators
could then get to work and, presently, tell Unthahorsten that the Box
had briefly visited 1,000,000 A. D., 1,000 A. D., or 1 A. D., as the case
might be.

Not that it mattered, except to Unthahorsten. But he was childish in
many respects.

There was little time to waste. The Box was beginning to glow and
shiver. Unthahorsten stared around wildly, fled into the next glossatch,
and groped in a storage bin there. He came up with an armful of pecul-
iar-looking stuff. Uh-huh. Some of the discarded toys of his son Snowen,
which the boy had brought with him when he had passed over from
Earth, after mastering the necessary technique. Well, Snowen needed
this junk no longer. He was conditioned, and had put away childish
things. Besides, though Unthahorsten's wife kept the toys for sentimental reasons, the experiment was more important.

Unthahorsten left the glossatch and dumped the assortment into the
Box, slamming the cover shut just before the warning signal flashed.
The Box went away. The manner of its departure hurt Unthahorsten's
eyes.

He waited.

And he waited.

Eventually he gave up and built another time machine, with identical results. Snowen hadn't been annoyed by the loss of his old toys, nor had Snowen's mother, so Unthahorsten cleaned out the bin and dumped the remainder of his son's childhood relics in the second time machine's Box.

According to his calculations, this one should have appeared on Earth, in the latter part of the nineteenth century, A. D. If that actually occurred, the device remained there.

Disgusted, Unthahorsten decided to make no more time machines. But the mischief had been done. There were two of them, and the first—

Scott Paradine found it while he was playing hooky from the Glendale Grammar School. There was a geography test that day, and Scott saw no sense in memorizing place names—which in 1942 was a fairly sensible theory. Besides, it was the sort of warm spring day, with a touch of coolness in the breeze, which invited a boy to lie down in a field and stare at the occasional clouds till he fell asleep. Nuts to geography! Scott dozed.

About noon he got hungry, so his stocky legs carried him to a nearby store. There he invested his small hoard with penurious care and a sublime disregard for his gastric juices. He went down by the creek to feed.

Having finished his supply of cheese, chocolate, and cookies, and having drained the soda-pop bottle to its dregs, Scott caught tadpoles and studied them with a certain amount of scientific curiosity. He did not persevere. Something tumbled down the bank and thudded into the muddy ground near the water, so Scott, with a wary glance around, hurried to investigate.

It was a box. It was, in fact, the Box. The gadgetry hitched to it meant little to Scott, though he wondered why it was so fused and burnt. He pondered. With his jackknife he pried and probed, his tongue sticking out from a corner of his mouth— Hm-m-m. Nobody was around. Where had the box come from? Somebody must have left it here, and sliding soil had dislodged it from its precarious perch.

"That's a helix," Scott decided, quite erroneously. It was helical, but it wasn't a helix, because of the dimensional warp involved. Had the thing been a model airplane, no matter how complicated, it would have held few mysteries to Scott. As it was, a problem was posed. Something told Scott that the device was a lot more complicated than the spring motor he had deftly dismantled last Friday.

But no boy has ever left a box unopened, unless forcibly dragged away. Scott probed deeper. The angles on this thing were funny. Short circuit, probably. That was why—*uh!* The knife slipped. Scott sucked his thumb and gave vent to experienced blasphemy.

Maybe it was a music box.

Scott shouldn't have felt depressed. The gadgetry would have given Einstein a headache and driven Steinmetz raving mad. The trouble was, of course, that the box had not yet completely entered the space-time continuum where Scott existed, and therefore it could not be opened. At any rate, not till Scott used a convenient rock to hammer the helical non-helix into a more convenient position.

He hammered it, in fact, from its contact point with the fourth dimension, releasing the space-time torsion it had been maintaining. There was a brittle snap. The box jarred slightly, and lay motionless, no longer only partially in existence. Scott opened it easily now.

The soft, woven helmet was the first thing that caught his eye, but he discarded that without much interest. It was just a cap. Next he lifted a square, transparent crystal block, small enough to cup in his palm—much too small to contain the maze of apparatus within it. In a moment Scott had solved that problem. The crystal was a sort of magnifying glass, vastly enlarging the things inside the block. Strange things they were, too. Miniature people, for example—

They moved. Like clockwork automatons, though much more smoothly. It was rather like watching a play. Scott was interested in their costumes, but fascinated by their actions. The tiny people were deftly building a house. Scott wished it would catch fire, so he could see the people put it out.

Flames licked up from the half-completed structure. The automatons, with a great deal of odd apparatus, extinguished the blaze.

It didn't take Scott long to catch on. But he was a little worried. The manikins would obey his thoughts. By the time he discovered that, he was frightened, and threw the cube from him.

Halfway up the bank, he reconsidered and returned. The crystal block lay partly in the water, shining in the sun. It was a toy; Scott sensed that, with the unerring instinct of a child. But he didn't pick it up immediately. Instead, he returned to the box and investigated its remaining contents.

He found some really remarkable gadgets. The afternoon passed all too quickly. Scott finally put the toys back in the box and lugged it home, grunting and puffing. He was quite red-faced by the time he arrived at the kitchen door.

His find he hid at the back of a closet in his own room upstairs. The crystal cube he slipped into his pocket, which already bulged with string, a coil of wire, two pennies, a wad of tinfoil, a grimy defense stamp, and a chunk of feldspar. Emma, Scott's two-year-old sister, waddled unsteadily in from the hall and said hello.

"Hello, Slug," Scott nodded, from his altitude of seven years and some months. He patronized Emma shockingly, but she didn't know the difference. Small, plump, and wide-eyed, she flopped down on the carpet and stared dolefully at her shoes.

"Tie 'em, Scotty, please?"

"Sap," Scott told her kindly, but knotted the laces. "Dinner ready yet?"

Emma nodded.

"Let's see your hands." For a wonder they were reasonably clean, though probably not aseptic. Scott regarded his own paws thoughtfully and, grimacing, went to the bathroom, where he made a sketchy toilet. The tadpoles had left traces.

Dennis Paradine and his wife Jane were having a cocktail before dinner, downstairs in the living room. He was a youngish, middle-aged man with gray-shot hair and a thinnish, prim-mouthed face; he taught philosophy at the university. Jane was small, neat, dark, and very pretty. She sipped her Martini and said:

"New shoes. Like 'em?"

"Here's to crime," Paradine muttered absently. "Huh? Shoes? Not now. Wait till I've finished this. I had a bad day."

"Exams?"

"Yeah. Flaming youth aspiring toward manhood. I hope they die. In considerable agony. *Insh'Allah!*"

"I want the olive," Jane requested.

"I know," Paradine said despondently. "It's been years since I've tasted one myself. In a Martini, I mean. Even if I put six of 'em in your glass, you're still not satisfied."

"I want yours. Blood brotherhood. Symbolism. That's why."

Paradine regarded his wife balefully and crossed his long legs. "You sound like one of my students."

"Like that hussy Betty Dawson, perhaps?" Jane unsheathed her nails. "Does she still leer at you in that offensive way?"

"She does. The child is a neat psychological problem. Luckily she isn't mine. If she were—" Paradine nodded significantly. "Sex consciousness and too many movies. I suppose she still thinks she can get a passing grade by showing me her knees. Which are, by the way, rather bony."

Jane adjusted her skirt with an air of complacent pride. Paradine uncoiled himself and poured fresh Martinis. "Candidly, I don't see the point of teaching those apes philosophy. They're all at the wrong age. Their habit-patterns, their methods of thinking, are already laid down. They're horribly conservative, not that they'd admit it. The only people who can understand philosophy are mature adults or kids like Emma and Scotty."

"Well, don't enroll Scotty in your course," Jane requested. "He isn't ready to be a *Philosophiae Doctor*. I hold no brief for child geniuses, especially when it's my son."

"Scotty would probably be better at it than Betty Dawson," Paradine grunted.

"'He died an enfeebled old dotard at five,'" Jane quoted dreamily. "I want your olive."

"Here. By the way, I like the shoes."

"Thank you. Here's Rosalie. Dinner?"

"It's all ready, Miz Pa'dine," said Rosalie, hovering. "I'll call Miss Emma 'n' Mista' Scotty."

"I'll get 'em." Paradine put his head into the next room and roared, "Kids! Come and get it!"

Small feet scuttered down the stairs. Scott dashed into view, scrubbed and shining, a rebellious cowlick aimed at the zenith. Emma pursued, levering herself carefully down the steps. Halfway she gave up the attempt to descend upright and reversed, finishing the task monkey-fashion, her small behind giving an impression of marvelous diligence upon the work in hand. Paradine watched, fascinated by the spectacle, till he was hurled back by the impact of his son's body.

"Hi, dad!" Scott shrieked.

Paradine recovered himself and regarded Scott with dignity. "Hi, yourself. Help me in to dinner. You've dislocated at least one of my hip joints."

But Scott was already tearing into the next room, where he stepped on Jane's new shoes in an ecstasy of affection, burbled an apology, and rushed off to find his place at the dinner table. Paradine cocked up an eyebrow as he followed, Emma's pudgy hand desperately gripping his forefinger.

"Wonder what the young devil's been up to?"

"No good, probably," Jane sighed. "Hello, darling. Let's see your ears."

"They're *clean*. Mickey licked 'em."

"Well, that Airedale's tongue is far cleaner than your ears," Jane pondered, making a brief examination. "Still, as long as you can hear, the dirt's only superficial."

"Fisshul?"

"Just a little, that means." Jane dragged her daughter to the table and inserted her legs into a high chair. Only lately had Emma graduated to the dignity of dining with the rest of the family, and she was, as Paradine remarked, all eat up with pride by the prospect. Only babies spilled food, Emma had been told. As a result, she took such painstaking care in conveying her spoon to her mouth that Paradine got the jitters whenever he watched.

"A conveyer belt would be the thing for Emma," he suggested, pulling out a chair for Jane. "Small buckets of spinach arriving at her face at stated intervals."

Dinner proceeded uneventfully until Paradine happened to glance at Scott's plate. "Hello, there. Sick? Been stuffing yourself at lunch?"

Scott thoughtfully examined the food still left before him. "I've had all I need, dad," he explained.

"You usually eat all you can hold, and a great deal more," Paradine said. "I know growing boys need several tons of foodstuff a day, but you're below par tonight. Feel O. K.?"

"Uh-huh. Honest, I've had all I need."

"All you *want?*"

"Sure. I eat different."

"Something they taught you at school?" Jane inquired.

Scott shook his head solemnly.

"Nobody taught me. I found it out myself. I use spit."

"Try again," Paradine suggested. "It's the wrong word."

"Uh . . . s-saliva. Hm-m-m?"

"Uh-huh. More pepsin? Is there pepsin in the salivary juices, Jane? I forget."

"There's poison in mine," Jane remarked. "Rosalie's left lumps in the mashed potatoes again."

But Paradine was interested. "You mean you're getting everything possible out of your food—no wastage—and eating less?"

Scott thought that over. "I guess so. It's not just the sp . . . saliva. I sort of measure how much to put in my mouth at once, and what stuff to mix up. I dunno. I just do it."

"Hm-m-m," said Paradine, making a note to check up later. "Rather a revolutionary idea." Kids often get screwy notions, but this one might not be so far off the beam. He pursed his lips. "Eventually I suppose people will eat quite differently—I mean the *way* they eat, as well as what. What they eat, I mean. Jane, our son shows signs of becoming a genius."

"Oh?"

"It's a rather good point in dietetics he just made. Did you figure it out yourself, Scott?"

"Sure," the boy said, and really believed it.

"Where'd you get the idea?"

"Oh, I—" Scott wriggled. "I dunno. It doesn't mean much, I guess."

Paradine was unreasonably disappointed. "But surely—"

"S-s-s-spit!" Emma shrieked, overcome by a sudden fit of badness. *"Spit!"* She attempted to demonstrate, but succeeded only in dribbling into her bib.

With a resigned air Jane rescued and reproved her daughter, while Paradine eyed Scott with rather puzzled interest. But it was not till after dinner, in the living room, that anything further happened.

"Any homework?"

"N-no," Scott said, flushing guiltily. To cover his embarrassment he took from his pocket a gadget he had found in the box, and began to unfold it. The result resembled a tesseract, strung with beads. Paradine didn't see it at first, but Emma did. She wanted to play with it.

"No. Lay off, Slug," Scott ordered. "You can watch me." He fumbled with the beads, making soft, interested noises. Emma extended a fat forefinger and yelped.

"Scotty," Paradine said warningly.

"I didn't hurt her."

"Bit me. It did," Emma mourned.

Paradine looked up. He frowned, staring. What in—

"Is that an abacus?" he asked. "Let's see it, please."

Somewhat unwillingly Scott brought the gadget across to his father's chair. Paradine blinked. The "abacus," unfolded, was more than a foot square, composed of thin, rigid wires that interlocked here and there. On the wires the colored beads were strung. They could be slid back and forth, and from one support to another, even at the points of jointure. But—a pierced bead couldn't cross *interlocking* wires—

So, apparently, they weren't pierced. Paradine looked closer. Each small sphere had a deep groove running around it, so that it could be revolved and slid along the wire at the same time. Paradine tried to pull one free. It clung as though magnetically. Iron? It looked more like plastic.

The framework itself— Paradine wasn't a mathematician. But the angles formed by the wires were vaguely shocking, in their ridiculous lack of Euclidean logic. They were a maze. Perhaps that's what the gadget was—a puzzle.

"Where'd you get this?"

"Uncle Harry gave it to me," Scott said on the spur of the moment. "Last Sunday, when he came over." Uncle Harry was out of town, a circumstance Scott well knew. At the age of seven, a boy soon learns that the vagaries of adults follow a certain definite pattern, and that they are fussy about the donors of gifts. Moreover, Uncle Harry would not return for several weeks; the expiration of that period was unimaginable to Scott, or, at least, the fact that his lie would ultimately be discovered meant less to him than the advantages of being allowed to keep the toy.

Paradine found himself growing slightly confused as he attempted to manipulate the beads. The angles were vaguely illogical. It was like a puzzle. This red bead, if slid along *this* wire to *that* junction, should reach *there*—but it didn't. A maze, odd, but no doubt instructive. Paradine had a well-founded feeling that he'd have no patience with the thing himself.

Scott did, however, retiring to a corner and sliding beads around with much fumbling and grunting. The beads *did* sting, when Scott chose the wrong ones or tried to slide them in the wrong direction. At last he crowed exultantly.

"I did it, dad!"

"Eh? What? Let's see." The device looked exactly the same to Paradine, but Scott pointed and beamed.

"I made it disappear."

"It's still there."

"That blue bead. It's gone now."

Paradine didn't believe that, so he merely snorted. Scott puzzled over the framework again. He experimented. This time there were no shocks, even slight. The abacus had showed him the correct method. Now it was up to him to do it on his own. The bizarre angles of the wires seemed a little less confusing now, somehow.

It was a most instructive toy—

It worked, Scott thought, rather like the crystal cube. Reminded of that gadget, he took it from his pocket and relinquished the abacus to

Emma, who was struck dumb with joy. She fell to work sliding the beads, this time without protesting against the shocks—which, indeed, were very minor—and, being imitative, she managed to make a bead disappear almost as quickly as had Scott. The blue bead reappeared— but Scott didn't notice. He had forethoughtfully retired into an angle of the chesterfield with an overstuffed chair and amused himself with the cube.

There were little people inside the thing, tiny manikins much enlarged by the magnifying properties of the crystal, and they moved, all right. They built a house. It caught fire, with realistic-seeming flames, and stood by waiting. Scott puffed urgently. "Put it *out!*"

But nothing happened. Where was that queer fire engine, with revolving arms, that had appeared before? Here it was. It came sailing into the picture and stopped. Scott urged it on.

This was fun. Like putting on a play, only more real. The little people did what Scott told them, inside of his head. If he made a mistake, they waited till he'd found the right way. They even posed new problems for him—

The cube, too, was a most instructive toy. It was teaching Scott, with alarming rapidity—and teaching him very entertainingly. But it gave him no really new knowledge as yet. He wasn't ready. Later—later—

Emma grew tired of the abacus and went in search of Scott. She couldn't find him, even in his room, but once there the contents of the closet intrigued her. She discovered the box. It contained treasure-trove —a doll, which Scott had already noticed but discarded with a sneer. Squealing, Emma brought the doll downstairs, squatted in the middle of the floor, and began to take it apart.

"Darling! What's that?"

"Mr. Bear!"

Obviously it wasn't Mr. Bear, who was blind, earless, but comforting in his soft fatness. But all dolls were named Mr. Bear to Emma.

Jane Paradine hesitated. "Did you take that from some other little girl?"

"I didn't. She's mine."

Scott came out from his hiding place, thrusting the cube into his pocket. "Uh—that's from Uncle Harry."

"Did Uncle Harry give that to you, Emma?"

"He gave it to me for Emma," Scott put in hastily, adding another stone to his foundation of deceit. "Last Sunday."

"You'll break it, dear."

Emma brought the doll to her mother. "She comes apart. See?"

"Oh? It . . . *ugh!*" Jane sucked in her breath. Paradine looked up quickly.

"What's up?"

She brought the doll over to him, hesitated, and then went into the dining room, giving Paradine a significant glance. He followed, closing the door. Jane had already placed the doll on the cleared table.

"This isn't very nice, is it, Denny?"

"Hm-m-m." It was rather unpleasant, at first glance. One might have expected an anatomical dummy in a medical school, but a child's doll—

The thing came apart in sections, skin, muscles, organs, miniature but quite perfect, as far as Paradine could see. He was interested. "Dunno. Such things haven't the same connotations to a kid—"

"Look at that liver. Is it a liver?"

"Sure. Say, I . . . this is funny."

"What?"

"It isn't anatomically perfect, after all." Paradine pulled up a chair. "The digestive tract's too short. No large intestine. No appendix, either."

"Should Emma have a thing like this?"

"I wouldn't mind having it myself," Paradine said. "Where on earth did Harry pick it up? No, I don't see any harm in it. Adults are conditioned to react unpleasantly to innards. Kids don't. They figure they're solid inside, like a potato. Emma can get a sound working knowledge of physiology from this doll."

"But what are those? Nerves?"

"No, these are the nerves. Arteries here; veins here. Funny sort of aorta—" Paradine looked baffled. "That . . . what's Latin for network? Anyway . . . huh? *Rita? Rata?*"

"*Rales,*" Jane suggested at random.

"That's a sort of breathing," Paradine said crushingly. "I can't figure out what this luminous network of stuff is. It goes all through the body, like nerves."

"Blood."

"Nope. Not circulatory, not neural—funny! It seems to be hooked up with the lungs."

They became engrossed, puzzling over the strange doll. It was made with remarkable perfection of detail, and that in itself was strange, in view of the physiological variation from the norm. "Wait'll I get that Gould," Paradine said, and presently was comparing the doll with anatomical charts. He learned little, except to increase his bafflement.

But it was more fun than a jigsaw puzzle.

Meanwhile, in the adjoining room, Emma was sliding the beads to and fro in the abacus. The motions didn't seem so strange now. Even when the beads vanished. She could almost follow that new direction—almost—

Scott panted, staring into the crystal cube and mentally directing, with many false starts, the building of a structure somewhat more complicated than the one which had been destroyed by fire. He, too, was learning—being conditioned—

Paradine's mistake, from a completely anthropomorphic standpoint, was that he didn't get rid of the toys instantly. He did not realize their significance, and, by the time he did, the progression of circumstances had got well under way. Uncle Harry remained out of town, so Paradine couldn't check with him. Too, the midterm exams were on, which meant arduous mental effort and complete exhaustion at night; and Jane was slightly ill for a week or so. Emma and Scott had free rein with the toys.

"What," Scott asked his father one evening, "is a wabe, dad?"

"Wave?"

He hesitated. "I . . . don't *think* so. Isn't wabe right?"

"Wab is Scot for web. That it?"

"I don't see how," Scott muttered, and wandered off, scowling, to amuse himself with the abacus. He was able to handle it quite deftly now. But, with the instinct of children for avoiding interruptions, he and Emma usually played with the toys in private. Not obviously, of course —but the more intricate experiments were never performed under the eye of an adult.

Scott was learning fast. What he now saw in the crystal cube had little relationship to the original simple problems. But they were fascinatingly technical. Had Scott realized that his education was being guided and supervised—though merely mechanically—he would probably have lost interest. As it was, his initiative was never quashed.

Abacus, cube, doll—and other toys the children found in the box—

Neither Paradine nor Jane guessed how much of an effect the contents of the time machine were having on the kids. How could they? Youngsters are instinctive dramatists, for purposes of self-protection. They have not yet fitted themselves to the exigencies—to them partially inexplicable—of a mature world. Moreover, their lives are complicated by human variables. They are told by one person that playing in the mud is permissible, but that, in their excavations, they must not uproot flowers or small trees. Another adult vetoes mud *per se*. The Ten Commandments are not carved on stone; they vary, and children are helplessly dependent on the caprice of those who give them birth and feed and clothe them. And tyrannize. The young animal does not resent that benevolent tyranny, for it is an essential part of nature. He is, however, an individualist, and maintains his integrity by a subtle, passive fight.

Under the eyes of an adult he changes. Like an actor on-stage, when he remembers, he strives to please, and also to attract attention to himself. Such attempts are not unknown to maturity. But adults are less obvious—to other adults.

It is difficult to admit that children lack subtlety. Children are different from the mature animal because they think in another way. We can more or less easily pierce the pretenses they set up—but they can do the same to us. Ruthlessly a child can destroy the pretenses of an adult. Iconoclasm is their prerogative.

Foppishness, for example. The amenities of social intercourse, exaggerated not quite to absurdity. The gigolo—

"Such *savoir faire!* Such punctilious courtesy!" The dowager and the blond young thing are often impressed. Men have less pleasant comments to make. But the child goes to the root of the matter.

"You're *silly!*"

How can an immature human understand the complicated system of social relationships? He can't. To him, an exaggeration of natural courtesy is silly. In his functional structure of life-patterns, it is rococo. He is an egotistic little animal, who cannot visualize himself in the position of another—certainly not an adult. A self-contained, almost perfect natural unit, his wants supplied by others, the child is much like a unicellular creature floating in the blood stream, nutriment carried to him, waste products carried away—

From the standpoint of logic, a child is rather horribly perfect. A baby may be even more perfect, but so alien to an adult that only superficial standards of comparison apply. The thought processes of an infant are completely unimaginable. But babies think, even before birth. In the womb they move and sleep, not entirely through instinct. We are conditioned to react rather peculiarly to the idea that a nearly-viable embryo may think. We are surprised, shocked into laughter, and repelled. Nothing human is alien.

But a baby is not human. An embryo is far less human.

That, perhaps, was why Emma learned more from the toys than did Scott. He could communicate his thoughts, of course; Emma could not, except in cryptic fragments. The matter of the scrawls, for example—

Give a young child pencil and paper, and he will draw something which looks different to him than to an adult. The absurd scribbles have little resemblance to a fire engine, but it *is* a fire engine, to a baby. Perhaps it is even three-dimensional. Babies think differently and see differently.

Paradine brooded over that, reading his paper one evening and watching Emma and Scott communicate. Scott was questioning his sister. Sometimes he did it in English. More often he had resource to gibberish and sign language. Emma tried to reply, but the handicap was too great.

Finally Scott got pencil and paper. Emma liked that. Tongue in cheek, she laboriously wrote a message. Scott took the paper, examined it, and scowled.

"That isn't right, Emma," he said.

Emma nodded vigorously. She seized the pencil again and made more scrawls. Scott puzzled for a while, finally smiled rather hesitantly, and got up. He vanished into the hall. Emma returned to the abacus.

Paradine rose and glanced down at the paper, with some mad thought that Emma might abruptly have mastered calligraphy. But she hadn't. The paper was covered with meaningless scrawls, of a type familiar to any parent. Paradine pursed his lips.

It might be a graph showing the mental variations of a manic-depressive cockroach, but probably wasn't. Still, it no doubt had meaning to Emma. Perhaps the scribble represented Mr. Bear.

Scott returned, looking pleased. He met Emma's gaze and nodded. Paradine felt a twinge of curiosity.

"Secrets?"

"Nope. Emma . . . uh . . . asked me to do something for her."

"Oh." Paradine, recalling instances of babies who had babbled in unknown tongues and baffled linguists, made a note to pocket the paper
when the kids had finished with it. The next day he showed the scrawl
to Elkins at the university. Elkins had a sound working knowledge of
many unlikely languages, but he chuckled over Emma's venture into
literature.

"Here's a free translation, Dennis. Quote. I don't know what this
means, but I kid the hell out of my father with it. Unquote."

The two men laughed and went off to their classes. But later Paradine
was to remember the incident. Especially after he met Holloway. Before
that, however, months were to pass, and the situation to develop even
further toward its climax.

Perhaps Paradine and Jane had evinced too much interest in the toys.
Emma and Scott took to keeping them hidden, playing with them only
in private. They never did it overtly, but with a certain unobtrusive caution. Nevertheless, Jane especially was somewhat troubled.

She spoke to Paradine about it one evening. "That doll Harry gave
Emma."

"Yeah?"

"I was downtown today and tried to find out where it came from. No
soap."

"Maybe Harry bought it in New York."

Jane was unconvinced. "I asked them about the other things, too.
They showed me their stock—Johnsons's a big store, you know. But
there's nothing like Emma's abacus."

"Hm-m-m." Paradine wasn't much interested. They had tickets for a
show that night, and it was getting late. So the subject was dropped for
the nonce.

Later it cropped up again, when a neighbor telephoned Jane.

"Scotty's never been like that, Denny. Mrs. Burns said he frightened
the devil out of her Francis."

"Francis? A little fat bully of a punk, isn't he? Like his father. I
broke Burns' nose for him once, when we were sophomores."

"Stop boasting and listen," Jane said, mixing a highball. "Scott
showed Francis something that scared him. Hadn't you better—"

"I suppose so." Paradine listened. Noises in the next room told him
the whereabouts of his son. "Scotty!"

"Bang," Scott said, and appeared smiling. "I killed 'em all. Space
pirates. You want me, dad?"

"Yes. If you don't mind leaving the space pirates unburied for a few
minutes. What did you do to Francis Burns?"

Scott's blue eyes reflected incredible candor. "Huh?"

"Try hard. You can remember, I'm sure."

"Uh. Oh, that. I didn't do nothing."

"Anything," Jane corrected absently.

"Anything. Honest. I just let him look into my television set, and it
. . . it scared him."

"Television set?"

Scott produced the crystal cube. "It isn't really that. See?"

Paradine examined the gadget, startled by the magnification. All he
could see, though, was a maze of meaningless colored designs.

"Uncle Harry—"

Paradine reached for the telephone. Scott gulped. "Is . . . is Uncle
Harry back in town?"

"Yeah."

"Well, I gotta take a bath." Scott headed for the door. Paradine met
Jane's gaze and nodded significantly.

Harry was home, but disclaimed all knowledge of the peculiar toys.
Rather grimly, Paradine requested Scott to bring down from his room
all of the playthings. Finally they lay in a row on the table, cube,
abacus, doll, helmetlike cap, several other mysterious contraptions. Scott
was cross-examined. He lied valiantly for a time, but broke down at last
and bawled, hiccuping his confession.

"Get the box these things came in," Paradine ordered. "Then head for
bed."

"Are you . . . *hup!* . . . gonna punish me, daddy?"

"For playing hooky and lying, yes. You know the rules. No more
shows for two weeks. No sodas for the same period."

Scott gulped. "You gonna keep my things?"

"I don't know yet."

"Well . . . g'night, daddy. G'night, mom."

After the small figure had gone upstairs, Paradine dragged a chair to
the table and carefully scrutinized the box. He poked thoughtfully at
the fused gadgetry. Jane watched.

"What is it, Denny?"

"Dunno. Who'd leave a box of toys down by the creek?"

"It might have fallen out of a car."

"Not at that point. The road doesn't hit the creek north of the rail-
road trestle. Empty lots—nothing else." Paradine lit a cigarette. "Drink,
honey?"

"I'll fix it." Jane went to work, her eyes troubled. She brought Paradine a glass and stood behind him, ruffling his hair with her fingers. "Is
anything wrong?"

"Of course not. Only—where did these toys come from?"

"Johnsons's didn't know, and they get their stock from New York."

"I've been checking up, too," Paradine admitted. "That doll"—he
poked it—"rather worried me. Custom jobs, maybe, but I wish I knew
who'd made 'em."

"A psychologist? That abacus—don't they give people tests with such
things?"

Paradine snapped his fingers. "Right! And say! There's a guy going
to speak at the university next week, fellow named Holloway, who's a

child psychologist. He's a big shot, with quite a reputation. He might know something about it."

"Holloway? I don't—"

"Rex Holloway. He's . . . hm-m-m! He doesn't live far from here. Do you suppose he might have had these things made himself?"

Jane was examining the abacus. She grimaced and drew back. "If he did, I don't like him. But see if you can find out, Denny."

Paradine nodded. "I shall."

He drank his highball, frowning. He was vaguely worried. But he wasn't scared—yet.

Rex Holloway was a fat, shiny man, with a bald head and thick spectacles, above which his thick, black brows lay like bushy caterpillars. Paradine brought him home to dinner one night a week later. Holloway did not appear to watch the children, but nothing they did or said was lost on him. His gray eyes, shrewd and bright, missed little.

The toys fascinated him. In the living room the three adults gathered around the table, where the playthings had been placed. Holloway studied them carefully as he listened to what Jane and Paradine had to say. At last he broke his silence.

"I'm glad I came here tonight. But not completely. This is very disturbing, you know."

"Eh?" Paradine stared, and Jane's face showed her consternation. Holloway's next words did not calm them.

"We are dealing with madness."

He smiled at the shocked looks they gave him. "All children are mad, from an adult viewpoint. Ever read Hughes' 'High Wind in Jamaica'?"

"I've got it." Paradine secured the little book from its shelf. Holloway extended a hand, took it, and flipped the pages till he had found the place he wanted. He read aloud:

" 'Babies of course are not human—they are animals, and have a very ancient and ramified culture, as cats have, and fishes, and even snakes; the same in kind as these, but much more complicated and vivid, since babies are, after all, one of the most developed species of the lower vertebrates. In short, babies have minds which work in terms and categories of their own which cannot be translated into the terms and categories of the human mind.' "

Jane tried to take that calmly, but couldn't. "You don't mean that Emma—"

"Could you think like your daughter?" Holloway asked. "Listen: 'One can no more think like a baby than one can think like a bee.' "

Paradine mixed drinks. Over his shoulder he said, "You're theorizing quite a bit, aren't you? As I get it, you're implying that babies have a culture of their own, even a high standard of intelligence."

"Not necessarily. There's no yardstick, you see. All I say is that babies think in other ways than we do. Not necessarily *better*—that's a

question of relative values. But with a different manner of extension—"
He sought for words, grimacing.

"Fantasy," Paradine said, rather rudely, but annoyed because of
Emma. "Babies don't have different senses from ours."

"Who said they did?" Holloway demanded. "They use their minds in
a different way, that's all. But it's quite enough!"

"I'm trying to understand," Jane said slowly. "All I can think of is
my Mixmaster. It can whip up batter and potatoes, but it can squeeze
oranges, too."

"Something like that. The brain's a colloid, a very complicated machine. We don't know much about its potentialities. We don't even know
how much it can grasp. But it *is* known that the mind becomes conditioned as the human animal matures. It follows certain familiar theorems, and all thought thereafter is pretty well based on patterns taken
for granted. Look at this." Holloway touched the abacus. "Have you experimented with it?"

"A little," Paradine said.

"But not much. Eh?"

"Well—"

"Why not?"

"It's pointless," Paradine complained. "Even a puzzle has to have
some logic. But those crazy angles—"

"Your mind has been conditioned to Euclid," Holloway said. "So
this—thing—bores us, and seems pointless. But a child knows nothing
of Euclid. A different sort of geometry from ours wouldn't impress him
as being illogical. He believes what he sees."

"Are you trying to tell me that this gadget's got a fourth-dimensional
extension?" Paradine demanded.

"Not visually, anyway," Holloway denied. "All I say is that our
minds, conditioned to Euclid, can see nothing in this but an illogical
tangle of wires. But a child—especially a baby—might see more. Not at
first. It'd be a puzzle, of course. Only a child wouldn't be handicapped
by too many preconceived ideas."

"Hardening of the thought-arteries," Jane interjected.

Paradine was not convinced. "Then a baby could work calculus better
than Einstein? No, I don't mean that. I can see your point, more or less
clearly. Only—"

"Well, look. Let's suppose there are two kinds of geometry—we'll
limit it, for the sake of the example. Our kind, Euclidean, and another,
which we'll call x. X hasn't much relationship to Euclid. It's based on
different theorems. Two and two needn't equal four in it; they could
equal y_2, or they might not even *equal*. A baby's mind is not yet conditioned, except by certain questionable factors of heredity and environment. Start the infant on Euclid—"

"Poor kid," Jane said.

Holloway shot her a quick glance. "The basis of Euclid. Alphabet blocks. Math, geometry, algebra—they come much later. We're familiar with that development. On the other hand, start the baby with the basic principles of our x logic."

"Blocks? What kind?"

Holloway looked at the abacus. "It wouldn't make much sense to us. But we've been conditioned to Euclid."

Paradine poured himself a stiff shot of whiskey. "That's pretty awful. You're not limiting to math."

"Right! I'm not limiting it at all. How can I? I'm not conditioned to x logic."

"There's the answer," Jane said, with a sigh of relief. "Who is? It'd take such a person to make the sort of toys you apparently think these are."

Holloway nodded, his eyes, behind the thick lenses, blinking. "Such people may exist."

"Where?"

"They might prefer to keep hidden."

"Supermen?"

"I wish I knew. You see, Paradine, we've got yardstick trouble again. By our standards these people might seem super-doopers in certain respects. In others they might seem moronic. It's not a quantitative difference; it's qualitative. They *think* different. And I'm sure we can do things they can't."

"Maybe they wouldn't want to," Jane said.

Paradine tapped the fused gadgetry on the box. "What about this? It implies—"

"A purpose, sure."

"Transportation?"

"One thinks of that first. If so, the box might have come from anywhere."

"Where—things are—*different?*" Paradine asked slowly.

"Exactly. In space, or even time. I don't know; I'm a pyschologist. Unfortunately I'm conditioned to Euclid, too."

"Funny place it must be," Jane said. "Denny, get rid of those toys."

"I intend to."

Holloway picked up the crystal cube. "Did you question the children much?"

Paradine said, "Yeah. Scott said there were people in that cube when he first looked. I asked him what was in it now."

"What did he say?" The psychologist's eyes widened.

"He said they were building a place. His exact words. I asked him who—people? But he couldn't explain."

"No, I suppose not," Holloway muttered. "It must be progressive. How long have the children had these toys?"

"About three months, I guess."

"Time enough. The perfect toy, you see, is both instructive and mechanical. It should do things, to interest a child, and it should teach, preferably unobtrusively. Simple problems at first. Later—"

"*X* logic," Jane said, white-faced.

Paradine cursed under his breath. "Emma and Scott are perfectly normal!"

"Do you know how their minds work—now?"

Holloway didn't pursue the thought. He fingered the doll. "It would be interesting to know the conditions of the place where these things came from. Induction doesn't help a great deal, though. Too many factors are missing. We can't visualize a world based on the *x* factor—environment adjusted to minds thinking in *x* patterns. This luminous network inside the doll. It could be anything. It could exist inside us, though we haven't discovered it yet. When we find the right stain—" He shrugged. "What do you make of this?"

It was a crimson globe, two inches in diameter, with a protruding knob upon its surface.

"What could anyone make of it?"

"Scott? Emma?"

"I hadn't even seen it till about three weeks ago. Then Emma started to play with it." Paradine nibbled his lip. "After that, Scott got interested."

"Just what do they do?"

"Hold it up in front of them and move it back and forth. No particular pattern of motion."

"No Euclidean pattern," Holloway corrected. "At first they couldn't understand the toy's purpose. They had to be educated up to it."

"That's horrible," Jane said.

"Not to them. Emma is probably quicker at understanding *x* than is Scott, for her mind isn't yet conditioned to this environment."

Paradine said, "But I can remember plenty of things I did as a child. Even as a baby."

"Well?"

"Was I—mad—then?"

"The things you don't remember are the criterion of your madness," Holloway retorted. "But I use the word 'madness' purely as a convenient symbol for the variation from the known human norm. The arbitrary standard of sanity."

Jane put down her glass. "You've said that induction was difficult, Mr. Holloway. But it seems to me you're making a great deal of it from very little. After all, these toys—"

"I *am* a psychologist, and I've specialized in children. I'm not a layman. These toys mean a great deal to me, chiefly because they mean so little."

"You might be wrong."

"Well, I rather hope I am. I'd like to examine the children."

Jane rose in arms. "How?"

After Holloway had explained, she nodded, though still a bit hesitantly. "Well, that's all right. But they're not guinea pigs."

The psychologist patted the air with a plump hand. "My dear girl! I'm not a Frankenstein. To me the individual is the prime factor—naturally, since I work with minds. If there's anything wrong with the youngsters, I want to cure them."

Paradine put down his cigarette and slowly watched blue smoke spiral up, wavering in an unfelt draft. "Can you give a prognosis?"

"I'll try. That's all I can say. If the undeveloped minds have been turned into the x channel, it's necessary to divert them back. I'm not saying that's the wisest thing to do, but it probably is from our standards. After all, Emma and Scott will have to live in this world."

"Yeah. Yeah. I can't believe there's much wrong. They seem about average, thoroughly normal."

"Superficially they may seem so. They've no reason for acting abnormally, have they? And how can you tell if they—think differently?"

"I'll call 'em," Paradine said.

"Make it informal, then. I don't want them to be on guard."

Jane nodded toward the toys. Holloway said, "Leave the stuff there, eh?"

But the psychologist, after Emma and Scott were summoned, made no immediate move at direct questioning. He managed to draw Scott unobtrusively into the conversation, dropping key words now and then. Nothing so obvious as a word-association test—co-operation is necessary for that.

The most interesting development occurred when Holloway took up the abacus. "Mind showing me how this works?"

Scott hesitated. "Yes, sir. Like this—" He slid a bead deftly through the maze, in a tangled course, so swiftly that no one was quite sure whether or not it ultimately vanished. It might have been merely legerdemain. Then, again—

Holloway tried. Scott watched, wrinkling his nose.

"That right?"

"Uh-huh. It's gotta go *there*—"

"Here? Why?"

"Well, that's the only way to make it work."

But Holloway was conditioned to Euclid. There was no apparent reason why the bead should slide from this particular wire to the other. It looked like a random factor. Also, Holloway suddenly noticed, this wasn't the path the bead had taken previously, when Scott had worked the puzzle. At least, as well as he could tell.

"Will you show me again?"

Scott did, and twice more, on request. Holloway blinked through his glasses. Random, yes. And a variable. Scott moved the bead along a different course each time.

Somehow, none of the adults could tell whether or not the bead vanished. If they had expected to see it disappear, their reactions might have been different.

In the end nothing was solved. Holloway, as he said good night, seemed ill at ease.

"May I come again?"

"I wish you would," Jane told him. "Any time. You still think—"

He nodded. "The children's minds are not reacting normally. They're not dull at all, but I've the most extraordinary impression that they arrive at conclusions in a way we don't understand. As though they used algebra while we used geometry. The same conclusion, but a different method of reaching it."

"What about the toys?" Paradine asked suddenly.

"Keep them out of the way. I'd like to borrow them, if I may—"

That night Paradine slept badly. Holloway's parallel had been ill-chosen. It led to disturbing theories. The x factor— The children were using the equivalent of algebraic reasoning, while adults used geometry.

Fair enough. Only—

Algebra can give you answers that geometry cannot, since there are certain terms and symbols which cannot be expressed geometrically. Suppose x logic showed conclusions inconceivable to an adult mind?

"Damn!" Paradine whispered. Jane stirred beside him.

"Dear? Can't you sleep either?"

"No." He got up and went into the next room. Emma slept peacefully as a cherub, her fat arm curled around Mr. Bear. Through the open doorway Paradine could see Scott's dark head motionless on the pillow.

Jane was beside him. He slipped his arm around her.

"Poor little people," she murmured. "And Holloway called them mad. I think we're the ones who are crazy, Dennis."

"Uh-huh. We've got jitters."

Scott stirred in his sleep. Without awakening, he called what was obviously a question, though it did not seem to be in any particular language. Emma gave a little mewling cry that changed pitch sharply.

She had not wakened. The children lay without stirring.

But Paradine thought, with a sudden sickness in his middle, it was exactly as though Scott had asked Emma something, and she had replied.

Had their minds changed so that even—sleep—was different to them?

He thrust the thought away. "You'll catch cold. Let's get back to bed. Want a drink?"

"I think I do," Jane said, watching Emma. Her hand reached out blindly toward the child; she drew it back. "Come on. We'll wake the kids."

They drank a little brandy together, but said nothing. Jane cried in her sleep, later.

Scott was not awake, but his mind worked in slow, careful building. Thus—

"They'll take the toys away. The fat man . . . listava dangerous maybe. But the Ghoric direction won't show . . . evankrus dun-hasn't-them. Intransdection . . . bright and shiny. Emma. She's more kho-

pranik-high now than . . . I still don't see how to . . . thavarar lixery
dist—"

A little of Scott's thoughts could still be understood. But Emma had
become conditioned to x much faster.

She was thinking, too.

Not like an adult or a child. Not even like a human. Except, perhaps,
a human of a type shockingly unfamiliar to *genus homo*.

Sometimes Scott himself had difficulty in following her thoughts.

If it had not been for Holloway, life might have settled back into an
almost normal routine. The toys were no longer active reminders. Emma
still enjoyed her dolls and sand pile, with a thoroughly explicable de-
light. Scott was satisfied with baseball and his chemical set. They did
everything other children did, and evinced few, if any, flashes of abnor-
mality. But Holloway seemed to be an alarmist.

He was having the toys tested, with rather idiotic results. He drew
endless charts and diagrams, corresponded with mathematicians, engineers, and other psychologists, and went quietly crazy trying to find
rhyme or reason in the construction of the gadgets. The box itself, with
its cryptic machinery, told nothing. Fusing had melted too much of the
stuff into slag. But the toys—

It was the random element that baffled investigation. Even that was
a matter of semantics. For Holloway was convinced that it wasn't really
random. There just weren't enough known factors. No adult could work
the abacus, for example. And Holloway thoughtfully refrained from letting a child play with the thing.

The crystal cube was similarly cryptic. It showed a mad pattern of
colors, which sometimes moved. In this it resembled a kaleidoscope. But
the shifting of balance and gravity didn't affect it. Again the random
factor.

Or, rather, the unknown. The x pattern. Eventually Paradine and
Jane slipped back into something like complacence, with a feeling that
the children had been cured of their mental quirk, now that the con-
tributing cause had been removed. Certain of the actions of Emma and
Scott gave them every reason to quit worrying.

For the kids enjoyed swimming, hiking, movies, games, the normal
functional toys of this particular time-sector. It was true that they failed
to master certain rather puzzling mechanical devices which involved
some calculation. A three-dimensional jigsaw globe Paradine had picked
up, for example. But he found that difficult himself.

Once in a while there were lapses. Scott was hiking with his father one
Saturday afternoon, and the two had paused at the summit of a hill. Beneath them a rather lovely valley was spread.

"Pretty, isn't it?" Paradine remarked.

Scott examined the scene gravely. "It's all wrong," he said.

"Eh?"

"I dunno."

"What's wrong about it?"

"Gee—" Scott lapsed into puzzled silence. "I dunno."

The children had missed their toys, but not for long. Emma recovered first, though Scott still moped. He held unintelligible conversations with his sister, and studied meaningless scrawls she drew on paper he supplied. It was almost as though he was consulting her, anent difficult problems beyond his grasp.

If Emma understood more, Scott had more real intelligence, and manipulatory skill as well. He built a gadget with his Meccano set, but was dissatisfied. The apparent cause of his dissatisfaction was exactly why Paradine was relieved when he viewed the structure. It was the sort of thing a normal boy would make, vaguely reminiscent of a cubistic ship.

It was a bit too normal to please Scott. He asked Emma more questions, though in private. She thought for a time, and then made more scrawls with an awkwardly clutched pencil.

"Can you read that stuff?" Jane asked her son one morning.

"Not read it, exactly. I can tell what she means. Not all the time, but mostly."

"Is it writing?"

"N-no. It doesn't mean what it *looks* like."

"Symbolism," Paradine suggested over his coffee.

Jane looked at him, her eyes widening. "Denny—"

He winked and shook his head. Later, when they were alone, he said, "Don't let Holloway upset you. I'm not implying that the kids are corresponding in an unknown tongue. If Emma draws a squiggle and says it's a flower, that's an arbitrary rule—Scott remembers that. Next time she draws the same sort of squiggle, or tries to—well!"

"Sure," Jane said doubtfully. "Have you noticed Scott's been doing a lot of reading lately?"

"I noticed. Nothing unusual, though. No Kant or Spinoza."

"He browses, that's all."

"Well, so did I, at his age," Paradine said, and went off to his morning classes. He lunched with Holloway, which was becoming a daily habit, and spoke of Emma's literary endeavors.

"Was I right about symbolism, Rex?"

The psychologist nodded. "Quite right. Our own language is nothing but arbitrary symbolism now. At least in its application. Look here." On his napkin he drew a very narrow ellipse. "What's that?"

"You mean what does it represent?"

"Yes. What does it suggest to you? It could be a crude representation of—what?"

"Plenty of things," Paradine said. "Rim of a glass. A fried egg. A loaf of French bread. A cigar."

Holloway added a little triangle to his drawing, apex joined to one end of the ellipse. He looked up at Paradine.

"A fish," the latter said instantly.

"Our familiar symbol for a fish. Even without fins, eyes or mouth, it's recognizable, because we've been conditioned to identify this particular shape with our mental picture of a fish. The basis of a rebus. A symbol, to us, means a lot more than what we actually see on paper. What's in your mind when you look at this sketch?"

"Why—a fish."

"Keep going. What do you visualize—everything!"

"Scales," Paradine said slowly, looking into space. "Water. Foam. A fish's eye. The fins. The colors."

"So the symbol represents a lot more than just the abstract idea *fish*. Note the connotation's that of a noun, not a verb. It's harder to express actions by symbolism, you know. Anyway—reverse the process. Suppose you want to make a symbol for some concrete noun, say *bird*. Draw it."

Paradine drew two connected arcs, concavities down.

"The lowest common denominator," Holloway nodded. "The natural tendency is to simplify. Especially when a child is seeing something for the first time and has few standards of comparison. He tries to identify the new thing with what's already familiar to him. Ever notice how a child draws the ocean?" He didn't wait for an answer; he went on.

"A series of jagged points. Like the oscillating line on a seismograph. When I first saw the Pacific, I was about three. I remember it pretty clearly. It looked—tilted. A flat plain, slanted at an angle. The waves were regular triangles, apex upward. Now I didn't *see* them stylized that way, but later, remembering, I had to find some familiar standard of comparison. Which is the only way of getting any conception of an entirely new thing. The average child tries to draw these regular triangles, but his co-ordination's poor. He gets a seismograph pattern."

"All of which means what?"

"A child sees the ocean. He stylizes it. He draws a certain definite pattern, symbolic, to him, of the sea. Emma's scrawls may be symbols, too. I don't mean that the world looks different to her—brighter, perhaps, and sharper, more vivid and with a slackening of perception above her eye level. What I do mean is that her thought-processes are different, that she translates what she sees into abnormal symbols."

"You still believe—"

"Yes, I do. Her mind has been conditioned unusually. It may be that she breaks down what she sees into simple, obvious patterns—and realizes a significance to those patterns that we can't understand. Like the abacus. She saw a pattern in that, though to us it was completely random."

Paradine abruptly decided to taper off these luncheon engagements with Holloway. The man was an alarmist. His theories were growing more fantastic than ever, and he dragged in anything, applicable or not, that would support them.

Rather sardonically he said, "Do you mean Emma's communicating with Scott in an unknown language?"

"In symbols for which she hasn't any words. I'm sure Scott understands a great deal of those—scrawls. To him, an isosceles triangle may represent any factor, though probably a concrete noun. Would a man who knew nothing of algebra understand what H_2O meant? Would he realize that the symbol could evoke a picture of the ocean?"

Paradine didn't answer. Instead, he mentioned to Holloway Scott's curious remark that the landscape, from the hill, had looked all wrong. A moment later, he was inclined to regret his impulse, for the psychologist was off again.

"Scott's thought-patterns are building up to a sum that doesn't equal this world. Perhaps he's subconsciously expecting to see the world where those toys came from."

Paradine stopped listening. Enough was enough. The kids were getting along all right, and the only remaining disturbing factor was Holloway himself. That night, however, Scott evinced an interest, later significant, in eels.

There was nothing apparently harmful in natural history. Paradine explained about eels.

"But where do they lay their eggs? Or do they?"

"That's still a mystery. Their spawning grounds are unknown. Maybe the Sargasso Sea, or the deeps, where the pressure can help them force the young out of their bodies."

"Funny," Scott said, thinking deeply.

"Salmon do the same thing, more or less. They go up rivers to spawn." Paradine went into detail. Scott was fascinated.

"But that's *right,* dad. They're born in the river, and when they learn how to swim, they go down to the sea. And they come back to lay their eggs, huh?"

"Right."

"Only they wouldn't *come* back," Scott pondered. "They'd just send their eggs—"

"It'd take a very long ovipositor," Paradine said, and vouchsafed some well-chosen remarks upon oviparity.

His son wasn't entirely satisfied. Flowers, he contended, sent their seeds long distances.

"They don't guide them. Not many find fertile soil."

"Flowers haven't got brains, though. Dad, why do people live. *here?"*

"Glendale?"

"No—*here.* This whole place. It isn't all there is, I bet."

"Do you mean the other planets?"

Scott was hesitant. "This is only—part—of the big place. It's like the river where the salmon go. Why don't people go on down to the ocean when they grow up?"

Paradine realized that Scott was speaking figuratively. He felt a brief chill. The—ocean?

The young of the species are not conditioned to live in the completer world of their parents. Having developed sufficiently, they enter that world. Later they breed. The fertilized eggs are buried in the sand, far up the river, where later they hatch.

And they learn. Instinct alone is fatally slow. Especially in the case of a specialized genus, unable to cope even with this world, unable to feed or drink or survive, unless someone has foresightedly provided for those needs.

The young, fed and tended, would survive. There would be incubators and robots. They would survive, but they would not know how to swim downstream, to the vaster world of the ocean.

So they must be taught. They must be trained and conditioned in many ways.

Painlessly, subtly, unobtrusively. Children love toys that do things— and if those toys teach at the same time—

In the latter half of the nineteenth century an Englishman sat on a grassy bank near a stream. A very small girl lay near him, staring up at the sky. She had discarded a curious toy with which she had been playing, and now was murmuring a wordless little song, to which the man listened with half an ear.

"What was that, my dear?" he asked at last.

"Just something I made up, Uncle Charles."

"Sing it again." He pulled out a notebook.

The girl obeyed.

"Does it mean anything?"

She nodded. "Oh, yes. Like the stories I tell you, you know."

"They're wonderful stories, dear."

"And you'll put them in a book some day?"

"Yes, but I must change them quite a lot, or no one would understand. But I don't think I'll change your little song."

"You mustn't. If you did, it wouldn't mean anything."

"I won't change that stanza, anyway," he promised. "Just what does it mean?"

"It's the way out, I think," the girl said doubtfully. "I'm not sure yet. My magic toys told me."

"I wish I knew what London shop sold those marvelous toys!"

"Mamma bought them for me. She's dead. Papa doesn't care."

She lied. She had found the toys in a box one day, as she played by the Thames. And they were indeed wonderful.

Her little song— Uncle Charles thought it didn't mean anything. (He wasn't her real uncle, she parenthesized. But he was nice.) The song meant a great deal. It was the way. Presently she would do what it said, and then—

But she was already too old. She never found the way.

Paradine had dropped Holloway. Jane had taken a dislike to him, naturally enough, since what she wanted most of all was to have her fears calmed. Since Scott and Emma acted normally now, Jane felt satisfied.

It was partly wishful-thinking, to which Paradine could not entirely subscribe.

Scott kept bringing gadgets to Emma for her approval. Usually she'd shake her head. Sometimes she would look doubtful. Very occasionally she would signify agreement. Then there would be an hour of laborious, crazy scribbling on scraps of note paper, and Scott, after studying the notations, would arrange and rearrange his rocks, bits of machinery, candle ends, and assorted junk. Each day the maid cleaned them away, and each day Scott began again.

He condescended to explain a little to his puzzled father, who could see no rhyme or reason in the game.

"But why this pebble right here?"

"It's hard and round, dad. It *belongs* there."

"So is this one hard and round."

"Well, that's got vaseline on it. When you get that far, you can't *see* just a hard round thing."

"What comes next? This candle?"

Scott looked disgusted. "That's toward the end. The iron ring's next."

It was, Paradine thought, like a Scout trail through the woods, markers in a labyrinth. But here again was the random factor. Logic halted—familiar logic—at Scott's motives in arranging the junk as he did.

Paradine went out. Over his shoulder he saw Scott pull a crumpled piece of paper and a pencil from his pocket, and head for Emma, who was squatted in a corner thinking things over.

Well—

Jane was lunching with Uncle Harry, and, on this hot Sunday afternoon there was little to do but read the papers. Paradine settled himself in the coolest place he could find, with a Collins, and lost himself in the comic strips.

An hour later a clatter of feet upstairs roused him from his doze. Scott's voice was crying exultantly, "This is it, Slug! Come on—"

Paradine stood up quickly, frowning. As he went into the hall the telephone began to ring. Jane had promised to call—

His hand was on the receiver when Emma's faint voice squealed with excitement. Paradine grimaced. What the devil was going on upstairs?

Scott shrieked, "Look out! This way!"

Paradine, his mouth working, his nerves ridiculously tense, forgot the phone and raced up the stairs. The door of Scott's room was open.

The children were vanishing.

They went in fragments, like thick smoke in a wind, or like movement in a distorting mirror. Hand in hand they went, in a direction Paradine could not understand, and as he blinked there on the threshold, they were gone.

"Emma!" he said, dry-throated. *"Scotty!"*

On the carpet lay a pattern of markers, pebbles, an iron ring—junk. A random pattern. A crumpled sheet of paper blew toward Paradine.

He picked it up automatically.

"Kids. Where are you? Don't hide—

"Emma! SCOTTY!"

Downstairs the telephone stopped its shrill, monotonous ringing. Paradine looked at the paper he held.

It was a leaf torn from a book. There were interlineations and marginal notes, in Emma's meaningless scrawl. A stanza of verse had been so underlined and scribbled over that it was almost illegible, but Paradine was thoroughly familiar with "Through the Looking Glass." His memory gave him the words—

> 'Twas brillig, and the slithy toves
> Did gyre and gimbel in the wabe.
> All mimsy were the borogoves,
> And the mome raths outgrabe.

Idiotically he thought: Humpty Dumpty explained it. A wabe is the plot of grass around a sundial. A sundial. Time— It has something to do with time. A long time ago Scotty asked me what a wabe was. Symbolism.

'Twas brillig—

A perfect mathematical formula, giving all the conditions, in symbolism the children had finally understood. The junk on the floor. The toves had to be made slithy—vaseline?—and they had to be placed in a certain relationship, so that they'd gyre and gimbel.

Lunacy!

But it had not been lunacy to Emma and Scott. They thought differently. They used x logic. Those notes Emma had made on the page— she'd translated Carroll's words into symbols both she and Scott could understand.

The random factor had made sense to the children. They had fulfilled the conditions of the time-space equation. *And the mome raths outgrabe—*

Paradine made a rather ghastly little sound, deep in his throat. He looked at the crazy pattern on the carpet. If he could follow it, as the kids had done— But he couldn't. The pattern was senseless. The random factor defeated him. He was conditioned to Euclid.

Even if he went insane, he still couldn't do it. It would be the wrong kind of lunacy.

His mind had stopped working now. But in a moment the stasis of incredulous horror would pass— Paradine crumpled the page in his fingers. "Emma, Scotty," he called in a dead voice, as though he could expect no response.

Sunlight slanted through the open windows, brightening the golden pelt of Mr. Bear. Downstairs the ringing of the telephone began again.

TIME AND TIME AGAIN

BLINDED by the bomb-flash and numbed by the narcotic injection, he could not estimate the extent of his injuries, but he knew that he was dying. Around him, in the darkness, voices sounded as through a thick wall.

"They mighta left mosta these Joes where they was. Half of them won't even last till the truck comes."

"No matter; so long as they're alive, they must be treated," another voice, crisp and cultivated, rebuked. "Better start taking names, while we're waiting."

"Yes, sir." Fingers fumbled at his identity badge. "Hartley, Allan; Captain, G5, Chem. Research AN/73/D. Serial, SO-23869403J."

"Allan Hartley!" The medic officer spoke in shocked surprise. "Why, he's the man who wrote 'Children of the Mist,' 'Rose of Death,' and 'Conqueror's Road'!"

He tried to speak, and must have stirred; the corpsman's voice sharpened.

"Major, I think he's part conscious. Mebbe I better give him 'nother shot."

"Yes, yes; by all means, sergeant."

Something jabbed Allan Hartley in the back of the neck. Soft billows of oblivion closed in upon him, and all that remained to him was a tiny spark of awareness, glowing alone and lost in a great darkness.

The Spark grew brighter. He was more than a something that merely knew that it existed. He was a man, and he had a name, and a military rank, and memories. Memories of the searing blue-green flash, and of what he had been doing outside the shelter the moment before, and memories of the month-long siege, and of the retreat from the north, and memories of the days before the War, back to the time when he had been little Allan Hartley, a schoolboy, the son of a successful lawyer, in Williamsport, Pennsylvania.

His mother he could not remember; there was only a vague impression of the house full of people who had tried to comfort him for something he could not understand. But he remembered the old German woman who had kept house for his father, afterward, and he remembered his bedroom, with its chintz-covered chairs, and the warm-colored patch quilt on the old cherry bed, and the tan curtains at the windows, edged with dusky red, and the morning sun shining through them. He could almost see them, now.

He blinked. He *could* see them!

For a long time, he lay staring at them unbelievingly, and then he deliberately closed his eyes and counted ten seconds, and as he counted, terror gripped him. He was afraid to open them again, lest he find himself blind, or gazing at the filth and wreckage of a blasted city, but when he reached ten, he forced himself to look, and gave a sigh of relief. The sunlit curtains and the sun-gilded mist outside were still there.

He reached out to check one sense against another, feeling the rough monk's cloth and the edging of maroon silk thread. They were tangible as well as visible. Then he saw that the back of his hand was unscarred. There should have been a scar, souvenir of a rough-and-tumble brawl of his cub reporter days. He examined both hands closely. An instant later, he had sat up in bed and thrown off the covers, partially removing his pajamas and inspecting as much of his body as was visible.

It was the smooth body of a little boy.

That was ridiculous. He was a man of forty-three; an army officer, a chemist, once a best-selling novelist. He had been married, and divorced ten years ago. He looked again at his body. It was only twelve years old. Fourteen, at the very oldest. His eyes swept the room, wide with wonder. Every detail was familiar: the flower-splashed chair covers; the table that served as desk and catch-all for his possessions; the dresser, with its mirror stuck full of pictures of aircraft. It was the bedroom of his childhood home. He swung his legs over the edge of the bed. They were six inches too short to reach the floor.

For an instant, the room spun dizzily, and he was in the grip of utter panic, all confidence in the evidence of his senses lost. Was he insane? Or delirious? Or had the bomb really killed him; was this what death was like? What was that thing, about "ye become as little children"? He started to laugh, and his juvenile larynx made giggling sounds. They seemed funny, too, and aggravated his mirth. For a little while, he was on the edge of hysteria and then, when he managed to control his laughter, he felt calmer. If he were dead, then he must be a discarnate entity, and would be able to penetrate matter. To his relief, he was unable to push his hand through the bed. So he was alive; he was also fully awake, and, he hoped, rational. He rose to his feet and prowled about the room, taking stock of its contents.

There was no calendar in sight, and he could find no newspapers or dated periodicals, but he knew that it was prior to July 18, 1946. On that day, his fourteenth birthday, his father had given him a light .22 rifle, and it had been hung on a pair of rustic forks on the wall. It was not there now, nor ever had been. On the table, he saw a boys' book of military aircraft, with a clean, new dustjacket; the flyleaf was inscribed: *To Allan Hartley, from his father, on his thirteenth birthday, 7/18 '45.* Glancing out the window at the foliage on the trees, he estimated the date at late July or early August, 1945; that would make him just thirteen.

His clothes were draped on a chair beside the bed. Stripping off his pajamas, he donned shorts, then sat down and picked up a pair of lemon-colored socks, which he regarded with disfavor. As he pulled one on, a church bell began to clang. St. Boniface, up on the hill, ringing for early Mass; so this was Sunday. He paused, the second sock in his hand.

There was no question that his present environment was actual. Yet, on the other hand, he possessed a set of memories completely at variance with it. Now, suppose, since his environment were not an illusion, everything else were? Suppose all these troublesome memories were no more than a dream? Why, he was just little Allan Hartley, safe in his room on a Sunday morning, badly scared by a nightmare! Too much science fiction, Allan; too many comic books!

That was a wonderfully comforting thought, and he hugged it to him contentedly. It lasted all the while he was buttoning up his shirt and pulling on his pants, but when he reached for his shoes, it evaporated. Ever since he had wakened, he realized, he had been occupied with thoughts utterly incomprehensible to any thirteen-year-old; even thinking in words that would have been so much Sanscrit to himself at thirteen. He shook his head regretfully. The just-a-dream hypothesis went by the deep six.

He picked up the second shoe and glared at it as though it were responsible for his predicament. He was going to have to be careful. An unexpected display of adult characteristics might give rise to some questions he would find hard to answer credibly. Fortunately, he was an only child; there would be no brothers or sisters to trip him up. Old Mrs. Stauber, the housekeeper, wouldn't be much of a problem; even in his normal childhood, he had bulked like an intellectual giant in comparison to her. But his father—

Now, there the going would be tough. He knew that shrewd attorney's mind, whetted keen on a generation of lying and reluctant witnesses. Sooner or later, he would forget for an instant and betray himself. Then he smiled, remembering the books he had discovered, in his late 'teens, on his father's shelves and recalling the character of the openminded agnostic lawyer. If he could only avoid the inevitable unmasking until he had a plausible explanatory theory.

Blake Hartley was leaving the bathroom as Allan Hartley opened his door and stepped into the hall. The lawyer was bare-armed and in slippers; at forty-eight, there was only a faint powdering of gray in his dark hair, and not a gray thread in his clipped mustache. The old Merry Widower, himself, Allan thought, grinning as he remembered the white-

haired but still vigorous man from whom he'd parted at the outbreak of
the War.

"'Morning, Dad," he greeted.

"'Morning, son. You're up early. Going to Sunday school?"

Now there was the advantage of a father who'd cut his first intellectual tooth on Tom Paine and Bob Ingersoll; attendance at divine services was on a strictly voluntary basis.

"Why, I don't think so; I want to do some reading, this morning."

"That's always a good thing to do," Blake Hartley approved. "After
breakfast, suppose you take a walk down to the station and get me a
Times." He dug in his trouser pocket and came out with a half dollar.
"Get anything you want for yourself, while you're at it."

Allan thanked his father and pocketed the coin.

"Mrs. Stauber'll still be at Mass," he suggested. "Say I get the paper
now; breakfast won't be ready till she gets here."

"Good idea." Blake Hartley nodded, pleased. "You'll have three-
quarters of an hour, at least."

So far, he congratulated himself, everything had gone smoothly. Finishing his toilet, he went downstairs and onto the street, turning left at
Brandon to Campbell, and left again in the direction of the station. Before he reached the underpass, a dozen half-forgotten memories had re-
vived. Here was a house that would, in a few years, be gutted by fire.
Here were four dwellings standing where he had last seen a five-story
apartment building. A gasoline station and a weed-grown lot would
shortly be replaced by a supermarket. The environs of the station itself
were a complete puzzle to him, until he oriented himself.

He bought a New York *Times*, glancing first of all at the date line.
Sunday, August 5, 1945; he'd estimated pretty closely. The battle of
Okinawa had been won. The Potsdam Conference had just ended. There
was still pictures of the B-25 crash against the Empire State Building,
a week ago Saturday. And Japan was still being pounded by bombs from
the air and shells from off-shore naval guns. Why, tomorrow, Hiroshima
was due for the Big Job! It amused him to reflect that he was probably
the only person in Williamsport who knew that.

On the way home, a boy, sitting on the top step of a front porch,
hailed him. Allan replied cordially, trying to remember who it was. Of
course; Larry Morton! He and Allan had been buddies. They probably had been swimming, or playing Commandos and Germans, the
afternoon before. Larry had gone to Cornell the same year that Allan
had gone to Penn State; they had both graduated in 1954. Larry had
gotten into some Government bureau, and then he had married a Pitts-
burgh girl, and had become twelfth vice-president of her father's firm.
He had been killed, in 1968, in a plane crash.

"You gonna Sunday school?" Larry asked, mercifully unaware of the
fate Allan foresaw for him.

"Why, no. I have some things I want to do at home." He'd have to watch himself. Larry would spot a difference quicker than any adult. "Heck with it," he added.

"Golly, I wisht I c'ld stay home from Sunday school whenever I wanted to," Larry envied. "How about us goin' swimmin', at the Canoe Club, 'safter?"

Allan thought fast. "Gee, I wisht I c'ld," he replied, lowering his grammatical sights. "I gotta stay home, 'safter. We're expectin' comp'ny; coupla aunts of mine. Dad wants me to stay home when they come."

That went over all right. Anybody knew that there was no rational accounting for the vagaries of the adult mind, and no appeal from adult demands. The prospect of company at the Hartley home would keep Larry away, that afternoon. He showed his disappointment.

"Aw, jeepers creepers!" he blasphemed euphemistically.

"Mebbe t'morrow," Allan said. "If I c'n make it. I gotta go, now; ain't had breakfast yet." He scuffed his feet boyishly, exchanged so-longs with his friend, and continued homeward.

As he had hoped, the Sunday paper kept his father occupied at breakfast, to the exclusion of any dangerous table talk. Blake Hartley was still deep in the financial section when Allan left the table and went to the library. There should be two books there to which he wanted badly to refer. For a while, he was afraid that his father had not ac-quired them prior to 1945, but he finally found them, and carried them onto the front porch, along with a pencil and a ruled yellow scratch pad. In his experienced future—or his past-to-come—Allan Hartley had been accustomed to doing his thinking with a pencil. As reporter, as novelist plotting his work, as amateur chemist in his home laboratory, as scien-tific warfare research officer, his ideas had always been clarified by making notes. He pushed a chair to the table and built up the seat with cushions, wondering how soon he would become used to the proportional disparity between himself and the furniture. As he opened the books and took his pencil in his hand, there was one thing missing. If he could only smoke a pipe, now!

His father came out and stretched in a wicker chair with the *Times* book-review section. The morning hours passed. Allan Hartley leafed through one book and then the other. His pencil moved rapidly at times; at others, he doodled absently. There was no question, any more, in his mind, as to what or who he was. He was Allan Hartley, a man of forty-three, marooned in his own thirteen-year-old body, thirty years back in his own past. That was, of course, against all common sense, but he was easily able to ignore that objection. It had been made before: against the astronomy of Copernicus, and the geography of Columbus, and the biology of Darwin, and the industrial technology of Samuel Colt, and the military doctrines of Charles de Gaulle. Today's common sense had a habit of turning into tomorrow's utter nonsense. What he needed, right now, but bad, was a theory that would explain what had happened to him.

Understanding was beginning to dawn when Mrs. Stauber came out to announce midday dinner.

"I hope you von't mind haffin' it so early," she apologized. "Mein sister, Jennie, offer in Nippenose, she iss sick; I vant to go see her, dis afternoon, yet. I'll be back in blenty time to get supper, Mr. Hartley."

"Hey, Dad!" Allan spoke up. "Why can't we get our own supper, and have a picnic, like? That'd be fun, and Mrs. Stauber could stay as long as she wanted to."

His father looked at him. Such consideration for others was a most gratifying deviation from the juvenile norm; dawn of altruism, or something. He gave hearty assent.

"Why, of course, Mrs. Stauber. Allan and I can shift for ourselves, this evening; can't we, Allan? You needn't come back till tomorrow morning."

"*Ach,* t'ank you! T'ank you so mooch, Mr. Hartley."

At dinner, Allan got out from under the burden of conversation by questioning his father about the War and luring him into a lengthy dissertation on the difficulties of the forthcoming invasion of Japan. In view of what he remembered of the next twenty-four hours, Allan was secretly amused. His father was sure that the War would run on to mid-1946.

After dinner, they returned to the porch, Hartley *père* smoking a cigar and carrying out several law books. He only glanced at these occasionally; for the most part, he sat and blew smoke rings, and watched them float away. Some thrice-guilty felon was about to be triumphantly acquitted by a weeping jury; Allan could recognize a courtroom masterpiece in the process of incubation.

It was several hours later that the crunch of feet on the walk caused father and son to look up simultaneously. The approaching visitor was a tall man in a rumpled black suit; he had knobby wrists and big, awkward hands; black hair flecked with gray, and a harsh, bigoted face. Allan remembered him. Frank Gutchall. Lived on Campbell Street; a religious fanatic, and some sort of lay preacher. Maybe he needed legal advice; Allan could vaguely remember some incident—

"Ah, good afternoon, Mr. Gutchall. Lovely day, isn't it?" Blake Hartley said.

Gutchall cleared his throat. "Mr. Hartley, I wonder if you could lend me a gun and some bullets," he began, embarrassedly. "My little dog's been hurt, and it's suffering something terrible. I want a gun, to put the poor thing out of its pain."

"Why, yes; of course. How would a 20-gauge shotgun do?" Blake Hartley asked. "You wouldn't want anything heavy."

Gutchall fidgeted. "Why, er, I was hoping you'd let me have a little gun." He held his hands about six inches apart. "A pistol, that I could put in my pocket. It wouldn't look right, to carry a hunting gun on the Lord's day; people wouldn't understand that it was for a work of mercy."

The lawyer nodded. In view of Gutchall's religious beliefs, the objection made sense.

"Well, I have a Colt .38-special," he said, "but you know, I belong to this Auxiliary Police outfit. If I were called out for duty, this evening, I'd need it. How soon could you bring it back?"

Something clicked in Allan Hartley's mind. He remembered now, what that incident had been. He knew, too, what he had to do.

"Dad, aren't there some cartridges left for the Luger?" he asked.

Blake Hartley snapped his fingers. "By George, yes! I have a German automatic I can let you have, but I wish you'd bring it back as soon as possible. I'll get it for you."

Before he could rise, Allan was on his feet.

"Sit still, Dad; I'll get it. I know where the cartridges are." With that, he darted into the house and upstairs.

The Luger hung on the wall over his father's bed. Getting it down, he dismounted it, working with rapid precision. He used the blade of his pocketknife to unlock the endpiece of the breechblock, slipping out the firing pin and buttoning it into his shirt pocket. Then he reassembled the harmless pistol, and filled the clip with 9-millimeter cartridges from the bureau drawer.

There was an extension telephone beside the bed. Finding Gutchall's address in the directory, he lifted the telephone, and stretched his handkerchief over the mouthpiece. Then he dialed Police Headquarters.

"This is Blake Hartley," he lied, deepening his voice and copying his father's tone. "Frank Gutchall, who lives at . . . take this down"—he gave Gutchall's address—"has just borrowed a pistol from me, ostensibly to shoot a dog. He has no dog. He intends shooting his wife. Don't argue about how I know; there isn't time. Just take it for granted that I do. I disabled the pistol—took out the firing pin—but if he finds out what I did, he may get some other weapon. He's on his way home, but he's on foot. If you hurry, you may get a man there before he arrives, and grab him before he finds out the pistol won't shoot."

"O.K., Mr. Hartley. We'll take care of it. Thanks."

"And I wish you'd get my pistol back, as soon as you can. It's something I brought home from the other War, and I shouldn't like to lose it."

"We'll take care of that, too. Thank you, Mr. Hartley."

He hung up, and carried the Luger and the loaded clip down to the porch.

"Look, Mr. Gutchall; here's how it works," he said, showing it to the visitor. Then he slapped in the clip and yanked up on the toggle loading the chamber. "It's ready to shoot, now; this is the safety." He pushed it on. "When you're ready to shoot, just shove it forward and up, and then pull the trigger. You have to pull the trigger each time; it's loaded for eight shots. And be sure to put the safety back when you're through shooting."

"Did you load the chamber?" Blake Hartley demanded.

"Sure. It's on safe, now."

"Let me see." His father took the pistol, being careful to keep his finger out of the trigger guard, and looked at it. "Yes, that's all right." He repeated the instructions Allan had given, stressing the importance of putting the safety on after using. "Understand how it works, now?" he asked.

"Yes, I understand how it works. Thank you, Mr. Hartley. Thank you, too, young man."

Gutchall put the Luger in his hip pocket, made sure it wouldn't fall out, and took his departure.

"You shouldn't have loaded it," Hartley *père* reproved, when he was gone.

Allan sighed. This was it; the masquerade was over.

"I had to, to keep you from fooling with it," he said. "I didn't want you finding out that I'd taken out the firing pin."

"You what?"

"Gutchall didn't want that gun to shoot a dog. He has no dog. He meant to shoot his wife with it. He's a religious maniac; sees visions, hears voices, receives revelations, talks with the Holy Ghost. The Holy Ghost probably put him up to this caper. I'll submit that any man who holds long conversations with the Deity isn't to be trusted with a gun, and neither is any man who lies about why he wants one. And while I was at it, I called the police, on the upstairs phone. I had to use your name; I deepened my voice and talked through a handkerchief."

"You—" Blake Hartley jumped as though bee-stung. "Why did you have to do that?"

"You know why. I couldn't have told them, 'This is little Allan Hartley, just thirteen years old; please, Mr. Policeman, go and arrest Frank Gutchall before he goes root-toot-toot at his wife with my pappa's Luger.' That would have gone over big, now, wouldn't it?"

"And suppose he really wants to shoot a dog; what sort of a mess will I be in?"

"No mess at all. If I'm wrong—which I'm not—I'll take the thump for it, myself. It'll pass for a dumb kid trick, and nothing'll be done. But if I'm right, you'll have to front for me. They'll keep your name out of it, but they'd give me a lot of cheap boy-hero publicity, which I don't want." He picked up his pencil again. "We should have the complete returns in about twenty minutes."

That was a ten-minute underestimate, and it was another quarter-hour before the detective-sergeant who returned the Luger had finished congratulating Blake Hartley and giving him the thanks of the Department. After he had gone, the lawyer picked up the Luger, withdrew the clip, and ejected the round in the chamber.

"Well," he told his son, "you were right. You saved that woman's life." He looked at the automatic, and then handed it across the table. "Now, let's see you put that firing pin back."

Allan Hartley dismantled the weapon, inserted the missing part, and put it together again, then snapped it experimentally and returned it to his father. Blake Hartley looked at it again, and laid it on the table.

"Now, son, suppose we have a little talk," he said softly.

"But I explained everything," Allan objected innocently.

"You did not," his father retorted. "Yesterday you'd never have thought of a trick like this; why, you wouldn't even have known how to take this pistol apart. And at dinner, I caught you using language and expressing ideas that were entirely outside anything you'd ever known before. Now, I want to know—and I mean this literally."

Allan chuckled. "I hope you're not toying with the rather medieval notion of obsession," he said.

Blake Hartley started. Something very like that must have been flitting through his mind. He opened his mouth to say something, then closed it abruptly.

"The trouble is, I'm not sure you aren't right," his son continued. "You say you find me—changed. When did you first notice a difference?"

"Last night, you were still my little boy. This morning—" Blake Hartley was talking more to himself than to Allan. "I don't know. You were unusually silent at breakfast. And come to think of it, there was something . . . something strange . . . about you when I saw you in the hall, upstairs. . . . Allan!" he burst out, vehemently. "What has happened to you?"

Allan Hartley felt a twinge of pain. What his father was going through was almost what he, himself, had endured, in the first few minutes after waking.

"I wish I could be sure, myself, Dad," he said. "You see, when I woke, this morning, I hadn't the least recollection of anything I'd done yesterday. August 4, 1945, that is," he specified. "I was positively convinced that I was a man of forty-three, and my last memory was of lying on a stretcher, injured by a bomb explosion. And I was equally convinced that this had happened in 1975."

"Huh?" His father straightened. "Did you say nineteen *seventy*-five?" He thought for a moment. "That's right; in 1975, you will be forty-three. A bomb, you say?"

Allan nodded. "During the siege of Buffalo, in the Third World War," he said, "I was a captain in G5—Scientific Warfare, General Staff. There'd been a transpolar air invasion of Canada, and I'd been sent to the front to check on service failures of a new lubricating oil for combat equipment. A week after I got there, Ottawa fell, and the retreat started. We made a stand at Buffalo, and that was where I copped it. I remember being picked up, and getting a narcotic injection. The next thing I knew, I was in bed, upstairs, and it was 1945 again, and I was back in my own little thirteen-year-old body."

"Oh, Allan, you just had a nightmare to end nightmares!" his father assured him, laughing a trifle too heartily. "That's all!"

"That was one of the first things I thought of. I had to reject it; it just wouldn't fit the facts. Look; a normal dream is part of the dreamer's own physical brain, isn't it? Well, here is a part about two thousand per cent greater than the whole from which it was taken. Which is absurd."

"You mean all this Battle of Buffalo stuff? That's easy. All the radio commentators have been harping on the horrors of World War III, and you couldn't have avoided hearing some of it. You just have an undigested chunk of H. V. Kaltenborn raising hell in your subconscious."

"It wasn't just World War III; it was everything. My four years at high school, and my four years at Penn State, and my seven years as a reporter on the Philadelphia *Record*. And my novels: 'Children of the Mist,' 'Rose of Death,' 'Conqueror's Road.' They were no kid stuff. Why, yesterday I'd never even have thought of some of the ideas I used in my detective stories, that I published under a *nom-de-plume*. And my hobby, chemistry; I was pretty good at that. Patented a couple of processes that made me as much money as my writing. You think a thirteen-year-old just dreamed all that up? Or, here; you speak French, don't you?" He switched languages and spoke at some length in good conversational slang-spiced Parisian. "Too bad you don't speak Spanish, too," he added, reverting to English. "Except for a Mexican accent you could cut with a machete, I'm even better there than in French. And I know some German, and a little Russian."

Blake Hartley was staring at his son, stunned. It was some time before he could make himself speak.

"I could barely keep up with you, in French," he admitted. "I can swear that in the last thirteen years of your life, you had absolutely no chance to learn it. All right; you lived till 1975, you say. Then, all of a sudden, you found yourself back here, thirteen years old, in 1945. I suppose you remember everything in between?" he asked. "Did you ever read James Branch Cabell? Remember Florian de Puysange, in 'The High Place'?"

"Yes. You find the same idea in 'Jurgen' too," Allan said. "You know, I'm beginning to wonder if Cabell mightn't have known something he didn't want to write."

"But it's impossible!" Blake Hartley hit the table with his hand, so hard that the heavy pistol bounced. The loose round he had ejected from the chamber toppled over and started to roll, falling off the edge. He stooped and picked it up. "How can you go back, against time? And the time you claim you came from doesn't exist, now; it hasn't happened yet." He reached for the pistol magazine, to insert the cartridge, and as he did, he saw the books in front of his son. "Dunne's 'Experiment with Time,'" he commented. "And J. N. M. Tyrrell's 'Science and Psychical Phenomena.' Are you trying to work out a theory?"

"Yes." It encouraged Allan to see that his father had unconsciously adopted an adult-to-adult manner. "I think I'm getting somewhere, too. You've read these books? Well, look, Dad; what's your attitude on precognition? The ability of the human mind to exhibit real knowledge, apart from logical inference, of future events? You think Dunne is telling the truth about his experiences? Or that the cases in Tyrrell's book are properly verified, and can't be explained away on the basis of chance?"

Blake Hartley frowned. "I don't know," he confessed. "The evidence is the sort that any court in the world would accept, if it concerned ordinary, normal events. Especially the cases investigated by the Society for Psychical Research; they *have* been verified. But how can anybody know of something that hasn't happened yet? If it hasn't happened yet, it doesn't exist, and you can't have real knowledge of something that has no real existence."

"Tyrrell discusses that dilemma, and doesn't dispose of it. I think I can. If somebody has real knowledge of the future, then the future must be available to the present mind. And if any moment other than the bare present exists, then all time must be totally present; every moment must be perpetually coexistent with every other moment," Allan said.

"Yes. I think I see what you mean. That was Dunne's idea, wasn't it?"

"No. Dunne postulated an infinite series of time dimensions, the entire extent of each being the bare present moment of the next. What I'm postulating is the perpetual coexistence of every moment of time in this dimension, just as every graduation on a yardstick exists equally with every other graduation, but each at a different point in space."

"Well, as far as duration and sequence go, that's all right," the father agreed. "But how about the 'Passage of Time'?"

"Well, time *does* appear to pass. So does the landscape you see from a moving car window. I'll suggest that both are illusions of the same kind. We imagine time to be dynamic, because we've never viewed it from a fixed point, but if it is totally present, then it must be static, and in that case, we're moving through time."

"That seems all right. But what's your car window?"

"If all time is totally present, then you must exist simultaneously at every moment along your individual life span," Allan said. "Your physical body, and your mind, and all the thoughts contained in your mind, each at its appropriate moment in sequence. But what is it that exists only at the bare moment we think of as *now?*"

Blake Hartley grinned. Already, he was accepting his small son as an intellectual equal.

"Please, teacher; what?"

"Your consciousness. And don't say, 'What's that?' Teacher doesn't know. But we're only conscious of one moment; the illusory *now*. This is 'now,' and it was 'now' when you asked that question, and it'll be 'now' when I stop talking, but each is a different moment. We imagine that all those nows are rushing past us. Really, they're standing still, and our consciousness is whizzing past them."

His father thought that over for some time. Then he sat up. "Hey!" he cried, suddenly. "If some part of our ego is time-free and passes from moment to moment, it must be extraphysical, because the physical body exists at every moment through which the consciousness passes. And if it's extraphysical, there's no reason whatever for assuming that it passes out of existence when it reaches the moment of the death of the body. Why, there's logical evidence for survival, independent of any alleged spirit communication! You can toss out Patience Worth, and Mrs. Osborne Leonard's Feda, and Sir Oliver Lodge's son, and Wilfred Brandon, and all the other spirit-communicators, and you still have evidence."

"I hadn't thought of that," Allan confessed. "I think you're right. Well, let's put that at the bottom of the agenda and get on with this time business. You 'lose consciousness' as in sleep; where does your consciousness go? I think it simply detaches from the moment at which you go to sleep, and moves backward or forward along the line of moment-sequence, to some prior or subsequent moment, attaching there."

"Well, why don't we know anything about that?" Blake Hartley asked. "It never seems to happen. We go to sleep tonight, and it's always tomorrow morning when we wake; never day-before-yesterday, or last month, or next year."

"It never . . . or almost never . . . *seems* to happen; you're right there. Know why? Because if the consciousness goes forward, it attaches at a moment when the physical brain contains memories of the previous, consciously unexperienced, moment. You wake, remembering the evening before, because that's the memory contained in your mind at that moment, and back of it are memories of all the events in the interim. See?"

"Yes. But how about backward movement, like this experience of yours?"

"This experience of mine may not be unique, but I never heard of another case like it. What usually happens is that the memories carried back by the consciousness are buried in the subconscious mind. You know how thick the wall between the subconscious and the conscious mind is. These dreams of Dunne's, and the cases in Tyrrell's book, are leakage. That's why precognitions are usually incomplete and distorted, and generally trivial. The wonder isn't that good cases are so few; it's surprising that there are any at all." Allan looked at the papers in front of him. "I haven't begun to theorize about how I managed to remember everything. It may have been the radiations from the bomb, or the effect of the narcotic, or both together, or something at this end, or a combination of all three. But the fact remains that my subconscious barrier didn't function, and everything got through. So, you see, I am obsessed—by my own future identity."

"And I'd been afraid that you'd been, well, taken over by some . . . some outsider." Blake Hartley grinned weakly. "I don't mind admitting, Allan, that what's happened has been a shock. But that other . . . I just couldn't have taken that."

"No. Not and stayed sane. But really, I am your son; the same entity I was yesterday. I've just had what you might call an educational short cut."

"I'll say you have!" His father laughed in real amusement. He discovered that his cigar had gone out, and re-lit it. "Here; if you can remember the next thirty years, suppose you tell me when the War's going to end. This one, I mean."

"The Japanese surrender will be announced at exactly 1901—7:01 P.M. present style—on August 14. A week from Tuesday. Better make sure we have plenty of grub in the house by then. Everything will be closed up tight till Thursday morning; even the restaurants. I remember, we had nothing to eat in the house but some scraps."

"Well! It is handy, having a prophet in the family! I'll see to it Mrs. Stauber gets plenty of groceries in. . . . Tuesday a week? That's pretty sudden, isn't it?"

"The Japs are going to think so," Allan replied. He went on to describe what was going to happen.

His father swore softly. "You know, I've heard talk about atomic energy, but I thought it was just Buck Rogers stuff. Was that the sort of bomb that got you?"

"That was a firecracker to the bomb that got me. That thing exploded a good ten miles away."

Blake Hartley whistled softly. "And that's going to happen in thirty years! You know, son, if I were you, I wouldn't like to have to know about a thing like that." He looked at Allan for a moment. "Please, if you know, don't ever tell me when I'm going to die."

Allan smiled. "I can't. I had a letter from you just before I left for the front. You were seventy-eight, then, and you were still hunting, and fishing, and flying your own plane. But I'm not going to get killed in any Battle of Buffalo, this time, and if I can prevent it, and I think I can, there won't be any World War III."

"But— You say all time exists, perpetually coexistent and totally present," his father said. "Then it's right there in front of you, and you're getting closer to it, every watch tick."

Allan Hartley shook his head. "You know what I remembered, when Frank Gutchall came to borrow a gun?" he asked. "Well, the other time, I hadn't been home. I'd been swimming at the Canoe Club, with Larry Morton. When I got home, about half an hour from now, I found the house full of cops. Gutchall talked the .38 officers' model out of you, and gone home; he'd shot his wife four times through the body, finished her off with another one back of the ear, and then used his sixth shot to blast his brains out. The cops traced the gun; they took a very poor view of your lending it to him. You never got it back."

"Trust that gang to keep a good gun," the lawyer said.

"I didn't want us to lose it, this time, and I didn't want to see you lose face around City Hall. Gutchalls, of course, are expendable," Allan said. "But my main reason for fixing Frank Gutchall up with a padded cell was that I wanted to know whether or not the future could be altered. I have it on experimental authority that it can be. There must be additional dimensions of time; lines of alternate probabilities. Something like William Seabrook's witch-doctor friend's Fan-Shaped Destiny. When I brought memories of the future back to the present, I added certain factors to the causal chain. That set up an entirely new line of probabilities. On no notice at all, I stopped a murder and a suicide. With thirty years to work, I can stop a world war. I'll have the means to do it, too."

"The means?"

"Unlimited wealth and influence. Here." Allan picked up a sheet and handed it to his father. "Used properly, we can make two or three million on that, alone. A list of all the Kentucky Derby, Preakness, and Belmont winners to 1970. That'll furnish us primary capital. Then, remember, I was something of a chemist. I took it up, originally, to get background material for one of my detective stories; it fascinated me, and I made it a hobby, and then a source of income. I'm thirty years ahead of any chemist in the world, now. You remember *I. G. Farbenindustrie?* Ten years from now, we'll make them look like pikers."

His father looked at the yellow sheet. "Assault, at eight to one," he said. "I can scrape up about five thousand for that— Yes; in ten years— Any other little operations you have in mind?" he asked.

"About 1950, we start building a political organization, here in Pennsylvania. In 1960, I think we can elect you President. The world situation will be crucial, by that time, and we had a good-natured nonentity in the White House then, who let things go till war became inevitable. I think President Hartley can be trusted to take a strong line of policy. In the meantime, you can read Machiavelli."

"That's my little boy, talking!" Blake Hartley said softly. "All right, son; I'll do just what you tell me, and when you grow up, I'll be president. . . . Let's go get supper, now."

HARRY WALTON

HOUSING SHORTAGE

"IT'S not an ordinary sort of house," the skinny man said. "Not exactly a honeymoon cottage, I know. But then, I built it to suit myself."

"It's divine," said Josie. "Besides, our honeymoon is over. We'll take it."

Of course we would. The place was roomy, comfortable, and—for these days—a steal at the rent asked. But I had to act as if I had *something* to say about it.

"Just a minute. You're offering it furnished, but what about this in the ad—'no radio'? That means there's none in the house, or you won't have one brought in?"

The skinny guy, who'd said his name was Professor Dalrymple, turned his bifocals back on me.

"I have no objection to radios. But there is a good reason why I have not included one in the furnishings. It would be inoperative."

"Huh? Oh, it wouldn't work? Why not?"

The professor sighed. "If I knew that, Mr. Gates, I should have solved one of the great mysteries of the electromagnetic spectrum. The skip phenomenon is known to every radio engineer. My house seems to be in a blind spot so far as radio reception is concerned. You would be unable to listen to your favorite programs—or any others."

"No singing commercials?" I cracked. "We'll take the place. Say, why the high fence along the driveway outside?"

"To insure myself privacy," the professor explained. "Since I may some day wish to live here again, I can rent the house only on condition that the fences—and other things—be left exactly as they are."

"Sure. Sure." The fence meant nothing to me. We weren't renting the place to throw garden parties, and three months of house-hunting had pretty well worn the edges off our choosiness. But Josie, womanlike, had to have the last word after I was ready to sign on the dotted.

"Please, professor," she wheedled. "Can't we have real . . . I mean plain glass . . . windows just in a couple of rooms. If we buy the glass, and Joe puts it in?"

I started to nix that. As a handy man I'm all bruised thumbs. But the professor rallied around faster than I could.

"The windows must remain just as they are. My own tests prove that transparent windows distract the attention and injure eyesight by excessive glare. The house being air-conditioned, it is never necessary to open windows, while the translucent panes admit ample light."

He rattled it off like reading from a book—or saying something he'd had lots of practice saying.

"But a woman wants to look out of her home," Josie began a flank attack. "It's so cozy to look out when it's raining outdoors."

The professor blinked behind his glasses. "I appreciate the sentiment, and I do hope you will feel under no obligation to rent the house. It will be easy to repeat my advertisement in tomorrow's—"

"Don't bother. We'll take it right now," I said, stepping delicately on Josie's number fives. We were all standing on the front step, and I'd just spotted another car pulling up.

"Of course we'll take it," she gasped. "I really don't care about the windows. Not a bit."

We signed the lease right there, before the other house hunters came close enough to show the gleam in their eyes.

The professor wasn't kidding when he said a radio wouldn't work. I had a battery portable Josie'd given me one Christmas, so the first chance I had I unpacked it and put in new batteries. Not a peep. I walked toward the door with it, and just as I got past the bend in the vestibule it broke into the tune of "Onesy Twosy." Two steps back, and it quit dead.

"Hey, Josie," I yelled. "We can have a radio, if we hook it up in the vestibule and turn it up loud."

So I did that—left the portable turned on in the vestibule and stepped back into the living room.

Quiet. Just like that.

"Fine time for it to quit," I squawked, walking back.

"Threesy, foursy," came back the portable.

I jumped a foot—backward.

Dead silence.

"The acoustics in this place," I announced, "are out of this world." But I didn't know what I was talking about then.

Windows are things you expect to look through. But ours were frosted; light could come in, but you couldn't see out. Josie said they got on her nerves, and nagged me until I tried to open one.

It couldn't be done. The frames weren't made to slide. They might as well have been solid with the walls. But the air conditioning was fine. We really had no more use for an open window than Gypsy Rose Lee has for a whalebone corset.

The house stood on about an acre of ground, but there were so many trees and hedges you never saw all of it at once. In fact, the professor had fixed things so you couldn't walk around a corner of the house. One iron fence ran along the driveway from the road right up to the north corner, and another fence like it stretched from the east corner until it lost itself in more trees. There were hedges behind hedges. I figured the professor sure did like privacy.

"Joe," the wife said a few weeks after we'd moved in, "I don't like it."

"Among other things, what?" I came back, trying to read the newspaper.

"Well, I'm not sure."

I laid the paper down. This from Josie was like Comrade Stalin saying he wasn't so sure about Communism. What Josie likes and doesn't like, she knows.

"Well—the neighbors, for one," she said when I kept looking at her.

"Best we ever had," I came back. "Never borrow sugar, don't beg for rides, have no dogs, throw no late parties, and best of all don't live near by. That makes them ideal neighbors."

"Well, I heard them."

I picked up the paper. "Josie, they've got a right to make a little noise in their own yard, even if you are walking by."

"But I wasn't."

I gave up trying to read. "Look, Love, are we talking about the same thing? The nearest house is half a mile away. You couldn't hear anything less than a boiler explosion from there. With that fixed in mind, let's start over."

"I heard them," she said.

"O.K. O.K. Who and where?"

"Don't know. A woman and a man, out on our front step."

"Now it makes sense. Did you ask them in?"

"They weren't . . . oh, Joe, you're mixing me all up. They weren't on our front step. I was, when I heard them."

"Then *they* must have been passing by, although you've pretty good ears to hear them all the way from the road. It's two hundred feet away."

"*They* weren't," she snapped. "They were just . . . just like around the corner of the house. Anyway, close to it."

The Sherlock in me popped up. "Then there must be a short cut behind all those trees and things, back of the house."

Josie shook her head.

"Why not?" I yelled. "And why get excited about it anyhow? What were they talking about, murder and arson?"

"No. First he said, 'Good-by, Honey.' And a few seconds later she called out, louder, 'Bring some butter back if you can find any.' And he called, still louder, 'Sure will . . . if.' As though they'd been together and then he'd gone off."

"And that's your mystery?" I asked. "Simple. You heard this, I'll bet, between eight and eight-thirty in the morning. I will also deduce, like a detective, that they are probably husband and wife, and that he was just leaving to go to work."

Even as I talked I felt something didn't fit, that I was the one talking nonsense, not Josie. I looked at her. She looked at me.

"And then, children," she said, "the lady went back inside the magic oak, and shut the door."

"You win," I admitted. "It's not the right dialogue for a short cut across lots. Unless, of course, she was walking part way with him. That could be it."

"Of course," said Josie. "And she must have brought the door with her. Because I heard it slam."

Josie didn't mention the neighbors again, and I made a resolution to go around the hedges some Sunday and find the short cut. But the first week we went to the beach, and the next it was raining, and after that it didn't seem important.

It was raining this Saturday night too, and I got in dripping wet and hungry.

"What're you cooking for the man who brings home the bacon, Love?" I asked, barging into the kitchen.

It was spare ribs, which I like. But I was wet and wanted sympathy.

"You're lucky you didn't have to go out today. Look at me, soaked to the skin while you don't even know it's raining."

She gave me what was a dirty look in any language.

"Don't get sore, Love. I'm glad you *are* comfortable. Just feed me and you'll find me tolerably human."

"I'm not sore," she said in a tone of voice that said she was. "And I'm glad you think I'm comfortable, for I don't."

"But why not? The place is as comfy as you could ask, the air conditioning's perfect, it's dry and warm inside. Why, you'd never guess it's pouring outside."

She gave me a queer look. "No, you wouldn't—today. I hope it clears up tomorrow. Now come and sit down. Dinner's ready."

But it didn't clear up. The moment I woke Sunday morning I knew it was still raining. Up on the second floor you could hear it plainly—on the windows, on the roof, on the gutters. I rolled over for an extra snooze, but Josie had other ideas.

"You promised to drive me to Madge's and play golf with Henry while we two visit. Remember?"

"In this weather? Have a heart. No golf in this rain. Make it next week."

"I will if it's still raining when we leave," she agreed. "But you've got to get ready."

I argued, but took the count. All the time we dressed and had breakfast it rained, but loud.

"Funny we couldn't hear it last night," I said. "Anyway, Henry and Madge won't expect us."

Josie smiled the way the Mona Lisa does.

"Remember you promised to play fair. Dress as though we *are* going, and if it's still raining when we step out the door, we stay home."

Grumbling, I dragged out my raincoat.

"Be logical," said Josie. "If we go, you won't need that. Just take your clubs."

We must have looked silly, standing there in our sunny Sunday morning best, me with a bag of golf clubs and she in a flowery dress that looked as if a heavy fog could wash it away, while all around us the rain played drumsticks on the house.

"Listen to it come down," I said. "You're not going to see this through to the bitter end, are you?"

She smiled like a little girl who knows a secret. I walked angrily to the door, opened it, and went out. At first I didn't see anything but the half-bitter little grin on her face. Then it hit me.

It wasn't raining. Old Sol was blazing out of the kind of blue sky they write songs about. The world looked as though it had been washed, starched, and thoroughly dried.

When I came to I laid down my bag of clubs and went back inside. Rain. Rain beating against glass. Rain on the roof. Hissing, pattering, thumping, noisy rain. It was a sound I'd have sworn could be nothing else.

But I went out again, locked the door, and picked up my clubs. "Darned funny," I admitted. "Must be something wrong with the air-conditioning plant, and the noise gets piped all over the house. Sure funny how it sounds like rain."

Josie looked at me, grinning a little like somebody who doesn't think things are a bit funny.

"You're a sweet liar, Joe," she said. "But it *is* rain."

I lost all nine holes to Henry, thinking about it.

There was nothing wrong with the air-conditioning equipment. I went into the basement that night and looked at it. It was a big, box-like affair, all housed so thoroughly there really was nothing to see. But it made only a low, humming sound. The rain noise had stopped by the time we got back, so my snooping didn't prove anything. Maybe the machinery went out of whack just occasionally, and was on its good behavior again.

That's what I finally sold myself.

Somehow I didn't want to go to work next morning, but rather than argue with Josie—and my boss—I went. What I did manage was to get home early, while it was still daylight—late afternoon of a sunny, clear day.

And the minute I got in the house I heard it again. That sound that couldn't be anything but rain pelting against roof and windows. I kissed Josie without concentrating, and as soon as she went back to the kitchen I ducked downstairs.

No noise. No soap.

But I noticed something else, something I wasn't looking for, something that sneaked up on me.

I'd been all around the air conditioner, seen it from every side. And nowhere was there a switch, a fuse box, a manual control, a shutoff dingus. Three or four thick BX cables came out of the concrete wall and floor and ran into the gadget. No controls.

A week before I wouldn't have given it two thoughts. The thing ran fine. It needed no attention. It was fixed so you couldn't monkey with it. So what?

Only that things aren't built that way. Even automatic machines aren't fixed to run *regardless*. They've always got some gimmick you can shut them off by. Even the fixit man has to turn off the juice somewhere. But this gadget had nothing, and I had a wild idea, suddenly, that any serviceman would tear his hair if asked to fix it.

It was still raining—with sound effects. I had to get closer to the sound, from inside the house.

"Now don't go away again," Josie called as I started up the stairs. "Supper's almost ready and I don't want it getting cold."

But nothing could have kept me out of the attic just then. Nothing but the hatchway door. There was a square cut out of the ceiling in one bedroom, and a panel closing it—the kind that usually lifts up. Not this one. After I found the screws set in the edges I got the six-in-one combination tool I keep in my dresser drawer—because it's strictly useless where you really need tools—and got out the screws. Then I lifted the panel and hoisted myself up.

They say if you think you're crazy you're sane as they come. Which was reassuring just then, because I thought I was nuts until I remembered that. For up here it was raining—but hard. It was rain on the roof. The kind of splashy, spattery, hard-driving kind of rain that sounds like what it is and nothing else.

Maybe I'd expected it. Maybe if I hadn't found it I really would have gone goony. But finding it didn't answer anything; it asked a thousand questions more, all whispering at me from out of the darkness. There were no attic windows; it was pitch black except for a little round dot of daylight up under the ridgepole at one end, where maybe a shingle had fallen off.

So I threw my flashlight around, having brought it just in case. It showed me an ordinary, run-of-the-mill attic, with the look all attics have. But what didn't belong was the network of wires that ran all around, up and down the rafters, crisscross at both ends, and into two BX cables that ducked back into the floor.

And before I could think myself out of that, there was the other thing. Another six inches to one side with the torch and I'd never have seen it. I wish I hadn't. Because I'll never forget it, and it isn't a pretty thing to remember.

A snake, and not a big one either. Not more than a foot long. An ugly, flattish head. Fangs an inch long that overlay its lower jaw so you could see them even when its mouth was closed. And wings.

A winged snake, lying there in the disk of light my flashlight threw. A *feathered* snake. Stretched out, the wings would have been eighteen inches across. It had no tail such as a bird has; it was all wing and body. Staring at it, I wondered if it balanced in flight by shifting the curve of its snake tail fore and aft. As if that mattered.

As if anything mattered but the crazy fact that this thing which didn't exist—which couldn't exist—lay dead at my feet.

Sure, I know that birds and snakes may have started from the same root way back, or so they think. But that's theory, and this was fact. It must have slipped into the attic through that hole where the shingle was missing, and then batted around in the dark, unable to find its way out again, until it died of starvation.

You think about things like that when you face the impossible. You explain the things that would be clear to a four-year-old, because that helps you think you've still got all your marbles. I even noticed that the rain wasn't coming down as hard. It was only a whisper.

Then a new sound—a slithering, scratching noise just outside the thin shingles. And suddenly a *swack*—sharp, impatient. And silence.

A thing like this, or bigger? A feathered snake, crawling along the roof, its wing slapping the shingles as it took off? Or something else, something that could claw off those shingles to get inside if it knew there was food to be had?

Why had the professor put blind windows all over the house?

I went back through the hatch and tightened the screws holding the panel as hard as they'd go. Then I changed my shirt to keep Josie from asking questions. It was soaking wet anyhow.

Next day I tried to find the professor. We'd been paying the rent to his bank. At the bank they told me he was traveling, couldn't be reached.

So I went home, very quiet. There wasn't a smell of supper in the place. No Josie in the kitchen. Nothing cooking. Something tightened up inside me, because no matter what, Josie always has supper ready. Yelling her name, I went upstairs three steps at a time.

She was lying across the bed, dressed, as though she'd lain down for a nap and overslept. My nightmares about winged snakes ten feet long smashing windows to get in began to look silly. I woke her a special way we have, and she sighed a bit and came to.

"Joe," she said. "Oh, Joe, I'm awfully glad to see you."

"What's the matter, Love? Not feeling well?"

She sat up, not sleepy, but alert the way you are when you remember something you'd rather forget.

"It was a dream, Joe. A nightmare, I guess. It seemed so real—terrible." She shivered, but went on. "It seemed I went out to go shopping—I meant to today, you know. I got out of the house and as far as the azalea bush. But there wasn't any azalea bush."

"Call that a nightmare?" I kidded.

"No, but that made me look around. And—Joe, nothing was right. The sky, even. It was too pink. And our concrete walk wasn't there. Nor was the fence, nor the trees. It was just a big plain, except for the mushrooms. At least they looked like mushrooms—big ones, all colors."

"Just like Alice in Wonderland. Which side did you eat?"

"Alice was a little girl, Joe. When a grown-up thinks she sees things like that, it isn't cute any more. It was as if the world had gone all wrong. A pink sky, and mushrooms big as a table. Not just written down to be read about, but there as something real. And *I* was what didn't belong."

"It's still just a dream, Love," I said, wishing I could explain my feathered snake the same way.

"And you know how dreams are," she went on. "How you know you ought to run, or wake up, before something awful happens. But you don't. I knew I should run back in the house, but I didn't. I walked around, looking, and terribly afraid. Once something like a bee buzzed around me. Then it lit on a flower—a green daisy—and I got a good look at it. The thing that buzzed was a bird. A bird no bigger than my thumbnail, Joe."

And a snake with wings up in the attic, just a few feet away.

"The bird was beautiful, but it frightened me more than the pink sky or the mushrooms. I must have stretched out my hand, because it flew away. And then—I picked the daisy.

"Joe, that daisy was as big as a soup plate and green as moss—green petals on a red stem with red leaves. Picking it was like taking along part of a nightmare to wake up with. You see—everything seemed so real in the dream, I was afraid I was crazy. So I had to pick it to prove to myself, later, that I wasn't."

"O.K., Love. So you dreamed you picked it. And then?"

"I ran back to the house, and put the daisy in a vase, and put the vase on the piano. Then I ran up here and lay down, and was awfully scared. And I still am."

"Forget it, Love. You're awake now. Want to go out to dinner?"

"Joe, suppose I didn't—"

"Come on. It'll do you good to eat out."

"No, I mean suppose I didn't dream it."

"My aunt's foot! Go down and look on the piano."

She looked me right in the eye.

"Joe, that's why I've been waiting. *You* look."

My spine wriggled.

"Oh, sure," I said loudly. "I'll go look."

I got up and tramped downstairs, making plenty of noise. I went into the living room. There was the piano. There was the vase. And in it—

A green daisy, big as a soup plate.

It was hot that night inside the house, but we wouldn't have been comfortable anyway, so the fact that the air conditioner wasn't working right didn't register. Josie cooked a snack we hardly touched, and we went to bed.

We had a fight in the morning. Not about giving up the house—we'd agreed on that, but I wanted to take Josie with me, and come back for our stuff together later. But she "just couldn't." There were so many things to pack, and curtains to take down, and she'd be perfectly all right inside the house. A woman's argument. So of course it won.

And not a word about what we were both thinking of all the time—what we'd see when we opened the front door.

Giant mushrooms or azalea bush?

You understand we had to make out like it was any other morning. Shave, dress for the office, have breakfast, kiss the wife, and put my hat on by the door, the door we didn't want to open.

But when I did, the world was pouring rain, rain that spattered on the leaves and dripped from every stem of the azalea bush.

The most wonderful rain on the most wonderful bush in the most wonderful world in all the universe.

So I kissed Josie once more, concentrating this time, and went out. Not knowing I'd wish I had knocked her cold and dragged her along. Not dreaming of the nightmare I had coming up.

I told the fellow at the bank, who was to collect the rent, that we were leaving. But I didn't tell him why.

"We don't like not being able to look out of the windows, and if we could, we wouldn't want to see mushrooms the size of a table. And there's a winged snake in the attic. It's dead, but we don't like it. Daisies shouldn't be green, and the birds are the wrong size, and neighbors who aren't there can be heard on our front step."

You see why I didn't tell him? I just gave notice and asked to see Dalrymple. But I got the same answer as the day before.

I couldn't find an apartment, but by great good luck the furnished room we'd left happened to be vacant, and I took it. Then I headed back to get Josie, whistling as I turned into the driveway. Who's afraid of the big green daisy?

But the trees screened the house until you were right on top of it, and before I saw it I knew I was really scared. Of nothing—and everything. Scared that the house mightn't be there, or that a feathered snake might be sitting on the azalea bush.

Instead, everything looked just as I'd left it. I unlocked the door because I knew Josie would be busy. Three steps inside, I felt my knees jellyfish under me.

Not that there was much wrong that you could see—just the furniture. It wasn't the right kind, and it wasn't in the right places, and to me that meant this wasn't the room I'd left a few hours ago.

"Josie!" I yelled. And other things, running from one room to another. All were different. Not a stick of furniture was the same. In the living room there was no piano, no vase, no green daisy. And no Josie anywhere.

I tore upstairs, still yelling. Something wrapped itself around my neck just as I turned at the landing. I clawed at it while it turned me around. It was a big, blondish man, dressed in the kind of uniform laundry drivers and delivery men wear.

"Gotcha now! What've you done with Greta? Answer me or I'll break your neck."

"Where's Josie?" I squeaked between his ten fingers.

"If you done any harm to Greta—" he bellowed.

With that kind of talk we weren't getting anywhere. He saw it, luckily, and instead of choking me just shook me. He was that big.

"What's goin' on here? What's happened to my Greta?"

"Don't know," I gasped. "Never saw her. I left Josie here—"

He shook me again.

"Drop the double talk. You're here, ain't you? You got to know—"

From downstairs came the sound of a slammed door. He let go of me so suddenly I almost dropped. Then we ran neck and neck down the stairs, reaching the dining room in a dead heat.

It was a little fellow with a scrubby mustache, carrying a briefcase. He just stood and stared at us for half a minute.

"I'm sorry," he said at last. "I guess . . . I guess I'm sick. Could somebody tell me how to get to 16 Bonita Road?"

"What you want there?" the big man asked.

"I live there," answered the little guy, looking around the room like he'd lost his way.

"What's your address?" I asked the big blond.

"Gravesend Avenue, and I ain't lost. Not till I got in here, I wasn't."

"Just around the next street from me," I said. "We're on Kendrick Road."

I had a feeling, but didn't know why, that the addresses were important. Bonita, Gravesend, and Kendrick were the three sides of a square. So what?

"I must be going," said the little man. "Helen . . . my wife . . . will be waiting for me."

"No you don't—" began the big fellow. But I put a hand on his arm, and we both watched little Milquetoast head for the kitchen. We followed him. When he opened the back door—there wasn't any in the house Josie and I'd rented—we could see a flagstone walk and part of the row of maples on Bonita Road.

But he didn't go out. He turned around in the door and looked at us. Then he began to cry like a kid—big, gulping sobs that it hurt to watch. Slowly things began to click in my head; they didn't make sense, but what did? I took the little guy's briefcase away, led him to a chair, and put a glass of water in front of him.

"If you love your wife," I said, "don't go away."

The big guy tagged along as I went to the living room. There was a foyer leading off it that I'd never seen before.

"Is this the way you come in from Gravesend Avenue?" I asked.

"Sure. But something's phony—"

. "Shut up. I'm getting an idea. Is this your house, with the furniture all wrong?"

He just nodded. My mind kept racing along a lot of blind alleys and back again to a house that belonged to three other people. I took time out to look around more carefully. The furniture wasn't only different; it was thrown around where it would do the most good, regardless of looks. No woman would have arranged it this way.

I went to the old-fashioned desk, neat in a fussy sort of way, but not pretty. A bundle of pigeon-holed bills interested me. They were made out to James Dalrymple. One of them, for electricity, was up in the high brackets.

"What do we do now?" the big guy asked suddenly. "I don't care about the house. All I want is to find Greta."

The fight was out of him now that there was nothing he could lick into, and he answered questions in a willing, hopeless sort of way. They'd rented the house from an agent and lived here three months. Greta didn't go out much, but she wished you could look out of the windows. Check.

"You've been upstairs, and there's nobody there," I said finally. "So if the guy we want to see is around, he must be in the cellar."

We had to go back through the kitchen, so we picked up Milquetoast on the way. The door at the bottom of the cellar steps opened easily. There was another, locked, behind it. I knocked hard on it, but nobody answered.

"We ain't waiting," said the big man. "Out of the way."

He slammed his weight against the panels. On the fourth try the lock got tired and he went through, me right behind and Milquetoast trailing.

There was a bigger air conditioner than I remembered, ten times as many cables, and a panel board against one wall that should have been in an Edison substation. The air smelled the way it does after a thunderstorm sometimes, and in a far corner an electric arc spotlighted the figure of a man welding something to a mess of bus bars.

We three went up to him—and didn't do a thing. There was something about the way he was working—as if neither he nor we mattered —that stopped even the big blond guy. And then with a snap the arc went out, and the welder took the mask off his face. It was the professor.

"I've been expecting you," he said, sort of tired. "What time is it?"

I got it from a fancy sort of clock with four hands hung on the wall. "Quarter to six."

"I know what you're wondering," he said. "Your wives—I can promise two of you that they are safe for the present."

Something tight in my chest told me I was the third.

"We knew last night," I managed to say. "She won't leave the house. Will that help?"

"Yes. She's safe indoors so long as the house stands. The crucial time phase occurs at 6:22. Help me with this grid."

The big fellow helped me jockey the bus bars into position, and the professor showed us how to take out another set. We forgot all about Milquetoast. Later we wished we hadn't.

"You already know too much," the professor said as we worked. "You have a right to know the rest."

He fished three cables from somewhere and clamped terminals to them in a way that showed he'd had plenty of practice.

"I don't suppose you know anything of the structure of time, or that you've studied the brilliant theories of Dunne as given in his book 'The Serial Universe.' He suggested a second time rate or flow as being necessary to measure the passage of Time One, the time our clocks measure. Further, he postulated a third time flow to gauge the passage of this second time rate, or Time Two. And so on."

Remember the condensed milk can with a picture of itself on the label, and that picture having a smaller picture in it, and how you wondered where the thing would stop?

"The sequence is infinite," the professor went on, as if I'd asked him. "I cannot explain the new physics by which I was able to check Dunne's theories and later to measure the cycles and synchronization of several time states. I found each linked with its own three-dimensional space. I learned that the entropy of these regressive states was greater than that of ours, so that I could reach them physically and even reproduce material objects in them."

"Such as houses," I said. "You mean Josie's marooned in the past somewhere?"

He was pulling still another bus-bar grid from what I thought of as the air conditioner. It was fused as if it had been in a furnace.

"No! These time states are parallel. Your wives are in the present, but in regressive time states. To travel back through Time One would involve all the paradoxes pointed out in fiction, but to enter a regressive time proved all too easy. The drop in energy, the entropy difference, supplied the power. I had only to trigger the fall. The discovery was tempting, for I was short of money. Another man might have thought of a hundred ways to earn more with the means at hand. I could imagine only one."

"You sent this house into three different times," I said.

He nodded. "I needed it for myself, but if I could generate others like it, and gain an income to carry on my work, where was the harm in that? The shortage of housing space not only made it easy, but even seemed to justify it."

A slow shudder went over the big blond fellow. He looked at the professor strangely, while the hands that were holding the grid tightened until the knuckles showed white.

"Get her back," he said slowly. "If I don't get Greta back, I'll kill you."

It was the wrong tune just then. I knew that nobody but the professor could help us, and if anything had to be settled it ought to wait.

"One house, and four entrances," I said to ease things up. "Each hidden from the others, with fences between so the tenants wouldn't go visiting, or notice each other. Each of us came home, stepped through a doorway, and into a different house."

The professor nodded. "Each entrance was a miniature time grid. You, for instance, entered Time Four whenever you passed through, and re-entered Time One whenever you left the house. The necessary equipment was housed with the air-conditioning unit, which was needed because I could not allow windows to be opened. The regressive universes are—unearthly. But inside the four walls all was normal."

"Until yesterday?" I asked.

He nodded. "I take full blame. You can do what you like with me when we are finished. But the breakdown was pure mischance, not negligence, nor miscalculation. I overrated every part, allowed a great safety factor. It could not have been foreseen."

"What's it like—where Greta is?" croaked the big man.

"Strange, but not unpleasant. While the life forms are odd, they are not dangerous in either Time Two or Time Three. That is why I said your wives would be safe, as they will be even if—"

He looked at me, and I knew it was Josie who wouldn't be safe *if*—

"Finish it," I croaked.

"If we can't restore the full capacity of the time grid by 6:22," he explained, "the temporal extensions of this house will collapse. Remember that they exist only because *it* exists—in Time One. The bridge has been broken for nine hours. But I think we shall have the grid working in time."

We worked. At 6:12 the professor stepped back, turned up a couple of controllers, and stared at a flock of meters for what seemed an age. I didn't seem to breathe while we waited. Then he turned to us.

"The bridge is restored. You can go back upstairs and get your wives. Go out by the doorway you are accustomed to, then go back in."

I know how they feel when the Marines arrive. I could have hugged the professor, even if he had shot six innocent people into three different hangouts of old Father Time. The blond guy showed it too, before he ran out.

And Milquetoast?

We'd forgotten him, the guy with the zero personality, the little man who wasn't there. But he had gone the color of ripe cheese, and was muttering something we couldn't make out.

"It's all right," I said. "You've got her back. Helen's waiting for you upstairs."

He stared at us with eyes that didn't seem to belong to him. When he talked, it was like chalk squeaking against a slate.

"She was always waiting. Until I came home. Then she argued. She nagged, until I couldn't stand it."

"She'll be glad to see you now," I said, talking as to a kid.

"She won't see me. When I couldn't go on any longer, I did something. This morning I killed her."

Just saying it seemed to stiffen him inside.

"She would never have believed I could do it, but I did. It was easier than I thought. Just one shot. I had kept an old letter in which she threatened to kill herself. It was worded just right. I left it and the gun near her."

The professor and I just stared at him, but we didn't doubt. Nobody could have.

"All day something bothered me—something I'd forgotten, or done wrong. Only an hour ago it came to me. I had wiped my fingerprints off the gun, but I hadn't put hers on it. Hers had to be on, or it couldn't be suicide. I had to come back and put them on. And then—"

And then he'd found house and corpse both gone. And, once the shock was over, the most perfect out for murder anybody ever had. No wonder he hadn't helped us rebuild those grids.

"I had to tell you," he mumbled. "I was crazy to tell. But they can't convict me *if the body is gone.*"

It's always a mistake to underrate the other fellow. That's what we'd done with Milquetoast. He was small, but fast. Before the professor or I could move, as if shoved by built-in springs, he jumped for the panel board, grabbed the controls, and swung them clear around.

The professor howled. We both jumped for the little guy, but he'd already grabbed two of the smaller cables on the board. There were two blue arcs as he yanked them free.

I reached him first with a haymaker to the jaw. Even after he was limp I hit him a second time—for Josie.

Meanwhile the professor had swung the controls back, grabbed the cables, and was holding them to their terminals. I knew he couldn't connect them without cutting off the juice altogether. Meter needles were still pulsing wildly, but settling back to something like rest.

"We can't stop to reconnect now," he gasped. "Another break and we'll lose synchronism. Get your wife out."

I could see he meant but quick. Milquetoast was still on ice and looked safe enough. I took the cellar stairs three steps at a time—and went out the kitchen door because that was nearest.

The row of maples on Bonita Road. High fences between, and a good quarter of a mile the long way around to Kendrick Road. I couldn't expect the professor to hang on that long. I went back into the kitchen.

Another kitchen. The wrong house. The color scheme was different. There were dirty dishes in the sink and more on the table. I'd stepped out of Time One.

Into Milquetoast's house!

Swearing—or praying—and seeing the professor sweating under the strain of those cables, I ran into the dining room. That was where our entrance was—Josie's and mine.

No foyer, no street door in this dining room. Of course not. Only the Time One house would have all four entrances. I headed back for the kitchen through the living room. That's where I saw her.

It's no good speaking ill—but she looked as if maybe Milquetoast had had to kill her. Big, with a face that had spoiled and selfish written all over it even in death. The gun lay beside her. But I had no time to waste. There was no entrance in the living room.

My thoughts were racing like mad. If I went out by the kitchen entrance—the only one this house had—I'd get back to Time One all right. But to reach my own entrance I'd have to go clear around, unless I could climb a fence—and I knew I couldn't. Go back into the kitchen, and I'd land in this house of the dead again. Dead end.

Sometimes things click just as you get desperate, or because you are. I grabbed up a chair, smashed a kitchen window, and caught a glimpse of red grass and cone-shaped, feathery trees outside. Taking the chair along, I went out the door. Green grass and Bonita Road with its maples.

The window, from outside, wasn't broken. From inside, I'd smashed only the Time Two window. So I used the chair again, from outside. Then I jumped up on it and climbed through into the house. The kitchen was different again. Having side-stepped the time grid, I'd got back into the kitchen of Time One, where we'd met Milquetoast. I didn't stop, but raced through into the dining room and out of the house again. On the step I about-faced and went back in. Into the house we'd called home.

"Josie!" I yelled.

She ran out of the kitchen to meet me, hair stringy and apron cockeyed and the loveliest thing I ever saw. Not giving her time to talk, I grabbed her and yanked her out the door. We stood panting together by the azalea bush.

"Joe Gates," she said, "you let me loose this minute or your supper will be burnt to a crisp."

But I didn't let her go, just held her, thinking how close a thing it had been—no supper, no house, no Josie.

"We're going out to dinner," I came back, "to celebrate how lucky I am to have you back, which I will explain later. And now I have to see a man about a murder, and I want you to promise you will not go back into the house even for a second, no matter what."

She looked at me, and I guess it was what she saw or guessed that made her promise. So I went to the nearest cellar window and kicked the glass in. After looking to make sure it was the Time One house I was getting into, I climbed down.

The professor was still hanging on, but his arms shook. I yelled at him to say we were O.K. He turned toward me, haggard with strain.

"Can't hold much longer. Have to make sure—the others got out."

What could you do in a case like that? I ran upstairs again, made sure I was picking the right entrance—the living room one this time—and walked out and in. The blond man was taking it easy in a big chair with a brunette on his lap. Greta? I didn't stop to ask.

"Get out," I yelled.

The big guy may have been slow, but he got that all right. He heaved himself out of the chair, Greta and all, and carried her right along. We left the house in a dead heat, and then, as if we expected something to happen to it, turned and looked.

Nothing happened.

"Don't go back in," I warned them. "The professor is in trouble."

It meant breaking another cellar window, because we were on a different side of the house. Again I dropped into the Time One cellar. Again I yelled at the professor that he could let go, we were all out.

But a shadow hunched itself on the floor. It jumped and hit the professor like a tackler on a football field. There was an awful glare of juice gone wild, a snap and crackle of arcing currents. Against the light two figures stood out for a split second—the professor's and Milquetoast's. And suddenly I couldn't see them any more. It was dark again, and my eyes felt the way they do when you go into a movie in broad day.

Then the light of half a dozen yellow bulbs came back, and I could see what I couldn't believe.

Half of the air conditioner—or time grid—was lopped off as if a knife had cut it. The half where I'd seen the figures last. The ends of cables and bus bars, cut clean across, shone in the break. Of Milquetoast and the professor there wasn't a sign.

So the little man who had to kill got away from the police. Whether there are worse things in the time state he landed in I don't know. As for the professor, he just might manage to find his way back again some day.

But I don't think he will.

After a last look around, I went upstairs and walked out to meet Josie by the azalea bush. Then we walked the long way around—even though I knew the time grids were dead I couldn't go back in then—and told Greta and her husband how things were. When I told him where he could find a furnished room, he went right over to clinch it.

Me and Josie, we don't like furnished rooms. So we told the bank we'd changed our minds and would stay. Josie stored the professor's stuff in the attic, bought some of our own furniture, and made me put in clear windows all around, some of them hinged to open. So it's now a pretty comfortable house even though the air conditioning doesn't work.

After all, there *is* a housing shortage.

ROBERT MOORE WILLIAMS

FLIGHT OF THE DAWN STAR

THE port lock opened with a slight hiss, and Technician Jack Graham stepped out. He sucked in great mouthfuls of the wine-rich air of this new planet, and it flooded through his being like a draught of an ageless life-giving elixir, which somehow seemed to heal and soothe the fear that had been—and still was—a black shadow weighing heavily on his mind.

There was a sun of sorts overhead—an ancient, yellowish sun, bathing in its beneficent glow the long rolling sweep of the garden land. Quietly flowing streams wound placidly through green meadows and among green trees. His eyes followed the horizon round and he gasped at what he saw. Turning, he called within the ship.

Ruddy Sarl, navigator and amateur astronomer, answered: "What is it? I'm coming as fast as I can."

Ruddy Sarl stood in the lock, with one hand shading his eyes against the glow of the sun while he followed his comrade's pointing hand.

He whistled softly, and there was surprise and awe and a lack of understanding in what he did not say, but mostly there was awe. Awe tells the story where words leave off, and magnificent, and supreme, and mighty, and colossal, and all the other adjectives would not have described the city half as well as the words Ruddy Sarl did not use. He looked. His eyes brought him evidence of stupendous height, of story piled on story that reached up to the clouds themselves, of graceful lines and sweeping curves, an edifice wrought by the patient toil of uncounted generations laboring to create in material things a city adequate to their vast dreaming. And his eyes also told him that the dream had failed—for the city had crumbled and was still crumbling to the ground. His eyes stopped seeing at that point and his mind took up the task, wondering what had happened to the men who had built that city, what *could* have happened to thwart the ambitions of a race capable of such construction? War? Pestilence? Famine? Flood? Back on Earth —with a shock and a wrench he realized it was the Earth he would never see again—those four factors took inevitable toll of the ambitious construction of men. War? Pestilence? Famine? Flood? Barbaric hobgoblins of a civilization in the state of barbarism!

But here, on this unknown planet, some mighty race had risen above barbarism. The evidence was irrefutable. The race that built that city could not have been involved in war or threatened by pestilence or flood. What, then, had happened?

"Perhaps—" Graham showed where his thoughts were running. "Perhaps there are people here somewhere who can help us—"

Reluctantly Sarl forced himself to think of the present.

"Yes—yes, there may be—still. There once was, no doubt of it. But— well, no telling how many years have passed since the inhabitants left that city. Ten thousand—hundred thousand—a million. The place seems built to last forever, but forever is so long—" There was an odd touch of pathos in his voice. He was thinking of the wasted materials and labor. And most of all, of the wasted dreams, so adequately expressed in the gray ruin towering toward the yellow sun.

"You are certain," Graham anxiously inquired, "that you don't know where we are?"

Sarl shrugged eloquent shoulders. "Last night, as we were dropping down to this planet, you saw the stars. Did you recognize any of them, or any of the constellations?"

Graham shivered. When the warp had released them they had hurried to the ports, and all around them, stretching away for lightyear after lightyear, infinitely distant, had been the stars, pin points of exploding light against the black fabric of dead space. Stars—and as far as the eye could reach—more stars, until all conception of their number was lost, and in that vast expanse of space no constellation that they even remotely recognized.

Home—home— The green hills of Earth so far away that even the stout atomic engines of the *Dawn Star* could not push them there. Graham swallowed, then tried to grin. "Well, we can make the best of it— What do you say we go look?"

"All we can do," Sarl answered, stepping lithely to the ground. They had not taken a dozen steps before Graham slapped at his hip.

"Fools!" he growled. "To go running around a strange planet without a gun of any kind. We've learned better than that."

He turned on his heel and strode rapidly back to the ship. When he returned he was buckling a positron gun to his body. He handed a second weapon to Sarl, who silently gazed at it.

"Put it on," Graham snapped.

"All right—only—well, this world looks so confounded peaceful that even the thought of a gun is somehow revolting."

"Yes, but no matter how things look, I *know* it's peaceful after I've turned this thing loose on it."

Staring at the city, Sarl buckled on the gun. The city was so huge and the gun so small—yet he could blast an awful hole in the city as the stream of released positrons combined with the electrons of the building material—or any other material—blasting the electrons into nothingness and releasing a flood of gamma rays. A very efficient little weapon. Men of the Solar System found a use for them. When Mars raided Jupiter or Jupiter raided Venus or either of them raided Earth, the positron gun was a handy thing to have, for it blasted men and raiding ships out of space. Occasionally, when its own confined force field failed, it blasted the user. But that was only a regrettable accident.

Perhaps it would be needed. Sarl hoped not. The men who could build such a city could build weapons, too. Only—from the way the city looked, weapons had never been used on it.

Walking over fields soft with grass, where they could not hear the sound of their own footsteps, under trees and across streams, they approached the city. Their eyes fastened on it, yet the occasional hurried glances over the land revealed what each was thinking. What had become of the descendants of the race that built those sky-high towers? There was no sign of them. Had they vanished into the vast void of forgotten things? Had they sought a new home elsewhere? Had the natural resources of their plant failed—little by little—until there was not enough left to support the inhabitants? Who could tell? The city had seen them go, but it was steeped in silence. Somehow it did not seem to be a sorrowing silence. More it seemed an empty nest, from which the nestlings, having no longer a use for it, had flown—

They walked on, and the city climbed high above them, rising tier on tier into the sky, yearning toward the vault above.

"No one here," Sarl said thoughtfully. "In this quiet air such a city would last for eternity, forever and forever—and then a day." His voice trailed off.

"It does not seem possible," Graham protested, "that a race intelligent enough, strong enough, to build this city would have perished. But it has." And he thought of Nineveh and Karnak and Thebes and the ruins of Baalbek, festering under Earth's sun off yonder somewhere in the vast void of space.

As if in refutation, the air was suddenly vibrant with the note of a voice. Then another voice took up the sound and another and another, and the voices laughed together, happily, and the air vibrated with a pleasing sound. They could not see its source, but with one accord they stepped to the protection of a huge tree and hid behind it, seeking the origin of the laughter suddenly filling the air.

"Someone *is* here," said Graham.

"Look," Sarl breathed. "No— Not at the city. At that meadow there."

There was a flash of bronze in the meadow, and laughing and dancing from the shadow of the trees came a figure. Naked, it was, and seemingly it needed no clothing. Following the first figure were others, all repeating the steps of a rhythmic dance.

"Children," Sarl whispered. "No—youths."

"Playing——" Jack Graham said to himself.

His voice was heavy with wonder. In the shadow of the greatest city he had ever seen, the youth of a race was playing. While the creation of their ancestors corroded into ruin around them, they played silly dancing games, waving their arms and tossing their bodies in the sunlight, carelessly indifferent of the labor of long generations of workers who had toiled and dreamed for them. Or was this true? Perhaps the race of builders had perished and these youths belonged to another emerging race, a group beginning the slow climb upward from savagery to civilization? Graham did not understand. If they were an emerging race, how could they play when that mighty city was there, brooding over lost secrets, challenging the imagination of any fertile mind to solve its mysteries——

Sarl stepped out from behind the tree and waved his arms at the dancers and Graham swore at him and lifted his positron gun.

"Put it down," said Sarl, glancing at the weapon.

"How do we know they're friendly?" Graham argued. "I'm not taking any chances."

The dancers stopped. They seemed to freeze in their positions while they stared at the two strange figures who had so suddenly appeared. Then they were running, dancing over the meadow toward them, and

Graham was gripping his gun, his finger on the trigger. He had never known a form of life that was not at war with all other forms of life. It was the law of evolution—a grim, gray law grown hoary through unforgotten ages of survival.

Then the dancers were on them and the air was filled with the chatter of voices that were somehow friendly and not at all curious. Graham eased the pressure on the trigger and waited. With the exception of minor differences, they seemed like seventeen-year-old youths from Earth. Their bodies were slender and utterly naked. Their limbs were well-formed, symmetrical and graceful. Their eyes were wide and smiling. They carried themselves with a sureness, with a certainty that was full of meaning——

Sarl stood there smiling, a little ahead of Graham, and the five youths danced to within ten feet of him, and then stopped, suddenly. Their eyes went wide and the smile on their faces died out. Curiosity replaced the smile and then a mild wonder, and mixed with the wonder was an awe in which there showed a trace of fear.

"We thought——"

Graham dropped his gun. His own brain talked to him!

"We thought you were Ulvan and Dar—but you aren't. Who are you?"

"Strangers from a far land," Sarl answered, unperturbed, and Graham, flushing, picked up his gun. He had been on Mars often enough to know the possibilities of telepathy, but he had not expected it here. The Martians were an old race, an ancient, learned race. But these people were young. Obviously they belonged to a race on its way up, whereas telepathy was something that only a very old race could use. Controlled telepathy took brain power, and brain power meant untold years of evolution. Or it worked that way in the Solar System. Perhaps—— But they were asking questions.

"Strangers? There are no strangers here."

Sarl, navigator and amateur astronomer, tried to explain. Only he knew how hard a task he had. Even if this race did have the ability to use telepathy, how could he explain a space warp to them? Yet he knew he had to explain it. They wanted to know. He had the feeling that if the explanation was not adequate—but it was only a feeling. Graham kept the gun ready, and listened.

"We shoved off from Mercury, the planet nearest our sun, and just for the hell of it, mostly, but also because I wanted to check the bending of light rays under the Sun's mass, we poked our ship in toward the Sun. You know, we wanted to see how close we could get without being burned. I had an idea—but no matter. We went in as close as we dared, to the point where the gravity of the mighty mass had us in such a tight grip that our engines could scarcely pull us out—when something happened. I think a sunspot exploded under us. Anyhow—there was a flash of blinding light and then everything was black. The ship creaked and groaned and popped and the engines had no effect. Everything was black for hours, and then a sort of dim grayness filtered through the ports. Again there was a click, and we were floating in space—with a new universe around us———"

They were listening very attentively to Sarl, Graham thought—just as though they understood it all, when even Sarl didn't understand it. He was just guessing, but it sounded like a good guess, as good as any. And here they were, which somehow seemed to prove that Sarl was right. Graham choked up inside. They would never see the rolling plains of Earth again—never. But he kept his finger on the gun.

The five bronze youths conferred. Graham got the idea that they were sorry for Sarl and him, that they would help if they could. Only they couldn't. There wasn't any way to help. It was impossible. Time wasn't long enough.

The nearest youth smiled at Sarl. "I am Nard," he said. "Your story has interested us. What happened is really very simple. You were twisted out of your space and into another space, and then back into your own space, but you didn't come out where you went in. You looped through hyper-space for an untold distance. It is unfortunate—we are sorry."

Graham blinked. They understood. And they answered Sarl. Not in words, but in pure ideas. The words they used to each other were an obscure but hauntingly familiar chatter—meaningless——— But they knew about space. They knew. It seemed impossible——— Graham glanced at the city climbing up toward the sky and back at the five slender striplings. He could not understand. There was a nebulous thought in his mind——— He took his finger off the trigger.

Nard smiled at him. He nodded toward the city. "You are wondering about that? Our forbears built it, in the long ago———" He used a term that indicated time, but it carried no meaning to Graham. Too vast. But he felt a strange nostalgic touch of envy.

Sarl was asking questions. Sarl wanted to know. Where were their elders? What had happened to make them desert their cities? Were there other people like them on this planet? Were there girls? Did people—die here? Foolish questions. But Nard answered them smilingly.

From the answers there emerged a meaning that Graham could not quite comprehend, and Sarl, too, knitted his brows in perplexity.

There were no elders, Nard said. They were the elders, these striplings, these bronzed and careless youths. They never grew any older than that. It was puzzling. They grew older in years but not in physical development. Here, the decrepitude of old age did not exist. They had merely arrested physical change. Nard talked of molecules and atoms and waves and vibrations. He dug deep into the structure of matter, and Sarl nodded for a time and then stopped nodding as the explanation went beyond him. And Graham did not follow that far, but he knew that Nard had told him why they never grew old.

Yes, there were girls here, and people died, too—though only through accident, and there were many others like them.

Sarl suggested to Nard and his companions that they return with them to visit their ship. They went. The *Dawn Star* rested softly on the deep grass. Nard went through it, with his fellows, and Sarl explained how it operated, and they were politely interested, but they were not astonished at all.

"There are ships somewhat like this one over there in the city," Nard explained. "Their principle of operation is different, but the result is the same: they fly."

"Don't you ever use them?" Graham asked.

"Oh, no. Our ancestors flew everywhere and learned everything, and if we wanted to know anything we would go into the cities and look in the libraries and the answer would be there. But we rarely need to know anything," he added naïvely.

"No need to know?" Sarl gasped.

"Why should we? We have everything we need, and nothing"—he paused and groped for the meaning he wanted—"troubles us."

"But," Sarl exploded, "how can you stand it? I would go mad with nothing to do."

"We play and we think. That is enough."

It was enough, Graham and Sarl saw in the days that followed. It sounded stupid and silly, but it wasn't. There wasn't any objective left for the descendants of this lost race to seek. So they played, and they encouraged Jack Graham and Ruddy Sarl to play with them. But the Earthlings could not master the intricacies of the games. They were clumsy and they stumbled. And the positron gun which Graham wore constantly got in his way. And when the inhabitants were tired of playing and withdrew to think, the Earthlings could not follow them at all. For this was done one by one. The bronzed youths or equally bronzed girls simply slipped away from their comrades to stretch out on the grass, staring fixedly at nothing. They did not work. Why should they? A pleasant-tasting, strangely satisfying fruit grew on the trees and this was all they ate. Sarl examined the trees and the fruit and muttered to himself and Nard explained that there was a perfect balance between food supply and inhabitants. Back in the long past all that had been planned. Graham muttered that everything seemed to have been planned. He did not like it.

Nard had difficulty in understanding what they wanted to know, when Graham asked about government. Government? He didn't know what that was—the idea of one man having power over other men. Finally he understood.

"There is no government. Each one does as he pleases. Our fathers struggled a very long time that we might be ungoverned. It was one of their dreams."

"But don't you have disputes?"

"Disputes? No. We are civilized. We are intelligent."

It struck Graham that this was the perfect answer. In a truly intelligent civilization there would be no cause for disputes. But——

Days passed. Graham and Sarl tried to understand and to participate, but it was hard. Both of them looking at the city, the ancient city sleeping peacefully in the yellow sun—— Nard had said that there were libraries there—libraries where all facts were gathered.

Little by little Graham and Sarl realized that nostalgia was growing on them. Here was heaven, but they had little use for it. Here was peace and intelligence, but more and more often they looked at the city——

They were Earthlings, and life on Earth was a rushing, fighting, jostling, scurrying affair—they were not ready for peace. Peace and understanding came through long centuries, through thousands and hundreds of thousands of years. They were barbarians, Graham and Sarl, young barbarians out of their era. Off yonder, somewhere in space, was a newer solar system, where the last problem had not been solved, where the last spaceship had not made its final flight and settled home forever. And yet this strange planet on which they landed was somehow a dream world, a haven dimly sought——

They looked more often at the city.

Nard came to them. "You want to go home," he stated quietly.

"Lord, yes!" Graham almost sobbed, and Sarl nodded slowly.

"We had hoped you would prefer to stay here. In time, we believe we could teach you to love it. But here we do as we please, and it is your will to return home. We will go to the city."

"It is not possible to return home," said Sarl flatly. "We are not only lost, but the distance is much too vast—light-years——"

Nard continued smiling. "The distance is not difficult. We can project you into hyper-space and hurl you outward at a speed infinitely greater than that of light. But there may be some difficulty in knowing where to send you. Space is so large——"

"You tell me——" Graham whispered, but Sarl spoke flatly.

"It is not possible to return home. How can you select our sun from the infinite number of suns lost in space? Our sun may be out of vision entirely."

"Come," Nard answered. "We shall see."

They went to the city. It towered above them, dreaming in the vault of heaven. They were ants—they were less than ants crawling in the shadow of the Matterhorn——

Nard led them to an opening, and into a tunnel. They turned and twisted; lights flashed on to light their way and turned off after they had passed.

"My people," said Nard—and there was pride in the way he said it—"planned all this."

They came to a vast room. Lights winked on around them. Down this room were aisle after aisle of tablelike boards covered with myriads of tiny buttons.

"Here we will see if we can discover where to send you."

Sarl faced him. "Do you realize what you are saying? You are telling us that the solution of the Problem of Multiple Bodies is here. It is not possible——"

Graham knew that back on Earth the astronomers and mathematicians were still struggling to discover the equations that would completely represent the behavior of three bodies. The mathematicians knew there was an answer—because the problem was solved in nature—but they had not been able to find the equations. They were seeking them desperately. They would answer the most important question of the Solar System—how to predict the behavior of more than two bodies.

"My ancestors solved the problem of three bodies and of more than three bodies. Then—in order to facilitate the practical solution of that problem—they built a machine to do the work for them. They were great on building machines," he added.

Sarl took a deep breath. "Those ancestors of yours must have been a great people."

"Perhaps they were. It is so difficult to know, from this distance. At any rate, they had ambitions——

"Now will you give me some pertinent facts about your solar system? I doubt if they included all the facts about your system—if they mapped it at all—but they probably knew about your sun, and fitted it into their machine. If it is a large sun, they did—otherwise they would not have obtained correct answers to their problems."

"What do you mean by pertinent facts?"

"Weight, for one. Rate of radiation, for another. Those things are part of the problem, and are especially important if the time involved is very great, since the weight and the radiation rate shrink. Time—time——" Nard paused, perplexed. "I had almost forgotten," he apologized. "This machine has not been used in a very long time." He pointed to the shadowy framework in the room.

Nard moved a lever. The great framework above them started moving. Graham and Sarl stared at it.

"You see," Nard explained as the framework shifted, "this is a miniature representation of the known universe. But when we came in, it had not been used for some thousands of years, and the time factor had to be brought up to date. The data you have on your sun would not be correct for several thousand years ago, and the machine would never locate your sun for us.

"The people who built this machine took an arbitrary point in space for their starting point. They drew imaginary lines dividing space into four quadrants. Then they placed all the stars where they belonged at that moment, with machinery to move them. The operator can then follow the stars through all space and all time, even to the end of time."

"How can that be?" Sarl asked.

Nard explained. Vibration and interwoven vibration, energy and negative energy levels—— Graham watched the framework turn above them. He did not hear the words. Nard was groping, anyhow, trying to explain in primitive ideas something that only a mathematician could grasp. Graham watched the framework as it turned.

It stopped. "It has reached the present," said Nard.

He went down the tables, punching buttons, feeding into the machine the facts Sarl had given him. He pressed a master switch. The lights went out——

Graham heard his own voice crying in the darkness. Involuntarily he jerked the positron gun from his belt.

On a black screen in front of them appeared a tiny sun, a white-hot flaming sun. For a second it looked like—and during that second wild hope was in Graham's heart, and then he saw the three tiny points of lights moving around it, and he knew it was not Sol——

"No," he heard Sarl whisper in the darkness. "That is not our system."

"We will examine the series above and below it," Nard answered, manipulating the controls.

There was another sun framed in the black velvet screen that somehow looked like space—and might be space, for the men who could build this machine might do that, too. But it was not Sol—there were no planets. Sarl whispered in the darkness and Nard whispered in reply and there was another sun, but there were no planets around it either. And Graham knew how it felt to have hope die out. Earth—smiling Mother Earth— I will not return to you—ever—forever—and forever.

There were more whispers and more flaming points of light, and Graham could tell that Nard was perplexed and in doubt and he wondered why he did not screen all the suns in space, for that way they would surely stumble on the right one. But he knew they had only one lifetime in which to do it, and generation after generation of men had labored building this machine and putting the suns there. To show them all would take—he did not know how many years. There were so many stars.

And Nard sighed and the lights came on again, and Graham knew that Nard had given up. Why should he spend a lifetime trying to help two strangers return home?

But Nard was talking again to Sarl, asking him questions—asking him more about the space warp and how it acted. There was an odd perplexed light in Nard's eyes. And then there was a shining light in his eyes and the lights in the room were gone——

Graham could feel the shifting of the framework over him as time moved again, as the factor governing time shifted the framework that moved the suns, and he knew that minutes had passed. He stirred protestingly and Nard whispered to him to be patient. The minutes moved into hours and still the time factor shifted. And it was suddenly very lonely in the vast room.

There was a sun on the screen and Sarl was counting joyously—"Six —seven—eight! It's the Solar System! It's there."

Graham heard himself shouting. Out toward the edge of the screen were—unmistakable sign—the rings of Saturn! The one thing that nature had never duplicated. And third out from the Sun was—Earth!

Home—— Graham gulped and fumbled in the darkness for Sarl and pounded him on the back and Sarl was hugging him and he was hugging Sarl. He was a barbarian and he belonged back on that barbaric Earth, back in that barbaric age. He had never known how much he really belonged there until this moment.

And Nard had said that he could send them back, that the return would be easy, that only the knowing where to return them had been difficult——

Home—home again! His shout echoed and reëchoed through the mighty vault above.

The light came on, and there was Nard—but he wasn't smiling, and his eyes weren't shining, either. His eyes were misty and Nard turned away as they watched.

Graham and Sarl knew that something was wrong.

They leaped to the side of the bronze youth, roughly turned him around, and Graham fumbled for his positron gun. Then they saw the drawn, pinched look on his face. They released him——

"Nard—you don't mean—you don't—you can't help us return? You said you could."

Nard lifted his shoulders—a gesture strangely Earthly—and he shook his head.

"I am sorry. I can't return you. You are already there."

"There!" Graham gabbled. "This city on Earth! You—this strange peaceful race on barbaric Earth? No!" His voice thundered.

"This is Earth. This is Earth—but more than a million years after you left it. I should have known you were Earth-sired. Your bodies—a dozen things should have told me. But you unintentionally misled me into thinking about distance in space instead of in time."

"But——" Graham tried to say, and he saw Sarl's face. Somehow Sarl understood.

"That warp," said Sarl slowly.

"—was a time warp and not a space warp. You went along with the Sun as it moved, and when you came through again, the stars had shifted until you couldn't recognize them. You thought you had been shifted in space. You had been, of course, but there are an infinite number of spaces, of possible spaces. You were warped into one where time had almost stopped. You took over the time-rate of the space where you were, and over a million years passed. When I couldn't locate your sun, I suspected the truth, and I set the controls on our sun and sent the time factor backward. There is no doubt——"

"Then we'll never—get home?" Graham's voice was a whisper.

Nard shook his head.

"No. I could send you through space, but not back through time. It is not possible."

Graham fingered his gun, doubtful, hesitant, frightened, as Nard led them out of the city. They were out of the tunnel. The city towered sky-high above them, and they looked up at it.

"Our descendants—not exactly ours—but the descendants of our race, built that," said Sarl, and pride grew strong in his voice, and Graham heard the note of pride and finally understood. "Somehow we skipped all of the work and arrived at the goal of our dreaming. I can see it now. Back on Earth, we dreamed of peace and quiet, a land without hunger and without cold—Eden—The Happy Isles—Paradise. Well, it is good to know—that the race won through to the realization of its dreams."

Sarl looked at Graham. Jack Graham had laid his gun on the ground, and one by one he was removing his garments, tossing them carelessly away, as though he would never need them again. And Nard looked, and Nard smiled. And Sarl started removing his clothes, too.

They walked over the green meadows toward the shade of the friendly trees——

LAWRENCE O'DONNELL

VINTAGE SEASON

THREE people came up the walk to the old mansion just at dawn on a perfect May morning. Oliver Wilson in his pajamas watched them from an upper window through a haze of conflicting emotions, resentment predominant. He didn't want them there.

They were foreigners. He knew only that much about them. They had the curious name of Sancisco, and their first names, scrawled in loops on the lease, appeared to be Omerie, Kleph and Klia, though it was impossible as he looked down upon them now to sort them out by signature. He hadn't even been sure whether they would be men or women, and he had expected something a little less cosmopolitan.

Oliver's heart sank a little as he watched them follow the taxi driver up the walk. He had hoped for less self-assurance in his unwelcome tenants, because he meant to force them out of the house if he could. It didn't look very promising from here.

The man went first. He was tall and dark, and he wore his clothes and carried his body with that peculiar arrogant assurance that comes from perfect confidence in every phase of one's being. The two women were laughing as they followed him. Their voices were light and sweet, and their faces were beautiful, each in its own exotic way, but the first thing Oliver thought of when he looked at them was, "Expensive!"

It was not only that patina of perfection that seemed to dwell in every line of their incredibly flawless garments. There are degrees of wealth beyond which wealth itself ceases to have significance. Oliver had seen before, on rare occasions, something like this assurance that the earth turning beneath their well-shod feet turned only to their whim.

It puzzled him a little in this case, because he had the feeling as the three came up the walk that the beautiful clothing they wore so confidently was not clothing they were accustomed to. There was a curious air of condescension in the way they moved. Like women in costume. They minced a little on their delicate high heels, held out an arm to stare at the cut of a sleeve, twisted now and then inside their garments as if the clothing sat strangely on them, as if they were accustomed to something entirely different.

And there was an elegance about the way the garments fitted them which even to Oliver looked strikingly unusual. Only an actress on the screen, who can stop time and the film to adjust every disarrayed fold so that she looks perpetually perfect, might appear thus elegantly clad. But let these women move as they liked, and each fold of their clothing followed perfectly with the moment and fell perfectly into place again. One might almost suspect the garments were not cut of ordinary cloth, or that they were cut according to some unknown, subtle scheme, with many artful hidden seams placed by a tailor incredibly skilled at his trade.

They seemed excited. They talked in high, clear, very sweet voices, looking up at the perfect blue and transparent sky in which dawn was still frankly pink. They looked at the trees on the lawn, the leaves translucently green with an under color of golden newness, the edges crimped from constriction in the recent bud.

Happily and with excitement in their voices they called to the man, and when he answered his own voice blended so perfectly in cadence with theirs that it sounded like three people singing together. Their voices, like their clothing, seemed to have an elegance far beyond the ordinary, to be under a control such as Oliver Wilson had never dreamed of before this morning.

The taxi driver brought up the luggage, which was of a beautiful pale stuff that did not look quite like leather, and had curves in it so subtle it seemed square until you saw how two or three pieces of it fitted together when carried, into a perfectly balanced block. It was scuffed, as if from much use. And though there was a great deal of it, the taxi man did not seem to find his burden heavy. Oliver saw him look down at it now and then and heft the weight incredulously.

One of the women had very black hair, and a skin like cream, and

smoke-blue eyes heavy-lidded with the weight of her lashes. It was the
other woman Oliver's gaze followed as she came up the walk. Her hair
was a clear, pale red, and her face had a softness that he thought would
be like velvet to touch. She was tanned to a warm amber darker than her
hair.

Just as they reached the porch steps the fair woman lifted her head
and looked up. She gazed straight into Oliver's eyes and he saw that hers
were very blue, and just a little amused, as if she had known he was
there all along. Also they were frankly admiring.

Feeling a bit dizzy, Oliver hurried back to his room to dress.

"We are here on a vacation," the dark man said, accepting the keys.
"We will not wish to be disturbed, as I made clear in our correspondence.
You have engaged a cook and housemaid for us, I understand? We will
expect you to move your own belongings out of the house, then, and—"

"Wait," Oliver said uncomfortably. "Something's come up. I—" He
hesitated, not sure just how to present it. These were such increasingly
odd people. Even their speech was odd. They spoke so distinctly, not
slurring any of the words into contractions. English seemed as familiar
to them as a native tongue, but they all spoke as trained singers sing,
with perfect breath control and voice placement.

And there was a coldness in the man's voice, as if some gulf lay between him and Oliver, so deep no feeling of human contact could bridge
it.

"I wonder," Oliver said, "if I could find you better living quarters
somewhere else in town. There's a place across the street that—"

The dark woman said, "Oh, no!" in a lightly horrified voice, and all
three of them laughed. It was cool, distant laughter that did not include
Oliver.

The dark man said: "We chose this house carefully, Mr. Wilson. We
would not be interested in living anywhere else."

Oliver said desperately, "I don't see why. It isn't even a modern
house. I have two others in much better condition. Even across the street
you'd have a fine view of the city. Here there isn't anything. The other
houses cut off the view, and—"

"We engaged rooms here, Mr. Wilson," the man said with finality.
"We expect to use them. Now will you make arrangements to leave as
soon as possible?"

Oliver said, "No," and looked stubborn. "That isn't in the lease. You
can live here until next month, since you paid for it, but you can't put
me out. I'm staying."

The man opened his mouth to say something. He looked coldly at
Oliver and closed it again. The feeling of aloofness was chill between
them. There was a moment's silence. Then the man said,

"Very well. Be kind enough to stay out of our way."

It was a little odd that he didn't inquire Oliver's motives. Oliver was
not yet sure enough of the man to explain. He couldn't very well say,

"Since the lease was signed, I've been offered three times what the house is worth if I'll sell it before the end of May." He couldn't say, "I want the money, and I'm going to use my own nuisance-value to annoy you until you're willing to move out." After all, there seemed no reason why they shouldn't. After seeing them, there seemed doubly no reason, for it was clear they must be accustomed to surroundings infinitely better than this time-worn old house.

It was very strange, the value this house had so suddenly acquired. There was no reason at all why two groups of semi-anonymous people should be so eager to possess it for the month of May.

In silence Oliver showed his tenants upstairs to the three big bedrooms across the front of the house. He was intensely conscious of the red-haired woman and the way she watched him with a sort of obviously covert interest, quite warmly, and with a curious undertone to her interest that he could not quite place. It was familiar, but elusive. He thought how pleasant it would be to talk to her alone, if only to try to capture that elusive attitude and put a name to it.

Afterward he went down to the telephone and called his fiancée.

Sue's voice squeaked a little with excitement over the wire.

"Oliver, so early? Why, it's hardly six yet. Did you tell them what I said? Are they going to go?"

"Can't tell yet. I doubt it. After all, Sue, I did take their money, you know."

"Oliver, they've got to go! You've got to do something!"

"I'm trying, Sue. But I don't like it."

"Well, there isn't any reason why they shouldn't stay somewhere else. And we're going to need that money. You'll just have to think of something, Oliver."

Oliver met his own worried eyes in the mirror above the telephone and scowled at himself. His straw-colored hair was tangled and there was a shining stubble on his pleasant, tanned face. He was sorry the red-haired woman had first seen him in this untidy condition. Then his conscience smote him at the sound of Sue's determined voice and he said:

"I'll try, darling. I'll try. But I did take their money."

They had, in fact, paid a great deal of money, considerably more than the rooms were worth even in that year of high prices and high wages. The country was just moving into one of those fabulous eras which are later referred to as the Gay Forties or the Golden Sixties—a pleasant period of national euphoria. It was a stimulating time to be alive—while it lasted.

"All right," Oliver said resignedly. "I'll do my best."

But he was conscious, as the next few days went by, that he was not doing his best. There were several reasons for that. From the beginning the idea of making himself a nuisance to his tenants had been Sue's, not Oliver's. And if Oliver had been a little less compliant or Sue a little less determined the whole project would never have got under way. Reason was on Sue's side, but—

For one thing, the tenants were so fascinating. All they said and did had a queer sort of inversion to it, as if a mirror had been held up to ordinary living and in the reflection showed strange variations from the norm. Their minds worked on a different basic premise, Oliver thought, from his own. They seemed to derive covert amusement from the most unamusing things; they patronized, they were aloof with a quality of cold detachment which did not prevent them from laughing inexplicably far too often for Oliver's comfort.

He saw them occasionally, on their way to and from their rooms. They were polite and distant, not, he suspected, from anger at his presence but from sheer indifference.

Most of the day they spent out of the house. The perfect May weather held unbroken and they seemed to give themselves up whole-heartedly to admiration of it, entirely confident that the warm, pale-gold sunshine and the scented air would not be interrupted by rain or cold. They were so sure of it that Oliver felt uneasy.

They took only one meal a day in the house, a late dinner. And their reactions to the meal were unpredictable. Laughter greeted some of the dishes, and a sort of delicate disgust others. No one would touch the salad, for instance. And the fish seemed to cause a wave of queer embarrassment around the table.

They dressed elaborately for each dinner. The man—his name was Omerie—looked extremely handsome in his dinner clothes, but he seemed a little sulky and Oliver twice heard the women laughing because he had to wear black. Oliver entertained a sudden vision, for no reason, of the man in garments as bright and as subtly cut as the women's, and it seemed somehow very right for him. He wore even the dark clothing with a certain flamboyance, as if cloth-of-gold would be more normal for him.

When they were in the house at other meal times, they ate in their rooms. They must have brought a great deal of food with them, from whatever mysterious place they had come. Oliver wondered with increasing curiosity where it might be. Delicious odors drifted into the hall sometimes, at odd hours, from their closed doors. Oliver could not identify them, but almost always they smelled irresistible. A few times the food-smell was rather shockingly unpleasant, almost nauseating. It takes a connoisseur, Oliver reflected, to appreciate the decadent. And these people, most certainly, were connoisseurs.

Why they lived so contentedly in this huge, ramshackle old house was a question that disturbed his dreams at night. Or why they refused to move. He caught some fascinating glimpses into their rooms, which appeared to have been changed almost completely by additions he could not have defined very clearly from the brief sights he had of them. The feeling of luxury which his first glance at them had evoked was confirmed by the richness of the hangings they had apparently brought with them, the half-glimpsed ornaments, the pictures on the walls, even the whiffs of exotic perfume that floated from half-open doors.

He saw the women go by him in the halls, moving softly through the brown dimness in their gowns so uncannily perfect in fit, so lushly rich, so glowingly colored they seemed unreal. That poise born of confidence in the subservience of the world gave them an imperious aloofness, but more than once Oliver, meeting the blue gaze of the woman with the red hair and the soft, tanned skin, thought he saw quickened interest there. She smiled at him in the dimness and went by in a haze of fragrance and a halo of incredible richness, and the warmth of the smile lingered after she had gone.

He knew she did not mean this aloofness to last between them. From the very first he was sure of that. When the time came she would make the opportunity to be alone with him. The thought was confusing and tremendously exciting. There was nothing he could do but wait, knowing she would see him when it suited her.

On the third day he lunched with Sue in a little downtown restaurant overlooking the great sweep of the metropolis across the river far below. Sue had shining brown curls and brown eyes, and her chin was a bit more prominent than is strictly accordant with beauty. From childhood Sue had known what she wanted and how to get it, and it seemed to Oliver just now that she had never wanted anything quite so much as the sale of this house.

"It's such a marvelous offer for the old mausoleum," she said, breaking into a roll with a gesture of violence. "We'll never have a chance like that again, and prices are so high we'll need the money to start housekeeping. Surely you can do *something*, Oliver!"

"I'm trying," Oliver assured her uncomfortably.

"Have you heard anything more from that madwoman who wants to buy it?"

Oliver shook his head. "Her attorney phoned again yesterday. Nothing new. I wonder who she is."

"I don't think even the attorney knows. All this mystery—I don't like it, Oliver. Even those Sancisco people— What did they do today?"

Oliver laughed. "They spent about an hour this morning telephoning movie theaters in the city, checking up on a lot of third-rate films they want to see parts of."

"Parts of? But why?"

"I don't know. I think . . . oh, nothing. More coffee?"

The trouble was, he thought he did know. It was too unlikely a guess to tell Sue about, and without familiarity with the Sancisco oddities she would only think Oliver was losing his mind. But he had from their talk, a definite impression that there was an actor in bit parts in all these films whose performances they mentioned with something very near to awe. They referred to him as Golconda, which didn't appear to be his name, so that Oliver had no way of guessing which obscure bit-player it was they admired so deeply. Golconda might have been the name of a character he had once played—and with superlative skill, judging by the comments of the Sanciscoes—but to Oliver it meant nothing at all.

"They do funny things," he said, stirring his coffee reflectively. "Yesterday Omerie—that's the man—came in with a book of poems published about five years ago, and all of them handled it like a first edition of Shakespeare. I never even heard of the author, but he seems to be a tin god in their country, wherever that is."

"You still don't know? Haven't they even dropped any hints?"

"We don't do much talking," Oliver reminded her with some irony.

"I know, but— Oh, well, I guess it doesn't matter. Go on, what else do they do?"

"Well, this morning they were going to spend studying 'Golconda' and his great art, and this afternoon I think they're taking a trip up the river to some sort of shrine I never heard of. It isn't very far, wherever it is, because I know they're coming back for dinner. Some great man's birthplace, I think—they promised to take home souvenirs of the place if they could get any. They're typical tourists, all right—if I could only figure out what's behind the whole thing. It doesn't make sense."

"Nothing about that house makes sense any more. I do wish—"

She went on in a petulant voice, but Oliver ceased suddenly to hear her, because just outside the door, walking with imperial elegance on her high heels, a familiar figure passed. He did not see her face, but he thought he would know that poise, that richness of line and motion, anywhere on earth.

"Excuse me a minute," he muttered to Sue, and was out of his chair before she could speak. He made the door in half a dozen long strides, and the beautifully elegant passer-by was only a few steps away when he got there. Then, with the words he had meant to speak already half uttered, he fell silent and stood there staring.

It was not the red-haired woman. It was not her dark companion. It was a stranger. He watched, speechless, while the lovely, imperious creature moved on through the crowd and vanished, moving with familiar poise and assurance and an equally familiar strangeness as if the beautiful and exquisitely fitted garments she wore were an exotic costume to her, as they had always seemed to the Sancisco women. Every other woman on the street looked untidy and ill-at-ease beside her. Walking like a queen, she melted into the crowd and was gone.

She came from *their* country, Oliver told himself dizzily. So someone else nearby had mysterious tenants in this month of perfect May weather. Someone else was puzzling in vain today over the strangeness of the people from that nameless land.

In silence he went back to Sue.

The door stood invitingly ajar in the brown dimness of the upper hall. Oliver's steps slowed as he drew near it, and his heart began to quicken correspondingly. It was the red-haired woman's room, and he thought the door was not open by accident. Her name, he knew now, was Kleph.

The door creaked a little on its hinges and from within a very sweet voice said lazily, "Won't you come in?"

The room looked very different indeed. The big bed had been pushed back against the wall and a cover thrown over it that brushed the floor all around looked like soft-haired fur except that it was a pale blue-green and sparkled as if every hair were tipped with invisible crystals. Three books lay open on the fur, and a very curious-looking magazine with faintly luminous printing and a page of pictures that at first glance appeared three-dimensional. Also a tiny porcelain pipe encrusted with porcelain flowers, and a thin wisp of smoke floating from the bowl.

Above the bed a broad picture hung, framing a square of blue water so real Oliver had to look twice to be sure it was not rippling gently from left to right. From the ceiling swung a crystal globe on a glass cord. It turned gently, the light from the windows making curved rectangles in its sides.

Under the center window a sort of chaise longue stood which Oliver had not seen before. He could only assume it was at least partly pneumatic and had been brought in the luggage. There was a very rich-looking quilted cloth covering and hiding it, embossed all over in shining metallic patterns.

Kleph moved slowly from the door and sank upon the chaise longue with a little sigh of content. The couch accommodated itself to her body with what looked like delightful comfort. Kleph wriggled a little and then smiled up at Oliver.

"Do come on in. Sit over there, where you can see out the window. I love your beautiful spring weather. You know, there never was a May like it in civilized times." She said that quite seriously, her blue eyes on Oliver's, and there was a hint of patronage in her voice, as if the weather had been arranged especially for her.

Oliver started across the room and then paused and looked down in amazement at the floor, which felt unstable. He had not noticed before that the carpet was pure white, unspotted, and sank about an inch under the pressure of the feet. He saw then that Kleph's feet were bare, or almost bare. She wore something like gossamer buskins of filmy net, fitting her feet exactly. The bare soles were pink as if they had been rouged, and the nails had a liquid gleam like tiny mirrors. He moved closer, and was not as surprised as he should have been to see that they really were tiny mirrors, painted with some lacquer that gave them reflecting surfaces.

"Do sit down," Kleph said again, waving a white-sleeved arm toward a chair by the window. She wore a garment that looked like short, soft down, loosely cut but following perfectly every motion she made. And there was something curiously different about her very shape today. When Oliver saw her in street clothes, she had the square-shouldered, slim-flanked figure that all women strive for, but here in her lounging robe she looked—well, different. There was an almost swanlike slope to

her shoulders today, a roundness and softness to her body that looked
unfamiliar and very appealing.

"Will you have some tea?" Kleph asked, and smiled charmingly.

A low table beside her held a tray and several small covered cups,
lovely things with an inner glow like rose quartz, the color shining
deeply as if from within layer upon layer of translucence. She took up
one of the cups—there were no saucers—and offered it to Oliver.

It felt fragile and thin as paper in his hand. He could not see the contents because of the cup's cover, which seemed to be one with the cup
itself and left only a thin open crescent at the rim. Steam rose from the
opening.

Kleph took up a cup of her own and tilted it to her lips, smiling at
Oliver over the rim. She was very beautiful. The pale red hair lay in
shining loops against her head and the corona of curls like a halo above
her forehead might have been pressed down like a wreath. Every hair
kept order as perfectly as if it had been painted on, though the breeze
from the window stirred now and then among the softly shining strands.

Oliver tried the tea. Its flavor was exquisite, very hot, and the taste
that lingered upon his tongue was like the scent of flowers. It was an
extremely feminine drink. He sipped again, surprised to find how much
he liked it.

The scent of flowers seemed to increase as he drank, swirling through
his head like smoke. After the third sip there was a faint buzzing in his
ears. The bees among the flowers, perhaps, he thought incoherently—
and sipped again.

Kleph watched him, smiling.

"The others will be out all afternoon," she told Oliver comfortably.
"I thought it would give us a pleasant time to be acquainted."

Oliver was rather horrified to hear himself saying, "What makes you
talk like that?" He had had no idea of asking the question; something
seemed to have loosened his control over his own tongue.

Kleph's smile deepened. She tipped the cup to her lips and there was
indulgence in her voice when she said, "What do you mean by that?"

He waved his hand vaguely, noting with some surprise that at a
glance it seemed to have six or seven fingers as it moved past his face.

"I don't know—precision, I guess. Why don't you say 'don't', for instance?"

"In our country we are trained to speak with precision," Kleph explained. "Just as we are trained to move and dress and think with precision. Any slovenliness is trained out of us in childhood. With you, of
course—" She was polite. "With you, this does not happen to be a national fetish. With us, we have time for the amenities. We like them."

Her voice had grown sweeter and sweeter as she spoke, until by now
it was almost indistinguishable from the sweetness of the flower-scent in
Oliver's head, and the delicate flavor of the tea.

"What country do you come from?" he asked, and tilted the cup
again to drink, mildly surprised to notice that it seemed inexhaustible.

Kleph's smile was definitely patronizing this time. It didn't irritate him. Nothing could irritate him just now. The whole room swam in a beautiful rosy glow as fragrant as the flowers.

"We must not speak of that, Mr. Wilson."

"But—" Oliver paused. After all, it was, of course, none of his business. "This is a vacation?" he asked vaguely.

"Call it a pilgrimage, perhaps."

"Pilgrimage?" Oliver was so interested that for an instant his mind came back into sharp focus. "To—what?"

"I should not have said that, Mr. Wilson. Please forget it. Do you like the tea?"

"Very much."

"You will have guessed by now that it is not only tea, but an euphoriac."

Oliver stared. "Euphoriac?"

Kleph made a descriptive circle in the air with one graceful hand, and laughed. "You do not feel the effects yet? Surely you do?"

"I feel," Oliver said, "the way I'd feel after four whiskeys."

Kleph shuddered delicately. "We get our euphoria less painfully. And without the after-effects your barbarous alcohols used to have." She bit her lip. "Sorry. I must be euphoric myself to speak so freely. Please forgive me. Shall we have some music?"

Kleph leaned backward on the chaise longue and reached toward the wall beside her. The sleeve, falling away from her round tanned arm, left bare the inside of the wrist, and Oliver was startled to see there a long, rosy streak of fading scar. His inhibitions had dissolved in the fumes of the fragrant tea; he caught his breath and leaned forward to stare.

Kleph shook the sleeve back over the scar with a quick gesture. Color came into her face beneath the softly tinted tan and she would not meet Oliver's eyes. A queer shame seemed to have fallen upon her.

Oliver said tactlessly, "What is it? What's the matter?"

Still she would not look at him. Much later he understood that shame and knew she had reason for it. Now he listened blankly as she said:

"Nothing . . . nothing at all. A . . . an inoculation. All of us . . . oh, never mind. Listen to the music."

This time she reached out with the other arm. She touched nothing, but when she had held her hand near the wall a sound breathed through the room. It was the sound of water, the sighing of waves receding upon long, sloped beaches. Oliver followed Kleph's gaze toward the picture of the blue water above the bed.

The waves there were moving. More than that, the point of vision moved. Slowly the seascape drifted past, moving with the waves, following them toward shore. Oliver watched, half-hypnotized by a motion that seemed at the time quite acceptable and not in the least surprising.

The waves lifted and broke in creaming foam and ran seething up a sandy beach. Then through the sound of the water music began to breathe, and through the water itself a man's face dawned in the frame, smiling intimately into the room. He held an oddly archaic musical instrument, lute-shaped, its body striped light and dark like a melon and its long neck bent back over his shoulder. He was singing, and Oliver felt mildly astonished at the song. It was very familiar and very odd indeed. He groped through the unfamiliar rhythms and found at last a thread to catch the tune by—it was "Make-Believe," from "Showboat," but certainly a showboat that had never steamed up the Mississippi.

"What's he doing to it?" he demanded after a few moments of outraged listening. "I never heard anything like it!"

Kleph laughed and stretched out her arm again. Enigmatically she said, "We call it kyling. Never mind. How do you like this?"

It was a comedian, a man in semiclown make-up, his eyes exaggerated so that they seemed to cover half his face. He stood by a broad glass pillar before a dark curtain and sang a gay, staccato song interspersed with patter that sounded impromptu, and all the while his left hand did an intricate, musical tattoo of the nailtips on the glass of the column. He strolled around and around it as he sang. The rhythms of his fingernails blended with the song and swung widely away into patterns of their own, and blended again without a break.

It was confusing to follow. The song made even less sense than the monologue, which had something to do with a lost slipper and was full of allusions which made Kleph smile, but were utterly unintelligible to Oliver. The man had a dry, brittle style that was not very amusing, though Kleph seemed fascinated. Oliver was interested to see in him an extension and a variation of that extreme smooth confidence which marked all three of the Sanciscoes. Clearly a racial trait, he thought.

Other performances followed, some of them fragmentary as if lifted out of a completer version. One he knew. The obvious, stirring melody struck his recognition before the figures—marching men against a haze, a great banner rolling backward above them in the smoke, foreground figures striding gigantically and shouting in rhythm, "Forward, forward the lily banners go!"

The music was tinny, the images blurred and poorly colored, but there was a gusto about the performance that caught at Oliver's imagination. He stared, remembering the old film from long ago. Dennis King and a ragged chorus, singing "The Song of the Vagabonds" from—was it "Vagabond King?"

"A very old one," Kleph said apologetically. "But I like it."

The steam of the intoxicating tea swirled between Oliver and the picture. Music swelled and sank through the room and the fragrant fumes and his own euphoric brain. Nothing seemed strange. He had discovered how to drink the tea. Like nitrous oxide, the effect was not cumulative. When you reached a peak of euphoria, you could not increase the peak. It was best to wait for a slight dip in the effect of the stimulant before taking more.

Otherwise it had most of the effects of alcohol—everything after awhile dissolved into a delightful fog through which all he saw was uniformly enchanting and partook of the qualities of a dream. He questioned nothing. Afterward he was not certain how much of it he really had dreamed.

There was the dancing doll, for instance. He remembered it quite clearly, in sharp focus—a tiny, slender woman with a long-nosed, dark-eyed face and a pointed chin. She moved delicately across the white rug —knee-high, exquisite. Her features were as mobile as her body, and she danced lightly, with resounding strokes of her toes, each echoing like a bell. It was a formalized sort of dance, and she sang breathlessly in accompaniment, making amusing little grimaces. Certainly it was a portrait-doll, animated to mimic the original perfectly in voice and motion. Afterward, Oliver knew he must have dreamed it.

What else happened he was quite unable to remember later. He knew Kleph had said some curious things, but they all made sense at the time, and afterward he couldn't remember a word. He knew he had been offered little glittering candies in a transparent dish, and that some of them had been delicious and one or two so bitter his tongue still curled the next day when he recalled them, and one—Kleph sucked luxuriantly on the same kind—of a taste that was actively nauseating.

As for Kleph herself—he was frantically uncertain the next day what had really happened. He thought he could remember the softness of her white-downed arms clasped at the back of his neck, while she laughed up at him and exhaled into his face the flowery fragrance of the tea. But beyond that he was totally unable to recall anything, for awhile.

There was a brief interlude later, before the oblivion of sleep. He was almost sure he remembered a moment when the other two Sanciscoes stood looking down at him, the man scowling, the smoky-eyed woman smiling a derisive smile.

The man said, from a vast distance, "Kleph, you know this is against every rule—" His voice began in a thin hum and soared in fantastic flight beyond the range of hearing. Oliver thought he remembered the dark woman's laughter, thin and distant too, and the hum of her voice like bees in flight.

"Kleph, Kleph, you silly little fool, can we never trust you out of sight?"

Kleph's voice then said something that seemed to make no sense. "What does it matter, *here?*"

The man answered in that buzzing, faraway hum. "—matter of giving your bond before you leave, not to interfere. You know you signed the rules—"

Kleph's voice, nearer and more intelligible: "But here the difference is . . . it does not matter *here!* You both know that. How could it matter?"

Oliver felt the downy brush of her sleeve against his cheek, but he saw nothing except the slow, smoke-like ebb and flow of darkness past his eyes. He heard the voices wrangle musically from far away, and he heard them cease.

When he woke the next morning, alone in his own room, he woke with the memory of Kleph's eyes upon him very sorrowfully, her lovely tanned face looking down on him with the red hair falling fragrantly on each side of it and sadness and compassion in her eyes. He thought he had probably dreamed that. There was no reason why anyone should look at him with such sadness.

Sue telephoned that day.

"Oliver, the people who want to buy the house are here. That madwoman and her husband. Shall I bring them over?"

Oliver's mind all day had been hazy with the vague, bewildering memories of yesterday. Kleph's face kept floating before him, blotting out the room. He said, "What? I . . . oh, well, bring them if you want to. I don't see what good it'll do."

"Oliver, what's wrong with you? We agreed we needed the money, didn't we? I don't see how you can think of passing up such a wonderful bargain without even a struggle. We could get married and buy our own house right away, and you know we'll never get such an offer again for that old trash-heap. Wake up, Oliver!"

Oliver made an effort. "I know, Sue—I know. But—"

"Oliver, you've got to think of something!" Her voice was imperious.

He knew she was right. Kleph or no Kleph, the bargain shouldn't be ignored if there were any way at all of getting the tenants out. He wondered again what made the place so suddenly priceless to so many people. And what the last week in May had to do with the value of the house.

A sudden sharp curiosity pierced even the vagueness of his mind today. May's last week was so important that the whole sale of the house stood or fell upon occupancy by then. Why? *Why?*

"What's going to happen next week?" he asked rhetorically of the telephone. "Why can't they wait till these people leave? I'd knock a couple of thousand off the price if they'd—"

"You would not, Oliver Wilson! I can buy all our refrigeration units with that extra money. You'll just have to work out some way to give possession by next week, and that's that. You hear me?"

"Keep your shirt on," Oliver said pacifically. "I'm only human, but I'll try."

"I'm bringing the people over right away," Sue told him. "While the Sanciscoes are still out. Now you put your mind to work and think of something, Oliver." She paused, and her voice was reflective when she spoke again. "They're . . . awfully odd people, darling."

"Odd?"

"You'll see."

It was an elderly woman and a very young man who trailed Sue up the walk. Oliver knew immediately what had struck Sue about them. He was somehow not at all surprised to see that both wore their clothing with the familiar air of elegant self-consciousness he had come to know so well. They, too, looked around them at the beautiful, sunny afternoon with conscious enjoyment and an air of faint condescension. He knew before he heard them speak how musical their voices would be and how meticulously they would pronounce each word.

There was no doubt about it. The people of Kleph's mysterious country were arriving here in force—for something. For the last week of May? He shrugged mentally; there was no way of guessing—yet. One thing only was sure: all of them must come from that nameless land where people controlled their voices like singers and their garments like actors who could stop the reel of time itself to adjust every disordered fold.

The elderly woman took full charge of the conversation from the start. They stood together on the rickety, unpainted porch, and Sue had no chance even for introductions.

"Young man, I am Madame Hollia. This is my husband." Her voice had an underrunning current of harshness, which was perhaps age. And her face looked almost corsetted, the loose flesh coerced into something like firmness by some invisible method Oliver could not guess at. The make-up was so skillful he could not be certain it was make-up at all, but he had a definite feeling that she was much older than she looked. It would have taken a lifetime of command to put so much authority into the harsh, deep, musically controlled voice.

The young man said nothing. He was very handsome. His type, apparently, was one that does not change much no matter in what culture or country it may occur. He wore beautifully tailored garments and carried in one gloved hand a box of red leather, about the size and shape of a book.

Madame Hollia went on. "I understand your problem about the house. You wish to sell to me, but are legally bound by your lease with Omerie and his friends. Is that right?"

Oliver nodded. "But—"

"Let me finish. If Omerie can be forced to vacate before next week, you will accept our offer. Right? Very well. Hara!" She nodded to the young man beside her. He jumped to instant attention, bowed slightly, said, "Yes, Hollia," and slipped a gloved hand into his coat.

Madame Hollia took the little object offered on his palm, her gesture as she reached for it almost imperial, as if royal robes swept from her outstretched arm.

"Here," she said, "is something that may help us. My dear"—she held it out to Sue—"if you can hide this somewhere about the house, I believe your unwelcome tenants will not trouble you much longer."

Sue took the thing curiously. It looked like a tiny silver box, no more than an inch square, indented at the top and with no line to show it could be opened.

"Wait a minute," Oliver broke in uneasily. "What is it?"

"Nothing that will harm anyone, I assure you."

"Then what—"

Madame Hollia's imperious gesture at one sweep silenced him and commanded Sue forward. "Go on, my dear. Hurry, before Omerie comes back. I can assure you there is no danger to anyone."

Oliver broke in determinedly. "Madame Hollia, I'll have to know what your plans are. I—"

"Oh, Oliver, please!" Sue's fingers closed over the silver cube. "Don't worry about it. I'm sure Madame Hollia knows best. Don't you *want* to get those people out?"

"Of course I do. But I don't want the house blown up or—"

Madame Hollia's deep laughter was indulgent. "Nothing so crude, I promise you, Mr. Wilson. Remember, we want the house! Hurry, my dear."

Sue nodded and slipped hastily past Oliver into the hall. Outnumbered, he subsided uneasily. The young man, Hara, tapped a negligent foot and admired the sunlight as they waited. It was an afternoon as perfect as all of May had been, translucent gold, balmy with an edge of chill lingering in the air to point up a perfect contrast with the summer to come. Hara looked around him confidently, like a man paying just tribute to a stage-set provided wholly for himself. He even glanced up at a drone from above and followed the course of a big transcontinental plane half dissolved in golden haze high in the sun. "Quaint," he murmured in a gratified voice.

Sue came back and slipped her hand through Oliver's arm, squeezing excitedly. "There," she said. "How long will it take, Madame Hollia?"

"That will depend, my dear. Not very long. Now, Mr. Wilson, one word with you. You live here also, I understand? For your own comfort, take my advice and—"

Somewhere within the house a door slammed and a clear, high voice rang wordlessly up a rippling scale. Then there was the sound of feet on the stairs, and a single line of song. *"Come hider, love, to me—"*

Hara started, almost dropping the red leather box he held.

"Kleph!" he said in a whisper. "Or Klia. I know they both just came on from Canterbury. But I thought—"

"Hush." Madame Hollia's features composed themselves into an imperious blank. She breathed triumphantly through her nose, drew back upon herself and turned an imposing facade to the door.

Kleph wore the same softly downy robe Oliver had seen before, except that today it was not white, but a pale, clear blue that gave her tan an apricot flush. She was smiling.

"Why, Hollia!" Her tone was at its most musical. "I thought I recognized voices from home. How nice to see you. No one knew you were coming to the—" She broke off and glanced at Oliver and then away again. "Hara, too," she said. "What a pleasant surprise."

Sue said flatly, "When did *you* get back?"

Kleph smiled at her. "You must be the little Miss Johnson. Why, I did not go out at all. I was tired of sight-seeing. I have been napping in my room."

Sue drew in her breath in something that just escaped being a disbelieving sniff. A look flashed between the two women, and for an instant held—and that instant was timeless. It was an extraordinary pause in which a great deal of wordless interplay took place in the space of a second.

Oliver saw the quality of Kleph's smile at Sue, that same look of quiet confidence he had noticed so often about all of these strange people. He saw Sue's quick inventory of the other woman, and he saw how Sue squared her shoulders and stood up straight, smoothing down her summer frock over her flat hips so that for an instant she stood posed consciously, looking down on Kleph. It was deliberate. Bewildered, he glanced again at Kleph.

Kleph's shoulders sloped softly, her robe was belted to a tiny waist and hung in deep folds over frankly rounded hips. Sue's was the fashionable figure—but Sue was the first to surrender.

Kleph's smile did not falter. But in the silence there was an abrupt reversal of values, based on no more than the measureless quality of Kleph's confidence in herself, the quiet, assured smile. It was suddenly made very clear that fashion is not a constant. Kleph's curious, out-of-mode curves without warning became the norm, and Sue was a queer, angular, half-masculine creature beside her.

Oliver had no idea how it was done. Somehow the authority passed in a breath from one woman to the other. Beauty is almost wholly a matter of fashion; what is beautiful today would have been grotesque a couple of generations ago and will be grotesque a hundred years ahead. It will be worse than grotesque; it will be outmoded and therefore faintly ridiculous.

Sue was that. Kleph had only to exert her authority to make it clear to everyone on the porch. Kleph was a beauty, suddenly and very convincingly, beautiful in the accepted mode, and Sue was amusingly old-fashioned, an anachronism in her lithe, square-shouldered slimness. She did not belong. She was grotesque among these strangely immaculate people.

Sue's collapse was complete. But pride sustained her, and bewilderment. Probably she never did grasp entirely what was wrong. She gave Kleph one glance of burning resentment and when her eyes came back to Oliver there was suspicion in them, and mistrust.

Looking backward later, Oliver thought that in that moment, for the first time clearly, he began to suspect the truth. But he had no time to ponder it, for after the brief instant of enmity the three people from—elsewhere—began to speak all at once, as if in a belated attempt to cover something they did not want noticed.

Kleph said, "This beautiful weather—" and Madame Hollia said, "So fortunate to have this house—" and Hara, holding up the red leather box, said loudest of all, "Cenbe sent you this, Kleph. His latest."

Kleph put out both hands for it eagerly, the eiderdown sleeves falling back from her rounded arms. Oliver had a quick glimpse of that mysterious scar before the sleeve fell back, and it seemed to him that there was the faintest trace of a similar scar vanishing into Hara's cuff as he let his own arm drop.

"Cenbe!" Kleph cried, her voice high and sweet and delighted. "How wonderful! What period?"

"From November 1664," Hara said. "London, of course, though I think there may be some counterpoint from the 1347 November. He hasn't finished—of course." He glanced almost nervously at Oliver and Sue. "A wonderful example," he said quickly. "Marvelous. If you have the taste for it, of course."

Madame Hollia shuddered with ponderous delicacy. "That man!" she said. "Fascinating, of course—a great man. But—so *advanced!*"

"It takes a connoisseur to appreciate Cenbe's work fully," Kleph said in a slightly tart voice. "We all admit that."

"Oh yes, we all bow to Cenbe," Hollia conceded. "I confess the man terrifies me a little, my dear. Do we expect him to join us?"

"I suppose so," Kelph said. "If his—work—is not yet finished, then of course. You know Cenbe's tastes."

Hollia and Hara laughed together. "I know when to look for him, then," Hollia said. She glanced at the staring Oliver and the subdued but angry Sue, and with a commanding effort brought the subject back into line.

"So fortunate, my dear Kleph, to have this house," she declared heavily. "I saw a tridimensional of it—afterward—and it was still quite perfect. Such a fortunate coincidence. Would you consider parting with your lease, for a consideration? Say, a coronation seat at—"

"Nothing could buy us, Hollia," Kleph told her gaily, clasping the red box to her bosom.

Hollia gave her a cool stare. "You may change your mind, my dear Kleph," she said pontifically. "There is still time. You can always reach us through Mr. Wilson here. We have rooms up the street in the Montgomery House—nothing like yours, of course, but they will do. For us, they will do."

Oliver blinked. The Montgomery House was the most expensive hotel in town. Compared to this collapsing old ruin, it was a palace. There was no understanding these people. Their values seemed to have suffered a complete reversal.

Madame Hollia moved majestically toward the steps.

"Very pleasant to see you, my dear," she said over one well-padded shoulder. "Enjoy your stay. My regards to Omerie and Klia. Mr. Wilson—" she nodded toward the walk. "A word with you."

Oliver followed her down toward the street. Madame Hollia paused halfway there and touched his arm.

"One word of advice," she said huskily. "You say you sleep here? Move out, young man. Move out before tonight."

Oliver was searching in a half-desultory fashion for the hiding place Sue had found for the mysterious silver cube, when the first sounds from above began to drift down the stairwell toward him. Kleph had closed her door, but the house was old and strange qualities in the noise overhead seemed to seep through the woodwork like an almost visible stain.

It was music, in a way. But much more than music. And it was a terrible sound, the sounds of calamity and of all human reaction to calamity, everything from hysteria to heartbreak, from irrational joy to rationalized acceptance.

The calamity was—single. The music did not attempt to correlate all human sorrows; it focused sharply upon one and followed the ramifications out and out. Oliver recognized these basics to the sounds in a very brief moment. They were essentials, and they seemed to beat into his brain with the first strains of the music which was so much more than music.

But when he lifted his head to listen he lost all grasp upon the meaning of the noise and it was sheer medley and confusion. To think of it was to blur it hopelessly in the mind, and he could not recapture that first instant of unreasoning acceptance.

He went upstairs almost in a daze, hardly knowing what he was doing. He pushed Kleph's door open. He looked inside—

What he saw there he could not afterward remember except in a blurring as vague as the blurred ideas the music roused in his brain. Half the room had vanished behind a mist, and the mist was a three-dimensional screen upon which were projected— He had no words for them. He was not even sure if the projections were visual. The mist was spinning with motion and sound, but essentially it was neither sound nor motion that Oliver saw.

This was a work of art. Oliver knew no name for it. It transcended all art-forms he knew, blended them, and out of the blend produced subtleties his mind could not begin to grasp. Basically, this was the attempt of a master-composer to correlate every essential aspect of a vast human experience into something that could be conveyed in a few moments to every sense at once.

The shifting visions on the screen were not pictures in themselves, but hints of pictures, subtly selected outlines that plucked at the mind and with one deft touch set whole chords ringing through the memory. Perhaps each beholder reacted differently, since it was in the eye and the mind of the beholder that the truth of the picture lay. No two would be aware of the same symphonic panorama, but each would see essentially the same terrible story unfold.

Every sense was touched by that deft and merciless genius. Color and shape and motion flickered in the screen, hinting much, evoking unbearable memories deep in the mind; odors floated from the screen and touched the heart of the beholder more poignantly than anything visual could do. The skin crawled sometimes as if to a tangible cold hand laid upon it. The tongue curled with remembered bitterness and remembered sweet.

It was outrageous. It violated the innermost privacies of a man's mind, called up secret things long ago walled off behind mental scar tissue, forced its terrible message upon the beholder relentlessly though the mind might threaten to crack beneath the stress of it.

And yet, in spite of all this vivid awareness, Oliver did not know what calamity the screen portrayed. That it was real, vast, overwhelmingly dreadful he could not doubt. That it had once happened was unmistakable. He caught flashing glimpses of human faces distorted with grief and disease and death—real faces, faces that had once lived and were seen now in the instant of dying. He saw men and women in rich clothing superimposed in panorama upon reeling thousands of ragged folk, great throngs of them swept past the sight in an instant, and he saw that death made no distinction among them.

He saw lovely women laugh and shake their curls, and the laughter shriek into hysteria and the hysteria into music. He saw one man's face, over and over—a long, dark, saturnine face, deeply lined, sorrowful, the face of a powerful man wise in worldliness, urbane—and helpless. That face was for awhile a recurring motif, always more tortured, more helpless than before.

The music broke off in the midst of a rising glide. The mist vanished and the room reappeared before him. The anguished dark face for an instant seemed to Oliver printed everywhere he looked, like after-vision on the eyelids. He knew that face. He had seen it before, not often, but he should know its name—

"Oliver, Oliver—" Kleph's sweet voice came out of a fog at him. He was leaning dizzily against the doorpost looking down into her eyes. She, too, had that dazed blankness he must show on his own face. The power of the dreadful symphony still held them both. But even in this confused moment Oliver saw that Kleph had been enjoying the experience.

He felt sickened to the depths of his mind, dizzy with sickness and revulsion because of the superimposing of human miseries he had just beheld. But Kleph—only appreciation showed upon her face. To her it had been magnificence, and magnificence only.

Irrelevantly Oliver remembered the nauseating candies she had enjoyed, the nauseating odors of strange food that drifted sometimes through the hall from her room.

What was it she had said downstairs a little while ago? Connoisseur, that was it. Only a connoisseur could appreciate work as—as *advanced* —as the work of someone called Cenbe.

A whiff of intoxicating sweetness curled past Oliver's face. Something cool and smooth was pressed into his hand.

"Oh, Oliver, I am so sorry," Kleph's voice murmured contritely. "Here, drink the euphoriac and you will feel better. Please drink!"

The familiar fragrance of the hot sweet tea was on his tongue before he knew he had complied. Its relaxing fumes floated up through his brain and in a moment or two the world felt stable around him again. The room was as it had always been. And Kleph—

Her eyes were very bright. Sympathy showed in them for him, but for herself she was still brimmed with the high elation of what she had just been experiencing.

"Come and sit down," she said gently, tugging at his arm. "I am so sorry—I should not have played that over, where you could hear it. I have no excuse, really. It was only that I forgot what the effect might be on one who had never heard Cenbe's symphonies before. I was so impatient to see what he had done with . . . with his new subject. I am so very sorry, Oliver!"

"What was it?" His voice sounded steadier than he had expected. The tea was responsible for that. He sipped again, glad of the consoling euphoria its fragrance brought.

"A . . . a composite intepretation of . . . oh, Oliver, you know I must not answer questions!"

"But—"

"No—drink your tea and forget what it was you saw. Think of other things. Here, we will have music—another kind of music, something gay—"

She reached for the wall beside the window, and as before, Oliver saw the broad framed picture of blue water above the bed ripple and grow pale. Through it another scene began to dawn like shapes rising beneath the surface of the sea.

He had a glimpse of a dark-curtained stage upon which a man in a tight dark tunic and hose moved with a restless, sidelong pace, his hands and face startlingly pale against the black about him. He limped; he had a crooked back and he spoke familiar lines. Oliver had seen John Barrymore once as the Crook-Backed Richard, and it seemed vaguely outrageous to him that any other actor should essay that difficult part. This one he had never seen before, but the man had a fascinatingly smooth manner and his interpretation of the Plantagenet king was quite new and something Shakespeare probably never dreamed of.

"No," Kleph said, "not this. Nothing gloomy." And she put out her hand again. The nameless new Richard faded and there was a swirl of changing pictures and changing voices, all blurred together, before the scene steadied upon a stage-full of dancers in pastel ballet skirts, drifting effortlessly through some complicated pattern of motion. The music that went with it was light and effortless too. The room filled up with the clear, floating melody.

Oliver set down his cup. He felt much surer of himself now, and he thought the euphoriac had done all it could for him. He didn't want to blur again mentally. There were things he meant to learn about. Now. He considered how to begin.

Kleph was watching him. "That Hollia," she said suddenly. "She wants to buy the house?"

Oliver nodded. "She's offering a lot of money. Sue's going to be awfully disappointed if—" He hesitated. Perhaps, after all, Sue would not be disappointed. He remembered the little silver cube with the enigmatic function and he wondered if he should mention it to Kleph. But the euphoriac had not reached that level of his brain, and he remembered his duty to Sue and was silent.

Kleph shook her head, her eyes upon his warm with—was it sympathy?

"Believe me," she said, "you will not find that—important—after all. I promise you, Oliver."

He stared at her. "I wish you'd explain."

Kleph laughed on a note more sorrowful than amused. But it occurred to Oliver suddenly that there was no longer condescension in her voice. Imperceptibly that air of delicate amusement had vanished from her manner toward him. The cool detachment that still marked Omerie's attitude, and Klia's, was not in Kleph's any more. It was a subtlety he did not think she could assume. It had to come spontaneously or not at all. And for no reason he was willing to examine, it became suddenly very important to Oliver that Kleph should not condescend to him, that she should feel toward him as he felt toward her. He would not think of it.

He looked down at his cup, rose-quartz, exhaling a thin plume of steam from its crescent-slit opening. This time, he thought, maybe he could make the tea work for him. For he remembered how it loosened the tongue, and there was a great deal he needed to know. The idea that had come to him on the porch in the instant of silent rivalry between Kleph and Sue seemed now too fantastic to entertain. But some answer there must be.

Kleph herself gave him the opening.

"I must not take too much euphoriac this afternoon," she said, smiling at him over her pink cup. "It will make me drowsy, and we are going out this evening with friends."

"More friends?" Oliver asked. "From your country?"

Kleph nodded. "Very dear friends we have expected all this week."

"I wish you'd tell me," Oliver said bluntly, "where it is you come from. It isn't from here. Your culture is too different from ours—even your names—" He broke off as Kleph shook her head.

"I wish I could tell you. But that is against all the rules. It is even against the rules for me to be here talking to you now."

"What rules?"

She made a helpless gesture. "You must not ask me, Oliver." She leaned back on the chaise longue that adjusted itself luxuriously to the motion, and smiled very sweetly at him. "We must not talk about things like that. Forget it, listen to the music, enjoy yourself if you can—" She closed her eyes and laid her head back against the cushions. Oliver saw the round tanned throat swell as she began to hum a tune. Eyes still closed, she sang again the words she had sung upon the stairs. *"Come hider, love, to me—"*

A memory clicked over suddenly in Oliver's mind. He had never heard the queer, lagging tune before, but he thought he knew the words. He remembered what Hollia's husband had said when he heard that line of song, and he leaned forward. She would not answer a direct question, but perhaps—

"Was the weather this warm in Canterbury?" he asked, and held his breath. Kleph hummed another line of the song and shook her head, eyes still closed.

"It was autumn there," she said. "But bright, wonderfully bright. Even their clothing, you know . . . everyone was singing that new song, and I can't get it out of my head." She sang another line, and the words were almost unintelligible—English, yet not an English Oliver could understand.

He stood up. "Wait," he said. "I want to find something. Back in a minute."

She opened her eyes and smiled mistily at him, still humming. He went downstairs as fast as he could—the stairway swayed a little, though his head was nearly clear now—and into the library. The book he wanted was old and battered, interlined with the penciled notes of his college days. He did not remember very clearly where the passage he wanted was, but he thumbed fast through the columns and by sheer luck found it within a few minutes. Then he went back upstairs, feeling strange emptiness in his stomach because of what he almost believed now.

"Kleph," he said firmly, "I know that song. I know the year it was new."

Her lids rose slowly; she looked at him through a mist of euphoriac. He was not sure she had understood. For a long moment she held him with her gaze. Then she put out one downy-sleeved arm and spread her tanned fingers toward him. She laughed deep in her throat.

"Come hider, love, to me," she said.

He crossed the room slowly, took her hand. The fingers closed warmly about his. She pulled him down so that he had to kneel beside her. Her other arm lifted. Again she laughed, very softly, and closed her eyes, lifting her face to his.

The kiss was warm and long. He caught something of her own euphoria from the fragrance of the tea breathed into his face. And he was startled at the end of the kiss, when the clasp of her arms loosened about his neck, to feel the sudden rush of her breath against his cheek. There were tears on her face, and the sound she made was a sob.

He held her off and looked down in amazement. She sobbed once more, caught a deep breath, and said, "Oh, Oliver, Oliver—" Then she shook her head and pulled free, turning away to hide her face. "I . . .

I am sorry," she said unevenly. "Please forgive me. It does not matter
. . . I *know* it does not matter . . . but—"

"What's wrong? What doesn't matter?"

"Nothing. Nothing . . . please forget it. Nothing at all." She got a
handkerchief from the table and blew her nose, smiling at him with an
effect of radiance through the tears.

Suddenly he was very angry. He had heard enough evasions and mystifying half-truths. He said roughly, "Do you think I'm crazy? I know
enough now to—"

"Oliver, please!" She held up her own cup, steaming fragrantly.
"Please, no more questions. Here, euphoria is what you need, Oliver.
Euphoria, not answers."

"What year was it when you heard that song in Canterbury?" he demanded, pushing the cup aside.

She blinked at him, tears bright on her lashes. "Why . . . what year
do you think?"

"I know," Oliver told her grimly. "I know the year that song was
popular. I know you just came from Canterbury—Hollia's husband said
so. It's May now, but it was autumn in Canterbury, and you just came
from there, so lately the song you heard is still running through your
head. Chaucer's Pardoner sang that song sometime around the end of the
fourteenth century. Did you see Chaucer, Kleph? What was it like in
England that long ago?"

Kleph's eyes fixed his for a silent moment. Then her shoulders
drooped and her whole body went limp with resignation beneath the soft
blue robe. "I am a fool," she said gently. "It must have been easy to trap
me. You really believe—what you say?"

Oliver nodded.

She said in a low voice, "Few people do believe it. That is one of our
maxims, when we travel. We are safe from much suspicion because people before The Travel began will not believe."

The emptiness in Oliver's stomach suddenly doubled in volume. For
an instant the bottom dropped out of time itself and the universe was
unsteady about him. He felt sick. He felt naked and helpless. There was
a buzzing in his ears and the room dimmed before him.

He had not really believed—not until this instant. He had expected
some rational explanation from her that would tidy all his wild half-
thoughts and suspicions into something a man could accept as believable. Not this.

Kleph dabbed at her eyes with the pale-blue handkerchief and smiled
tremulously.

"I know," she said. "It must be a terrible thing to accept. To have all
your concepts turned upside down— We know it from childhood, of
course, but for you . . . here, Oliver. The euphoriac will make it
easier."

He took the cup, the faint stain of her lip rouge still on the crescent
opening. He drank, feeling the dizzy sweetness spiral through his head,

and his brain turned a little in his skull as the volatile fragrance took effect. With that turning, focus shifted and all his values with it.

He began to feel better. The flesh settled on his bones again, and the warm clothing of temporal assurance settled upon his flesh, and he was no longer naked and reeling in the vortex of unstable time.

"The story is very simple, really," Kleph said. "We—travel. Our own time is not terribly far ahead of yours. No, I must not say how far. But we still remember your songs and poets and some of your great actors. We are a people of much leisure, and we cultivate the art of enjoying ourselves.

"This is a tour we are making—a tour of a year's seasons. Vintage seasons. That autumn in Canterbury was the most magnificent autumn our researchers could discover anywhere. We rode in a pilgrimage to the shrine—it was a wonderful experience, though the clothing was a little hard to manage.

"Now this month of May is almost over—the loveliest May in recorded times. A perfect May in a wonderful period. You have no way of knowing what a good, gay period you live in, Oliver. The very feeling in the air of the cities—that wonderful national confidence and happiness —everything going as smoothly as a dream. There were other Mays with fine weather, but each of them had a war or a famine, or something else wrong." She hesitated, grimaced and went on rapidly. "In a few days we are to meet at a coronation in Rome," she said. "I think the year will be 800—Christmastime. We—"

"But why," Oliver interrupted, "did you insist on this house? Why do the others want to get it away from you?"

Kleph stared at him. He saw the tears rising again in small bright crescents that gathered above her lower lids. He saw the look of obstinacy that came upon her soft, tanned face. She shook her head.

"You must not ask me that." She held out the steaming cup. "Here, drink and forget what I have said. I can tell you no more. No more at all."

When he woke, for a little while he had no idea where he was. He did not remember leaving Kleph or coming to his own room. He didn't care, just then. For he woke to a sense of overwhelming terror.

The dark was full of it. His brain rocked on waves of fear and pain. He lay motionless, too frightened to stir, some atavistic memory warning him to lie quiet until he knew from which direction the danger threatened. Reasonless panic broke over him in a tidal flow; his head ached with its violence and the dark throbbed to the same rhythms.

A knock sounded at the door. Omerie's deep voice said, "Wilson! Wilson, are you awake?"

Oliver tried twice before he had breath to answer. "Y-yes—what is it?"

The knob rattled. Omerie's dim figure groped for the light switch and the room sprang into visibility. Omerie's face was drawn with strain, and he held one hand to his head as if it ached in rhythm with Oliver's.

It was in that moment, before Omerie spoke again, that Oliver remembered Hollia's warning. "Move out, young man—move out before tonight." Wildly he wondered what threatened them all in this dark house that throbbed with the rhythms of pure terror.

Omerie in an angry voice answered the unspoken question.

"Someone has planted a subsonic in the house, Wilson. Kleph thinks you may know where it is."

"S-subsonic?"

"Call it a gadget," Omerie interpreted impatiently. "Probably a small metal box that—"

Oliver said, "Oh," in a tone that must have told Omerie everything.

"Where is it?" he demanded. "Quick. Let's get this over."

"I d-don't know." With an effort Oliver controlled the chattering of his teeth. "Y-you mean all this—all this is just from the little box?"

"Of course. Now tell me how to find it before we all go crazy."

Oliver got shakily out of bed, groping for his robe with nerveless hands. "I s-suppose she hid it somewhere downstairs," he said. "S-she wasn't gone long."

Omerie got the story out of him in a few brief questions. He clicked his teeth in exasperation when Oliver had finished it.

"That stupid Hollia—"

"Omerie!" Kleph's plaintive voice wailed from the hall. "Please hurry, Omerie! This is too much to stand! Oh, Omerie, please!"

Oliver stood up abruptly. Then a redoubled wave of the inexplicable pain seemed to explode in his skull at the motion, and he clutched the bedpost and reeled.

"Go find the thing yourself," he heard himself saying dizzily. "I can't even walk—"

Omerie's own temper was drawn wire-tight by the pressure in the room. He seized Oliver's shoulder and shook him, saying in a tight voice, "You let it in—now help us get it out, or—"

"It's a gadget out of your world, not mine!" Oliver said furiously.

And then it seemed to him there was a sudden coldness and silence in the room. Even the pain and the senseless terror paused for a moment. Omerie's pale, cold eyes fixed upon Oliver a stare so chill he could almost feel the ice in it.

"What do you know about our—world?" Omerie demanded.

Oliver did not speak a word. He did not need to; his face must have betrayed what he knew. He was beyond concealment in the stress of this nighttime terror he still could not understand.

Omerie bared his white teeth and said three perfectly unintelligible words. Then he stepped to the door and snapped, "Kleph!"

Oliver could see the two women huddled together in the hall, shaking violently with involuntary waves of that strange, synthetic terror. Klia, in a luminous green gown, was rigid with control, but Kleph made no effort whatever at repression. Her downy robe had turned soft gold tonight; she shivered in it and the tears ran down her face unchecked.

"Kleph," Omerie said in a dangerous voice, "you were euphoric again yesterday?"

Kleph darted a scared glance at Oliver and nodded guiltily.

"You talked too much." It was a complete indictment in one sentence. "You know the rules, Kleph. You will not be allowed to travel again if anyone reports this to the authorities."

Kleph's lovely creamy face creased suddenly into impenitent dimples.

"I know it was wrong. I am very sorry—but you will not stop me if Cenbe says no."

Klia flung out her arms in a gesture of helpless anger. Omerie shrugged. "In this case, as it happens, no great harm is done," he said, giving Oliver an unfathomable glance. "But it might have been serious. Next time perhaps it will be. I must have a talk with Cenbe."

"We must find the subsonic first of all," Klia reminded them, shivering. "If Kleph is afraid to help, she can go out for awhile. I confess I am very sick of Kleph's company just now."

"We could give up the house!" Kleph cried wildly. "Let Hollia have it! How can you stand this long enough to hunt—"

"Give up the house?" Klia echoed. "You must be mad! With all our invitations out?"

"There will be no need for that," Omerie said. "We can find it if we all hunt. You feel able to help?" He looked at Oliver.

With an effort Oliver controlled his own senseless panic as the waves of it swept through the room. "Yes," he said. "But what about me? What are you going to do?"

"That should be obvious," Omerie said, his pale eyes in the dark face regarding Oliver impassively. "Keep you in the house until we go. We can certainly do no less. You understand that. And there is no reason for us to do more, as it happens. Silence is all we need to impose. It is all we promised when we signed our travel papers."

"But—" Oliver groped for the fallacy in that reasoning. It was no use. He could not think clearly. Panic surged insanely through his mind from the very air around him. "All right," he said. "Let's hunt."

It was dawn before they found the box, tucked inside the ripped seam of a sofa cushion. Omerie took it upstairs without a word. Five minutes later the pressure in the air abruptly dropped and peace fell blissfully upon the house.

"They will try again," Omerie said to Oliver at the door of the back bedroom. "We must watch for that. As for you, I must see that you remain in the house until Friday. For your own comfort, I advise you to let me know if Hollia offers any further tricks. I confess I am not quite sure how to enforce your staying indoors. I could use methods that would make you very uncomfortable. I would prefer to accept your word on it."

Oliver hesitated. The relaxing of pressure upon his brain had left him exhausted and stupid, and he was not at all sure what to say.

Omerie went on after a moment. "It was partly our fault for not insuring that we have the house to ourselves," he said. "Living here with us, you could scarcely help suspecting. Shall we say that in return for your promise, I reimburse you in part for losing the sale price on this house?"

Oliver thought that over. It would pacify Sue a little. And it meant only two days indoors. Besides, what good would escaping do? What could he say to outsiders that would not lead him straight to a padded cell?

"All right," he said wearily. "I promise."

By Friday morning there was still no sign from Hollia. Sue telephoned at noon. Oliver knew the crackle of her voice over the wire when Kleph took the call. Even the crackle sounded hysterical; Sue saw her bargain slipping hopelessly through her grasping little fingers.

Kleph's voice was soothing. "I am sorry," she said many times, in the intervals when the voice paused. "I am truly sorry. Believe me, you will find it does not matter. I know . . . I am sorry—"

She turned from the phone at last. "The girl says Hollia has given up," she told the others.

"Not Hollia," Klia said firmly.

Omerie shrugged. "We have very little time left. If she intends anything more, it will be tonight. We must watch for it."

"Oh, not tonight!" Kleph's voice was horrified. "Not even Hollia would do that!"

"Hollia, my dear, in her own way is quite as unscrupulous as you are," Omerie told her with a smile.

"But—would she spoil things for us just because she can't be here?"

"What do you think?" Klia demanded.

Oliver ceased to listen. There was no making sense out of their talk, but he knew that by tonight whatever the secret was must surely come into the open at last. He was willing to wait and see.

For two days excitement had been building up in the house and the three who shared it with him. Even the servants felt it and were nervous and unsure of themselves. Oliver had given up asking questions—it only embarrassed his tenants—and watched.

All the chairs in the house were collected in the three front bedrooms. The furniture was rearranged to make room for them, and dozens of covered cups had been set out on trays. Oliver recognized Kleph's rose-quartz set among the rest. No steam rose from the thin crescent-openings, but the cups were full. Oliver lifted one and felt a heavy liquid move within it, like something half-solid, sluggishly.

Guests were obviously expected, but the regular dinner hour of nine came and went, and no one had yet arrived. Dinner was finished; the servants went home. The Sanciscoes went to their rooms to dress, amid a feeling of mounting tension.

Oliver stepped out on the porch after dinner, trying in vain to guess what it was that had wrought such a pitch of expectancy in the house. There was a quarter moon swimming in haze on the horizon, but the stars which had made every night of May this far a dazzling translucency, were very dim tonight. Clouds had begun to gather at sundown, and the undimmed weather of the whole month seemed ready to break at last.

Behind Oliver the door opened a little, and closed. He caught Kleph's fragrance before he turned, and a faint whiff of the fragrance of the euphoriac she was much too fond of drinking. She came to his side and slipped a hand into his, looking up into his face in the darkness.

"Oliver," she said very softly. "Promise me one thing. Promise me not to leave the house tonight."

"I've already promised that," he said a little irritably.

"I know. But tonight—I have a very particular reason for wanting you indoors tonight." She leaned her head against his shoulder for a moment, and despite himself his irritation softened. He had not seen Kleph alone since that last night of her revelations; he supposed he never would be alone with her again for more than a few minutes at a time. But he knew he would not forget those two bewildering evenings. He knew too, now, that she was very weak and foolish—but she was still Kleph and he had held her in his arms, and was not likely ever to forget it.

"You might be—hurt—if you went out tonight," she was saying in a muffled voice. "I know it will not matter, in the end, but—remember you promised, Oliver."

She was gone again, and the door had closed behind her, before he could voice the futile questions in his mind.

The guests began to arrive just before midnight. From the head of the stairs Oliver saw them coming in by twos and threes, and was astonished at how many of these people from the future must have gathered here in the past weeks. He could see quite clearly now how they differed from the norm of his own period. Their physical elegance was what one noticed first—perfect grooming, meticulous manners, meticulously controlled voices. But because they were all idle, all in a way, sensation-hunters, there was a certain shrillness underlying their voices, especially when heard all together. Petulance and self-indulgence showed beneath the good manners. And tonight, an all-pervasive excitement.

By one o'clock everyone had gathered in the front rooms. The teacups had begun to steam, apparently of themselves, around midnight, and the house was full of the faint, thin fragrance that induced a sort of euphoria all through the rooms, breathed in with the perfume of the tea.

It made Oliver feel light and drowsy. He was determined to sit up as long as the others did, but he must have dozed off in his own room, by the window, an unopened book in his lap.

For when it happened he was not sure for a few minutes whether or not it was a dream.

The vast, incredible crash was louder than sound. He felt the whole
house shake under him, felt rather than heard the timbers grind upon
one another like broken bones, while he was still in the borderland of
sleep. When he woke fully he was on the floor among the shattered
fragments of the window.

How long or short a time he had lain there he did not know. The world
was still stunned with that tremendous noise, or his ears still deaf from
it, for there was no sound anywhere.

He was halfway down the hall toward the front rooms when sound
began to return from outside. It was a low, indescribable rumble at
first, prickled with countless tiny distant screams. Oliver's eardrums
ached from the terrible impact of the vast unheard noise, but the numbness was wearing off and he heard before he saw it the first voices of the
stricken city.

The door to Kleph's room resisted him for a moment. The house had
settled a little from the violence of the—the explosion?—and the
frame was out of line. When he got the door open he could only stand
blinking stupidly into the darkness within. All the lights were out, but
there was a breathless sort of whispering going on in many voices.

The chairs were drawn around the broad front windows so that everyone could see out; the air swam with the fragrance of euphoria. There
was light enough here from outside for Oliver to see that a few onlookers still had their hands to their ears, but all were craning eagerly
forward to see.

Through a dreamlike haze Oliver saw the city spread out with impossible distinctness below the window. He knew quite well that a row of
houses across the street blocked the view—yet he was looking over the
city now, and he could see it in a limitless panorama from here to the
horizon. The houses between had vanished.

On the far skyline fire was already a solid mass, painting the low
clouds crimson. That sulphurous light reflecting back from the sky
upon the city made clear the rows upon rows of flattened houses with
flame beginning to lick up among them, and farther out the formless
rubble of what had been houses a few minutes ago and was now nothing
at all.

The city had begun to be vocal. The noise of the flames rose loudest,
but you could hear a rumble of human voices like the beat of surf a long
way off, and the staccato noises of screaming made a sort of pattern that
came and went continuously through the web of sound. Threading it in
undulating waves the shrieks of sirens knit the web together into a terrible symphony that had, in its way, a strange, inhuman beauty.

Briefly through Oliver's stunned incredulity went the memory of that
other symphony Kleph had played here one day, another catastrophe
retold in terms of music and moving shapes.

He said hoarsely, "Kleph—"

The tableau by the window broke. Every head turned, and Oliver
saw the faces of strangers staring at him, some few in embarrassment

avoiding his eyes, but most seeking them out with that avid, inhuman curiosity which is common to a type in all crowds at accident scenes. But these people were here by design, audience at a vast disaster timed almost for their coming.

Kleph got up unsteadily, her velvet dinner gown tripping her as she rose. She set down a cup and swayed a little as she came toward the door, saying, "Oliver . . . Oliver—" in a sweet, uncertain voice. She was drunk, he saw, and wrought up by the catastrophe to a pitch of stimulation in which she was not very sure what she was doing.

Oliver heard himself saying in a thin voice not his own, "W-what was it, Kleph? What happened? What—" But *happened* seemed so inadequate a word for the incredible panorama below that he had to choke back hysterical laughter upon the struggling questions, and broke off entirely, trying to control the shaking that had seized his body.

Kleph made an unsteady stoop and seized a steaming cup. She came to him, swaying, holding it out—her panacea for all ills.

"Here, drink it, Oliver—we are all quite safe here, quite safe." She thrust the cup to his lips and he gulped automatically, grateful for the fumes that began their slow, coiling surcease in his brain with the first swallow.

"It was a meteor," Kleph was saying. "Quite a small meteor, really. We are perfectly safe here. This house was never touched."

Out of some cell of the unconscious Oliver heard himself saying incoherently, "Sue? Is Sue—" he could not finish.

Kleph thrust the cup at him again. "I think she may be safe—for awhile. Please, Oliver—forget about all that and drink."

"But you *knew!*" Realization of that came belatedly to his stunned brain. "You could have given warning, or—"

"How could we change the past?" Kleph asked. "We knew—but could we stop the meteor? Or warn the city? Before we come we must give our word never to interfere—"

Their voices had risen imperceptibly to be audible above the rising volume of sound from below. The city was roaring now, with flames and cries and the crash of falling buildings. Light in the room turned lurid and pulsed upon the walls and ceiling in red light and redder dark.

Downstairs a door slammed. Someone laughed. It was high, hoarse, angry laughter. Then from the crowd in the room someone gasped and there was a chorus of dismayed cries. Oliver tried to focus upon the window and the terrible panorama beyond, and found he could not.

It took several seconds of determined blinking to prove that more than his own vision was at fault. Kleph whimpered softly and moved against him. His arms closed about her automatically, and he was grateful for the warm, solid flesh against him. This much at least he could touch and be sure of, though everything else that was happening might be a dream. Her perfume and the heady perfume of the tea rose together in his head, and for an instant, holding her in this embrace that must certainly be the last time he ever held her, he did not care that something had gone terribly wrong with the very air of the room.

It was blindness—not continuous, but a series of swift, widening ripples between which he could catch glimpses of the other faces in the room, strained and astonished in the flickering light from the city.

The ripples came faster. There was only a blink of sight between them now, and the blinks grew briefer and briefer, the intervals of darkness more broad.

From downstairs the laughter rose again up the stairwell. Oliver thought he knew the voice. He opened his mouth to speak, but a door nearby slammed open before he could find his tongue, and Omerie shouted down the stairs.

"Hollia?" he roared above the roaring of the city. "Hollia, is that you?"

She laughed again, triumphantly. "I warned you!" her hoarse, harsh voice called. "Now come out in the street with the rest of us if you want to see any more!"

"Hollia!" Omerie shouted desperately. "Stop this or—"

The laughter was derisive. "What will you do, Omerie? This time I hid it too well—come down in the street if you want to watch the rest."

There was angry silence in the house. Oliver could feel Kleph's quick, excited breathing light upon his cheek, feel the soft motions of her body in his arms. He tried consciously to make the moment last, stretch it out to infinity. Everything had happened too swiftly to impress very clearly on his mind anything except what he could touch and hold. He held her in an embrace made consciously light, though he wanted to clasp her in a tight, despairing grip, because he was sure this was the last embrace they would ever share.

The eye-straining blinks of light and blindness went on. From far away below the roar of the burning city rolled on, threaded together by the long, looped cadences of the sirens that linked all sounds into one.

Then in the bewildering dark another voice sounded from the hall downstairs. A man's voice, very deep, very melodious, saying:

"What is this? What are you doing here? Hollia—is that you?"

Oliver felt Kleph stiffen in his arms. She caught her breath, but she said nothing in the instant while heavy feet began to mount the stairs, coming up with a solid, confident tread that shook the old house to each step.

Then Kleph thrust herself hard out of Oliver's arms. He heard her high, sweet, excited voice crying, "Cenbe! Cenbe!" and she ran to meet the newcomer through the waves of dark and light that swept the shaken house.

Oliver staggered a little and felt a chair seat catching the back of his legs. He sank into it and lifted to his lips the cup he still held. Its steam was warm and moist in his face, though he could scarcely make out the shape of the rim.

He lifted it with both hands and drank.

When he opened his eyes it was quite dark in the room. Also it was silent except for a thin, melodious humming almost below the threshold of sound. Oliver struggled with the memory of a monstrous nightmare. He put it resolutely out of his mind and sat up, feeling an unfamiliar bed creak and sway under him.

This was Kleph's room. But no—Kleph's no longer. Her shining hangings were gone from the walls, her white resilient rug, her pictures. The room looked as it had looked before she came, except for one thing.

In the far corner was a table—a block of translucent stuff—out of which light poured softly. A man sat on a low stool before it, leaning forward, his heavy shoulders outlined against the glow. He wore earphones and he was making quick, erratic notes upon a pad on his knee, swaying a little as if to the tune of unheard music.

The curtains were drawn, but from beyond them came a distant, muffled roaring that Oliver remembered from his nightmare. He put a hand to his face, aware of a feverish warmth and a dipping of the room before his eyes. His head ached, and there was a deep malaise in every limb and nerve.

As the bed creaked, the man in the corner turned, sliding the earphones down like a collar. He had a strong, sensitive face above a dark beard, trimmed short. Oliver had never seen him before, but he had that air Oliver knew so well by now, of remoteness which was the knowledge of time itself lying like a gulf between them.

When he spoke his deep voice was impersonally kind.

"You had too much euphoriac, Wilson," he said, aloofly sympathetic. "You slept a long while."

"How long?" Oliver's throat felt sticky when he spoke.

The man did not answer. Oliver shook his head experimentally. He said, "I thought Kleph said you don't get hangovers from—" Then another thought interrupted the first, and he said quickly, "Where is Kleph?" He looked confusedly toward the door.

"They should be in Rome by now. Watching Charlemagne's coronation at St. Peter's on Christmas Day a thousand years from here."

That was not a thought Oliver could grasp clearly. His aching brain sheered away from it; he found thinking at all was strangely difficult. Staring at the man, he traced an idea painfully to its conclusion.

"So they've gone on—but you stayed behind. Why? You . . . you're Cenbe? I heard your—symphonia, Kleph called it."

"You heard part of it. I have not finished yet. I needed—this." Cenbe inclined his head toward the curtains beyond which the subdued roaring still went on.

"You needed—the meteor?" The knowledge worked painfully through his dulled brain until it seemed to strike some area still untouched by the aching, an area still alive to implication. "The *meteor?* But—"

There was a power implicit in Cenbe's raised hand that seemed to push Oliver down upon the bed again. Cenbe said patiently, "The worst of it is past now, for awhile. Forget it if you can. That was days ago. I said you were asleep for some time. I let you rest. I knew this house would be safe—from the fire at least."

"Then—something more's to come?" Oliver only mumbled his question. He was not sure he wanted an answer. He had been curious so long, and now that knowledge lay almost within reach, something about his brain seemed to refuse to listen. Perhaps this weariness, this feverish, dizzy feeling would pass as the effect of the euphoriac wore off.

Cenbe's voice ran on smoothly, soothingly, almost as if Cenbe too did not want him to think. It was easiest to lie here and listen.

"I am a composer," Cenbe was saying. "I happen to be interested in interpreting certain forms of disaster into my own terms. That is why I stayed on. The others were dilettantes. They came for the May weather and the spectacle. The aftermath—well why should they wait for that? As for myself—I suppose I am a connoisseur. I find the aftermath rather fascinating. And I need it. I need to study it at first hand, for my own purposes."

His eyes dwelt upon Oliver for an instant very keenly, like a physician's eyes, impersonal and observant. Absently he reached for his stylus and the note pad. And as he moved, Oliver saw a familiar mark on the underside of the thick, tanned wrist.

"Kleph had that scar, too," he heard himself whisper. "And the others."

Cenbe nodded. "Inoculation. It was necessary, under the circumstances. We did not want disease to spread in our own time-world."

"Disease?"

Cenbe shrugged. "You would not recognize the name."

"But, if you can inoculate against disease—" Oliver thrust himself up on an aching arm. He had a half-grasp upon a thought now which he did not want to let go. Effort seemed to make the ideas come more clearly through his mounting confusion. With enormous effort he went on.

"I'm getting it now," he said. "Wait. I've been trying to work this out. You can change history? You can! I know you can. Kleph said she had to promise not to interfere. You all had to promise. Does that mean you really could change your own past—our time?"

Cenbe laid down his pad again. He looked at Oliver thoughtfully, a dark, intent look under heavy brows. "Yes," he said. "Yes, the past can be changed, but not easily. And it changes the future, too, necessarily. The lines of probability are switched into new patterns—but it is extremely difficult, and it has never been allowed. The physiotemporal course tends to slide back to its norm, always. That is why it is so hard to force any alteration." He shrugged. "A theoretical science. We do not change history, Wilson. If we changed our past, our present would be altered, too. And our time-world is entirely to our liking. There may be a few malcontents there, but they are not allowed the privilege of temporal travel."

Oliver spoke louder against the roaring from beyond the windows. "But you've got the power! You could alter history, if you wanted to—wipe out all the pain and suffering and tragedy—"

"All of that passed away long ago," Cenbe said.

"Not—*now!* Not—*this!*"

Cenbe looked at him enigmatically for awhile. Then— "This, too," he said.

And suddenly Oliver realized from across what distances Cenbe was watching him. A vast distance, as time is measured. Cenbe was a composer and a genius, and necessarily strongly emphatic, but his psychic locus was very far away in time. The dying city outside, the whole world of *now* was not quite real to Cenbe, falling short of reality because of that basic variance in time. It was merely one of the building blocks that had gone to support the edifice on which Cenbe's culture stood in a misty, unknown, terrible future.

It seemed terrible to Oliver now. Even Kleph—all of them had been touched with a pettiness, the faculty that had enabled Hollia to concentrate on her malicious, small schemes to acquire a ringside seat while the meteor thundered in toward Earth's atmosphere. They were all dilettantes, Kleph and Omerie and the others. They toured time, but only as onlookers. Were they bored—sated—with their normal existence?

Not sated enough to wish change, basically. Their own time-world was a fulfilled womb, a perfection made manifest for their needs. They dared not change the past—they could not risk flawing their own present.

Revulsion shook him. Remembering the touch of Kleph's lips, he felt a sour sickness on his tongue. Alluring she had been; he knew that too well. But the aftermath—

There was something wrong about this race from the future. He had felt it dimly at first, before Kleph's nearness had drowned caution and buffered his sensibilities. Time traveling purely as an escape mechanism seemed almost blasphemous. A race with such power—

Kleph—leaving him for the barbaric, splendid coronation at Rome a thousand years ago—*how had she seen him?* Not as a living, breathing man. He knew that, very certainly. Kleph's race were spectators.

But he read more than casual interest in Cenbe's eyes now. There was an avidity there, a bright, fascinated probing. The man had replaced his earphones—he was different from the others. He was a connoisseur. After the vintage season came the aftermath—and Cenbe.

Cenbe watched and waited, light flickering softly in the translucent block before him, his fingers poised over the note pad. The ultimate connoisseur waited to savor the rarities that no non-gourmet could appreciate.

Those thin, distant rhythms of sound that was almost music began to be audible again above the noises of the distant fire. Listening, remembering, Oliver could very nearly catch the pattern of the symphonia as he had heard it, all intermingled with the flash of changing faces and the rank upon rank of the dying—

He lay back on the bed letting the room swirl away into the darkness behind his closed and aching lids. The ache was implicit in every cell of his body, almost a second ego taking possession and driving him out of himself, a strong, sure ego taking over as he himself let go.

Why, he wondered dully, should Kleph have lied? She had said there was no aftermath to the drink she had given him. No aftermath—and yet this painful possession was strong enough to edge him out of his own body.

Kleph had not lied. It was no aftermath to drink. He knew that—but the knowledge no longer touched his brain or his body. He lay still, giving them up to the power of the illness which was aftermath to something far stronger than the strongest drink. The illness that had no name—yet.

Cenbe's new symphonia was a crowning triumph. It had its premiere from Antares Hall, and the applause was an ovation. History itself, of course, was the artist—opening with the meteor that forecast the great plagues of the fourteenth century and closing with the climax Cenbe had caught on the threshold of modern times. But only Cenbe could have interpreted it with such subtle power.

Critics spoke of the masterly way in which he had chosen the face of the Stuart king as a recurrent motif against the montage of emotion and sound and movement. But there were other faces, fading through the great sweep of the composition, which helped to build up to the tremendous climax. One face in particular, one moment that the audience absorbed greedily. A moment in which one man's face loomed huge in the screen, every feature clear. Cenbe had never caught an emotional crisis so effectively, the critics agreed. You could almost read the man's eyes.

After Cenbe had left, he lay motionless for a long while. He was thinking feverishly—

I've got to find some way to tell people. If I'd known in advance, maybe something could have been done. We'd have forced them to tell us how to change the probabilities. We could have evacuated the city.

If I could leave a message—

Maybe not for today's people. But later. They visit all through time. If they could be recognized and caught somewhere, sometime, and made to change destiny—

It wasn't easy to stand up. The room kept tilting. But he managed it. He found pencil and paper and through the swaying of the shadows he wrote down what he could. Enough. Enough to warn, enough to save.

He put the sheets on the table, in plain sight, and weighted them down before he stumbled back to bed through closing darkness.

The house was dynamited six days later, part of the futile attempt to halt the relentless spread of the Blue Death.

PART SIX

From Outer Space

OSCAR J. FRIEND

OF JOVIAN BUILD

THE metal space ship, fallen to earth, was nested in a grove of trees. A thing of shimmering, golden scales about one hundred feet long, shaped somewhat like a blunted javelin, the craft looked like a beautiful, full-grown dragon to the men who had come upon it.

At first, the warriors were frightened. Then, as the strange thing gave no indication of life, their awe turned to curiosity. They ventured closer, gripping their spears and javelins nervously. The ship they thought was a dragon did not stir. At last one of the party drew near enough to touch the serpent experimentally with the point of the spear. The thing rang with a brazen sound. But still it stirred not.

Then it was that one, bolder than the rest, found odd steps, like horizontal gills, which led up the curving head to a level area. There was a glass aperture, like a bulging eye. Soon a dozen men were swarming about the head and staring into the eye. The window presented a most unusual picture. Through it the observer saw a man with large ears who sat in a curved armchair. He faced a metal wall studded with strange dials and knobs.

"Ho, Perexites," shouted one warrior as he pried with his short sword at a crevice at the base of the hemispherical eye, "methinks 'tis like Talus—another creation of Hephaestus. It is a dragon of metal."

"Have a care then that it doesn't wax hot and burn thy feet," laughed Perexites.

Others of the group clambered along the back of the strange creature while more than a few circled it on the ground, climbing over the felled trees crushed by the ship. Suddenly, the thing came to horrible and terrifying life. The picture of the man with the large ears moved. Wearily, slowly, like a tired man moving under water, the figure reached out one hand and pressed a series of the little buttons on the wall.

Shafts of flame leaped forth from an opening just below the globular eye, like a triple tongue. From the tip of one of the three forks issued a column of green vapor. Another stabbed forth bluish thunderbolts, and from the third fork flowed a pencil of reddish light. The great eye began to revolve upon that rounded head with a vibratory hum.

Death rays struck one man after another with deadly accuracy. The men toppled to the ground, lifeless. Those that escaped the blue death rays were enveloped by the lethal green gas. Others, caught by the red shaft of light, simply were disintegrated.

Soon all the men about the globular eye were dead or utterly annihilated. The metallic dragon was alone in the midst of the carnage it had wrought with poison gas, death ray, and electronic thunderbolt.

It was thus that Cadmus, founder of Thebes, discovered matters when he came in search of his followers. Brave beyond the usual courage of men, he drew his sword and charged forward to avenge the death of his followers, or die with them. He clambered up the side of the space ship, reached the window that seemed like a great eye.

Then the Greek halted in amazement. For inside the transparent eye of the metal dragon he saw a man imprisoned. Attacking the quartz window fearlessly, Cadmus was dismayed to have his weapon spring back from the blow he struck. Before he could strike again, the man within moved a finger and pressed against a projection of some sort within the spherical dome. A section of the dome split open, making a passageway into the interior.

Cadmus shortened his sword grip for a thrust into the vitals of any foe and strode forward. Within the dome, he knelt swiftly beside the imprisoned man who was breathing stertorously, his head now resting on his arm. Then Cadmus met with the greatest surprise of his life. Warm with life, this queer and suffering stranger had flesh as hard as bronze. When Cadmus attempted to roll him over onto his back, he found himself unable to budge the man.

He prepared to grip the heavily breathing stranger with both hands. And at this moment a voice spoke in his brain, and he was aware of a definite thought implanted in his mind.

"You cannot move me, my friend, for I weigh nearly three hundred and twenty times more than you think. The artificial gravitational field was put out of service in the crash. It was with the greatest effort that I manipulated the keys of the ray tubes and the conning turret. I am sorry to have killed your companions. I did so before I caught their simple thought waves."

At this calm admission Cadmus drew back and gripped his sword again, his face growing stern. The unknown man who was able to give his thoughts birth in the listener's brain managed to roll himself half over on his side, and he stared at the Greek warrior with agonized eyes.

"Your weapon, I know now, will avail you naught, since I understand its use from reading your mind. The present density of my mass is impenetrable to any weapon known to your kind. But since you desire my death so fiercely, know that I am dying—internally crushed by the shock of landing on your planet. I admitted you so you can heed and obey my message.

"I am Mentor 5X9378, sole navigator of the spatial vessel *Marduk*, leader of the expedition to explore the third planet of this System. My companions, because of the length of time required to make this journey, are each in a special casket in the main compartment below us in a state of suspended animation. They were thus cushioned and protected from the crash which has been the cause of my death. Once awake and free, they will be able to repair the gravitational field and proceed with the purpose of this expedition.

"You are wondering why I seem so heavy to you. The world I come from has a surface gravity two and one-half times that of this planet. Our astronomers made the astounding discovery that this planet is a carefully scaled miniature of ours. Hence, if we were to explore it successfully, we would have to be reduced in size.

"Savant 2X1470, using his atom and mass impactor, reduced us to one-hundred-and-one-sixteenth our normal size. Thus, the cellular structure of my entire body has been condensed until I am nearer a true solid than any other body you have ever seen."

Cadmus stared in bewilderment.

"I see you follow my statements with difficulty, and my time grows short. Push this lever to the forward end of its slot. That opens the way to the storage deck below. Then shove that second and third lever and twist the wheel there as far as it will go to the right. That opens the ports on the storage level to light and air."

Cadmus reached out and manipulated the proper levers and twisted the shining and spoked wheel. He was conscious at once of a vibratory hum somewhere below him. A section of the floor of the dome moved downward out of sight, revealing a flight of metal steps. Urged by the dying man, Cadmus slowly descended the stairs. At the bottom of the stairs, a strange sight met his eyes. There were polished caskets of gray metal lining the interior of this metal dragon like gigantic teeth in the belly of a whale.

Cadmus became conscious of the ghost voice flooding his brain with an explanation. Each tooth encased a slumbering man like the stranger beneath the dome of the huge glass eye. A tiny seam traced a symmetrical oval upon the face of each tooth from top to bottom. On the face of this panel was a lever and a tiny wheel.

In obedience to the summons within his brain, Cadmus halted before the first great casket, twisted the lever, spun the tiny wheel, and stood back to observe results.

The door of the casket opened outward, slowly but smoothly. Within the padded interior was a man with big ears like the dying man above. On his breast was a single drop of bright red blood where a fang had pricked him deeply. A glance at the inner side of the panel showed Cadmus the cause of the phenomenon.

"You observe the method of revival," the thought explained itself in his mind. "Hasten and open the other caskets!"

But Cadmus did not stir for a moment, because the sleeper did. The man quivered, stirred, began breathing in a stertorous sound like the man above. Then he opened his eyes and gazed blankly. Slowly, heavily, he moved his arms up from his sides to his face. Cadmus was on the verge of offering a helping hand when the voice in his brain deterred him.

"You cannot help him. Go quickly and open the remaining receptacles!"

Impelled by this urge, Cadmus zigzagged his way along the huge chamber, manipulating levers and wheels as he went. At the far end of this storage deck was a casket that looked like a double tooth. It was just as he reached this last casket that he heard a heavy noise behind him. He whirled about and stared. The first man had fallen headlong out of his shell.

As the Greek warrior watched, others began to follow suit. And then the crowning horror dawned on him. The first man he had released, and who was gasping his last, was no longer four cubits in height. *He was nearly eight cubits tall!* In less than an hour, he had doubled his stature. The others had grown also in proportion to the length of time they had been out of their chrysalis.

With a fearful cry, Cadmus raced madly for the stairs to the eye above. He found the first man grown to a full ten cubits! Thinking the creature was dead, Cadmus leaped over the gigantic form and plunged headlong through the open section of the dragon eye. Even as he fled, he was conscious of a last faint mental message.

"The composition of the atmosphere of the third planet has proven fatal. Due to unforeseen contingencies, our expedition has proven a failure, and there is none to report to the savants. There remains only annihilation."

But Cadmus did not remain to watch that heavy hand drop in a final effort upon a dial that was oddly different from the others on the wall. He was far out of the grove when the terrific explosion came—a blast that shook the earth and knocked him senseless upon the plain of Panope.

When he later came to examine the ruins, there was nothing left of his own companions, the dragon, or of the heavy men from another world—save a memory.

It was in 1981 that Dr. John Graham, archeologist, discovered the thing. His expedition was exploring the subsoil of the north Mediterranean littoral that had once been ancient Greece. The eminent scientist himself was manipulating the Fore Televisor when the queerly shaped object came into focus.

"Teague! Oh, Teague!" Dr. Graham called to his technical engineer and general assistant.

"Yes, Doctor," answered the young man, hastening forward at the sound of the excitement in the other's voice. "What's wrong?"

"Have a look at this," said Graham, his voice trembling as he motioned toward the eye-pieces of special quartz. "I have the dials set at one hundred and three feet, and unless the ray has gone crazy, I've discovered a metallic object that's fully eight feet long, and nearly as wide. I can't believe it. There's no evidence that the ancient Greeks worked with metals on that scale."

Larry Teague glanced quickly at the adjustments on the Fore Televisor and then fitted his face to the hoodlike eyepieces. At once he became fully as excited as his superior.

"You're right, Dr. Graham!" he exclaimed without removing his eyes from the hood. "It's a double object of some kind. It looks like—like the old twin elk's tooth charm my grandfather wore. What do you think it is? What shall we do?"

"We'll excavate at once," decided Graham promptly. "This is distinctly a find of the first magnitude."

It took three weeks to get down to the object. From its resting place beneath the accumulation of centuries of erosion and disintegrating rock shot with myriad flecks of an unknown silvery metal the odd find was exhumed and returned to the light of day. A casual examination revealed that the gray metal was smooth and unaffected by its years underground. It was artificially made, and the metal was unlike any ever found before on Earth.

"Unquestionably from a meteorite," decided Dr. Graham, and Teague concurred. "This thing came here from space, I'm quite positive. And do you notice the odd shape, Teague? It's like a double casket with the same base, a sort of mausoleum for a man and a woman."

"The old scientific theory of the coming of Adam and Eve, eh?" remarked the young man. Then he shrugged his shoulders. "Silly talk, of course. The only way to learn about the thing is to examine it carefully. I'll have it out of this hole in a jiffy."

They went back to the surface, but Teague did not have the cryptlike container out in a jiffy. After breaking three winches and two steel cables without budging the thing, Teague finally solved the problem by descending with a small Morris-Hayden degravitator which he attached to the base of the object with cables. After turning on the current, the nullification of gravity made it absurdly easy to lift the peculiarly heavy thing out of the bottom of that shaft they had sunk to reach it.

Closer examination showed that an oval line, a lever, and an oddly figured dial were in and on the face of each half of the casket. Dr. Graham's comment about a casket took the popular fancy. Some unknown reporter promptly named the find the Hellenic Chrysalis, and the name stuck.

The first thing Dr. Graham did was to compute the weight of the chrysalis. The answer was stunning. The Hellenic Chrysalis weighed nearly one hundred tons! Leaving the degravitator attached, Graham promptly abandoned the expedition and towed the chrysalis back to his New York laboratory in the wake of his air liner.

Back in the laboratory, leaving the degravitator on the chrysalis because of the thing's tremendous weight, the two scientists resolutely shut out the world and proceeded to exhaust every known test on the crypt. At last they found themselves no wiser than at the outset. So they decided to chance disaster and attempt to open one-half of the double casket.

Having pored in vain over the odd configurations of the circular dial, Dr. Graham found that it moved only in a clockwise direction, and he recklessly turned it as far as it would go. Then, as nothing happened, he twisted the lever. And both men stood back and trembled a little as they awaited they knew not what.

There was a vibratory hum within the lid. In due time the cover swung ponderously open to reveal the figure of a man in a state of perfect preservation. He was clad in the short skirt, helmet, greaves and sandals of an ancient Greek warrior. In one hand was a jewel-headed scepter.

"A Greek soldier!" cried out Teague in amazement. "Perfectly embalmed."

"Look!" said Graham, pointing with a trembling finger to the man's breast where a single drop of red blood glistened moistly. "Listen! He is breathing. He's alive, Teague! Great God, he lives!"

"Suspended animation!" whispered the younger man disbelievingly. "But, Doctor, the ancient Greeks knew nothing of that theory."

"He isn't a Greek, Teague," said Graham, his voice hoarse.

"What is he, then?"

"I don't know," said the scientist slowly. "But I intend finding out. Look at his exceptionally large ears. The costume is not quite right for Grecian identification. And the idea of suspended animation! Teague, I'm positive this is not an Earthman. Can't you feel his strangeness? Don't you sense an alien atmosphere about him?"

Before the young assistant could reply, the man in the chrysalis opened his eyes and stared blankly at them. His breathing gradually grew louder and more stertorous, but his lungs seemed to lift and lower his chest quite easily. Then quick intelligence came into his face, and he gripped his queer rod, felt of himself, and shifted in his casket. He opened his mouth and spoke in a terrifically heavy voice which seemed to penetrate his listeners like a rasp. But the words were incomprehensible.

Dr. Graham, encouraged by the highly intelligent look on the man's face, addressed him in one language after another. All to no avail. No answering spark of understanding kindled in the casket man's eyes. He frowned in concentration as he wondered where this strange being could have come from—and to his great astonishment an answer to this unspoken question formed thought images within his brain.

He stared with wide, startled eyes at Teague, and saw that his assistant was experiencing the same sort of shock. There could be but one answer. This strange being was communicating with them in thought images without the use of the media of speech.

"True, I am not of this planet," was the substance of the thought which seemed to be born within their brains. "I come from the fifth planet in this System—if this is the planet we set out to explore. Where is Mentor 5X9378? Where is the *Marduk?* Where are my companions?"

The two Americans looked at each other.

"Jupiter!" murmured Graham in awe. "Teague, he came from *Jupiter!*"

"Yes," the thought wave rolled through their brains. "The fifth planet is my world. But where are my comrades?"

Dr. Graham concentrated on a thought response.

"You were alone when we found you buried under a hundred feet of soil. You must have been there in a state of suspended animation for at least five thousand years! How did you come here from Jupiter?"

"Five thousand of your years?" groaned the man from the chrysalis. "Then all is lost. It has been nearly five hundred of our Mardukian years. Marduk has passed safely through the poison gas belt by now or has perished. But Mentor 5X9378 would never have abandoned me. Some catastrophe must have overtaken him. He destroyed the *Marduk,* or was forced to flee after unloading all the sleepers. But where are they?"

"Try to think!" urged Graham mentally. "We are your friends—Graham and Teague. We want to help you, but you must help us. What is your name? Tell us what you can!"

A faint smile of understanding lit up the features of the being in the casket. He lightly raised one hand and pointed to the drop of blood drying on his chest and then to the mechanism fitted to the under side of the casket-lid.

"An injection was made into my heart muscle and stimulating gas was forced in and out of my lungs when you opened this casket. There were fifty of us brought to your world in this state. Only Mentor 5X9378 was left conscious to direct the *Marduk,* our spatial ship which was named after our planet. When the savants discovered that Marduk was due to pass through a poison gas belt that would miss the inferior planets, the savants began planning a wholesale migration sunward. Three expeditions were sent out first. Ours was one of them. We had less than two hundred years to prepare.

"Our astronomers had learned that this planet, queerly enough, was almost a scaled miniature of Marduk, with animal life and flora quite similar to ours and in same proportion to this planet as we are to Marduk. But Marduk has one hundred and sixteen times the surface area of planet three. A company of men, each a hundred and sixteen times the height of you, would overrun this planet. So we were reduced in size to be comparable to your world. The last I remember was the sleep-inducing injection given me on Marduk just before being subjected to the impactor and then being placed and sealed in my crypt here."

Quite interested in his own thoughts, the strange being gripped the edge of his casket and stepped easily out upon the laboratory floor. As he passed beyond the nullifying effect of the Morris-Hayden degravitator an amazing thing happened. He fell heavily to his hands and knees with a force that shook the sturdily constructed building. The flooring buckled and splintered beneath his hands. In one place his foot went through. He strained every muscle to keep from being crushed to the floor, his breathing was horribly labored.

"Merciful heavens!" ejaculated Dr. Graham, instantly realizing what had happened. "They reduced their volume but not their mass. This man still has his normal Jovian weight—close to thirty tons, I should judge—and he's only six feet tall to carry that tremendous tonnage. There's not enough bearing surface to his hands and feet; his muscles have not adequate leverage to lift such a load."

"He should weigh only forty percent of his Jovian weight on Earth," commented Teague. "The gravity of Jupiter is two and a half times that of Earth."

"You mean he should be conscious of only forty percent; the actual weight is the same," corrected Graham. "But his tremendous reduction in size sets his muscular strength at naught. Help me get him back to his casket—the degravitator nullifies Earth's effects on him."

In unison they grasped the arms of the man from Jupiter to assist him to his feet. It was like gripping warm iron that was rigid to their touch, but which kneaded slowly with a life of its own. And they were unable to budge him. Teague turned to the chrysalis which, thanks to the purring degravitator, was practically weightless. Quickly he pushed it out onto the floor beside the fallen man.

"Help us!" he concentrated. "Get back into your casket where your weight is nullified."

The Jovian understood. Painfully he gripped the rim of his mausoleum with one clutching hand. Dragging himself slowly into the sheltering protection of the casket, the change in his control of his muscles was marked. His breathing became easier, and he pulled himself upright to stand comfortably at ease. But something frightful had happened.

He no longer fitted in the chrysalis! His head and shoulders were outside the casket! He was growing at the rate of an inch a minute— and the rate was visibly accelerating.

"My God!" cried Teague in alarm. "What's happened?"

"Somehow the change in gravity, coupled with something, must have counteracted the force that reduced him in size," said Graham, reflecting deeply on this alarming circumstance. "Possibly the state of suspended animation for thousands of years—"

"Main gas in your atmosphere," the thought of the Jovian impinged on his consciousness. "You call it—ni-troo-jene? The savants knew of its presence. Not particularly poisonous to me. Marduk has it, too. But with impacted cellular structure and gravity of this planet, it seems to boil my blood. I am returning to my own size."

"What shall we do, Dr. Graham?" exclaimed Teague, anxiously eyeing the visibly increasing giant and surveying the size of the laboratory. "He'll be crowded here in less than ten minutes at this rate. Can't we stop him?"

"Impossible! We haven't had time enough even to learn his name. We've got to get him out of here, or he'll be crushed to death and destroy the building, too."

"A new Alice in Wonderland," said Teague, laughing hysterically.

"Snap out of that!" said Graham sharply. "Ring for the freight elevator, and let's get him out in the open before it's too late."

The young assistant recovered himself and did as bid. In frantic haste they pushed the Hellenic Chrysalis to the lift. Too late! The case would have made it nicely, but the Jovian so far overflowed its confines that he could not get into the cage. Dr. Graham considered things despairingly.

The laboratory was about a hundred feet long and on the fifth floor or top floor of a loft building.

"Get an ax!" he cried. "We've got to enlarge a window and let him go down the fire escape."

"Will it hold his weight?" demanded Teague.

"He'll have to chance it. It's better than expanding in here."

Madly they shoved the chrysalis back through the laboratory and to the windows overlooking the alley. By this time the Jovian was nearly twenty feet tall. They could have crammed him in the elevator without the mausoleum if they had been strong enough to handle him. But he would likely have died from the unbearable weight of gravity before he reached his proper size.

The giant sprawled quietly on his casket and watched their actions with grave eyes. Suddenly understanding their intentions, he waved them back from the row of windows. Raising his scepterlike rod that he had never released from his hand, he aimed it at the wall of the building and pressed a stud at the rear of the queer metal tube. At once a reddish glow leaped out from the end to play on the row of windows. Before their eyes the glass and stone and metal melted away like so much snow beneath a tropic sun. In a moment there was only open space where there had been substantial wall.

"Did you see that?" whispered Dr. Graham. "A disintegrating ray! We must save this man at all costs. We can learn so much from him."

The Jovian, still growing at an alarming rate, shut off his ray and smiled at the two little men.

"I—I grow faint with vertigo," his thought informed them, "but my strength seems to be returning in ratio to my return to my normal size. I shall be all right as soon as I can stand."

"My God, Doctor!" groaned Larry Teague, moving out of the way of one of the Jovian's expanding legs. "He'll be wrecking the laboratory in another minute. Where can we hide him?"

"*How* can we hide him?" returned the worried scientist. "How can we feed him?"

There was no time for further speculation. The Jovian had reached the limit of the confines of the huge laboratory. Various paraphernalia and equipment around the walls began to shatter, break, or overturn as he crowded them. The two scientists were crouching in a corner near the window area now. Dr. Graham concentrated on a message to the one-hundred-foot giant.

"Have you strength enough to get out through the opening you made?" he demanded.

For answer the Jovian pointed his wand upward toward the roof and snapped on the red ray. Before their eyes the roof melted away, leaving them under the blue vault of sky with a brightly shining sun. The giant sat up, shading his eyes from the glare of the sun.

He was nearly two hundred feet tall by now.

"We make artificial sunlight on Marduk," he explained.

He didn't take time to think anything else. He was staring about in wonder as the great city unfolded about him. The two men, lost below him in the shadow of one foot, heard the gradual rise of wild pandemonium as the populace of the city became aware of the Gulliver who was rising from their midst.

Panic reigned in a moment. Fire whistles began to scream, and the shouts of frenzied people grew like the howling of demons in a bad dream.

There were car wrecks and tie-ups of traffic. People lost their lives in the wild stampedes. A few hardy souls stood in office building windows and stared in amazement or disbelief at the growing giant of a man. And the Jovian slowly got to his feet, moving carefully so as not to crush the building beneath him.

New York went mad.

It was like a disturbed anthill. And when the Jovian stepped down to street level, crushing in a couple of delivery trucks with his heavily sandaled foot, a flying squadron of police came onto the scene and began firing at the feet and lower limbs of the giant. The shots must have stung him, for he jumped away angrily, making a havoc of the street and the buildings on both sides for the length of a block.

He was now over five hundred feet tall.

Alarmed and bewildered by the din around him, completely out of touch with the only two men he knew, still expanding as he grew to his full height of seven hundred feet, the Jovian was panic-stricken.

Then the municipal government ordered down all commercial aircraft and sent up a fleet of armed fliers with four-inch guns. The result was horrible.

The black fighting planes with the domed turrets and flaming guns swarmed around the giant's head and shoulders. Wounded in several places by these things, the Jovian swatted a number of them out of existence with his huge hand as a simple matter of self-protection. From the roof garden atop one of the buildings he swooped up a handful of people to hold them close to his head while he attempted to send out thought impulses asking them to stop the attack on him.

A sudden blow in his shoulder where a four-inch shell struck home made him jerk convulsively and tighten his hand involuntarily. He crushed the handful of people like insects. Then the giant started running toward the open water that was the upper Bay. Every step he took spelled disaster and ruin and death for New York. He toppled over the Woolworth Building with his shoulder as he passed. He staggered, wrecking the other side of the street before he could recover.

At last he was free. He sank a couple of freighters and one ferry as he plunged into the ocean and caused a tidal wave to sweep over Staten Island as he waded breast-high out to sea.

And all the time, back at his wrecked laboratory, Dr. John Graham was trying to get in touch with the authorities by telephone to explain matters and have the senseless attack on the Jovian stopped.

All to no avail. The eastern seacoast was in an uproar within twenty-four hours. Dr. John Graham and his assistant were summarily jailed until such time as their share in this catastrophe could be investigated. The Atlantic fleet was just steaming northward to put in at New York. The president of the United States ordered the fleet to drive north and east until it found the terrible giant and destroyed him.

This was done. The Jovian was found in a semi-exhausted condition swimming eastward, bleeding copiously from a bad wound in the shoulder. The super-dreadnoughts opened up on the target with big guns, torpedoes, and depth bombs. The result was inevitable.

Having lost his ponderous density of mass by a return to his proper height, the Jovian fell an easy prey to the weapons of the Lilliputian world which warred upon him without parley. He died in the North Atlantic ocean, friendless, alone, and bewildered—millions of miles away from his own world, and thousands of years away from his own time—sinking ingloriously to the bottom of the ocean to feed the deep sea fishes of an inferior planet.

It was some days later that Dr. Graham was released from custody— far too late for anything save explanations, as is the engaging and ingenious custom of mankind. His trial, unique in a long history of unique trials, excited world comment. He was finally absolved from blame of the tragedy, and the press of the world poured contumely upon the unreasoning panic of little earthworms whose frantic terror had caused the destruction of the most sensational figure ever seen upon the planet.

Scientists all but wept and wrung their hands at thought of the irreparable loss to mankind of knowledge which transcended that of Earth. And then the world went mad with joy upon learning that the final remaining tooth of the ancient dragon of Cadmus had escaped the general holocaust and was still safe in the midst of the ruins of the Graham laboratory.

Under the auspices of the Federal Government, guarded by a convoy of battleships, Dr. Graham and a bevy of world-famous scientists were established with the ponderous chrysalis upon an island in an isolated portion of the Pacific Ocean. No expense was spared in the making of that final experiment a success. The last survivor of that ill-fated spatial expedition from Jupiter was destined to be received in cordial and royal style. Elaborate plans were made to set up intelligent communication with the forthcoming Jovian, and preparations for his—or her—comfort and well being outrivaled the fabulous treatment of Gulliver at the hands of the Lilliputians.

The Hellenic Chrysalis was at last opened. Instead of a man or woman from Jupiter, the last tooth contained only a machine of intricate design and strange potentialities. A metal plate affixed to one side appeared to be a set of instructions addressed to one Mentor 5X9378, in indecipherable characters.

After months of laborious experimentation, Dr. Graham and his eminent colleagues came to an astounding conclusion. Ironically enough, they pointed out, the strange thing was a machine equipped to maintain Jovians at the Earthly stature of six feet! Poor little giant!

POLTON CROSS

WINGS ACROSS THE COSMOS

MY name is Amos Latham, and I am, I hope, a reasonably intelligent man. I know nearly all the subjects encompassed in a modern education, but I must admit my knowledge fell far short on the day that I found an object resembling the half shell of a walnut lying at the bottom of a neatly drilled five-foot hole in my best sweet pea bed.

My job? In a way, I'm a farmer. I like to experiment in grafting, pursue if possible hybrid experiments on the lines laid down by Mendel.

I found the walnut on June 7th, 1961, just six days ago. It was a perplexing puzzle in itself to decide how an object so small, unless it were a meteorite, had got to such a depth overnight—but the puzzle deepened when I found that by no means at hand could I begin to budge it!

I began to suspect the thing had some sort of underpart that went down like a shaft into the ground at the bottom of the hole it had burrowed—that what I saw was only the upper part of some sort of buried spear. That being so, the only thing to do was to clear the sides of the thin shaft and dig the object out.

It took me half a day to make the shaft wide enough to permit me getting down it, but even then I was no better off. I could see clearly enough that the walnut was simply a hemisphere of shell-like substance —but of a vastly incredible weight! I strained and tugged at it until my fingers ached. But I couldn't shift it in the slightest. I just couldn't convince myself that such a fact was true—but it was.

To say my curiosity was aroused is putting it mildly. I went into the garage and brought out a block and tackle. I erected it on a pretty stout scaffolding tripod and fixed the chain clamp around the inch-square lump. The tripod snapped, but the object didn't budge!

That settled it. Beyond question I'd happened on something that was outside all normal laws, at least in the matter of weight. I remembered something about electrons and protons in contact—neutrons—and went inside the house to telephone Bradley.

Bradley is a physicist, in the employ of the Bureau of Standards. He arrived late that afternoon. Bradley, with his usual foresight, had brought along a powerful breakdown truck, complete with crane, trailing behind his car.

I greeted him warmly as he came toward the house, but as he returned the greeting there was a doubt in his closely set gray eyes.

"Where is this walnut of yours?" he asked, after we had had a drink.

I took him out to the sweet pea bed, or rather what was left of it after my excavational work.

The thing was still there, and the faint smile vanished from Bradley's face as he tried vainly to shift it.

"Boy, you have got onto something!" he whistled in amazement. "If that stuff belongs on this world I'm clean crazy. Anyway, we'll soon see."

Scrambling back to the top of the small crater he signaled the truckmen. They backed their conveyance clumsily into the garden and watched curiously as they lowered the crane chain. Finally we managed to encompass the walnut in the clamp and gave the pullway order.

A terrific strain was thrown on the chain as it slowly creaked and groaned over the winch. Powerful though the truck's engine was it took every vestige of it to lift that absurdly tiny thing from the ground. Very slowly it rose up, inch by inch. We saw that the underside was apparently like the rest of it. Brad was watching the thing keenly.

Finally, we had the object deposited on a huge stone block that had once been part of a well at the bottom of the garden. There the task of the astounded truckmen ended. They went off round-eyed and puzzled in a settling haze of dust, leaving us both to our own devices.

Smoking pensively, Bradley studied the object for a while, then turned to me.

"Dense as hell," he said bluntly. "Pretty similar to the stuff that must exist at the core of Earth, though infinitely denser than even that."

I nodded slowly and waited for him to continue.

"That lump came from somewhere out in space," he resumed. "Where, we don't know, but we can hazard a guess—probably from the region of the giant star areas. Specks of substance like this floating around in space probably made up the cores of the very worlds around us—stuff so densely packed that it had an unbelievable weight. It may be a fragment from a sun where matter is densely packed."

"You mean a white dwarf?" I suggested.

He nodded.

"That's it. Take the Companion of Sirius, for example. That is a white dwarf, and Adams at Mount Wilson Observatory proved long ago that the density there is two thousand times greater than that of platinum. Take a matchbox full of the stuff and it would require a derrick to raise it. That's the kind of thing we've got here. That's why it ploughed so deep into the earth when it arrived. Strange it didn't burn up; can't quite figure out that angle."

I pondered. Physics isn't entirely in my line; but Brad hadn't finished talking. He studied the object more closely for a while, then went on.

"Come to think of it, this substance might not be from a sun, but from a cooled world. Eddington tells us that heat is not entirely necessary for compressibility of matter. It is not essential to have a temperature of about ten million degrees in order to smash atoms. Terrific pressure alone will suffice.

"The shell of satellite electrons which can be broken by the attacks of X-rays, or the fierce collisions going on in the interior of a star, can also break by the application of continued pressure on a dense world. This produces an almost bare nucleus with the heavier atoms retaining a few of the closest electrons, forming a structure of perhaps one hundredth of a complete atom.

"The consequent compression produces vast weight by comparison with sizes to which we're accustomed. Take the example in physics: in a monatomic gas like helium a thirty-two fold increase in pressure gives an eight fold increase of density, if the heat of compression is retained in the gas. There you have an example of heat pressure—but on a world that is a child of a compressed sun—the Companion of Sirius for example—the very pressure of that world would produce similar, even far greater results. At the very roughest estimate this thing here weighs about one ton to the cubic inch—and that's plenty heavy!"

"And now that it's here what do we do with it?" I asked quietly.

He shrugged.

"Nothing we can do, except give it to the meteorite section of the museum. I'll make arrangements for it to be picked up. It'll be about two weeks, though; I've a special Government job waiting for me."

Talking, we went into the house and had dinner. It was late when Brad finally left with the promise to return in two weeks. Once I'd seen him off I strolled over in the moonlight calm to survey again that uncanny lump.

But it had changed! I got quite a shock as the rays of the amber moon smote now upon a tiny, tortoiselike head. Bent legs, exceptionally powerful, jutted outward from the shell. The legs moved slowly as I went toward the thing, but it stopped on the stone. Perhaps it realized that to fall off would mean another five foot plunge into the ground.

I studied the creature from a distance, observing the viciously curved scar of a mouth. Its resemblance to a tortoise was now quite remarkable. It was smaller, of course, and incredibly heavier!

I shall never know if it was impulse or plain curiosity that prompted me to extend an ingratiating hand toward it. Not knowing what type of intelligence the thing possessed that seemed the only way I could show friendship.

A second later I regretted it. The tiny head shot forward toward my out-stretched hand, faster than the striking paw of a cat. Before I knew it the creature's terrible mouth had scissored open and shut. There was a momentary gleam of small, needle-pointed teeth. Then I was gazing at a numbed, crimsoned finger from which the top, to the first knuckle, had been completely severed!

For a second or two I hardly knew what to think, the shock stunned me. I blundered back into the house, cauterized and bandaged the numbed member. Then, fuming with anger both at the hostility of my visitor and my own stupidity, I sat down to figure the thing out.

I didn't get very far. I couldn't understand how a thing like the walnut had traveled through the void of space and arrived with an impact that had buried it five feet in the ground—yet could live here in an atmosphere of oxygen and hydrogen. Either it was completely adaptable to both space and air, or else it had traveled in some kind of protecting case that had fallen away at the frictional heat of our upper atmosphere.

I meditated once upon killing the infernal thing, but I refrained for two reasons. The bullet would probably glance off such armor-plated density. Secondly, the object was going to interest the scientists. I made up my mind to call Bradley the next day.

My sleep was strangely disturbed—physically by the burning pain of returning sensation in my injured finger, and mentally by the memory of the walnut and the realization in my occasional wakeful spells that it was still outside, a densely heavy, vicious-jawed devil.

At times I dreamed, but they were dreams of a quality surely denied to any sane man. I beheld a world of intense darkness lying still and airless under a sky powdered with unfamiliar nebulae and constellations. There was a sense of vast loneliness and incompleteness, of enormous stretches of time occupied by an abstract state that I could only roughly determine as meditation. Meditation? By the walnut? Well, that was how it looked.

As though to substantiate my guess I glimpsed the walnut upon this darkly empty plain, surrounded by the outlines of what dimly appeared to be a city—but a city with no earthly similarity, ruled by machines and yet deserted. In the midst of these perplexing immensities the walnut brooded alone—

Suddenly I was awake, feverishly hot, with a name burning in my brain, the oddest, most astounding name. It sounded like—Yithan Kan.

I screamed it out three times, then suddenly remembered where I was. Dazedly I looked through the window toward the dawn light. That ton weight dark object was still on the block of stone. I shuddered. The memory of that ghastly dream with its terrific sense of weight and loneliness was still seared into my mind.

I felt ill as I got up and dressed. My finger had ceased bleeding but was anything but healthy to look at. It had taken on a curious brittle appearance most unusual for normal coagulation. The finger itself felt curiously different—leaden is the only way to describe it.

I thought once of phoning Doc Shaw to come over. Then, mainly because I detest the fussiness of physicians and because of my complete faith in my own first aid efforts, I let the idea drop. Instead I phoned New York, but to my annoyance Bradley was already in Washington.

It occurred to me with a sudden panicky feeling that for another two weeks I would be alone with this atrocity from an unknown world— unless of course I took the obvious course and left.

I decided against that. Don't ask me why: I can only put it down to the same lure that drives perfectly sane men into absolute danger by the very force of some intangible fascination. I went outside and watched the walnut in the hot morning sunshine. Its capacity for motionlessness amazed me. It did not seem to have budged a thirty-second of an inch since it had been placed there.

Keeping a respectable distance away I decided to call out that absurd name.

"Yithan Kan! Yithan Kan," I shouted, "can you hear me? Can you understand me?"

The beady eyes, like microscopic garnets, studied me unwaveringly, and I returned the stare like a man hypnotized by a snake. That very act did something to me. I could feel a groping and plucking at the neurones and receptive cells of my brain.

That which followed was not exactly an exchange of communications —in fact I do not believe my brain was developed enough to pass any coherent thought. It was more a series of mental images from which I gathered that this weird object, on arrival, had been stunned by the terrific impact. Only its super hardness and density had saved its life.

It was, as I had guessed, perfectly adaptable to any conditions. Its natural environment was one of intense cold—interstellar cold. Here on Earth it had apparently adapted itself immediately to the drastic change in conditions. I have heard of plants with such amazing adaptability, but the idea of an intelligent organism with similar abilities was unbelievable. Much to my surprise I learned that Yithan Kan was the female of its species.

So much I gathered on that first communication, then the spell was broken by some slight sound made by the wind. Disturbed in both mind and body I went into the house and tried to figure out what I ought to do, particularly how to improve my physical condition. I felt bone weary, and for no apparent reason.

It occurred to me that I might have been poisoned by the bite, but a second examination of my injured finger and a study of a droplet of blood through my microscope revealed no such signs. I wasn't poisoned; it was something else that had gripped me—something subtly different.

Several times I wondered if I ought to feed the walnut, then decided it didn't seem necessary. From what I could gather it absorbed energy directly—probably from the shorter cosmic rays which abound freely in space and also to a good extent on Earth.

With the passage of time my conviction of illness increased. From my injured finger the leaden sensation had traveled the entire length of my arm, changing it from normal color to a stone gray hue. I began to become really alarmed.

As I prepared lunch, though I did it more from force of habit than because I was hungry, I received another shock. I'd decided on canned beans to go with some cold meat, and in the most natural fashion possible I grabbed the tin with my injured hand to pull it from the shelf.

The can felt like pulp in my grasp—I found myself staring in amazement as juice and squashed beans spurted from the cracks in the tin, so tightly had I gripped it! I doubt if a hammer could have flattened it more effectively. I dropped the battered can in stupefied horror, then looked at my hand. It wasn't scarred or cut by the can's sharp edges— only weighted, almost without feeling, horribly numb. I flexed my fingers that I could hardly feel—all save the injured one which wouldn't move at all.

I forgot all about a meal; the complexity of this new happening forced me to start pacing around, trying to figure out what had occurred.

From a sense of horror I graduated by easy stages to one of interest, even triumph. I spent some time testing my strength on the hardest things I could find, felt a certain joy in discovering that most metals would bend easily in my one-handed grip, that even small stones crushed into powder as though cramped in a vise.

Of course, I knew that the walnut was at the bottom of it. But how had this thing come about? Had the bite it had given me started some condition of matter such as could only exist on the unknown, unimaginably heavy world from which the creature had come? What was the explanation?

Man, clearly, is what the scientists vaguely call a "fortuitous concourse of atoms in the shape of a man," a concourse that has the mystic power of thinking. He is in effect a very definite movable knot of energy condensed into a visible form. In the beginning of time some cosmic radiation changed a free energy state into a definite material build-up called protoplasm, and after the intermediate stages it became Man.

Somewhere, the enigmatic occurrence of mutations had come about— the definite change from one species into another effected by—Just what? Science is still hazy on that. Maybe radiations once again— unseen, undetectable, operating upon material structures at certain intervals of time.

These radiations have produced through the ages a change so enormous as to elevate protoplasm into living man. Nothing has been destroyed because nothing in the universe *can* be destroyed: only change is possible. Unseen forces altered atoms into a new concourse, formed a new pattern, and ultimately built them into the shape of Man.

But if this entity possessed—as was highly probable—many of these spatial radiations as part of its natural make-up, it was also possible that in the fashion of radium's hideously destructive emanations, a good deal of radiation had entered my body at the moment of that finger severance. And, since this creature was infinitely more powerful than I, representing a far mightier state of condensed matter, it would be possible to bend me entirely to its own matter state just as a strong will can overpower a weak one.

In that case the atoms and electrons of my body were even now undergoing a change! Pressures and radiations, operating on an infinitely small scale, were at work within me, changing my whole natural formation into a new condition of matter!

My strength! The dead weight increasing in my arm! The crawling numbness creeping around my shoulders and neck!

"God!" I cried hoarsely, leaping up as the searing truth struck home to me. "God—" I brought my hand down bitterly on the table with the intensity of my thoughts. The tabletop splintered as though split with an ax.

I scarcely heeded it. I had become accustomed by now to the frightful power of that left arm. With every hour it was growing heavier, tauter, more unwieldy—yet as the same conviction of strain passed around my shoulders I began to feel an awareness of new balance. I felt less one-sided. It could only mean that my new weight was distributing itself equally by slow degrees.

Struck with a sudden thought I hunted up a tape line and, standing flat against a wall, measured myself. I felt a queer sensation at my heart when I discovered I was two inches shorter in height! Then a compressing, contracting effect was in force! My mass was becoming smaller and denser . . .

Frightened, I went outside and tried to communicate with the walnut, but my brain emanations were useless. Nor did the thing attempt to communicate with me, though it watched me with motionless intentness.

But the reason for it all? That was what I could not understand. That bite had been deliberate; the walnut had purposely impregnated me, but to what purpose? Sheer malice? No: an intelligence so profound would not stoop to so earthly a thing as malice. There was another reason—perhaps it lay somewhere in the realms of those weird, disturbing dreams I had had.

And still no thought of leaving entered my head, or if it did I refused to heed it. I believe the creature itself was responsible for that, holding me by some indefinable shackle of will power, forcing me onward into a state I could only guess at, but which savored with every passing hour of a place unworldly, lying across inconceivable distances.

Quite suddenly, toward evening, the sickly feeling that had persisted with me all day passed off. I became ravenously hungry. I had an appetite that would have done credit to a lumberjack.

In the space of an hour I had emptied my small but well stocked refrigerator, but even then I only felt vaguely satisfied. I knew that it would not be long before I would have to eat again.

Energy, of course—strange, mysterious changes within me that demanded a sudden terrific influx of supply to keep pace with my rate of increasing strength. Very similar, I decided, to the tautness of a spring governing the exact amount of potential energy it must possess.

By the time I went to bed—after a final dubious look at the motionless walnut in the rising moonlight—I was feeling very top heavy indeed. The effect seemed to be working downward from my arms and shoulder—for my other arm was now likewise affected to the lower extremities.

The bed creaked noisily as I lay upon it. I was asleep almost immediately and once again strange, incredible dreams penetrated my mind. But this time my brain was much clearer, remarkably sharpened. I saw the things that were offered to me by some kind of extra sensory reception. Records of a strange race buried in a long-lost antiquity on a world of huge weight, were laid bare before me.

I saw again that dark, unfriendly airless world with its vaulted dome of unfamiliar stars. This time I saw others of the Walnut race—spawning thousands. Through flickering, kaleidoscopic flashes I watched a strange disease, apparently an unfavorable radiation from outer space, attack one after another of the beings, wipe them out with the efficiency that lethal gas kills a man.

I realized more clearly than ever that these beings did sustain themselves by radiations. To them, a sudden influx of abnormal radiation was a perfect cosmic Black Plague, absolutely fatal in effect. I saw the death of thousands upon thousands of the creatures until there could not have been more than five remaining.

Here the disease stopped, but four of the five died slowly from after-effects, leaving only one—Yithan Kan!

One, a female of the species, surrounded by the glory of a magnificently intelligent race's discoveries, yet unable alone to do anything with them. Unable to mate, unable to perpetuate the superb science of her species.

She seemed to meditate over the perplexity of this problem for years. I saw her study machines that had no earthly meaning. Telescopes of surpassing power revealed to her the unrevealed depths of the cosmos on polished mirrors of floating mercury. The dead worlds of Sirius, the half-formed worlds of Arcturus, the rich but lifeless worlds whirling around vast Antares and Betelgeuse—these she studied, without avail.

Then the instruments' powers reached out across immeasurable light years to the regions of the dwarf G-type suns, to the Solar System. Mercury, Venus, Mars, and the outer planets were mirrored perfectly in the instruments, but Yithan Kan found no traces of life in any of them. That seemed to be the treasured possession of the third world alone.

Yithan Kan seemed to come to a decision. Her head and legs folded inside her shell-like body. She generated gravity neutralization as simply as a spider spins its web, and hurtled bullet-like into the swirling, dusty emptinesses overhead. . . .

I awoke suddenly with visions of galaxies, suns and planets whirling before my vision. It was morning, and I was no longer in bed. No! The bed had collapsed under my weight in the night, precipitating me onto a floor that was showing signs of cracking.

My heaviness now was a terrific burden. During the night I had changed incredibly, was literally half my previous size with an energy and strength beyond belief.

Hunger, terror, wonderment—these three things battled in my mind as I lumbered creakingly across the cracking floor. I gained the doorway safely enough, but I fell through the staircase and landed in the kitchen below! I wasn't hurt. No indeed! Where I had struck myself against the woodwork it had splintered and left my hardened, stone-gray flesh untouched!

I went into the yard, strangled a dozen chickens one after the other and ate them raw. I was no longer Amos Latham; I was something metamorphosing into an unknown state for an equally unknown purpose. I knew now how Yithan Kan had come to Earth, but the *why* still defeated me.

I knew, too, that if she wanted she could easily get off that stone block without dropping to the ground. Her natural power of gravity neutralization would accomplish that. Only when she had been unconscious from her great fall had she weighed her normal ton to the cubic inch.

Her wine-red little eyes watched me as I ravenously ate the fowls. I didn't try to communicate: I had all my work cut out to master my own movements and control my will power. Going back into the house I thought of the idea of recording my experiences, and up to now I think I have managed to maintain a certain coherency.

It is not easy to write this because I have to have my hand fastened to a rope slung to a beam in the garage roof so that the weight of my arm and hand does not interfere with writing. If this writing is thick and heavy it is because I am constantly wearing down the pencil point, frequently breaking the pencils themselves. The very lightest of pressure suffices.

I feel now that I may revert to the present tense because I have caught up with my experiences to date. There is nothing for me now but to state events as they happen, and I have the oddest conception that they will happen soon.

I have been resting. At least I call it that for want of a better term. In truth, it was more a comatose condition occasioned, I think, by exhaustion. The vast change in my make-up, the enigmatic forcing together of electronic spaces by unconjecturable radiations, the consequent denser packing of materials by scientific powers that I can hardly guess at, tires me with amazing rapidity. But during that sleep, if sleep it was, I dreamed again.

Yithan Kan is more than a mere scientist. She has the knowledge of a brilliant race at her command. The forces of light, space, gravitation and pressure are solved riddles to her mind. I have learned that my earlier hypothesis—that a matter formation can be altered by radiation into what is possibly a new and unthought of state—is correct. By radiations from her own body she has mastered mine, literally is bending its formation to conform with her wishes.

I have eaten again, and now I feel that that huge hunger is abating, maybe by the establishment of some new level of change. I am smaller, infinitely smaller, yet the mass of my body is infinitely increased, compressed to an unbelievable weight.

I no longer dare to go inside the house. Floors and furniture splinter under my weight. . . . I have substituted a chain for a rope to support the pencil, but live in fear that the beam, a foot thick though it is, will smash in two if I do not stop writing. . . . Yet I must go on.

I think I have been unconscious again—it seems to me that days have drifted by. Perhaps it is a good thing I am so far from town; people rarely pass around here. With my last awakening I became conscious of a new sense, which still persists.

I can sense the inflow of cosmic radiations such as are quite undetectable to normal human beings. They give me life, strength, an abounding energy that is both glorious and yet oddly terrifying.

Around me is a world of giantism. The garage seems to me like a vast hall; this very pencil is far bigger than I. I am forced to work it like a lever—but now it is simpler because I have taken on a neutralizing power. The radiations I absorb from space I can convert within myself to neutralizing uses.

You wonder? Why should you? A plant breaks down nitrogen: a human being inhales oxygen and hydrogen and exhales, by the use of inner chemistry, carbon dioxide. Is it so wonderful that I absorb energies and transmit them in their most needed form—for the nullification of weight? No, it is not so impossible but—I forget! I am no longer human, therefore I no longer think properly along human lines.

Do not ask me to explain the full state of my metamorphosis; I have tried to do that already, to tell by the stages through which it happened how Yithan Kan reassembled my bodily atoms so completely as to give me a body no more than an inch in diameter, yet weighing very nearly a ton, without neutralization.

All this she has accomplished without causing death, as easily indeed as in my own experiments I have grafted cuttings from one tree onto another without killing either. Organic life is truly indeed simply an arrangement—in the higher states—of living, thinking matter which, by a mind clever enough, can be altered into a new and entirely un-predictable state.

From this doorway I can see Yithan Kan very clearly. She is as big as I, high atop a mighty block of stone—a stone that was only an ordi-nary block on the day she was first put there. I am like a microscopic tortoise, hardly visible. I am no longer an Earth being, for I am not breathing—only absorbing radiations. The entity of Amos Latham has gone and instead I am—*What?*

At last I grasp the purpose of Yithan Kan's visit. I can feel her mental radiations coming to me, and with those radiations the faint leftover human traces of my mind evince a certain admiration for the nobility, the relentless purpose, of her aim.

For the perpetuation of her race and science she needs a mate—a male. I am still a male. She metamorphosed me into a being identical with herself save in the matter of sex—as easily as a sculptor can model a piece of clay into a woman and then into a dog without changing the clay. He merely reforms the atoms and molecules of the clay into a new shape.

And what does he use for his tools? Basically, force! In like manner, but fully understanding the absolute nature of the force *behind* force, Yithan Kan has remoulded me.

She needs me . . . and I need her! I know I do. I feel it. She is compelling to me now—fascinating. Our children on that far distant world beyond Sirius will carry on the heritage of a race entirely elimi-nated excepted for this indomitable one—Yithan Kan. Afterward, the nucleus of a new race, a reaching upward toward achievement.

I must go to Yithan Kan. Earth no longer holds me. At will I can, and shall, leave it behind—wing across the cosmos with Yithan Kan to her distant planet.

I shall go. I must go. Now!

THE EMBASSY

"I CAME to New York," said Grafius, "because I am sure that there are Martians here." He leaned back to blow a smoke ring, followed it to its dissolution in the air-conditioning outlet with his cool, gray eyes.

"Iron Man!" bawled Broderick, quick as the snap of a relay. He backed around behind his chair as the office door opened and the formidable Mr. Doolan appeared, fists cocked on the ready.

"It's a whack," declared Broderick, pointing at Grafius. "It says there are Martians in New York."

Doolan, probably the most muscular, certainly the dumbest, cop ever kicked out of the police department, eyed Grafius dimly as he clamped the caller's shoulder in a colossal vise of a hand. "Make with the feet," he said, groping for his words. "Hit the main, but heavy."

"He means 'get out,'" explained Broderick. "I echo his sentiments completely."

Grafius, rising leisurely, fished in his breast pocket and chucked a sharkskin wallet onto the desk. "Look it over," he said. "Well worth your time." He stood impassively as Broderick drew from the wallet several large bills.

"Holy-holy," whispered the inspector general as he fingered the money. "I didn't think you cared." Briskly he seated himself again and waved away Doolan.

"Naturally," he explained, toying with Grafius' card, "I'm loath to part with all this lettuce. Your remark about our little speckled friends, the Martians, I shall ignore. This is a small, young agency, new to the art of private investigation. Martians are outside our ken at this moment of the year 1942, but if there's anything in a more conventional line we can do for you—"

"Nothing at all, thank you," said Grafius of Springfield. He recovered his wallet and card from the desk. "However, if you'd care to listen with an open mind—"

"Open wider than the gates of hell," said the private detective, his eyes on the vanishing currency. "Tell your tale."

Grafius crushed out his cigar. "Suppose you were a Martian," he said.

Broderick snickered. "One of the small ones with three tails, or the nasty size with teeth to match?" he asked amiably.

"I'm sorry," said the man from Springfield. "My data doesn't go as far as that, but in a moment I'll give you a reasonable description of the Martians that are in New York.

"When I say Martian, of course, the meaning is 'extraterrestrial of greater civilization than ours.' They may not be Martians. They may even be from another galaxy. But assume you are what I call a Martian, and that you want to keep in touch with Earthly civilization and advancement. Just where would you go?"

"Coney Island?" helplessly suggested the detective.

"Naturally not," said Grafius severely. "Nor to Sea Breeze, Kansas. Nor to Nome, Alaska. Nor to Equatorial Africa. You wouldn't go to some small town. You wouldn't go to some out-of-the-way part of the world where living is anywhere from twenty to several hundred years behind human progress. This will eliminate Asia and Africa. It will eliminate almost all of Europe and South America."

"I get it," said Broderick. "The Martians would head for the U. S. A."

"Exactly. The United States today is the most technically and culturally advanced nation on Earth. And, further, if you came to the United States, you'd come to New York. You would come because it's the largest human concentration on the globe. It's the economic capital of the continent—the very hemisphere! You agree?"

"Sure," said Broderick. "And you wouldn't be in London because of the war. You can't observe human culture while the shells are popping."

"Exactly. But I still haven't proved anything. To continue: it's quite clear to me that we Earth people aren't the only intelligent, civilized race in the Universe. Out of the infinitude of stars and planets there most definitely, mathematically *must* be others. Mars—to continue with my example—is older than Earth geologically; if there were Martians, and if their evolutionary history corresponded with ours, they would certainly be further advanced than we.

"And I will make one more hypothesis: it is that we Earth people are today on the verge of space conquest, and that any race further advanced than we must have already mastered space flight."

"Go on," said Broderick, who was beginning to look scared. He was a naturally apprehensive type, and the thought that Martians might be just around the corner didn't help him.

"Certainly. But you needn't look so worried, for the Martians won't show up in your office. They must work strictly under cover, since from their point of view—advanced, you will remember—it would be foolish to make themselves known to us as long as we humans are a military, predatory race. It would be a risk which no advanced mentality would take."

"How long has this been going on?" asked Broderick agitatedly.

"Judging from the geology of Mars, some hundreds of years," replied Grafius dreamily. "They've been watching, waiting—"

"You said you could describe them," snapped the detective. "What do they look like?"

"I can't describe their appearance," said Grafius, down to Earth again. "But this is what they most probably are: a group of ordinary-appearing people who live together. In downtown New York, close to newspapers, publishers, news cables, communication centers and the financial powers of Wall Street. They would have no obvious means of support, for all their time must be taken up with the observation that is their career. They almost certainly live in a private house, without prying janitors who would get curious about their peculiar radio equipment.

"And our best bet—they are sure to receive every major paper and magazine, in all the languages of the world."

"I get it," said Broderick. "Very sweet and simple. But what's your reason for wanting to meet up with the Martians, social, if I may ask?"

"Call it curiosity," smiled Grafius. "Or an inflated ego. Or merely the desire to check my logic."

"Sure," said Broderick. "I can offer you the following services of my bureau: bodyguard—that's Iron Man, outside. Think you'll need him?"

"Certainly not," said Grafius of Springfield. "You have no right to suppose that the Martians would stoop to violence. Remember their advanced mentality."

"I won't insist," said the detective. "Second, I can check on all subscription departments of the big papers and magazines. Third, the radio parts lead. Fourth, renting agents. Fifth, sixth and seventh, correlation of these. Eighth, incidentals. It should come to about—" He named a figure. The remainder of the interview was purely financial in character.

Iron Man Doolan wasn't very bright. He knew how to walk, but occasionally he forgot and would try to take both feet off the ground at once. This led to minor contusions of the face and extremities, bruises and gashes that the ex-cop never noticed. He was underorganized.

It taxed him seriously, this walking about in a strange neighborhood. There were hydrants and traffic signals in his way, and each one was a problem in navigation to be solved. Thus it took him half an hour to walk the city block he had been shown to by Broderick, who was waiting nervously, tapping his feet, in a cigar store.

"He's dull—very dull," confided the detective to Grafius, who sipped a coke at the soda fountain. "But the only man for a job like this. Do you think they'll make trouble for him?"

Grafius gurgled through the straw apologetically. "Perhaps," he said. "If it is No. 108—" He brooded into his glass, not finishing the sentence.

"It certainly is," said Broderick decidedly. "What could it be but the Martian embassy that takes everything from *Pic* to the Manchester *Guardian?*"

"Polish revolutionaries," suggested the man from Springfield. "Possibly an invalid. We haven't watched the place for more than a couple of weeks. We really haven't any data worth the name."

The detective hiccupped with nervousness, hastily swallowed a pepsin tablet. Then he stared at his client fixedly. "You amaze me," he stated at last. "You come at me with a flit-git chain of possibilities that you're staking real cash on. And once we hit a solid train you refuse to believe your own eyes. Man, what do you want—a sworn statement from your Martians that they live in No. 108?"

"Let's take a look," said Grafius. "I hope your Mr. Doolan gets a bite."

"Iron Man, I repeat, is not very bright. But he's pushed buttons before, and if somebody answers the door he's going to push the button on his minicam. I drilled that into his—"

He broke off at the sound of a scream, a shriek, a lance of thin noise that sliced down the street. Then there was a crash of steel on concrete. The two dashed from the shop and along the sidewalk.

They stopped short at the sight of Iron Man Doolan's three hundred pounds of muscle grotesquely spattered and slimed underneath a ponderous safe. A colored girl, young and skinny, was wailing in a thin monotone, to herself: "First he squashed and then it fell. First he squashed and then—"

Broderick grabbed her by the shoulders. "What happened?" he yelled hoarsely. "What did you see?"

She stopped her wail and looked directly and simply at him. In an explanatory tone she said: "First he squashed—and *then* it fell." Broderick, feeling sick, let go of her, vaguely heard her burst into hysterical tears as he took Grafius by the arm and walked him away down the street.

Somewhere on Riverside Drive that evening the detective declared: "I know it sounds like a damned childish trick, but I'm going to get drunk, because I had a lot of affection for Doolan. He would understand it as a fitting tribute."

"He was, in his way, the perfect expression of a brutal ideal," mused Grafius. "In an earlier, less sophisticated day he would have been a sort of deity. I'll go with you, if you don't mind."

In a place whose atmosphere was Chinese they drank libations to the departed Iron Man, then moved on down the street. Midnight found Broderick pie-eyed, but with a tense control over his emotions that he was afraid to break through.

It was Grafius at last who suggested calmly: "They are a menace. What shall we do about them?"

Broderick knew just exactly what the man from Springfield meant. With a blurred tongue he replied: "Lay off of them. Keep out of their way. If we make trouble, it's curtains for us—what they did to Doolan is all the proof I need. I know when I'm licked."

"Yes," said Grafius. "That's the trouble with you. Doolan didn't know—" He collapsed softly over the table. Broderick stared at him for a long moment, then gulped the rest of his drink and poked his client in the shoulder.

Grafius came up fighting. "Martians," he shrilled. "Dirty, dusty, dry sons of—"

"Take it easy," said the detective. He eyed a girl sitting solo at a nearby table, who eyed him back with a come-on smile.

Grafius stared at the interchange broodingly. "Keep away from her," he said at last. "She may be one of the Martians—filth they are—unspeakable things—bone-dry monsters from an undead world—" He canted over the table again.

The liquor hit Broderick then like a padded tent maul. He remembered conducting a fantastically polite Gallup poll of the customers in the saloon, inquiring their precise sentiments toward "our little feathered friends of the Red Planet."

He should have known better than to act up in Skelley's Skittle House. Skelley was a restaurateur slow to wrath, but he had his license to take care of, as well as his good name. And Skelley, like so many of his kind, got a big kick out of seeing what a Micky Finn could do.

Grafius was completely unconscious when Broderick, with elaborate protestations of gratitude, accepted the "last one on the house." He tossed down the rye and quaffed the chaser. Skelley, ever the artist, had stirred the chloral into the larger glass.

The stuff took effect on Broderick like a keg of gunpowder. After the first few spasms he was utterly helpless, poisoned to within an inch of his life, lying heaving on the floor, his eye whites rolling and yellowed, pouring sweat from every hair, actually and literally wishing he were dead and out of his internal agony. That is what a skilled practitioner can do with the little bottle behind the bar.

He saw the waiter and Skelley go through Grafius' pockets, calling for witnesses among the customers that they were taking no more than their due. The customers heartily approved; a woman whose face was baggy and chalked said: "Peeble wh' dunno hodda drink li' gennlem'n shunt drink 't all!" She hiccupped violently, and a waitress led her to the powder room for treatment.

Skelley laboriously read the calling card in Grafius' vest. "That ain't no help," he declared wittily. "It don't say which Springfield."

Broderick saw and felt himself being rolled over, his pockets being dipped into. The spasms began again, ending suddenly as he heard the voice of his host declare: "No. 108! Snooty neighborhood for a lush like that."

The detective tried to explain, tried to tell the man that it wasn't his address but the address of the Martians he'd chanced on in his pockets. But all the voice he could summon up was a grunt that broke to a peep of protest as he was hauled up and carried out in Skelley's strong and practiced arms.

He and Grafius were dumped into a taxi; between spasms he heard the restaurateur give the hackie the Martians' address.

Broderick was going through a physical and mental hell, lying there in the back of the cab. He noted through his nauseous haze the street lights sliding by, noted the passage of Washington Square, sensed the auto turning up Fifth Avenue. His agony lessened by Fiftieth Street, and for a moment he could talk. Hoarsely he called to the cabby to stop. Before he could amplify and explain, the retching overtook him again, and he was helpless.

He passed out completely at a long traffic-light stop; he never felt the car turn right. The next thing he knew the cabby was bundling him out of the rear, leaning him beside Grafius against the door of No. 108. The cabby leaned against the buzzer for a moment, then drove off.

Broderick could only stare with dumb agony as the door opened. "Dear, dear!" said the soft, shocked voice of a woman.

"Are they anyone we know, Florence?" demanded a man.

"Unfortunate creatures, whoever they are," said the woman.

Broderick got a glimpse of a handsome, ruddy face as the man carried him into the hall, the woman following with Grafius. The man from Springfield awoke suddenly, stared into the face of the woman, then set up a shrill screaming that did not end until she had punched him twice in the jaw.

"Shame!" she declared. "We're kind enough to take you two sots in out of the cold and then you get the D. T.'s!" There was a warm smile lurking in the corners of her mouth.

The man opened a door somewhere, and Broderick apprehended a smooth, continuous clicking sound, very much faster and more rhythmical than a typewriter.

"There's something familiar about this boy, Florence," declared the man as he studied the helpless detective.

She wrinkled her brows prettily. "Of course!" she cried at last with a delighted smile. "It's that Broderick!"

"Yes. That Broderick," said the man. "And this other one—"

"Oh!" cried the woman, in tones of ineffable loathing. "*Oh!*" She turned her head away as though sickened.

"Yes," said the man, his face wrinkled and writhing with unspeakable disgust. "This other one is the Grafius he was so often thinking about."

The woman turned again, her face raging angry, black with the blackest passion. Her high French heels ground into the face of the dead-drunk Grafius again and again; the man had to pull her off at last. It was plain that he himself was exercising will power of the highest order in control of an impulse to smash and mangle the despised one.

"Grafius!" he said at last, as though the word were a lump of vileness in his mouth. "That Venusian!" He spat.

The woman broke free from his grasp, kicked the mutilated face. Broderick heard the teeth splintering in the abused mouth.

LESTER DEL REY

DARK MISSION

THE rays of the Sun lanced down over the tops of the trees and into the clearing, revealing a scene of chaos and havoc. Yesterday there had been a wooden frame house there, but now only pieces of it remained. One wall had been broken away, as by an explosion, and lay on the ground in fragments; the roof was crushed in, as if some giant had stepped on it and passed on.

But the cause of the damage was still there, lying on the ruins of the house. A tangled mass of buckled girders and metal plates lay mixed with a litter of laboratory equipment that had been neatly arranged in one room of the house, and parts of a strange engine lay at one side. Beyond was a tube that might have been a rocket. The great metal object that lay across the broken roof now only hinted at the sleek cylinder it had once been, but a trained observer might have guessed that it was the wreck of a rocketship. From the former laboratory, flames were licking up at the metal hull, and slowly spreading toward the rest of the house.

In the clearing, two figures lay outstretched, of similar size and build, but otherwise unlike. One was of a dark man of middle age, completely naked, with a face cut and battered beyond all recognition. The odd angle of the head was unmistakable proof that his neck was broken. The other man might have been a brawny sea viking of earlier days, both from his size and appearance, but his face revealed something finer and of a higher culture. He was fully clothed, and the slow movement of his chest showed that there was still life in him. Beside him, there was a broken beam from the roof, a few spots of blood on it. There was more blood on the man's head, but the cut was minor, and he was only stunned.

Now he stirred uneasily and groped uncertainly to his feet, shaking his head and fingering the cut on his scalp. His eyes traveled slowly across the clearing and to the ruins that were burning merrily. The corpse claimed his next attention, and he turned it over to examine the neck. He knit his brows and shook his head savagely, trying to call back the memories that eluded him.

They would not come. He recognized what his eyes saw, but his mind produced no words to describe them, and the past was missing. His first memory was of wakening to find his head pounding with an ache that was almost unbearable. Without surprise, he studied the rocket and saw that it had come down on the house, out of control, but it evoked no pictures in his mind, and he gave up. He might have been in the rocket or the house at the time; he had no way of telling which. Probably the naked man had been asleep at the time in the house.

Something prickled gently in the back of his mind, growing stronger and urging him to do something. He must not waste time here, but must fulfill some vital mission. What mission? For a second, he almost had it, and then it was gone again, leaving only the compelling urge that must be obeyed. He shrugged and started away from the ruins toward the little trail that showed through the trees.

Then another impulse called him back to the corpse, and he obeyed it because he knew of nothing else to do. Acting without conscious volition, he tugged at the corpse, found it strangely heavy, and dragged it toward the house. The flames were everywhere now, but he found a place where the heat was not too great and pulled the corpse over a pile of combustibles.

With the secondary impulse satisfied, the first urge returned, and he set off down the trail, moving slowly. The shoes hurt his feet, and his legs were leaden, but he kept on grimly, while a series of questions went around his head in circles. Who was he, where, and why?

Whoever had lived in the house, himself or the corpse, had obviously chosen the spot for privacy; the trail seemed to go on through the woods endlessly, and he saw no signs of houses along it. He clumped on mechanically, wondering if there was no end, until a row of crossed poles bearing wires caught his eye. Ahead, he made out a broad highway, with vehicles speeding along it in both directions, and hastened forward, hoping to meet someone.

Luck was with him. Pulled up at the side of the road was one of the vehicles, and a man was doing something at the front end of the car. Rough words carried back to him suggesting anger. He grinned suddenly and hastened toward the car, his eyes riveted on the man's head. A tense feeling shot through his brain and left, just as he reached the machine.

"Need help?" The words slipped out unconsciously, and now other words came pouring into his head, along with ideas and knowledge that had not been there before. But the sight of the man, or whatever had restored that section of his memory, had brought back no personal knowledge, and that seemed wrong somehow. The driving impulse he felt was still unexplained.

The man had looked up at his words, and relief shot over the sweating face. "Help's the one thing I need," he replied gratefully. "I been fussing with this blasted contraption darned near an hour, and nobody's even stopped to ask, so far. Know anything about it?"

"Um-m-m." The stranger, as he was calling himself for want of a better name, tested the wires himself, vaguely troubled at the simplicity of the engine. He gave up and went around to the other side, lifting the hood and inspecting the design. Then sureness came to him as he reached for the tool kit. "Probably the . . . um . . . timing pins," he said.

It was. A few minutes later the engine purred softly and the driver turned to the stranger. "O. K. now, I guess. Good thing you came along; worst part of the road, and not a repair shop for miles. Where you going?"

"I—" The stranger caught himself. "The big city," he said, for want of a better destination.

"Hop in, then. I'm going to Elizabeth, right on your way. Glad to have you along; gets so a man talks to himself on these long drives, unless he has something to do. Smoke?"

"Thank you, no. I never do." He watched the other light up, feeling uncomfortable about it. The smell of the smoke, when it reached him, was nauseous, as were the odor of gasoline and the man's own personal effluvium, but he pushed them out of his mind as much as possible. "Have you heard or read anything about a rocketship of some kind?"

"Sure. Oglethorpe's, you mean? I been reading what the papers had to say about it." The drummer took his eyes off the road for a second, and his beady little eyes gleamed. "I been wondering a long time why some of these big-shot financiers don't back up the rockets, and finally Oglethorpe does. Boy, now maybe we'll find out something about this Mars business."

The stranger grinned mechanically. "What does his ship look like?"

"Picture of it in the *Scoop,* front page. Find it back of the seat, there. Yeah, that's it. Wonder what the Martians look like?"

"Hard to guess," the stranger answered. Even rough halftones of the picture showed that it was not the ship that had crashed, but radically different. "No word of other rockets?"

"Nope, not that I know of. You know, I kinda feel maybe the Martians might look like us. Sure." He took the other's skepticism for granted without looking around. "Wrote a story about that once, for one of these science-fiction magazines, but they sent it back. I figured out maybe a long time ago there was a civilization on Earth—Atlantis, maybe—and they went over and settled on Mars. Only Atlantis sunk on them, and there they were, stranded. I figured maybe one day they came back, sort of lost out for a while, but popped up again and started civilization humming. Not bad, eh?"

"Clever," the stranger admitted. "But it sounds vaguely familiar. Suppose we said instead there was a war between the mother world and Mars that wrecked both civilizations, instead of your Atlantis sinking. Wouldn't that be more logical?"

"Maybe, I dunno. Might try it, though mostly they seem to want freaks— Darned fool, passing on a hill!" He leaned out to shake a pudgy fist, then came back to his rambling account. "Read one the other day with two races, one like octopuses, the others twenty feet tall and all blue."

Memory pricked tantalizingly and came almost to the surface. Blue— Then it was gone again, leaving only a troubled feeling. The stranger frowned and settled down in the seat, answering in monosyllables to the other's monologue, and watching the patchwork of country and cities slip by.

"There's Elizabeth. Any particular place you want me to drop you?"

The stranger stirred from the half-coma induced by the cutting ache in his head, and looked about. "Any place," he answered. Then the urge in the back of his mind grabbed at him again, and he changed it. "Some doctor's office."

That made sense, of course. Perhaps the impulse had been only the logical desire to seek medical aid, all along. But it was still there, clamoring for expression, and he doubted the logic of anything connected with it. The call for aid could not explain the sense of disaster that accompanied it. As the car stopped before a house with a doctor's shingle, his pulse was hammering with frenzied urgency.

"Here we are." The drummer reached out toward the door handle, almost brushing one of the other's hands. The stranger jerked it back savagely, avoiding contact by a narrow margin, and a cold chill ran up his back and quivered its way down again. If that hand had touched him— The half-opened door closed again, but left one fact impressed on him. Under no conditions must he suffer another to make direct contact with his body, lest something horrible should happen! Another crazy angle, unconnected with the others, but too strong for disobedience.

He climbed out, muttering his thanks, and made up the walk toward the office of Dr. Lanahan, hours 12:00 to 4:00.

The doctor was an old man, with the seamed and rugged good-nature of the general practitioner, and his office fitted him. There was a row of medical books along one wall, a glass-doored cabinet containing various medicaments, and a clutter of medical instruments. He listened to the stranger's account quietly, smiling encouragement at times, and tapping the desk with his pencil.

"Amnesia, of course," he agreed, finally. "Rather peculiar in some respects, but most cases of that are individual. When the brain is injured, its actions are usually unpredictable. Have you considered the possibility of hallucinations in connection with those impulses you mention?"

"Yes." He had considered it from all angles, and rejected the solutions as too feeble. "If they were ordinary impulses, I'd agree with you. But they're far deeper than that, and there's a good reason for them, somewhere. I'm sure of that."

"Hm-m-m." The doctor tapped his pencil again and considered. The stranger sat staring at the base of his neck, and the tense feeling in his head returned, as it had been when he first met the drummer. Something rolled around in his mind and quieted. "And you have nothing on you in the way of identification?"

"Uh!" The stranger grunted, feeling foolish, and reached into his pockets. "I hadn't thought of that." He brought out a package of cigarettes, a stained handkerchief, glasses, odds and ends that meant nothing to him, and finally a wallet stuffed with bills. The doctor seized on that and ran through its contents quickly.

"Evidently you had money. . . . Hm-m-m, no identification card, except for the letters L. H. Ah, here we are; a calling card." He passed it over, along with the wallet, and smiled in self-satisfaction. "Evidently you're a fellow physician, Dr. Lurton Haines. Does that recall anything?"

"Nothing." It was good to have a name, in a way, but that was his only response to the sight of the card. And why was he carrying glasses and cigarettes for which he had no earthly use?

The doctor was hunting through his pile of books, and finally came up with a dirty red volume. "Who's Who," he explained. "Let's see. Hm-m-m! Here we are. 'Lurton R. Haines, M. D.' Odd, I thought you were younger than that. Work along cancer research. No relatives mentioned. The address is evidently that of the house you remember first—'Surrey Road, Danesville.' Want to see it?"

He passed the volume over, and the stranger—or Haines—scanned it carefully, but got no more out of it than the other's summary, except for the fact that he was forty-two years old. He put the book back on the desk, and reached for his wallet, laying a bill on the pad where the other could reach it.

"Thank you, Dr. Lanahan." There was obviously nothing more the doctor could do for him, and the odor of the little room and the doctor were stifling him; apparently he was allergic to the smell of other men. "Never mind the cut on the head—it's purely superficial."

"But—"

Haines shrugged and mustered a smile, reached for the door, and made for the outside again. The urge was gone now, replaced by a vast sense of gloom, and he knew that his mission had ended in failure.

They knew so little about healing, though they tried so hard. The entire field of medicine ran through Haines' mind now, with all its startling successes and hopeless failures, and he knew that even his own problem was beyond their ability. And the knowledge, like the sudden return of speech, was a mystery; it had come rushing into his mind while he stared at the doctor, at the end of the sudden tenseness, and a numbing sense of failure had accompanied it. Strangely, it was not the knowledge of a specialist in cancer research, but such common methods as a general practitioner might use.

One solution suggested itself, but it was too fantastic for belief. The existence of telepaths was suspected, but not ones who could steal whole pages of knowledge from the mind of another, merely by looking at him. No, that was more illogical than the sudden wakening of isolated fields of memory by the sight of the two men.

He stopped at a corner, weary under the load of despondency he was carrying, and mulled it over dully. A newsboy approached hopefully. *"Time* a' *News* out!" the boy singsonged his wares. *"Scoop* 'n' *Juhnal!* Read awl about the big train wreck! Paper, mister?"

Haines shrugged dully. "No paper!"

"Blonde found moidehed in bathtub," the boy insinuated. "Mahs rocket account!" The man must have an Achilles' heel somewhere.

But the garbled jargon only half registered on Haines' ears. He started across the street, rubbing his temples, before the second driving impulse caught at him and sent him back remorselessly to the paper boy. He found some small change in his pocket, dropped a nickel on the pile of papers, disregarding the boy's hand, and picked up a copy of the *Scoop.* "Screwball," the boy decided aloud, and dived for the nickel.

The picture was no longer on the front page of the tabloid, but Haines located the account with some effort. "Mars Rocket Take-off Wednesday," said the headline in conservative twenty-four-point type, and there was three-quarters of a column under it. "Man's first flight to Mars will not be delayed, James Oglethorpe told reporters here today. Undismayed by the skepticism of the scientists, the financier is going ahead with his plans, and expects his men to take off for Mars Wednesday, June 8, as scheduled. Construction has been completed, and the rocket machine is now undergoing tests."

Haines scanned down the page, noting the salient facts. The writer had kept his tongue in his cheek, but under the faintly mocking words there was the information he wanted. The rocket might work; man was at last on his way toward the conquests of the planets. There was no mention of another rocket. Obviously then, that one must have been built in secret in a futile effort to beat Oglethorpe's model.

But that was unimportant. The important thing was that he must stop the flight! Above all else, man must not make that trip! There was no sanity to it, and yet somehow it was beyond mere sanity. It was his duty to prevent any such voyage, and that duty was not to be questioned.

He returned quickly to the newsboy, reached out to touch his shoulder, and felt his hand jerk back to avoid the touch. The boy seemed to sense it, though, for he turned quickly. "Paper?" he began brightly before recognizing the stranger. "Oh, it's you. Watcha want?"

"Where can I find a train to New York?" Haines pulled a quarter from his pocket and tossed it on the pile of papers.

The boy's eyes brightened again.

"Four blocks down, turn right, and keep going till you come to the station. Can't miss it. Thanks, mister."

The discovery of the telephone book as a source of information was Haines' single major triumph, and the fact that the first Oglethorpe he tried was a colored street cleaner failed to take the edge off it. Now he trudged uptown, counting the numbers that made no sense to him; apparently the only system was one of arithmetical progression, irrespective of streets.

His shoulders were drooping, and the lines of pain around his eyes had finally succeeded in drawing his brows together. A coughing spell hit him, torturing his lungs for long minutes, and then passed. That was a new development, as was the pressure around his heart. And everywhere was the irritating aroma of men, gasoline, and tobacco, a stale mixture that he could not escape. He thrust his hands deeper into his pockets to avoid chance contact with someone on the street, and crossed over toward the building that bore the number for which he was searching.

Another man was entering the elevator, and he followed mechanically, relieved that he would not have to plod up the stairs. "Oglethorpe?" he asked the operator, uncertainly.

"Fourth floor, Room 405." The boy slid the gate open, pointing, and Haines stepped out and into the chromium-trimmed reception room. There were half a dozen doors leading from it, but he spotted the one marked "James H. Oglethorpe, Private," and slouched forward.

"Were you expected, sir?" The girl popped up in his face, one hand on the gate that barred his way. Her face was a study in frustration, which probably explained the sharpness of her tone. She delivered an Horatius-guarding-the-bridge formula. "Mr. Oglethorpe is busy now."

"Lunch," Haines answered curtly. He had already noticed that men talked more freely over food.

She flipped a little book in her hand and stared at it. "There's no record here of a luncheon engagement, Mr.—"

"Haines. Dr. Lurton Haines." He grinned wryly, wiggling a twenty-dollar bill casually in one hand. Money was apparently the one disease to which nobody was immune. Her eyes dropped to it, and hesitation entered her voice as she consulted her book.

"Of course, Mr. Oglethorpe might have made it some time ago and forgotten to tell me—" She caught his slight nod, and followed the bill to the corner of the desk. "Just have a seat, and I'll speak to Mr. Oglethorpe."

She came out of the office a few minutes later, and winked quickly. "He'd forgotten," she told Haines, "but it's all right now. He'll be right out, Dr. Haines. It's lucky he's having lunch late today."

James Oglethorpe was a younger man than Haines had expected, though his interest in rocketry might have been some clue to that. He came out of his office, pushing a Homburg down on curly black hair, and raked the other with his eyes. "Dr. Haines?" he asked, thrusting out a large hand. "Seems we have a luncheon engagement."

Haines rose quickly and bowed before the other had a chance to grasp his hand. Apparently Oglethorpe did not notice, for he went on smoothly. "Easy to forget these telephone engagements, sometimes. Aren't you the cancer man? One of your friends was in a few months ago for a contribution to your work."

They were in the elevator then, and Haines waited until it opened and they headed for the lunchroom in the building before answering. "I'm not looking for money this time, however. It's the rocket you're financing that interests me. I think it may work."

"It will, though you're one of the few that believes it." Caution, doubt, and interest were mingled on Oglethorpe's face. He ordered before turning back to Haines. "Want to go along? If you do, there's still room for a physician in the crew."

"No, nothing like that. Toast and milk only, please—" Haines had no idea of how to broach the subject, with nothing concrete to back up his statements. Looking at the set of the other's jaw and the general bulldog attitude of the man, he gave up hope and only continued because he had to. He fell back on imagination, wondering how much of it was true.

"Another rocket made that trip, Mr. Oglethorpe, and returned. But the pilot was dying before he landed. I can show you the wreck of his machine, though there's not much left after the fire—perhaps not enough to prove it was a rocketship. Somewhere out on Mars there's something man should never find. It's—"

"Ghosts?" suggested Oglethorpe, brusquely.

"Death! I'm asking you—"

Again Oglethorpe interrupted. "Don't. There was a man in to see me yesterday who claimed he'd been there—offered to show me the wreck of *his* machine. A letter this morning explained that the Martians had visited the writer and threatened all manner of things. I'm not calling you a liar, Dr. Haines, but I've heard too many of those stories; whoever told you this one was either a crank or a horror-monger. I can show you a stack of letters that range from astrology to zombies, all explaining why I can't go, and some offer photographs for proof."

"Suppose I said I'd made the trip in that rocket?" The card in the wallet said he was Haines, and the wallet had been in the suit he was wearing; but there had also been the glasses and cigarettes for which he had no use.

Oglethorpe twisted his lips, either in disgust or amusement. "You're an intelligent man, Dr. Haines; let's assume I am, also. It may sound ridiculous to you, but the only reason I had for making the fortune I'm credited with was to build that ship, and it's taken more work and time than the layman would believe. If a green ant, seven feet high, walked into my office and threatened Armageddon, I'd still go."

Even the impossible impulse recognized the impossible. Oglethorpe was a man who did things first and worried about them when the mood hit him—and there was nothing moody about him. The conversation turned to everyday matters and Haines let it drift as it would, finally dragging out into silence.

At least, he was wiser by one thing: he knew the location of the rocket ground and the set-up of guards around it—something even the newspapermen had failed to learn, since all pictures and information had come through Oglethorpe. There could no longer be any question of his ability to gain desired information by some hazy telepathic process. Either he was a mental freak, or the accident had done things to him that should have been surprising but weren't.

Haines had taken a cab from the airport, giving instructions that caused the driver to lift his eyebrows; but money was still all-powerful. Now they were slipping through country even more desolate than the woods around Haines' house, and the end of the road came into view, with a rutted muddy trail leading off, marked by the tires of the trucks Oglethorpe had used for his freighting. The cab stopped there.

"This the place?" the driver asked uncertainly.

"It is." Haines added a bill to what had already been paid and dismissed him. Then he dragged his way out to the dirt road and followed it, stopping for rest frequently. His ears were humming loudly now, and each separate little vertebra of his back protested at his going on. But there was no turning back; he had tried that, at the airport and found the urge strong enough to combat his weakening will.

"Only a little rest!" he muttered thickly, but the force in his head lifted his leaden feet and sent them marching toward the rocket camp. Above him the gray clouds passed over the Moon, and he looked up at Mars shining in the sky. Words from the lower part of the drummer's vocabulary came into his throat, but the effort of saying them was more than the red planet merited. He plowed on in silence.

Mars had moved over several degrees in the sky when he first sighted the camp, lying in a long, narrow valley. At one end were the shacks of the workmen, at the other a big structure that housed the rocket from chance prying eyes. Haines stopped to cough out part of his lungs, and his breath was husky and labored as he worked his way down.

The guards should be strung out along the edge of the valley. Oglethorpe was taking no chances with the cranks who had written him letters and denounced him as a godless fool leading his men to death. Rockets at best were fragile things, and only a few men would be needed to ruin the machine once it was discovered. Haines ran over the guards' positions, and skirted through the underbrush, watching for periods when the Moon was darkened. Once he almost tripped an alarm, but missed it in time.

Beyond, there was no shrubbery, but his suit was almost the shade of the ground in the moonlight, and by lying still between dark spells, he crawled forward toward the rocket shed, undetected. He noticed the distance of the houses and the outlying guards and nodded to himself; they should be safe from any explosion.

The coast looked clear. Then, in the shadow of the building, a tiny red spark gleamed and subsided slowly; a man was there, smoking a cigarette. By straining his eyes, Haines made out the long barrel of a rifle against the building. This guard must be an added precaution, unknown to Oglethorpe.

A sudden rift in the thickening clouds came, and Haines slid himself flat against the ground, puzzling over the new complication. For a second he considered turning back, but realized that he could not—his path now was clearly defined, and he had no choice but to follow it. As the Moon slid out of sight again, he came to his feet quietly and moved toward the figure waiting there.

"Hello!" His voice was soft, designed to reach the man at the building but not the guards behind in the outskirts. "Hello, there. Can I come forward? Special inspector from Oglethorpe."

A beam of light lanced out from the shadow, blinding him, and he walked forward at the best pace he could muster. The light might reveal him to the other guards, but he doubted it; their attention was directed outward, away from the buildings.

"Come ahead," the answer came finally. "How'd you get past the others?" The voice was suspicious, but not unusually so. The rifle, Haines saw, was directed at his mid-section, and he stopped a few feet away, where the other could watch him.

"Jimmy Durham knew I was coming," he told the guard. According to the information he had stolen from Oglethorpe's mind, Durham was in charge of the guards. "He told me he hadn't had time to notify you, but I took a chance."

"Hm-m-m. Guess it's all right, since they let you through; but you can't leave here until somebody identifies you. Keep your hands up." The guard came forward cautiously to feel for concealed weapons. Haines held his hands up out of the other's reach, where there was no danger of a direct skin to skin contact. "O. K., seems all right. What's your business here?"

"General inspection; the boss got word there might be a little trouble brewing and sent me here to make sure guard was being kept, and to warn you. All locked up here?"

"Nope. A lock wouldn't do much good on this shack; that's why I'm here. Want I should signal Jimmy to come and identify you so you can go?"

"Don't bother." Conditions were apparently ideal, except for one thing. But he would not murder the guard! There must be some other way, without adding that to the work he was forced to do. "I'm in no hurry, now that I've seen everything. Have a smoke?"

"Just threw one away. 'Smatter, no matches? Here."

Haines rubbed one against the friction surface of the box and lit the cigarette gingerly. The raw smoke stung against his burning throat, but he controlled the cough, and blew it out again; in the dark, the guard could not see his eyes watering, nor the grimaces he made. He was waging a bitter fight with himself against the impulse that had ordered the smoke to distract the guard's attention, and he knew he was failing. "Thanks!"

One of the guard's hands met his, reaching for the box. The next second the man's throat was between the stranger's hands, and he was staggering back, struggling to tear away and cry for help. Surprise confused his efforts for the split second necessary, and one of Haines' hands came free and out, then chopped down sharply to strike the guard's neck with the edge of the palm. A low grunt gurgled out, and the figure went limp.

Impulse had conquered again! The guard was dead, his neck broken by the sharp blow. Haines leaned against the building, catching his breath and fighting back the desire to lose his stomach's contents. When some control came back, he picked up the guard's flashlight, and turned into the building. In the darkness, the outlines of the great rocketship were barely visible.

With fumbling fingers Haines groped forward to the hull, then struck a match and shaded it in his hands until he could make out the airport, standing open. Too much light might show through a window and attract attention.

Inside, he threw the low power of the flashlight on and moved forward, down the catwalk and toward the rear where the power machinery would be housed. It had been simple, after all, and only the quick work of destruction still remained.

He traced the control valves easily, running an eye over the uncovered walls and searching out the pipes that led from them. From the little apparatus he saw, this ship was obviously inferior to the one that had crashed, yet it had taken years to build and drained Oglethorpe's money almost to the limit. Once destroyed, it might take men ten more years to replace it; two was the minimum, and in those two years—

The thought slipped from him, but some memories were coming back. He saw himself in a small metal room, fighting against the inexorable exhaustion of fuel, and losing. Then there had been a final burst from the rockets, and the ship had dropped sickeningly through the atmosphere. He had barely had time to get to the air locks before the crash. Miraculously, as the ship's fall was cushioned by the house, he had been thrown free into the lower branches of a tree, to catch, and lose momentum before striking Earth.

The man who had been in the house had fared worse; he had been thrown out with the wrecked wall, already dead. Roughly, the stranger remembered a hasty transfer of clothing from the corpse, and then the beam had dropped on him, shutting out his memory in blackness. So he was not Haines, after all, but someone from the rocket, and his story to Oglethorpe had been basically true.

Haines—he still thought of himself under that name—caught himself as his knees gave under him, and hauled himself up by the aid of a protruding bar. There was work to be done; after that, what happened to his own failing body was another matter. It seemed now that from his awakening he had expected to meet death before another day, and had been careless of the fact.

He ran his eyes around the rocket room again, until he came to a tool kit that lay invitingly open with a large wrench sticking up from it. That would serve to open the valves. The flashlight lay on the floor where he had dropped it, and he kicked it around with his foot to point at the wall, groping out for the wrench. His fingers were stiff as they clasped around the handle.

And, in the beam of light, he noticed his hand for the first time in hours. Dark-blue veins rose high on flesh that was marked with a faint pale-blue. He considered it dully, thrusting out his other hand and examining it; there, too, was the blue flush, and on his palms, as he turned them upward, the same color showed. Blue!

The last of his memory flashed through his brain in a roaring wave, bringing a slow tide of pictures with it. With one part of his mind, he was working on the valves with the wrench, while the other considered the knowledge that had returned to him. He saw the streets of a delicate, fairy city, half deserted, and as he seemed to watch, a man staggered out of a doorway, clutching at his throat with blue hands, to fall writhing to the ground! The people passed on quickly, avoiding contact with the corpse, fearful even to touch each other.

Everywhere, death reached out for the people. The planet was riddled with it. It lay on the skin of an infected person, to be picked up by the touch of another, and passed on to still more. In the air, a few seconds sufficed to kill the germs, but new ones were being sent out from the pores of the skin, so that there were always a few active ones lurking there. On contact, the disease began an insidious conquest, until, after months without a sign, it suddenly attacked the body housing it, turned it blue, and brought death in a few painful hours.

Some claimed it was the result of an experiment that had gone beyond control, others that it had dropped as a spore from space. Whatever it was, there was no cure for it on Mars. Only the legends that spoke of a race of their people on the mother world of Earth offered any faint hope, and to that they had turned when there was no other chance.

He saw himself undergoing examinations that finally resulted in his being chosen to go in the rocket they were building feverishly. He had been picked because his powers of telepathy were unusual, even to the mental science of Mars; the few remaining weeks had been used in developing that power systematically, and implanting in his head the duties that he must perform, so long as a vestige of life remained to him.

Haines watched the first of the liquid from the fuel pipes splash out, and dropped the wrench. Old Leán Dagh had doubted his ability to draw knowledge by telepathy from a race of a different culture, he reflected; too bad the old man had died without knowing of the success his methods had met, even though the mission had been a failure, due to man's feeble knowledge of the curative sciences. Now his one task was to prevent the race of this world from dying in the same manner.

He pulled himself to his feet again and went staggering down the catwalk, muttering disconnected sentences. The blue of his skin was darker now, and he had to force himself across the space from the ship to the door of the building, grimly commanding his failing muscles, to the guard's body that still lay where he had left it.

Most of the strength left him was useless against the pull of this heavier planet and the torture movement had become. He tried to drag the corpse behind him, then fell on hands and knees and backed toward the ship, using one arm and his teeth on the collar to pull it after him. He was swimming in a world that was bordering on unconsciousness, now, and once darkness claimed him; he came out of it to find himself inside the rocket, still dragging his burden, the implanted impulses stronger than his will.

Bit by bit, he dragged his burden behind him down the catwalk, until the engine room was reached, and he could drop it on the floor, where the liquid fuel had made a thin film. The air was heavy with vapors, and chilled by the evaporation, but he was only partly conscious of that. Only a spark was needed now, and his last duty would be finished.

Inevitably, a few of the dead on Mars would be left unburned, where men might find the last of that unfortunate race, and the germs would still live within them. Earthmen must not face that. Until such a time as the last Martian had crumbled to dust and released the plague into the air to be destroyed, the race of Earth must remain within the confines of its own atmosphere, and safe.

There was only himself and the corpse he had touched left here to carry possible germs, and the ship to carry the men to other sources of infection; all that was easily remedied.

The stranger from Mars groped in his pocket for the guard's match box, smiling faintly. Just before the final darkness swept over him, he drew one of the matches from the box and scraped it across the friction surface. Flame danced from the point and outward—

PART SEVEN

Far Traveling

THE ETHICAL EQUATIONS

IT is very, very queer. The Ethical Equations, of course, link conduct with probability, and give mathematical proof that certain patterns of conduct increase the probability of certain kinds of coincidences. But nobody ever expected them to have any really practical effect. Elucidation of the laws of chance did not stop gambling, though it did make life insurance practical. The Ethical Equations weren't expected to be even as useful as that. They were just theories, which seemed unlikely to affect anybody particularly. They were complicated, for one thing. They admitted that the ideal pattern of conduct for one man wasn't the best for another. A politician, for example, has an entirely different code—and properly—from a Space Patrol man. But still, on at least one occasion—

The thing from outer space was fifteen hundred feet long, and upward of a hundred and fifty feet through at its middle section, and well over two hundred in a curious bulge like a fish's head at its bow. There were odd, gill-like flaps just back of that bulge, too, and the whole thing looked extraordinarily like a monster, eyeless fish, floating in empty space out beyond Jupiter. But it had drifted in from somewhere beyond the sun's gravitational field—its speed was too great for it to have a closed orbit—and it swung with a slow, inane, purposeless motion about some axis it had established within itself.

The little spacecruiser edged closer and closer. Freddy Holmes had been a pariah on the *Arnina* all the way out from Mars, but he clenched his hands and forgot his misery and the ruin of his career in the excitement of looking at the thing.

"No response to signals on any frequency, sir," said the communications officer, formally. "It is not radiating. It has a minute magnetic field. Its surface temperature is just about four degrees absolute."

The commander of the *Arnina* said, "Hrrrmph!" Then he said, "We'll lay alongside." Then he looked at Freddy Holmes and stiffened. "No," he said, "I believe you take over now, Mr. Holmes."

Freddy started. He was in a very bad spot, but his excitement had made him oblivious of it for a moment. The undisguised hostility with which he was regarded by the skipper and the others on the bridge brought it back, however.

"You take over, Mr. Holmes," repeated the skipper bitterly. "I have orders to that effect. You originally detected this object and your uncle asked Headquarters that you be given full authority to investigate it. You have that authority. Now, what are you going to do with it?"

There was fury in his voice surpassing even the rasping dislike of the voyage out. He was a lieutenant commander and he had been instructed to take orders from a junior officer. That was bad enough. But this was humanity's first contact with an extrasolar civilization, and Freddy Holmes, lieutenant junior grade, had been given charge of the matter by pure political pull.

Freddy swallowed.

"I . . . I—" He swallowed again and said miserably, "Sir, I've tried to explain that I dislike the present set-up as much as you possibly can. I . . . wish that you would let me put myself under your orders, sir, instead of—"

"No!" rasped the commander vengefully. "You are in command, Mr. Holmes. Your uncle put on political pressure to arrange it. My orders are to carry out your instructions, not to wet-nurse you if the job is too big for you to handle. This is in your lap! Will you issue orders?"

Freddy stiffened.

"Very well, sir. It's plainly a ship and apparently a derelict. No crew would come in without using a drive or allow their ship to swing about aimlessly. You will maintain your present position with relation to it. I'll take a spaceboat and a volunteer, if you will find me one, and look it over."

He turned and left the bridge. Two minutes later he was struggling into a spacesuit when Lieutenant Bridges—also junior grade—came briskly into the spacesuit locker and observed:

"I've permission to go with you, Mr. Holmes." He began to get into another spacesuit. As he pulled it up over his chest he added blithely: "I'd say this was worth the price of admission!"

Freddy did not answer. Three minutes later the little spaceboat pulled out from the side of the cruiser. Designed for expeditionary work and tool-carrying rather than as an escapecraft, it was not inclosed. It would carry men in spacesuits, with their tools and weapons, and they could breathe from its tanks instead of from their suits, and use its power and so conserve their own. But it was a strange feeling to sit within its spidery outline and see the great blank sides of the strange object draw near. When the spaceboat actually touched the vast metal wall it seemed impossible, like the approach to some sorcerer's castle across a monstrous moat of stars.

It was real enough, though. The felted rollers touched, and Bridges grunted in satisfaction.

"Magnetic. We can anchor to it. Now what?"

"We hunt for an entrance port," said Freddy curtly. He added: "Those openings that look like gills are the drive tubes. Their drive's in front instead of the rear. Apparently they don't use gyros for steering."

The tiny craft clung to the giant's skin, like a fly on a stranded whale. It moved slowly to the top of the rounded body, and over it, and down on the other side. Presently the cruiser came in sight again as it came up the near side once more.

"Nary a port, sir," said Bridges blithely. "Do we cut our way in?"

"Hm-m-m," said Freddy slowly. "We have our drive in the rear, and our control room in front. So we take on supplies amidships, and that's where we looked. But this ship is driven from the front. Its control room might be amidships. If so, it might load at the stern. Let's see."

The little craft crawled to the stern of the monster.

"There!" said Freddy.

It was not like an entrance port on any vessel in the solar system. It slid aside, without hinges. There was an inner door, but it opened just as readily. There was no rush of air, and it was hard to tell if it was intended as an air lock or not.

"Air's gone," said Freddy. "It's a derelict, all right. You might bring a blaster, but what we'll mostly need is light, I think."

The magnetic anchors took hold. The metal grip shoes of the spacesuits made loud noises inside the suits as the two of them pushed their way into the interior of the ship. The spacecruiser had been able to watch them, until now. Now they were gone.

The giant, enigmatic object which was so much like a blind fish in empty space floated on. It swung aimlessly about some inner axis. The thin sunlight, out here beyond Jupiter, smote upon it harshly. It seemed to hang motionless in mid-space against an all-surrounding background of distant and unwinking stars. The trim Space Patrol ship hung alertly a mile and a half away. Nothing seemed to happen at all.

Freddy was rather pale when he went back to the bridge. The pressure mark on his forehead from the spacesuit helmet was still visible, and he rubbed at it abstractedly. The skipper regarded him with a sort of envious bitterness. After all, any human would envy any other who had set foot in an alien spaceship. Lieutenant Bridges followed him. For an instant there were no words. Then Bridges saluted briskly:

"Reporting back on board, sir, and returning to watch duty after permitted volunteer activity."

The skipper touched his hat sourly. Bridges departed with crisp precision. The skipper regarded Freddy with the helpless fury of a senior officer who has been ordered to prove a junior officer a fool, and who has seen the assignment blow up in his face and that of the superior officers who ordered it. It was an enraging situation. Freddy Holmes, newly commissioned and assigned to the detector station on Luna which keeps track of asteroids and meteor streams, had discovered a small object coming in over Neptune. Its speed was too high for it to be a regular member of the solar system, so he'd reported it as a visitor and suggested immediate examination. But junior officers are not supposed to make discoveries. It violates tradition, which is a sort of Ethical Equation in the Space Patrol. So Freddy was slapped down for his presumption. And he slapped back, on account of the Ethical Equations' bearing upon scientific discoveries. The first known object to come from beyond the stars ought to be examined. Definitely. So, most unprofessionally for a Space Patrol junior, Freddy raised a stink.

The present state of affairs was the result. He had an uncle who was a prominent politician. That uncle went before the Space Patrol Board and pointed out smoothly that his nephew's discovery was important. He demonstrated with mathematical precision that the Patrol was being ridiculous in ignoring a significant discovery simply because a junior officer had made it. And the Board, seething at outside interference, ordered Freddy to be taken to the object he had detected, given absolute command of the spacecruiser which had taken him there, and directed to make the examination he had suggested. By all the laws of probability, he would have to report that the hunk of matter from beyond the solar system was just like hunks of matter in it. And then the Board would pin back both his and his uncle's ears with a vengeance.

But now the hunk of matter turned out to be a fish-shaped artifact from an alien civilization. It turned out to be important. So the situation was one to make anybody steeped in Patrol tradition grind his teeth.

"The thing, sir," said Freddy evenly, "is a spaceship. It is driven by atomic engines shooting blasts sternward from somewhere near the bow. Apparently they steer only by hand. Apparently, too, there was a blow-up in the engine room and they lost most of their fuel out the tube vents. After that, the ship was helpless though they patched up the engines after a fashion. It is possible to calculate that in its practically free fall to the sun it's been in its present state for a couple of thousand years."

"I take it, then," said the skipper with fine irony, "that there are no survivors of the crew."

"It presents several problems, sir," said Freddy evenly, "and that's one of them." He was rather pale. "The ship is empty of air, but her tanks are full. Storage spaces containing what look like supplies are only partly emptied. The crew did not starve or suffocate. The ship simply lost most of her fuel. So it looks like they prepared the ship to endure an indefinite amount of floating about in free space and"—he hesitated —"then it looks like they went into suspended animation. They're all on board, in transparent cases that have—machinery attached. Maybe they thought they'd be picked up by sister ships sooner or later."

The skipper blinked.

"Suspended animation? They're alive?" Then he said sharply: "What sort of ship is it? Cargo?"

"No, sir," said Freddy. "That's another problem. Bridges and I agree that it's a fighting ship, sir. There are rows of generators serving things that could only be weapons. By the way they're braced, there are tractor beams and pressor beams and—there are vacuum tubes that have grids but apparently work with cold cathodes. By the size of the cables that lead to them, those tubes handle amperages up in the thousands. You can figure that one out, sir."

The skipper paced two steps this way, and two steps that. The thing was stupendous. But his instructions were precise.

"I'm under your orders," he said doggedly. "What are you going to do?"

"I'm going to work myself to death, I suppose," said Freddy unhappily, "and some other men with me. I want to go over that ship backwards, forwards, and sideways with scanners, and everything the scanners see photographed back on board, here. I want men to work the scanners and technicians on board to direct them for their specialties. I want to get every rivet and coil in that whole ship on film before touching anything."

The skipper said grudgingly:

"That's not too foolish. Very well, Mr. Holmes, it will be done."

"Thank you," said Freddy. He started to leave the bridge, and stopped. "The men to handle the scanners," he added, "ought to be rather carefully picked. Imaginative men wouldn't do. The crew of that ship—they look horribly alive, and they aren't pretty. And . . . er . . . the plastic cases they're in are arranged to open from inside. That's another problem still, sir."

He went on down. The skipper clasped his hands behind his back and began to pace the bridge furiously. The first object from beyond the stars was a spaceship. It had weapons the Patrol had only vainly imagined. And he, a two-and-a-half striper, had to stand by and take orders for its investigation from a lieutenant junior grade just out of the Academy. Because of politics! The skipper ground his teeth—

Then Freddy's last comment suddenly had meaning. The plastic cases in which the alien's crew lay in suspended animation opened from the inside. From the inside!

Cold sweat came out on the skipper's forehead as he realized the implication. Tractor and pressor beams, and the ship's fuel not quite gone, and the suspended-animation cases opening from the inside—

There was a slender, coaxial cable connecting the two spacecraft, now. They drifted in sunward together. The little cruiser was dwarfed by the alien giant.

The sun was very far away; brighter than any star, to be sure, and pouring out a fierce radiation, but still very far from a warming orb. All about were the small, illimitably distant lights which were stars. There was exactly one object in view which had an appreciable diameter. That was Jupiter, a new moon in shape, twenty million miles sunward and eighty million miles farther along its orbit. The rest was emptiness.

The spidery little spaceboat slid along the cable between the two craft. Spacesuited figures got out and clumped on magnetic-soled shoes to the air lock. They went in.

Freddy came to the bridge. The skipper said hoarsely:

"Mr. Holmes, I would like to make a request. You are, by orders of the Board, in command of this ship until your investigation of the ship yonder is completed."

Freddy's face was haggard and worn. He said abstractedly:

"Yes, sir. What is it?"

"I would like," said the *Arnina's* skipper urgently, "to send a complete report of your investigation so far. Since you are in command, I cannot do so without your permission."

"I would rather you didn't, sir," said Freddy. Tired as he was, his jaws clamped. "Frankly, sir, I think they'd cancel your present orders and issue others entirely."

The skipper bit his lip. That was the idea. The scanners had sent back complete images of almost everything in the other ship, now. Everything was recorded on film. The skipper had seen the monsters which were the crew of the extrasolar vessel. And the plastic cases in which they had slumbered for at least two thousand years did open from the inside. That was what bothered him. They did open from the inside!

The electronics technicians of the *Arnina* were going about in silly rapture, drawing diagrams for each other and contemplating the results with dazed appreciation. The gunnery officer was making scale, detailed design-drawings for weapons he had never hoped for, and waking up of nights to feel for those drawings and be sure that they were real. But the engineer officer was wringing his hands. He wanted to take the other ship's engines apart. They were so enormously smaller than the *Arnina's* drive, and yet they had driven a ship with eighty-four times the *Arnina's* mass—and he could not see how they could work.

The alien ship was ten thousand years ahead of the *Arnina*. Its secrets were being funneled over to the little Earth-ship at a rapid rate. But the cases holding its still-living crew opened from the inside.

"Nevertheless, Mr. Holmes," the skipper said feverishly, "I must ask permission to send that report."

"But I am in command," said Freddy tiredly, "and I intend to stay in command. I will give you a written order forbidding you to make a report, sir. Disobedience will be mutiny."

The skipper grew almost purple.

"Do you realize," he demanded savagely, "that if the crew of that ship is in suspended animation, and if their coffins or containers open only from inside—do you realize that they expect to open them themselves?"

"Yes, sir," said Freddy wearily. "Of course. Why not?"

"Do you realize that cables from those containers lead to thermobatteries in the ship's outer plating? The monsters knew they couldn't survive without power, but they knew that in any other solar system they could get it! So they made sure they'd pass close to our sun with what power they dared use, and went into suspended animation with a reserve of power to land on and thermobatteries that would waken them when it was time to set to work!"

"Yes, sir," said Freddy, as wearily as before. "They had courage, at any rate. But what would you do about that?"

"I'd report it to Headquarters!" raged the skipper. "I'd report that this is a warship capable of blasting the whole Patrol out of the ether and smashing our planets! I'd say it was manned by monsters now fortunately helpless, but with fuel enough to maneuver to a landing. And I'd asked authority to take their coffins out of their ship and destroy them! Then I'd—"

"I did something simpler," said Freddy. "I disconnected the thermobatteries. They can't revive. So I'm going to get a few hours' sleep. If you'll excuse me—"

He went to his own cabin and threw himself on his bunk.

Men with scanners continued to examine every square inch of the monster derelict. They worked in spacesuits. To have filled the giant hull with air would practically have emptied the *Arnina's* tanks. A spacesuited man held a scanner before a curious roll of flexible substance, on which were inscribed symbols. His headphones brought instructions from the photo room. A record of some sort was being duplicated by photography. There were scanners at work in the storerooms, the crew's quarters, the gun mounts. So far no single article had been moved from the giant stranger. That was Freddy's order. Every possible bit of information was being extracted from every possible object, but nothing had been taken away. Even chemical analysis was being done by scanner, using cold-light spectrography applied from the laboratory on the cruiser.

And Freddy's unpopularity had not lessened. The engineer officer cursed him luridly. The stranger's engines, now— They had been patched up after an explosion, and they were tantalizingly suggestive. But their working was unfathomable. The engineer officer wanted to get his hands on them. The physiochemical officer wanted to do some analysis with his own hands, instead of by cold-light spectrography over a scanner. And every man, from the lowest enlisted apprentice to the skipper himself, wanted to get hold of some artifact made by an alien, nonhuman race ten thousand years ahead of human civilization. So Freddy was unpopular.

But that was only part of his unhappiness. He felt that he had acted improperly. The Ethical Equations gave mathematical proof that probabilities and ethics are interlinked, so that final admirable results cannot be expected from unethical beginnings. Freddy had violated discipline—which is one sort of ethics—and after that through his uncle had interjected politics into Patrol affairs. Which was definitely a crime. By the Equations, the probability of disastrous coincidences was going to be enormous until corrective, ethically proper action was taken to cancel out the original crimes. And Freddy had been unable to devise such action. He felt, too, that the matter was urgent. He slept uneasily despite his fatigue, because there was something in the back of his mind which warned him stridently that disaster lay ahead.

Freddy awoke still unrefreshed and stared dully at the ceiling over his head. He was trying discouragedly to envision a reasonable solution when there came a tap on his door. It was Bridges with a batch of papers.

"Here you are!" he said cheerfully, when Freddy opened to him. "Now we're all going to be happy!"

Freddy took the extended sheets.

"What's happened?" he asked. "Did the skipper send for fresh orders regardless, and I'm to go in the brig?"

Bridges, grinning, pointed to the sheets of paper in Freddy's hand. They were from the physiochemical officer, who was equipped to do exact surveys on the lesser heavenly bodies.

"*Elements found in the alien vessel*," was the heading of a list. Freddy scanned the list. No heavy elements, but the rest was familiar. There had been pure nitrogen in the fuel tank, he remembered, and the engineer officer was going quietly mad trying to understand how they had used nitrogen for atomic power. Freddy looked down to the bottom. Iron was the heaviest element present.

"Why should this make everybody happy?" asked Freddy.

Bridges pointed with his finger. The familiar atomic symbols had unfamiliar numerals by them. H^3, Li^5, Gl^8— He blinked. He saw N^{15}, F^{18}, $S^{34,35}$— Then he stared. Bridges grinned.

"Try to figure what that ship's worth!" he said happily. "It's all over the *Arnina*. Prize money isn't allowed in the Patrol, but five percent of salvage is. Hydrogen three has been detected on Earth, but never isolated. Lithium five doesn't exist on Earth, or glucinium eight, or nitrogen fifteen or oxygen seventeen or fluorine eighteen or sulphur thirty-four or thirty-five! The whole ship is made up of isotopes that simply don't exist in the solar system! And you know what pure isotopes sell for! The hull's practically pure iron fifty-five! Pure iron fifty-four sells for thirty-five credits a gram! Talk about the lost treasures of Mars! For technical use only, the stripped hull of this stranger is worth ten years' revenue of Earth government! Every man on the *Arnina* is rich for life. And you're popular!"

Freddy did not smile.

"Nitrogen fifteen," he said slowly. "That's what's in the remaining fuel tank. It goes into a queer little aluminum chamber we couldn't figure out, and from there into the drive tubes. I see—"

He was very pale. Bridges beamed.

"A hundred thousand tons of materials that simply don't exist on Earth! Pure isotopes, intact! Not a contamination in a carload! My dear chap, I've come to like you, but you've been hated by everyone else. Now come out and bask in admiration and affection!"

Freddy said, unheeding:

"I've been wondering what that aluminum chamber was for. It looked so infernally simple, and I couldn't see what it did—"

"Come out and have a drink!" insisted Bridges joyously. "Be lionized! Make friends and influence people!"

"No," said Freddy. He smiled mirthlessly. "I'll be lynched later anyhow. Hm-m-m. I want to talk to the engineer officer. We want to get that ship navigating under its own power. It's too big to do anything with towlines."

"But nobody's figured out its engines!" protested Bridges. "Apparently there's nothing but a tiny trickle of nitrogen through a silly chamber that does something to it, and then it flows through aluminum baffles into the drive tubes. It's too simple! How are you going to make a thing like that work?"

"I think," said Freddy, "it's going to be horribly simple. That whole ship is made up of isotopes we don't have on Earth. No. It has aluminum and carbon. They're simple substances. Theirs and ours are just alike. But most of the rest—"

He was pale. He looked as if he were suffering.

"I'll get a couple of tanks made up, of aluminum, and filled with nitrogen. Plain air should do—And I'll want a gyro-control. I'll want it made of aluminum, too, with graphite bearings—"

He grinned mirthlessly at Bridges.

"Ever hear of the Ethical Equations, Bridges? You'd never expect them to suggest the answer to a space-drive problem, would you? But that's what they've done. I'll get the engineer officer to have those things made up. It's nice to have known you, Bridges—"

As Bridges went out, Freddy Holmes sat down, wetting his lips, to make sketches for the engineer officer to work from.

The control room and the engine room of the monster ship were one. It was a huge, globular chamber filled with apparatus of startlingly alien design. To Freddy, and to Bridges too, now, there was not so much of monstrousness as at first. Eight days of familiarity, and knowledge of how they worked, had made them seem almost normal. But still it was eerie to belt themselves before the instrument board, with only their hand lamps for illumination, and cast a last glance at the aluminum replacements of parts that had been made on some planet of another sun.

"If this works," said Freddy, and swallowed, "we're lucky. Here's the engine control. Cross your fingers, Bridges."

The interior of the hulk was still airless. Freddy shifted a queerly shaped lever an infinitesimal trace. There was a slight surging movement of the whole vast hull. A faint murmuring came through the fabric of the monster ship to the soles of their spacesuit boots. Freddy wet his lips and touched another lever.

"This should be lights."

It was. Images formed on the queerly shaped screens. The whole interior of the ship glowed. And the whole creation had been so alien as somehow to be revolting, in the harsh white light of the hand lamps the men had used. But now it was like a highly improbable fairy palace. The fact that all doors were circular and all passages round tubes was only pleasantly strange, in the many-colored glow of the ship's own lighting system. Freddy shook his head in his spacesuit helmet, as if to shake away drops of sweat on his forehead.

"The next should be heat," he said more grimly than before. "We do not touch that! Oh, definitely! But we try the drive."

The ship stirred. It swept forward in a swift smooth acceleration that was invincibly convincing of power. The *Arnina* dwindled swiftly, behind. And Freddy, with compressed lips, touched controls here, and there, and the monstrous ship obeyed with the docility of a willing, well-trained animal. It swept back to clear sight of the *Arnina*.

"I would say," said Bridges in a shaking voice, "that it works. The Patrol has nothing like this!"

"No," said Freddy shortly. His voice sounded sick. "Not like this! It's a sweet ship. I'm going to hook in the gyro controls. They ought to work. The creatures who made this didn't use them. I don't know why. But they didn't."

He cut off everything but the lights. He bent down and hooked in the compact little aluminum device which would control the flow of nitrogen to the port and starboard drive tubes.

Freddy came back to the control board and threw in the drive once more. And the gyro control worked. It should. After all, the tool work of a Space Patrol machinist should be good. Freddy tested it thoroughly. He set it on certain fine adjustment. He threw three switches. Then he picked up one tiny kit he had prepared.

"Come along," he said tiredly. "Our work's over. We go back to the *Arnina* and I probably get lynched."

Bridges, bewildered, followed him to the spidery little spaceboat. They cast off from the huge ship, now three miles or more from the *Arnina* and untenanted save by its own monstrous crew in suspended animation. The Space Patrol cruiser shifted position to draw near and pick them up. And Freddy said hardly:

"Remember the Ethical Equations, Bridges? I said they gave me the answer to that other ship's drive. If they were right, it couldn't have been anything else. Now I'm going to find out about something else."

His spacegloved hands worked clumsily. From the tiny kit he spilled out a single small object. He plopped it into something from a chest in the spaceboat—a mortar shell, as Bridges saw incredulously. He dropped that into the muzzle of a line-mortar the spaceboat carried as a matter of course. He jerked the lanyard. The mortar flamed. Expanding gases beat at the spacesuits of the men. A tiny, glowing, crimson spark sped toward outer space. Seconds passed. Three. Four. Five—

"Apparently I'm a fool," said Freddy, in the grimmest voice Bridges had ever heard.

But then there was light. And such light! Where the dwindling red spark of a tracer mortar shell had sped toward infinitely distant stars, there was suddenly an explosion of such incredible violence as even the proving-grounds of the Space Patrol had never known. There was no sound in empty space. There was no substance to be heated to incandescence other than that of a half-pound tracer shell. But there was a flare of blue-white light and a crash of such violent static that Bridges was deafened by it. Even through the glass of his helmet he felt a flash of savage heat. Then there was—nothing.

"What was that?" said Bridges, shaken.

"The Ethical Equations," said Freddy. "Apparently I'm not the fool I thought—"

The *Arnina* slid up alongside the little spaceboat. Freedy did not alight. He moved the boat over to its cradle and plugged in his communicator set. He talked over that set with his helmet phone, not radiating a signal that Bridges could pick up. In three minutes or so the great lock opened and four spacesuited figures came out. One wore the crested four-communicator helmet which only the skipper of a cruiser wears when in command of a landing party. The newcomers to the outside of the *Arnina's* hull crowded into the little spaceboat. Freddy's voice sounded again in the headphones, grim and cold.

"I've some more shells, sir. They're tracer shells which have been in the work boat for eight days. They're not quite as cold as the ship, yonder—that's had two thousand years to cool off in—but they're cold. I figure they're not over eight or ten degrees absolute. And here are the bits of material from the other ship. You can touch them. Our spacesuits are as nearly nonconductive of heat as anything could be. You won't warm them if you hold them in your hand."

The skipper—Bridges could see him—looked at the scraps of metal Freddy held out to him. They were morsels of iron and other material from the alien ship. By the cold glare of a handlight the skipper thrust one into the threaded hollow at the nose of a mortar shell into which a line-end is screwed when a line is to be thrown. The skipper himself dropped in the mortar shell and fired it. Again a racing, receding speck of red in emptiness. And a second terrible, atomic blast.

The skipper's voice in the headphones:

"How much more of the stuff did you bring away?"

"Three more pieces, sir," said Freddy's voice, very steady now. "You see how it happens, sir. They're isotopes we don't have on Earth. And we don't have them because in contact with other isotopes at normal temperatures, they're unstable. They go off. Here we dropped them into the mortar shells and nothing happened, because both isotopes were cold—down to the temperature of liquid helium, or nearly. But there's a tracer compound in the shells, and it burns as they fly away. The shell grows warm. And when either isotope, in contact with the other, is as warm as . . . say . . . liquid hydrogen . . . why . . . they destroy each other. The ship yonder is of the same material. Its mass is about a hundred thousand tons. Except for the aluminum and maybe one or two other elements that also are nonisotopic and the same in both ships, every bit of that ship will blast off if it comes in contact with matter from this solar system above ten or twelve degrees absolute."

"Shoot the other samples away," said the skipper harshly. "We want to be sure—"

There were three violent puffs of gases expanding into empty space. There were three incredible blue-white flames in the void. There was silence. Then—

"That thing has to be destroyed," said the skipper, heavily. "We couldn't set it down anywhere, and its crew might wake up anyhow, at any moment. We haven't anything that could fight it, and if it tried to land on Earth—"

The alien monster, drifting aimlessly in the void, suddenly moved. Thin flames came from the gill-like openings at the bow. Then one side jetted more strongly. It swung about, steadied, and swept forward with a terrifying smooth acceleration. It built up speed vastly more swiftly than any Earthship could possibly do. It dwindled to a speck. It vanished in empty space.

But it was not bound inward toward the sun. It was not headed for the plainly visible half-moon disk of Jupiter, now barely seventy million miles away. It headed out toward the stars.

"I wasn't sure until a few minutes ago," said Freddy Holmes unsteadily, "but by the Ethical Equations something like that was probable. I couldn't make certain until we'd gotten everything possible from it, and until I had everything arranged. But I was worried from the first. The Ethical Equations made it pretty certain that if we did the wrong thing we'd suffer for it . . . and by we I mean the whole Earth, because any visitor from beyond the stars would be bound to affect the whole human race." His voice wavered a little. "It was hard to figure out what we ought to do. If one of our ships had been in the same fix, though, we'd have hoped for—friendliness. We'd hope for fuel, maybe, and help in starting back home. But this ship was a warship, and we'd have been helpless to fight it. It would have been hard to be friendly. Yet, according to the Ethical Equations, if we wanted our first contact with an alien civilization to be of benefit to us, it was up to us to get it started back home with plenty of fuel."

"You mean," said the skipper, incredulously, "you mean you—"

"Its engines use nitrogen," said Freddy. "It runs nitrogen fifteen into a little gadget we know how to make, now. It's very simple, but it's a sort of atom smasher. It turns nitrogen fifteen into nitrogen fourteen and hydrogen. I think we can make use of that for ourselves. Nitrogen fourteen is the kind we have. It can be handled in aluminum pipes and tanks, because there's only one aluminum, which is stable under all conditions. But when it hits the alien isotopes in the drive tubes, it breaks down—"

He took a deep breath.

"I gave them a double aluminum tank of nitrogen, and by-passed their atom smasher. Nitrogen fourteen goes into their drive tubes, and they drive! And . . . I figured back their orbit, and set a gyro to head them back for their own solar system for as long as the first tank of nitrogen holds out. They'll make it out of the sun's gravitational field on that, anyhow. And I reconnected their thermo-batteries. When they start to wake up they'll see the gyro and know that somebody gave it to them. The double tank is like their own and they'll realize they have a fresh supply of fuel to land with. It . . . may be a thousand years before they're back home, but when they get there they'll know we're friendly and . . . not afraid of them. And meanwhile we've got all their gadgets to work on and work with—"

Freddy was silent. The little spaceboat clung to the side of the *Arnina,* which with its drive off was now drifting in sunward past the orbit of Jupiter.

"It is very rare," said the skipper ungraciously, "that a superior officer in the Patrol apologizes to an inferior. But I apologize to you, Mr. Holmes, for thinking you a fool. And when I think that I, and certainly every other Patrol officer of experience, would have thought of nothing but setting that ship down at Patrol Base for study, and when I think what an atomic explosion of a hundred thousand tons of matter would have done to Earth . . . I apologize a second time."

Freddy said uncomfortably:

"If there are to be any apologies made, sir, I guess I've got to make them. Every man on the *Arnina* has figured he's rich, and I've sent it all back where it came from. But you see, sir, the Ethical Equations—"

When Freddy's resignation went in with the report of his investigation of the alien vessel, it was returned marked *"Not Accepted."* And Freddy was ordered to report to a tiny, hard-worked spacecan on which a junior Space Patrol officer normally gets his ears pinned back and learns his work the hard way. And Freddy was happy, because he wanted to be a Space Patrol officer more than he wanted anything else in the world. His uncle was satisfied, too, because he wanted Freddy to be content, and because certain space-admirals truculently told him that Freddy was needed in the Patrol and would get all the consideration and promotion he needed without any politicians butting in. And the Space Patrol was happy because it had a lot of new gadgets to work with which were going to make it a force able not only to look after interplanetary traffic but defend it, if necessary.

And, for that matter, the Ethical Equations were satisfied.

IT'S GREAT TO BE BACK

HOME—back to Earth again! Josephine MacRae's heart was pounding. She said, "Hurry up, Allan!" and fidgeted while her husband
checked over the apartment. Earth-Moon freight rates made it silly to
ship their belongings; except for the bag he carried, they had converted
everything to cash. Satisfied, he joined her at the lift; they went on up
to the administration level and there to a door marked: Luna City
Community Association—*Anna Stone, Service Manager.*

Miss Stone accepted their apartment keys grimly. "Mr. and Mrs.
MacRae. So you're actually leaving us?"

Josephine bristled. "Think we'd change our minds?"

The manager shrugged. "No. I knew nearly three years ago that you
would go back—from your complaints."

"By my comp— Miss Stone, I don't blame you personally, but this
pressurized rabbit warren would try the patience of a—"

"Take it easy, Jo!" her husband cautioned her.

Josephine flushed. "Sorry, Miss Stone."

"Never mind. We just see things differently. I was here when Luna
City was three air-sealed Quonset huts, with tunnels you had to crawl
through." She stuck out a square hand. "I honestly hope you'll enjoy
being groundhogs. Hot jets, good luck and safe landing."

Back in the lift, Josephine sputtered, " 'Groundhogs' indeed! Just
because we prefer fresh air and our own native planet—"

"You use the term," Allan pointed out.

"But I use it about people who have never been off Terra."

"We've both said more than once that we wished we had had sense
enough never to have left Earth. We're groundhogs at heart, Jo."

"Yes, but—Allan, you're being obnoxious. This is the happiest day
of my life. Aren't you glad to be going home? Aren't you?"

"Sure I am. It'll be great to be back. Golf. Skiing."

"And opera. Real live grand opera. Allan, we've simply got to have
a week or two in Manhattan before going to the country."

"I thought you wanted to feel rain on your face?"

"I want that too. I want it all at once, and I can't wait. Oh, darling, it's like getting out of jail." She clung to him.

He unwound her as the lift stopped. "Don't blubber."

"Allan, you're a beast," she said dreamily. "I'm so happy."

In bankers' row, the clerk in Trans-America had their transfer of account ready. "Going home, eh? I envy you. Hunting, fishing."

"Surf bathing is more my style. And sailing."

"I," said Jo, "simply want to see green trees and blue sky."

The clerk nodded. "I know. Well, have fun. Are you taking three months or six?"

"We're not coming back," Allan stated flatly. "Three years of living like a fish in an aquarium is enough."

"So?" The clerk's face became impassive. "Well, hot jets."

"Thanks." They went on up to subsurface and took the crosstown slidewalk out to the rocket port. Its tunnel broke surface at one point, becoming a pressurized shed; a window on the west looked out on the surface of the Moon, and, beyond the hills, the Earth.

The sight of it, great and green and bountiful, against black lunar sky and harsh, unwinking stars, brought quick tears to Jo's eyes. Home— that lovely planet was hers! Allan looked at it more casually, noting the Greenwich. The sunrise line had just touched South America— must be about eight-twenty; better hurry.

They stepped off the slidewalk into the arms of waiting friends. "Hey, you lugs are late! The Gremlin blasts off in seven minutes."

"But we aren't going in it," MacRae answered. "No, siree."

"What? Not going? Did you change your minds?"

Josephine laughed. "Pay no attention to him, Jack. We're going in the express instead. So we've got twenty minutes yet."

"Well! A couple of rich tourists, eh?"

"Oh, the extra fare isn't bad. Why make two changes and sweat out a week in space?" She rubbed her bare middle significantly.

"She can't take free flight, Jack," her husband explained.

"Well, neither can I; I was sick the whole trip out. Still, I don't think you'll be sick, Jo. You're used to Moon weight now."

"Maybe," she agreed, "but there is a lot of difference between one sixth gravity and no gravity."

Jack Crail's wife cut in, "Josephine MacRae, are you going to risk your life in an atomic-powered ship?"

"Why not, darling? You work in an atomics laboratory!"

"It's not the same thing. In the lab we take precautions. The Commerce Commission should never have licensed the expresses."

"Now, Emma," Crail objected, "they've worked the bugs out of those ships."

"Humph! I may be old-fashioned, but I'll go back the way I came, via Terminal and Supra-New-York, in good old reliable fuel rockets."

"Never mind," Allan interrupted. "It's done, and we've got to get over to the express-launching site. Good-by, everybody! It's been grand knowing you. If you come back to God's country, look us up."

"Good-by, Jo. . . . Good-by, Allan!" "Give my regards to Broadway!" "Be sure to write!" "Aloha, hot jets!"

They showed their tickets, entered the air lock and climbed into the pressurized shuttle used between Leyport proper and the express-launching site.

"Hang on, folks," the driver called back over his shoulder; Jo and Allan hurriedly settled into the cushions. The lock opened to the airless tunnel ahead. Six minutes later they climbed out twenty miles away, beyond the hills shielding Luna City's roof from the radioactive splash of the express.

In the Sparrowhawk they shared a compartment with a missionary family. The Reverend Doctor Simmons seemed to want to explain why he was traveling in luxury. "It's for the child," he told them, as his wife strapped their baby girl into a small acceleration couch rigged between her parents' couches. They all strapped down at the warning siren. Jo felt her heart begin to pound. At last—at long last!

The jets took hold, mashing them into the cushions. Jo had not known she could feel so heavy—much worse than the trip out. The baby cried all through acceleration, in wordless terror and discomfort. After a weary time they were suddenly weightless, as the ship went into free flight. When the terrible binding weight was free of her chest, Jo's heart felt as light as her body. Allan threw off his upper strap. "How do you feel, kid?"

"Oh, I feel fine!" Jo unstrapped and faced him. Then she hiccuped. "That is, I think I do."

Five minutes later she was not in doubt; she merely wished to die. Allan swam out of the compartment and located the ship's surgeon, who gave her a hypo. Allan waited until the drug had made her more comfortable, then left for the lounge to try his own cure for spacesickness— Mothersill's Seasick Remedy washed down with champagne. Presently he regretted having mixed them.

Little Gloria Simmons was not spacesick. She thought being weightless was fun, and went bouncing off floor plate, overhead and bulkhead like a dimpled balloon. Jo feebly considered strangling the child, if she floated within reach, but it was too much effort.

Deceleration, logy as it made them feel, was welcome relief after nausea—except to little Gloria. She cried again, while her mother tried to explain. Her father prayed. After a long, long time came a slight jar and the sound of the siren.

Jo managed to raise her head. "What's the matter? Is there an accident?"

"I don't think so. I think we've landed."

"We can't have! We're still braking—I'm heavy as lead."

Allan grinned feebly. "So am I. Earth gravity, remember?"

The baby continued to cry.

They said good-by to the missionary family and staggered out of the ship, supporting each other.

"It can't be just the gravity," Jo protested. "I've taken earth-normal weight in the centrifuge at the Y, back home—I mean back in Luna City. We're weak from spacesickness."

Allan steadied himself. "That's it. No food for two days."

"Allan, didn't you eat anything either?"

"No. Not permanently, so to speak. Are you hungry?"

"Starving."

"How about dinner at Keen's Chop House?"

"Wonderful. Oh, Allan, we're back!" Her tears started again.

After chuting down the Hudson Valley and into Grand Central Station, they glimpsed the Simmonses again. While waiting at the dock for their bag, Jo saw the reverend doctor climb heavily out of a tube capsule, carrying his daughter and followed by his wife. He set the child down carefully. She stood for a moment, trembling on her pudgy legs, then collapsed to the dock. She lay there, crying thinly.

A spaceman—a pilot, by his uniform—stopped and looked pityingly at the child. "Born in the Moon?" he asked.

"Uh? What? Why, yes, she was, sir."

"Pick her up and carry her. She'll have to learn to walk all over again." The spaceman shook his head sadly and glided away.

Simmons looked still more troubled, then sat down on the dock beside his child, careless of the dirt. Jo felt too weak to help. She looked around for Allan, but he was busy; their bag had arrived. He started to pick it up, then felt suddenly silly. It seemed nailed to the dock. He knew what was in it—rolls of microfilm and color film, souvenirs, toilet articles, irreplaceables—fifty pounds of mass. It couldn't weigh what it seemed to. But it did. He had forgotten what fifty pounds weigh on Earth.

"Porter, mister?" The speaker was gray-haired and thin, but he scooped the bag up casually.

Allan called, "Come along, Jo," and followed him sheepishly.

The porter slowed to match his labored steps. "Just down from the Moon?" he asked. "You got a reservation?"

"Why, no."

"Stick with me. I got a friend on the desk at the Commodore." He led them to the Concourse slidewalk and into the hotel.

They were too weary to dine out; Allan had dinner sent up. Afterward, Jo fell asleep in a hot tub and he had trouble getting her out and into bed—she liked the support the water gave her.

She woke up, struggling, about four in the morning. "Allan!"

"Huh? What's the matter?" He fumbled for the light switch.

"Uh . . . nothing, I guess. I dreamt I was back in the ship. The jets had run away with her. What makes it so stuffy? My head is splitting."

"Huh? It can't be stuffy. This joint is air-conditioned." He sniffed the air. "I've got a headache too," he admitted.

"Well, do something. Open a window."

He stumbled up and did so, shivered when the outer air hit him, and hurried back to bed. He was wondering whether he could get to sleep with the roar of the city pouring in through the open window, when his wife spoke again, "Allan, I'm cold. May I crawl in with you?"

The sunlight streamed in the window, warm and mellow. When it touched his eyes, he woke and found his wife awake beside him.

She sighed and snuggled. "Oh, darling, look! Blue sky! We're home. I'd forgotten how lovely it is."

"It's great to be back, all right." He threw off the covers.

Jo squealed and jerked them back. "Don't do that!"

"Huh?"

"Mamma's great big boy is going to climb out and close that window while mamma stays under the covers."

"Well, all right." He found he could walk more easily, but it was good to get back into bed. Once there, he faced the telephone and shouted at it, "Service!"

"Order, please," it answered in a sweet contralto.

"Orange juice and coffee for two—extra coffee—six eggs, scrambled medium, and whole-wheat toast. And please send up a *Times* and *The Saturday Evening Post.*"

The delivery cupboard buzzed while he was shaving. He answered it and served Jo in bed. Breakfast over, he put down his paper and said, "Can you pull your nose out of that magazine?"

"Glad to. The darn thing is too big and heavy to hold."

"Why don't you have the *stat* edition mailed to you from Luna City? Wouldn't cost more than eight or nine times as much."

"Don't be silly. What's on your mind?"

"Climb out of that frowsty little nest and we'll go shopping."

"Unh-uh. No. I am not going outdoors in a moonsuit."

"'Fraid of being stared at? Getting prudish in your old age?"

"No, me lord; I simply refuse to expose myself in six ounces of nylon. I want some warm clothes." She squirmed farther under the covers.

"The perfect pioneer woman. Going to have fitters sent up?"

"We can't afford that—not while we're living on our savings. Look, you're going anyway. Buy me any old rag, so long as it's warm."

MacRae looked stubborn. "I've tried shopping for you before."

"Just this once, please. Run over to Saks and pick out a street dress in a blue wool jersey, size twelve. And a pair of nylons."

"Well, all right."

"That's a lamb. I won't be loafing; I have a list as long as your arm of people I've promised to call up, look up, have lunch with."

He shopped for himself first; his sensible shorts and singlet felt as inadequate as a straw hat in a snowstorm. It was really quite balmy, but it seemed cold after Luna City's unfailing seventy-two degrees. He stayed underground mostly or stuck to the roofed-over stretch of Fifth Avenue. He suspected that the salesmen were outfitting him in clothes that made him look like a yokel. But they were warm. They were also heavy, adding to the pain in his chest and making him even more unsteady. He wondered when he would regain his ground legs.

A motherly saleswoman took care of Jo's order and sold him a warm cape for her as well. He headed back, stumbling under his load, and trying futilely to flag a ground taxi. Everyone seemed in such a hurry!

He got back, aching all over and thinking about a hot bath. He did not get it; Jo had a visitor. "Mrs. Appleby, my husband. . . . Allan, this is Emma Crail's mother."

"Oh, how do you do, doctor—or should it be professor?"

"Mister."

"When I heard you were in town I just couldn't wait to hear all about my poor darling. How is she? Does she look well? These modern girls —I've told her time and time again that she must get outdoors. I walk in the park every day, and look at me. She sent me a picture—I have it here somewhere; at least I think so—and she doesn't look a bit well, undernourished. Those synthetic foods—"

"She doesn't eat synthetic foods, Mrs. Appleby."

"—must be quite impossible, I'm sure, not to mention the taste. What were you saying?"

"Your daughter doesn't live on synthetic foods," Allan repeated. "Fresh fruits and vegetables are one thing we have almost too much of in Luna City. The air-conditioning plant, you know."

"That's just what I was saying. I confess I don't see just how you get food out of air-conditioning machinery on the Moon—"

"In the Moon, Mrs. Appleby."

"—but it can't be healthy. Our air conditioner is always breaking down and making the most horrible smells. Simply ghastly, my dears. You'd think they could build a simple little thing like an air conditioner so that—"

"Mrs. Appleby," MacRae said desperately, "the air-conditioning plant in Luna City is a hydroponic farm, tanks of green growing plants. The plants take carbon dioxide out of the air and put oxygen back in."

"But— Are you quite sure, doctor? I'm sure Emma said—"

"Quite sure."

"Well, I don't pretend to understand these things; I'm the artistic type. Poor Herbert often said— Herbert was Emma's father; simply wrapped up in his engineering, though I always saw to it that he heard good music and saw the reviews of the best books. Emma takes after her father, I'm afraid. I do wish she would give up that silly work. Hardly the thing for a lady, do you think, Mrs. MacRae? All those atoms and neuters and things floating around in the air. I read all about it in the Science Made Simple column in the—"

"She's quite good at it and she seems to like it."

"Well, perhaps that's the important thing—to be happy in what you do, no matter how silly. But I worry about the child, buried away from civilization, no one of her own sort to talk with, no theaters, no cultural life, no society."

"Luna City has stereo transcriptions of every successful Broadway play." Jo's voice had a slight edge.

"Oh! Really? But it's not just the plays, my dear; it's the society of gentle folk. Now, when I was a girl, my parents—"

Allan butted in, "One o'clock. Have you had lunch, my dear?"

Mrs. Appleby sat up with a jerk. "Oh, heavenly days! I simply must fly. My dress designer—a tyrant, but a genius. I'll give you her address. It's been charming, my dears, and I can't thank you too much for telling me all about my poor child. I do wish she would be sensible like you two; I'm always ready to make a home for her—and her husband, for that matter. Do come and see me often. I love to talk to people who've been on the Moon."

"In the Moon."

"It makes me feel closer to my darling. Good-by, then."

When the door closed behind her, Jo said, "Allan, I need a drink."

"I'll join you."

Jo cut her shopping short; it was too tiring.

By four o'clock they were driving in Central Park, enjoying the autumn scenery to the lazy clop-clop of horses' hoofs. The helicopters, the pigeons, the streak in the sky where the Antipodes rocket had passed, made a scene idyllic in beauty and serenity.

Jo whispered huskily, "Isn't it lovely?"

"Sure is. Say, did you notice they've torn up Forty-second Street again?"

Back in their room, Jo collapsed on her bed, while Allan took off his shoes. He sat rubbing his feet, and remarked, "I'm going barefooted all evening. Golly, how my feet hurt!"

"So do mine. But we're going to your father's, my sweet."

"Huh? Oh, damn, I forgot. Jo, whatever possessed you? Call him up and postpone it. We're still half dead from the trip."

"But, Allan, he's invited a lot of your friends."

"Balls of fire and cold mush! I haven't any real friends in New York. Make it next week."

" 'Next week.' H'm'm—look, Allan; let's go to the country right away." Jo's parents had left her a tiny, wornout farm in Connecticut.

"What happened to your yen for plays and music?"

"I'll show you." She went to the window, open since noon. "Look at that window sill." She drew their initials in the grime. "Allan, this city is filthy."

"You can't expect ten million people not to kick up dust."

"Luna City was never like this. I could wear a white outfit there till I got tired of it. Here one wouldn't last a day."

"Luna City has a roof, and precipitrons in every air duct."

"Well, Manhattan ought to have! I either freeze or smother."

"You wanted to feel rain on your face."

"Don't be tiresome. I want it out in the clean, green country."

"Okay. I want to start my book anyhow. I'll call your agent."

"I called this morning. We can move in any time."

It was a stand-up supper at his father's house, though Jo sat down and let food be fetched. Allan, as guest of honor, had to stay on his aching feet. His father led him to the buffet. "Here, son, try this goose liver. It should go well after a diet of green cheese."

Allan agreed that it was good.

"See here, son, you really ought to tell these folks about your trip."

"No speeches, dad. Let 'em read the *National Geographic*."

"Nonsense!" He turned around. . . . "Quiet, everybody! Allan is going to tell us how the Lunatics live."

Allan bit his lip. To be sure, the citizens of Luna City used that term to each other, but it did not sound the same here. "Oh, shucks, I haven't anything to say. Go on and eat."

"You talk, we'll eat."

"Tell about Looney City."

"Did you see the Man in the Moon?"

"Go on, what's it like to live on the Moon?"

"Not 'on the Moon'; in the Moon."

"What's the difference?"

"Why, none, I guess." There was no way to explain why Moon colonists emphasized that they lived under the surface, but it irritated him the way "Frisco" irritates a San Franciscan. " 'In the Moon' is the way we say it. We don't spend much time on the surface, except the staff at Shapley Observatory, and the prospectors, and so forth. The living quarters are underground, naturally."

"Why 'naturally'? Afraid of meteors?"

"No more than you are afraid of lightning. We go underground for insulation against heat and cold and as support for pressure sealing. Both are cheaper and easier underground. The soil is easy to work and its pores act like vacuum in a vacuum jug. It *is vacuum*."

"But, Mr. MacRae," a serious-looking lady inquired, "doesn't it hurt your ears to live under pressure?"

Allan fanned the air. "It's the same here—fifteen pounds."

She looked puzzled. "I suppose so, but it's hard to imagine. It would terrify me to be sealed up in a cave. Suppose it blew out?"

"Fifteen pounds of pressure is no problem; engineers work in thousands of pounds per square inch. Anyhow, Luna City is compartmented like a ship. The Dutch live behind dikes; down South they have levees. Subways, ocean liners, aircraft—they're all artificial ways to live. Luna City seems strange just because it's far away."

She shivered. "It scares me."

A pretentious little man pushed his way forward. "Mr. MacRae, granted that it is nice for science and all that, why should taxpayers' money be wasted on a colony on the Moon?"

"You seem to have answered yourself," Allan told him slowly.

"Then how do you justify it? Tell me that, sir."

"It doesn't need justifying; the Luna colony has paid its cost many times over. The Lunar companies are all paying propositions. Artemis Mines, Spaceways, Spaceways Provisioning Corporation, Diana Recreations, Electronics Research Company, Lunar Bio Labs, not to mention all of Rutherford—look 'em up. I'll admit the Cosmic Research Project nicks the taxpayer a little, since it's a joint enterprise of the Harriman Foundation and the Government."

"Then you admit it. It's the principle of the thing."

Allan's feet were hurting him very badly. "What principle? Historically, research has always paid off. Take it up with your senator." He turned his back and looked for more goose liver.

A man touched him on the arm; Allan recognized an old schoolmate. "Allan, congratulations on ticking off old Beetle. He's been needing it; I think he's some sort of a radical."

Allan grinned. "I shouldn't have lost my temper."

"A good job you did. Say, Allan, I'm taking a couple of out-of-town buyers around to the hot spots tomorrow night. Come along."

"Thanks a lot, but we're going out in the country."

"Oh, you mustn't miss this party. After all, you've been buried on the Moon; you need relaxation after all that monotony."

Allan felt his cheeks getting warm. "Thanks just the same, but— Ever seen the Earth-View Room in Hotel Moon Haven?"

"No. Plan to take the trip when I've made my pile, of course."

"Well, there's a night club! Ever see a dancer leap thirty feet into the air and do slow rolls? Or a juggler work in low gravity? Ever try a lunacy cocktail?" Jo caught his eye across the room. "Er—excuse me, old man. My wife wants me." As he turned away he added, "Moon Haven itself isn't just a spacemen's dive, by the way; it's recommended by the Duncan Hines Association."

Jo was very pale. "Darling, you've got to get me out of here. I'm suffocating. I'm really ill."

"Suits." They made their excuses.

Jo woke up with a stuffy cold, so they took a cab directly to her country place.

There were low-lying clouds under them, but the weather was fine above. The sunshine and the drowsy beat of the rotors regained for them the joy of homecoming.

Allan broke the lazy reverie. "Here's a funny thing, Jo. You couldn't hire me to go back to the Moon, but last night I found myself defending the Loonies every time I opened my mouth."

She nodded. "I know. Honest to heaven, some people act as if the

Earth were flat. Some of them don't really believe in anything, and some are so matter-of-fact that you know they don't really understand —and I don't know which sort annoys me the more."

It was foggy when they landed, but the house was clean, the agent had laid a fire and stocked the refrigerator. In ten minutes they were sipping hot punch and baking the weariness from their bones.

"This," said Allan, stretching, "is okay. It really is great to be back."

"Uh-huh. All except the new highway." They could hear the big Diesels growling on the grade, fifty yards from their door.

"Forget it. Turn your back and you're looking into the woods."

They soon had their ground legs well enough to enjoy little walks in the woods during a long, warm Indian summer. Allan worked on the results of three years' research, preparatory to starting his book. Jo helped him with the statistical work, got reacquainted with the delights of cooking, daydreamed and rested.

It was on the day of the first frost that the toilet stopped up. The village plumber did not show up until the next day. Meanwhile they resorted to a drafty, spider-infested little building of another era, still standing out beyond the woodpile.

The plumber was not encouraging. "New septic tank. New sile pipe. Pay you to get new fixtures. Five, six hundred dollars. Have to calculate."

"That's all right," Allan told him. "Can you start today?"

The man laughed. "I can see plainly, mister, that you don't know what it is to get materials and labor today. Next spring, maybe."

"That's impossible, man. Never mind the cost. Get it done."

The native shrugged. "Sorry not to oblige you. Good day."

When he left, Jo exploded, "Allan, he doesn't want to help us."

"Well, maybe. I'll try for help from Norwalk or even from the city. You can't trudge through snow out to that Iron Maiden all winter."

"I hope not."

"You must not. You've had one cold." He stared morosely at the fire. "I suppose I brought it on by my misplaced sense of humor."

"What do you mean?"

"Well, you know we've taken a lot of kidding ever since it got around that we were colonials. Harmless, but some of it rankled. You remember I went into the village alone last Saturday?"

"Yes. What happened?"

"They started in on me in the barbershop. I let it ride at first, then the worm turned. I pitched some double-talk about the Moon—corny old stuff like the vacuum worms and petrified air. When they finally realized I was ribbing them, nobody laughed. Our rustic sanitary engineer was in the group. I'm sorry."

"Don't be." She kissed him. "I'm glad you paid them back."

The plumber from Norwalk was helpful, but rain, and then sleet, slowed the work. They both caught colds. On the ninth miserable day,

Allan was working at his desk when he heard Jo come in the back door, returning from shopping. Presently he became aware that she had not come in to say "Hello." He went to investigate.

He found her slumped on a kitchen chair, crying quietly. "Darling," he said urgently, "honey baby, whatever is the matter?"

She looked up. "I did't bead to led you doe."

"Blow your nose. Then wipe your eyes. What do you mean, 'you didn't mean to let me know'? What happened?"

She let it out, punctuated by sniffles. First, the grocer had said he had no cleansing tissues; then, when she had pointed to them, had stated that they were sold. Finally, he had mentioned "bringing in outside labor and taking the bread out of the mouths of honest folk."

Jo had blown up and had rehashed the incident of Allan and the barbershop wits. The grocer had simply grown more stiff. " 'Lady,' he said to me, 'I don't know or care whether you and your husband have been to the Moon. I don't take much stock in such things. In any case, I don't need your trade.' Oh, Allan, I'm so unhappy."

"Not so unhappy as he's going to be! Where's my hat?"

"Allan, you're not leaving this house! I won't have you fighting!"

"I won't have him bullying you."

"He won't again. Oh, my dear, I've tried so hard, but I can't stand it here. It's not just the villagers; it's the cold and the cockroaches and always having a runny nose. I'm tired out and my feet hurt all the time." She started to cry again.

"There, there! We'll leave, honey. We'll go to Florida. I'll finish my book while you lie in the sun."

"Oh, I don't want to go to Florida. I want to go home!"

"Huh? You mean . . . back to Luna City?"

"Yes. Oh, dearest, I know you don't want to, but I can't help it. I could put up with the dirt and cold and the comic-strip plumbing, but it's not being understood that gets me. These groundhogs don't know anything."

He grinned at her. "Keep sending, Kid; I'm on your frequency."

"Allan!"

He nodded. "I found out I was a Loony at heart quite a while ago, but I was afraid to tell you. My feet hurt, too, and I'm sick of being treated like a freak. I've tried to be tolerant, but I can't stand groundhogs. I miss the civilized folks in dear old Luna."

She nodded. "I guess it's prejudice, but I feel the same way."

"It's not prejudice. Be honest. What does it take to get to Luna City?"

"A ticket."

"Smarty pants! Not as a tourist, but to get a job there. You know the answer: Intelligence. It costs a lot to send a man to the Moon and more to keep him there. To pay off, he has to be worth a lot. High I.Q., good compatibility index, superior education—everything that makes a person pleasant and interesting to have around. We're spoiled; the human cussedness that groundhogs take for granted, we now find intolerable, because Loonies are different. The fact that Luna City is the most comfortable environment that man ever built for himself is unimportant; it's people who count. Let's go home."

He went to the phone—an antique, speech-only rig—and called the Foundation's New York office. While he waited, truncheon-like receiver to his ear, she said, "Suppose they won't have us?"

"That's what worries me." They knew that the Lunar enterprises rarely rehired personnel who had once quit; the physical examination was rumored to be much harder to pass the second time.

"Hello? Foundation? May I speak to the recruiting office? Hello. I *can't* turn on my view plate; this instrument is a hangover from the dark ages. This is Allan MacRae, physical chemist. Contract Number One-three-four-oh-seven-two-nine. And Josephine MacRae, One-three-four-oh-seven-three-oh. We want to sign up again. I said we want to sign up again. . . . Okay, I'll wait."

"Pray, darling, pray!"

"I'm praying. . . . How's that? My appointment's still vacant? Fine, fine! How about my wife?" He listened with a worried look; Jo held her breath. Then he cupped the speaker. "Hey, Jo, your job's filled. They offer you an interim job as a junior accountant."

"Tell 'em, 'Yes!'"

"That'll be fine. When can we take our exams? . . . Swell. Thanks! Good-by." He hung up and turned to his wife. "Physical and psycho as soon as we like; professional exams waived."

"What are we waiting for?"

"Nothing." He dialed the Norwalk Copter Service. "Can you send a cab? . . . Good grief, don't you have radar? Okay, g'by!" He snorted. "Grounded by the weather. I'll call New York for a modern cab."

Ninety minutes later they landed on top of Harriman Tower.

The psychologist was cordial. "We'll get this over before you have your chests thumped. Sit down. Tell me about yourselves." He drew them out skillfully. "I see. Did you get the plumbing repaired?"

"Well, it was being fixed."

"I can sympathize with your foot trouble, Mrs. MacRae; my arches always bother me here. That's the real reason, isn't it?"

"Oh, no!"

"Now, Mrs. MacRae—"

"Really it's not—truly. I want people to talk to who know what I mean. I'm homesick for my own sort. I want to go home, and I've got to have this job to do it. I'll steady down, I know I will."

The doctor looked grave. "How about you, Mr. MacRae?"

"Well, it's about the same story. I've been trying to write a book, but I can't work. I'm homesick. I want to go back."

Doctor Feldman suddenly smiled. "It won't be too difficult."

"You mean we're in? If we pass the physical?"

"Never mind that; your discharge examinations are recent enough.

Of course, you'll go out to Arizona for reconditioning and quarantine. Maybe you're wondering why it's been so easy, when it's supposed to be so hard. It's simple: we don't want people lured back by the high pay. We do want people who will be happy and as permanent as possible. Now that you're 'Moonstruck,' we want you back." He got up and stuck out his hand.

Back in the Commodore that night, Jo was struck by a thought. "Allan, do you suppose we could get our own apartment back?"

"I don't know. We could send a radio. . . . No! We'll telephone."

It took ten minutes to put the call through. Miss Stone's face softened a little when she recognized them.

"Miss Stone, we're coming home!"

There was the usual three-second lag, then, "Yes, I know. It came over the tape twenty minutes ago."

"Oh. Say, Miss Stone, is our old flat vacant?" They waited.

"I've held it; I knew you'd come back. Welcome home, Loonies."

When the screen cleared, Jo said, "Allan, how did she know?"

"Does it matter? We're in, kid! Members of the lodge."

"I guess you're right. . . . Oh, Allan, look!" she had stepped to the window; scudding clouds had just uncovered the Moon. It was three days old and *Mare Fecunditatis*—the roll of hair at the back of the Lady in the Moon's head—was cleared by the sunrise line. Near the right-hand edge of that great, dark sea was a tiny spot, visible only to their inner eyes—Luna City.

The crescent hung, serene and silvery, over the tall buildings. "Darling, isn't it beautiful?"

"Certainly is. It'll be great to be back. Don't get your nose all runny."

CLIFFORD D. SIMAK

TOOLS

VENUS had broken many men. Now it was breaking Harvey Boone, and the worst of it was that Boone knew it was breaking him and couldn't do a thing about it.

Although it wasn't entirely Venus. Partly it was Archie—Archie, the thing in the talking jar. Perhaps it wasn't right calling Archie just a "thing." Archie might have been an "it" or "they." No one knew. In fact, no one knew much of anything about Archie despite the fact men had talked to him and studied him for almost a hundred years.

Harvey Boone was official observer for the Solar Institute, and his reports, sent back with every rocketload of radium that streaked out to Earth, were adding to the voluminous mass of data assembled on Archie. Data that told almost nothing at all.

Venus itself was bad enough. Men died when a suit cracked or radium shields broke down. Although that wasn't the usual way the planet killed. Venus had a better—perhaps, more accurately—a worse way.

Any alien planet is hard to live on and stay sane. Strangeness is a word that doesn't have much meaning until a man stands face to face with it and then it smacks him straight between the eyes.

Venus was alien—plus. One always had a sense that eyes were watching him, watching all the time. And waiting. Although one didn't have the least idea what they were waiting for.

On Venus, something always stalked a man—something that trod just on the outer edge of shadow. A sense of not belonging, of being out of place, of being an intruder. A baffling psychological something that drove men to their deaths or to living deaths that were even worse.

Harvey Boone huddled on a chair in one corner of the laboratory, nursing a whiskey bottle, while Archie chuckled at him.

"Nerves," said Archie. "Your nerves are shot to hell."

Boone's hand shook as he tilted the whiskey bottle up. His hate-filled eyes glared at the lead-glass jar even as he gulped.

Boone knew what Archie said was true. Even through his drink-fogged brain, the one fact stood out in bright relief—he was going crazy. He had seen Johnny Garrison, commander of the dome, watching him. And Doc Steele. Doc was the psychologist, and when Doc started watching one it was time to pull up and try to straighten oneself out. For Doc's word was law. It had to be law.

A knock sounded on the door and Boone called out an invitation. Doc Steele strode in.

"Good morning, Boone," he said. "Hello, Archie."

Archie's voice, mechanical and toneless, returned the greeting.

"Have a drink," said Boone.

Doc shook his head, took a cigar from his pocket and with a knife cut it neatly in two. One half he stuck back in his pocket, the other half in his mouth.

"Don't you ever light those things?" demanded Boone irritably.

"Nope," Doc replied cheerfully. "Always dry-smoke them."

He said to Archie: "How are you today, Archie?"

Despite its mechanical whir, Archie's reply sounded almost querulous: "Why do you always ask me that, doctor? You know there's nothing wrong with me. There never could be. I'm always all right."

Doc chuckled. "I seem to keep forgetting about you. Wish the human race was like that. Then there wouldn't be any need for chaps like me."

"I'm glad you came," Archie grated. "I like to talk to you. You never make me feel you're trying to find out something."

"He says that to get my goat," snapped Boone.

"I wouldn't let him do it," Doc declared. To Archie he said: "I suppose it does get tiresome after a hundred years or so. But it doesn't seem to have done much good. No one seems to have found out much about you."

He swiveled the cigar across his face. "Maybe they tried too hard."

"That," said Archie, "might be true. You remind me of Masterson. You're different from the ones who come out to watch me now."

"You don't like them?" Doc winked at Boone and Boone glowered back.

"Why should I like them?" asked Archie. "They regard me as a freak, a curiosity, something to be observed, an assignment to be done. Masterson thought of me as life, as a fellow entity. And so do you."

"Why, bless my soul," said Doc, "and so I do."

"The others pity me," Archie stated.

"You don't catch me pitying you," Doc declared. "Sometimes I catch myself wishing I were you. I suspect I might enjoy your kind of philosophy."

"The human race," protested Archie, "couldn't understand my philosophy. I doubt if I could explain it to them. The language doesn't have the words. Just as I had a hard time understanding a lot of your Terrestrial philosophy and economics. I've studied your history and your economics and your political science. I've kept up with your current events. And sometimes, many times, it doesn't make sense to me. Sometimes I think it's stupid, but I try to tell myself that it may be because I don't understand. I miss something, perhaps. Some vital quirk of mind, some underlying factor."

Doc sobered. "I don't think you miss much, Archie. A lot of the things we do are stupid, even by our own standards. We lack foresight so often."

Doc lifted his eyes to the large oil portrait that hung on the wall above Boone's desk, and he had quite forgotten Boone. From the portrait, kindly gray eyes smiled out of the face. The brows were furrowed, the wavy white hair looked like a silver crown.

"We need more men like him," said Doc. "More men with vision."

The portrait was of Masterson, the man who had discovered intelligent life existing in the great clouds of radon that hung over the vast beds of radium ore. Masterson had been more than a man of vision. He had been a genius and a glutton for work.

From the moment he had discerned, by accident, what he thought were lifelike properties in some radon he was studying, he had labored unceasingly with but one end in view. In this very laboratory he had carried out his life work, and there, in the lead-glass jar on the table, lay the end product—Archie.

Masterson had confined radon under pressure in a shielded jar equipped with a delicate system of controls. Failing time after time, never admitting defeat, he had taught radon in the jar to recognize certain electrical impulses set up within the jar. And the radon, recognizing these impulses as intelligent symbols, finally had learned to manipulate the controls which produced the voice by which it spoke.

It had not been as easy as it sounded, however. It took many grueling years. For both Masterson and Archie were groping in the dark, working without comparable experience, without even a comparable understanding or a comparable mode of thinking. Two alien minds—

"Does it seem a long time, Archie?" Doc asked.

"That's hard to say," the speaker boomed. "Time doesn't have a great deal of meaning to something that goes on and on."

"You mean you are immortal?"

"No, perhaps not immortal."

"But do you know?" snapped Doc.

Archie did, then, the thing which had driven observer after observer close to madness. He simply didn't answer.

Silence thrummed in the room. Doc heard the click of sliding doors elsewhere in the dome, the low hum of powerful machinery.

"That's the way he is," yelled Boone. "That's the way he always is. Shuts up like a clam. Sometimes I'd like to—"

"Break it up, Archie," commanded Doc. "You don't have to play dead with me. I'm not here to question you. I'm just here to pass the time of day. Is there anything I can do for you?"

"You might bring in the latest newspapers and read to me," said Archie.

"That," declared Doc, "would be a downright privilege."

"But not the funnies," cautioned Archie. "Somehow I can't appreciate the funnies."

Outside the dome, the week-long night had fallen and it was snowing again—great, white sheets driven by gusty blasts of wind. Not real snow, but paraformaldehyde, solidified formaldehyde. For that was the stuff of which the mighty cloud banks which forever shielded the planet from space were composed.

Harvey Boone, clad in space gear, stood on the barren ridge above the dome and looked down at the scene spread before his eyes.

There lay the dome, with the flicker of shadows playing over it as the great batteries of lamps set in the radium pits swung to and fro.

In the pits labored mighty machines—specialized machines operating with "radon brains," using, in simplified form, the same principles of control as were used to communicate with Archie. Brains that could receive and understand orders, execute them through the medium of the machinery which they controlled—but which, unlike Archie, did not hold human knowledge accumulated over the course of a hundred years.

Here and there were men. Men incased in shining crystal armor to protect them against the hell's brew that was Venus' atmosphere. Carbon dioxide and not a trace of oxygen. Once there had been plenty of free oxygen, some water vapor. But the oxygen had gone to form carbon dioxide and formaldehyde, and the water vapor had combined to solidify the formaldehyde.

Harvey Boone shivered as a blast of hot wind swirled a blanket of solidified formaldehyde around him, shutting off the view. For a moment he stood isolated in a world of swirling white and through the whiteness something seemed to stalk him. Something that might have been fear, and yet more stark than fear, more subtle than panic, more agonizing than terror.

Boone was on the verge of cringing horror before the wind whipped the cloud of snow away. The gale hooted and howled at him. The dancing snow made ghostly patterns in the air. The banks of lights in the pits below weaved fantastically against the sweeping, wind-driven clouds of white.

Unaccountable panic gripped him tight. Mocking whispers danced along the wind. The rising wind shrieked malignantly and a burst of snow swished at him.

Harvey Boone screamed and ran, unseen terror trotting at his heels.

But the closing lock did not shut out the horror of the outdoors. It wasn't something one could get rid of as easily as that.

Stripped of space gear, he found his hands were shaking.

"I need a drink," he told himself.

In the laboratory he took the bottle out of his desk, tilted it.

A mocking laugh sounded behind him. Nerves on edge, he whirled about.

A face was leering at him from the glass jar on the table. And that was wrong. For there wasn't any face. There wasn't anything one could see inside the jar. Nothing but Archie—radon under pressure. One doesn't see radon—not unless one looks at it through a spectroscope.

Boone passed his hand swiftly before his eyes and looked again. The face was gone.

Archie chortled at him. "I'm getting you. I almost got you then. You'll crack up pretty soon. What are you waiting for? Why are you hanging on? In the end I'll get you!"

Boone strangled with rage.

"You're wrong," he mouthed. "I'm the one that's got you." He slapped a pile of notes that lay on his desk. "I'm the one who's going to crack you. I'll bust you wide open. I'll let them know what you really are."

"Oh, yeah!" crowed Archie.

Boone set down the bottle. "Damn you," he said thickly, "I have half a notion to settle you once and for all. You've deviled me long enough. I'm going to let you die."

"You'll do what?" demanded Archie.

"I'll let you die," stormed Boone. "All I have to do is forget to pump more radon in. In another week you'll be polonium and—"

"You wouldn't dare," taunted Archie. "You know what would happen to you then. The Institute would have your scalp for that."

The face was in the jar again. A terrible face. One that sent fear and loathing and terrifying anger surging through the scientist.

With a shriek of rage, Boone grabbed the bottle off the desk and hurled it. It missed Archie, shattered against the wall, spraying the glass jar with liquor.

Archie tittered and a hand materialized before the face, waggling its fingers in an obscene gesture.

With a hoarse whoop, Boone leaped forward and snatched up a heavy stool. Archie's laughter rang through the room—terrible laughter.

Boone screamed in insane rage and babbled. The stool came up and smashed downward. The jar splintered under the crashing impact.

Searing radiations lanced through the room. The spectrographic detectors flamed faintly. Fans whined, rose to a piercing shriek, sweeping the air, throwing the radon outside the dome. Atmosphere hissed and roared.

But Harvey Boone knew none of this, for Harvey Boone was dead. Incredible pain had lashed at him in one searing second and he had dropped, his face and hands burned to a fiery red, his eyes mere staring holes.

Radon, in its pure state, weight for weight, is one hundred thousand times as active as radium.

"But Archie couldn't have had anything to do with it," protested Johnny Garrison. "Hypnotism! That's incredible. He couldn't hypnotize a person. There's nothing to support such a belief. We've observed Archie for a hundred years—"

"Let's not forget one thing," interrupted Doc. "In Archie we were observing something that was intelligent. Just how intelligent we had no way of knowing. But we do know this: His intelligence was not human intelligence. It couldn't be. True, we bridged the gap, we talked with him. But the talk was carried on in human terms, upon a human basis."

Doc's cigar traveled from east to west. "Does that suggest anything to you?"

The dome commander's face was white. "I'd never thought of that. But it means—it would have to mean—that Archie was intelligent enough to force his thought processes into human channels."

Doc nodded. "Could man have done the same? Could man have forced himself to think the way Archie thinks? I doubt it. Archie's thought processes probably would be too alien for us to even grasp. What is more, Archie recognized this. It all boils down to this: We furnished the mechanical set-up, Archie furnished the mental set-up."

"You make it sound frightening," said Garrison.

"It is frightening," Doc assured him.

Garrison stood up. "There's no use beating around the bush. Both of us are thinking the same thing."

Doc said: "I'm afraid so. There's nothing else to think."

"All of them know," said Garrison, "all of them, or it, or whatever is out there—they know as much as Archie knew."

"I'm sure they do," Doc agreed. "Archie never lost his identity, even though we had to pump in new radon every few days. It was always the same Archie. Tests with the radon brains on the machines, however, revealed merely an intelligence very poorly versed in human knowledge. The same radon, mind you, and yet the radon that was used to replenish Archie becomes Archie, while all the other radon remained an intelligence that had none of Archie's human knowledge."

"And now," said Garrison, "it's all Archie. I told Mac he'd have to shut down the machines when the radon ran low in the brains. We simply can't take a chance. There'll be hell to pay. R. C. will blast space wide open. We're behind schedule now—"

He stared out the port with haggard face, watching the snow sweep by.

"Take it easy, Johnny," counseled Doc. "The home office has been riding you again. You're behind schedule and you're getting jumpy. You're remembering some of the things you've seen happen to men who couldn't keep the wheels of industry moving and the banners of Radium, Inc., waving high. You're thinking of R. C.'s secret police and charges of sabotage and God knows what."

"Look, Doc," said Garrison desperately, almost pleadingly, "this is my big chance—my last chance. I'm not too young any more, and this chance has to click. Make good here on Venus and I'm set for life. No more third-rate wilderness posts out on the Jovian moons, no more stinking tricks on the Martian desert. It'll be Earth for me—Earth and an easy-chair."

"I know how it is," said Doc. "It's the old system of fear. You're afraid of the big boys and Mac is afraid of you and the men are afraid of Mac. And all of us are afraid of Venus. Radium, Inc., owns the Solar System, body and soul. The radium monopoly, holding companies, interlocking directories—it all adds up to invisible government, not too invisible at that. R. C. Webster owns us all. He owns us by virtue of Streeter's secret police and his spies. He owns us because radium is power and he owns the radium. He owns us because there isn't a government that won't jump when he snaps his fingers. His father and grandfather owned us before this, and his son and grandson will own us after a while."

He chuckled. "You needn't look so horrified, Johnny. You're the only one that's hearing me, and you won't say a word. But you know it's the truth as well as I. Radium is the basis of the power that holds the Solar System in thrall. The wheels of the System depend on radium from Venus. It was the price the people of Earth had to pay for solar expansion, for a solar empire. Just the cost of wheeling a ship from one planet to another is tremendous. It takes capital to develop a solar empire, and when capital is called on it always has a price. We paid that price, and this is what we got."

Garrison reached out with trembling hands to pick up a bottle of brandy. The liquor splashed as he poured it in a tumbler.

"What are we going to do, Doc?"

"I wish I knew," said Doc.

A bell jangled and Garrison lifted the phone.

The voice of the chief engineer shouted at him.

"Chief, we have to fill those brains again. Either that or shut down. The radon is running low."

"I thought I told you to shut them down," yelled Garrison. "We can't take a chance. We can't turn those machines over to Archie."

Mac howled in anguish. "But we're way behind schedule. Shut them down and—"

"Shut them down!" roared Garrison. "Sparks is trying to get through to Earth. I'll let you know."

He hung the speaker back in its cradle, lifted it again and dialed the communications room.

"How's the call to Earth coming?"

"I'm trying," yelped Sparks, "but I'm afraid. We're nearing the Sun, you know. Space is all chopped. . . . Hey, wait a minute. Here we are. I'll tie you in—"

Static crackled and snapped. A thin voice was shouting.

"That you, Garrison? Hello, Garrison!"

Garrison recognized the voice, distorted as it was, and grimaced. He could envision R. C. Webster, president of Radium, Inc., bouncing up and down in his chair, furious at the prospect of more trouble on Venus.

"Yes, R. C., this is Garrison."

"Well," piped R. C., "what's the trouble now? Speak up, man, what's gone wrong this time?"

Swiftly Garrison told him. Twice static blotted out the tight beam and Sparks worked like a demon to re-establish contact.

"And what are you afraid of?" shrieked the man on Earth.

"Simply this," explained Garrison, wishing it didn't sound so silly. "Archie has escaped. That means all the radon knows as much as he did. If we pump new radon into the brains, we'll be pumping in intelligence radon—that is, radon that knows about us—that is—"

"Poppycock," yelled R. C. "That's the biggest lot of damn foolishness I've ever heard."

"But, R. C.—"

"Look here, young man," fumed the voice, "we're behind schedule, aren't we? You're out there to dig radium, aren't you?"

"Yes," admitted Garrison, hopelessly.

"All right, then, dig radium. Get back on schedule. Fill up those brains and tear into it—"

"But you don't understand—"

"I said to fill up those brains and get to work. And keep working!"

"Those are orders?" asked Garrison.

"Those are orders!" snapped R. C.

Static howled at them derisively.

Garrison watched the ship roar away from the surface, lose itself in the driving whiteness of solidified formaldehyde. Beside him, Mac rubbed armored hands together in exultation.

"That almost puts us on schedule," he announced.

Garrison nodded, staring moodily out over the field. It was night again, and little wind devils of formaldehyde danced and jigged across the ground. Night and a snowstorm, and the mercury at one hundred forty degrees above Fahrenheit. During the week-long day it got hotter.

He heard the clicking of the mighty brain-controlled machines as they dug ore in the pits, the whine of wind around the dome and in the jagged hills, the snicking of the refrigerator units in his suit.

"How soon will you have Archie's jar done, Mac?" he asked. "The new Institute observer is getting anxious to see what he can get out of him."

"Just a few hours more," said Mac. "It took us a long time to figure out some of the things about it, but I've had the robots on it steady."

"Rush it over soon as you get it done. We've tried to talk to some of the radon brains in the machines, but it's no dice."

"There's just one thing bothers me," said Mac.

"What is that?" Garrison asked sharply.

"Well, we didn't figure out exactly all the angles on that jar. Some of the working parts are mighty complicated and delicate, you know. But we thought we'd get started at least and let the Institute stooge take over when he got here. But when those robots—"

"Yes?" said Garrison.

"When those robots got to the things we couldn't understand, they tossed the blueprints to one side and went right ahead. So help me, they didn't even fumble."

The two men looked at one another, faces stolid.

"I don't like it," Mac declared.

"Neither do I," said Garrison.

He turned and walked slowly toward the dome, while Mac went back to the pits.

In Garrison's office, Doc had cornered Roger Chester, the new Institute observer.

"The Institute has mountains of reports," Chester was saying. "I tried to go through them before I came out. Night and day almost. Ever since I knew I was going to replace Boone."

Doc carefully halved a new cigar, tucked one piece in his pocket, the other in his mouth.

"What were you looking for?" he asked.

"A clue. You see, I knew Boone. For years. He wasn't the kind of fellow who would break. It would have taken more than Venus. But I didn't find a thing."

"Boone himself might have furnished that clue," Doc suggested quietly. "Did you look through his reports?",

"I read them over and over," Chester admitted. "There was nothing there. Some of his reports were missing. The last few days—"

"Those last few days can be canceled out," said Doc. "The lad wasn't himself. I wouldn't be surprised he didn't write any reports those last few days."

Chester said: "That would have been unlike him."

Doc wrangled the cigar viciously. "Find anything else?"

"Not much. Not much more than Masterson knew. Even now—after all these years, it's hard to believe—that radon could be alive."

"If any gas could live," said Doc, "it would be radon. It's heavy. Molecular weight of 222. One hundred eleven times as heavy as hydrogen, five times as heavy as carbon dioxide. Not complicated from a molecular standpoint, but atomically one of the most complicated known. Complicated enough for life. And if you're looking for the unbalance necessary for life, it's radioactive. Chemically inert, perhaps, but terrifically unstable physically—"

The door of the office opened and Garrison walked in.

"Still chewing the fat about Archie?" he asked.

He strode to his desk and took out a bottle and glasses.

"It's been two weeks since Archie got away," he said. "And nothing's happened. We're sitting on top of a volcano, waiting for it to go sky high. And nothing happens. What is Archie doing? What is he waiting for?"

"That's a big order, Garrison," declared Chester. "Let us try to envision a life which had no tools because it couldn't make them, would be useless to it even if it did have them because it couldn't use them. Man's rise, you must remember, is largely, if not entirely, attributable to his use of tools. An accident that made his thumb opposing gave him a running start—"

The phone on the desk blared. Garrison snatched it up, and Mac's voice shrieked at him.

"Chief, those damn robots are running away! So are the machines in the pit—"

Cold fingers seemed to clamp around the commander's throat.

Mac's voice was almost sobbing. "—hell for leather out here. But they left Archie's jar. Must have forgotten that."

"Mac," yelled Garrison, "jump into a tractor and try to follow them. Find out where they're going."

"But, chief—"

"Follow them!" shouted Garrison.

He slammed down the hand piece, lifted it and dialed.

"Sparks, get hold of Earth!"

"No soap," said Sparks laconically.

"Damn it, try to get them. It's a matter of life and death!"

"I can't," wailed Sparks. "We're around the Sun. We can't get through."

"Get the ship, then."

"It won't do any good," yelped Sparks. "They're hugging the Sun to cut down distance. It'll be days before they can relay a message."

"O. K.," said Garrison wearily. "Forget it."

He hung up and faced Chester.

"You don't have to imagine Archie without tools any longer," he said. "He has them now. He just stole them from us."

Mac dragged in hours later.

"I didn't find a thing," he reported. "Not a single thing."

Garrison studied him, red-eyed from worry. "That's all right, Mac. I didn't think you would. Five miles from here and you're on unknown ground."

"What are we going to do now, chief?"

Garrison shook his head. "I don't know. Sparks finally got a message through. Managed to pick up Mercury, just coming around the Sun. Probably they'll shoot it out to Mars to be relayed to Earth."

Chester came out of the laboratory and sat down.

Doc swiveled his cigar.

"What has Archie to say?" he asked.

Chester's face grew red. "I pumped the radon into the jar. But there was no response. Practically none, that is. Told me to go to hell."

Doc chuckled at the man's discomfiture. "Don't let Archie get you down. That's what he did to Boone. Got on his nerves. Drove him insane. Archie had to get out some way, you see. He couldn't do anything while he was shut up in one place. So he forced Boone to let him out. Boone didn't know what was going on, but Archie did—"

"But what is Archie doing now?" exploded Garrison.

"He's playing a game of nerves," said Doc. "He's softening us up. We'll be ready to meet his terms when he's ready to make them."

"But why terms? What could Archie want?"

Doc's cigar swished back and forth. "How should I know? We might not even recognize what Archie is fighting for—and, again, we might. He might be fighting for his existence. His life depends upon those radium beds. No more radium, no more radon, no more Archie."

"Nonsense," Chester broke in. "We could have dug those beds for a million years and not made a dent in them."

"A million years," objected Doc, "might be only a minute or two for Archie."

"Damn you, Doc," snapped Garrison, "what are you grinning for? What is so funny about it?"

"It's amusing," Doc explained. "Something I've often wondered about—just what Earthmen would do if they ran up against something that had them licked forty ways from Sunday."

"But he hasn't got us licked," yelled Mac. "Not yet."

"Anything that can keep radium from Earth can lick us," Doc declared. "And Archie can do that—don't you ever kid yourself."

"But he'll ruin the Solar System," shouted Garrison. "Machines will have to shut down. Mines and factories will be idle. Spaceships will stop running. Planets will have to be evacuated—"

"What you mean," Doc pointed out, "is that he'll ruin Radium, Inc. Not the Solar System. The System can get along without Radium, Inc. Probably even without radium. It did for thousands of years, you know. The only trouble now is that the System is keyed to radium. If there isn't any radium, it means the economic framework that was built on radium must be swept away or some substitute must be found. And if no substitute is found, we must start over again and find some other way of life—perhaps a better way—"

Chester leaped to his feet.

"That's treason!" he shouted.

Silence struck the room like a thunderclap. Three pairs of eyes stared at the standing man. The air seemed to crackle with an electric aliveness.

"Sit down," Doc snapped.

Chester sank slowly into his chair. Mac's hands opened and closed, as if he were kneading someone's throat.

Doc nodded. "One of R. C.'s agents. He didn't smell quite like an Institute man to me. He said it was hard to believe radon could be alive. With an Institute man that wouldn't be belief, it would be knowledge."

"A dirty, snooping stooge," said Mac. "Sent out to see what was wrong on Venus."

"But not too good a one," Doc observed. "He lets his enthusiasm for Radium, Inc., run away with him. Of course, all of us were taught that enthusiasm ourselves—in school. But we soon got over it."

Chester ran his tongue over his lips.

"When Radium, Inc., can monkey with the Institute," said Doc, "it means one of two things. R. C. is getting pretty sure of himself or he's getting desperate. The Institute was the one thing that stood out against him. Up to now he hasn't dared to lay a finger on it."

Garrison had said nothing, but now he spoke: "By rights, Chester, we ought to kill you."

"You wouldn't dare," said Chester thinly.

"What difference does it make?" asked Garrison. "If we don't, another one of R. C.'s men will. You've slipped up. And R. C. doesn't give his men a chance to slip a second time."

"But you were talking treason," Chester insisted.

"Call it treason," snarled Garrison. "Call it anything you like. It's the language that's being talked up and down the System. Wherever men work out their hearts and strangle their conscience in hope of scraps thrown from Radium, Inc.'s table, they're saying the same thing we are saying."

The phone blared and Garrison put forth his hand, lifted the set and spoke.

"It's R. C.," Sparks yelled at the other end. "It's sort of weak, but maybe you can hear. Mars and Mercury are relaying."

"Hello, R. C.," said Garrison.

Static screamed in deafening whoops, and then R. C.'s voice sifted through, disjointed and reedy.

"—sit tight. We're sending men, ten shiploads of them."

"Men!" yelped Garrison. "What will we do with men?"

"Machines, too," scratched R. C.'s voice. "Manually operated machines—" More howls and screeches drowned out the rest.

"But R. C., you can't do that," yelled Garrison. "The men will die like flies. It'll be mass murder. It'll be like it was before—in the early days, before Masterson developed the radon brains. Men can't work in those radium pits—not work and live."

"That's a lot of damn tripe," raved R. C. "They'll work—"

"They'll revolt!" shrieked Garrison.

"Oh, no, they won't. I'm sending police along."

"Police!" stormed Garrison. "Some of Streeter's bloody butchers?"

"I'm sending Streeter himself. Streeter and some of his picked men. They'll keep order—"

"Look, R. C.," said Garrison bitterly, "you'd better send a new commander, too. I'll be damned if I'll work with Streeter."

"Take it easy, Garrison. You're doing all right. Just a bunch of bad breaks. You'll make out all right."

"I won't work those men," snapped Garrison. "Not the way they'll have to work. Radium isn't worth it."

"You will," yelled R. C., "or I'll have Streeter sock you down in the pits yourself. Radium has to move. We have to have it."

"By the way," said Garrison, suddenly calm, his eyes on Chester, "you remember that Institute chap who came to replace Boone?"

"Yes, I seem to remember—"

"He's lost," said Garrison. "Walked out into the hills. We've combed them, but there's no sign of him."

Chester rose from the chair in a smooth leap, hurling himself at Garrison, one hand snatching at the phone. The impact of his body staggered Garrison, but the commander sent him reeling with a shove.

"What was that you said, R. C.? I didn't hear. The static."

"I said to hell with him. Don't waste time looking for him. There are more important things."

Chester was charging in again on Garrison, intent on getting the phone. Mac moved with the speed of lightning, one huge fist knotted and pulled far back. It traveled in a looping, powerful arc, caught the charging man flush on the chin. Chester's head snapped back, his feet surged clear of the floor, his body smashed against the wall. He slid into a heap, like a doll someone had tossed into a corner.

Doc crossed the room and knelt beside him.

"You hit too hard," he said.

"I meant to hit hard," growled Mac.

"He's dead," said Doc. "You broke his neck."

Outside, the eternal snowstorm howled, sweeping the jagged hills and lamp-lighted pits.

Doc stood in front of a port and watched the scurrying activity that boiled within the mine. Hundreds of armored men and hundreds of laboring machines. Three spaceships, stationed beside the stock pile, were being loaded. Streeter's police, with ready guns, patrolled the sentry towers that loomed above the pits.

The door opened and Garrison came in with dragging feet.

"How many this shift?" asked Doc.

"Seven," Garrison answered hoarsely. "A screen blew up."

Doc sucked at the dead cigar. "This has to stop, Johnny. It has to stop or something is bound to crack. It's a death sentence for any man to be sent out here. The last replacements were criminals, men shanghaied off the street."

Garrison angrily sloshed the liquor in his glass.

"Don't look at me," he snapped. "It's out of my hands now. I'm acting only in an administrative capacity. Those are the exact words. Administrative capacity. Streeter is the works out here. He's the one that's running the show. He's the one that's working the men to death. And when they start to raise a little hell, those babies of his up in the towers open up on them."

"I know all that," admitted Doc. "I wasn't trying to blame you, Johnny. After all, we needn't kid ourselves. If we don't walk the line, Streeter will open up on us as well."

"You're telling me," said Garrison. He gulped the liquor. "Streeter knows that something happened to Chester. That yarn about his being lost out in the hills simply didn't click."

"We never meant it should," Doc declared. "But so long as we serve our purpose, so long as we throw no monkey wrenches, so long as we're good little boys, we can go on living."

Archie's voice grated from beyond the open laboratory door.

"Doctor, will you please come here?"

"Sure, Archie, sure. What can I do for you?"

"I would like to talk to Captain Streeter."

"Captain Streeter," warned Doc, "isn't a nice man. If I were you, I'd keep away from him."

"But nevertheless," persisted Archie, "I would like to talk to him. I have something that I'm sure will interest him. Will you call him, please?"

"Certainly," agreed Doc.

He strode out into the office and dialed the phone.

"Streeter speaking," said a voice.

"Archie wants to talk to you," said the Doc.

"Archie!" stormed Streeter. "Tell that lousy little hunk of gas to go chase himself."

"Streeter," said Doc, "it doesn't make any difference to me what you do; but, if I were in your place, I would talk to Archie. In fact, I'd come running when he called me."

Doc replaced the phone, cutting off the sounds of rage coming from the other end.

"Well?" asked Garrison.

"He'll come," said Doc.

Ten minutes later Streeter did come, cold anger in his eyes.

"I wish you gentlemen would tend to small details yourselves," he snarled.

Doc jerked his thumb toward the open door. "In there," he said.

Boots clumping angrily, Streeter strode into the laboratory.

"What is it?" his voice boomed.

"Captain Streeter," grated Archie's voice, "I don't like your way of doing things. I don't like Radium, Inc.'s way of doing things."

"Oh, so you don't," said Streeter, words silky with rage.

"So," continued Archie, "I'm giving you and your men half an hour to get out of here. Out of the mine and off this planet."

There were strangling sounds as the police captain fought to speak. Finally he rasped: "And if we don't?"

"If you don't," said Archie, "I shall force you to move. If the mine is not vacated within half an hour, I shall start bombardment."

"Bombardment!"

"Exactly. This place is ringed with cannon. It is a barbaric thing to do, but it's the only way you'd understand. I could use other methods, but the cannon probably are the best."

"You're bluffing," shrieked Streeter. "You haven't any cannon."

"Very well," said Archie. "Do what you wish. It's immaterial to me. You have thirty minutes."

Streeter swung around and stamped out into the office.

"You heard?" he asked.

Doc nodded. "If I were you, Streeter, I'd pull stakes. Archie isn't fooling."

"Cannon!" snorted the captain.

"Exactly," said Garrison. "And don't you ever think Archie doesn't have them. When the machines ran away they took along our tools."

Streeter's face hardened. "Let's say he has them, then. All right, he has them. So have we. We'll fight him!"

Doc laughed. "You'll play hell. Fighting Archie is a joke. Where are you going to find him? How are you going to corner him? There isn't any way to hit him, no way to come to grips with him. You can't defeat him. You can't destroy him. So long as there are radium beds there will always be an Archie."

"I'm calling Earth," said Streeter, grimly. "It's time the army took over."

"Call in your army," said Doc, "but remember one thing. The only thing you can fight is Archie's weapons. You may destroy his guns, but you can't hurt Archie. All he has to do is build some more. And those weapons won't be easy to hit. Because, you see, those guns will be intelligent. They won't depend on brass hats and military orders. They'll have brains of their own. You'll be fighting deadly intelligent machines. I tell you, Streeter, you haven't got a chance!"

Streeter turned to Garrison with bleak eyes.

"You think the same?" he challenged and the menace in his voice was scarcely hidden.

"Archie isn't bluffing," Garrison insisted. "He can make guns, tanks, ships . . . in fact, he can duplicate anything we have—with improvements. He's got our tools and our knowledge and he's got something we haven't got. That's his knowledge, the knowledge he never shared with us."

"You both are under technical arrest," snapped Streeter. "You will remain inside the dome. If you venture out—"

"Get out of here," yelled Garrison. "Get out of here before I break your neck!"

Streeter got out, with Garrison's laughter ringing in his ears.

Doc glanced at his watch. "Fifteen minutes gone. I wonder what Streeter will do."

"He won't do anything," Garrison predicted. "He's pigheaded. He'll put in a call to Earth, have an expeditionary force sent out as a precautionary measure. But even now he doesn't believe what Archie told him."

"I do," said Doc. "You better put in a call to Mac. Tell him to hustle over here. I'd hate to have him get caught in the fireworks."

Garrison nodded and reached for the phone. Doc got up and walked into the laboratory.

"Well, Archie, how are you feeling now?"

"Why do you always ask me that, doctor?" Archie demanded irritably. "I'm feeling all right. I always feel all right. There's nothing to go wrong with me."

"Thought you might feel a bit different—starting a war."

"It isn't a war," insisted Archie. "It isn't even an adventure. At least, not the kind of an adventure the human race would understand. It is a part of a carefully studied plan."

"But why are you doing it, Archie? Why are you messing into this at all? The human race can't touch you. You could, if you wanted to, just go on disregarding them."

"You might be able to understand," said Archie.

"I sure would try," Doc promised.

"You know about me," said Archie. "You probably can imagine the sort of life I lived before the Earthmen came. For eons I was a thing without physical life. My life was mental. I developed mentally. I specialized in mentality, you see, because I didn't have a body to worry about. I thought and speculated and that was all right, because it was the only kind of life I knew. It was a good life, too, free of so many of the worries and annoyances of physical being. Sometimes I wish it could have continued.

"I didn't have any enemies. I didn't even have neighbors to fight with. For I could be one or I could be many; I was sufficient to myself.

"I realized there was such a thing as physical being, of course, because I observed the few tiny animals that are able to survive on Venus. Pitifully inadequate physical life as compared with the life on Earth, but physical life nevertheless.

"I wondered about that life. I attempted to formulate a behavioristic pattern for such a type of life endowed with my mentality. Starting with small imaginings, I built that idea up into the pattern of a hypothetical civilization, a civilization that paralleled Earth's in some ways, differed from it vastly in others. It couldn't be the same, you know, because my philosophy was a far cry from the kind of thought that you developed."

The grating voice died and then began again—"I, myself, of course, can never live a life like that."

"But Earthmen could," suggested Doc, the çigar dangling in his mouth.

"You're right, doctor," Archie said. "Earthmen could."

"If you could force them to."

"I will force no one to do anything," Archie grated. "I am experimenting."

"But would the experiment be good for Earth? Would your way of life, your hypothetical civilization, be the right one for Earth to follow?"

"Frankly, doctor," said Archie, "I don't give a damn."

"Well, well," said Doc.

"There's something else, doctor," said Archie. "You and Garrison and Mac are in trouble."

"Trouble," admitted Doc, "doesn't rightly express it. We're in a mess clear up to our ears."

"There is a ship waiting for you," said Archie. "Back in the hills north of the dome. It is the fastest thing ever built for space."

"A ship!" cried Doc. "Where did the ship come from?"

"I built it," Archie said.

"You—"

What Doc had meant to say was engulfed by a wave of sound that seemed to rock the dome.

"There it goes!" yelled Garrison.

Doc ran into the office and through the port he saw debris still flying through the air—the tangled wreckage of machines and blasted ore.

The radium pits disrupted in another flash of blue-white flame and again thunder blanketed and rocked the dome. The two remaining watch towers vanished in the upheaval and disintegrated in the blast, losing their identity in the clouts of flung-up earth.

"He's using high explosives," yelled Garrison.

"Of course," gasped Doc. "He wouldn't dare use radioactive stuff or he'd blast the planet to bits. No one would dare use anything but high explosives in a war on Venus."

The door swung open and Mac stumbled in.

"Thanks for the call," he said.

Men were running now out in the pits, scurrying like frightened ants, heading for the one spaceship which had escaped the shells.

The dust settled slowly over the battered field, now plunged in gloom with the shattering of the lights. And, as if by signal, the howling wind swept a sheet of snow down to blot out the sight.

When the snow cleared, the pits were empty of life—there was no movement in the blasted gouges. Fire spurted from the launching rockets of the one undamaged spaceship, the dome vibrating to the monster's take-off. Momentarily a trail of flame climbed into the clouds and then silence and grayness clamped down over the deserted mine and dome.

"That settles it," Mac commented. "We're left alone. We'll have to wait until the military comes and then—"

"You're wrong," said Doc. "There's a ship waiting out north in the hills for you two fellows. A ship that Archie built. Better take Sparks along with you. He's probably still around."

"For the two of us?" asked Mac. "Why not all of us?"

"I can't go," said Doc, "I have to stay. I have a job to do."

"Forget it, Doc," urged Garrison. "Archie really built that ship for you. You were the one he liked. You were the only one he liked."

Doc shook his head stubbornly. "No, I've thought it out. I can't go along. Archie says the ship is fast. If I were you, I'd head for the asteroids. Stick around there for a while. Maybe after a time you can come out. Things are apt to be different then."

"You're afraid of what R. C. would do to you if he caught you," jeered Mac.

"No. I'm not afraid of that," Doc protested. "He couldn't do any more to me then than if he had me now. And, anyhow, R. C. is through. He doesn't know it yet, but he's through for good and all."

"Mac," said Garrison, "let's tie the stubborn old fool up and take him along whether he wants to go or not."

"Look, Johnny," declared Doc. "I'd never forgive you if you did. Take my word for it. I have to stay."

"O.K.," said Mac. "If the benighted old goat doesn't want to go, let the rest of us get moving. I'll go hunt up Sparks. We don't want to have that war fleet Streeter called for pick us up as they are coming in."

Garrison nodded dumbly and moved toward the door. With the knob in his hand, he turned back.

"I don't suppose I'll be seeing you again, Doc."

"I don't imagine you will. I'm sorry the way things turned out, Johnny. It was a dirty shame. And you so near to Earth and that easy-chair."

"Aw, hell," said Garrison, "who cares for easy-chairs?"

Doc watched through the port until he saw the flare of a ship painting the northern hills. His gaze followed the streak of flame that climbed up and out toward the Sun.

Up and out toward the Sun. Out where one could see the stars. Out to take their place with a race that could conquer those stars. A race that could stretch out its hand and handiwork to the farthest reaches of the Universe. A race that could trace new pathways between the galaxies. A race that could hang its signposts on distant solar systems.

But a race that needed leadership to do it—a leadership that would strike off its shackles, shackles such as Radium, Inc., would weave. Shackles born of hate and greed and jealousies.

Perhaps Man had gotten off on the wrong foot. Perhaps his philosophy had been all wrong even from the start. Perhaps a bit of alien philosophy, weird as it might seem at first, would be good for him.

With a sigh, Doc turned back to the room.

A mournful silence hung there. Machinery still throbbed and occasionally there was a whine of fans, but aside from that there was no other sound.

Doc selected a fresh cigar from his vest pocket and carefully cut it in two. One half he stuck in his mouth, the other went back into the pocket.

He headed for the laboratory, shutting the door behind him.

"Howdy, Archie," he said.

"You're a fool," said Archie.

"What's the matter now?"

"I gave you a chance," rasped Archie. "You threw it away. Don't blame me for anything that happens now."

"I had to have a little talk with you," said Doc.

"You could have had it before."

"No," persisted Doc. "This one had to be private. No chance for anyone to hear."

"All right," said Archie, impatiently, "go ahead and spill it."

"I just wanted to tell you something," Doc explained. "Something that might make you easy in your mind. I destroyed those notes Boone made before he died."

"You did what?"

"I destroyed them. I didn't want to see you vulnerable. Because as soon as anything becomes vulnerable to the human race it's a goner, sure as shooting."

"Why didn't you tell me this before?" Archie rumbled.

"Because I couldn't make up my mind," Doc told him. "I had to think it out."

"You had a long time to make it up."

Doc swiveled the cigar from east to west. "Yeah, that's right. But somehow I couldn't seem to do it. I made the decision just a little while ago."

"What decided you?"

"A spaceship," said Doc. "A spaceship that you made."

"I understand," said Archie.

"You aren't as tough as you would like to have us think," declared Doc. "You might not have had them before, but since Masterson found you, you've absorbed some conception of human emotions. The spaceship proved it."

"I like you, doctor," Archie said. "You remind me of Masterson."

"I'm giving you the human race to carry out your experiment," said Doc. "It can be a great experiment. You have good material to work with. All you need to do is handle it right. Point it toward the stars and keep it going straight. I'm backing you against Radium, Inc. I think the human race will get a better break from you. Don't disappoint me, Archie."

"I hadn't thought of that," Archie rumbled. "Maybe your race does deserve a break."

"They aren't such bad folks. And, anyhow," Doc chuckled, "if they don't like the way you do things they can turn their backs on you. If they don't insist on radium, you have no hold on them. But if Radium, Inc., could beat you, there'd be no hope for them. They'd only fall deeper and deeper into slavery."

"Why are you telling me this?" Archie grumbled. "You had the knowledge that would have broken me. You haven't used it. You say you aren't going to. Why not let it go at that?"

"If you were a man," declared Doc, "I'd slap you down for that. I'm not trying to pose as a hero. There is something else."

"Yes?"

"Look, Boone was the only man who stumbled on the clue. Even he, perhaps, didn't realize all he had. But he might have. Given time, he certainly would have. But you killed him first. You had intended to all along as a means of escaping yourself. But his stumbling on the clue made you hurry up the job."

"I was defending myself," Archie declared.

"Those notes were dangerous," said Doc. "They gave the human race an angle for attack."

"But you destroyed the notes. I'm safe now."

Doc shook his head. "No, Archie, you aren't. For, you see, I know."

"But you wouldn't tell."

"Oh, yes, I would," said Doc. "I couldn't help but tell. R. C.'s police have ways to make one talk. Slick ways. Unpleasant ways. I'm a psychologist. I should know. And they suspect I may know more than I've ever told. Chester was curious about Boone's reports—"

"But if you had escaped with the others, you could have hidden—"

"Even then, there would have been the chance they would have found me," Doc declared. "Just an outside chance—but in a thing like this you can't take any chance at all."

He walked across the room, picked up the heavy stool.

"This is the only way to do it, Archie. There's no other thing to do. It's the only way we can fool them—you and I."

Archie's voice was cold, mechanical. "You don't have to do it that way, doctor. There are other ways."

Doc chuckled. "Psychological effect, Archie. First Boone, now me. Makes you sinister. After two accidents like this no one will want to study you too much—or too closely."

He weighed the heavy stool in his hand, getting the feel of it.

His cigar traveled across his face. He lifted the stool and crashed it down.

ARTHUR C. CLARKE

RESCUE PARTY

WHO was to blame? For three days Alveron's thoughts had come back to that question, and still he had found no answer. A creature of a less civilized or a less sensitive race would never have let it torture his mind, and would have satisfied himself with the assurance that no one could be responsible for the working of fate. But Alveron and his kind had been lords of the Universe since the dawn of history, since that far distant age when the Time Barrier had been folded round the cosmos by the unknown powers that lay beyond the Beginning. To them had been given all knowledge—and with infinite knowledge went infinite responsibility. If there were mistakes and errors in the administration of the Galaxy, the fault lay on the heads of Alveron and his people. And this was no mere mistake: it was one of the greatest tragedies in history.

The crew still knew nothing. Even Rugon, his closest friend and the ship's deputy captain, had been told only part of the truth. But now the doomed worlds lay less than a billion miles ahead. In a few hours, they would be landing on the third planet.

Once again Alveron read the message from Base: then, with a flick of a tentacle that no human eye could have followed, he pressed the "General Attention" button. Throughout the mile-long cylinder that was the Galactic Survey Ship *S9000*, creatures of many races laid down their work to listen to the words of their captain.

"I know you have all been wondering," began Alveron, "why we were ordered to abandon our survey and to proceed at such an acceleration to this region of space. Some of you may realize what this acceleration means. Our ship is on its last voyage: the generators have already been running for sixty hours at Ultimate Overload. We will be very lucky if we return to Base under our own power.

"We are approaching a sun which is about to become a Nova. Detonation will occur in seven hours, with an uncertainty of one hour, leaving us a maximum of only four hours for exploration. There are ten planets in the system about to be destroyed—*and there is a civilization on the third*. That fact was discovered only a few days ago. It is our tragic mission to contact that doomed race, and if possible to save some of its members. I know that there is little we can do in so short a time with this single ship. No other machine can possibly reach the system before detonation occurs."

There was a long pause during which there could have been no sound or movement in the whole of the mighty ship as it sped silently towards the worlds ahead. Alveron knew what his companions were thinking and he tried to answer their unspoken question.

"You will wonder how such a disaster, the greatest of which we have any record, has been allowed to occur. On one point I can reassure you. The fault does not lie with the Survey.

"As you know, with our present fleet of under twelve thousand ships, it is possible to re-examine each of the eight thousand million solar systems in the Galaxy at intervals of about a million years. Most worlds change very little in so short a time as that.

"Less than four hundred thousand years ago, the survey ship *S5060* examined the planets of the system we are approaching. It found intelligence on none of them, though the third planet was teeming with animal life and two other worlds had once been inhabited. The usual report was submitted and the system is due for its next examination in six hundred thousand years.

"It now appears that in the incredibly short period since the last survey, intelligent life has appeared in the system. The first intimation of this occurred when unknown radio signals were detected on the planet Kulath in the system X29.35, Y34.76, Z27.93. Bearings were taken on them and they were found to come from the system ahead.

"Kulath is two hundred light-years from here, so those radio waves had been on their way for two centuries. Thus for at least that period of time a civilization has existed on one of these worlds—a civilization that can generate electromagnetic waves and all that that implies.

"An immediate telescopic examination of the system was made and it was then found that the sun was in the unstable prenova stage. Detonation might occur at any moment, and indeed might have done so while the light waves were on their way to Kulath.

"There was a slight delay while the supervelocity scanners on Kulath II were focused on to the system. They showed that the explosion had not yet occurred but was only a few hours away. If Kulath had been a fraction of a light-year further from this sun, we should never have known of its civilization until it had ceased to exist.

"The Administrator of Kulath contacted Sector Base immediately, and I was ordered to proceed to the system at once. Our object is to save what members we can of the doomed race, if indeed there are any left. But we have assumed that a civilization possessing radio could have protected itself against any rise of temperature that may have already occurred.

"This ship and the two tenders will each explore a section of the planet. Commander Torkalee will take Number One, Commander Orostron Number Two. They will have just under four hours in which to explore this world. At the end of that time, they *must* be back in the ship. It will be leaving then, with or without them. I will give the two commanders detailed instructions in the control room immediately.

"That is all. We enter atmosphere in two hours."

On the world once known as Earth the fires were dying out: there was nothing left to burn. The great forests that had swept across the planet like a tidal wave with the passing of the cities were now no more than glowing charcoal and the smoke of their funeral pyres still stained the sky. But the last hours were still to come, for the surface rocks had not yet begun to flow. The continents were dimly visible through the haze, but their outlines meant nothing to the watchers in the approaching ship. The charts they possessed were out of date by a dozen Ice Ages and more deluges than one.

The *Sgooo* had driven past Jupiter and seen at once that no life could exist in those half-gaseous oceans of compressed hydrocarbons, now erupting furiously under the sun's abnormal heat. Mars and the outer planets they had missed, and Alveron realized that the worlds nearer the sun than Earth would be already melting. It was more than likely, he thought sadly, that the tragedy of this unknown race was already finished. Deep in his heart, he thought it might be better so. The ship could only have carried a few hundred survivors, and the problem of selection had been haunting his mind.

Rugon, Chief of Communications and Deputy Captain, came into the control room. For the last hour he had been striving to detect radiation from Earth, but in vain.

"We're too late," he announced gloomily. "I've monitored the whole spectrum and the ether's dead except for our own stations and some two-hundred-year-old programs from Kulath. Nothing in this system is radiating any more."

He moved towards the giant vision screen with a graceful flowing motion that no mere biped could ever hope to imitate. Alveron said nothing: he had been expecting this news.

One entire wall of the control room was taken up by the screen, a great black rectangle that gave an impression of almost infinite depth. Three of Rugon's slender control tentacles, useless for heavy work but incredibly swift at all manipulation, flickered over the selector dials and the screen lit up with a thousand points of light. The star field flowed swiftly past as Rugon adjusted the controls, bringing the projector to bear upon the sun itself.

No man of Earth would have recognized the monstrous shape that filled the screen. The sun's light was white no longer: great violet-blue clouds covered half its surface and from them long streamers of flame were erupting into space. At one point an enormous prominence had reared itself out of the photosphere, far out even into the flickering veils of the corona. It was as though a tree of fire had taken root in the surface of the sun—a tree that stood half a million miles high and whose branches were rivers of flame sweeping through space at hundreds of miles a second.

"I suppose," said Rugon presently, "that you are quite satisfied about the astronomers' calculations. After all—"

"Oh, we're perfectly safe," said Alveron confidently. "I've spoken to Kulath Observatory and they have been making some additional checks through our own instruments. That uncertainty of an hour includes a private safety margin which they won't tell me in case I feel tempted to stay any longer."

He glanced at the instrument board.

"The pilot should have brought us to the atmosphere now. Switch the screen back to the planet, please. Ah, there they go!"

There was a sudden tremor underfoot and a raucous clanging of alarms, instantly stilled. Across the vision screen two slim projectiles dived towards the looming mass of Earth. For a few miles they traveled together: then they separated, one vanishing abruptly as it entered the shadow of the planet.

Slowly the huge mother ship, with its thousand times greater mass, descended after them into the raging storms that already were tearing down the deserted cities of Man.

It was night in the hemisphere over which Orostron drove his tiny command. Like Torkalee, his mission was to photograph and record, and to report progress to the mother ship. The little scout had no room for specimens or passengers. If contact was made with the inhabitants of this world, the *Sqooo* would come at once. There would be no time for parleying. If there was any trouble the rescue would be by force and the explanations could come later.

The ruined land beneath was bathed with an eerie, flickering light, for a great auroral display was raging over half the world. But the image on the vision screen was independent of external light, and it showed clearly a waste of barren rock that seemed never to have known any form of life. Presumably this desert land must come to an end somewhere. Orostron increased his speed to the highest value he dared risk in so dense an atmosphere.

The machine fled on through the storm, and presently the desert of rock began to climb towards the sky. A great mountain range lay ahead, its peaks lost in the smoke-laden clouds. Orostron directed the scanners towards the horizon, and on the vision screen the line of mountains seemed suddenly very close and menacing. He started to climb rapidly. It was difficult to imagine a more unpromising land in which to find civilization and he wondered if it would be wise to change course. He decided against it. Five minutes later, he had his reward.

Miles below lay a decapitated mountain, the whole of its summit sheared away by some tremendous feat of engineering. Rising out of the rock and straddling the artificial plateau was an intricate structure of metal girders, supporting masses of machinery. Orostron brought his ship to a halt and spiraled down towards the mountain.

The slight Doppler blur had now vanished, and the picture on the screen was clear-cut. The lattice-work was supporting some scores of great metal mirrors, pointing skywards at an angle of forty-five degrees to the horizontal. They were slightly concave, and each had some complicated mechanism at its focus. There seemed something impressive and purposeful about the great array; every mirror was aimed at precisely the same spot in the sky—or beyond.

Orostron turned to his colleagues.

"It looks like some kind of observatory to me," he said. "Have you ever seen anything like it before?"

Klarten, a multitentacled, tripedal creature from a globular cluster at the edge of the Milky Way, had a different theory.

"That's communication equipment. Those reflectors are for focusing electromagnetic beams. I've seen the same kind of installation on a hundred worlds before. It may even be the station that Kulath picked up —though that's rather unlikely, for the beams would be very narrow from mirrors that size."

"That would explain why Rugon could detect no radiation before we landed," added Hansur II, one of the twin beings from the planet Thargon.

Orostron did not agree at all.

"If that *is* a radio station, it must be built for interplanetary communication. Look at the way the mirrors are pointed. I don't believe that a race which has only had radio for two centuries can have crossed space. It took my people six thousand years to do it."

"We managed it in three," said Hansur II mildly, speaking a few seconds ahead of his twin. Before the inevitable argument could develop, Klarten began to wave his tentacles with excitement. While the others had been talking, he had started the automatic monitor.

"Here it is! Listen!"

He threw a switch, and the little room was filled with a raucous whining sound, continually changing in pitch but nevertheless retaining certain characteristics that were difficult to define.

The four explorers listened intently for a minute; then Orostron said: "Surely that can't be any form of speech! No creature could produce sounds as quickly as that!"

Hansur I had come to the same conclusion.

"That's a television program. Don't you think so, Klarten?"

The other agreed.

"Yes, and each of those mirrors seems to be radiating a different program. I wonder where they're going? If I'm correct, one of the other planets in the system must lie along those beams. We can soon check that."

Orostron called the *Sooo* and reported the discovery. Both Rugon and Alveron were greatly excited, and made a quick check of the astronomical records.

The result was surprising—and disappointing. None of the other nine planets lay anywhere near the line of transmission. The great mirrors appeared to be pointing blindly into space.

There seemed only one conclusion to be drawn, and Klarten was the first to voice it.

"They *had* interplanetary communication," he said. "But the station must be deserted now, and the transmitters no longer controlled. They haven't been switched off, and are just pointing where they were left."

"Well, we'll soon find out," said Orostron. "I'm going to land."

He brought the machine slowly down to the level of the great metal mirrors, and past them until it came to rest on the mountain rock. A hundred yards away, a white stone building crouched beneath the maze of steel girders. It was windowless, but there were several doors in the wall facing them.

Orostron watched his companions climb into their protective suits and wished he could follow. But someone had to stay in the machine to keep in touch with the mother ship. Those were Alveron's instructions, and they were very wise. One never knew what would happen on a world that was being explored for the first time, especially under conditions such as these.

Very cautiously, the three explorers stepped out of the air lock and adjusted the antigravity field of their suits. Then, each with the mode of locomotion peculiar to his race, the little party went towards the building, the Hansur twins leading and Klarten following close behind. His gravity control was apparently giving trouble, for he suddenly fell to the ground, rather to the amusement of his colleagues. Orostron saw them pause for a moment at the nearest door—then it opened and they disappeared from sight.

So Orostron waited, with what patience he could, while the storm rose around him and the light of the aurora grew ever brighter in the sky. At the agreed times he called the mother ship and received brief acknowledgments from Rugon. He wondered how Torkalee was faring, halfway round the planet, but he could not contact him through the crash and thunder of solar interference.

It did not take Klarten and the Hansurs long to discover that their theories were largely correct. The building was a radio station, and it was deserted. It consisted of one tremendous room with a few small offices leading from it. In the main chamber, row after row of electrical equipment stretched into the distance; lights flickered and winked on hundreds of control panels, and a dull glow came from the elements in a great avenue of vacuum tubes.

But Klarten was not impressed. The first radio sets his race had built were now fossilized in strata a thousand million years old. Man, who had possessed electrical machines for only a few centuries, could not compete with those who had known them for half the lifetime of the Earth.

Nevertheless, the party kept their recorders running as they explored the building. There was still one problem to be solved. The deserted station was broadcasting programs—but where were they coming from? The central switchboard had been quickly located. It was designed to handle scores of programs simultaneously, but the source of those programs was lost in a maze of cables that vanished underground. Back in the *Sqooo*, Rugon was trying to analyze the broadcasts and perhaps his researches would reveal their origin. It was impossible to trace cables that might lead across continents.

The party wasted little time at the deserted station. There was nothing they could learn from it, and they were seeking life rather than scientific information. A few minutes later the little ship rose swiftly from the plateau and headed towards the plains that must lie beyond the mountains. Less than three hours were still left to them.

As the array of enigmatic mirrors dropped out of sight, Orostron was struck by a sudden thought. Was it imagination, or had they all moved through a small angle while he had been waiting, as if they were still compensating for the rotation of the Earth? He could not be sure, and he dismissed the matter as unimportant. It would only mean that the directing mechanism was still working, after a fashion.

They discovered the city fifteen minutes later. It was a great, sprawling metropolis, built around a river that had disappeared leaving an ugly scar winding its way among the great buildings and beneath bridges that looked very incongruous now.

Even from the air, the city looked deserted. But only two and a half hours were left—there was no time for further exploration. Orostron made his decision, and landed near the largest structure he could see. It seemed reasonable to suppose that some creatures would have sought shelter in the strongest buildings, where they would be safe until the very end.

The deepest coves—the heart of the planet itself—would give no protection when the final cataclysm came. Even if this race had reached the outer planets, its doom would only be delayed by the few hours it would take for the ravening wavefronts to cross the Solar System.

Orostron could not know that the city had been deserted not for a few days or weeks, but for over a century. For the culture of cities, which had outlasted so many civilizations, had been doomed at last when the helicopter brought universal transportation. Within a few generations the great masses of mankind, knowing that they could reach any part of the globe in a matter of hours, had gone back to the fields and forests for which they had always longed. The new civilization had machines and resources of which earlier ages had never dreamed, but it was essentially rural and no longer bound to the steel and concrete warrens that had dominated the centuries before. Such cities that still remained were specialized centers of research, administration or entertainment; the others had been allowed to decay where it was too much trouble to destroy them. The dozen or so greatest of all cities, and the ancient university towns, had scarcely changed and would have lasted for many generations to come. But the cities that had been founded on steam and iron and surface transportation had passed with the industries that had nourished them.

And so while Orostron waited in the tender, his colleagues raced through endless empty corridors and deserted halls, taking innumerable photographs but learning nothing of the creatures who had used these buildings. There were libraries, meeting places, council rooms, thousands of offices—all were empty and deep with dust. If they had not seen the radio station on its mountain eyrie, the explorers could well have believed that this world had known no life for centuries.

Through the long minutes of waiting, Orostron tried to imagine where this race could have vanished. Perhaps they had killed themselves knowing that escape was impossible; perhaps they had built great shelters in the bowels of the planet, and even now were cowering in their millions beneath his feet, waiting for the end. He began to fear that he would never know.

It was almost a relief when at last he had to give the order for the return. Soon he would know if Torkalee's party had been more fortunate. And he was anxious to get back to the mother ship, for as the minutes passed the suspense had become more and more acute. There had always been the thought in his mind: "What if the astronomers of Kulath have made a mistake?" He would begin to feel happy when the walls of the *Sgooo* were around him. He would be happier still when they were out in space and this ominous sun was shrinking far astern.

As soon as his colleagues had entered the air lock, Orostron hurled his tiny machine into the sky and set the controls to home on the *Sgooo*. Then he turned to his friends.

"Well, what have you found?" he asked.

Klarten produced a large roll of canvas and spread it out on the floor.

"This is what they were like," he said quietly. "Bipeds, with only two arms. They seem to have managed well, in spite of that handicap. Only two eyes as well, unless there are others in the back. We were lucky to find this; it's about the only thing they left behind."

The ancient oil painting stared stonily back at the three creatures regarding it so intently. By the irony of fate, its complete worthlessness had saved it from oblivion. When the city had been evacuated, no one had bothered to move Alderman John Richards, 1909—1974. For a century and a half he had been gathering dust while far away from the old cities the new civilization had been rising to heights no earlier culture had ever known.

"That was almost all we found," said Klarten. "The city must have been deserted for years. I'm afraid our expedition has been a failure. If there are any living beings on this world, they've hidden themselves too well for us to find them."

His commander was forced to agree.

"It was an almost impossible task," he said. "If we'd had weeks instead of hours we might have succeeded. For all we know, they may even have built shelters under the sea. No one seems to have thought of that."

He glanced quickly at the indicators and corrected the course.

"We'll be there in five minutes. Alveron seems to be moving rather quickly. I wonder if Torkalee has found anything?"

The *Sgooo* was hanging a few miles above the seaboard of a blazing continent when Orostron homed upon it. The danger line was thirty minutes away and there was no time to lose. Skillfully, he maneuvered the little ship into its launching tube and the party stepped out of the air lock.

There was a small crowd waiting for them. That was to be expected, but Orostron could see at once that something more than curiosity had brought his friends here. Even before a word was spoken, he knew that something was wrong.

"Torkalee hasn't returned. He's lost his party and we're going to the rescue. Come along to the control room at once."

From the beginning, Torkalee had been luckier than Orostron. He had followed the zone of twilight, keeping away from the intolerable glare of the sun, until he came to the shores of an inland sea. It was a very recent sea, one of the latest of Man's works, for the land it covered had been desert less than a century before. In a few hours it would be desert again, for the water was boiling and clouds of steam were rising to the skies. But they could not veil the loveliness of the great white city that overlooked the tideless sea.

Flying machines were still parked neatly round the square in which Torkalee landed. They were disappointingly primitive, though beautifully finished, and depended on rotating airfoils for support. Nowhere was there any sign of life, but the place gave the impression that its inhabitants were not very far away. Lights were still shining from some of the windows.

Torkalee's three companions lost no time in leaving the machine. Leader of the party, by seniority of rank and race was T'sinadree, who like Alveron himself had been born on one of the ancient planets of the Central Suns. Next came Alarkane, from a race which was one of the youngest in the Universe and took a perverse pride in the fact. Last came one of the strange beings from the system of Palador. It was nameless, like all its kind, for it possessed no identity of its own, being merely a mobile but still dependent cell in the consciousness of its race. Though it and its fellows had long been scattered over the Galaxy in the exploration of countless worlds, some unknown link still bound them together as inexorably as the living cells in a human body.

When a creature of Palador spoke, the pronoun it used was always "We." There was not, nor could there ever be, any first person singular in the language of Palador.

The great doors of the splendid building baffled the explorers, though any human child would have known their secret. T'sinadree wasted no time on them but called Torkalee on his personal transmitter. Then the three hurried aside while their commander maneuvered his machine into the best position. There was a brief burst of intolerable flame; the massive steelwork flickered once at the edge of the visible spectrum and was gone. The stones were still glowing when the eager party hurried into the building, the beams of their light projectors fanning before them.

The torches were not needed. Before them lay a great hall, glowing with light from lines of tubes along the ceiling. On either side, the hall opened out into long corridors, while straight ahead a massive stairway swept majestically towards the upper floors.

For a moment T'sinadree hesitated. Then, since one way was as good as another, he led his companions down the first corridor.

The feeling that life was near had now become very strong. At any moment, it seemed, they might be confronted by the creatures of this world. If they showed hostility—and they could scarcely be blamed if they did—the paralyzers would be used at once.

The tension was very great as the party entered the first room, and only relaxed when they saw that it held nothing but machines—row after row of them, now stilled and silent. Lining the enormous room were thousands of metal filing cabinets, forming a continuous wall as far as the eye could reach. And that was all; there was no furniture, nothing but the cabinets and the mysterious machines.

Alarkane, always the quickest of the three, was already examining the cabinets. Each held many thousand sheets of tough, thin material, perforated with innumerable holes and slots. The Paladorian appropriated one of the cards and Alarkane recorded the scene together with some close-ups of the machines. Then they left. The great room, which had been one of the marvels of the world, meant nothing to them. No living eye would ever again see that wonderful battery of almost human Hollerith analyzers and the five thousand million punched cards holding all that could be recorded of each man, woman and child on the planet.

It was clear that this building had been used very recently. With growing excitement, the explorers hurried on to the next room. This they found to be an enormous library, for millions of books lay all around them on miles and miles of shelving. Here, though the explorers could not know it, were the records of all the laws that Man had ever passed, and all the speeches that had ever been made in his council chambers.

T'sinadree was deciding his plan of action when Alarkane drew his attention to one of the racks a hundred yards away. It was half empty, unlike all the others. Around it books lay in a tumbled heap on the floor, as if knocked down by someone in frantic haste. The signs were unmistakable. Not long ago, other creatures had been this way. Faint wheel marks were clearly visible on the floor to the acute sense of Alarkane, though the others could see nothing. Alarkane could even detect footprints, but knowing nothing of the creatures that had formed them he could not say which way they led.

The sense of nearness was stronger than ever now, but it was nearness in time, not in space. Alarkane voiced the thoughts of the party.

"Those books must have been valuable, and someone has come to rescue them—rather as an afterthought, I should say. That means there must be a place of refuge, possibly not very far away. Perhaps we may be able to find some other clues that will lead us to it."

T'sinadree agreed, but the Paladorian refused to be enthusiastic.

"That may be so," it said, "but the refuge may be anywhere on the planet, and we have just two hours left. Let us waste no more time if we hope to rescue these people."

The party hurried forward once more, pausing only to collect a few books that might be useful to the scientists at Base—though it was doubtful if they could ever be translated. They soon found that the great building was composed largely of small rooms, all showing signs of recent occupation. Most of them were in a neat and tidy condition, but one or two were very much the reverse. The explorers were particularly puzzled by one room—clearly an office of some kind—that appeared to have been completely wrecked. The floor was littered with papers, the furniture had been smashed, and smoke was pouring through the broken windows from the fires outside.

T'sinadree was rather alarmed.

"Surely no dangerous animal could have got into a place like this!" he exclaimed, fingering his paralyzer nervously.

Alarkane did not answer. He began to make that annoying sound which his race called "laughter." It was several minutes before he would explain what had amused him.

"I don't think any animal has done it," he said. "In fact, the explanation is very simple. Suppose you had been working all your life in this room, dealing with endless papers, year after year. And suddenly, you are told that you will never see it again, that your work is finished, and that you can leave it forever. More than that—no one will come after you. *Everything* is finished. How would you make your exit, T'sinadree?"

The other thought for a moment.

"Well, I suppose I'd just tidy things up and leave. That's what seems to have happened in all the other rooms."

Alarkane laughed again.

"I'm quite sure you would. But some individuals have a different psychology. I think I should have liked the creature that used this room."

He did not explain himself further, and his two colleagues puzzled over his words for quite a while before they gave it up.

It came as something of a shock when Torkalee gave the order to return. They had gathered a great deal of information, but had found no clue that might lead them to the missing inhabitants of this world. That problem was as baffling as ever, and now it seemed that it would never be solved. There were only forty minutes left before the *Sgooo* would be departing.

They were halfway back to the tender when they saw the semi-circular passage leading down into the depths of the building. Its architectural style was quite different from that used elsewhere, and the gently sloping floor was an irresistible attraction to creatures whose many legs had grown weary of the marble staircases which only bipeds could have built in such profusion. T'sinadree had been the worst sufferer, for he normally employed twelve legs and could use twenty when he was in a hurry—though no one had ever seen him perform this feat.

The party stopped dead and looked down the passageway with a single thought. *A tunnel, leading down into the depths of the earth.* At its end, they might yet find the people of this world and rescue some of them from their fate. For there was still time to call the mother ship if the need arose.

T'sinadree signaled to his commander and Torkalee brought the little machine immediately overhead. There might not be time for the party to retrace its footsteps through the maze of passages, so meticulously recorded in the Paladorian mind that there was no possibility of going astray. If speed were necessary, Torkalee could blast his way through the dozen floors above their head. In any case, it should not take long to find what lay at the end of the passage.

It took only thirty seconds. The tunnel ended quite abruptly in a very curious cylindrical room with magnificently padded seats along the walls. There was no way out save that by which they had come and it was several seconds before the purpose of the chamber dawned on Alarkane's mind. It was a pity, he thought, that they would never have time to use this. The thought was suddenly interrupted by a cry from T'sinadree. Alarkane wheeled around, and saw that the entrance had closed silently behind them.

Even in that first moment of panic, Alarkane found himself thinking with some admiration: "Whoever they were, they knew how to build automatic machinery!"

The Paladorian was the first to speak. It waved one of its tendrils towards the seats.

"We think it would be best to be seated," it said. The multiplex mind of Palador had already analyzed the situation and knew what was coming.

They did not have long to wait before a low-pitched hum came from a grille overhead, and for the very last time in history a human, even if lifeless, voice was heard on Earth. The words were meaningless, though the trapped explorers could guess their message clearly enough.

"Choose your stations, please, and be seated."

Simultaneously, a wall panel at one end of the compartment glowed with light. On it was a simple map, consisting of a series of a dozen circles connected by a line. Each of the circles had writing alongside it, and beside the writing were two buttons of different colors.

Alarkane looked questioningly at his leader.

"Don't touch them," said T'sinadree. "If we leave the controls alone, the doors may open again."

He was wrong. The engineers who had designed the automatic subway had assumed that anyone who entered it would naturally wish to go somewhere. If they selected no intermediate station, their destination could only be the end of the line.

There was another pause while the relays and thyratrons waited for their orders. In those thirty seconds, if they had known what to do, the party could have opened the doors and left the subway. But they did not know, and the machines geared to a human psychology acted for them.

The surge of acceleration was not very great; the lavish upholstery was a luxury, not a necessity. Only an almost imperceptible vibration told of the speed at which they were traveling through the bowels of the earth, on a journey the duration of which they could not even guess. And in thirty minutes, the *Sqooo* would be leaving the Solar System.

There was a long silence in the speeding machine. T'sinadree and Alarkane were thinking rapidly. So was the Paladorian, though in a different fashion. The conception of personal death was meaningless to it, for the destruction of a single unit meant no more to the group mind than the loss of a nail-paring to a man. But it could, though with great difficulty, appreciate the plight of individual intelligences such as Alarkane and T'sinadree, and it was anxious to help them if it could.

Alarkane had managed to contact Torkalee with his personal transmitter, though the signal was very weak and seemed to be fading quickly. Rapidly he explained the situation, and almost at once the signals became clearer. Torkalee was following the path of the machine, flying above the ground under which they were speeding to their unknown destination. That was the first indication they had of the fact that they were traveling at nearly a thousand miles an hour, and very soon after that Torkalee was able to give the still more disturbing news that they were rapidly approaching the sea. While they were beneath the land, there was a hope, though a slender one, that they might stop the machine and escape. But under the ocean—not all the brains and the machinery in the great mother ship could save them. No one could have devised a more perfect trap.

T'sinadree had been examining the wall map with great attention. Its meaning was obvious, and along the line connecting the circles a tiny spot of light was crawling. It was already halfway to the first of the stations marked.

"I'm going to press one of those buttons," said T'sinadree at last. "It won't do any harm, and we may learn something."

"I agree. Which will you try first?"

"There are only two kinds, and it won't matter if we try the wrong one first. I suppose one is to start the machine and the other is to stop it."

Alarkane was not very hopeful.

"It started without any button pressing," he said. "I think it's completely automatic and we can't control it from here at all."

T'sinadree could not agree.

"These buttons are clearly associated with the stations, and there's no point in having them unless you can use them to stop yourself. The only question is, which is the right one?"

His analysis was perfectly correct. The machine could be stopped at any intermediate station. They had only been on their way ten minutes, and if they could leave now, no harm would have been done. It was just bad luck that T'sinadree's first choice was the wrong button.

The little light on the map crawled slowly through the illuminated circle without checking its speed. And at the same time Torkalee called from the ship overhead.

"You have just passed underneath a city and are heading out to sea. There cannot be another stop for nearly a thousand miles."

Alveron had given up all hope of finding life on this world. The *Sgooo* had roamed over half the planet, never staying long in one place, descending ever and again in an effort to attract attention. There had been no response; Earth seemed utterly dead. If any of its inhabitants were still alive, thought Alveron, they must have hidden themselves in its depths where no help could reach them, though their doom would be none the less certain.

Rugon brought news of the disaster. The great ship ceased its fruitless searching and fled back through the storm to the ocean above which Torkalee's little tender was still following the track of the buried machine.

The scene was truly terrifying. Not since the days when Earth was born had there been such seas as this. Mountains of water were racing before the storm which had now reached velocities of many hundred miles an hour. Even at this distance from the mainland the air was full of flying debris—trees, fragments of houses, sheets of metal, anything that had not been anchored to the ground. No airborne machine could have lived for a moment in such a gale. And ever and again even the roar of the wind was drowned as the vast water-mountains met head-on with a crash that seemed to shake the sky.

Fortunately, there had been no serious earthquakes yet. Far beneath the bed of the ocean, the wonderful piece of engineering which had been the world president's private vacuum-subway was still working perfectly, unaffected by the tumult and destruction above. It would continue to work until the last minute of the Earth's existence, which, if the astronomers were right, was not much more than fifteen minutes away—though precisely how much more, Alveron would have given a great deal to know. It would be nearly an hour before the trapped party could reach land and even the slightest hope of rescue.

Alveron's instructions had been precise, though even without them he would never have dreamed of taking any risks with the great machine that had been intrusted to his care. Had he been human, the decision to abandon the trapped members of his crew would have been desperately hard to make. But he came of a race far more sensitive than Man, a race that so loved the things of the spirit that long ago, and with infinite reluctance, it had taken over control of the Universe since only thus could it be sure that justice was being done. Alveron would need all his superhuman gifts to carry him through the next few hours.

Meanwhile, a mile below the bed of the ocean Alarkane and T'sinadree were very busy indeed with their private communicators. Fifteen minutes is not a long time in which to wind up the affairs of a lifetime. It is indeed, scarcely long enough to dictate more than a few of those farewell messages which at such moments are so much more important than all other matters.

All the while the Paladorian had remained silent and motionless, saying not a word. The other two, resigned to their fate and engrossed in their personal affairs, had given it no thought. They were startled when suddenly it began to address them in its peculiarly passionless voice.

"We perceive that you are making certain arrangements concerning your anticipated destruction. That will probably be unnecessary. Captain Alveron hopes to rescue us if we can stop this machine when we reach land again."

Both T'sinadree and Alarkane were too surprised to say anything for a moment. Then the latter gasped, "How do you know?"

It was a foolish question for he remembered at once that there were several Paladorians—if one could use the phrase—in the *Sgooo*, and consequently their companion knew everything that was happening in the mother ship. So he did not wait for an answer but continued: "Alveron can't do that! He daren't take such a risk!"

"There will be no risk," said the Paladorian. "We have told him what to do. It is really very simple."

Alarkane and T'sinadree looked at their companion with something approaching awe, realizing now what must have happened. In moments of crisis, the single units comprising the Paladorian mind could link together in an organization no less close than that of any physical brain. At such moments they formed an intellect more powerful than any other in the Universe. All ordinary problems could be solved by a few hundred or thousand units. Very rarely millions would be needed, and on two historic occasions the billions of cells of the entire Paladorian consciousness had been welded together to deal with emergencies that threatened the race. The mind of Palador was one of the greatest mental resources of the Universe; its full force was seldom required, but the knowledge that it was available was supremely comforting to other races. Alarkane wondered how many cells had co-ordinated to deal with this particular emergency. He also wondered how so trivial an incident had ever come to its attention at all.

To that question he was never to know the answer, though he might have guessed it had he known that the chillingly remote Paladorian mind possessed an almost human streak of vanity. Long ago, Alarkane had written a book trying to prove that eventually all intelligent races would sacrifice individual consciousness and that one day only groupminds would remain in the Universe. Palador, he had said, was the first of those ultimate intellects, and the vast, dispersed mind had not been displeased.

They had no time to ask any further questions before Alveron himself began to speak through their communicators.

"Alveron calling! We're staying on this planet until the detonation wave reaches it, so we may be able to rescue you. You're heading towards a city on the coast which you'll reach in forty minutes at your present speed. If you cannot stop yourselves then, we're going to blast the tunnel behind and ahead of you to cut off your power. Then we'll sink a shaft to get you out—the chief engineer says he can do it in five minutes with the main projectors. So you should be safe within an hour, unless the sun blows up before."

"And if that happens, you'll be destroyed as well! You mustn't take such a risk!"

"Don't let that worry you; we're perfectly safe. When the sun detonates, the explosion wave will take several minutes to rise to its maximum. But apart from that, we're on the night side of the planet, behind an eight-thousand-mile screen of rock. When the first warning of the explosion comes, we will accelerate out of the Solar System, keeping in the shadow of the planet. Under our maximum drive, we will reach the velocity of light before leaving the cone of shadow, and the sun cannot harm us then."

T'sinadree was still afraid to hope. Another objection came at once into his mind.

"Yes, but how will you get any warning, here on the night side of the planet?"

"Very easily," replied Alveron. "This world has a moon which is now visible from this hemisphere. We have telescopes trained on it. If it shows any sudden increase in brilliance, our main drive goes on automatically and we'll be thrown out of the system."

The logic was flawless. Alveron, cautious as ever, was taking no chances. It would be many minutes before the eight-thousand-mile shield of rock and metal could be destroyed by the fires of the exploding sun. In that time, the *Sqooo* could have reached the safety of the velocity of light.

Alarkane pressed the second button when they were still several miles from the coast. He did not expect anything to happen then, assuming that the machine could not stop between stations. It seemed too good to be true when, a few minutes later, the machine's slight vibration died away and they came to a halt.

The doors slid silently apart. Even before they were fully open, the three had left the compartment. They were taking no more chances. Before them a long tunnel stretched into the distance rising slowly out of sight. They were starting along it when suddenly Alveron's voice called from the communicators.

"Stay where you are! We're going to blast!"

The ground shuddered once, and far ahead there came the rumble of falling rock. Again the earth shook—and a hundred yards ahead the passageway vanished abruptly. A tremendous vertical shaft had been cut clean through it.

The party hurried forward again until they came to the end of the corridor and stood waiting on its lip. The shaft in which it ended was a full thousand feet across and descended into the earth as far as the torches could throw their beams. Overhead, the storm clouds fled beneath a moon that no man would have recognized, so luridly brilliant was its disk. And, most glorious of all sights, the *Sqooo* floated high above, the great projectors that had drilled this enormous pit still glowing cherry red.

A dark shape detached itself from the mother ship and dropped swiftly towards the ground. Torkalee was returning to collect his friends. A little later, Alveron greeted them in the control room. He waved to the great vision screen and said quietly:

"You see, we were only just in time."

The continent below them was slowly settling beneath the mile-high

waves that were attacking its coasts. The last that anyone was ever to
see of Earth was a great plain, bathed with the silver light of the abnormally brilliant moon. Across its face the waters were pouring in a glittering flood towards a distant range of mountains. The sea had won its
final victory, but its triumph would be short-lived for soon sea and land
would be no more. Even as the silent party in the control room watched
the destruction below, the infinitely greater catastrophe to which this
was only the prelude came swiftly upon them.

It was as though dawn had broken suddenly over this moonlit landscape. But it was not dawn: it was only the moon, shining with the brilliance of a second sun. For perhaps thirty seconds that awesome, unnatural light burnt fiercely on the doomed land beneath. Then there
came a sudden flashing of indicator lights across the control board. The
main drive was on. For a second Alveron glanced at the indicators and
checked their information. When he looked again at the screen, Earth
was already gone.

The magnificent, desperately overstrained generators quietly died
when the *S9000* was passing the orbit of Persephone. It did not matter,
the sun could never harm them now, and although the ship was speeding helplessly out into the lonely night of interstellar space, it would
only be a matter of days before rescue came.

There was irony in that. A day ago, they had been the rescuers, going
to the aid of a race that now no longer existed. Not for the first time Alveron wondered about the world that had just perished. He tried, in
vain, to picture it as it had been in its glory, the streets of its cities
thronged with life. Primitive though its people had been, they might
have offered much to the Universe later in history. If only they could
have made contact! Regret was useless: long before their coming, the
people of this world must have buried themselves in its iron heart. And
now they and their civilization would remain a mystery for the rest of
time.

Alveron was glad when his thoughts were interrupted by Rugon's entrance. The chief of communications had been very busy ever since the
take-off, trying to analyze the programs radiated by the transmitter
Orostron had discovered. The problem was not a difficult one, but it demanded the construction of special equipment, and that had taken time.

"Well, what have you found?" asked Alveron.

"Quit a lot," replied his friend. "There's something mysterious here,
and I don't understand it.

"It didn't take long to find how the vision transmissions were built
up, and we've been able to convert them to suit our own equipment. It
seems that there were cameras all over the planet, surveying points of
interest. Some of them were apparently in cities, on the tops of very
high buildings. The cameras were rotating continuously to give panoramic views. In the programs we've recorded there are about twenty
different scenes.

"In addition, there are a number of transmissions of a different kind, neither sound nor vision. They seem to be purely scientific—possibly instrument readings or something of that sort. All these programs were going out simultaneously on different frequency bands.

"Now there must be a reason for all this. Orostron still thinks that the station simply wasn't switched off when it was deserted. But these aren't the sort of programs such a station would normally radiate at all. It was certainly used for interplanetary relaying—Klarten was quite right there. So these people must have crossed space, since none of the other planets had any life at the time of the last survey. Don't you agree?"

Alveron was following intently.

"Yes, that seems reasonable enough. But it's also certain that the beam was pointing to none of the other planets. I checked that myself."

"I know," said Rugon. "What I want to discover is why a giant interplanetary relay station is busily transmitting pictures of a world about to be destroyed—*pictures that would be of immense interest to scientists and astronomers*. Someone had gone to a lot of trouble to arrange all those panoramic cameras. I am convinced that those beams were going *somewhere*."

Alveron started up.

"Do you imagine that there might be an outer planet that hasn't been reported?" he asked. "If so, your theory's certainly wrong. The beam wasn't even pointing in the plane of the Solar System. And even if it were—just look at this."

He switched on the vision screen and adjusted the controls. Against the velvet curtain of space was hanging a blue-white sphere, apparently composed of many concentric shells of incandescent gas. Even though its immense distance made all movement invisible, it was clearly expanding at an enormous rate. At its center was a blinding point of light —the white dwarf star that the sun had now become.

"You probably don't realize just how big that sphere is," said Alveron. "Look at this."

He increased the magnification until only the center portion of the nova was visible. Close to its heart were two minute condensations, one on either side of the nucleus.

"Those are the two giant planets of the system. They have still managed to retain their existence—after a fashion. And they were several hundred million miles from the sun.

"The nova is still expanding—but it's already twice the size of the Solar System."

Rugon was silent for a moment.

"Perhaps you're right," he said, rather grudgingly. "You've disposed of my first theory. But you still haven't satisfied me."

He made several swift circuits of the room before speaking again. Alveron waited patiently, he knew the almost intuitive powers of his friend, who could often solve a problem when mere logic seemed insufficient.

Then, rather slowly, Rugon began to speak again.

"What do you think of this?" he said. "Suppose we've completely underestimated this people? Orostron did it once—he thought they could never have crossed space, since they'd only known radio for two centuries. Hansur II told me that. Well, Orostron was quite wrong. Perhaps we're all wrong. I've had a look at the material that Klarten brought back from the transmitter. He wasn't impressed by what he found, but it's a marvelous achievement for so short a time. There were devices in that station that belonged to civilizations thousands of years older. *Alveron, can we follow that beam to see where it leads?*"

Alveron said nothing for a full minute. He had been more than half expecting the question, but it was not an easy one to answer. The main generators had gone completely. There was no point in trying to repair them. But there was still power available, and while there was power, anything could be done in time. It would mean a lot of improvisation, and some difficult maneuvers, for the ship still had its enormous initial velocity. Yes, it could be done, and the activity would keep the crew from becoming further depressed, now that the reaction caused by the mission's failure had started to set in. The news that the nearest heavy repair ship could not reach them for three weeks had also caused a slump in morale.

The engineers, as usual, made a tremendous fuss. Again as usual, they did the job in half the time they had dismissed as being absolutely impossible. Very slowly, over many hours, the great ship began to discard the speed its main drive had given it in as many minutes. In a tremendous curve, millions of miles in radius, the *S9000* changed its course and the star fields shifted round it.

The maneuver took three days, but at the end of that time the ship was limping along a course parallel to the beam that had once come from Earth. They were heading out into emptiness, the blazing sphere that had been the sun dwindling slowly behind them. By the standards of interstellar flight, they were almost stationary.

For hours Rugon strained over his instruments, driving his detector beams far ahead into space. There were certainly no planets within many light-years; there was no doubt of that. From time to time Alveron came to see him and always he had to give the same reply: "Nothing to report." About a fifth of the time Rugon's intuition let him down badly; he began to wonder if this were such an occasion.

Not until a week later did the needles of the mass-detectors quiver feebly at the ends of their scales. But Rugon said nothing, not even to his captain. He waited until he was sure, and he went on waiting until even the short-range scanners began to react, and to build up the first faint pictures on the vision screen. Still he waited patiently until he could interpret the images. Then, when he knew that his wildest fancy was even less than the truth, he called his colleagues into the control room.

The picture on the vision screen was the familiar one of endless star fields, sun beyond sun to the very limits of the Universe. Near the center of the screen a distant nebula made a patch of haze that was difficult for the eye to grasp.

Rugon increased the magnification. The stars flowed out of the field; the little nebula expanded until it filled the screen and then—it was a nebula no longer. A simultaneous gasp of amazement came from all the company at the sight that lay before them.

Lying across league after league of space, ranged in a vast three dimensional array of rows and columns with the precision of a marching army, were thousands of tiny pencils of light. They were moving swiftly; the whole immense lattice holding its shape as a single unit. Even as Alveron and his comrades watched, the formation began to drift off the screen and Rugon had to recenter the controls.

After a long pause, Rugon started to speak.

"This is the race," he said softly, "that has only known radio for two centuries—the race that we believed had crept to die in the heart of its planet. I have examined those images under the highest possible magnification.

"That is the greatest fleet of which there has ever been a record. Each of those points of light represents a ship larger than our own. Of course, they are very primitive—what you see on the screen are the jets of their rockets. Yes, they dared to use rockets to bridge interstellar space! You realize what that means. It would take them centuries to reach the nearest star. The whole race must have embarked on this journey in the hope that its descendants would complete it, generations later.

"To measure the extent of their accomplishment, think of the ages it took us to conquer space, and the longer ages still before we attempted to reach the stars. Even if we were threatened with annihilation, could we have done so much in so short a time? Remember, this is the youngest civilization in the Universe. Four hundred thousand years ago it did not even exist. What will it be a million years from now?"

An hour later, Orostron left the crippled mother ship to make contact with the great fleet ahead. As the little torpedo disappeared among the stars, Alveron turned to his friend and made a remark that Rugon was often to remember in the years ahead.

"I wonder what they'll be like?" he mused. "Will they be nothing but wonderful engineers, with no art or philosophy? They're going to have such a surprise when Orostron reaches them—I expect it will be rather a blow to their pride. It's funny how all isolated races think they're the only people in the Universe. But they should be grateful to us—we're going to save them a good many hundred years of travel."

Alveron glanced at the Milky Way, lying like a veil of silver mist across the vision screen. He waved towards it with a sweep of a tentacle that embraced the whole circle of the Galaxy, from the Central Planets to the lonely suns of the Rim.

"You know," he said to Rugon, "I feel rather afraid of these people. Suppose they don't like our little Federation?" He waved once more towards the star-clouds that lay massed across the screen, glowing with the light of their countless suns.

"Something tells me they'll be very determined people," he added. "We had better be polite to them. After all, we only outnumber them about a thousand million to one."

Rugon laughed at his captain's little joke.

Twenty years afterwards, the remark didn't seem so funny.